# Betsy the Vampire Queen

# Betsy the Vampire Queen

Undead and Unwed
Undead and Unemployed
Undead and Unappreciated
Undead and Unreturnable

## MaryJanice Davidson

Barbara—
you're right about
the cover!

*[signature]*

SFBC
FANTASY

# Betsy the Vampire Queen

# Contents

# Undead and Unwed

*This book is dedicated to
Anthony Alongi,
my editor, my partner, my bearded nemesis,
and my friend.
All praise to my darling husband.*

# Acknowledgments

There's really no need to thank anyone; I did this *all myself*. Okay, that was a rather large lie. While I did the actual writing, many people helped in ways they might not be aware of.

First, thanks to my husband, who edited every word I wrote, and kept the kids out of my hair while I was on deadline. Thanks also to Angela Knight, who was kind enough to mention my work to the fabulous Cindy Hwang; Tina Engler, who gave me the thumbs-up to write an obscure e-book about a dead secretary; and Martha Punches, who edited a rough draft for free.

Thanks also to my book club, the Magic Widows, who often gave me great ideas for dialogue, and special thanks to Cathleen Barkmeier for the information on G.A.D.

I'd also like to thank my friends on the Cape: Curt, Andrea, Guy, Vana, and Jon. Anthony brought a Midwestern redneck around, and they welcomed her from day one.

Finally, I'd like to thank my family: Al, Sharon, Yvonne, Paul, Bill, Elinor, Julie Kathryn, Thomas, Betsy, Scott, and Daniel. They have paid me the ultimate compliment of being unsurprised at my success. Or they've hidden their surprise very well. Either way, I'm grateful.

# Chapter 1

T H E day I died started out bad and got worse in a hurry

I hit my snooze alarm a few too many times and was late for work. Who wouldn't hit the snooze to get another nine minutes of sleep? No one, that's who. Subsequently, I almost always oversleep. Stupid snooze button.

I didn't have time for breakfast. Instead, I gobbled a pair of chocolate Pop Tarts while waiting for the bus. Mmmm . . . chocolate. My mom would have approved (who do you think got me hooked on the darned things?), but a nutritionist would have smacked me upside the head with her calorie counter.

The bus was, of course, late. You gotta love the Minnesota Transit system. Six buses for a population area of a quarter million. When they weren't late, they were early—I'd lost count of the number of times I'd stepped outside only to see my bus disappearing down the street. Schedule? What schedule?

When the bus, late again, finally did lumber into sight, I climbed on and sat down . . . in gum.

At a nine A.M. meeting (to which I arrived at 9:20) I found out the recession (the one the economists have been denying for years) had hit me right between the eyes: I had been laid off. Not unexpected—the last time good old Hamton & Sons had been profitable I'd been in high school—but it hurt, just the same. Losing a job is the worst. You know, beyond a shadow of a doubt, that somebody doesn't want you. Doesn't matter if the reasons are personal, financial, or practical. They just don't want you.

Hamton & Sons, realizing about a year too late that they had to slash costs, decided administrative layoffs were the way to go as opposed to, say, cutting the six figure salaries of senior management. The clerks and secretaries had been deemed expendable. But vengeance would be ours. Without us, those twits couldn't even send a fax, much less run the company.

With this cheerful thought, I cleaned out my desk, ignored the way my coworkers were avoiding looking at me, and scuttled home. I consoled myself by stopping at Dairy Queen for a blueberry milkshake. Signs of spring: robins, new grass, and Dairy Queen opening for the season.

As I walked through my front door, still slurping, I saw my answering machine light winking at me like a small black dragon. The message was from my stepmonster, and from the racket in the background, she was calling from her salon: "Your father and I won't be able to make it to your party tonight . . . I'm on new medication and I—we—just can't. Sorry." *Sure you are, jerk.* "Have fun without us." *No problem.* "Maybe you'll meet someone tonight." Translation: Maybe some poor slob will marry you.

My stepmonster had, from day one, related to me in only one way: as a rival for her new husband's affections. Worse, she never hesitated to play the depression card to get out of something that was important to me. This ceased bothering me about a week after I met her, so I suppose it was just as well.

I went into the kitchen to feed my cat, and that's when I noticed she'd run away again. Always looking for adventure, my Giselle (although it's more like I'm her Betsy).

I looked at the clock. My, my. Not even noon. Time to do laundry and gouge out my eyes, and the day would be complete.

Happy birthday to me.


AS it turned out, we had a freak April snowstorm, and my party was postponed. Just as well . . . I didn't feel like going out, putting on a happy face, and drinking too many daiquiris. The Mall of America is a terrific place, but I've got to be in the mood for overpriced retail merchandise, rowdy weekend crowds, and six-dollar drinks.

Nick called around eight P.M., and that was my day's sole bright spot. Nick Berry was a superfine detective who worked out of St. Paul. I'd been attacked a couple of months before, and . . .

Okay, well, "attacked" is putting it mildly. Like using the word "unfortunate" to describe World War II. I don't like to talk about it—to *think* about it—but what happened was, a bunch of creeps jumped me as I was leaving Khan's Mongolian Barbecue (all you can eat for $11.95, including salad, dessert, and free refills—quite the bargain if you don't mind your clothes reeking of garlic for hours).

I have no idea what my attackers wanted—they didn't take my purse or try to rape me or even babble about government conspiracies.

They came out of nowhere—literally. One minute I was yawning and fumbling for my keys, the next I was surrounded. They clawed and bit at me like a bunch of rabid squirrels while I fended them off with the toes of my Manolo Blahniks and screamed for help as loud as I could . . . so loud I couldn't speak above a whisper for three days. They stank—worse than my kitchen that time I went to the Cape for two weeks and forgot to empty my garbage before I left. They all had long hair and funny-colored eyes and they never talked to me.

Help didn't come, but the bad guys ran away. Maybe they were rattled by my voice—when I scream, dogs howl. Or maybe they didn't like the way I stank of garlic. Whatever the reason, they ran away—skittered away, actually. While I leaned against my car, concentrating on not passing out, I glanced back and it looked like a few of them were on all fours. I struggled mightily not to yark up my buffet, ginger tea, and sesame bread—no way was I pissing away that $11.95—and then called 911 on my cell phone.

Detective Nick was assigned to the case, and he interviewed me in the hospital while they were disinfecting the bite marks. All fifteen of them. The intern who took care of me smelled like cilantro and kept humming the theme from *Harry Potter and the Chamber of Secrets*. Off-key. This was actually more annoying than the sting of the antiseptic.

That was last fall. Since then, more and more people—they didn't discriminate between women and men—were being attacked. The last two had turned up dead. So, yeah, I was freaked out by what happened, and I'd sworn off Khan's until the bad guys were caught, but mostly I was grateful it hadn't been worse.

Anyway, Detective Nick called and we chatted and, long story short, I promised to come in to look through the Big Book o' Bad Guys one more time. And I would. For myself, to feel empowered, but mostly to see Nick, who was exactly my height (six feet), with dark blond hair cut regulation-short, light blue eyes, a swimmer's build, and dimples! He looked like an escapee from a Mr. Hardbody calendar. I've broken the law, Officer, take me in.

Making Nick my eye candy would be the closest I'd gotten to getting laid in . . . what year was it? Not that I'm a prude. I'm just picky. Really, really picky. I treat myself to the nicest, most expensive shoes I can get my hands on, which isn't easy on a secretary's budget, and never mind all the money my dad keeps trying to throw at me. If I used his money, they wouldn't be my shoes. They'd be his. Anyway, I save up for months to buy the dumb things, and they only have to go on my feet.

Yep, that's me in a nutshell: Elizabeth Taylor (don't start! I've heard 'em all), single, dead-end job (well, not anymore), lives with her cat. And I'm so dull, the fucking cat runs away about three times a month just to get a little excitement.

And speaking of the cat . . . was that her telltale *Ri-aaaooowwwww!* from the street? Well, super. Giselle hated the snow. She had probably been looking for a little spring lovin' and got caught in the storm. Now she was outside waiting for rescue. And when I *did* rescue her, she'd be horribly affronted and wouldn't make eye contact for the rest of the week.

I slipped into my boots and headed into the yard. It was still snowing, but I could see Giselle crouched in the middle of the street like a small blob of shadow, one with amber-colored eyes. I wasted ten seconds calling her—*why* do I call cats?—then clomped through my yard into the street.

Normally this wouldn't be a problem, as I live at the end of the block and it's a quiet street. However, in the snow on icy roads, the driver didn't see me in time. When he did, he did the absolute worst thing: slammed on his brakes. That pretty much sealed my doom.

Dying doesn't hurt. I know that sounds like a crock, some touchy-feely nonsense meant to make people feel better about biting the big one. But the fact is, your body is so traumatized by what's happening, it shuts down your nerve endings. Not only did dying not hurt, I didn't even feel the cold. And it was only ten degrees that night.

I handled it badly, I admit. When I saw he was going to plow into me, I froze like a deer in headlights. A big, dumb, blond deer who had just paid for touch-up highlights. I couldn't move, not even to save my life.

Giselle certainly could; the ungrateful little wretch scampered right the hell out of there. Me, I went flying. The car hit me at forty miles an hour, which was survivable, and knocked me into a tree, which was not.

It didn't hurt, as I said, but there was tremendous pressure, all over my body. I heard things break. I heard my own skull shatter—it sounded like someone was chewing ice in my ear. I felt myself bleed, felt liquid pouring from everywhere. I felt my bladder let go involuntarily for the first time in twenty-six years. In the dark, my blood on the snow looked black.

The last thing I saw was Giselle sitting on my porch, waiting for me to let her in. The last thing I heard was the driver, screaming for help.

Well, not the *last*. But you know what I mean.

# Chapter 2

BEING dead really makes you think. Mostly, it makes you think about all the stuff you screwed up, or didn't do.

It's not that I had this tremendously exciting life or anything, but jeez, I would have liked to have lived more than a measly thirty years. And when I thought of the way I wasted the last year . . . the last ten years . . . ugh.

I was never a genius. Strictly C-plus average, which was just fine. Who could worry about Geometry and Civics and Chemistry when I had to work on my talent number for the Miss Burnsville pageant? Not to mention keeping three or four fellas on the hook without them realizing they were on the hook . . . sometimes I was exhausted by lunchtime.

Anyway, I tolerated high school, hated college (just like high school, only with ashtrays and beer kegs), flunked out, modeled for a bit, got bored with *that* . . . people never believed me when I told them modeling was about as interesting as watching dust bunnies. But it was true. The money was okay, but that was the only good thing about it.

Modeling, contrary to the idea projected by the media, wasn't the least bit glamorous. You spend your days going to cattle calls with your portfolio tucked under one arm and a desperate smile on your pretty face. You get maybe one job in ten . . . if you're lucky. Then you get up at 5:30 in the morning to do that job, and often work an eighteen-hour day. Then, maybe five weeks later, you finally get paid. And that's after your agent holds the check for ten days to make sure it clears.

Still, I had some fun in the beginning. Runway shows were

made for the strut. It was a kick to tell people what I did for a living—this is America, after all, land of the shallow. Announcing the way I earned my money was always good for a free drink or three. God knows, men were certainly impressed.

Print ads were awful, though . . . shot after shot after shot and smile, smile, smile, and sometimes you were on your feet for ten hours at a stretch. And the attitude—smile big, honey, then sit on Daddy's lap—was worse.

And don't get me started on the male models! Much more vain than the ladies. To this day I can't watch *Zoolander;* it just hits too damned close to home. I'm sure Ben Stiller thought he was making a comedy, but it was really more like a documentary.

It was tough work, dating someone who spent more on hair products than I did. And never being able to catch their eye because they were always checking out their reflection. And a lot of them were hounds—turn your back to get a drink, and you were likely to find your dates du jour chatting up some other bim . . . or feeling her up. Or feeling up the waiter. I hated being the last to know I was a beard. So embarrassing!

About two years into it, I'd had enough. All at once. I was sitting in a room full of tall blond women with long legs and hair . . women with my height and coloring. And it occurred to me that the men waiting in the back to interview me didn't care that I loved steak and risotto, and scary movies (with the exception of *Zoolander*) and my mom. They didn't care that I was a member of P.E.T.A. and a registered Republican (contrary to popular belief, the two aren't mutually exclusive). Hell, they didn't care if I was a wanted felon. The *only* thing they cared about was my face and my body.

I remember thinking, *What am I doing here?*

Excellent question. I got up and walked out. Didn't even take my portfolio home with me. My friend Jessica has called me a woman of instant decision and I guess there's some truth in that. Once I make up my mind, that's it.

Anyway, I started temping around the Twin Cities, which, like all the jobs I ever had, was fun until I mastered the situation and got bored. Eventually I had so much experience as a secretary they made me a supersecretary . . . excuse me, an executive assistant.

Which brought me to Hamton & Sons, where my job was fraught with excitement and danger. Excitement because there was rarely enough money to pay the company's bills. Danger because I was often worried I'd succumb to the urge to throttle my boss, and go down for homicide. Triple homicide, if the brokers got in my way.

Most people complain about their bosses—it's the American way—but I was serious: I truly despised him. Worse, I didn't respect him. And there were days when I wondered if he was really crazy.

Last week had been typical. I got to work just in time to be met at the door by wide-eyed brokers who had, in the ten minutes they'd been unsupervised, broken the copy machine. The *brand-new* copy machine. I swear they were like children. Little children whom you cannot turn your back on. Little chain-smoking children.

"It's not working," Todd, the head of the broker posse, informed me. "We'll just have to send it back. I told you we didn't need a new one."

"The old one got so overheated all our copies were brown and smelled like smoke. What'd you do?" I said, hanging up my coat.

"Nothing. I was making copies and then it clanked and then it stopped."

"What. Did. You. Do."

"Well . . . I tried to fix it. I didn't want to bother you," he hurried on at my murderous expression.

He tried to scurry away but I grabbed his arm and tugged him toward the machine, which was making an ominous wheezing sound. I pointed to the poster taped on the wall. "Read it."

"Betsy, I'm really busy, the market just opened and I have to—ow! Okay, okay. Don't pinch. It says 'If anything goes wrong, do not under ANY circumstances fix it yourself . . . find Betsy or Terry.' There, okay?"

"Just wanted to make sure you hadn't forgotten how to read." I let go of his arm before I gave in to the urge to pinch him again. "Go away, I'll fix it."

Twenty minutes and one ruined skirt later (stupid toner!), the machine was up and running. So I started to go through my mail, only to stop dead at the now familiar monthly letter from the I.R.S.

I marched straight into my boss, Tom's, office. He looked up when I shut the door behind me, spearing me with the dead stare of the classic sociopath. Or maybe he learned it in business school.

I shook the letter at him. "The I.R.S. is still—still!—looking for our payroll taxes."

"I can't deal with that right now," Tom said testily. He was of medium height—and resented the hell out of the fact that I was taller—and smoked like cigarettes were going to be outlawed within the week. Despite the strict Minnesota Clean Indoor Air Act, his office smelled like an ashtray. "Talk to me when the market's closed."

"Tom, we're almost a year behind! That money is our employees', to be paid to the government. You know, state and federal taxes? We can't keep using it to pay our bills. We already owe the government over a hundred thousand dollars!"

"After the market closes," he said, and turned back to his computer. Dismissed. And of course, at 3:01 P.M., he'd be out the door, avoiding any tedious meetings with me.

I stomped out. Not a day went by that Tom didn't try something sneaky. He either lied to his customers, lied to his employees, or used their money without telling them. If caught, he would blame me. And he had the uncanny knack of being able to convince people it wasn't his fault. He was a hell of a salesman, I'd give him that. Even I, who knew him well, could often be fooled by his enthusiasm.

I hated being his enforcer, writing up disciplinary reports for the brokers while he got to do the raises—Tom was strictly a fun-stuff guy. And I hated it when he made me lie to his clients. They were nice people and had no idea they were trusting a sociopath with their money.

But, damn it, the money was great. Even better, I was able to work four ten-hour days, which meant three-day weekends. Three days was just about long enough to muster the courage to go back to the office on Monday. It was tough to give up. Any other secretarial job and I'd have to save for a lot longer to get my shoes. I guess that meant I was a sellout.

I stayed until 5:00 P.M. and, as usual, I was the only one. The receptionist went home at 4:30, and everyone else left at 3:30, after the markets were closed. But Tom lived in fear of missing a vital phone call, so I stayed until 5:00 every night. Well, it was a good way to catch up on my reading.

I left at 5:00 to meet my date . . . Todd's nephew, of all people. He assured me we'd get along swimmingly. Normally I avoided blind dates like they were split ends, but I was lonesome, and hadn't met anyone new in over a year. I was too old for club-hopping, and too young for bingo. So I went.

Big mistake. Todd's nephew was a foot shorter than I was.

This didn't bother me—most men were shorter than I was. But some fellows seemed to take it personally, like I'd gotten tall just to spite them. All part of my diabolical plan.

The nephew, Gerry, was one of these. He kept looking up at me, then would glance away, and then, helplessly, look up at me again. It was like he was dazzled—or horrified—by my long legs.

After he'd made several off-color jokes, regaled me with the tales of how he defeated all the grasping, greedy Jews at his accounting firm with wit and cunning, and informed me that the United States should just blow up all the Third World countries and end terrorism at a stroke (presumably with terrorism), I'd had enough. Soul mates we were not. It served me right. I hated dating.

I submitted to a good night kiss only because I wanted to see how he'd reach. He stood on his tiptoes and I bent down. Soft moist lips hit the area between my cheek and my mouth, and I got a whiff of beer and garlic. I didn't mind the garlic, but I positively hated beer. I practically broke my wrist ramming the key through the lock so I could get into the house.

So, a day in the life. My life. What a waste. And now I was done. I never did anything. Not one thing.

# Chapter 3

$\mathcal{I}$ opened my eyes to pure darkness. When I was a kid I read a short story about a preacher who went to hell, and when he got there he discovered the dead didn't have eyelids, so they couldn't close their eyes to block out the horror. Right away I knew I wasn't in hell, since I couldn't see a thing.

I wriggled experimentally. I was in a small, closed space. I was lying on something hard, but the sides of my little cage were padded. If this was a hospital room, it was the strangest one ever. And the drugs were spectacular . . . I didn't hurt anywhere. And where was everybody? Why was it so quiet?

I wriggled some more, then had a brainstorm and sat up. My head banged into something firm but yielding, which gave way when I shoved. Then I was sitting up, blinking in the gloom.

At first I thought I was in a large, industrial kitchen.

Then I realized I was sitting in a coffin. A white coffin with gold scrolling on the sides, lined in plush pink satin (ugh!). It had been placed on a large, stainless steel table. The table was in the middle of the room, and there was a row of sinks against the far wall. Not a stove in sight. Just several strange-looking instruments, and an industrial-sized makeup kit. Which meant this wasn't a kitchen, this was—

I nearly broke something scrambling out. As it was, I moved too quickly and the coffin and I tumbled off the table and onto the floor. I felt the shock in my knees as I hit but didn't care. In a flash I shoved the coffin off my back and was on my feet and running.

I burst through the swinging doors and found myself in a large, wood-paneled entryway. It was even gloomier in here; there were no windows that I could see, just rows and rows of coat racks. At the far end of the entry was a tall, wild-eyed blonde dressed in an absurd pink suit. She might have been pretty if she wasn't wearing orange blusher and too much blue eye shadow. Her brownish-rose lipstick was all wrong for her face, too. Just about any makeup would have been wrong for her, as she was so shockingly pale.

The blonde wobbled toward me on cheap shoes—Payless, buy one pair get the second at half price—and I saw her hair was actually quite nice: shoulder length, with a cute flip at the ends and interesting streaky highlights.

Interesting Shade #23 Lush Golden Blonde highlights. Heyyyyyyy . . .

The woman in the awful suit was me. The woman in the *cheap shoes* was me!

I staggered closer to the mirror, wide-eyed. Yes, it was really me, and yes, I looked this awful. I really was in hell!

I forced myself to calm down. When that didn't work, I slapped myself, smearing blush on my palm. Clearly I was wrong; this wasn't hell. Hell wasn't a wood-paneled entryway with a mirror on one end and a coffin on the other. It made sense that I looked so repugnant. I was dead. That silly ass in the Pontiac Aztek, doubtless conspiring with my cat, had killed me. The perfect end to a perfect day.

I was dead but too dumb to lie down. Dead and walking around inside the funeral home in a cheap suit and fake leather shoes. The funeral must be tomorrow . . . later today, I amended, looking at the clock.

Who had picked out this outfit for me? And these shoes?

I slipped one of the shoes off, looked at the inside.

*Property of Antonia O'Neill Taylor.*

I knew it. My stepmother! The bitch meant to bury me wearing her cast-off shoes! This bothered me more than being driven into a tree while my cat watched. I nearly threw the wretched shoe at the mirror but instead reluctantly forced it back onto my foot. It was cold outside and I'd need the protection. But at such a price! If Giselle could see me now—if anyone I had ever known could see me now . . .

My cat! Who was going to look after the little monster? Jessica, probably, or maybe my mother . . . yes, probably my mother.

My mother. She'd have been devastated when she got the news. My father, too . . . he might even take the whole day off work for my funeral. My stepmother—well, I doubted she'd much care. She thought I was a headstrong spoiled brat, and I thought she was a conniving, dishonest, gold-digging bitch. And the fact that we were both right and had been since we laid eyes on each other didn't help at all.

It occurred to me that I should seek out my grieving friends and family and tell them I had no intention of being buried. I had to find a new job, for crying out loud, I couldn't hang out in a coffin six feet under. I had to pay my bills or they'd shut off my cable.

Then sanity returned. I was dead. I'd been zombified or whatever, and needed to finish the job the guy in the Aztek had started. Or maybe this was purgatory, a task set for me, something I had to finish before God opened the gate.

I had the fleeting thought that the doctors in the ER had made a mistake, but shook it off. I remembered, too well, the sound of my skull shattering. If it hadn't killed me, I'd be in an ICU now with more tubes than a chemistry classroom. Not dolled up like a . . .

*(dead)*

. . . whore wearing cheap castoffs on my . . .

*(dead)*

. . . feet.

All that aside, to be brutally honest, I couldn't bear for anyone to see me looking the way I did. I would literally rather be dead. Again.

I gave my reflection one final incredulous once-over, then walked to the end of the hallway, found the stairwell, and started climbing. The funeral home was three stories high—and what they needed the other two stories for I was *not* going to think about—which should be high enough, since I planned to go head-first. My nasty shoes clack-clacked on the stairs. I wouldn't let myself look down at my feet.

At first I thought the door was locked, but with a good hard shove it obligingly opened with a shriek of metal on metal. I stepped outside.

It was a beautiful spring night—all traces of snow from the storm had melted. The air smelled wet and warm, like fertility. I had the oddest feeling that if I were to scatter seeds on the cement rooftop, they would take hold and grow. A night had never, ever smelled so sweetly, not even the day I moved into my own place.

City lights twinkled in the distance, reminding me of Christmas. Reminding me all my Christmases were done. There were a few cars moving on the street below, and, far off, I could hear a woman laughing. Well, at least someone was having a good time.

As I stepped onto the ledge, I ignored the not inconsiderable twinge of apprehension that raced up my spine. Even though I was dead, I didn't like looking down at the street. I stifled the urge to step back to safety.

Safety, ha! What was that?

This wasn't my last night on earth. That had been a couple of days ago. There was nothing to feel sad about. I had been a good girl in life, and now I was going to my reward, damn it. I was *not* going to stumble around like a zombie, scaring the hell out of people and pretending I still had a place in the world.

"God," I said, teetering for balance, "it's me, Betsy. I'm coming to see you now. Make up the guest room."

I dove off the roof, fought the urge to curl into a cannonball, and hit the street below, headfirst, exactly as I had planned. What was *not* in the plan was the smashing, crunching pain in my head when I hit, and how I didn't even lose consciousness, much less see my pal God.

Instead I groaned, clutched my head, then finally stood when the pain abated. Only to get creamed by an early morning garbage truck. I looked up in time to see the horror-struck driver mouthing *"Jesus Christ, lady, look out!"* something, then my forehead made brisk contact with the truck's front grille. I slid down it like road kill and hit the street, ass first. That hurt less than hitting the grille, but not by much.

I lay in the street for a long moment, seriously debating whether or not to get up. Finally I decided I couldn't lie there forever—clearly I was bad at just lying anywhere—and slowly got to my feet.

When I stood, brushing dirt from my cheap skirt and blowing my hair out of my face, the driver slammed the truck in reverse and got the hell out of Dodge. Not that I could blame him—I was probably a gruesome sight. But who ever heard of a hit-and-run garbage truck?

# Chapter 4

$\mathcal{I}$ am nothing if not persistent. Flinging myself into the Mississippi didn't work: I found I no longer needed to breathe. I trudged around on the muddy river bottom for half an hour, patiently waiting to drown, before giving up and slogging my way back to shore. Interestingly, I couldn't feel the cold, though it couldn't have been more than forty-five degrees, and I was supersoaked.

Grounding myself while I held onto a live power line didn't work, either (though it did *awful* things to my hair).

I drank a bottle of bleach, and the only consequence was a startling case of dry mouth . . . I was *so* thirsty!

I shoplifted a butcher knife from the nearby Wal-Mart—the place to shop if you're dead, it's three A.M., and you don't have any credit cards—and stabbed myself in the heart: nothing. A small trickle of blood flowed sluggishly and, while I watched in horrified fascination, slowed and stopped. In another few minutes the only sign I'd stabbed myself was the cut in my suit and a modest bloodstain.

I was trudging down Lake Street, trying to figure out how to decapitate myself, when I heard low voices and what sounded like muffled crying. I almost moved on—didn't I have enough problems of my own?—when good sense returned and I walked through the alley and around the corner.

I took in the scene at once: three men hulking around a woman in a sort of sinister half-moon. She was holding hands with a big-eyed girl. The girl looked about six or so. Fear made the woman look about fifty. Her purse was lying on the ground between them. Nobody moved to get it, and I had a quick, clear thought: She tossed it at them, and tried to run, and they cornered her. They don't want her purse. They want—

"Please," she said, almost whispered, and I thought the acoustics must be very good for me to have heard them from almost a block away. "Don't do anything to me in front of my daughter. I'll go with you—I'll do whatever you want, just please, please—"

"Mommy, don't leave me here by myself!" The girl's eyes were light brown, almost whiskey-colored, and when they filled with tears I felt something lurch inside my dead heart. "Just—you go away! Leave my mommy alone, you—you—you stinkers!"

"Shhh, Justine, shhh . . ." The woman was trying to pry her daughter's fingers free and made a ghastly attempt at a laugh. "She's tired—it's late—I'll go with you—"

"Don't want *you*," one of the men said, his eyes on the girl. Justine burst into fresh tears, but not before kicking the ground, raining pebbles and grit on the man's feet. Even in the midst of my shock at witnessing such a horrid scene, I admired the hell out of the girl.

"I'll take you back to my car—the engine's dead but I could—with all of you, just don't—don't—"

"Hey, assholes!" I said cheerfully. All five of them jumped, which surprised me . . . I wasn't the world's quietest walker. I couldn't believe I was doing this. I wasn't exactly the confrontational type. On the other hand, what did I possibly have to lose? "Er . . . you three assholes. Not the lady and the kid. Fellas, could you come over here and kill me, please?" While they were busy killing me, the two of them could run for it. Everyone wins!

Relieved, Justine smiled at me, revealing the gap where she'd lost one of her baby teeth. Then the men moved forward, and Justine grabbed her mom's hand and started dragging her toward the relative safety of Lake Street.

"I'll—"

"Come *on*, Mommy!"

"—get help!"

"Don't you dare," I snapped. "If you mess up my murder, I'll be furious." One of the men had grabbed my arm and was dragging me back toward Justine and her mom. "Just a minute, pal, I've got to—" He poked me, hard, and without thought I shoved.

The rest of it happened awfully fast. Jerkoff number one hadn't poked me, he'd stabbed me, for all the good it did. And when I shoved, his feet left the ground and he sailed back as if hurricane-force winds had blown him. When he finally touched ground he rolled for a good ten feet before he got to his feet and ran like he'd had one too many chimichangas and needed a bathroom.

While I was staring and making my usual vocalization when I didn't understand ("What . . . ?"), the other two moved in. I reached up and grabbed them by the backs of their dirty necks, then banged their heads together. I did this entirely without thinking about it—my usual reaction to stressful situations. There was a sickening crunch, and I heard—yech!—their skulls cave in. It was the sound I'd heard at my cousin's wedding when the bratty ring bearer threw the melon boat on the floor, sort of a muffled squishy sound. The bad guys dropped to the ground, deader than disco. Their faces were frozen in eternal expressions of pissed-off.

I nearly threw up into their staring faces. "Oh, shit!"

"Thank you thank you thank you!" Justine's mom was in my arms, reeking of fear and Tiffany perfume.

Ack, a witness to my felony! "Oh, shit!"

She was clutching me with not inconsiderable strength and babbling into my hair. I wriggled, trying to extricate myself without hurting her. "Ohmygod I thought they were going to rape me kill me hurt Justine kill Justine thank you thank you thank you—"

"I can't believe this! Did you see what I did? I can't believe I did it! How did I do it?"

"—thank you thank you thank you so so so much!" She kissed me on the mouth, a hearty smack.

"Whoa! Ixnay the issing-kay . . . we hardly know each other. Also, I'm so straight I could be a ruler. Leggo now, there's a nice hysteric."

She let go of me, still babbling, staggered a few feet away, and threw up. I couldn't blame her—I sort of felt like it myself, though if I hadn't puked after drinking the bleach, I probably never would. She finished retching, wiped her mouth with the back of one trembling hand, knelt, and started picking up the items that had fallen from her purse.

Weirdly, all of a sudden I wanted to grab her back, pukey breath and all. Something about her—the blood, the—she had scraped herself, or one of the men had cut her, and she was bleeding, the blood was flowing beneath her shirt, on the inside of her upper arm, and it trickled steadily and suddenly I was so thirsty I couldn't breathe. Not that I'd been breathing. But you know what I mean.

Justine was staring up at me. She had sidled close to me while her mother was shouting at the floor, so to speak. Her tears had dried, making her cheeks shine in the moonlight. She looked very, very thoughtful. And about six years older than she'd looked five minutes ago.

She pointed. "Doesn't that hurt like crazy?"

I looked down, then jerked the knife out of my side. Very little blood again. Sluggish flow that was already stopping. Again. Urgh. "No. Thanks. Uh . . . don't be scared. Anymore, I mean."

"Why'd you ask them to kill you?"

Normally I wouldn't share unpleasant confidences with a strange child, but what could I say? It had been one of those nights. Plus, she *had* pointed out the knife sticking out of my ribs; I felt obliged to give her an honest answer. "I'm a zombie," I explained, except I was having trouble talking, all of a sudden. "I'm trying to thtay dead."

"You're not a zombie." She pointed at my mouth. "You're a vampire. A good one, so that's all right," she added.

My hand came up so quickly I actually bit myself. I felt the sharp tips of new fangs, fangs that had come out when I'd smelled her mother's blood, fangs that seemed to be taking up half my mouth.

"A vampire? How ith that pothible? I died in a car ackthident, for God'th thake! Aw, thon of a bith!"

"Are you going to suck our blood?" Justine asked curiously.

"Ugh! Blood maketh me throw up. Even the thight of it—ugh!"

"Not anymore, I bet," she said. This was the most level-headed first-grader I'd ever met. Maybe I could take her under my wing and make her my evil sidekick. "It's okay. You can if you want to. You saved us. My mom," she said, her tone dropping to turn low, confidential, "was really scared."

*She's not the only one, sugar . . . and by the way, I bet you'd taste like electricity, all that youth and energy coursing through your bloodstream.*

I clapped both hands over my mouth and started backing away. "Run," I said, but I didn't have to bother; Justine's mama had finished gathering up her things, taken one look at my new dentition, picked up her daughter, and galloped away in the opposite direction. Justine managed a wave while bouncing on her mother's hip.

"There'th a gath thtathion at the end of this block!" I yelled after her. "You can call triple A!" I stuck my fingers in my mouth. My lisp was going away, and so were my fangs. "And what were you thinking, having your daughter out at four o'clock in the morning?" I shouted after her, freshly annoyed. "Dope!"

People think because Minneapolis is in the Midwest, rapes and murders and burglaries don't happen there. They do, just not as often in cold weather. I'd bet a thousand bucks the car that had broken down on them was a rental.

Well, the mystery was solved. I was a vampire. How, I had no idea. Car accident victims did not rise from the dead. So I'd always thought, anyway.

In the movies, some bim was always stalked by a tall, dark creature of the night, and she'd swoon into his arms and wake up ravenous three days later. But nothing like that had happened to me. The last tall, dark creature of the night I'd met had been the janitor at work. And he hadn't bitten me, just told me to use the men's room so he could clean the women's room.

There just wasn't any explanation for what had happened to me. Unless . . . could it have something to do with my attack a few months ago? The attackers had been savage, snarling, barely human. Until tonight, it had been the most surreal thing to happen to me, and that included the tax audit and my parents' divorce. Could the attackers have infected me?

And why was I still me? Now that I was a ravenous member of the undead, I should be sucking little girls dry and then lunching on their mamas. I should be a ruthless predator of the night, caring for nothing but my own unnatural fiendish hunger.

The men in the alley had been asshole predators, but I was still horrified when I accidentally killed two of them. I'd let Justine and her mom go—had *ordered* them to go. I was thirstier than I'd ever been in my . . . uh . . . life, but it wasn't ruling me. I wasn't an animal. I was still me, Betsy, disgusted with my current footwear and ready to give my eyeteeth (or my new fangs) for Colin Farrell's autograph.

Colin Farrell . . . now *there* was someone who'd make a delightful snack.

# Chapter 5

"**FATHER**," I said, "you have to help me."

"I'll be glad to, but I'm not a priest."

"I'm going to hell, and I didn't do a damned thing to deserve being damned. Except for that whole double homicide thing. But it was an accident! Plus, I should get points for saving Justine and her mom."

"I said I'm not a priest, miss. I'm the janitor. And this isn't a Catholic church—we're Presbyterians."

"Fine, you'll do in a pinch. Can you burn me up with holy water?" I had the man by the shirt and was pulling him up on his toes—he was about three inches shorter than me. "Poke me to death with your crucifix?" I shook him like a rat. "Pelt me with communion wafers?"

He gifted me with a sweet, loopy grin. "You're pretty."

Surprised, I let go of him. He did a shocking thing, then: He flung his arms around me and kissed me. Hard. Really very hard, and he put a lot into it, too; his tongue was poking into my mouth and something hard and firm was poking against my lower belly. He tasted like Wheaties.

"Gluk!" I said, or something like it. I gently pushed him away, but even so he flew over the pew and landed with a jarring thud near the pulpit. The grin didn't waver and neither, unfortunately, did his erection; I could see the small tent in his chinos. "Do it again," he sighed, head lolling back on his shoulders.

"Oh, for—just—sleep it off!" I snapped and, to my surprise, his head dropped onto his shoulder and he started to snore. Drunk, then . . . sure. I should have smelled it on him.

I took another look and cursed myself—of course he was the janitor; he was dressed in tan chinos and a T-shirt that read "D&E Cleaning: We'll Wipe Your Mess!" In my keyed-up panic, I'd grabbed the first person I had seen when I walked into the church. He'd grabbed me back, but that was only fair.

I was still surprised I had managed to get inside the church without bursting into flame. Not that I'd been a rabid churchgoer before I died. I mean, I used to go when I was a kid, but that was mostly to get away from my stepmonster for a couple of hours. That, and the free grape juice. But since I'd moved out of my dad's house, I hadn't been except for the occasional religious holiday. I was strictly an Easter-and-Christmas Christian.

And now, a dead Christian. So I was amazed I was able to enter the sanctuary without exploding. But nothing like that had happened. The door had opened easily and the church was the way they all were: forbidding, yet comforting, like a beloved but stern grandparent.

I cautiously sat down on a pew, expecting a severe ass burning. Nothing happened. I touched the Bible in front of me . . . nothing. Rubbed the Bible all over my face—nope.

Damn it! Okay, I was a vampire. Shocking, but I was getting used to it. Except vampire rules weren't applying! I should be a writhing tower of flame, not sitting impatiently in a pew waiting for God to send my soul to hell.

I glanced at the clock on the far wall. It was after four in the morning; the sun would be up soon. Maybe a morning stroll would finish me off.

I sighed and slumped back against the pew. "What's going on, God?" I whined. "Sure, I haven't exactly been a frequent flyer for church, but what'd I do to deserve this? I was a pretty good gal. I was kind to children and dumb animals. I even volunteered at soup kitchens, for Christ's sake! Okay, so, yeah, I was kind of materialistic, but quality costs. I don't think it's a sin to want the best shoes money can buy. For one thing, they last forever. For another—pride of ownership. Am I right? So, come on. If Hitler wasn't a vampire, how come I am? Well?"

"My dear?"

"Yeeeaaaggghhhh!" I shot to my feet and nearly fell out of the pew.

A little late, I smelled starch, old cotton, and aftershave, and spun to see the minister walking down the aisle toward me. He was a man in his early fifties, completely bald on top with a white

monk's fringe around the sides and back of his head. He wore
black slacks and a black short-sleeved shirt, and there was a small
cross pinned to his collar. His cheeks were pink from where he
had shaved, and he wore thick glasses and sported a heroic Roman
nose. A wedding band gleamed on the third finger of his left hand.
He was about twenty pounds too heavy for his height, which
meant he probably gave the most excellent hugs.

"You scared me," I said reproachfully. "I thought you were
God."

"Not quite, dear." He took in the scene at a glance: Cleaning
Guy passed out and snoring on the floor, and Dead Girl standing
in the pew looking like baked dog shit.

He smiled at me. "It must be Monday."

I ended up telling him the whole story while he fixed coffee
in the fellowship hall, then sat down across from me and listened
patiently.

After the night I'd had, the chairs were sinfully comfortable. I
drank three cups of coffee with lots of cream and sugar (no need
to worry about the waistline anymore) and finished with, "Then I
came here, but none of the doors or Bibles or anything are hurting
me." I left out the part about the cleaning guy trying to mack on
me in front of the pulpit—no need to get anyone in trouble. "You
don't have a cross on you, do you?" I added hopefully.

He unpinned the small silver cross on his collar and handed it
to me. I closed my fingers around it, tightly, wincing in anticipa-
tion, but nothing happened. I shook it. Was this thing on? Still
nothing.

I handed it back. "Thanks, but never mind."

"You can have it," he said.

"No, that's all right."

"No, really! I want you to have it."

His cheeks were flushed, and the color deepened as I grabbed
his hand, pressed the cross into it, and folded his fingers closed.
"Thanks, but it's yours. You shouldn't give it to a stranger."

"A beautiful stranger."

"What?" First the cleaning guy, now the minister! Hitting on
the *dead* girl . . . ewwww!

As if in response to my shocked thought, he blinked and
slowly shook his head. "Forgive me. I don't know what's come
over me." He touched his wedding ring absently, and that seemed
to give him the strength to look me in the eyes. "Please continue."

"There's nothing else. I'm lost," I finished. "I don't have the faintest idea what to do. I'm sure you think I'm nuts, and I sure don't blame you, but could you just pretend to believe me and give me some advice?"

"You're not nuts, and I don't think you're lying," he soothed. He had a faint southern accent which put me in mind of grits and magnolias. "It's obvious you've had a terrible experience and you need—you just need to talk to someone. And maybe rest."

Sure, rest. In the grave? I wish. Instead, now I was looking at a nice long rest in a nice place where you can make nice baskets and potholders, and the walls have nice padding. I was too tired to stab myself in the heart with my coffee spoon to prove my point. I just nodded and stared at my coffee cup. Maybe if I broke it into pieces and ate it . . . ?

"As to why the Bible didn't hurt you, that's quite obvious, dear—God still loves you."

"Or the rules don't apply to me," I pointed out, but even as I said it I realized how arrogant and ridiculous that was. God's rules applied to each and every person on the planet . . . except Betsy Taylor! Shyeah. I mean, I was vain, but even *I* couldn't go *that* far. "So you're saying I should stop with the attempts at self-immolation?"

"At once." He was still touching his ring, and his voice was stronger now, less dreamy. "You said yourself you helped that woman and her little girl, and you haven't bitten anybody. You're clearly in possession of your soul." He hesitated, then plunged. "A parishioner of mine works for a—a nice place in downtown Minneapolis. Could I give you her card? If you don't have a car I'll be glad to drive—"

"I'll be glad to take the card," I said, then added the lie: "I'll call her later this morning."

The minister and I—he'd told me his name but I had forgotten it—parted on good terms, and when I left he was shaking the janitor awake.

I headed home. The minister had thought I was a nut-job, but that didn't negate his advice. My old life was over, but I was beginning to see that maybe . . . maybe I could make a new one.

I was a heartless denizen of the realm of the ravenous undead, and the urge to drink blood (ew!) was getting stronger, but there were ways and ways, and I didn't have to be a lamprey on legs if I didn't want to. For one thing, there were at least six blood banks in this city.

And God still loved me. I had it on good authority, because ministers can't lie. It was like a law.

God loved me (and so, apparently, did the janitor and the minister). It seemed pretty obvious to me now, and I wondered why it hadn't occurred to me earlier tonight: When you try to kill yourself nine or ten different ways, and none of them works, obviously you're meant to be around for a while.

Incredibly, amazingly, I'd been given a second chance. Me, of all people! And I had no plans to waste it. Anymore, anyway.

I was able to flag down a taxi not even two blocks from the church. Since this was Minneapolis as opposed to Boston or New York, taxis were a rare and wonderful thing. Like a helpful Neiman Marcus employee!

I spotted the taxi at the end of the block, going away from me, and lifted my hand in a halfhearted wave. I heard the shriek of tires gripping pavement, and then the cab was swinging around in an illegal U-turn and zooming up to the curb. The driver leapt out and wrenched open the passenger door for me.

"Uh . . . thanks. D'you mind driving to Edina?"

Nothing. Not even a nod. He just stared at me. He was an older man, about my dad's age, with a paunch from too much sitting down, and crumbs in his beard. His shirt buttons strained over his belly, but he looked nice. He was smiling, anyway. Actually grinning goofily, but I didn't want to walk twenty miles, and was in no position to be picky.

I climbed in and we were off. And let me tell you something, if I'd still been looking to die a horrible death, I should have flagged the taxi as soon as I left the mortuary. Beyond any cliché, this guy was nuts. It didn't help that he kept staring at me in his rearview mirror. The blare of horns or the cursing of an early pedestrian would usually bring his attention—briefly—back to the road.

After he'd nearly creamed a bread truck, a newspaper van, a station wagon full of early morning commuters, and a bus, I'd had enough. I might be invulnerable (probably) to a hideously mangling car crash, but my intrepid driver likely wasn't.

"Stop looking at me!" I snapped, cringing as the bus driver laid on the horn. The sonorous bellow filled my eardrums, my world. "Pay attention to the road."

He instantly obeyed, snapping his gaze back to the street. And we didn't have any more problems.

I belatedly realized, when he pulled up to my house, that I had no way of paying the fare. What had I been thinking when I flagged this guy down? I'd been thinking about a nap and a drink, not necessarily in that order.

"Um . . . if you'll wait a minute, I can run inside and—" And what? If memory served, I had exactly forty-eight cents in my wallet. And two tokens for a free car wash at Insty-Lube. Since my birthday party had been canceled, I hadn't gone to a cash machine that day. "Will you take a check? Or maybe no charge, out of the goodness of your heart?" I joked.

He gave me a loopy smile. "Yes, ma'am."

Ma'am? The guy was twice my age, damnit! I had a horrible thought: Had being dead given me wrinkles?

"Well, okay, then," I said doubtfully, covertly feeling my face for crow's feet. "Thanks for the ride."

He zoomed off, still looking at me out his window. I winced as he bounced over the curb and knocked over a mailbox, then scurried up my driveway so I wouldn't have to see more carnage. It was amazing how easy it was in this state to get a driver's license

My house looked exactly the same on the outside, but as soon as I walked in—some boob had left the door unlocked (oh, wait, that was me)—I saw a real mess. Quite a few of my things had been packed into boxes, which were stacked haphazardly all over my living room. The lights had been left on in the kitchen . . . and how much had that cost me while I was being dolled up in the funeral home? I smelled my stepmother's perfume (Dune, and she used too much of it) on the air and had a horrible thought.

I rushed to my bedroom. There were more boxes back here, and several of my dresses were thrown across my bed. A few had fallen off and were crumpled on the floor in puddles of polyester, silk, and cotton.

I flung open the closet door and my worst fears were realized. Some of my clothes were there, and so were my Stride Rites and the cheap flats I'd bought for casual days at the office. But my babies, the Manolo Blahniks, the Pradas, the Ferragamos, the Guccis, and Fendis . . . all gone.

My stepmother had told the mortician to dress me in one of her old suits, slapped a pair of her used knockoffs on my feet, then headed to my house and grabbed my good shoes for herself.

Let me say that again: She slapped a pair of her used knockoffs on my feet, then *headed to my house and grabbed my good shoes for herself*.

While I was still processing this information, I heard a tentative *meow* and looked up in time to see Giselle peeking at me from the doorway. Cool, she made it back okay. I forced a smile and took a step toward her—who knew when she'd been fed last? And what was she still doing here?—only to see her puff up to twice her size and run away so quickly she hit the far wall, bounced off, and kept going.

I sat down on my bed and cried.

CRYING'S okay while it lasts, but you can only do it for so long. Toward the end, you always feel a little silly, like, "Am I still making this noise?" And it's weird to do it when you can't make tears anymore. I could sob, but not a tear in sight. Did this mean I wouldn't pee or sweat, either? I was in no rush to go to the bathroom and find out.

Anyway, eventually you're done, and you have to figure out what to do next. Whether it was to break up with the guy in question, stab the boss, shrug off the stepmother's cattiness, or figure out how to get along as a vampire, something has to come next.

I flopped belly down on my bed, limp as a noodle and completely exhausted. And *thirsty*. But I wasn't going to do anything about that now. Except maybe snack on Giselle—no, I wasn't going to do that, either. I was just going to lie here—my room faced east—and let the sun finish me off.

If I woke up dead again, I'd take it as a sign that I was supposed to move on. If I didn't wake up . . . well, at least that was one problem solved. Hell couldn't be worse than a Wal-Mart after midnight, right?

With that thought in my head, I fell asleep.

# Chapter 6

ℐ awakened instantly, as I had in the funeral home. This was a definite departure from the norm; usually it took me an hour, a shower, two cups of coffee, and the morning commute to wake all the way up. Not anymore. One minute I was dead (ha!) to the world, the next I was wide awake and rising from my coffin. Well, my bed with Laura Ashley sheets.

I felt perfectly awake, perfectly clear. You know how when you take a nap in the middle of the afternoon, you're groggy for, like, two hours afterward? There was none of that. I felt like I'd just had three Frappucinos. With extra sugar!

The first thing I saw was Giselle, perched imperiously at the foot of my bed. She had apparently done plenty of corpse-sniffing during the day and had decided I would do. So the first thing I did was feed her. Just that simple action—something I'd done twice a day for years—was incredibly comforting. Then I took a shower, brushed my teeth, changed into clean, comfortable clothes, and slipped into my tennis shoes.

I was here, I was dead, get used to it . . . or however the chant for vampire rights went. No more suicide games. It was time to adjust and deal. How, I had no idea, but it was important to get started. Momentum usually helped me figure out the rest of the plan.

Step one: Get my shoes back.

𝒜 few words about my stepmother. I could have forgiven her for marrying my father. I could have forgiven her for seeing me as a rival rather than a member of the family. I could *not* forgive her for chasing my father while he was married, bringing him down like a wounded gazelle, and then marrying the carcass.

My father wasn't a saint—still isn't—but Antonia did everything she could to help him fall from grace. You know how some people are born artists or born accountants? The Ant was a born home-wrecker. She even had the right build: falsely augmented breasts constantly swelling out the v-neck of her too-tight sweaters, black miniskirts, bare legs (even in winter! in Minnesota!), and fuck-me pumps.

To complete the stereotype, she was stupid. And blond. She once asked me if lesbians had periods. I managed to choke back the gales of humiliating laughter that wanted to pour forth and explained. "Well, that doesn't make any sense," she had snapped back.

My mother got the house and the humiliation that comes from your family and friends knowing your husband traded you in for a younger, thinner model. My father got Ant and a promotion—she was the definitive trophy wife, and, I'll give her this much, was a great help to his career. I got a twenty-eight-year-old stepmother, at the tender age of thirteen.

The first thing she ever said to me was, "Be careful of my suit." The second was, "Don't touch that." "That" was one of my mother's antique vases, which she'd given to me before Antonia muscled her out.

Yep, she took prisoners and moved in. As for myself, I'll tell the truth and shame the devil: I made no effort to get to know her. I had zero interest in building a relationship with the woman who had destroyed my mother's marriage. Plus, it's hard to be nice to someone when you instantly realize they don't like you. I was everything that was a threat to her: a smart, moody teenager my father loved with all his tiny heart.

About a week after she moved in, when I overheard her referring to my mother as "that cow from the suburbs," I tossed her gold ingot necklace into the blender. Over the sound of my stepmother's screams, I pressed "puree." This was followed by my first trip to a therapist's office.

The Ant was a big believer in therapists. Professionals paid to listen to every complaint you could think up . . . what bliss! Very early on, she proudly explained to me she had been diagnosed with depression, but it was the oddest mental illness I had seen. Medication didn't help, but jewelry did. She would be too depressed to attend one of my school plays, but could always rally for an expensive night out on the town with my dad.

My father, the drone, just tried to keep his head down. To his credit, he never gave in to the Ant's demands that I live full-time with my mother. He had been granted shared custody, and by God he would share me. Instead he kept her quiet with trinkets, and bought me off with shoes, and went to a *lot* of out-of-town seminars. I took the shoes, and tried to get along. Antonia never insulted Mom in my hearing again, and I never again had to toss precious metals into our KitchenAid. But I had little sympathy for either of them. They had made their choices.

I pulled up outside their absurdly large house. It was three stories high, with a red brick exterior and more skylights than a greenhouse. I stared at it, as always surprised by the sheer size—do two people really need thirty-five hundred square feet?—and hopped out of my car. It was a relief to be driving my own car as opposed to being at the mercy of the public transportation system.

Apparently, neither my house nor my car had been sold; nothing of my estate—pitiful as it was—had been settled yet. Well, heck, I'd only been dead a day or two. My family—well, my mom and dad, at least—were doubtless still in shock.

I pushed open the front door in time to hear my stepmother's dulcet tones: "Godammit, Arnie, you should sue their asses off! *They lost your daughter's body!* Now the funeral's been delayed who knows how long, we're going to have to postpone our vacation—Jesus Christ!"

A clink as my father dropped an ice cube into his glass of Dewar's. "I'm mad, too, Toni, but let's give the funeral place a chance. I know they're doing everything they can. If they haven't found—" Here his voice broke a bit, and I instantly forgave him for most of my adolescence. "—haven't found Betsy by tomorrow, I'll make some phone calls."

"If we cancel, we lose the cruise deposit," the Ant warned. Gads! Trapped on a boat with that woman! What the *hell* was my father thinking? "That's three grand, down the drain."

"That's really not my main concern right now," my dad said, very quietly. Oh, now she was in trouble. I could count on one hand how often I'd heard *that* tone.

The Ant, a creature of pure instinct, had the grace to pause. "Oh. Well. Maybe I'll just go on ahead, and you can stay here and—you know. Take care of things."

"Jesus, Toni! I know you and Betsy didn't get along, but for

God's sake, your stepdaughter is *dead*. And all you can think about is that fucking vacation." I heard a few noisy gulps as my dad drained his cocktail. "What's the matter with you?"

"Nothing," the Ant said quickly. "I'm just—in shock, I guess. I wasn't thinking about what I said. I'm sorry, Honey Bear. You look so sad! Poor poor baby. Come here and let Mama fix it."

I gagged and nearly galloped down the hallway before I had to listen to more foreplay. "Stop!" I said, walking into the living room with both hands firmly over my eyes. "You guys aren't naked, are you? Because I've put up with a lot in the last twenty-four hours, but I draw the line at that."

I spread my fingers and looked. My father was slumped in his Laz-E-Boy, and the Ant was frozen in the act of crouching over him and running her fingers through his combover. The look on my stepmother's face was well worth the misery of dying and coming back. "Oh, good, you're still dressed. Anyway. Here I am. Ant, where the *hell* are my shoes?"

Dead (ha!) silence, broken by the crash of breaking glass as the stepmonster's wineglass hit the floor. The color drained from her face all at once, and for the first time I noticed she had a fine network of crow's feet around each eye. She was fifteen years older than me, and right then she looked every minute of it.

"B-Betsy?" My father was trying to smile, but the corners of his mouth trembled and I knew he was afraid. It was awful—my own dad, scared of me!—but I wasn't going to do something about it right that second. I kept walking toward his wife.

"You gave the mortuary a pink suit when you know damn well I hate pink. You gave them your shitty castoffs when you know how much I love designer shoes. Then you snuck in my house and *stole* my good shoes. And then you were going to take a cruise! After seducing my father—again! *On the day of my funeral*." I was having trouble figuring out what made me the maddest.

She'd backed up all the way to the mantel, and in another few seconds would probably crawl into the fireplace. I didn't stop until we were nose-to-nose. Her breath smelled like lobster. Nice! A celebratory dinner on the day of the stepdaughter's funeral. "Now. Where are they?"

"Toni, you really did that?" my father asked. This was typical. He always overlooked the giant, insurmountable issue (daughter returning from the grave) and focused on something more manageable (bitch wife stealing dead daughter's footwear). "You know how long she saved up to buy—"

"She was *dead,* for Christ's sake!" Even now, my stepmonster managed to sound affronted and harassed.

"Hi, Dad," I said. Then, "Antonia, that is irrelevant!" I heard something break behind me, but didn't turn. "Where are they?"

"Elizabeth—I—you—you aren't—you aren't yourself and that's all there is to it!"

"Ant, you treacherous cow, you've never spoken truer words Better tell me where my shoes are." I leaned in closer and grinned at her. She blanched and I heard her breathing stop. "You should see what happened to the last two guys who pissed me off."

"Check her bedroom," a voice said softly from behind me. I turned and there was my best friend, Jessica Watkins, standing in the entryway. Her eyes were red-rimmed. She was wearing a long black see-through skirt over black leggings, a black turtleneck, and her hair was skinned back in a bun so tight it forced her eyebrows up into a look of perpetual surprise. She had forgone makeup to show she was in mourning. I hadn't seen Jessica without mascara since seventh grade. "Mrs. Taylor would have wasted no time in putting them away, you know. So, like I said, you should check her closet." Then she burst into noisy tears. "Oh, Liz, I thought you were dead! We all thought you were dead!"

"Don't call me that. You know I hate that. And I sort of am." I said as she rushed toward me. Before she hit my embrace, I put a hand on my stepmonster's face and shoved very, very gently—she flew sideways and her ass hit the Laz-E-Boy, rapidly vacated by my father. "It's a long story. Prepare to be regaled."

Then my oldest friend wept against my neck while I steered her toward the back bedroom. I glanced back and saw my stepmother staring in stunned silence while my father fumblingly fixed himself another drink.

# Chapter 7

"AND then I decided to get my shoes back and here I am. Honey, can you let go of me for a minute?"

Jess had been clutching my hand with both of hers the entire time I told her what had happened, and reluctantly let go. I flexed it to get the feeling back.

"I can't believe it," she kept saying, shaking her head so hard it gave me a headache to watch. "I just can't believe it."

We were on our knees in the Ant's walk-in closet. I was carefully inspecting my shoes for scuffs and putting them inside the skirt of my stepmother's fourteen-hundred-dollar ball gown (what forty-five-year-old woman needs a ball gown?). My father and stepmother were hiding in the living room, too afraid to come back and talk to me, to find out what happened. I could smell their fear and unease—it was like burning plastic—and while not having to face them any longer was a relief, I felt bad all the same.

And what was up with all the smelling? Suddenly I was Super Sniffer. I mean, since when did emotions have scents? But now I was effortlessly relying on my nose as much as my eyes and ears. I was the Undead Bloodhound! It was weird, but cool.

"I just can't believe it," Jess said again.

"*You* can't believe it? Try waking up dead and attempting to grasp the situation. It's taken me almost two days to get used to the idea. Or at least to start to get used to the idea. And I'm not even sure how it happened, or what I'm supposed to—"

"I don't give a *shit*," Jessica said. "You're alive—sort of—walking and talking, anyway, and that's all I care about." She threw her arms around me again. She weighed about ninety pounds and it was like being grabbed by a bundle of sticks. "Liz. I'm so happy you're here! Today was the worst day of my whole life!"

"What a coincidence!" I cried, and we both got the giggles. I added, "And don't call me Liz, you *know* I hate it."

"Or you'll suck my blood?"

"I'm trying to put that off," I admitted, but couldn't help but dart a glance at her long, ebony neck. "The thought of it makes me want to yark. Repeatedly. Besides, I hate dark meat."

That earned me a sharp poke. I needled Jess whenever I could, because it was a best friend's privilege and also because she was grossly prejudiced. She thought all whites were greedy and treacherous, with the possible exception of yours truly. Admittedly, this could sometimes be a hard case to argue against.

When we met in seventh grade, her first words to me were, "Drop dead twice, you privileged whitemeat schmuck." The fact that she was saying this while clutching a Gucci bag didn't seem to be relevant. My response ("Go cry in a bag of money, sweetie.") startled her into becoming my friend. That's how I made most of my friends: the element of surprise.

"Now that you're undead," Jessica went on, "I expect you to stop repressing me and others of my racial persuasion," which was as big a laugh as I'd had that day. Jessica was about as repressed as Tipper Gore.

"Noted."

"Are you being driven insane with the unholy urge to feed?" she asked in a "would you like cream with that?" tone of voice.

I couldn't help grinning. "Not insane, but I'm super, super thirsty. Like, jump out of bed and work out for an hour thirsty. Dancing at the club all night thirsty. I woke up that way and it's pretty constant."

"Well, stay the hell away . . . I'd hate to have to pepper-spray my best friend."

"Right. After throwing myself off the roof, getting run over by a garbage truck, electrocuting myself, drinking bleach, and committing a double homicide and felonious assault, I sure wouldn't want to be pepper-sprayed."

She smiled. "You're unkillable now. Good. I don't need another phone call like I got last week. And it sounded like those two asswipes got what was coming to them, messing with a mom and her kid in the middle of the night."

"I'm trying not to think about it," I said guiltily.

"I'm just saying, you don't have anything to feel bad about."

"Believe it or not, my new status as vigilante-murderess is the least of my problems. Now, how long have I been dead? What's been going on? I can't ask *them*," I said, jerking my head toward the living room. "He's in shock and she's useless. More worried about losing the cruise deposit than my untimely demise."

Jessica's eyes went all narrow and squinty, but she didn't say anything. What was the point? She'd known the Ant as long as I had. "Well," she began slowly, folding her legs beneath her and clasping her fingers together. She looked like a black praying mantis. "Your dad called me Thursday night. I reacted to the news of your death by calling him a fucking honky liar and slamming the phone down. FYI, I've never called anyone a honky in my life; it's *so* twentieth century. Then I burst into tears. Also very twentieth century. This lasted about eight hours. I talked to Officer Stud—"

"Nick Berry?"

"He called to ask about funeral information. I guess he found out about the accident because he's a cop and all. He was at the funeral," she added slyly. She'd been teasing me about my nonexistent affair for months.

"Oooh, details, who else?"

"Umm . . . most of the gang from work. And John."

"Eww, the guy who picks his nose and wipes it on the walls of his cube?"

"The same. Don't worry, I kept a close eye on Booger Boy. And your former boss was there! He lays you off, you *die*, and the colossal prick had the nerve to be all sad-eyed at your funeral. *And* ask me if I knew where you'd kept the phone number for the copy machine repair guy, and if I knew if you'd taken care of the Carroll shipment before you died."

I burst out laughing.

"Of course, there wasn't actually a funeral . . . they lost your body!" Jessica was warming to her subject; her eyes had a frightening sparkle. "Picture it: We're all standing around, waiting for things to get started, making small talk with people we absolutely hate—"

"The mind reels."

"—and the head mortician guy comes in and tells us there's been 'a slight problem.' Which I thought was weird until I walked into this house and got a look at what weird really was. And speaking of weird, weren't you embalmed? I mean, did it just not affect you, or did your folks cheap out and skip that step, or what?"

"You're asking *me?* How the hell should I know?" I barely suppressed a shudder. The thought of liposuction creeped me out, to say nothing of tubing and embalming fluid. A riddle I was in no hurry to solve, and that was a fact. "Why are you here, anyway? Not that I mind, because you probably saved me from wringing the Ant's neck. But you hate my parents. Don't tell me—you bought up their mortgage from the bank and came over to foreclose on them."

"I wish. Thanks for the idea, though, maybe I'll do that next weekend."

"Jessica . . ."

"I got a look at Mrs. Taylor's footgear at the funeral is all. I knew those weren't her Pradas. So I figured I'd come over and try to get them back."

"It's so stupid," I complained. "She's a whole size smaller than me! They don't even fit her, and she wants them anyway."

"Trash," Jessica said with a shrug. "Who can fathom?"

I smiled at her. She looked like an Egyptian queen, and fought for her friends like a cobra. She positively despised my father and his wife, but braved Hell House the day of my funeral to get my shoes back. "Oh, Jess . . . why? I was dead, for all you knew. I didn't need them anymore."

"Well, *I* did," she said tartly. Which was a lie; Jessica has feet like Magic Johnson. "Besides, it wasn't right. That jerk had to have swiped your dad's keys, snuck into your house, and stole! I knew you wouldn't have wanted her to have them. I figured I'd donate them to the Foot."

I nodded. In her spare time (which was to say, fifty hours a week), Jessica ran The Right Foot. The Foot gave interviewing tips, advice, résumé assistance, and hand-me-down suits and accessories to disadvantaged women to use for job interviews.

"Awesome idea, and bless your heart for thinking of it." I bundled the rest of my shoes into the ball gown, making a sack out of the dress and slinging it over my shoulder like a vampiric Santa. "Of course, there'll be none of that now that I'm back from the dead. If I ever needed fabulous shoes, it's now. Let's book."

I scooped up Antonia's jewelry box, stopped in the kitchen, and handed the sack of shoes to Jess, who looked on with wide-eyed interest as I dumped the Ant's jewelry into the blender, clapped the top on, and hit "liquefy."

The grinding, jarring, and screeching brought her on the run. My father went to hide in his den, comforted by his proximity to old whiskey and new porn.

After a few seconds, during which we all stared at the mightily vibrating blender, I let the whirling blades groan to a halt. I could hear the Ant grinding her teeth, but she didn't say a single word. Just stared at me with equal parts hate and fear.

I liked that just fine.

"Listen carefully, Ant. Pretend—oh, pretend your life depends on it! Don't you *ever* go into my home again without permission. Touch my things again, whether I'm dead or not, and I'll kick your ass up into your shoulder blades." I said this perfectly pleasantly while I yanked the handle off the fridge and handed it to her. "Got it? Super. See you at Easter."

We left. The sight of Antonia O'Neill Taylor shrinking back from me as I passed her was one I'll treasure forever.

# Chapter 8

AFTER some argument, Jessica and I parted ways, and I drove to my mother's house. Now that I had decided to make a new life for myself (not that I had any idea how), I couldn't let another minute go by with Mama thinking I was still dead.

"That's fine," Jessica said, "but you might have explained to Papa and Mrs. Taylor that the reason you're walking around is because you're a vampire." Her voice broke on "vampire" and she smothered a giggle. I couldn't blame her. It did sound ludicrous.

"You saw them," I retorted. "Did they look like they were up for any explanations? Dad wouldn't even come out to say goodbye. And the Ant was busy fishing her mangled jewelry out of the blender."

"Good point."

I had asked Jessica to share the news with whomever she thought needed to hear it, but she was horrified by the idea. "In the movies, the vampire always goes underground," she argued. "Stays dead to their friends and family."

"A, this isn't the movies, and B, I'm not having my friends and family think I'm dead when I'm walking around. This is not a secret! I'm not skulking around in the shadows like some anemic idiot for the next two hundred years. Give me a break."

"What about the government? Scientists? What if they want to capture you or study you? Plus, you've got a death certificate. So your social security number doesn't work, your credit's no good . . . you can't just pick up where you left off. Betsy, think it over."

Those thoughts hadn't occurred to me. How was I going to

make a living? Maybe I could be a clerk on the night shift at a motel, or something. "I—I haven't thought that out yet," I admitted. "Give me a break, forty-eight hours ago I was naked on a slab."

"Ooooh, you finally had a date?"

"Har-de-fucking-har. I'll worry about that stuff later. I've got to get to Mom."

Jessica nodded. "Fair enough. I'll come with you."

"Forget it. It's gonna be hard enough telling her I'm back from the dead without you cracking wise in the background."

"You shouldn't be alone," she protested.

"What could possibly happen to me?"

There was a pause, followed by a grudging, "Good point."

I climbed into my car, slammed the door, and rolled down the window. "Tell or don't tell, it's all the same to me. I'm just saying, I'm not keeping it a deep dark secret. How'd you like it if I hadn't told you?"

"That's different. We're practically sisters."

"People can tell," I said brightly, "by the close family resemblance."

Jessica rolled her eyes. "I'm just saying, you don't have to tell *everybody*. Your family and me, I think. Maybe Officer Nick."

"Detective Nick."

She ignored the correction. "You could invite him over . . . have seductive music playing—something awful by Sade, maybe—and then pounce! He could be your first meal."

I shied away from the thought, even while part of me surged hungrily at the mental image of Detective Nick being my first. "You're ill," I told her. "Also, I hate Sade. Go home and get some sleep."

"I'm not ill. I'm freaked out. Which is a good problem to have, given the alternative. Say hi to Mama Taylor for me. And think it over, blabbermouth. The movies can't be wrong about everything."

Which just goes to show, Jessica hardly ever goes to the movies.


I was parked outside my mom's small, two-story house in Hastings, a small town thirty miles outside St. Paul. Although it was almost midnight, all the lights on the lower level were blazing. My mom suffered from insomnia at the best of times. Which this certainly wasn't.

I bounded up the porch steps, knocked twice, then turned the knob. Unlocked—one of the things I loved about Hastings.

I stepped into the living room and saw an old woman sitting in my mother's chair. She had my mother's curly white hair (Mom had started going gray in high school), and was wearing my mom's black suit, and my mom's pearls—a wedding gift from her parents.

"Who—?" (the hell are you?) I almost asked, but of course it was her. Shock and grief had put twenty years on her face. She'd gotten pregnant with me one month out of high school, and we'd often been mistaken for sisters. Not today.

Mom stared. She tried to speak but her mouth trembled and made speech impossible. She gripped the arms of her rocking chair so hard I heard her bones creak. I rushed across the room and threw myself at the foot of her chair. She looked so dreadful I was terrified. "Mom, it's me—it's okay! I'm okay!"

"This is the worst dream I've ever had," she remarked to no one in particular. I felt her hand come up and gently touch the top of my head. "Yes indeed."

"It's not a dream, Mom." I grabbed her hand, pressed it to my cheek. "See? It's real." I pinched her leg through the skirt, hard enough to make her yelp. "See?"

"You wretched child, I'm going to have a bruise the size of a plum." I felt her tears dripping down on my face. "You awful, awful child. Such a burden. Such a—" She started to cry in earnest and couldn't finish the familiar, well-loved fake complaints.

We held each other for a long time.


"DON'T be scared," I said about half an hour later, "but I'm a vampire."

"As Jessica would say, I don't give a *shit*. Also, you move faster than the human eye can track."

"What?"

Mom tossed a handful of freshly grated Parmesan into the risotto and stirred. "When you ran to me. I blinked and you were at my feet. You moved faster than I could follow. It was like watching a movie that had been speeded up."

"That's not the least of it—I've got a nose like a bloodhound. I could smell your perfume the second I walked in the house, and it's not like you dump the stuff on." I didn't tell her that I could smell emotions, too. Her relief and joy smelled like tea roses.

"Interesting. Either you've been involved in some sort of secret scientific government-sponsored experiment and never mentioned it—"

"No, but that's a good one. I'll have to remember it."

"Or there's a supernatural explanation."

I blinked. Mom had always had a strong practical streak, but she was adjusting to my undead status with unbelievable aplomb.

She must have read my expression, because she said, "Sweetie, you were dead. I was at the morgue. I saw. And now you're back. Do I care why? Not remotely. My prayers have been answered. Not that I prayed. I've spent the last few days positively furious with God."

I was silent, picturing her agony. The long walk down the sterile-smelling hallway . . . sterile, with a faint whiff of death underneath. Burning fluorescent lights. A professionally sympathetic doctor. Then, the identification: "Yes, that's my daughter. What's left of her."

"Just about every culture has legends about vampires," Mom continued. "I've often thought there must be some truth in the stories . . . else why would there be so many of them?"

"By that logic," I said, "I can assume the Easter Bunny will be stopping by this month?"

"Funny girl. Risotto?"

"Please." Mom had stopped crying, washed her face, changed out of the suit she wore to my funeral, and cooked my favorite meal: pork loin with risotto. Like Jessica, she couldn't stop touching me. Like I minded! "I'm *so* hungry, and that smells terrific."

I wolfed it down in about thirty seconds. Then I spent five minutes in the bathroom throwing it all up. Mom held my hair back from my face and, when I finished and slumped dispiritedly on the bathroom tile, she handed me a damp washcloth.

I started to cry, that odd tearless crying that was now my specialty. "I can't have regular food anymore! No more risotto, shrimp cocktail, lobster, prime rib—"

"Cancer, AIDS, death by mugging, rape, homicide . . ."

I looked up in mid-sniffle. Mom looked down at me with the combination of compassion and practicality that was her trademark. I'd seen that look when I told her I was going to flunk out of college. She loved me more than she loved herself, but that never stopped her from telling the truth. No matter how little I wanted to hear it.

"I'd like to be more sympathetic," she said kindly, "but I'm so happy to have you back, Elizabeth. As awful as it's been for you, you have no idea what the last three days have been like for me, for your father and your friends—I thought Jessica was going to collapse at the funeral home. I didn't think the girl *could* cry, but she practically melted today. Your father didn't even recognize me, he was in such a daze. Your stepmother was—er—upset."

I shook my head at the truth, and the lie. "Oh . . . Mom."

"But I never have to worry about going to the morgue again, unless you trip on a stake on the way home. As to the rest of it: We'll deal, as the kids say. Haven't we been doing just that since you were thirteen?"

I scowled. "I don't think people who can eat risotto should have an opinion."

"Silly child. It's just fuel. In the big scheme of things, this is a minor one indeed. Brush your fangs, and then we'll talk some more." She turned to leave, but not before I saw the smirk.

"Very funny!" I yelled after her.

# Chapter 9

$\mathcal{I}$ pulled into my driveway at 4:30 in the morning. I was still feeling vaguely ill after eating real food, but I was immensely cheered by my mom's rah-rah-be-the-best-vamp-you-can-be speech. It had been a long night, but a productive one, and I was ready to drink a gallon of water—not that it would help my thirst—and go to bed.

There was a strange car parked in my driveway, a white Taurus. Sighing, I parked on the street and, as I walked up my driveway, I peeked inside the car and saw the bubble light. Cop. And when I entered my house (lugging the Ant's ball gown and my shoes), I could smell Detective Nick Berry's clean, distinctive scent. Which, by the way, I'd never been able to do before. Whenever I saw him at the station, all I could smell were stale croissants (the doughnut thing is a myth) and old coffee.

He hurried out of my kitchen—what had he been doing, making himself a snack?—and stopped dead when he saw me. His jaw sagged and he made a motion toward the gun in his shoulder holster.

"Oh, *that's* nice," I snapped, slamming the door behind me and dropping the ball gown. "Don't you dare pull a gun on me in my own house. And where's your warrant?"

"I didn't need one, seeing as how you're dead. Also, you didn't lock your front door again."

"I had a few other things on my mind when I left," I grumbled. "Boy, Jessica just couldn't *wait* to tell you, could she?" I'd strangle her the next time I saw her. I said my undeath wasn't a secret, but I didn't mean she should run to the cops first thing. Her match-making was going to be the end of me. Well, probably not. "That jerk . . . friends are the quintessential mixed blessing."

He was staring at me like a dog zooming in on a pork chop. "I didn't believe her—figured it was a rotten joke—but promised her I'd check it out."

"The fact that her family owns two thirds of the state probably didn't figure into your decision," I said dryly.

"The chief had me put it pretty high on my list," Nick admit-ted. He blinked rapidly. "I can't believe I'm discussing this with a dead girl."

"*You* can't?"

"Did you know it's against the law to fake your own death? The D.A.'s gonna be pissed."

"Believe it or not, Nick, that is the least of my problems right now. And I didn't fake anything."

He'd been gaping at me while we talked, and as I kicked off my tennis shoes he crossed the room. To my complete astonish-ment, he pulled me into his arms like a hero in a romance novel.

"Eh? Leggo."

"God," he said, staring into my eyes. We were exactly the same height, so it was a little unnerving. His eyes were light blue, with gold flecks. His pupils were huge. I could see myself staring in them, mouth hanging open. "You're so beautiful."

I was frozen with amazement. Nick had touched me a few times—mostly to shake my hand, and once our fingers brushed when he handed me a Milky Way—but he'd always been cool, pleasant, and nice. Nice Guy nice. I had sensed zero interest, which is why I'd never pursued him, and why Jessica's hints and intimations were so annoying. But now—

"God," he said again, and kissed me. Except it was more like he was trying to swallow me. His tongue jumped into my mouth— at least that's what it felt like—and suddenly I was breathing his breath. This was startling, but not unpleasant. Then: "Ow!" He jerked back and touched his lower lip, where a tiny drop of blood welled. "You bit me."

"Sorry—you thtartled me. I mean, you took me by thurprithe. Oh, thit." I could *not* look away from that tiny little crimson drop. It gleamed. It beckoned. It begged to be tasted. "Nick, you thould go. Right now."

"But you're so beautiful," he whispered, and kissed me again, more gently. I tasted his blood, and that was that. Had I thought I was thirsty before? The strongest, most compelling craving I had ever known completely took me over.

I kissed him back and sucked on his lower lip, which was plump and tasty. Mmmm, the better to eat you with, my dear! Then he was tearing at my clothes like a horny teenager. I heard the "clunk" of his holster hitting the floor, prayed his gun wouldn't misfire, heard the jingle of the coins in his pockets as his slacks hit the floor in a polyester puddle, heard the riiiiiip that meant I'd need to buy a new T-shirt. I had no idea what had happened to my leggings. He could have eaten them for all I would have noticed.

I tore my mouth from his, jerked his face to the side, and bit him on the side of the neck. I wasn't remotely horrified. There was no reticence at all, no maidenly shrinking at the thought of drinking his blood like it was a cranberry spritzer. I couldn't wait. I *wouldn't* wait.

I'd been prepared to really bite down, but my fangs slid through his skin like a laser scalpel, and then his blood was flooding my mouth. My knees buckled as my body truly came alive for the first time since that Aztek knocked me into a tree. Everything was suddenly loud and bright and vivid; Nick's heartbeat thundered in my ears and the dim lighting in the room seemed more like a stadium lit up at night. I could smell his lust—like crisp shavings of cedar.

Nick had gone rigid in my fiendish embrace, but given the firm length I could feel against my belly, he didn't seem to find this objectionable at all. Thank God, because I couldn't stop. He was fumbling at his tidy whities, but couldn't seem to get them pulled down—he'd try and then he'd squirm and shudder against me.

Now, I can count the number of sexual partners I've had on one hand. Okay, on three fingers. Madame Slut I was not. And with every one, as with most women, it took time and manipulation to make me come. Not to mention I had to be naked! That whole three strokes and it's time to ride the orgasm train thing is a pure myth, and I feel sorry for women who believe it and then think there's something wrong with them when they need more than a slap and tickle to get off.

That said, when Nick groaned and shuddered against me while his blood was in my mouth, I was instantly jolted into orgasm, and his dick wasn't anywhere near me. It was still swaddled in his cotton Jockeys, and I still had my Friday underpants on (yech! I was pretty sure it was Tuesday).

It was a shallow orgasm, the kind you get when you're diddling with yourself and squeeze your knees together at just the right moment, but a come is a come (I should stitch that on a sampler sometime). Drinking blood had made everything more *there,* all sensations were more intense and opened a vein of sensuality I never dreamed existed.

His broad swimmer's chest was pressed up against mine hard enough to flatten my breasts. He was sweating and panting, and I abruptly realized I didn't need to drink anymore. My thirst was gone and I felt better than I ever had. I felt like jumping over the house. Maybe I even could.

I stopped drinking and pulled back, licking the bite mark to get the last few drops. Nick clutched me with both hands while he fought to keep his feet; his eyes were rolling and there were beads of sweat on his upper lip. I could still hear his heartbeat hammering in my ears—it sounded like his pulse was about one-sixty. I was shocked—I could have run (and won) a marathon, and poor Nick looked half dead.

"Oh, Jesus—"

"Don't," he whispered against my neck.

"Nick, I'm so sorry, I—"

"Don't stop," he managed. "Do more. Bite me. Again."

The full impact of his request hit me, and in my horror I nearly dropped him. I suddenly remembered the church janitor . . .

*(you're pretty)*

. . . and the minister . . .

*(a beautiful stranger)*

. . . and how odd they'd seemed; odd but, as I was having such a strange night myself, I'd shrugged off their reactions. Now here was Nick, a perfectly pleasant man who had showed no interest in me except as a witness, Nick with his clothes in ruins and blood on his throat, Nick who wanted me to bite him again. *Again!*

Not only could I live through car crashes and electrocution, not only could I toss grown men like they were magazines, but I could make men want me. Me! I mean, I was cute in high school, and carefully maintained my cuteness as an adult, but the boys certainly never fell all over themselves trying to be with me. They did that to Jessica, usually after they got a look at her checkbook.

But now . . . now they looked at me and wanted me, didn't

care if I drained them dry as long as they could hold onto me while I did it.

I got ready to yowl with horror and frustration, when I got a grip *(you've overreacted enough the last two days)* and instead picked Nick up and carried him to my room like he was a blond male Scarlett and I was an undead Rhett.

"SO it's true."

"What is, Nick?"

"Vampires."

"Yes. It's true. I'm really, really sorry." I threw my arm over my eyes. I couldn't look at him. Now that I had satiated my evil thirst, I was thoroughly embarrassed. Talk about your first date faux pas!

He propped himself up on an elbow and looked down at me. I knew this because I peeked. We'd been lying in bed, side by side, for about five minutes, in silence. I was both relieved and frightened when he started talking.

"Don't be sorry. That was the best of my life. I mean, not that we actually . . . never mind. Did you—" He paused. "Did you get enough to . . . um . . . eat?"

I winced. "Yes. I'm fine. Thank you." And now, the incredible awkwardness that happens between two acquaintances who got too intimate too soon and now have to chat. "Uh . . . are *you* okay?"

He touched his neck. I was amazed to see the bite mark was almost entirely healed. "It hardly even hurts." Then he blushed like a kid. It was really charming—weird to see it perfectly in the dark, but charming. "And I came in my pants. Haven't done that since—"

"Last week?" I asked brightly.

"Very funny." He was still feeling his neck. "This is amazing. I can't even feel where you bit me!"

"Like a dog, I apparently have an enzyme in my saliva that speeds up healing."

He burst out laughing. Oh, thank goodness. Then he was rolling over on top of me and nibbling my throat. "Time for another drink?" he asked, and the naked eagerness in his voice made my heart lurch.

"No." I pushed him, but he immediately settled back on top of me. "Absolutely not."

"I don't mind—"

"Dammit! You do, I bet, way down deep inside you, you probably mind plenty. Nick, I *bit* you! I drank your blood and I didn't even ask."

"You never have to ask," he said quietly. "Besides, I wanted you to. I was grabbing onto you just as much as you were grabbing onto me. You didn't have much choice, the way I see it."

I snorted. "You couldn't have hurt me and you sure as shit can't force me. I think you're having trouble figuring out who the victim is here." Did vampirism encourage Stockholm syndrome?

He was still lying on top of me and I could feel his groin pressing against mine; he was throbbing and hard as a pipe. Amazing! The guy had to be in his forties. "I don't feel like a victim. Come on," he coaxed. "Let me in . . . and I'll let you in."

"No no *no*. Never again, Detective Berry, absolutely not. It'd be like rape. It *is* rape. Also, you have to go home and take a shower. Seriously."

He laughed at me, but stopped when I asked, "How'd you feel about me before I died?"

"Uh . . . I thought you were great. Really cute. I mean, beautiful."

"Ever want to slam me up against a wall and try to screw the bejeezus out of me while I drank your blood?"

"Uh . . ."

"Exactly. But you're ready for all that now, suddenly. You don't even mind if I *drink your blood* while we grope. Hello? This is not normal behavior. It's not me you want. It's—it's whatever makes me a vampire. A supernatural gift or whatever—but it's not *me*. It's my undead pheromones. And that's why we're done."

He protested, but I turned a deaf ear, helped him reholster his gun, so to speak, reassembled his clothes, and pushed him out my front door. Even so, he hammered on it for fifteen minutes, begging to be let back in.

I fled to my bedroom and put a pillow over my head, but I could still hear him for a long time.

In the movies, vampires are always these all-powerful jerks who use people like Kleenex. Now I could see why. A clean-cut boy next door who lets you drink his blood, then begs for more of the same, will let you do anything.

Anything at all.

# Chapter 10

"Die, bloodsucking hellspawn!"

My eyes flashed open and I saw the stake descending. Whoever was holding it was probably moving pretty fast, but to me it looked like slow motion. I grabbed the wrist holding the stake and tugged.

The woman flew over my head and sailed across the room. I got a whiff of Chanel No. 5 and steak sauce as she soared through the air with the greatest of ease. She could have been hurt, but she landed on the futon mattress, clearly dragged in while I was sleeping the sleep of the sated animal.

"Dammit, Jessica!"

She crouched on the mattress, almost giggling. "And now," she boomed, her voice artificially deep, "the bloodsucking fiend rises from her grave to mete out harsh punishment to the mere mortal who dared try to end her unnatural life!"

"What the hell is wrong with you?"

She bounced up from the mattress, grinning. "That's the only thing you've got to worry about now, kiddo. Where there be vampires, there be vampire hunters. *They* don't know you're one of the good guys. I figured we could do some drills." For the first time—I never said I was a genius, or even especially quick—I noticed she was wearing jeans, a heavy sweatshirt, kneepads, elbow pads, and a biker's helmet. She looked like an armadillo. "You know, get your anti-stake reflexes really humming."

"Coffee," I groaned, staggering toward the bathroom. I was perfectly awake—and I certainly didn't need to pee—but I was determined to maintain some sort of routine. "And get lost!"

"No way. Now that you're back from the dead, I'm doing everything I can to keep you from biting the big one again. I'm not going through last week again. Liz, are you prepared to *deal with THIS?*" She yowled that last as she leaped toward my back. I had plenty of time to sidestep her, and she hit the wall like a bug and bounced off, landing on her padded knees in front of my dresser. "Ooh, nice!" she said approvingly. "You didn't even turn. We'll add superhearing to the list."

"Please go away," I begged. "I plan to stay inside and wallow in guilt all day. Night, I mean."

"Why?"

Good question. I couldn't tell her about Nick. I was too embarrassed. Plus, since Nick had—err—finished, in Jessica's mind it would count as a CA (carnal act). She'd probably whip out the Sex Calendar and update it on the spot. As a goad to upping the frequency of my CAs, she had started to keep track. The pitiful number I racked up last year was especially humiliating. "Because I'm now an unnatural creature, that's why. Buzz off."

"No way! We're going to fight crime tonight."

"We are, huh?"

"Yup. Also, you're kind of clammy. I tried to take your pulse when I got here, and your wrist is chilly. I know! Let's take your temperature."

I shuddered at the thought. Was I room temperature? Cold-blooded like a snake? Ugh. "Let's not."

"You were impossible to wake up. I made plenty of noise coming in, and you never budged. I even shook you a coupla times—nothing. You were sleeping like the dea—like someone really tired out."

"Well, how come I woke up when you were swinging a stake at my head?"

She pointed wordlessly out the window. It was quite dark. "Waited until sunset."

I shrugged. I was in the bathroom by now, staring at the toilet. I had absolutely no urge to sit on it. Time to think up a new use for it. Maybe unhook it, empty the water out, and plant irises in the bowl?

I took a shower, but it didn't do a thing for me. I mean, it got me clean, but I didn't have that oh-this-is-so-refreshing feeling I usually got from a hot shower in the morning. Evening.

I dried off, quickly got dressed, and found Jessica putzing around in the kitchen. I found out Miss Stabs-A-Lot had been busy while I was resting (it was too deep, dreamless and, let's face it, deathlike, to call it sleeping). She'd set up my computer to download all the pertinent news stories of the day, so when I *(rose)* got up I'd see what had been happening in the world during the day. She'd also bought my house.

"My house," I said slowly.

"Yeah, house, it's a noun. As in, the place you live." She must have noticed my expression remained blank, because she elaborated. "Hey, it was going on the market at the end of the month. You're dead, remember? You don't live here anymore, and since you still had eleven years to go on your mortgage, the bank was kind of interested in getting it back." She handed me a thick sheaf of papers. "It's all taken care of."

I blinked down at the paperwork. "Jess . . . I don't know what to say. This was so thoughtful . . . and *smart*. I hadn't even started thinking about stuff like my house and car—"

"Which I also bought," she added helpfully.

"So quickly? I haven't even been dead a week. How could you do all this stuff in a day?"

"It helps to be ridiculously wealthy," she said modestly. "Also, duh, I'm the executor of your estate, remember?"

"I thought you were joking."

"All the paperwork you signed, you thought that was part of the joke?"

"D'you blame me? I mean, *what* estate?"

She snorted. "Anyway. I started the stuff the day you died. It—it gave me something to do. Besides, I didn't want Mrs. Taylor doing something rotten with your things. Figured I'd legally own it all, have plenty of time to sort through everything, then put it back on the market once everything was—you know—settled."

I shook my head. "No wonder you kicked my ass on the SATs. Okay, well, I suppose I can make my house and car payments to you instead of the bank—"

"Uh-oh, no way."

"Jessica—"

"Forget it."

"You can't just spend all that money—"

"You're dead, I can't heeeeear youuuu . . ."

"—and not get anything ba—"

"La la la la la *la la la la.*" Her hands were clapped over her ears and her eyes were squeezed shut.

I kicked her ankle, very very gently. "Fine, fine, *fine!*"

She opened her eyes and smiled at me, then bent and rubbed her ankle. "Good. And ouch! Besides, it's not a gift. You're not going to have much income coming in for a while, but you'll be ambushing bad guys at night—"

"I haven't decided *what* I'm going to be doing at night."

"So it evens out," she finished with trademark stubbornness. "You shouldn't have to worry about house payments on top of everything else."

"Well . . . thanks. I really don't know what to say. You're too good."

"Damn right I am. I'm gonna be your rich anonymous backer while you go out at night and kick ass for the side of goodness and right. And Lord knows you can't do that on what *you* make. Made, I mean."

I knew I should have fought her more, but the fact was, Jessica could have paid off the homes of everyone we went to high school with, and still have about a billion dollars left over. It was stupid to protest when she had the bucks and the inclination. But I'd find a nonmonetary way to make it up to her.

*Look her in the eyes and tell her to take your money,* a treacherous inner voice whispered. It sounded alarmingly like my stepmother. *Make her bend.*

I shoved the thought away, horrified, and told myself it wouldn't work: Jessica was a woman, and had no interest in seeing what color underpants I had on.

*You can make her be interested.*

"No!"

"No what? Cracking up already? Heck, it's only 7 30. Way too early for hysterics." My phone started ringing. "I'll get it, dead girl . . . we better figure out the phones, too."

I stared into my fridge and thought about how thirsty I was (and tried not to think about all the pints of yummy blood coursing through my energetic pal). Eggs? No. Leftover pasta salad? No, it had been spoiled *before* I died. An orange? That might not be too bad. I could cut it into quarters and suck out the juice.

Jessica trotted back into the kitchen. "Your mom says howdy and to be careful fighting crime. *Man,* she's cool! If anyone else came back from the dead, their folks'd still be in a rubber room. How'd it go last night?"

"I didn't do anything!"

"To your mom? I should hope not."

"Oh. Right. Uh—she was incredibly cool about it. A real one-eighty from Dad and the Ant. Very 'oh, you're a vampire, that's nice, dear, watch out for holy water' . . . like that. Which was surprising, even for her. I guess she took my death really hard. She was really, really happy to see me, and beyond that, didn't give a fig for the details."

"That's how I feel, too. Plus, I can't help it, I think it's so *neat*."

"Please. You sound like a cheerleader."

"Well, I was one. But I can't get over your mom . . . man, I'd give anything to—" I heard her teeth clack together as she made herself stop talking, and I turned my back on her. It was ostensibly to cut up my orange, but actually, it was to give her a few seconds to collect herself.

Jessica was loyal, loving, and marvelous in nearly all ways, but she had the temper of an Everglades gator whose eggs were threatened. And the thing that made her crazy, made her absolutely nuts, was when people fucked with kids. Because, as a kid, she'd been thoroughly fucked with.

Her father invented some dumb little circuit board that every computer in the world needed to work right, and he owned the patent . . . Mr. Watkins was probably the only person on the planet who'd been able to outsmart Bill Gates. The money poured in. He was one of the richest men in the world; he made more in one year than Oprah made in ten. He contributed generously to charities, political campaigns, and cities (six parks, four schools, and seventeen athletic fields had been named after him in this state alone).

When he wasn't accepting worship from the press and public, he studiously ignored his only child. So they lived under the same roof but never really interacted, until she hit adolescence. Then he took an interest. An extreme one.

Jessica went to her mother first, asking her to please "tell Daddy I don't like all the grabbing and stuff, and he tickles too hard." Mrs. Watkins, a former Vegas showgirl—Jessica wasn't beautiful and scrawny by accident—ignored her. She had no intention of upsetting the gravy train.

She tried her mother again when her father started coming into her room dressed only in his tidy whities. She got slapped for telling lies.

The night Mr. Watkins came to her room wearing his birthday suit, Jessica was waiting for him with a baseball bat—the only weapon she'd been able to smuggle to her room without being noticed.

She nearly killed him. Then she threw the bat out the window, called the police, got dressed, and calmly waited. The police were the ones who called the ambulance for her father.

At the station, Jessica told them everything.

Due to the power of the Watkins name, most of the details were kept out of the newspapers. Months went by, months of painful physical therapy for Mr. Watkins, while neighbors took care of Jessica, who had retained a lawyer and was going about the business of becoming an emancipated minor. Mr. and Mrs. Watkins were served with the papers the day Mr. Watkins had been told it was safe for him to eat solid foods again.

Mr. Watkins was so enraged at the thought of his daughter, his property, getting away from him for good with the help of the courts he had expected to control, he drove too recklessly to his favorite four-star restaurant, and plowed into the south side of the Pillsbury building. Neither he nor his wife were wearing seatbelts. Mrs. Watkins was killed instantly. Mr. Watkins hung on for three weeks through sheer rage, then someone mercifully pulled the plug and it was over.

Jessica, at the age of fourteen, inherited everything

She didn't go to the funerals.

"So, I'm gonna try an orange, see if I can keep that down," I said, forcing myself out of the unpleasant reverie. Jessica deserved a mom like mine—everyone did. But there was nothing to be done about it. "Did I tell you I throw up solid foods?"

"A fine party trick. Also, breakfast is served." Jessica held out a glass. One whiff and I knew it wasn't brimming with V-8. There was a green leaf stuck artfully to the side of the glass, which had been chilled, and its rim had been dipped in coarse salt. "It's O negative . . . the universal drink."

"You have garnished my glass of blood," I observed, "with basil and margarita salt."

"Sure. This is no drive-thru McDonald's blood. Aquavit closed!"

"Seriously. Where'd you get it?"

"I'll never tell. But we should set up a minibank or something for you here, so you don't have to prowl alleys looking for a fix. I've got a guy working on that right now. He thinks I'm an eccentric heiress who's setting up her own blood storage in case of a national shortage." She chortled. "He's right, of course. Cheers!"

I took the glass with all the enthusiasm I'd have shown if she was offering me a glass of pureed rattlesnake. The smell was making my head swim, and not in a good way. While Jess looked on, I took a tentative sip and nearly gagged. It was like drinking a dead battery, fallen leaves, a candle that had burned down to nothing. That's what it tasted like. nothing. And that's what it was doing for me, too. I was just as thirsty as I had been when I woke up ten minutes ago.

I handed the glass back, shaking my head. "Nope. It's got to be live."

Her face fell. "Nuts. So much for that plan. You really can't— uh—get nutrients out of it, or whatever? Metabolize it?"

"It's like gulping down a vitamin and saying that's supper. You'd starve to death pretty quick. But thanks for going to all the trouble," I added, because she looked so crestfallen. I had to admit I was pretty disappointed myself. Now I'd have to hunt.

I thought of Nick. *Give him a call, why don't you? He'll be here in a heartbeat.* Then I made the thought go away.

The phone rang again, but I put up a hand to stop Jess from bounding back into the other room. "I'll get it. It's probably my dad, anyway. He's had a day to get over the shock." I walked into my living room, and saw that Jessica had thoughtfully unpacked the boxes and put my things back. She was an exhausting pal, but I was damned lucky to have her on my side. I would do well to keep that in mind. "Hello?"

"Is this Elizabeth Taylor?"

"Yes. And don't joke about my name; I've heard them all."

"Elizabeth Taylor of seven-two-one-seven-five Louis Lane in Apple Valley?"

I yawned and covertly felt my teeth. Nope; fangless. "Yes, and I'm perfectly satisfied with my long-distance service. Thanks anyway."

"Why," the voice—male, sounded like he was in his early twenties—demanded, "are you answering the phone?"

"Because it rang, dope. Now, I'm really very busy, so if—"

"But you're dead!"

I paused. How best to handle this? Who was this guy? Visa? Xcel Energy? "Don't believe everything you read," I said finally. "Also, the checks are in the mail, but since I just got laid off I'd like to make payment arrangements—"

"You're a vampire and you're in your own house answering your phone? Get *out* of there!"

I nearly dropped the receiver. "A, how did you know that, and

B, fat chance! Plus, the mortgage is paid off. I'm not going anywhere. Nighty-night."

I hung up, but almost immediately the phone rang again. If a
phone could ring angrily, mine was furious. Or maybe I was just
picking up the emotions of the person on the other end. Either
way, the phone practically jumped into my hand. "Hello?"

*"Why are you answering your phone?"*

"Because it keeps ringing!" Why, why, *why,* didn't I get caller
I.D. when I had the chance? "Now stop bugging me before I star-
six-nine your ass."

"Wait! Don't hang up!"

Like I would. Could this be another vampire? Even if he
wasn't, he knew I *was.* Maybe he could tell me what's been going
on, give me some pointers. Anything was better than spending the
next ten years finding things out the hard way. "Well," I said coyly,
"I'm very busy."

"Look: Come to the downtown Barnes and Noble . . . you
know where that is?"

"Sure." Hard not to; it took up an entire city block.

"After you feed, meet me in the cookbook section . . ."

"That's mean!" I protested.

"Okay, fine, the humor section."

"That's not much better," I grumbled. "What, are you allergic
to the romance section? And I don't have to feed. I'll just go
right now."

A long pause, so long I thought he'd hung up, when he practically whispered, "You don't need to feed? Have you had time this
evening?"

"It's no big deal. I can go a few days. I mean, so what, right?"

"What?"

"Which word didn't you understand? Are you listening to me?"

"What?"

Was this guy hard of hearing, or just dim? "What do you look
like? How about a codeword? Or a superduper secret undead
handshake we can use?"

"Don't bother," he said, and he sounded incredibly rattled. "I
know what you look like, Miss Taylor."

"Now, how d'you know that?"

"Your obituary. Nice picture, by the way. See you in an hour."
Click.

"Oooh, now that sounds ominous." I quit speaking to a dead

line and hung up. I hoped the Ant hadn't picked a picture for the newspaper that was too heinous.

"What was that about?" Jessica asked.

I just looked at her.

"Hellooooo? My lips are moving, can you understand what I'm saying? What. Was. That. About?"

Convincing Jessica I needed to meet a mysterious someone who knew I was dead—alone—wasn't going to be easy. Best to get it over with.

# Chapter 11

I love my cat. She's a pain in the ass, but she's dependable, and has never once told me to change my shirt because I look like a crack whore in periwinkle blue. Heck, the whole reason I was in this fix was, in part, because of Giselle, but I hadn't gotten rid of her, or even snacked on her. I was definitely a cat person.

Which was why it was unbelievably annoying to discover dogs now found me irresistible. Before I woke up in the funeral home, I had ignored dogs, and they had ignored me, and we'd gone about our separate business. No longer.

By the time I'd gotten out of my car and walked a block, nearly a dozen dogs were following me. They were relentless in their adoration. When I turned to kick them away, they darted closer and licked my ankles and grinned big goofy doggy grins. I don't know why it hadn't happened the other night when I was prowling around Lake Street trying to kill myself in a variety of ways. Maybe my vampire pheromones took time to kick in. Maybe there were more dogs in this neighborhood. Maybe I'd gone insane.

As if the slobbering pack wasn't bad enough, my ears were still ringing from the scolding Jessica had given me. To sum up, she thought going out alone to meet a stranger who knew I was a vampire was (a) crazy, and (b) stupid, and if I was going to do such a thing, I was (c) crazy and stupid. I pointed out that it'd be even nuttier to bring my fragile, mortal pal along for the ride.

When she threatened to follow me, I went out to my driveway and tipped her car over. It was so easy . . . I'd had more trouble, in my old life, opening a garage door. Jessica was impressed, but pissed. I'd never smelled a mixed emotion before, and it was weird as hell—chocolate pudding on fire.

When I left she was willfully messing up my cupboards. She knows it makes me nuts when I can't find things.

I had parked my car in a prohibitively expensive ramp and was getting close to Barnes and Noble when a filthy, mud-spattered black limousine screeched up beside me. The dogs (there were eight: three black labs, a corgi, a golden retriever, two fat poodles, and a mutt; they all had collars and were trailing leashes) were startled by the noise, and I took advantage of that to hiss, "Get lost!"

All the limo's doors popped open.

"Huh?"

And several pairs of hard hands grabbed me.

"Hey!"

And stuffed me inside. The door slammed shut, and off we went.

"I knew this would happen," I informed my captors. "Just so you know. I mean, that phone call was so obviously a trap." My captors—there were four seated across from me (whoa, big seats!) and they made The Rock look puny—were all holding large wooden crosses at arm's length to ward me off. One of them was agitating a small, stoppered bottle, which I took to be holy water. They were a little tense, but hardly stinking of fear. They'd done this before. "Which one of you fellas called me?"

Dead silence.

"Well, okay, be that way, but I'm not scared, y'know. Actually, this is sort of bringing me back to prom night. The rough handling, the over-the-top limo, the sullen expressions . . . ah, it all comes roaring back."

The one opposite me snorted, but the other three remained sphinxlike. They all looked like vague clones of one another: broad through the chest, well over six feet tall, with big hands and big smelly feet. They all needed a shave, they all had dirty-blond hair and brown eyes, and they all smelled like Old Spice mixed with cherry cough syrup.

"Are you guys brothers?" I asked. Nothing. "Well, then, do you all have cocker spaniels? Because you know that saying, about how people start to look like their pets after a while? Because you guys look like cocker spaniels, if spaniels could walk erect and shave most of the hair off of their bodies. And talk. Assuming you guys talk. Which I shouldn't assume, because none of you has said a word. It's just me doing all the chatting. Which is fine, I don't mind carrying the burden of conversation, though it's just this sort of thing that drives my stepmother up a tree. It—"

"Shut up," the one on the end said.

"Really is unbelievable, I mean, *she* can talk about clothes and dinner parties and pool maintenance ad nauseam but God forbid anybody else get a word in edgewise, it's really—"

"Shut up," they said in sullen unison.

I folded my arms across my chest. "Make me," I said, fearlessly if immaturely.

The spaniel on the end leaned and shoved his cross closer to me. I toyed with the idea of grabbing it, breaking it into a thousand toothpicks, and using one of the toothpicks to clean my teeth, but (a) there wasn't anything in my teeth; (b) it seemed vaguely disrespectful, and (c) I didn't want to tip my hand. They were holding crosses and holy water and they felt safe. I was in no hurry to disabuse them of their quaint notions about vampires.

Which was something to think about, so I thought about it. I assumed if crosses and Bibles didn't work on me, they didn't work on any vampires. But I must be wrong about that, else why the crucifix brigade?

What else didn't work on me, but worked on "normal" vampires? I would have to keep my eyes and ears open, and that was a fact.

As I decided this, I realized the spaniel was still brandishing his cross about four inches from the end of my nose. "No, ah, no, please, it burns," I said politely. And stopped talking, which is what they seemed to prefer. Well, it was nothing to me. I decided to enjoy the scenery.

I groaned when we pulled up outside . . . a cemetery! *Mwah-hah-hah!* Who knows . . . what evil . . . *lurks* . . . in the hearts . . . of men. Oh, puke.

"Come on, you guys," I complained as they prodded me from the limousine. "Must we live out every stereotype? If you're taking me to see a guy in a cape with a high collar, I'll be very upset."

We tromped through the sufficiently spooky cemetery, complete with de rigueur moonlit tombstones, eerie owl hoots (in Minneapolis?), and large, spooky, utterly silent mausoleums. We paused outside the largest and spookiest. According to the six-inch-high letters, this was the CARLSON family mausoleum, a pretty typical name for a region settled by Norwegians.

"Ooooh, the CARLSON mausoleum," I mocked, as the Cocker Boys struggled with the heavy door. "How sinister! What's next, a plate of lutefisk and square dancing? Need a hand with that?" They did not; the door was finally swinging open. "What, no scary creaking sound from rusty hinges? Better get that looked into, it totally ruins the spooky mood thing you've got going here—jeez, don't *shove*, I'm *going*."

I plodded down several steps, past the big stone (yuck!) coffins, through a stone archway, and down another dozen or so steps. Obviously underground, this room was well lit by—of course—torches. There were several people milling about the room, but my gaze went to one right away.

He was unbelievable. Easily the most amazing-looking man I'd ever seen outside of *Playgirl*. Not that I read such trash. Well, hardly ever.

Tall, very tall—at least four inches taller than me, and I'm not petite. He had thick, inky black hair that swept back from his face in lush waves. Not many men could have pulled off the Elvis hair swirl thing, but this guy had it. His features were classically handsome: strong nose, good chin, nice broad forehead. His eyes were beautiful and frightening: deepest black, with a hard glitter to them, like stars shining in the dark winter sky. And his mouth was saved from being tender by a cruel twist of the upper lip. He looked mean and he looked *bad*.

And his body! He was so broad through the shoulders I wondered how he'd fit through the door, and his arms looked thick and powerful. The charcoal suit superbly set off his long frame, and speaking of long, his fingers were slim and straight; they looked deft and capable. Pianist's hands. Surgeon's hands. His shoes were—whoa! Were those Ferragamos? It was a rare and wonderful thing to see a properly shod man in an underground mausoleum. Interestingly, the tips were wet, like he'd rushed through the dewy grass to get here. Which was weird, because he didn't look like the sort of guy who rushed any place.

I started to edge toward him to get another look, when I glanced at his face again. Almost as interesting as his incredible good looks was the fact that he looked as annoyed to be there as I was.

There were other people in the room, too. I guess. Who the hell cared?

"Ah, gentlemen, you bring our newest acolyte!"

The overly booming voice—not, sad to say, from the fella I was admiring—brought me back to myself in a hurry. Yes, there were other people in the room. Other pale people, in fact. Pale, with glittery eyes and white, sharp teeth. They were standing perfectly still, like they were all playing statues. Except they looked ill. Too pale, even for vampires (I guessed . . . what did I know?), and thin, and cold, and ragged. Every one of them had at least one stain on their clothing. That was just sad—being dead was no excuse to get sloppy.

They huddled together and stared at the speaker, and I kind of felt sorry for them. They would have been scary if they hadn't looked so pathetic.

"Now, Miss Taylor, as our newest supplicant, you will be allowed to feed in just a moment. All of you will, in fact."

At this, the horde looked absurdly grateful.

The speaker was approaching me from the far side of the chilly stone room. He wasn't nearly as impressive as the other guy: medium height for a guy, about a head shorter than me, slightly chubby around the middle, a cleft chin (what Jessica would call, with unfailing tact, an "ass face"), watery blue eyes. And—(*groan!*)—dressed in a black tuxedo. Not a cape, but almost as bad.

"Uh, hi," I said, staring at the walking stereotype. In the books and movies, all the vampires were righteously good-looking, even the villains. Guess this guy hadn't read any of the books.

He took one of my hands in his and gripped it tightly. His hand was cold—colder than mine. Then he kissed it with his icky cold lips. I managed not to vomit on top of his bent, balding head. Finally—thank God!—he straightened up and let go of my hand, which I instantly wiped on my leg. Rude, but I just couldn't help it. Being kissed by Bald Boy was like being kissed by a dead fish.

"First, however—and I require this of all new Undead Children—" That's just how he said it, too. You could hear the capital letters. "—You must get down on those dimpled knees of yours and swear fealty to me. Then we will feast, and you will rest at my side, our newest undead child, and my current favorite."

"Dimpled knees?" Who *was* this guy?

I didn't mean to. I didn't want to. But I started to laugh and just couldn't stop. Everyone else in the room stopped rustling and murmuring, and turned shocked gazes in my direction. Except Mr. Gorgeous in the corner. His eyebrows arched and his lips twisted, but he didn't smile. He just studied me with that perfect, icy gaze.

"Stop it!"

"I can't," I giggled.

"I command you to stop laughing! You will not be allowed to drink at the sacred throats of our—"

"Stop, stop, you're killing me!" I giggled and snorted and leaned against the stone bust of a Carlson so I wouldn't fall down. "Next you'll tell me there will be dire consequences for daring to mock your august self."

He pointed a finger at me. Nothing happened. This seemed to surprise him (had he expected me to turn to dust?), and it also pissed him off. "Gentlemen! Punish her!"

This set me off into gales of laughter again. The Cocker Boys approached me, brandishing crosses, and one of them hurled water into my face. I must have sucked some in from laughing, because I started to sneeze. And laugh. And sneeze. And laugh. When I finally had control of myself the Cocker Boys were backed in the far corner, behind Bald Tux Boy, and all the other vampires—except one—were wedged as far from me as they could get.

"Oh, dear," I said. I wiped my eyes. I hadn't actually cried, of course, but my face was wet with holy water. "Oh, that was really great. Well worth the price of parking downtown. And hardly anything is, you know. Except maybe dinner at the Oceanaire."

"You're a vampire," Tux Boy said, except he didn't thunder it majestically this time. It sort of squeaked out.

"Thanks for the news flash, but I figured that out when I woke up dead a couple of days ago."

"But . . . but you . . ."

"Yeah. Well! This has been superfun, not, but I think I'll be going now."

"But . . . but you . . ."

"But . . . but I was curious so I came along for the ride. I mean, if somebody calls you up and knows you're a vampire, and *you* only knew for a couple of days, wouldn't you take a ride?"

"Called you? I—"

"So here I am, and excuse me, but yuck! It's filthy down here. And boring, which is worse. If hanging with other vamps means I have to go the whole movie cliché route, then forget it. Cemeteries? Acolytes? Partying in chilly mausoleums? Pass."

"You—"

"Also, nobody wears a tux this time of year unless they're going to a wedding. You look like an escapee from the set of *Dracula Does Doris*."

I paused for rebuttal, but nobody said anything. They were all just staring at me with their big glittery eyes. I'd been stared at more in the last three days than in the last thirty years, and I couldn't decide if it was cool or annoying.

I shrugged and walked out of the room, climbed the steps, and was back outside in a jiffy. The evening had been mildly educational, but ultimately disappointing. I couldn't believe vampires were so boring and uncool. I had set trends when I was alive . . . apparently it was up to me to carry the coolness torch when I was dead, too. There was no rest for the fashionable.

"Wait." It wasn't a shout; it was a cool command. And, weirdly, my feet stopped moving like they'd been spiked to the ground. I looked down at them in annoyance. Traitors!

I turned. Tall, Dark, and Sinister was rapidly approaching. He'd been the only one not to cringe before me in the mausoleum. At the time, I'd kind of liked it. Now I wasn't so sure.

"What is it? I have to go; I've wasted enough time in this pit."

He ignored me and grabbed my face with both hands, pulling me toward him until our mouths were millimeters apart. I squeaked angrily and tried to pull away, but it was like trying to pull free of cement. I had thought my undead strength was spectacular, but this guy was easily twice my strength.

He was touching my face, examining me like I was a really fascinating specimen, touching my lips, peeling my upper lip back and looking at my teeth.

I snapped at his fingers, which made the corner of his mouth twitch. "Let go! Jeez! I knew I shouldn't have gotten up this morning. This evening, I mean." I kicked him in the shin, which hurt like hell. It was like kicking a boulder. And his reaction was about as animated. "You don't get a lot of second dates, do you, pal?"

"You *are* a vampire," he said. It wasn't a question. He released his grip, and I backed up so fast I fell down.

He blinked down at me, then extended a hand. I smacked it away as I jumped to my feet. "What do you want, a prize for figuring it out? Jeez. Trust me, being dead—"

"Undead."

"—is the only way I would have been hanging around a bunch of too-pale, poorly dressed weirdos. But that is *not* my scene and I'm outta here. Sooo nice to meet you," I added sarcastically.

His hand shot out and grabbed me above the elbow. "I am also taking my leave, but you'll accompany me, I think." The stone face cracked and he almost smiled. "I insist on the pleasure of your company. We have much to talk about."

"My ass!"

"If you wish, although I'd have to see it first to truly comment. If it's anything like the rest of you, I'm sure it's quite nice. Also . . ." He yanked me up against his chest with about as much trouble as I'd have tossing a tissue. That icy black gaze bored into me. I felt everything inside me turn cold. It was like being glared at by an evil yeti.

"You haven't fed tonight, and yet you're energetic. You don't look at all hungry. In fact, you look . . . quite nice. However did you manage that?"

I cleared my throat to work up some spit (tough work, when you don't make much in the way of bodily fluids anymore) and said, "First of all, mind your own business, and second, it's none of your damned business! Now." My voice went hard and cold. I'd never heard it sound like that before, not even when I told the Ant she couldn't send me to military school. "Remove the hand, while you can still count to five with it."

He stared at me for another second, then laughed. I'd never heard chuckles sound so humorless.

"Quit that," I snapped, trying not to show how unnerved I was.

"Yes," he said, almost purred, and my arm was numb from the strength of his grip, "you'll come to my home. And we'll talk. About all kinds of things. And really, girl, it's for your own safety."

"Sorry, but I already promised the Wolfman I'd be his girl. Now let go!" I tugged, furious that my strength, one of the few good things about being a vampire, was useless here.

His other hand was on my face again; his fingers forced my teeth apart and he stroked one of my canines with a thumb. Then he pushed, hard, and I felt a drop of blood hit my tongue. This was shocking, for several reasons: it was delicious—five times better than Nick's—it was cool to the taste, and I didn't think vampires bled.

"I wonder," he said in a low voice, more breath than words, and his thumb was pushing, forcing its way into my mouth, an odd kind of rape and as infuriating as it was exciting. "I wonder what you'll taste like?"

*Well, why don't you find out? Wait. What the hell am I think-ing? This is a very bad man.*

"That'th it. For the latht time, *get off me!*" I shoved as hard as I ever had in my life. And I could hardly believe what happened next.

Although the whole thing took little more than a second, I saw it in slow motion. Tall, Dark, and Psychotic flew away from me like he'd been fired out of a cannon. He crashed back into a monument—a large cross—and *through* it. Stone flew everywhere, because as soon as he hit the cross it blew up and the back of his suit began to smolder. But he kept going, until he smashed into the side of the mausoleum and collapsed to the ground like a sack of dirt.

I didn't wait around to find out if he was dead (again), or pissed, or what. I ran.

# Chapter 12

WHEN I finally slowed and looked around, I saw with amazement I'd trotted sixteen blocks in about three minutes. Summer Olympics, here I come. Assuming they held the races at night.

I was on one of the side streets behind Minneapolis General Hospital, and figured I should go inside and call a cab. Maybe I'd luck out and get a woman cab driver.

I sure as hell wasn't going back to the cemetery—I wasn't meeting up with any of those losers again. And if I *ever* saw that rat bastard Elvis wanna-be sociopath again, I'd have his eyeballs for . . . for something disgusting you'd use eyeballs for.

Every time I thought of his hands on me, his thumb in my mouth, I got hot. No, dammit. I got pissed. Really pissed. I should shove my fingers in *his* mouth, see how he likes it. I should shove my fingers into his windpipe! Up his ass! Around his—

By now I was really stomping down the street, and when a pair of dogs slunk out of the alley, they took one look at me and ran the other way. Well, good! Canines beware! I was not one to fuck with, by God. How dare that gorgeous creep put his hands on me? *Me?* I hardly ever kissed on the first date, much less allowed strange vampires to shove their digits into my mouth.

I was almost relieved when a dull voice cut through the light traffic and the other night noises: "See ya, world." Yes! Something to distract me from the unsettling events of the last hour.

I looked up. Six stories above, a guy a few years younger than me was standing on the ledge. I could see him as clearly as if he was standing six feet away. He was looking down, straight at me.

In a romance novel, it'd be something like "our gaze met and sparks jumped" or something silly, but in fact he looked tired and resolved, and I was gaping up at him with my mouth hanging open like a rube enjoying her first night in the big city.

I knew at once he was waiting until I got out of the way so he could jump without taking the chance of splattering himself all over me. I stopped walking.

The building he was standing on was an old one, built of rough brick, and as I put my hands on the wall, testing the texture, I had a thought—a brainstorm, really. They really are like storms for me—it's like there's this *crash* and then I've got a brand new idea from nowhere. Anyway, I pulled myself up and started to climb. In no time I was skittering up the side of the building like a big blond bug. I was still pissed about what had happened in the cemetery, and worried for the guy on the roof, but couldn't help also being elated at what I was doing. I was climbing *six stories* of vertical wall . . . me! I couldn't even climb that damned rope in gym class, not even the easy one with the rubber grips.

But this was easy. It was wonderful! It required about as much effort as opening a can of Pringles. I was fast, I was strong, I was . . . I was *SpiderVamp!*

I got to the top and gave a little jump, which sent me soaring a few feet in the air, then I landed on the roof and bowed. "Ta-da!"

He was really cute. Dressed in scrubs which—mmmm—smelled like dried blood (ewww! Did I just think *mmm*?). Here was another guy with deep black hair. Except while Finger Boy gave off an air of understated menace, this fella was throwing off vibes of exhausted despair.

His hair was cut so brutally short I could see the pale gleam of his skull. His eyes were dark green, and he had a goatee that made him look like a tired devil. He was almost as pale as I was and thin, almost too thin. He stared at me with eyes gone huge.

"What have you been eating?" he said at last.

I sat on the ledge beside him. "Let's not go there. It's a long story and you wouldn't believe me anyway."

"I must really be tired," he said, more to himself than to me.

"Nice try, but I'm no illusion. Although in these second-rate tennis shoes, I ought to be. You look like hell, if you'll pardon my saying so."

"Well," he said reasonably, "that makes sense, because I feel like hell."

"It's none of my business, but why d'you want to jump? What happened?"

He blinked at me and shifted his weight. He wasn't nervous to be talking to me, not at all. Probably thought he could jump long before I got to him. And he was *so* sad and unhappy; nothing was surprising him tonight. "I'm sick of kids dying; I'm in debt up to my tits for medical school; my dad's got cancer; I haven't had sex in two months; I'm being kicked out of my apartment because the owner sold his house; I have G.A.D. and my Valium has stopped working for me."

"What's gad?"

"G.A.D. General Anxiety Disorder."

"That's pretty bad," I admitted. "I mean, I don't know what G.A.D. means exactly, but that's a pretty impressive shit list. Except for the sex thing. Typical man, wanting to jump because you haven't dipped your wick in a measly eight weeks. I once went two years."

He pondered that for a minute, then shook his head. "What about you? What happened to you?"

I crossed my legs and got comfy. "Well, I died earlier this week, found out I can't die *again,* my stepmother stole all my good shoes, I can't eat any kind of food, I practically raped a perfectly nice guy last night, met a bunch of vampires who turned out to be every bad movie stereotype imaginable, threw a persistent date through a stone cross, and found out I'm now one of the fastest creatures on the planet. Then I saw you."

"So you're a vampire?"

"Yes. But don't be scared. I'm still a nice person."

"When you're not raping men."

"Right." I gave him my friendliest, most winning smile, the one that had cinched the Miss Congeniality sash for me in high school. Luckily the blood on his scrubs was dry and didn't smell too yummy, or there'd be fangs poking through my pageant smile. "How about we go get a cup of coffee, talk about why our lives suck?"

He hesitated. The wind riffled his scrubs, but his hair was too short and didn't move. He glanced down at the street, then back at me, then down at the street again.

"You know, once I make up my mind, I usually try to follow through . . ."

"Come on," I coaxed. "Vampires exist and you never had the faintest clue, right?"

"Well—"

"Right! Shoot, I know I didn't. I mean, come on! Vampires? Hello, are we trapped in a bad movie? But if we do exist, think of all the other amazing things out there you don't know about. What if—what if there's werewolves and fairies and witches and stuff like that? It's a little early to shut the book on your whole life, don't you think? What are you, twenty-five?"

"Twenty-seven. Are you just luring me down so you can feed on me to quench your unholy thirst?"

Why were people always asking me this sort of thing? "Noooo, I just don't want you to jump. I can wait a while for my next meal."

"I'll get down," he said slowly, "if you'll make *me* your next meal."

I nearly swooned at the excitement that simple statement brought. "What have you been smoking? You just met me! I'm a ghoulish member of the undead!"

"You're also too cute to be scary, and the last two minutes have been the most interesting in the last three years. So . . . ?"

Still inwardly preening over being called cute, I had to force myself to address the issue at hand. "Pal, you have no idea what you're asking." I tried to sound tough and cool, but since I gasped out the whole sentence I sounded more like a horny cheerleader.

"Sure I do. Part of the reason I'm up here is—"

"You're really, really bummed about your sex life?"

For that I got a ghost of a smile. "Among other things. You were right, I figured there's nothing new in the world except death and people being shitty to each other. I never should have been a doctor. Never wanted to be. But my dad—anyway. it's just death and paperwork and more death. And it feeds my anxiety, which makes work hard, which feeds my anxiety." He trailed off and I saw his eyes shine with unshed tears. He blinked them back. "Anyway. Sorry. So, prove me wrong. Prove a few more things, besides. I want to feel what it's like. I want to feel something besides—besides nothing."

I bit my lip. The poor guy! "Forget it." But I was sidling toward him. I was thirsty, and here was a perfectly sane specimen (or as sane as a clinically depressed suicidal man could be) offering to be my dinner. I was nuts to turn it down. The alternative was taking it by force from some poor jerk.

Why in the world would I hurt or scare someone, when there was a willing guy standing right in front of me? At least he wasn't all goo-goo-eyed and mumbling about my beauty. He was perfectly clear, and curious, and willing, and what was the harm? And why was I trying to convince myself? I had to eat, right? Why was I still talking to myself?

"Okay . . . if I do this, . . . you promise not to jump?" I did a fairly good imitation of a reluctant night stalker.

"Yes."

"Or leap in front of a truck or take a bath with your toaster or comb your hair with a chainsaw?"

He laughed. He looked years younger when he did that. He wasn't afraid at all. And that made up my mind for me. "I promise. Now do it, cutie, before I come to my senses."

I jumped down from the ledge, pulled him down to me, gently. Brought him to me like a lover. His scrubs top had a v-neck, so I just tugged him toward me and bit him. He gasped and went rigid in my arms, then his arms came around me in a strangler's grip.

He went up on his toes and his hips pistoned toward mine. His blood was slowly spilling into my mouth and it tasted like the lushest, most potent wine ever made. My unbearable thirst became—if possible—even more unbearable for a split second, then abruptly abated. Sounds were sharper, the light—such as it was—became brighter. His heartbeat pounded in my ears and he was breathing in ragged gasps. I could smell his sex, hard and urgent and pressing against me, the smell of musk, the smell of life.

I pulled away. Another thing the movies got wrong. Vampires didn't have to drain a person dry . . . heck, I'd probably had half a cup, if that much. And it would last me the rest of the night, easily. I could drink more, of course, but it would be for pure pleasure, not need. I bet that creep from the cemetery drank ten times a night, just because he could.

"No," my dinner gasped.

"Yes, that's all I need."

"Oh, no . . . more, please God, more."

"Thanks, but I don't think you're exactly yourself right now."

He proved me right by grabbing my elbows and glaring into my eyes. "Do it again."

"Don't be greedy. Uh—what are you—?"

He had let go of me and was fumbling at the drawstring of his pants, tugging, and then his pants were around his ankles and his erection filled his hand. He gripped himself so hard his knuckles went white and, while I watched in total stupefaction, pumped

once, twice, three times, and then he was coming and I leapt out of
the way.

We stared at each other for a long moment, then he hurriedly
put away his dick and pulled up his pants, and tied the drawstring
waist with fingers that trembled. He was breathing hard, almost
gasping. I felt like doing some gasping myself.

I blinked. "As God is my witness, I have no idea what to say
to you."

"Me? What the hell did you *do*?" He asked the question in a
tone of total admiration. "One minute I was miserable as hell, the
next all I could think of was—uh—the exact opposite of dying."
He colored, the blood rushing to his cheeks. I could almost hear it.
"I've never done that before in front of—I'm sorry. You have no
idea how weird that is for me."

"Pal, you should walk in my Beverly Feldmans for a day. Hey,
I'm not complaining. Now that I'm recovering from the shock, I
mean. It's no worse than what I did to you. Thanks for taking matters into your own hands, as opposed to trying to plant your dick
in me."

"You didn't practically rape that man," he insisted His gaze
was direct and scarily earnest; I found I couldn't look away. "If
you bit someone and they wanted more . . . it wasn't rape. He
wanted to. In fact, it was probably like he had to."

I didn't want to talk about that. Being overwhelmed by a
bloodsucker and needing to boink them didn't mean the bloodsucker wasn't the bad guy. Right? Right. "Never mind. Let's get
off this roof, what do you say, Doctor . . . um . . . ?"

"Marc."

"I'm Betsy."

"Betsy?"

"Don't start. I can't help it if I've got unholy powers and a
boring first name."

"I'm sorry, it's just—you know, the list is sort of surreal."

"List?"

"Vampire, undead, wicked denizen of the night, unholy thirst,
man-raper, and—Betsy?"

"You're right," I admitted. "The whole thing does sound pretty
ludicrous. What can I say? I didn't choose any of this. I'm just sort
of stuck with it. I guess you could call me Elizabeth if you wanted,
except no one does."

"Elizabeth . . ."

"Forget it."

"Oh, come on."

"Nope."

"How bad can it be?"

"Taylor. Elizabeth Taylor."

He laughed, as everyone does when they hear my name. It was the laugh that made us friends, which I thought was just fine.

# Chapter 13

"**YOU** need a sidekick," Marc announced. He'd just finished his second plateful of steak and eggs. I was sticking with tea and honey.

"I've already got one," I said gloomily. "My friend Jessica."

"I mean a badass, not someone from the secretarial pool."

I stuck a finger in his face. "First of all, do not mock secretaries, nor their pools. They're as badass as can be—you think *management* runs a company?"

"You know a lot about it?"

"I was a secretary until last week."

"Then you died?"

"No, I was laid off. *Then* I died. In fact, I should take a drive by the place . . . it's probably gone up in flames by now." I giggled evilly. "When they laid off the admin staff, they lost the capability to call their clients, make their computers work, make the sorter on the copy machine work, place orders for office supplies, update the database, cut checks, figure out the postage machine, calculate payroll, send overnight packages . . . oh, the humanity." I grinned at the mental image, then got back to business. "Second, Jessica is at least twice as smart as anyone sitting at this table. Third— cripes, how much are you going to eat?" During my scolding he'd again flagged down the waitress.

"I've been a little too depressed to eat lately," he said defensively. "And after what happened on the roof, I'm *starving*. Besides, you're just jealous."

"You're right about that." I moodily stirred my tea. "My mom fixed my favorite meal the other night and I threw it up all over her bathroom."

"But you can drink . . . ?" He nodded toward my tea.

"Apparently. Doesn't do a thing for me . . . sure doesn't make me less thirsty. But it's familiar, you know?"

"Sure. That's why I stay in the ER. It's depressing as hell and you get no closure, but at least I know where everything is."

"If you're so unhappy in that job, why not leave? Go work in a nice family clinic somewhere."

"In this economy?"

"Oh, come on. It's not like you're a bricklayer. You're a doctor, and people always need doctors."

He shrugged and looked down at his plate. "Yeah, well . . ."

"I mean, it must be hard. Working in a children's hospital."

"It's unbelievably awful," he said gloomily. "You would not *believe* the evil shit people do to children."

"I don't want to hear it," I said hurriedly.

"Actually, I want to talk to *you* about it. You've got to—to feed, right? Well, I could get you a list of abusive parents, the ones who like to use their babies for ashtrays, the ones who decide to press a hot iron to the kid's back because she slammed the door a little too hard. And you could—you know. Fix things."

"A blood-sucking vigilante?" I was horrified. And intrigued. But mostly horrified. "Did you not hear me? About how until last week I was a secretary?"

"Not anymore," Marc said smugly. Now that he'd thought he'd found a purpose, his entire demeanor—even his smell!—was different. Gone was the slump-shouldered sad-eyed boy. In his place was the Cisco Kid. "You told me you thought you'd fight crime to atone for your feeding habits, right? Well, where better to start?"

I just shook my head and stirred my tea.

"Well, what's your alternative? You don't seem the type to skulk in the shadows and lure the unwary into your fiendish embrace."

The mental image made me chuckle.

"And another thing—vampires don't giggle."

"This one does. And before I forget . . ." My hand shot out. I pulled him toward me and looked deeply into his eyes. Time to use my unholy sex appeal, for good instead of evil. "I'm glad you're feeling better, but if you should relapse, you won't. Kill. Yourself." I paused, then added for good measure, "I command it."

He stared back. His pupils were dots; the lights in the all-night café were ferocious. "I'll do . . . whatever. The hell. I want. But thanks. Anyway."

I stared harder. *Come on, vampire mojo. Do your thing.* "Don't. Kill. Yourself."

"Why. Are you. Talking. Like this?"

I dropped his hands in disgust. "Dammit! I've been able to make men do my bidding since I woke up dead. And more than a few did my bidding in high school, thank you very much. What's so special about *you?*"

"Thanks for sounding so disgusted. And I have no idea. I— uh—" His jaw sagged and I could practically hear his I.Q. dropping. He stared dreamily over my shoulder. I looked—and nearly fell out of the booth. The psychopath from the cemetery was standing in the doorway of the café, looking straight at me. Ack! His hair was a mess, I was happy to see. I couldn't see his back, but he smelled like burned cotton. Good!

"Oh my God," Marc rhapsodized. "Who is *that?*"

"An asshole," I mumbled, turning back to him and picking up my tea. I was so rattled I sloshed some of the hot liquid on my hand, but I didn't feel a thing.

"He's coming over here!" Marc squealed. "Oh my God, oh my God, ohmyGod!"

"Will you get a hold of yourself?" I hissed. "You sound like a girl with a crush. Ah-ha!" Realization hit, a little slowly as usual. "You're *gay!*" I realized I'd shouted it and everyone in the café was staring at us. Or maybe they were staring at Danger Boy, who was rapidly approaching.

"Duh."

"What, 'duh'? How was I supposed to know? I just assumed you were straight."

"Because you are." He was still staring over my shoulder, hurriedly trying to fix his hair which was so incredibly short it could never be mussed. "*I* always assume everyone is gay."

"Well, statistically that's pretty dumb."

"I don't have to take criticism from an undead breeder . . . helloooo," he cooed. I felt a weight drop on my shoulder: Jerkoff's hand. I shrugged it off and resisted the urge to bite him like a rabid coyote.

"Good evening," Jerkoff said. On top of everything else, he had a killer baritone.

"Fuck off," I said warmly.

He slid into the booth beside Marc. I heard a muffled gasp and thought Marc was going to swoon. "We meet again."

"Yippee fucking skippy."

"I don't believe we've been formally introduced."

"I was just about to take care of that when you stuck your finger in my mouth." I thought about throwing my tea in his face, but the jerk would probably use Marc as a living shield.

"Ah. Yes. Well, my name is Sinclair. And you are . . . ?"

"Really pissed at you."

"Is that a family name?"

Marc burst out laughing. Sinclair favored him with a warm smile. "Is this a friend of yours?"

"None of your fucking business."

"She talked me out of jumping to a grisly death," Marc informed my new archenemy. "Then we came here to plot about all the abusive parents we're going to put an end to."

"We did *not*."

"Did too!"

Sinclair's nostrils flared, he leaned in close for a good look at Marc's neck (a bruise was rapidly forming, but there were no signs of teeth marks), then he looked at me. "You have fed on this man?"

I blushed. Or at least, I felt like I blushed—who knew if I still could? "Again: none of your fucking business."

He drummed his fingers on the table. I tried not to stare. They were sooo long and slim, and I had a vague idea of the power in them. "Interesting. And here you both are now. Hmm."

"Want to join us?" Marc piped up. I groaned, but they both ignored me. "Have a cup of coffee or something?"

"I don't drink . . . coffee."

"Oh, very funny," I snapped. "What are you doing here, Sink Lair? If it's about the bill for your coat, too damned bad—you brought that on yourself."

"Indeed." His gaze was cool. Black eyes bored into mine. It was about as pleasant as it sounds. "A matter I will bring up with you shortly, but as to your question, I am here for your benefit, my dear."

"Don't call me that."

"You can call *me* that," Marc chirped helpfully.

"Nostro wants you dead for your actions tonight. The vampire who brings him your head will be richly rewarded."

"Who the hell is Noseo?"

"Nostro. He's—I suppose you would call him a tribal chief.

Sometimes—often—vampires band together, and the strongest is in charge."

"Why in the hell do they do that?" I griped. "Why don't they just go about their own business like they did before they died?"

"Because they are not allowed to. Vampires are usually forced to take sides."

"Nobody's forced me."

"We will attend to that later—"

"What?"

"—but to answer your question, the undead band together for protection. For a sense of security."

"So this guy Notso is torqued off because I didn't play the game?"

'That, and because of your peals of hysterical laughter when he challenged you."

Marc had been following the conversation closely, and now he stared at me. "The head vamp wanted you do to something, and you laughed at him?"

"For quite some time," Sink Lair added helpfully.

"Betsy, jeez! Didn't he try to off you or something? You're lucky to be here."

"He visited upon her the worst punishment a vampire can endure . . . and she laughed at that, as well." Then, "*Betsy?*"

"Yeah, Betsy, wanna make something of it?"

"Indeed, no." Was the asshole actually hiding a smirk? I looked, and he stared back, expressionless. Must have been my imagination.

"So you're here to try to bring Notso my head?"

"Nostro. And no, I am not. You're far too pretty to behead."

"Barf. Is Nostro short for Nostrodamus? Is the tubby twit that unimaginative?"

Sink Lair looked pained. "Yes, and yes."

"Ugh."

"I quite agree."

"So why *are* you here, Sink Lair?"

"It's SIN-clair, and I should think that would be obvious, even to you—"

"Hey!"

"You are newly undead and clearly a menace to yourself. You don't know any of the rules, and there is now a bounty on your head not seventy-two hours after you first rose . . . well done, by the way. I will take you under my protection."

"And in return . . . ?" I didn't mean to sound like there was a bug in my mouth, but I couldn't help it. I didn't trust this guy as far as I could throw him. Hmm . . . better come up with a new cliché. I already proved I could throw him pretty far. "I mean, there's no way you're doing this out of the kindness of your rock."

"In return, we will discover why you are so different from the rest of us. You should have been in agony when they flung holy water on you. Instead it gave you the sneezes. Once I deduce—"

"No thanks."

There was a long pause. Clearly he had expected just about any response but refusal. Awwww, poor baby.

"Really. I insist."

"I don't care! You're not my father—although you're probably old enough to be, creep, and—"

"How old are you?" Marc asked breathlessly.

Sinclair spared him a glance. "I was born the year World War II began."

I gasped in horror. To think I was attracted to this fossil! Well, it wasn't entirely my fault . . . Sinclair looked like he was in his early thirties. There wasn't so much as a speck of gray in his inky black hair, no wrinkles bracketing his fathomless dark eyes. "Ewwwww! So you're, like, ninety years old? Yuck! Do you have a truss under that suit?"

"You are the most ignorant, prideful, vainglorious—"

"It's more like he's in his early sixties," Marc interrupted hurriedly. "And both of you, mellow out. I don't want to be in the middle of a vampire fistfight."

"Indeed. Go to sleep."

"But I'm ggggzzzzzz . . ."

I shoved my hand out, so Marc's head connected with my palm instead of colliding with the table. I slowly pulled away and gave Sinclair a good glare. "What'd you do that for?" And *how* did you do that? I'd have to try that on the stepmonster sometime.

He looked back, cool as a baby lying on a pile of ice cubes. "It was inappropriate for him to hear so much about us. Which is another matter I mean to take up with you. Is it true that you have told your family you are still alive?"

"I'm not still alive, it's none of your business, how'd you find out?"

He ignored my questions. "You must not do such things. You endanger the very ones you would seek to protect."

"Yeah? What do you know about it?"

"Well, I—"

"I don't actually want an answer," I explained. "I'm starting a rant, here."

"Sorry."

"And another thing: Has anyone ever told you, you don't use contractions? Everything is 'you are' and 'I am' and 'you would'. Is this the way they talked during Dubya-Dubya-two?"

"Has anyone ever told you that you lack focus?"

"Sure," I said. I drained my tea and set it down, hard. Marc snored on, oblivious. "Now listen up. I don't appreciate being grabbed, I sure as shit didn't care for your greasy fingers in my mouth—"

"I am tempted to put something else in your mouth this minute," he said silkily.

"Shut up! And I don't like you following me and I don't like you putting my friends to sleep."

"He is not your friend. You only met this evening."

"He's a friend I haven't known very long, all right? Again: *not that it's any of your business.* Now buzz off. I can take care of myself, I don't need you, I don't want you—"

"All lies."

I felt my stomach tighten at his insinuation, but plunged ahead. "And I don't want your stupid vampire tribes, either. Just because I'm dead doesn't mean I can't have a life."

Sinclair blinked at that one, and I hurried on before he could interrupt again. "Yeah, I told my family I wasn't dead . . . why the hell not? They're not going to stake me in the middle of the night—well, my real parents won't. I'm coping as well as I can, and I don't plan on hooking up with any of you undead losers. So stop following me and stop bugging me."

"Finished?"

"Uh . . . let's see . . . can take care of myself . . . it's my business who I tell . . . undead losers . . . stop bugging me . . . yeah."

"We will speak again. There will come a time, Miss Rogue, when you will badly need my help. I will gladly give it. I hold no grudges." He grinned at me. It was terrifying . . . all white teeth and glowing eyes. His canines looked half an inch long. How'd he do that? No one was bleeding that *I* could smell. "Provided you let me put something in your mouth again."

"Ewwwww!"

"Good night."

Poof! Vanished. Or he moved so quickly I couldn't track him. Either way, the undead Houdini was gone, I was shaking with rage and—oh, no!—lust, and Marc was drooling on the formica.

# Chapter 14

A few days passed without incident, which was apparently too much for my old pain in the ass, Jessica, and my new pain, Marc. The excitement of my return from the dead had died down, no vampire baddies had come knocking, my relationship with my stepmother and father remained the same (she ignored me, he sent checks), and that was just too darned staid for my pals. Never mind that *I* was perfectly happy with the status quo.

I introduced them and, after they bristled at each other for an hour, they decided to share me. I stayed out of it. As long as they weren't fighting, I didn't care what the arrangements were.

Jessica was always threatened when I made a new friend. I'd tried to explain that, no, I did not love all my friends equally, that she was my absolute favorite and would be forever, amen, but it usually fell on deaf ears. And it was strictly a one-way street: Jessica had loads of society friends who wouldn't know me if I slapped them in the face. Which was just the way I liked it. As Michael Crichton wrote in *Jurassic Park,* "You know what assholes congenitally rich people are."

Dr. Marc Spangler, on the other hand, for all his renewed sense of purpose (and proposed conspiracy to assault child abusers), was still fragile and I wanted nothing said or done to him that might send him back up on the roof. He was staying with me while he looked for a new place, an arrangement that suited us nicely: I wanted a roomie who could move around during the day, and he needed a bed.

Before I'd died I never would have done such a thing. Not because I didn't care, but because I wouldn't dare. You just couldn't know about people, what was really in their hearts and what hid behind a smile. But along with an endless thirst for blood, I now had a pretty good radar. I just knew Marc was an all right guy.

And frankly, I had never cared for living alone, which is why I had rescued Giselle from the animal shelter. I'd watch too many scary movies and stay awake all night in terror, flinching at every creak. The thing that terrified me the most were zombie movies. After watching *Resident Evil* I had nightmares for a week. It was ironic, because now I was one of the unkillable monsters. Still didn't like living by myself, though.

Jessica grumbled a bit, but dropped it when I explained about Vamp Radar. And I laid it out for Marc his first night in my house.

"I gotta tell you, I'm kind of worried about you."

"Me? How come?" He was buttering a croissant—ugh! Like there's not enough butter in one already. "I'd think you would have plenty of other stuff on your mind than little old me." He blinked at me exaggeratedly and sucked down the croissant in one gulp.

"I have surprisingly little on my mind. That was not an invitation to slam me," I added when he opened his bread-filled mouth. "It's just—I'm afraid if I turn my back on you, I'll find you up on another roof."

"Never happen," he replied confidently, lightly spraying me. I brushed croissant crumbs out of my bangs. "How come?"

"Because I have an anxiety disorder, not suicidal ideation. And people like me almost never kill themselves. We're too anxious about death."

The absurdity of that statement struck me all at once and I burst out laughing. Marc just grinned at me and wolfed down the rest of the croissants.

The three of us were adjusting, but there was a kind of balancing act for me to maintain between Jess and Marc. And so, because I wanted to keep the two neurotics happy, midnight found me in a private exam room at Minneapolis General, instead of checking out the "Midnight Madness Shoe Sale" at Neiman Marcus. "Only for you," I had said to Jessica. "And I guess you," I'd added to Marc.

There was one thing they both agreed upon: I was not your garden-variety vampire, and the more we knew about my abilities, the better. Marc wanted to get a "baseline," whatever the hell that was, and Jessica was just plain curious, so Marc got us a room at the hospital and the exam began.

"I'm not taking off any of my clothes," I warned him.

Marc rolled his eyes. "Aw, gee, I guess no big thrill for me tonight."

"For any of us," Jessica said dryly. "The girl's the color of a toad's belly and she needs her roots done."

"I do not!" I said, shocked. "I had them done two weeks before I died. My roots are fine."

"I wonder what would happen if you cut your hair?" Marc asked thoughtfully, slipping a thermometer under my tongue. "Would it stay short forever? Would it grow back? *Could* it grow back? Would it magically reappear the next night?" He was staring so thoughtfully at my hair I leaned as far away from him as I could without falling off the table.

"So this Sinclair fella . . . he wants to take you under his wing?" Jessica asked. She was rocketing around the exam room on the doctor's stool. She'd zoom up to a wall, kick off, and careen to the other side. Marc was obviously used to odd antics during an exam, but it was making me claustrophobic as hell. She had officially given up mourning colors for me, and tonight she was sporting green leggings, a buttercup yellow T-shirt, a salmon-colored raincoat, and green flats. "Teach you the vamp ropes?"

"God, he is so *hot*," Marc muttered. By contrast, he was a moving pile of rags in torn jeans and a faded T-shirt with the logo "Drop Dead, Fred" . . . an alarming choice for a physician. "Unbelievably yummy. Hoo, boy, I—hmm."

He peered at the thermometer, cleared it, then promptly stuck it in my mouth again. "By the way, I tested all the equipment on myself before you guys got here, so we know it works . . .'

"This assumes *you* work," Jessica pointed out with a smirk.

"No one hit your buzzer, Rich Girl. Now what were we talking about? Oh, yeah—Sinclair. You should see this guy, Jessica. He looks like the prince of darkness and he moves like a matador. I was sweating just looking at him."

"Yum," Jessica said, impressed. "White boy, I suppose."

"You suppose right, and don't forget, he's a hundred years old," I sneered.

"More like sixty-three, so he's got a lifetime of wisdom and street smarts, not to mention years of experience fucking every which way a guy can think up, to go with a nice, hard, powerful, eternally young body. Jesus, I'm gonna have to quit talking about this before I need to sit down."

"Please," I said thinly. I hadn't thought about the experience factor minus the ick factor of a wrinkled, decrepit body. Which was probably hiding under those superbly tailored suits. "Besides, it doesn't matter a purple crap what Sinclair wants. I'm not playing vamp politics. I'm minding my own business, and he sure as shit better mind his."

"Or you'll throw him through a concrete cross again," Jessica added. "I wish I could have seen it!"

"No you don't," I said glumly. "The whole thing was alternately stupid and frightening. If that's what I can expect from being in a vamp tribe, count me out. I haven't been back and I don't plan to *go* back. It was lame *and* scary, a dreadful combo."

Meanwhile, Marc was holding out a plastic cup. "Fill this."

I stared at it. "Um. I can't."

"Don't worry, you'll have privacy in the—"

"No, I mean, I literally can't. I haven't needed to use a bathroom since I woke up dead."

"Oh. Well, that's fine." But clearly it wasn't; Marc seemed rattled and hurried onto the next part of the exam.

"Think of what you'll save on toilet paper," Jessica said brightly.

"Oh, yeah, that makes it all worthwhile."

Marc slipped the bell of his stethoscope under my shirt. "Deep breath."

"Uh . . ."

"Try," he said, exasperated.

"Hey, watch the attitude, pal! This isn't my idea of fun, you know."

"Both of you be nice. Marc's never done an exam on a talking dead girl before, give him a break."

"Puh-leeze."

"Try," Marc said again.

I did, and I got so dizzy I nearly passed out. And when my breath whooshed out of my dead lungs I nearly threw up.

"Easy, easy."

"*You* take it easy." I slumped over and crossed my arms protectively over my tits. "I'm not breathing again, so I hope you got what you needed."

He was already shining a light in my eye. "Uh-huh," he said, sounding exactly like every other doctor in the world. He shined it in my other eye. "Uh-*huh*."

He backed away from me, shut the light off—not that it made much difference to me; I could still see perfectly well—and looked at my pupils again.

"Jesus!"

I heard the clang as he dropped his eye-thingie. "What? What's wrong?"

"Nothing." He felt around the floor for a second. Because there were no windows in this little antechamber of hell, I guessed it was pretty dark. Jessica was standing stock-still, afraid to move lest she bang a knee into a drawer, and Marc kept groping. If I didn't say anything and they ran into each other, it could get interesting.

"It's about four inches from your left hand," I said.

Marc's fingers brushed the end of the eye-thingie and he grabbed it. Then he got the lights back on and the exam commenced. "Open wide," he said with forced cheer, and I obliged. Then, "Let's see 'em."

"What?"

"Your fangs. Come on, out with them."

I blinked at him. Jessica was edging closer, obviously interested in getting a look-see herself. "I can't."

"Sure you can. You're a restless nightstalker of the night."

"Nightstalker of the night?"

"You hush," he said to Jessica. "Come on, Bets. I want to compare them to your other teeth."

I strained. I even grunted a little. Nothing. "It's no good, I can't."

"Try harder. Think of blood!"

"*You* think of blood," I said, annoyed. "I'm telling you, I can't just make them come out. Maybe when I have a little more experience my teeth will do my bidding, but not this week." I seized his wrist before he could step away from the table. I knew exactly what he was thinking.

Wait, let me clarify. It's not like I read his mind, more like I read his body language and knew what he was going to do next. Another swell vampire trick I found pretty handy. "And don't cut yourself to make my teeth come out, either. There's only so much of this I'm gonna put up with," I warned.

"Okay, okay. Ease up." I let go and could see the fingermarks where I'd grabbed him. They were dead white. He massaged his wrist and glared at me. "Jesus, you've got a grip like an anaconda. Can we please finish this?"

"Oh, like this was my idea?"

Twenty minutes later, after much bitching on both our parts, Marc was finished. He was looking at me a little strangely, which I pretended not to notice. He had watched me climb a building

with little surprise, handled being my dinner well enough, and in-
sinuated himself into my home with no fuss, but the scientist in
him was finally facing black-and-white facts, and apparently that
was a little daunting.

"So, will she live?" Jessica laughed.

"Well." He cleared his throat. "Your blood pressure is ten over
five, your Babinski reflex is nonexistent, your temperature is
eighty—which is why your handshake is so darned clammy—
respirations are three, and your pulse is six. All incompatible with
life."

"Wow," Jessica said, impressed. "Girlfriend, you're incompatible with life!"

"And here I thought I was just incompatible with pink."

"Which means you have to watch your ass, Bets," he warned.
"If you're found during the day and somebody freaks and calls an
ambulance, a doctor is going to pronounce you at the scene, and
then you'll be back in the morgue."

Jessica was now staring at me. "You only take a breath three
times a minute?"

"I guess," I said defensively. "I don't think about it. I mean,
c'mon . . . do you think about your breathing, unless you've got a
cold or something?"

"And she's not clammy," she said loyally. "Touching her is—
is like lying in a cool shade."

"Clammy," I said glumly. "Nice save on the shade thing,
though."

"*But.* Although your vitals are incompatible with life, you're
superstrong, inhumanly agile, and on a liquid diet. Also, you still
have a PERRLA—"

"English, white boy," Jessica commanded.

"Pupils are Even, Round, and React to Light and Accommo-
dation."

"I could have gone to medical school," I said. "Except for all
the math and stuff."

"In fact, your pupils now have a field almost twice as large as
ordinary people. I've never seen anything like it."

"What can I say," I said modestly. "I was always special."

"Yes," Jessica said sweetly, "you even have your own
Olympics."

He ignored us. "There's very little activity at a cellular level—
so you've stopped aging. Not to mention excreting. You say you
haven't taken a piss since you died—which makes no sense, be-

cause you drink liquids all day long—you don't sweat, and you don't cry."

"She's a very freaky girl," Jessica sang off-key. "The kind you don't take home to muthuh . . ."

"Jessica said you can't drink canned blood." He was tapping the bell of his stethoscope against his teeth while he thought out loud. Yuck! I hope he doused it in rubbing alcohol before he clapped it against some other unsuspecting patient's chest. "So there must be something about fresh—living—blood that keeps you going. Is it the electrolytes? The pure energy found in living cells . . . ? I wonder if you harness the—"

"You can't use science to explain everything," Jessica broke in. "There's probably some mystical shit going on, too."

I laughed. "Mystical shit? Is that a technical term?"

We were shrugging into our coats, shutting off the lights, and heading out the side door as quietly as possible. Marc wasn't scheduled to work tonight, and he didn't feel up to answering awkward questions about the talking dead girl on the exam table.

"I don't know. I've never believed in this stuff. Not ever . . . shit, I don't even read science fiction. But some of the stuff I've seen at the hospital . . . as a species, we're incredibly adaptable. We can survive a lot of stuff that would kill just about anything else."

"Yeah?" I asked, impressed.

"Believe it. I've seen kids come into the ER with poles sticking out of their skulls. And the next day they have a huge breakfast and want candy for lunch. It's unbelievable and completely unpredictable. So there's an explanation for—for what you are now. Maybe you're a mutation. Maybe a vampire is just another word for—"

"Mutant freak. Very comforting."

"Man, oh man, the paper I could write about this," he said, eyes glowing with scary fanaticism. "I'd be famous . . . right before they checked me into the psych ward for a pleasant year of pureed apricots and finger painting."

That gave all of us the giggles. The door slammed behind us and we started walking through the alley toward the street, when all hell broke loose.

I sensed the problem before Jessica and Marc did—those two didn't have a clue until the bitch was on us—but I wasn't fast enough. There was a blur and then a small, dark-haired woman with the bluest eyes I'd ever seen had Marc. She'd locked a forearm across his neck and was bending him back so his throat was at the level of her mouth. Jessica was facedown in the snow—while grabbing Marc, Shorty had shoved her into the wall, knocking her out.

"The infamous Betsy," Shorty purred. She was small, probably about five feet tall. Maybe ninety pounds. And clearly as strong as an ox on steroids. Her face was unremarkable, even plain—average nose, bare bump of a chin, narrow forehead—but her eyes were astonishing and lovely. Large and the color of a spring sky, they were fringed with dark, sooty lashes. Her canines were growing while I watched. "At last we meet." Annoyingly, she did not lisp.

"Friend of yours?" Marc gurgled. Half of his air was being cut off and he was bent so far back he was staring at the stars. I could see all the little hairs on his forearms were standing straight up. He was scared shitless, but his tone was just right: casual, unconcerned. I was very, very proud of him. Frankly, I hadn't known he was brave until just then. "Maybe an old school—glkk!—chum?"

"I've never seen her before. Listen, Tootsie Roll, you want to let go of my friend before I jam a cross up your ass?"

She laughed and tightened her grip. Marc gasped, but didn't say anything. She licked the side of his throat and he shuddered, while at the same time he leaned into her. "Oh-ho, this one's had a taste, yes? No wonder you're keeping him close."

"He's *my* lunch. Go grab your own." I took a casual step forward, and she bit him. Savagely—there was none of my tentativeness or care. She ripped off an inch-wide swath of skin, spit it out, then gulped back the blood like a dog sucked down water on a hot day.

Marc screamed, a lost sound in the dark.

I did a little screaming of my own. "Stop it!" I was reeling from the suddenness of the confrontation. A minute earlier we were just stepping outside, for God's sake. Even the cemetery meeting hadn't been this alarming. "Just—quit it, okay? What do you want?"

She stopped drinking. Her pupils were huge. Was that what Marc meant? I shoved the thought away and tried to stay focused as she replied, "You, of course. Your presence is requested by my master."

"Nosehair?"

Her nostrils flared. Blood gleamed on her chin. I actually wanted to lick it off, how's that for sick and disgusting? I could

feel my teeth growing, seeming to fill my mouth. I was so embarrassed I couldn't look at Marc. "Nosehair? Is that supposed to be
a joke?"

"No! I'm jutht really bad at nameth."

"What's wrong with your voice?"

"Never mind. You were thaying about your mathter . . . ?"

"Nostro desires your company. He told me to use any means to
persuade you. Now, I will . . ."

"Okay."

She paused. "What?"

"Okay, I'll go with you. We can go right now. Just let go of
him, all right?"

"Don't you dare," Marc said to the sky.

"Marc, shut up."

"Do *not* disappear with this bitch, Betsy. Bad, bad plan."

*"Marc."*

"Yes, Marc." She gave him a squeeze and I heard his ribs
groan under the pressure. Or maybe that was Marc groaning.
"Shut up." She considered for a long moment. Obviously she'd
expected more resistance. "Well, then."

After what seemed like half an hour, she released Marc, who
just about broke something scrambling away from her. He went
immediately to Jessica, knelt, and fumbled at her neck for a pulse.
"Very well. Come with me now."

"Marc." My fangs were retracting . . . thank God. "You find a
pulse?"

He looked up at me, shivering from the adrenaline rush. His
eyes were huge, and all the color had fallen out of his face. "Yes, I
think she's all right—just knocked out."

Congratulations, Short Stuff, maybe you'll live through the
next hour. "Okay. Take her to the ER. Get her looked at, and have
somebody take a look at your neck. I'm sorry."

"It's not your fault. I'll make up something good. I'll tell the
attending we were mugged, or something."

"I'm sorry." I started walking out of the alley. Shorty watched,
a look of amused scorn on her nasty little face. "I'll be back later."

"Not necessarily," Short Stuff tittered.

"Shut the fuck up, you cunt." I'd never used the C word before
tonight, but she seemed an ideal representation of it. And the
shocked look on her face—as if I'd slapped her, which I sort of
had, only with a word instead of my hand—was almost worth how
awful I felt about what she had done to my friends. *And oh,*

*sweetie, you want to watch out if I catch you with your guard down . . .*

But she was a spear carrier, a soldier. Nostro had sent her to me, had told her to do whatever she could to gain my attendance. His was the hash I had to settle first.

# Chapter 15

"My master will—"

"Shut the fuck up."

"You cannot speak to—"

"Shut the fuck up."

She leaned forward and her eyes went the color of the sky right before sunset. "You don't wish to fight with *me* . . . Betsy."

Ooooh, eyes that change color when she's in a snit. Now I was *really* scared. "You bet I do, Tootsie Roll. Bring it, you cow! Let's see how you do when you're not hiding behind one of my friends."

I must have sounded almost as angry as I felt, because she hesitated. Then she crossed her arms over her chest, doing an admirable impression of someone who hadn't been momentarily frightened, sat back, and stared out the limo window.

Yep, I was back in one of Noseo's limos. It had been waiting at the mouth of the alley like a big black gas-guzzling omen of death. I snapped the antenna off, just for fun, and threw it at Tootsie Roll's head. She ducked—barely. The driver didn't say a word, just held the door for me.

"I am Shanara."

"Shut the fuck up." I fumbled with my pocket—stupid linen trousers, they were going to wrinkle like hell—and tossed her a five dollar bill. "And go buy yourself a real name."

She let the bill bounce off her nonexistent chest, unfolded her arms, and started tapping her long red fingernails on the armrest. She was starting to get pretty pissed but, interestingly, wasn't doing anything. Did Nostril's edict give her permission to hurt my friends, but not me?

Time to find out. "Long red slut nails are so five minutes ago," I informed her. "In fact, it's more like five years ago. Just because you're dead doesn't mean you have to be a fashion eyesore."

"*Un*dead," she snapped.

"Dead," I said implacably. "When was the last time you had a nice steak? Or even a salad? Shit, a piece of toast? Dead people don't eat. We don't eat. *Ergo,* we are dead."

"We have more power than mere mortals can—"

"Blah, blah, blah. Save it for the recruitment center. So, when did you die? You don't look a day over sixty."

Her flat bosom heaved in indignation. "I became gloriously transformed in 1972."

"That explains the nails and the bell bottoms."

"These are in again!" she nearly screamed, pointing to her Gap knockoffs.

"Nope, sorry. I know, I know, it can be hard to keep up. Most people aren't smart enough to pull it off." From the front I could hear a curiously muffled sound, almost like someone was strangling on their own laughter.

Shaloser turned and, quick as thought, slammed her palm against the partition separating us from the driver. The glass cracked but didn't break. "Just drive, oaf!"

"Touchy," I commented. "By the way, Shamu, if you ever touch one of my friends again, I'll bite off all your fingers and stick them up your nose." I smiled pleasantly. "And that goes for ol' Nostril, too."

I was all talk, of course . . . shit, I was a secretary, not an avenger. An out-of-work secretary, I might add. I could type like a son of a bitch, but I'd never thrown a punch.

But I could talk. I could yak until Judgment Day, if I had to.

"You'll pay," she said stonily. "You won't be like this tomorrow."

"Bored and pissed off? God, I hope not."

She flinched like I'd poked a fork toward one of her eyes. Odd, very odd. I quickly thought about what I'd just said: bored? Pissed? God?

"God," I said. Another flinch. "Jesus Christ. Lord. 'Our Father, who art in Heaven . . .' "

"Stop it, *stop it!*" She was practically climbing the door, trying to get away from me. "Don't say it, don't say *Those Words!*"

"Stop talking in capital letters and I won't."

"What? I don't understand you."

"No one with your footwear," I said with a meaningful glance at her Prada knockoffs, "ever could."

"ARE we there yet?"

"No."

"Are we there yet?"

"No."

"Are we there yet?"

"No." ·

"Are we there yet?"

"Shut up! I had to bring you to him but I should not have to listen to another word out of your stupid sheep's mouth! Stop it, stop it, *stop it!*"

"Okay, okay. Say it, don't spray it, bee-yatch." I waited a few seconds, then asked brightly, "Are we there yet?"

"Mercifully," she said through gritted fangs, "we are."

"Hey, neat trick, you're all toothy. Why? Hungry?"

She probably was. She looked ghastly. Too white, too thin, and sort of haggard. Of course, that could just be the residual effect of being trapped with me in a closed space for thirty minutes.

The Ant, my father, and I went on one cross-country trip by car when I was a teen.

One.

"Don't even think about snacking on *me*."

"You wish," she snapped. The limo came to a smooth stop, the door popped open, and Shanara grabbed my elbow and practically shoved me out of the car. "Come along."

"What, no cemetery?" We were standing outside a gigantic house on Lake Minnetonka. It was three stories high, dark green, with four white pillars. It looked like Tara gone bad. All the lights were out, of course. "I thought your boss really went for the stereotypes."

No answer. She just grabbed my elbow again and jerked me along. I could tell she really, really wanted to hurt me. A sensible, intelligent person would use this opportunity to keep quiet and look for escape.

"So, Shanockers, are you this guy's retriever or what? 'I want Betsy, bring me Betsy . . . fetch!' Is it like that? Or are you just such a loser you don't have a life of your own, so you hang onto this guy's coattails? Hey, watch the suit!" I was wearing a tan

linen Anne Klein pantsuit and last year's Helene Arpel flats. I was
glad I wasn't more dressed up, or wearing my good Arpels. I'd
hate for these assholes to think I was trying to look nice for them.

She was pulling me through the house, which, although dark,
seemed well lit to me. She brought me (well, dragged me) through
a set of French doors, which opened to a ballroom. I looked up
warily for the disco ball and was relieved not to see one.

The room was full of about twenty people, all dressed (natch)
in black. The women all wore lipsticks in various shades of red,
and the men were all in tuxedos. Ugh! Rented suits! Is there anything worse?

"Ahhhhhh, Elizabeth." Nostro stood up from a (groan!)
throne. An actual throne at the far side of the ballroom. Really
ugly, too, all gold-plated and shiny and gauche, with a big gold fan
where his head would rest. At least he wasn't wearing a crown.
"Thank you for bringing her, Shanara."

"Arf arf, good dog, that's a good little bitch," I muttered under
my breath.

Sounding like my mom's teakettle, she actually hissed at me
before replying. "Your slightest wish is my most urgent command,
Master."

I snorted. Sha-na-na shot me a look of purest venom. Which I
pointedly ignored. "Listen, why am I here? Why'd you set your
dog on me?"

"You left too quickly last time," Nostro said pleasantly. As he
got closer I was again struck by his nondescript looks. In the
books, the vampire villain is always some superurbane, gorgeous
guy (or stunningly beautiful woman), but old Nostro looked like a
mean-spirited monk, the kind who tortured mice when the other
monks were praying. "I'm very glad you've chosen to return."

"You're so full of shit," I said. There were several gasps, but
no one moved, or said anything.

Nostro forced a smile and went on as if I hadn't said anything.
"Now we can complete the ceremony, and you can join my fam-
ily." He swept his arm around, indicating the others in the room.
"They are most anxious to greet you."

"Yeah, they look like they'd be a laugh a minute. Listen, Nostro, I don't appreciate any of this. I didn't choose to come back
and you know it. Your knockoff-wearing henchwhore here hurt a
friend of mine to get me here. And I'm not participating in any
ceremony. And I want you to *leave me alone.*"

More gasps. Nostro looked around slowly, a cobra watching

for careless mice, but nobody made eye contact. They were all
staring at the floor. Except for me, of course. Too dumb to be
scared, I guess. Or too mad.

Nostro turned back to me and forced yet another smile: I was
amazed to see it. His pupils, I noticed for the first time, were
rimmed in red. It was quite a bit scarier than the big spooky house,
the dumb tux, the stupid throne, and the fake courteous manner-
isms. That stuff just made me want to laugh. The thing he couldn't
help—his creepy, creepy eyes—that was really scary.

"I must insist," he said silkily. "I require your participation in
the ceremony and I will *not* . . ." "Not" was screamed, actually
screamed; I jumped. He continued in a perfectly mild voice.
". . . tolerate you siding with Sinclair."

(Note to self: Either being undead drove this guy crazy, or he
was crazy first.)

"Sinclair?" I was ready to swoon with relief. Not that I was the
swooning type. "You're worried about me siding with *that* rat bastard? Don't sweat it, chief. I wouldn't go near him on a bet.
Yuck!"

Nostro blinked slowly, like a frog. A fat, mean, dead frog.
"You do not wish allegiance with my clan or Sinclair?"

"By jove, I think he's got it!" I said this too brightly, hoping
for a laugh, and was rewarded with silence. I coughed and elaborated. "No, I don't want to hang out with any of you. I don't want
ceremonies or vamp politics or my friends getting ambushed because someone's really hot to talk to me . . . I don't want any of it.
No offense," I added, seeing his expression darken.

"None taken," he said with completely fake sincerity.

I tried really hard to keep the sarcasm out of my tone as I continued. "I just want to live my death the way I lived my life." I
looked around the room, trying to make eye contact with somebody . . . anybody. "Oh, come on!" I said loudly. "I can't be the
only one who feels like this. Don't you guys want to see your
friends? Maybe find your old boss and scare the shit out of him?
Show your parents you're not taking a dirt nap? Why do we have
to huddle together in little undead covens?"

"For protection, for—"

"For bullshit. The stories aren't all true—we've managed to
hang onto our souls. Why can't we stay individuals? Why can't we
turn the goddamned lights on? Why are you all wearing black?
Why do you all look like extras from a B-movie vampire set? Seriously, what's *wrong* with all of you?"

Nostro flinched at "God," just like Shanara had, but other than that, he was completely unmoved by my rallying cry.

"Enough," he said, because a few of the others were looking at me with surprise and not a little curiosity. "I hate to use a cliché . . ."

"*You* do?"

". . . but you're either with us, or with Sinclair. Which is it?"

"Neither! I think you're both creeps with ridiculous names."

"Ridiculous names?"

"Nostro? Come on. I'll bet you a hundred bucks that's not the name on your birth certificate. What's your real name? George? Fred? I bet it's something really mundane. Because boy, oh boy, you are *really* overcompensating."

As soon as it was out of my mouth I knew I'd gone too far. He lunged for me, crossing the six or seven feet between us in a blink, his hands going to my throat, closing off my air. Which would have been a huge problem if I'd needed to breathe more than a few times a minute.

"Join me!" he screamed up into my face.

"Glkk!" I said, or something like it. I knew I should be more frightened than I was, but it was *so* hard to take this yahoo seriously. In the movies, at least, the villain was tall and towering and good-looking and sinister—like Sinclair! Being assaulted by Nostro was like being assaulted by a storefront Santa on a bad day.

He shook me like a maraca and, on cue, the horde descended on us. There were too many of them to do me much damage; all I really saw (and felt) was a flurry of fists. Nostro released his grip and I heard him say, "The pit for her!"

"The pit for me?" I croaked. "Puh-leeze. Do you hear yourself? Oh, wait, I get it, it's not the pit, it's The Pit! DUM-de-DUM-dum."

The mumbling horde bore me away. I didn't try to fight—why bother? The odds were twenty to one. Instead I focused on keeping my footing, which was tough because they were sweeping me along so fast and furiously my toes were barely skimming the floor.

Down, down, down the stairs we went, and before I could so much as get a look at the room they'd swept me into, I was flying through the air, from darkness to more darkness. And someone came down into the darkness with me.

# Chapter 16

THE someone was a girl. Well, she could have been a hundred years old for all I knew, but she looked as if she'd be carded for buying cigarettes. Although it was quite dark in the pit, my undead eyeballs were working just fine, and I could make out her delicate, pale features: blond hair, sharp chin, high cheekbones, and big dark eyes, even more impressive than Shaknocker's. Pansy eyes, I think they're called, large and pretty and fringed with beautifully sooty lashes. Me, I had to pile on the L'Oreal Luscious Lash to prove I even had eyelashes.

We stood in the pit and stared at each other. She looked so young, so fresh; if she'd whipped out a pair of pom-poms and started cheering I wouldn't have been surprised.

Instead, she dropped to her knees and bowed so low her forehead was scraping the pit's bottom. "Majesty, I beg your forgiveness . . . I couldn't help you upstairs, there were too many of them."

"Get up, don't call me that, and don't sweat it. Jeez, will you get up? This floor is disgusting." I shifted tentatively; yup. My shoes were definitely sticking. It was like being in a movie theater after a midnight showing of *The Rocky Horror Picture Show*. "Seriously, get up." I bent, seized her arm, pulled her upright.

"Majesty—"

"Betsy."

"Queen Betsy—"

"Bet. See."

She looked away from me, then shyly glanced back. "I can't. Could you call Elizabeth the Second *Betsy?*"

"Well, no," I admitted, "although someone probably should. And I'm not the queen."

"Not yet," she said mysteriously.

I let that pass. She was a cutie, if obviously deranged. "Where are we? I mean, why am I down here? Is this like the dungeon?"

"If only, Majesty."

"Stop calling—if only? What's that supposed to mean?"

"The Master keeps his Fiends down here."

"I don't suppose Fiends is his code name for bunnies, is it?"

"Even now he is rushing to pull the lever."

"There's a lever, huh? Figures. Is it just me, or are we stuck in yet another bad movie?"

She blinked at me, obviously rattled by all the interruptions. What can I say, I talk a lot more when I'm nervous. "The cage doors will go up," she explained as if talking to a very small, very retarded child, "and the Fiends will be upon us."

"Well, that's a helluva note." I was nervous, but not out-and-out terrified. Not yet. I found the cheerleader extremely interesting. Why did she jump in with me? And why did she have the idea in her head that I was a queen? I wasn't even a Leo. "The walls are pretty steep in here . . . I'm betting this is so we don't have time to climb out. Any suggestions?"

"Yes." The cheerleader was digging in her jeans pocket and came up with a small, thickly padded envelope, the kind you mail computer disks in. She practically threw it at me, so anxious was she to get rid of it. "For you. Only you can wield this."

"Uh . . . thanks. Gee, I don't have anything for you . . ." I opened the envelope and peeped inside. And smiled. I upended the envelope and felt the cool gold chain slide into my hand. It was a beautiful gold cross on a chain so fine even I, with my superorbs, had trouble seeing it in the gloom of the pit. Excuse me, The Pit. I put it on, feeling the teensy clasp with my fingers and getting it hooked around my neck after a few seconds of fumbling. "Thanks a lot. I left mine at home."

"This is why you're the queen. Or you will be. You were foretold, you know."

"No I don't know . . . and who are you, anyway?"

"I'm Tina."

"Thank goodness!" I said so loudly she stepped back. "No silly-ass overdone names for you, m'girl."

"It's short for Christina Caresse Chavelle."

"Well, you did the best you could."

I heard a creaking noise just then, a really obnoxious one. Hinges clotted with dirt were turning with torturous slowness The sound made me want to clap both hands over my ears. I didn't, though. No need to start losing coolness points with Tina who had, after all, jumped into a pitch-dark pit with me and brought me a present. "What the heck is that?"

"The gate is going up. The Fiends are out." Tina said this in a perfectly placid tone, but she was nibbling at her lower lip. "Don't be afraid."

"Are you talking to me, or yourself?"

"Both," she admitted.

"I s'pose we should have done less chatting and more climbing, and now it's too late. You know, if this was a movie, I'd be throwing popcorn at the screen and yelling at the dumbass heroine."

"I had to answer your questions, Majesty."

"Oh, so this is *my* fault? Sure, blame the monarch for everything," I cracked.

She glanced up at me—boy, she was tiny. Barely up to my shoulder, and just as cute as a bug. "They will come at you but over my body, Majesty."

I tried not to laugh. "Thank you, Tina, but that's not very Queen-ey, is it? Cowering behind someone smaller? I mean you're, what? Ninety pounds?"

There was a rushing noise, like wind through capes, and I saw their eyes in the dark, little sullen coals. I counted ten coals. Clearly The Pit had an entrance, other than the top. But the other end was blocked, or the Fiends would be gamboling out in the moonlight like big evil puppies. If we dealt with them (big freaking if), we'd probably have time to climb out, but what then?

Tina stepped in front of me just as the first Fiend reached us. For once I was sorry I could see so well in the dark. They were vaguely human—like the devil is vaguely human. Although they had two legs, they scrabbled about on all fours. Their hair was, to a man (or a woman . . . their sex was indistinguishable), long and lank and kept flopping into their eyes. Their mouths were all fangs: toothy and sharp and terrifying to contemplate. Their cheeks were so hollow they'd be the envy of any supermodel. They were wearing rags, unbelievably filthy and pitiful rags, and though they were there to put the hurt on me, I felt a stab of sympathy all the same. These things were Nostro's pets, and he wasn't taking good care of them.

"Back off, boys," I said, my voice booming around the small

walls. "You don't want to mess with an out-of-work secretary. We're real testy."

The Fiends cringed away from me, but I doubt it was because of my threat. And I suddenly realized I could see a lot better than a few seconds ago.

The cross. The cross around my neck was glowing.

Not much. Not blazing with a pure white light like in the movies. The glow was feeble and yellowish and the cross wasn't burning me, wasn't even warm, but the Fiends couldn't bear it. Neither could Tina; she'd thrown her arms over her face.

"Wait a minute!" The hair . . . the scrabbling motions . . . the way they were more animal than human . . . I knew these things. "You attacked me! You guys attacked me outside Khan's last fall!" I wanted to fall down. I wanted to kick them in their evil ribs. It was a shocking idea, unbelievable, but I suddenly knew how I'd come to be a vampire. These . . . *things* . . . had infected me. Then along came the Aztek a few months later, and whatever the Fiends had put into my bloodstream from the scratches and nips had become active.

Was that why most anti-vamp things didn't work on me? Because I didn't die by a vampire's hand, I'd only been infected by one? Or five?

I shook myself like a dog to get my head clear—I'd been standing there like a dummy, my mouth sprung ajar, but this wasn't the time. The Fiends were still cringing away from me, from the cross. I knew now why Nostro had thrown me down here—these ornery little fellows would have torn a regular newborn vamp to pieces. There but for the bravery of Tina would I be kibble for the Fiends.

"Get out of here," I said softly, and took a step forward. They scuttled back, then turned and fled.

"Come on, shortcake," I said. "Let's get out of this fucking hole. And I've got a few choice words for your boss."

"Nostro isn't my boss," Tina said, sounding mortally offended. I tucked the cross into my shirt and she slowly lowered her arms. "You are."

"We'll talk about it later. Come on."

It was short work for us to climb out of The Pit. The walls were made of brick, and there were plenty of vampire-friendly crevices. Nobody was standing guard—Nostro was pretty confident, then, we'd been chomped. Overconfident asshole—didn't he watch any James Bond movies? You never, *ever* take your eyes off the good guys.

Tina knew the back way out, and I followed her. A few people spotted us, but they were too scared to make a peep. Instead, they shrank back from us and looked everywhere but our faces. Interesting.

Though she'd saved my bacon and I was feeling warm and friendly toward her, I had a rather large problem with Tina's next suggestion.

"No fucking way!"

"Please, Majesty—"

"Betsy, dammit!"

"It's for your safety. Sinclair must know what Nostro tried to do. And what he could not do. This is the chance to band together and defeat him once and for all. If you join Sinclair, Nostro will be destroyed."

"I hate that creep."

"Which one?"

"Both, frankly, but especially that snooty jerkoff, Sink Lair."

"Well." I had the sense Tina was choosing her words carefully. "If you help us defeat Nostro, you will be the reigning queen. You could order the jerkoff to leave town."

"Now that's a little more like it," I said approvingly. "Although I have no queen qualifications."

"Untrue," she said quietly. "I saw. You were foretold."

Some fool had left his keys in a handy unlocked Lexus, so we climbed in and off we went. We drove steadily south. I didn't feel terribly bad—served him right for living in a vampire neighborhood, anyway. Probably *was* a vampire. Besides, I'd leave the car in a safe place. After what I'd been through this week, it was tough to break a sweat over a little grand theft auto.

"Foretold," I said, clutching the armrest as Tina took the turn nearly on two wheels. "You said that before."

"There's a book. We—vampires—call it the *Tabla Morto*. A thousand years ago, vampires knew you were coming. *'A Queen shall ryse, who has power beyond that of the vampyre. The thyrst shall not consume her, and the cross never will harm her, and the beasts will befryend her, and she will rule the dead.'*" Tina nodded in satisfaction.

"My!" I coughed. That bit about the beasts . . . it explained the dogs. During the short walk to the car, every dog in the neighborhood had broken free and come to see me. Tina was wide-eyed while I swore and scolded and tried gently to boot them away. When we drove off they were barking enthusiastically at our taillights. Real subtle getaway. "What a lovely story."

Tina didn't crack a smile. "That's you, Majesty. You're the first vampire in a thousand years who could hold a cross without screaming or throwing up or being burned."

"You should see my other party tricks."

"Nostro threw holy water in your face and you laughed. You laughed." She said this in a tone of complete admiration. "The dogs do your will—"

"The hell they do. They never leave when I tell them to. Just lick my ankles and slobber on my shoes. *My shoes!*"

She quirked a little smile at me. "They don't leave because they know you're not truly angry with them. They just want to be near you. Best get used to it."

"Super." And here I figured I'd had a lot to think about *before* I went in the pit! Tonight was blowing all my circuits. "If that's true, if I'm the foretold SuperVamp, how come you're the only one who knows it? Why were you the only one who came in the pit with me? And thank you, by the way. That was really brave. I didn't know what I was getting into, but you did, and you came down anyway." I touched her shoulder. "If you need a favor, sunshine, you come and see me first."

She gave me the biggest smile I'd ever seen. "Oh, Majesty, it was nothing! It was the very least I could do for you! If I could have gone in the pit alone, I would have." The smile disappeared as quickly as it had shown up. "As to your question, the reason I was the only one to come with you is because Nostro's followers are a pack of fucking cowards."

"Tina!" Not that I'd never heard the F word before, but it sounded especially bad coming out of that cute mouth, that sweet face. Plus, the way she switched from formal English to twenty-first-century jargon was jarring, to put it mildly.

"They won't fight," she said stubbornly. "They do only what he says. Even if it means hurting innocents. Also, you're more myth than reality. Like the second coming of You-Know-Who."

"Christ?"

She shuddered and the car swerved, and then she nodded. "Yes. Him. Everyone knows about it, but how many people really truly believe it? Or would recognize that person if He were to return? They talk about miracles, about walking on water and turning water into wine, but if I ever saw someone doing it, I'd be so afraid. So would a lot of people, I think. Well, that's like you, Majesty."

"Um . . . I don't think you should run around comparing me to

Christ. No offense. That's, y'know, not too cool. I mean, people got pretty pissed when the Beatles did it."

She ignored that. "Every vampire knows about you . . . but hardly anyone believes."

"What about Sinclair?"

"He was the first to suspect who you could be. One of his men called you, asked you to come to the bookstore . . . remember, the night you were kidnapped?"

"Which night?" I grumbled. "Getting hard to keep track." But I remembered. So Sinclair's henchman had called me, not Nostro's. But there was obviously a spy in camp, because Nostro's men got to me first. Sinclair must have busted a gut to get to the mausoleum before I did. I remembered noticing his shoes, trying to get a closer look at them. He'd been leaving wet tracks, as though he'd plowed through the dew and arrived only seconds before I did. "So you work for Sinclair?"

"Yes."

Hmm. That was interesting, if icky. Still, I couldn't help being a bit suspicious of Miss Tina—she knew the back way out of the bad guy's house? She knew how to get out of the pit? But she wasn't *with* the bad guy?

"So," I said encouragingly. "What's the deal with you and Captain Grabby?"

She didn't crack a smile. "Sinclair saved me from Nostro," she said simply. "If not for him, I'd be one of those spiritless creatures."

"I gotta tell you, Tina, it creeps me out that you work for ol' jerkoff. What, you're like his runner or something?"

"I'm his servant, yes."

Ah-ha! "So he's like Nostro."

"No."

Oh.

"I'm with him because I choose to be with him," she continued. "If I wanted to leave tomorrow and live in France and never do another thing for him, he wouldn't demur. I made him, you see."

The car seemed to shrink, suddenly. I stared at her, slowly freaking out, and she stared through the windshield. "You made Sinclair a vampire?" I practically squeaked it.

"Yes. I was desperate. Nostro hardly ever lets us feed, it's his way of controlling us, making sure no one gets stronger than him."

"Creep," I commented.

"Indeed. I found Sinclair in a cemetery at night. His parents

had died that week. Murdered. He was alone in the world. He saw
me . . . I was too hungry for stealth and he saw me."

Tina's voice was getting softer; she could hardly get the words
out. It was as if she was desperately ashamed of her actions that
night, so long ago. "He opened his arms. He invited me to him. He
knew I was one of the monsters and he didn't care. And I—I took
him. I killed him."

"Well . . . uh . . . that's what you guys do, right?"

She shook her head. "That's another thing forbidden . . . we're
only allowed to make more vampires if we have Nostro's permission, but I was starving and I didn't care. He—Nostro—fancies
himself a scientist, and that's why he's making the Fiends—never
mind, I'm getting off track. To sum up, I was careless, and Sinclair paid for it. I was waiting for him when he rose."

I digested that one for a while. I didn't like the story for a number of reasons, and big number one was because it made me feel
sorry for Sinclair. I could picture the scene—him in a black suit,
pale with grief, alone, not caring about anything anymore. And Tina
coming up to him, stick-thin and ghastly white and shaking with
hunger. And how he took her in at a glance and opened his arms to
her, welcomed her. Because he had lost everything, and nothing
else mattered, not even death by vampire. "Wow. That's . . . that's
really something. And he got you away from Nostro."

"Sinclair was strong the moment he awoke. Some—a very
few—are like that."

"How come?"

"Nobody knows. Why are some people born great painters or
great mathematicians?"

"Got me . . . I flunked trig."

"Sinclair's will . . . it's incredible. Nostro didn't want to mess
with him, nobody did. So he let Sinclair go—"

"Why not just kill him?"

"Among other things, Nostro's quite mad, which I'm sure you
could not help noticing," Tina said dryly, "and his judgment is
open to question. Perhaps he was curious. Perhaps he was afraid."

"Perhaps he's a flaming dumbass. This guy's *got* to watch
more James Bond movies. They're like Bad Guy 101. So he let
Sinclair go, and—"

"—Sinclair took me with him, yes. And that's how it's been,
for years and years."

"How old are you?"

"I was born," she said, taking a sharp left and driving down a dirt road—when had we left the city?—"the month and year the Civil War began."

"Wuh . . . hmm. Okay, my mom's really into the Civil War and she'll have about a thousand questions for you later, but meanwhile—how old is Nosehair?"

She giggled at that, but abruptly snapped off the sound, as if it was dangerous to laugh at him, even miles away from his lakeside lair. "No one knows. From his strength, I would guess at least four hundred years. Maybe more."

"Unbelievable." I shook my head. "He's a supreme badass, but I can't look at him without wanting to crack up."

"That has been a problem," Tina said dryly.

"Oh, come on! Don't tell me you're afraid of him."

"I've seen him at work. I watched him slaughter an entire first-grade class while I was too hungry and weak—all of us were—to stop him. I saw him crack their bones and suck out the marrow. I saw—"

"Okay, okay! Jeez, enough of that." I managed to overcome the urge to yark all over the fine leather upholstery. "Um, you said from his strength he must be really old—still can't get my head around that one—what did you mean by that?"

"I told you Sinclair was born strong, but for most vampires, strength is acquired. The longer you feed, the more you learn, and the stronger you become. An eighty-year-old man has more life experience than you, yes? They've—uh—been around the block? Now: Picture the old man in a young body that never gets tired, with limitless strength and speed."

"Gotcha." Unlike most of what had happened to me lately, this made perfect sense.

"So a three-hundred-year-old vampire is much, much stronger than the vampire who rose for the first time yesterday. I suspect Sinclair was an extraordinary man when he was alive, because he was strong so quickly after death."

"Ooooh, Tina! Sounds like you've got the hots for the boss."

She smiled at me. "No, Majesty. I admire him a great deal, but as for the rest . . . I gave that up a hundred years ago."

"That may be the most depressing thing I've heard this week, cutie. Uh . . . sorry." The woman was old enough to be my great-great-great-great grandma, even if she looked like she just made the pep squad. Time to eighty-six the condescending nicknames.

"Majesty, you may call me Mistress Retch if you prefer. It's a pure pleasure to just be in your company."

"That's enough of that." If I'd been able to blush, I would have. "And I still haven't agreed to go to Sinclair's house."

"We're here," she said apologetically, as the gates swung open. We scooted through, fast enough to press me back into my seat, but when I heard the gates crash closed I knew why.

"Damn! The guy doesn't leave the front door open very long, does he?"

"He's a careful man," was all she said.

I mumbled something in reply, and I'm pretty sure Tina caught the word "jackass," but she was too polite to comment.

We pulled right up to the front of the house—it was a gorgeous red Victorian, but after Nostro's palace and, of course, growing up with a zillionaire pal, I was getting pretty bored with grand beautiful manors. Why didn't any of these people live in tract housing?

Tina shut off the car, scooted around the front, then held my door open for me before I'd even realized we'd stopped. "Quit that," I said, stepping out.

"Like the dogs," she said with a smile, "I know you don't entirely mean it. Shall I carry you up the steps, Majesty?"

"Only if you want to feel my foot up your ass," I warned, and she grinned. I was glad to see it. Tina was a little intimidating. And old! Sure, Nostro was old, too, ditto Sinclair, but the difference was, I kind of liked Tina.

The door opened as she approached, and we were ushered inside by a man who was maybe an inch taller than Tina. He had a small, sleek head and a pencil-thin mustache. His eyes were small and set close together, and his features were almost delicate . . . he looked like a clever whippet. He was wearing a billowy white shirt, black tailored pants, and small leather boots. Superdapper. "Hi," I said to the top of his head, because when he saw me he went into a deep bow. "I'm Betsy."

That straightened him up in a hurry. "Betsy?"

"Dennis . . ." Tina warned.

"You mean the future queen of the undead—*my* future queen?—is named Betsy?"

"Hey, it's a family name," I said defensively. "Short for Elizabeth, but don't call me that, I don't like it."

"Elizabeth is eminently more suitable to your station."

"Who cares? And I'm not going to be the queen of anything; I've got enough problems of my own without taking responsibility for a bunch of two-legged parasites. And will somebody get these dogs away from me?" To add to Sinclair's odious qualities, he apparently kept a hundred dogs. On closer inspection, it was more like six, all big fat black Labs. All slobbery. Thank God I was wearing last year's shoes!

"It's just a shock, that's all," Dennis said, looking me up and down. "You're—different from what I expected." Then, "Did you just call me a two-legged parasite?"

"Hey, I know your voice! You're the guy who called me to get me to the bookstore."

He bowed again. "It was my pleasure to be of service."

"Yeah, nice work—I got snatched by Noseo's henchmen, the Cocker Spaniel Boys."

"Er—what?"

"So thanks for *nothing*," I finished triumphantly.

"Dennis, help me with the dogs," Tina ordered. She looked stern, but as soon as she hustled the dogs into the other room I heard her laughing. At me, Dennis, or the big stupid dogs, I had no idea. Probably all three.

I looked around the entryway. It was a room unto itself, with soaring ceilings and a glorious staircase that looked like it had been lifted from one of the houses in *Gone with the Wind*. God, I loved that book. How could I not? The heroine was a trendy, acquisitive, vain jerk. I read *GWTW* about ten times the year I stumbled across it in high school, and twice a year since then. Sinclair's staircase looked like the one at Twelve Oaks.

Tina came hurrying out, dogless. "If you'll stay here Maj-Miss Taylor, I'll let Sinclair know you're here. Dennis will get you anything you need."

"Yes, I surely will." Dennis had finally remembered his manners. "Tea? Coffee? Wine?"

"I'd love a glass of plum wine," I admitted.

He blinked, then smiled. "Of course. The boss likes that stuff, too. Not me, though. It's like drinking sugar syrup out of a wineglass."

I followed him to the wet bar in the corner. "That's why I like it. Most wines taste like sour grape juice to me. Plum's the only stuff that's sweet enough." I glanced up at the ceiling and saw the mirror over the wet bar. "Jeez, that mirror's bigger than my whole bedroom."

Dennis followed my gaze and lowered his voice. "I'll tell you,

Miss Betsy, I was shocked when I rose and found out I still cast a reflection. It took me days to get over it. I felt like all those movies had betrayed me."

"Why wouldn't we cast reflections?" He cracked a brand-new bottle for me, poured, and handed me the glass. I sniffed—yum! It smelled like sugar and dark purple plums bursting with ripeness. Unfortunately, like coffee and gasoline (don't ask), wine never tasted as good as it smelled.

"Well. Because of not having a soul."

"We have souls. Sure we do. Otherwise we'd do bad things all the time. You know, like politicians."

He dropped the trendy butler attitude and stared at me with what looked a lot like hope. It made him seem much younger. "Do you really think so?"

"I know so." I said this with complete conviction, and added, "Besides, a minister told me."

"A minister? When?"

"Right after I woke up dead. I went to a church to blow myself up, but nothing worked."

If Dennis's eyes got any wider, they were going to fall right out of his head. "You were standing in a—a holy place? You were able to get past the steps?"

"Yeah, yeah, but listen, that's not the point. That whole 'vampires don't cast reflections because they have no soul' makes no sense. I mean, look up." He obeyed. "D'you see the bar? How about the bottles? And the floor? And the chair in the corner? We can see those in the mirror. And dogs and cats. And babies and frogs. They all cast reflections."

"True. But that doesn't exactly make your case about vampires keeping their souls."

"*You* make my case. And so do I. I mean, you probably hated blue jeans before you died, right?"

He actually shuddered.

"Right, easy, don't barf all over the bar. Well, you're not sporting any now, right? You don't have a pile of Levi's squirreled away in the back of your closet, do you? The stuff that made you *you* . . . it's all still there. You're just on a liquid diet now." I took a gulp of my wine. "Like me!"

"You know, there's something there," he said thoughtfully, but he wasn't looking up at the mirror anymore, he was looking at me. He topped off my glass. "Some sort of odd charisma. Even when you're being a pill, I like listening to you."

"Uh . . . thank you?"

"Frankly, Sinclair and Tina are about the only vampires I can stand."

I thought about that for a minute. "I haven't been one very long. Maybe that's what it is."

"No, it's not," he said seriously, "because young vampires are the worst. All they can think about is how hungry they are. You can't have a civilized conversation with them for at least five years."

"Bummer! That's all they do? Eat?"

"And sleep, yes."

"So, they're like newborn babies, except with fangs and rotten tempers?"

"Exactly."

"Well, I'm glad that didn't happen to *me*."

"And that's the question, isn't it?" Dennis was looking at me very closely. "Why aren't you like them?"

"Um . . . clean living?" I guessed.

"No, it's something more."

Uncomfortable with the turn this conversation was taking— not to mention the way Dennis was staring at me like I was an amazing bug—I changed the subject. "Listen, what's taking Tina so long? Where's Sinclair?"

"I think he's feeding with his ladyfriends." He said it just like that, all one word. "I'll see if I can give Tina a hand." He put the bottle away, then hurried up the stairs. "Excuse me, I'll be right back," he said over his shoulder, then got to the top and disappeared around a corner.

I let a minute go by, then said, "Well, screw this." I drained my glass, put it down . . . and then I heard the scream.

I bolted up the stairs after Dennis.

# Chapter 17

It wasn't a bad scream. It was a good scream. It was, in fact, a scream of ecstasy, like when I find out Gucci is having a shoe sale. Sinclair's "ladyfriends"? Try harem.

It didn't take long to find the room, even in a palace like this. I just followed the gasps and groans. By now I was pretty sure whoever had screamed wasn't in trouble, but I was curious. And annoyed—if I was such a vampiric big shot, how come Sinclair the Fink was keeping me waiting?

I opened the door at the end of the hall and saw Tina standing before a large window. She turned, saw me, and spread her hands in apology. "They're very busy," she explained. "I didn't have much luck getting his attention. It should only be a few more minutes."

Curious, I walked over and stood beside her. The window was clear—it was like one of those rooms within a room you saw in police stations. And through the window I could see Sinclair and two—whoops, there was another set of tits—three women. They were writhing and groaning and purring in the middle of a bed that was, if possible, bigger than king-sized. I mean, that bed looked like a satin-covered acre.

It was a four-poster, and each poster was as big around as a tree trunk. The bed was covered in chocolate-colored satin sheets (well, at least they weren't red . . . soooooo last year's *Cosmo*), but the pillows—all nine—had been knocked to the floor.

Sinclair looked happy. He was almost smiling! And he ought to be, in the middle of a brunette nest like he was. The three women all had elbow-length dark hair and sturdy limbs . . . no anorexic models for this guy. One of them even had a gently rounded belly. Two of them were fair-skinned, and the third was the color of milk chocolate, with the high cheekbones of Egyptian royalty.

They were human. I was a little surprised at how easily I could tell. They had a glow, a vitality that Sinclair and Tina and I lacked. Maybe it was because their hearts had to beat so much faster, they had to take so many breaths.

I coughed. "Uh . . . should we be, like, spying on them?"

Tina looked surprised. "They can't hear us. This glass is three inches thick. Besides, Sinclair doesn't mind. This room usually has a watcher."

"That's sick!"

"No, that's common sense."

"Um, you know, I have a totally different definition of common sense."

"Do you know how many men of power have been killed between the sheets?"

"I can safely say that I have no idea."

"Well, it's a lot. I told you he was a careful man. He never lets his guard down. Not even during times like these."

I was (uncharacteristically) silent. That was one of the worst things I'd ever heard. If you couldn't relax during sex— particularly during a *Penthouse*-inspired fantasy like this—well, that didn't sound like much of a life. Being careful was one thing. Being buried alive was something else.

"Why can't he stop?" I grumbled, folding my arms across my chest. Uncomfortable? Me? Naw. "I mean, I don't mind being kept waiting if it's—you know—business you can conduct while fully clothed. But why do we have to hang around while he gets his undead jollies? I had the impression this was important."

"This is," Tina said seriously. "We're not like you, Betsy. We *have* to feed. We can't put it off for a day or two. Sometimes not even an hour or two. For Sinclair, this is vital. It's . . . it's as close to life-affirming as we can ever get. Nothing else takes precedence."

One of the women squealed.

"Life affirming?" I asked dryly. I glanced away before I saw something unfit for Christian eyes. Then, like Lot's wife, I looked back just in time to see Sinclair position himself behind one of the women. Though it pained me on several levels to admit it, the man had the best ass I had ever seen. Taut, muscular, and sweetly rounded in exactly the right places. Yum.

"How come we can hear them?" I croaked, and realized just how dry my mouth was.

Tina pointed wordlessly to our left; I looked and saw the speaker on the wall. "That's sick," I said again, and looked back at the scene to assure myself that the depravity was continuing. I mean, somebody had to pay attention to this stuff, be aware of just what a pig Sinclair was.

"They're so beautiful," Tina said softly. She rested her hand on the glass, palm down. "So alive and fresh and young."

Young? Tina was right, not a single woman in that room was hard on the eyes, but they were in their late thirties, early forties, at the least. They were beautiful but they looked like real women: soft bellies, heavy thighs, laugh lines. No nineteen-year-olds for Sinclair.

I sort of liked him for that.

After a minute, Sinclair pulled away, bent, and said something to one of the women, too low for me to hear. She gifted him with a sated smile and her eyes slipped to half-mast. Then he turned his attention to another woman.

It was really something to watch. Part of me was ordering myself to leave the room, give them some privacy. I mean, in life I didn't even like watching late-night Cinemax—not even with the sound off—much less real people doing the sweaty mambo.

But it was hard to look away. For one thing, it was really hot. Unbelievably hot. Part of it was Sinclair's stamina, but another was his three companions. There was no jealousy, no cattiness; they were happy just to be there, to take turns. It was unlike anything I'd ever imagined. I figured in a ménage a—shit, what was the French word for four? Well, anyway, I figured in any sort of ménage there were bound to be hurt feelings. Not here.

"You've got the best ass I've seen in fifty years," Sinclair told his partner of the moment. He wasn't out of breath. In fact, he sounded amused, and his tone instantly made my hackles rise. It wasn't like he was detached; it was more like any three women could have been in there with him. Any three at all. "At least fifty."

"A thousand years!" the one with the great ass declared, and the three women giggled in unison.

Sinclair snorted and pulled out. I gasped. I don't know why I was surprised. Sinclair was huge—big, broad shoulders, powerful arms and legs—well over six feet, easily two hundred pounds, and not a scrap of flab on him. I should have expected—err—other parts of him to be—uhh—larger than average. All the same, I couldn't help being shocked.

"Jesus Christ," I said. "No wonder he doesn't go for the nineteen-year-olds!" If some little club bunny saw *that* coming at her, she'd go for the whip and chair.

Tina, my little sex tour narrator, nodded. "Sinclair prefers older bed partners. If they're not . . . experienced . . . he could hurt them. He wouldn't mean to, and he'd be sorry later, but they'd be hurt, just the same."

Meanwhile, back in Sodom, Sinclair was still hungry. He was gentle enough, but firm; one minute one of the women was almost asleep, and the next Sinclair was gripping her arms, holding her easily, while he bit her on the side of the neck.

She convulsed against him, crying out, "Ah, God, again, again!" while he drank from her throat, while her head rolled back on her shoulders in ecstasy.

Sinclair stopped drinking. A small rill of blood ran down his chin, which he caught with his tongue. His dick wagged in the air, momentarily friendless. "Don't stop," he said. Then, when he saw his partner of the second had to stop, was in fact in a near-faint, he said, "Someone else."

Another woman was instantly kneeling in front of him, but he grabbed her hair and pulled her toward him, pushed her on her back, leaned in, spread her thighs with his big hands, and bit her in her femoral artery.

"These guys," I commented dryly, "are in great shape." I tried to sound cool and detached because, the fact was. I'd never been as turned on in my life. I could have watched them all day. Which explained why Tina had been so reluctant to separate them and tell Sinclair he had a visitor.

The new partner was moaning while Sinclair's mouth was busy on her plump thigh. She was stroking her breasts, squeezing them hard enough to leave white marks in her flesh, screaming "More, more, more, *more!*" at the ceiling.

*What are you doing?*

Dead or not, vamp or not, I was standing in a strange mansion watching a creep and his harem *have sex*. This wasn't me! Betsy Taylor did not watch soft porn, much less act like some icky voyeur.

"I-I have to go." I said this with a complete lack of conviction. "I mean, they'll finish up soon."

"Yes, Majesty."

"And then we can tell Sinclair what happened tonight."

"Yes."

"And figure out where to go from there."

"All right." Tina said this with all the animation of a store mannequin.

"You okay?"

"It's just that I have to kiss you now." She turned and pulled me toward her. Her pupils were huge. I looked down at her pretty, pretty face and tried to feel a little more shocked. I'd never kissed a woman in my life. Never even been curious. My stance on homosexuality was exactly the same as my stance on heterosexuality: If you were having sex with a consenting adult, it was none of my business. Just keep it out of my face.

"I must beg your indulgence," Tina was saying. She went up—up, up!—on her tiptoes. Her mouth was dark red, with matching lip liner (I approved; clashing lip liners were so twentieth century), and her top lip looked like a little bow. The mouth of an enchantress . . . hopefully a good one. "Just . . . one . . . kiss."

"Forget it!" I said loudly, breaking the spell. She had—it was like I'd been hypnotized for a few seconds. First a voyeur, now a lesbian? Don't think so! "My God, you people are sick, sick! Does he do this every night? *Don't answer that!* And you! You keep your hands to yourself, missy!"

I shoved her away. She had let go the second I resisted, so my shove sent her reeling across the room.

"I thought," I said numbly, because even though I'd been right, I felt bad, "I thought you gave that stuff up a hundred years ago."

"Men," she said, watching me sadly with her big dark eyes. "I gave up men. I'm very sorry. I couldn't help it. I haven't fed tonight and you're so beautiful. But I'm very sorry."

"Well . . ." Being called beautiful momentarily distracted me, and I fought the urge to bask. *Focus, damn you, focus!* "Being dead is one thing, but having to watch Finklair romp in his bed o' babes . . . and then you decide to bring my latent lesbian tendencies to the surface—real latent, by the way, because when I was alive the thought of lip locking with another woman never crossed my mind, although there was that one time at summer camp when Cheryl Cooper dared me to French kiss her because we were playing Truth or Dare and like a moron I picked Dare and I-I—where was I going with this?"

"I have no idea, Majesty."

"Forget it. Forget it! I'm out of here."

"Please don't go. It's my fault. All my fault. I'm so sorry." To my horror, she was sinking to her knees, and actually—was she? She was! She was kissing the toes of my shoes! "Please, Majesty, forgive my impertinence. Please!"

"Stop that!" I hissed, hopping back so her lips weren't touching my shoes, then jerking her to her feet. She wouldn't look at me, was cringing away from my anger. Which made me feel bad. Which made me even angrier. "Don't kiss my shoes ever again! Jesus Christ—" She moaned and flinched away. "—why do vampires have to be so *weird* about everything? Why am I the only one who wants to live a normal goddamned life?"

She cringed at goddamned. I gave way completely to the anger and worry that had been plaguing me since I woke up dead. "God! God! God!" I screamed into her face, taking grim pleasure in the way she cowered. "Enough of this weird shit, I've had enough! Do you realize I haven't even been dead a week?" I let go of her arm and stormed out. I practically knocked Dennis to the floor as I stomped down the stairs.

He jumped out of my way in a hurry. Lucky for him. "What's wrong, Miss Betsy?"

"Nothing. Everything. I gotta go."

"Please don't!" Tina cried from the top of the stairs. "Please stay! We need you!"

"Well, I don't need you," I said, practically running across the marble floor. "And I've never been more grateful for anything in my life."

I heard a swish, and suddenly Sinclair was standing in front of me, which efficiently scared the bejeezus out of me. "Aaggghhh!" I looked up. He'd obviously jumped from the floor above and landed in my path. "And *you*. Get out of my—hey!" He gripped my elbow and dragged me toward a door across the room. I set my feet, but it was no good. At least he'd wrapped a sheet around his waist.

He slammed the door, plunging us into near darkness (well, more like twilight since I had undead eyesight) and shutting Tina and Dennis on the other side. "Elizabeth," he said calmly, as if we'd met on the street. "So good of you to drop by."

"Ugh, ugh, *ugh!*" I hissed. I was trying to pry his fingers off my arm, with no luck. "Let go, you perv. I want out of this—this house of sin!"

"But I don't want you to leave," he said reasonably. "Not now."

"Too damned bad! I don't want anything to do with you! You—you slut!"

"Now, Elizabeth," he said, and he had the nerve to sound reproachful, "I don't come to your house and criticize your lifestyle, do I?"

"Eeewwwwww! Lifestyle? God, I can still smell them on you!"

"Jealous?"

I gagged. "Not hardly. Now let go; I'm out of here."

"You've upset Tina dreadfully."

"Get it through your head: You're disgusting, I don't care what you think, I could care less how upset Tina is, let the fuck go."

"In a minute," he said carelessly, and then, with that infuriating strength he'd shown in the cemetery, he pulled me to him and pressed his mouth to mine.

I opened my mouth to yell—or bite—which proved to be a tactical error, as he used it as an excuse to shove his tongue into my mouth. I made fists and hammered at his chest as hard as I could, and I actually heard something snap. He shrugged off the blows and deepened the kiss. My knees went weak, which was annoying beyond belief. I'd never been so attracted to someone I absolutely despised, and it was infuriating.

I could feel his hand on the small of my back, pressing me close to him, could feel his hard length against my stomach—how could he want anyone after what just went on upstairs? Didn't he need a nap? Or a shower?

He pulled back, so abruptly I staggered. "There," he said, sounding indecently satisfied. "Now you'll stay, and we'll chat."

The crack of my slap was very loud, and I was savagely thrilled to see him rock back on his heels.

"If you touch me again, I'll kill you." I was practically crying, I was so angry. I turned and fumbled for the doorknob, and practically ran out of the room.

I ignored Dennis's stare, Tina's anguished "Wait!" and yanked open the front door. "Take a good look," I said grimly, "because you'll never see me again."

Tina burst into tears, and I slammed the door on her dry sobs. And I didn't feel bad. Not one bit. Nope. Not at all.

No.

Damn you, Sinclair.

# Chapter 18

$\mathcal{I}$ got home, after committing grand theft auto. Again. Once out the front door I'd circled around to the side and found Finklair's garage. It was full of at least half a dozen shiny cars, and the keys were conveniently numbered and hanging from a board by the door. I grabbed the set for the Jaguar and off I went. Nobody tried to stop me. Lucky for them.

I drove like a madwoman, and disdained my seatbelt. Who cared? Like a car crash could do anything to me anyway. Like a trip through the windshield wouldn't be a vacation after the day I'd had. And the car was choice—black, with a sweet-smelling leather interior and a gas pedal that went all the way to the floor just as easy as you please. I made the forty mile trip in about twenty minutes.

I screeched into my driveway and hopped out, after leaving the keys in the ignition. Childish, but I really hoped someone would steal it. The thought of Sinclair sitting in a police station filling out report after report was immensely cheering.

I saw my door had a giant crack running through the middle, like someone had been kicking it for an hour or more, and stopped short on my front stoop.

I'll admit it—I wasn't much interested in finding out who had broken in. Nope, forget it, I'd had enough. Whoever it was, they were welcome to my cotton sheets, dirty dishes, and fluffy magenta bath mats.

I was turning away, possibly to go find my mom and cry on her shoulder for three or four hours, when . . .

"Bets! Is that you?" Jessica's voice.

"Get in here quick!" Marc's.

What fresh hell was this? I pushed the door open and slowly walked inside. At least Jess was okay—sounded okay, anyway. Shanara couldn't have hurt her too badly. Jeez, had she bushwhacked us in that alley only three hours ago? It felt like three years.

My friends were kneeling beside a big pile of rags in the middle of my bedroom floor. Marc had a neat white bandage on his neck and was still wearing the bracelet they'd given him at the hospital. Jessica looked perfectly fine. I felt so bad I'd forgotten about them, even for a few moments. "Are you guys okay?"

"Yeah. Are you, girlfriend? You look a little white around the gills. More so than usual," Jessica chortled. Then she sobered up and pointed to the rag pile. "You got problems, Betsy. I mean, besides the ones we've already been dealing with."

Marc gently prodded the pile . . . and it was Nick! He looked unbelievably bad—like he hadn't eaten in three days, slept in five, bathed in ten. His hair was a mess of greasy tangles. His eyes rolled toward mine. They were so deeply bloodshot they were more red than white. "More," he husked. "Moremoremore."

"No, oh no!" I rushed to him. "Jesus, Nick, what happened?"

"Um . . . we were sort of hoping *you'd* know," Marc said, fingering his bandage. "I mean, he doesn't exactly look like he's been through a garden-variety bad day. And he can't stop saying your name."

"Oh, shit, shit . . ." I trailed off and buried my face in my hands. "I can't deal with this, you guys. *I can't deal with this!* Not being able to eat and being dead and my dad scared of me and bad guy vamps throwing me into pits and Sinclair being a slut and a great kisser and Nick being traumatized and me being a car thief again—I've had enough!"

Jessica's eyebrows arched. "Err . . . who's a great kisser?"

"Who threw you into a pit?" Marc asked, interested. Then, "Car thief *again?*"

"More," Nick whispered. His lips were dry, cracked. He smelled like a garbage truck on fire. "Betsy. More. Betsy."

"Jesus, I was just hungry, I didn't mean—"

"This is fucked up," Marc said. "I mean, you chowed on me, too, but you don't see me turning into a puddle of yearning lust."

"No," Jessica said slowly, and there was a funny look on her face I didn't much like, "but you sure moved in just as quick as you could."

Marc blinked. Nick moaned. I stared. "What's that got to do with anything?" he asked, honestly puzzled.

"Well . . . don't you think it's kind of strange, seeing as how you're same-sex oriented, and—"

"Not now, you guys! We've got bigger problems. One great big problem lying in the middle of the floor." I covered my eyes with my palms. "Oh, shit, Nick—I didn't mean—what did I do? What did I do?"

"Exactly the opposite," Sinclair said thoughtfully, "of what I do."

I whirled and dropped my hands. Sinclair, Tina, and Dennis were standing just inside my bedroom. I'd never heard them come in. Never sensed their presence, never so much as heard the pitter-patter of their little vampire feet. Neither had Jessica and Marc, because they both let out little screams and practically leapt into each other's arms.

Nick was oblivious. He'd started rocking back and forth on the floor in an effort to soothe himself, and never looked away from my face. It was unbelievably horrible—like watching a crippled dog crawl after his master. You didn't know whether to shoot the dog out of kindness, or pet him out of pity.

"You *gotta* be Sink Lair," Jessica practically gasped. She was annoyingly wide-eyed.

"Hi, Mr. Sinclair!" Marc trilled. He even waved. "You guys drop by for a snack?"

"You three get out of here!" I snapped. "I've got enough problems right now, thanks."

Sinclair pointed to Nick. "That one is of your own making, I think . . . I can smell you on him. Under about six layers of dirt, that is." He said it so carelessly I wanted to kill him. My hand went to the cross Tina had given me. Would he sound so cool and detached if I jammed this little trinket in his ear?

But Sinclair was already striding toward us. "Tina," he said quietly, kneeling beside Nick, "help me." His actions were the diametric opposite of his words, which was really confusing.

"What's wrong with him?" I cried. "Is he becoming a vampire?"

"No. He craves you. He's an addict, now."

Tina was wide-eyed. "How many times did you feed off this one?"

"It was only one time."

"You *dog*." From Jessica, naturally. "And you never said a word, you bad girl."

"Once," Sinclair repeated.

"Yeah. Just once. I swear!"

"But you only fed on me once, too," Marc said. "I mean, don't get me wrong, it was great—really different and cool and sexy and weird and all—but that was it. Why's this guy such a wreck?"

"Once?" Tina said, pointing to Nick.

"Do I have to paint it on my forehead? Yeah, once, just the one time."

Skeptical silence, broken when Sinclair said, "You can't just have them and release them, Elizabeth. You fled my home after you saw a—a certain aspect of the vampire lifestyle. But I would never do to mine what you did to yours."

That stung. A lot. "He's not *mine*. I barely even know him!"

"Well." Dennis cleared his throat. He was crouching over us, resting his hands on his thighs. He looked like an undead umpire. "That's worse, you know."

"But I didn't know!"

"I warned you," Sinclair said. He was shrugging out of his topcoat and putting it over Nick's shivering form. "You don't know the rules. Most vampires would learn or die. But you were born strong, and you have few of our weaknesses. So while you're learning, the innocent are being hurt."

"Hey, leave her alone. *I* wasn't hurt." Bless Dr. Marc! "I mean, sure, I feel sort of lonely and vulnerable sometimes . . ."

"Shut up," Jessica said, biting her lip, hard, so she wouldn't smile.

Sinclair ignored them completely. "Is my offer of help still so completely unacceptable?"

Jessica and Marc looked at me. Despite their attempts to make me feel better, I felt the weight of their judgment.

"Okay, okay . . . tell me what to do. How to help Nick. And I'll—I'll take your Vampire 101 class, Sinclair. But only after Nick is better."

"Your word on it, Elizabeth."

"She already told you she'd let you help," Jessica said, her voice like ice. She might think Sinclair was yummier than a triple fudge sundae, but nobody was going to question her best friend's honor in her own home. "If that's not enough, Sink Lair, don't let the door hit you in your big white ass on the way out."

"Please don't pronounce my name like that," he sighed. He lifted Nick easily into his arms. Then, "Big white ass?"

"Bring him to the bathroom," Tina said. "Dennis and I can take care of him."

"But—" I closed my mouth with a snap. Nick was almost as tall as Sinclair, which made him two heads taller than Tina and Dennis. Never mind. They could probably muscle a Volkswagen into my bathroom if they had to.

Sinclair carried Nick to my bathroom and carefully laid him on the floor. Dennis stripped him, grimacing at the smell, while Tina started the shower. Meanwhile, Sinclair put a hand on my shoulder, turned me around, and marched me out. Of my own bathroom!

"Hands to yourself, buster," I warned.

"You—uh—want something to drink?" Jessica was standing in the bedroom doorway. She blushed, which isn't easy to tell with her. "I mean, like tea or something, Mr. Sinclair?"

I was shocked. That was a quick reversal, especially for Jessica "I can hold a grudge until the end of time" Watkins. Sinclair's undead sex appeal must work on women like mine did on men.

"Please call me Eric," the undead skunk was saying with convincing warmth. "After all, you're a friend of Elizabeth's."

"He likes plum wine, get him a glass of that," I said irritably.

"I'll get it!" Marc said. He'd gone to throw Nick's rags into my washing machine, but leapt for the doorway the instant Jessica did. They became jammed at the shoulder, Three Stooges style.

"No, I'll get it!"

"Fuck you, getting drinks should be beneath you, honey."

"Fuck *you*, this is my house. I paid for it, didn't I?"

They struggled, then both popped free of the doorframe. I heard pounding footsteps as they raced each other to the kitchen, and put a hand over my eyes. Friends . . . the ultimate mixed blessing.

"A pity you are not as fond of me as your companions are," Sinclair teased.

"They don't know what a creep you are," I said sourly. I was annoyed to see Giselle purring in his arms as he absently tickled her under the chin. Fickle feline tramp! I snatched her away and tossed her in the direction of the doorway. With a snooty backward glance, she went. "If they had the slightest clue how wretched and nasty and despicable you are . . ."

"Now, Elizabeth, how can you say that?" He blinked at me with innocent Bambi eyes. Cold, glittering Bambi eyes. "You know I tried to help you at the mausoleum, and I sent Tina to help you at Nostro's home tonight. If she hadn't given you my gift the Fiends would have torn you to pieces."

"Your gift?"

"The cross belonged to my sister."

My fingers went instantly to the necklace, fumbling to take it off, but he stopped me with a shake of his head. "Keep it. I certainly can't wear it, and it might help you again."

Shocked, I said, "Yeah, but . . . it was your sister's."

"Yes, I know that. And now it's yours."

"Well . . . thank you. But—and it's not that I'm not grateful—"

"Not that, never that," he said mockingly.

"—but if you're so concerned, why didn't you come yourself tonight?"

"I did come," he said innocently. "More than once, in fact. I thought you were watching."

I felt my face get red, a good trick, since I was dead. "Very funny! You know what I mean."

"Alas, too well. Unfortunately, one of the conditions of Tina's release from Nostro was that I never set foot in his territory."

"Okay, well, this probably isn't the time to play Q and A, but some stuff has really been bugging me. Like that—why did he even let Tina on his property? He must have known she'd tell you everything she could."

"He likes to flaunt his power," he replied simply. "Thus, although I can send envoys, I myself must stay clear, unless he violates my territory. And he relishes showing off for my people. You might say he lives for it. However, the mausoleum where you first met Nostro is neutral ground . . . any vampire, from any city in the world, is welcome there. There are such neutral territories all over the planet."

"So you could come to the mausoleum for the—the party, I guess it was?" Lamest party *ever,* but oh well.

"I had no intention of coming, until I heard you were going to be there."

"Oh." Dammit! Hearing more details about how he got Tina away from Noseo—and how he wanted to meet me—made me start to hate him not so much. Which was not a good way to feel about a character as slippery as this guy. My hand went instinctively to the cross again. "Well, I'd thank you—"

"My heart! Can it stand the strain?"

"—except I know you've got some sneaky motive for helping me out."

"My anti-Nostro, pro-Elizabeth stance has been clear for a few days, there's nothing sneaky about it."

"Sneaky's your middle name—"

"Actually, it's Astor."

"—which reminds me, what are you doing here, anyway?" And wasn't an astor a kind of flower? I made a note to lock that one up ASAP.

"You have my car," he pointed out. "I must insist upon its return. You don't strike me as a sensible and sane driver. And you were certainly in a dangerous rush to leave."

"Let's not talk about it."

"A prude born in the late twentieth century? I hadn't thought such creatures existed."

"Just because I don't think you should be gaily boinking multiple partners—at the same time!—doesn't mean I'm a prude."

He gestured toward the bathroom, where poor Nick was being ministered to by Tina and Dennis. "I don't think you're in any position to question my judgment. My ladyfriends know what they're getting into."

"You're still a pig," I said bitterly. "I saw you. It didn't matter which three women were there—you didn't care. They were for you to *use*. That's not how you treat a friend."

"Well." His brows arched in thought. "Perhaps I simply haven't met the right woman."

"Or perhaps you're a pig!" I threw my hands in the air. "Did you really *need* three of them? I mean, come on. Realistically. *Three?*"

"Well." He smiled slowly, and I felt my stomach tighten. "Does anyone ever really *need* a banana split, when a single scoop sundae would do?"

"These. Are. Human. Beings." I was pushing the words out past gritted teeth; I was so pissed my eyes were crossed. "Not. Ice cream. Sundaes. *Pig.*"

"Your tiresome preaching has made me see the light. I have the bargain of the century for you, Elizabeth. I will give up their friendship at once, and all others for all time. Tonight. *If* you take their place in my bed. For all time."

My mouth fell open and I gaped at him. A zillion emotions— outrage, curiosity, fear, lust, shock—screamed through my head in

half a second, and before I knew I was going to do it, my hand leaped
to his face and slapped him hard enough to snap his head back.

He felt his jaw and looked at me. His black eyes glittered and
I swallowed the phrase, *I take it back!* that wanted to come out.

"Nice," was all he said. "I didn't see that one coming. Though
I suppose I should have. You have, after all, done this before."

I tried to say something appropriately haughty and scathing,
but couldn't think of a thing.

"Thank you," he said, so polite, and took the glass Jessica was
offering him. Marc was right behind her with a tray of cocktail accessories: maraschino cherries, lemon slices, olives. They hadn't
seen the slap. Heck, I had barely seen it—it was like my hand had
moved quicker than thought.

"What was that noise?" Jessica asked.

"Never mind. All that stuff for wine?" I sighed, rolling my
eyes and rubbing my palm. Smacking Sinclair had been like
smacking a chunk of granite.

For spite, Sinclair carefully selected a lemon slice and
dropped it into his wine.

Jessica peeked into the bathroom, then hurried back to report.
"They got that boy stripped mother naked and they're scrubbing
him with your brand-new loofah."

I winced. Thirty-seven ninety-nine at The Body Shop, kaput.
"Fair enough. It's my fault he's in this mess. What happens after
he's clean, Sinclair?"

"Eric."

"Errrrrrric . . ." Jessica and Marc repeated in dreamy chorus.

"Don't you two have *anything* else to do?" I practically
screamed.

"This is the most interesting week of my entire life," Marc
pointed out. "Vampires! Alliances! Gorgeous good guys. Sneaky
bad guys. Fighting the good fight! Now we're scrubbing a delirious cop in your bathroom. What's next? Who knows? And why in
the world would we go find something else to do?"

"Possibly because the events happening here are none of your
business?" Sinclair asked smoothly.

Marc snorted. "I live here, pal. That makes it my business. Besides, what else am I going to do? Fight red tape at the hospital,
beg HMOs to do the right thing while a kid dies? And what's Jess
going to do—count her money?"

"Besides, we're the sidekicks. Part of the team. Anything that
involves Liz here involves all of us," Jessica added.

"I shall endeavor to keep that in mind. To answer your question, Liz—"

"Don't you dare."

"Then no more Sink Lair, yes?"

*Dammit!* "Yes."

"Very good. As I was saying, once Detective Berry has been purified, Tina or Dennis will relieve his immediate need by feeding on him. Then we will make him forget he ever knew you as a vampire. He'll wake up in his own bed, with a week's worth of stubble, feeling like he's recovered from the flu."

"But I don't want this to happen to anyone ever again," I said. "I mean, your plan sounds like a good one, and God knows you've had a lot of years to perfect your sinister ways, but I'm looking to treat the disease, not the symptoms."

Sinclair had winced at "God," but answered smoothly enough. "Then pick one—or two—or three lovers who don't mind sharing blood along with their bodies, and use them as often as you must. Or they wish."

"Don't even think of glancing in my direction, girlfriend," Jessica ordered.

"Seriously," Marc added. "Unless you've managed to grow a penis in the last couple days."

"Thanks for nothing, creeps. Listen, Sinclair, even if I did such a yucky thing—and don't hold your breath—how do I know they won't become like Nick?"

"Because they'll have access to you. You won't have fed once and then turned your back on them."

"It wasn't like that," I said quietly.

"As you say." He was practically sneering, the big creep.

"It's probably not as bad as he's making out," Marc said, comforting me. "I mean, *I'm* not a wreck. About this, anyway."

"He is a homosexual. He is affected differently."

" 'He' is also standing right here, hello?"

"And," Sinclair went on, "as Jessica pointed out, he lives here. With you."

"Hey, somebody's got to defrost the freezer."

I laughed. Sinclair ignored us and continued lecturing. "Pick two. Or three. And feed on them, and let them have their way with you. You will find it's quite a satisfactory arrangement."

I wasn't laughing anymore. "Well, that's one of the big differences between thee and me, Sinclair, because I disagree!"

"She's a poet," Marc informed us, "and she didn't know it."

I glared at him, but Marc smiled back and didn't budge. I turned back to Sinclair. "It's like—it's like making a human being your—your pet or something." I'd never forget the coolly amused look on his face while he took one of his ladyfriends, then the other, then the other. They could have been anyone—he absolutely didn't care who was in his bed. I'd never do that to a person, make them feel like they were interchangeable parts of someone's machine.

*Never.*

"Did you not eat meat before your accident?" he asked. "You were strong and to keep yourself strong, you used the weak. That's what predators do. That's what vampires do. Otherwise, you are like those fools in P.E.T.A., who think we should all nibble grass and drink nectar."

"Uh-oh, here we go," Jessica muttered. "Every dead guy for himself."

"*I'm* a member of P.E.T.A.," I said. "I ate meat, sure, but I don't think we should pour shaving cream down a rabbit's throat, or rub eye makeup onto a dog's eyeball so American women can have lush lashes. It's one thing if you need the protein, but it's another if you want to hang a big dead stuffed head on your wall, or design a deodorant that makes your armpit smell like a flower patch."

"A vampiric P.E.T.A. member." Sinclair couldn't quite keep the smile off his face.

"You're one of *them?*" Marc said, horrified. "Oh, cripes! I had no idea. Jesus, I feel dirty! Why didn't you tell me?"

I blinked. "My being a vampire doesn't bother you, but my giving money to P.E.T.A. does?"

"Hey, it was one thing when you were a soulless underling of Satan, I could work with that, but a tree-hugging marmoset lover . . . ugh! I've got my pride, dude."

Jessica got the giggles, then started to laugh. Before long she was having one of her gut-busters and hanging onto the wall to keep from falling over.

Sinclair smirked, watching me. I noticed he was careful to keep his teeth covered, probably so that Jessica and Marc wouldn't run screaming from the room.

"I'd better go check on the others," I said at last. I passed them on my way to the bathroom and ignored the evil-eye sign Marc forked at me.

Marc was still freaking out. "P.E.T.A.! Man, I'm gonna have

to sit down and think this one over. Didn't mind being the sidekick of a bride of Satan, but a tree-hugger who, like, blows up labs and stuff . . ."

"Perhaps you *should* sit down," Sinclair suggested solicitously.

I passed Dennis on my way in. "We'll need some clothes for your Nick," he said over his shoulder. "Something he can wear home, that he can't trace back to you."

"I've got some old sweatsuits I never wear anymore—bottom drawer on the left. They don't have my name on them or anything. They'll be a little small, but they'll get the job done." Then I was stepping into the bathroom.

Nick was looking a little livelier, and well he should, since his head was pillowed on Tina's breasts and she was slowly, luxuriously working soapy lather over the muscles in his back. He was, as a matter of fact, extremely happy to see her. This was a great relief to me. When I saw the wreck that was the former Detective Nick Berry on my bedroom floor, I was afraid he'd never be happy to see anyone again.

"How's it going in here?" I asked. Squeaked, actually—I was a little nervous to be talking to Tina. What if she lost control and tried to molest me with the soap on a rope?

"He'll be all right. Do you think you could help me? I would ask Sinclair or Dennis, but—"

"It's my mess. Yeah, I'll help." I slipped out of my clothes, then slid the shower door aside and stepped in. "What—uh—what do we do now?"

"Now I fall upon you with ravenous hunger and hump your brains out."

I burst out laughing. I *was* scooched as far away from her as I could get, and that was a fact. I also felt a little weird about being naked in front of a lesbian. I probably had been before, at one time or another—public showers, that sort of thing—but you don't know for sure, right? You just assume everyone else is straight, and if someone's staring at your tits you figure she's working up the nerve to ask who did your boob job. "Very funny. Sorry."

"I'm the one who's sorry. I abused your trust and put everything in jeopardy." Her voice was so bitter it shocked me. "All because I couldn't keep myself to myself."

"Hey, whoa, calm down, sunshine. You just wanted a kiss, it's not like you tried to knife my kitty. Besides, I owed you a favor, right? From the pit?"

She shifted Nick as easily as a grown woman shifted a baby.

"So," she said, straight-faced, "I risked my life and faced the prospect of a horrible death to save you, and in return you rebuffed my advances, and now we're even."

"Right." I smirked.

She rolled her eyes. "The devil help us if you really are the queen." But she said it with a smile, and I knew she was teasing to make me feel better. "Very well, then. To business. If you'll drink from his throat, I'll take him inside me. He'll have relief and then we'll be able to plant the suggestions we need to."

"Take him—oh. Oh! Ack! Right here? Now?" How how *how* did I get myself in these situations?

"He is dying," she said seriously.

"So you're going to have sex with him and poof! All better?"

"Mock if you will—"

"I'm being serious!"

"—but it's what he needs."

"But you don't—you don't like—I mean—oh, fuck."

She laughed. "All those things are true, but exceptions must be made."

"Yeah, but . . . like I said, it's my mess."

"Yes, but you don't want to do it. You never meant to in the first place, and don't want to now, particularly with several people waiting right outside the door—two of them with exceptional hearing—and that's fine." Seeing the look on my face, she softened her tone. "It's all right, Betsy. I truly don't mind. It's nothing to me, and everything to him. Besides . . . aren't you thirsty?"

I was. I hadn't fed yet tonight. Or last night, for that matter. But . . . "Why does it have to be both? Why do we have to drink *and* fuck?"

"*We* don't," she said, "but they do. If we take from them, they need us in the way that they've never needed anyone before. They can't drink, so they go for the next best thing—the best way to affirm life. I guess it's like—like masturbating but not letting yourself reach orgasm. What's the point? It's frustrating and leaves everyone unhappy. We could take and not give ourselves to them in return, but it's a rotten thing to do."

*Oh. Well. If you put it that way . . .*

"This is very disturbing, and time's a' wasting and my water heater is only so big, so we'd better get cracking, and I *am* thirsty, but if you do this for me I owe you another favor. All right?"

She looked at me, and her little pink tongue came out and tapped one of her canines thoughtfully. "A kissing favor," she said finally.

"Awww, Tina, I told you," I whined, "I don't play that way."

"Not in life, certainly. But vampires have to adjust to many things . . . and quite a few of us find that after death we are—ah—flexible."

*That* explained a lot. If a strange woman had tried to lay a lip lock on me two weeks ago, I'd have clobbered her with my purse. But here I was, extremely naked, with a gorgeous woman and a guy who wasn't exactly ugly, both of whom would have been thrilled to fuck me, and I was more than a little tempted to be the meat in their sandwich.

It was all very strange. Calgon, take me away!

"Okay," I said with a convincing display of reluctance. "We'll discuss this later."

"Of course," she assured me. "I'd want to wait until we had . . . leisure."

"You know, those pauses you and Sinclair do before you finish a sentence are really terrifying."

"Why do you think we do it? And who do you think taught *him?*" she asked merrily. She rinsed the last of the soap from Nick's body, then beckoned me closer. I ran my hands up his back, then put my hands on his shoulders, leaned in, and bit him. Hot salty life trickled into my mouth and Nick straightened up in a hurry, completely losing the apathy that had cloaked him all night. He tried to turn to face me, but I wouldn't let him.

"Here, to me," Tina said in her sweet, almost musical voice. Nick lunged forward, picked her up, and drove into her. Her back slammed against the tile and her legs were forced up and around his waist. Tina let out a squeak of pain, and Nick started thrusting against her so hard I lost my grip.

"Oh my God, ith he hurting you?" I was horrified. I was ready to pull him off her and put him through the shower door, and never mind that he was the victim.

"Nothing. It's nothing."

It occurred to me that a woman who didn't choose to couple with men was taking a pounding on my behalf, and didn't even have the pleasure of the drink to ease things. Because she wanted *me* to drink. Which I had, like the selfish cow I was.

It's just . . . I hadn't thought he'd be so rough! So—so brutal and mindless. Of course, he'd tried to be like that with me, but I'd given it right back to him and besides, I liked men. But Tina—

Nick seized her by the thighs and wrenched her further apart; she cried out before she could lock it back.

"Oh, thcrew *thith*," I said.

I started to pull him off her, but stopped at her sharp, "No! Else it's for nothing!"

So I held her hand instead. She squeezed back, tightening painfully as Nick speeded up toward his climax. Then he was done and collapsing to his knees, already half unconscious, and I caught Tina as she fell forward. "That's it, sweetheart," I told her, brushing damp tendrils of hair out of her eyes. "That's the last pounding you take on my behalf."

"Agreed."

We staggered out of the shower together. I remembered to turn off the water before Nick drowned. But I still felt like putting him through the wall—how's that for irrational?

# Chapter 19

"**WERE** coming, too," Jessica said stubbornly.

"Indeed, no," Sinclair said politely.

"Hey, sidekicks tag along. It's, like, the rule. Besides, I want to watch Vampire 101," Marc gushed.

Dennis and Tina both looked appalled. "It's against all our laws," Tina explained. "And—and—"

"It's completely inappropriate," Dennis said, offended. "We're not circus monkeys. We don't perform for breathers."

"This is a private thing," Tina added. "Between Her Majesty and us."

"About that 'Her Majesty' stuff," Jessica said. "I mean, the girl's something special, no doubt . . . I've always known it."

"Awwwwww," I said.

"Shut up. Anyway, it was more a personality thing than anything else. Why is she the queen? It *can't* be her brains."

"Yeah, that's a very good—oh, thanks, creep."

"Look, honey, you're just not the sharpest knife in the drawer, is all. There's no shame in it."

"Just because I don't have a 142 I.Q. like *some* rich bitches doesn't mean my arms drag on the floor when I walk."

Sinclair was scowling. And so was I! "I can assure you, she wasn't elected. *I* certainly wouldn't have voted for her."

"Did I miss the memo that declared today 'take a big steaming shit on Betsy' day?" I griped.

"S'not my fault you don't check your in-bin," Jessica retorted. "So anyway, Eric, what's the deal with Queenie here?"

"Ugh! Do not even *think* of getting in the habit of calling me that. Seriously."

Sinclair sighed. It was a good effect, since I knew he didn't have to hardly ever exhale. "It's a long story, it's none of your business, she's leaving with us, good night."

At "good night," Marc and Jessica both folded bonelessly to the floor. I leapt aside so as not to be crushed by their falling carcasses. "Hey! Will you stop doing that to my friends? And *how* do you do it? Because I've got Easter dinner coming up with my father and stepmother . . ."

Sinclair actually shuddered when I said Easter—not sure if it was the Jesus angle, or if he was battling some sort of phobia of rabbits—but he quickly recovered. "We will cover that later. Come, Tina. Dennis."

"Good dogs, arf, arf," I muttered.

Sinclair picked up the dozing, dried, and dressed Nick, slung him over one shoulder like a sack of grain, and took him out to the Jaguar. Ignoring my protests, he unceremoniously stuffed him into the trunk, slammed it shut, and got into the driver's seat. "Coming?" he asked politely, while Tina and Dennis got into the other car, a red Maserati.

"I must be out of my fucking mind," I muttered, climbing into the passenger seat. The neighbor's dog started to run up to the car, tongue already lolling and ready to lick, but I slammed the door in time. "Completely nutso bonkers."

Meanwhile, Sinclair's knees were up to his ears and he looked decidedly aggrieved as he fumbled for the seat latch. "You have completely destroyed my interior," he complained, fussing with the rearview mirror. "You look tall but you apparently have legs like a platypus."

"Jeez, whine some more. Sue me for wanting to reach the pedals."

He started the engine and jerked in his seat as Rob Zombie's "Living Dead Girl" blared through the speakers.

"This is intolerable," Sinclair shouted in a vain attempt to be heard over the music. He lunged for the volume control, then stabbed irritably at the preset buttons. The car was instantly flooded with—gag!—serene string quartet music.

"Yuck," I commented.

"You took the word right out of my mouth." He rubbed his ear. "For pity's sake, Betsy. You have enhanced hearing. There's no need to turn the music up so loud."

"Are we gonna take Nick home, or are you going to keep bitching?"

"I plan to do both," he said wryly, pulling out of my driveway so sharply I lurched forward.

In no time at all, we were pulling up outside a small ranch house I took to be Nick's. I wasn't about to ask how Sinclair knew where he lived. Some stuff I just didn't want to know. Actually, *most* stuff I just didn't want to know, but people kept telling me anyway.

Sinclair got out, pulled Nick from the trunk, took him inside, did whatever hypnosis trick he had in his pocket for such occasions, and we left Nick dozing.

To my alarm, Tina and Dennis did a fade. "You don't need all three of us to teach you how to hunt," Tina said, waving as Dennis pulled out of Nick's driveway. "Luck!"

"Don't leave me alone with this asshole!" I shouted at the retreating taillights. Then, "Hunt?"

"You did promise," he said silkily. "Come."

"Come. Sit. Stay."

"Oh, if only."

"VAMPIRES don't exist."

I blinked. "Er . . . sorry, wasn't listening. Did you just say we don't exist?"

"Pay attention. We are myth, legend, folklore."

"Like the Tooth Fairy," I suggested, "with fangs."

"No, not remotely like that, because many children believe in the Tooth Fairy."

"Did you?"

"I was never a child," he said soberly. "Now. Because we don't exist, we are allowed to operate at a level unparalleled anywhere else in the natural world. This is vital, as we—"

"Whoa, whoa. Back up, slick. Never a child?"

"Please, Elizabeth. Try to stay focused. Now, as vampires don't—"

"I *am* focused. Why were you never a child?"

He didn't say anything. We were walking through a nature reserve about seventy miles north of the Twin Cities. I could hear all sorts of life—squirrels, deer, rabbits, bats, bugs, gophers, snakes—rustling and fighting and fucking and eating and dying, all around me. It was interesting, if nerve-wracking. The forest was teeming with life and I could smell it as well as hear it.

"I was never a child," he said at last, "because from the very beginning life was a struggle. I was regularly putting meat on my family's table before I knew the alphabet."

"How?"

"I was too small to use a gun effectively, so I learned how to set traps. Snares, and the like. And I could fish."

"Huh." I had to admit, I was impressed. Even if I absolutely could not see Mr. Slick as a toddler wandering down to the local fishing hole with a pole over one shoulder and a creel over the other. Opie he wasn't. "What'd your parents do?"

"We were farmers."

"No shit!"

"Surprised?"

"Well, yeah. I mean, you're so—" Slick. Refined. Fancy. Rich. Slick. Non-farmeresque. Did I say slick? "You're—uh—"

"Farming," he went on as if I wasn't still stammering, "is back-breaking work. Even now, in this century."

"How d'you know what it's like in this century?"

"I own several local farms."

"Oh. How come? I mean, seems to me like you'd want to get away from it altogether, and—"

"After my parents were killed I couldn't—I did not have the financial resources to—I just wanted to have the farms, and never mind the why of it! Now, back to business. Since vampires don't exist, we are allowed certain freedoms. But access to those freedoms depends entirely on—"

"But we *do* exist," I interrupted. I could take a hint—Sinclair was as rattled as I'd ever seen him, talking about owning *farms*, for goodness sake. So he wanted to get off the subject—I was hip to that. But not if he was going to babble a bunch of fantasy. "Hello? We're walking in the woods, aren't we? Just as undead as hell, right?"

Sinclair sighed. "Lesson one: Vampires don't exist."

"Lesson one blows."

"The point is, we go about our business in secret."

"Why?"

"Because that is the rule."

"But *why* is it the rule?"

He stopped short, exasperated. "Really, Elizabeth, this is not unlike a conversation with a first-grader."

"Oh, blow it out your ass. You can teach Vampire 101—I

agreed, and I'm a girl of my word—but you have to make sense. That's *my* rule."

"Yes, and stubborn adherence to *your* rules is why the most powerful vampire in five hundred years wants your head on a plate."

I made a face and kicked at a pile of leaves on the forest floor. *Know-it-all creep.*

"We. Do not. Exist. We do not seek out our parents. We do not return to our houses. We do not explain to strangers that we are undead."

"Is that why *we* are such total losers?"

"That," he said grimly, "will be taken care of. Now, about stalking—"

"Oh, cripes. Stalking? Do you hear how you sound?"

"How else will you eat?"

"It hasn't been a problem," I replied haughtily.

"Tell that to your policeman friend."

He had me there, the crumb. "So," I said sulkily, "about stalking."

"We don't breathe, our hearts don't beat. Well . . . very often, anyway. And it's surprisingly easy to steal up on someone without their knowing."

"Yeah, the night I woke up in the funeral home—"

"A story you simply must tell me someday," he interrupted smoothly. "As I was saying, if you focus, and practice, you can slip up on anyone—even another vampire."

That was a cheerful thought. Maybe, if I got good enough, I could sneak up on Sinclair and give him a well-deserved wedgie. "So, how do we do it?"

"Do you see the deer?"

As a matter of fact, I did. There was a doe and a yearling, about twenty yards ahead. If I'd been alive I'd never have heard or seen them—it was dark out, for one thing, and they were pretty well hidden back in the woods, for another.

"Yup."

"Let's try to walk up on them. Try to touch the doe before she knows you're there."

"And give her a heart attack? Jeez, she's a mom. Heartless creep."

"The fawn, then," he said impatiently.

"Scare *Bambi?* Sinclair, I swear, if you weren't a vampire, you'd be burning in hell."

He put a hand over his eyes and was silent for a long moment, his lips pressed tightly together. I knew the look. It was one I'd gotten from my father, various teachers, and bosses over the years. He was probably concentrating very hard on not strangling me. Hey, I am what I am. He'd better get used to it.

"Besides," I added, "somebody's coming." A whole herd of somebodies, sounded like. The sound of leaves crunching was very loud; I wanted to clap my hands over my ears. It sounded like a giant chewing Rice Krispies. And their breathing sounded like a winded rhino. I watched fearfully, waiting for the hideous creature to emerge.

"Howdy there, folks. Lost?"

The hideous creature was the game warden, a man in his late forties. He was about my height, with thinning blond hair and watery blue eyes. He was sporting a pretty good tan for April, and wearing a brown uniform with patches bearing the logo of the Minnesota Game and Fish Commission.

"We were just taking a walk," Sinclair said smoothly, shaking his head a little as we heard the doe and her fawn bound away. "Young lovers, you know." He slung an arm around my shoulders and hauled me up against him.

"Ugh!" I said. "I mean, yeah. Young lovers."

"Well, I'm gonna have to ask you to leave," he told us sternly. "We're doing some checking—there's word that one or two of the deer in here might have CWD."

"Chronic Wasting Disease?" Sinclair asked. "Are you certain?"

"No, that's why we're checking. Go on, now," he added kindly.

"Good evening."

"Okay, bye," I said, struggling to remove Sinclair's arm from my shoulders without being too obvious. It was like trying to dislodge a tree limb.

When we were out of earshot I pulled away. "Chronic Wasting Disease? Isn't that like mad cow disease for deer?"

"Yes."

"Ewwww! And you were gonna have us stalk mad deer!"

"Per the WHO, there is no evidence that CWD can infect humans, much less vampires."

I wasn't about to ask who the hell WHO was. "Nice going, Stalker Boy! Sucking the blood and getting mad vampire disease . . . so *not* on my to do list for the week! Not that any of this bullshit is," I added in a mutter.

"Suck their blood?" Sinclair sounded appalled. "Absolutely not."

"Oh, they were good enough to sneak up on and scare the crap out of, but not good enough to eat?"

He was actually shuddering. I didn't think he could! "No. No. The animals were just practice. And don't ask why; you know why."

"Uh, no, I don't." *Guess I'm not as bright as he thought. Dammit!* "Why not drink from animals? It's got to be easier, not to mention less traumatic. For all of us!"

"Have you not noticed the . . . effect . . . your mouth has on men?"

The effect my mouth . . . oh. Oh! If it was that sensual, that much of a turn-on, then if I tried to bite Bambi, the poor little deer would likely be climbing all over—"Oh."

"Indeed."

"Ugh.

"Yes."

"So only people, huh?" I sighed.

"Yes. But never children."

"Well, *duh.*"

"As long as we're clear. What seems patently obvious to me often seems to take you quite by surprise."

"Look, if you think I'm a dumbass, why don't you just say it instead of pussyfooting around all the—"

"I think you are a dumbass."

"You *what?*" The nerve! "Jeez, you can't even pretend to be nice for five seconds?"

"Whenever I try to be—ah—nice, I get a broken rib for my pains." He patted his left side.

"You deserved that, throwing down a lip lock on me without permission. And after being with *them.*"

"I disagree. I was simply being a good host."

I sputtered while he laughed at me. "Sinclair, you're the worst—the—oh, cripes, I can't think of anything bad enough."

"Public education?" he asked sympathetically.

"Probably better than yours, farmer boy," I snapped back. "Where the hell is the car? I've had about enough of tromping around in the woods with you."

"It's up ahead. Now, you understand very clearly what I meant about taking blood?"

"Yeah, yeah, no need to whip out the hand puppets, I got it." I spotted the car as we emerged from the woods. "Well, it's not like I have to worry about it every night or anything." I cheered up. "Not even the next couple of nights."

Sinclair shook his head. "Truly amazing."

I preened.

"And entirely without precedent. Or merit."

"Cut it out, you're just jealous. Hey, can I drive back?"

"Absolutely not."

"Jeez, am I the Queen or not?"

"Queen you may be, but I draw the line at letting you behind the wheel again."

"Men and their toys . . ."

I climbed in and sulked all the way back to his place.

———

# Chapter 20

**W**HEN I woke up next to Sinclair, I was the most shocked person on earth. Plus, to increase the creep factor, he was lying on his side, head propped on his chin, watching me. His chest was covered with a mat of crisp black hair, and his—

"Jesus!" I sat bolt upright and grabbed myself. I was, thank goodness, fully clothed. "Don't *do* that! What am I doing here on hell's satin acre?" I started groping my way toward the edge. We were in the middle of his gigantic bed and, I was happy to see, the sheets had been changed. They were such a light gray they were almost silver.

"And good evening to you, too." He watched as I clambered off his bed with all the grace of a laboring hippo. "How is it that you weren't burned to a crisp this morning?"

"What, you're asking *me*? How the hell should I know?"

The sun had caught up with us as we raced to Sinclair's. I didn't think much of it—hadn't I been sleeping in my bed with the curtains open this whole week, and didn't my room face east? But Sinclair flipped out when I opened my car door.

"How was I supposed to know you had an underground route to your place?" I grumbled, squinting at myself in the mirror and combing my fingers through my hair. Did my hair grow now? Would I ever need to worry about booking Simone at Le Kindest Kut? My roots didn't seem to be getting darker. Of course, I'd have to see if that was the case two months from now . . .

"Betsy?"

"What?" Now, if I wanted to try red highlights again—they'd been in and out and now they were trendy again—would it take?

Shoulder-length hair was classically trendy, but what if it went out someday? Horrible thought! Locked into an unfashionable hair-style . . . for eternity! It'd be as bad as being turned into a vampire in the 1960s, stuck with the Mary Tyler Moore look. Ugh! I'd pre-fer to be staked, quite honestly.

"*Elizabeth.*"

"What?"

"We were discussing why you weren't immolated last night; *try* to stay focused."

"Calm down before you have a stroke. What's the big deal? I figured sunlight didn't bother you any more than it did me."

"Thank you for clarifying. Now back up. Sunlight does not bother you?"

"You were in my room, Sinclair. Remember, it faces east? And my curtains are white and filmy?"

"I assumed you had been resting in the basement." He was looking at me with such intensity I nearly squirmed. "Remark-able. Truly remarkable!"

"Well, yes. Anyway." I coughed modestly. "When you stopped the car, I assumed it was time to get out, not time to wait for the entrance to open for the bat-cave."

Sinclair held up his arm. It was an angry red, almost the color of a cooked lobster. When he'd reached out, grabbed me, and pulled me back into the car he'd given himself a hell of a burn. "Obviously, you were mistaken."

I shuddered at the memory. It was really embarrassing. There I'd stood, blinking in the sunlight and yawning. Then Sinclair, more white-faced than usual, was reaching for me, his arm com-ing out of the dark car like a hairy life preserver. "Oh, right," I'd said slowly, stupidly. Had I ever been so tired? "The sun, it burns, oh, the agony . . . oh, cruel rays of zzzzzzzz."

Sinclair cleared his throat, a harsh bark that jerked me back to the present. "Well," I said, staring at his burn. "I'm sorry about that. I didn't mean for you to get hurt. You know, none of this would have happened if you'd let me drive."

"Second-degree burns are a small price to pay, then."

"I would have jumped back in the car myself, but it was hard to think. I was *so* tired."

"And you *so* almost got me fried alive, as you would put it. How could you not have known this would happen to you?" His tone was equal parts impatience and admiration.

"I didn't know I'd pretty much pass out as soon as dawn hit," I griped. "I'm usually in bed before the sun comes up. And the next thing I know, poof—I'm wide awake and it's a brand new night."

"This is an excellent time for your lessons to resume."

"Why?"

"Because you promised."

"No, I mean, why do you care? Why do you want to teach me?"

"Because," he said simply, standing in one fluid movement (I was relieved to see navy boxer shorts), "if you are to be an effective queen, you must know the terms of the society you will rule."

"Oh, come on. You don't really believe all that Book of the Dead stuff, do you? Because you don't treat me like a revered monarch. Not that it would kill you to try," I added.

"If I hadn't known your true rank before last night, I would have when I saw you standing in sunlight and yawning, instead of doing what an ordinary vampire would have done, which is burst into flames."

"Aw, it was nothing," I said with totally fake modesty. "But why did you stick me in your bed? Don't tell me this place doesn't have about a hundred extra bedrooms."

He gave me a slow smile. It was like watching the moon come up. "Host's privilege."

"Pervert." But I was rattled. He really was yummy, dammit. Absolutely gorgeous—and a good boy, when he wanted to be. He certainly could have taken a few liberties. But he hadn't.

And why the hell hadn't he? As if any member of his harem was prettier—or had better toned thighs—than *me*. He could do a hell of a lot worse than the Queen of All Undead, thank you very much! What, royalty wasn't good enough for him? The former Miss Congeniality *and* Miss Burnsville? He didn't like ex-cheerleaders? Every man in America lusted after cheerleaders. And I hadn't been some squad bunny, either; I'd been the choreographer.

"Betsy, are you all right? You've got the oddest look on your face. Even for you."

I shoved the thoughts away. "Why were you awake before me? For that matter, why didn't you fall asleep in the car? We left the woods so late . . ."

"I wasn't worried about the time, provided we were under cover before the sun rose—"

"But why did *I* fall asleep? And why did you wake up before me?"

"I heard those questions the first time. If you'll let me finish . . ," He trailed off and raised his eyebrows. I glared. ". . . ah, compliance. Such a pleasant, early evening surprise." He must have heard my teeth gnashing together, because he added, "The plain truth is, I'm quite a bit older than you are. I don't have to rest all day if I don't wish."

"Oh. So that's one of those things that will eventually happen for me?"

He looked me over critically. I self-consciously straightened out my bangs. "Not all. Some must rest all day. Nostro, for example."

"No need to sound so smug," I said. Because he sure did. I could tell he was loving the fact that, although I could gargle with holy water, I couldn't stay up as late as he could. "So, back to our lessons, then. Yawn."

"But first . . ." Sinclair's grin was almost catlike in its insolence. "There's the little matter of what I told you at the diner a few nights ago."

I had a nasty suspicion, but was ready for him. I wandered toward the chest of drawers by the window. It was taller than I was. "What are you talking about?"

He stalked after me. "I told you there would come a time when you needed my help, and I would give it, provided you put something of mine in your mouth." His hands reached for my shoulders and gently turned me to face him. "Lady's choice, of course, but I do hope you'll—what's that?"

"One of your handkerchiefs," I said, pulling it out of the top drawer. I stuffed it into my mouth, chewed, and swallowed. "Where's the bathroom?" I asked thickly. "I'm going to be sick."

He stared at me for a long moment, then started to laugh. He was laughing so hard he could barely point to the bathroom, and I almost didn't make it in time.


WHILE Sinclair showered, I decided I wanted a cup of tea. Useless, really . . . it sure wouldn't quench my thirst. But I hated waking up in strange places, with strange vampires, with no access to eye liner, and a nice cuppa was just what I needed to soothe my jangled undead nerves.

Problem was, Sinclair's abode was about the size of the White House. I tried to follow my nose and ended up in a spa . . . one that used green tea in the whirlpool to rid the body of antioxidants. Argh!

I went back into the hallway and nearly ran over another woman. "Sorry," I said automatically. I recognized her, which was retty amazing because the last time I'd seen her she'd been naked and sweaty and having entirely too much fun with Sinclair.

"Oh," I added lamely. I wasn't sure I wanted her to know if I recognized her or not. "Um, hi." I mean, *I* wouldn't have wanted to be recognized. But I was kind of a prude about cheating on taxes, group sex, murder, and stuff.

She sized me up. You can always tell when a woman does it as opposed to a man. A woman checks your hair, your makeup job, your clothes, your shoes. If you're barelegged she checks to see if you've got alligator skin or if you are acquainted with moisturizer. Basically, she's seeing whether you're a player or not.

A man checks your tits, then your face. It's annoying, but much more straightforward.

"Huh," she said, blowing out her breath in what I assumed was disgust. That was it, just, "huh," and a snort. Nice! She didn't even know me! Usually people have two or three conversations with me before they blow me off.

She was handsome rather than conventionally pretty, with high cheekbones, a wide forehead, strong nose, and deep-set black eyes. They were so dark that, like Sinclair's, I couldn't see her pupils. On him it was scary, like you could fall into them. On her it was just weird, like Keanu Reeves's eyes. She was a good two or three inches taller than me, which meant she was one of the tallest women I'd ever seen. She was wearing a red bathrobe and not much else, and was sorely in need of a pedicure.

"Say, I wonder if you could tell me where the kitchen is," I said, when she appeared to be finished, both with the sizing-up and the conversation. "I'm trying like heck to find it in this place, but—"

Her nostrils flared. Since she had a—shall we say—heroic nose, the effect was startling. I nearly took a step back. When she spoke, her voice was surprisingly deep and throaty. "Oh, so because I'm a sister I know where the kitchen is?"

"I thought—"

"You thought because I'm a black woman in my bathrobe at eight o'clock at night, I must be kitchen help? Because you've got that all wrong. For your information, I don't know a frying pan from my own ass."

"Er—I'm sorry to hear that?"

"I'm not *the help*. I'm the boss's right-hand lady, and I know you know *that* shit, because I know you watched us and got your jollies."

I was flabbergasted. I don't think I'd ever been accused of

prejudice before. I mean, everybody who knows me knows Jes
sica's my best friend. And anybody who knows Jessica know.
she's smarter, prettier, thinner, and richer than I am. There's just
no comparison. If anything, I tended to assume blacks (*"Never
African Americans,"* Jessica had schooled me. "Shit, my grand-
parents were from Jamaica.") were smarter and more successful
than I was. Because the ones I knew *were*.

Having verbally ripped me a new asshole, my nice new friend
was turning away. She stopped when I spoke.

"First of all," I said, and I was *very* angry, so I kept my tone
light, "I thought you might know where the kitchen is because you
appear to live here. Unless bathrobes are suddenly considered
trendy evening wear, which I doubt, because there wasn't a whisper of it in this month's *Vogue*."

She opened her mouth but I plunged ahead. "Number two,
watching you guys explore each other's naughty places wasn't *my*
idea. Not that I care what you do with Sinclair, but bragging about
it is just gauche. I mean, like it's an accomplishment he's jumped
your bones? I'm sure he's got a *rigorous* application process," I
added sarcastically. "You have tits, so I guess you pass."

"Don't you talk to me like that," she said sullenly, fingering
the belt of her robe.

"Don't *you* talk to *me* like that. I asked you a perfectly nice
question and you went off. Maybe if you kept your legs closed
once in a while, you could find time to brush up on your manners."

Her arm came up to hit me—not an open-handed slap, I noticed with alarm, but a closed fist. Of course, I was dead and she
was human, so to me it looked like she was trying to slug me underwater, but it was alarming just the same.

"Don't you dare!" I snapped. I batted her hand away like it
was a pesky fly. Unfortunately, this knocked her back about three
feet. Oops. "If you don't want to hear nasty things, don't start.
And another thing. If you ever—*ever*—accuse me of being prejudiced again, I will knock you on your fat ass. If you've got a problem with someone who treated you wrong, go take it out on *them*."

I swept past her and marched down the hall. I was always up
for a good catfight, provided I had the right ammo. But dammit! I
still didn't know where the kitchen was, and now I was thirstier
than ever. Should have chomped on what's-her-face, see how she
liked *that*.

I turned the corner and heard slow, measured clapping. There
was another of Sinclair's harem, standing in the doorway to an-

other bedroom. She was dressed, at least. "Oh, really excellent," she said in a perfect British accent. I loved to listen to Brits talk. "Mitzi's been needing someone to do that for quite a while."

"That Amazon's name is Mitzi?"

She gave me a sly smile. She was a real cutie; short, blond hair in a pixie cut, sky blue eyes, and a teeny dimpled chin. She was wearing a pink T-shirt that did fabulous things for her complexion, and white clamdiggers. Her toes were painted shell pink. They looked like little mother-of-pearls. "You should talk . . . Betsy."

"Fair enough. Say, *you* don't know where the kitchen is, do you? And this isn't a slur on your ethnicity in any way . . ."

"Come along, then." She bebopped down the hall and I practically had to run to keep up with her.

"Is it a race?" I asked.

"Oh, sorry." She slowed her pace a fraction.

"So you guys—you live here?"

"Mm-hmm."

"Do you like it?"

She looked at me, surprised. "What's not to like? You *have* seen Eric Sinclair, right?"

"Uh, yeah." Sure, he was handsome . . . but wasn't he one of the monsters? Wasn't I? Why would she want to be his hors d'oeuvre? "Not that I make snap judgments based on appearances—much— but you don't strike me as the type to enjoy being—um—well—"

She smiled, and the corners of her eyes crinkled in a friendly way. "A raging slut, one of a harem, his breakfast, lunch, and dinner?"

"Well. Yeah."

"Eric Sinclair saved me. I know I don't look it, but he found me on the streets. I was turning tricks on my knees in back alleys. He came up with a much better solution."

"Oh. Oh!" If I'd been alive, my face would be beet red by now. "You don't look—I mean, you're so—"

"My mum had a saying: 'It takes all types to make a world.'"

I'd never talked to a former prostitute before. Oh, the questions I had! How was the money? Were the pimps as bad as they seemed in the movies? Was there a dental plan? Could she tell a cop from a john? Did she ever Do It for fun, or was it all work, work, work? Was pregnancy considered an on-the-job hazard by OSHA?

I jerked myself back to the conversation. "My mom says that, too. Well, I guess the only thing that matters is if you're happy here. That, and if the food's decent. The rest is nobody's business."

She laughed. "The food is wonderful. And it's not exactly a burden, keeping Sinclair well-fed."

We were going downstairs now, but these weren't the front stairs I'd seen before. "Yeah, yeah, so he's not exactly hard to look at. Big deal. And by the way, is there somewhere I can buy a map to this place?"

She laughed again. "You'll get used to it."

"Christ, I hope not."

She quit laughing. The sound snapped off like she was a radio and somebody hit her switch. "You—I thought you were a vampire."

"I am."

"Say Christ again."

"Christ."

"Say, 'Jesus meek and mild.' "

"Jesus meek and mild."

"Recite the Lord's prayer, if you please."

"Only if you give me a cookie when I'm done. 'Our Father, who art in Heaven, hallowed be Thy name; Thy kingdom come; Thy will—' "

"Stop it!" Dennis came rocketing up the stairs, meeting us halfway. His feet seemed to barely touch the floor, he was moving so quickly. His hands were clapped firmly over his ears. His eyes were rolling like a rabid dog's. "Stop it, Karen! I can't get my work done when you're doing that. *Stop making that fucking noise!*"

"It's not me, Dennis," she who I took to be Karen replied, shrinking back against the wall. She jerked a thumb in my direction. "It's her."

"Oh." Dennis slowly lowered his hands. I noticed he was nattily attired in dark chinos, black socks, and a crisp white Oxford shirt. No tie, but he buttoned it all the way up to his neck anyway. "Oh, it's you."

"Sorry about that," I said.

"You needn't apologize to *me*, Majesty."

"I think I do. You looked like you were going to stroke out." *Or wet your pants. Possibly simultaneously.* "Sorry again."

"I'm sorry, too," Karen said quickly. "I didn't think she'd do it. I didn't think she could." She turned to me. "But you're a vampire!"

"That's what they keep telling me. So, about that trip to the kitchen . . ."

"Right, right." She shook herself like a terrier. "This way, then."

Dennis slunk off after a final mistrustful glance over one shoulder. "I really am sorry," Karen said in a low voice. "I mean, I'd never have asked a regular person to do that. Not here, of all places."

"Does it hurt them?" I kept my voice low, too, knowing too well how good vampire hearing was.

"Tina told me it's like hearing metal nails being dragged down a chalkboard, times a thousand. And they hear it in their head, so plugging their ears doesn't do any good—not that they don't try."

"Ouch!"

"But how can you—how can you even say the words? How can you even think them? And what d'you mean, 'Does it hurt them'? *You're* them."

"It's a mystery, all right," I said, a little proudly. Hey, why not? I was a mystery wrapped in an enigma and drenched with Big Mac secret sauce. "Sinclair's trying to figure it out. That's why he's teaching me how to be a vampire."

"Seems like you're the one who could be doing the teaching," Karen said, and then blushed to her hairline. "You didn't hear that, right?"

"Hear what?"

"Thank you."

We went down a couple more hallways and through a swinging door, and lo! Unto us a kitchen appeared. "Jeez, finally," I complained. "If I were still alive, I'd have died of thirst by now."

Karen cleared her throat. "About that. Um. Do you need—I mean, should I get someone?"

"Sweetie, the only thing I need you to get me is a teapot."

She jumped toward a tower of cabinets, rooted around in one, and emerged with a bright red pot, the kind that shrieked bloody murder when the water boiled.

"Thanks." I walked twenty feet to the sink—Sinclair's kitchen was bigger than my dad's entire ground floor—and filled it. "Want some?"

"Let me see . . ." She rooted through another cupboard. "Yes, I think. They have leaves, not bags, today."

"What's wrong with bags? Oh, right, you're a Brit. You're picky about your boiled leaves." I snickered.

"Well, I am! The stuff in teabags is undrinkable. That's the leftovers, you know. They take the good leaves and put them in tins, and the dust that's leftover they stuff into little bags!"

"Calm down before you need your blood pressure checked. I don't care either way. Tell you what, though, I hate those little leaves floating in my tea. Some of them always escape the tea ball. What if they make me throw up?" I added anxiously.

"Throw up?"

I nodded glumly and took a seat at a counter that was long enough to slaughter a couple of cows on. "Yeah, if I try to eat solid food, I puke. Not a pretty sight." I buried my head in my hands. "I just realized! Desserts! No more crème brulée, chocolate cake, ice cream. Ixnay on zabaglione with raspberries, chocolate chip cookies, French silk pie! Oh, I'm gonna cry right now."

"Please don't," Karen said anxiously. She took the teapot from me, which I'd been swinging around in my agitation, and went to the smallest stove—the one with only eight burners. She pressed a button and blue flame popped to life. "Forgive me, but . . . you're only thinking of this now?"

"Give me a break! I've only been dead—er, what day is it? I died late last week."

There was a clang and a slosh as she dropped the pot. "You're—you're newly risen?" Was she . . . ? She was! She was actually backing away from me. "But you're not—you should be all over me. I—I can't stay in here with you, I'm sorry, you seem rather nice but I—"

"Quit it!" I snapped. "All that Hugh Grantesque stammering is making me nervous. I'm not going to bite you. I'm not thirsty. Okay, well, I am, but I can control it. Really, I can. Otherwise I would have jumped Mitzi in the hall, right?"

Karen was squished up against the far wall. I could barely see her. Stupid industrial-sized kitchen. "Well . . . I suppose . . . and you *are* interesting." She forced a smile. "And me without my crucifix."

"It wouldn't do any good," I said apologetically. "I can touch them. I can probably *eat* them. No problem. Shoot, I'm wearing one right now."

That got her out of her corner. "Really? You can control your thirst and touch crosses?"

"Haven't we gone over this already? Your attention span is as tiny as your feet. What can I say? I'm an enigma, wrapped in a riddle, drenched with—"

"None of that. Who *are* you?" She was very close now—crossed the kitchen floor pretty quick!—and staring into my face.

I shrugged. "I'm just . . . me, I guess. Just Betsy. At least, that's who I always was."

"Hmm. Well, I don't believe we've been properly introduced. I'm Karen Helmbolt." She gingerly offered me a hand, doubtless expecting me to bite it. Instead I shook it briefly.

"Nice to meet you."

"Likewise . . . I guess."

While I laughed at that, she bent, picked up the pot, refilled it, and walked back to put it on the stove. Then she found a towel and wiped up the water on the floor, keeping more than a casual eye on me the entire time. "Well, it's certainly been interesting meeting you. It's been awfully quiet around here lately. You're the most unique thing to happen around here in—er—" She trailed off.

"Pretty quiet place to live, huh?"

"Oh, yes. Thank God," she added solemnly. Then she flinched. "Sorry about that. Oh! Sorry about *that*. I forgot you didn't—"

"Jeez, get a grip, willya? I thought Brits were laid-back and cool all the time."

"Not on days like today," she said dryly.

# Chapter 21

AᏋᎢᏋᏒ tea, I asked Karen to show me to the library. Color me geek, but I wanted to see the sorts of books Sinclair had lying around. And if he had any history books, I wanted to see if I could find him, or Tina, or Dennis in them. Or even Nostro. Know your enemy and all that, even if your enemy was a pathetic drama queen with a beer belly. Or would that be a blood belly?

Surprise, surprise, the library was right out of a nineteenth-century catalog. Dark walls, lush wine-colored carpet which I sunk into up to my ankles, mahogany furniture, and shelves of books. The desk was big enough for three people to work at comfortably without their ever brushing elbows. Ridiculous! If I didn't know for a fact that Sinclair didn't have to compensate for a darned thing, I'd sure have wondered.

On the wall behind the desk was a framed photo. It was sepia-toned and looked very old. The two men in the photo both had Sinclair's fathomless eyes, except one was a teenager and the other a man in his fifties. The women were petite, dainty, with dark hair and tip-tilted eyes . . . since the photo was black and white, I couldn't tell what color. Only the girl was smiling. She looked about thirteen. *That's his family,* I thought. *His folks and his sister. All dead, now. I wonder if he thought he'd still be around in the twenty-first century when they took this little snapshot?*

It was the only photo in the room.

I started thumbing through the books on the shelves. Shakespeare, no surprise there. The entire James Herriot collection, which *was* a surprise. I hadn't pegged Sinclair as the type to curl up with a book about a Yorkshire veterinarian. On the other hand, he *had* lived on a farm.

The entire wall behind the desk was wall-to-floor CDs. I didn't bother to look at any of them—there was no hope, based on last night's car ride.

I turned to the books. There was a set of leather-bound encyclopedias that smelled terrific, from aardvark to zymogen. Atlases. *The Geography of the World* in thirty-two volumes . . . copyright 1922. A globe in the corner by the window . . . I wondered if it was the hokey type my dad had, the kind that opened to reveal a wet bar. *The Canterbury Tales,* uck . . . even Sinclair wasn't *that* old. Dante's *Inferno* . . . big shocker.

And what were these? The middle shelf had its own unique genre: *Back from Death; Vampires of Historic Note; Walking with the Undead; The Vampire's Guide to Man; The Church and the Undead: A History; Living Dead and Living Well.* Who were these people?

I pulled *Vampires of Historic Note* off the shelf and immediately saw it was well used. It fell open to a heavily marked page, and I saw a bad picture of Nostro scowling up at me. I nearly dropped it.

*Nostrodamus, formerly known as Frederick O'Neill. DOB: February 14, 1627. POB: London, England. DOD: December 26, 1656.*

Awwww! Old Noseo was a Valentine baby. How cute. Born on Valentine's, dead the day after Christmas. Ick. His name was Fred? Ha, I knew it! No wonder he changed it as fast as he could. And what had happened to his British accent? Maybe he lost it after living in America for two hundred years.

The book weighed a ton, and it was at least six inches thick. I shifted my weight and began to read.

*Little is known of Nostrodamus in life because of poor recordkeeping and his reclusive nature.*

*In death, however, his exploits are worth noting, to wit:*

*The Undead Uprising of 1658. While eventually defeated, this is a significant event, as Nostrodamus was able to rally six thousand vampires in a very short time. If not for the intervention and eventual aid of the Catholic Church, the Undead may well have taken London.*

He'd been dead for two years before leading an uprising? Ambitious little fucker.

*The Maypole Massacre of 1660. Again, Nostrodamus was eventually defeated by the Church, but only after egregious loss of life, and this case proves he learned from his earlier errors. In a stroke of cunning, Nostrodamus took the town's children and—*

I turned the page. No thanks. Did not want to know.

*The Plymouth Uprising, 1700. After journeying to the New World via the cargo compartment of the Queen Elizabeth, Nostrodamus quickly established a foothold in the Massachusetts Bay Colony. This time, he was able to keep control of the town for fifty-six years, before being driven out by settlers and Native Americans, who set fire to Plymouth during daylight hours and staked all who were left alive that night.*
    *This is the first known record of Native Americans and colonists uniting against vampires. Nostrodamus sacrificed most of his followers to ensure his escape. Many of them were left behind for the townspeople to—*

I slammed the book shut, appalled. Cripes, the guy never gave up. Just attack after attack, and he didn't care who got hurt and who got dead. He'd do anything to hold onto his territory.

But he moved. And kept moving . . . sure, after every defeat. Now he was entrenched, and likely wouldn't want to skulk away and pick up the pieces somewhere else. Too bad for us.

And now he was mad at *me*. For what? All I did was laugh at him. And not die a hideous death. And insult him in front of his followers. And get away.

"Fascinating reading, yes?"

I nearly dropped the book on my foot. Sinclair was standing in the doorway, looking like a million bucks in black slacks, a midnight blue shirt, and black shoes. His hair was still damp from the shower, and he smelled vaguely of fresh blood. At my stare, he said easily, "I ran into Mitzi after my shower. And you ran into her, so I hear."

"Yeah, you've got a real sweetheart in that one. Don't let her get away."

"She's quite terrified, you know," he said, sounding amused.

"She had no idea who you were when she challenged you. I had my hands full trying to end her hysterics."

I dismissed this absurdity. "Nothing scares her. Where do all these books come from? I've never heard of some of them."

"Well," he said, straight-faced, "Shakespeare was a famous writer who was born—"

"I know *him,* dolt. I mean these Vampire 101 texts."

"You think once we die, we lose our creativity, or thirst for knowledge?"

"No. I guess not. So there are vamp publishing houses?" I chuckled.

"Yes."

I stopped laughing. "Oh. Listen, can I borrow some of these? All my other research sources have been the fiction section of the library, and the movie theater."

He visibly shuddered. "Please. Help yourself. I insist."

"Great." I started grabbing books. "And I think I'm going."

"You gave your—"

"I *know*. Stop nagging. But last night we covered stalking—"

"Hardly."

"And now I've got all this homework. C'mon, let me get this reading done. I'll come back tomorrow night and you can quiz me."

"Really? What are the penalties for missed questions?"

"Um . . ."

"Kisses?"

"In a pig's eye."

"There's no accounting for taste."

"Have I mentioned I hate banter? I'm going," I said shortly, stomping across the floor and shouldering past him. The stubborn cuss didn't budge, not even when I shoved my body weight against his side. So I had to grunt and wiggle my way past, all the while knowing he was smiling.

"Oh, and I'll need to borrow a car," I called over my shoulder, and was gratified to see the grin drop off his face.


I downshifted, but not by much, and took the turn in third gear. The car fishtailed behind me and I wrestled with the wheel until it straightened out. The roar of the engine—actually, the car was so pricey it was more a purr than a roar—was music to my ears.

Ah, sweet freedom! So long, Sinclair. See ya, Tina. Bye-bye, Dennis and Mitzi and Karen. Well, maybe not Karen.

I had one hand on the steering wheel, and the other was buried in the CD holder up to the elbow. I groped, felt, and pulled. Soundtrack from *Amadeus*. Nope. I took my hand off the wheel long enough to hit the power button for the window, and out into the night air ole Wolfgang went.

*Beethoven: Violin Concerto*. Pass. I tossed it. *Sentimento*, Andrea Bocelli. Who the hell was she? Toss. *Mahler: Symphony Number Five*. It probably wasn't any better than symphonies one through four . . . buh-bye. *Chopin: 24 Études*. Et tu, Chopin? Kiss pavement.

Who did I have to bite to find something decent to listen to? And why did I pick the car that had a state-of-the-art CD stereo system but *no damned radio?* Stupid Sinclair. Even if he wasn't an arrogant cuss, I felt like giving him a kick for his musical taste alone.

The flashing red lights in my rearview reminded me that there were worse problems than being trapped in Sinclair's shiny Mercedes with a bunch of his lousy CDs. For example, there was being pulled over at 9:30 at night in a car that wasn't mine, when I didn't have my driver's license.

I pulled over as safely and slowly as I could—a good trick, as I'd been going ninety—and frantically straightened out my bangs while the Bear approached. The Minnesota governor kept slashing the state budget, but there always seemed to be plenty of state troopers around to torment me. They were firing VA nurses left and right, but kept plenty of cops on the road . . . tell me *that's* fair.

More nurses, less tickets. That's my motto.

He stopped just outside my door, and bent down a bit to look in. I gave him a big smile. Here it came: dumbass question number one.

"Good evening, ma'am. Do you know how fast you were going?"

Nope. Even though I was driving, and I'm the only one in the car, and the speedometer is translucent amber, I have no idea. Twenty-five miles an hour? Thirty?

"I'm sorry, Officer. I'm in a hurry to get home. I guess I wasn't paying attention." Blink, blink. The oops, silly me, but I'm not in the habit of breaking the law so how about you let me off, you big strong sweetie? routine had a sixty-seven percent success rate, particularly when I was wearing my suede miniskirt.

He was still bending down, still staring at me. I took the plunge to head off dumbass question number two. "I'm afraid I don't have my license—I left it at home. And I don't have the registration. This isn't my car, it belongs to—" To whom? My friendly enemy? Nemesis? Local jerk? Undead tormenter? Creep with lousy taste in music? "—um, I borrowed it."

The trooper gave me a sweet, goofy grin. "You're pretty."

*Yes!* Make that a one-hundred-percent success rate, now that I was postmortem.

For the first time, I had a real glimpse of the possibilities. There had to be a tradeoff if I was expected to give up chocolate. Never again would I be a slave to the speed limit!

"Pretty," the trooper said again, in case I missed it the first time. Like I would! "You're so so pretty. Ummmm."

"Thanks. Is it okay if I go?"

"Uh-huh."

"Okay."

He didn't move. I was afraid I'd run over his toes, so I ordered, "Step back. Get into your car. Don't set any more speed traps tonight."

Worked like a charm.

# Chapter 22

I staggered into my empty house. It's not that I wasn't strong enough to easily carry the books, but they were an awkward bundle, and I could barely see over them.

I let the books tumble to my coffee table. The flimsy structure shuddered but, fortunately, maintained its integrity. Then I went to the kitchen.

Time for more tea to distract myself from my raging thirst. I could ignore it a lot of the time, but it was getting harder and harder. When had I fed last? It had been at least two full nights, that was for sure. I'd have to give in and chomp eventually. Maybe when it got really late I'd take a stroll and let myself get mugged.

There was a note on the fridge, scribbled on a prescription sheet and smeared with marinara sauce—Marc simply would *not* use a napkin. It was unbelievable—he looked neat as a pin and was a total slob. I didn't think gays were allowed to be messy.

I came closer and read:

*Hello oh vampire queen. Hope lessons with what's-his-face went okay. If he gives you any shit, lemmee at him. Jessica's working late at the Foot tonight and I've got the midnight shift this week. Don't bother looking in the fridge, we drank all the milk. I might bring some patient files home for you to look over. Hungry?*

*—M.*

Oh, he was a sly one. He hadn't let go of his undead vigilante plan. And, if I was going to be honest with myself, as far as plans went, it wasn't such a bad one. If I could get past the whole felonious assault thing. And the fact that, if I fed on them and left them, there was a chance they'd waste away and die.

And what the hell did he mean, they drank all the milk? Dammit! I hated tea without milk, or at least cream.

I was drinking my third cup of milkless tea and deeply engrossed in *The Church and the Undead: A History* when Jessica walked in. She immediately burst out laughing, which wasn't unusual. I was sprawled across the couch in my sushi pajamas and slippers that looked like monster paws. The coffee table groaned under the weight of the books and I had *Gone with the Wind* playing on the DVD player. Best movie *ever*.

"Comfy?" she asked, grinning. She tossed her keys in the dish by the phone nook and dropped her briefcase in the corner where, tomorrow morning, she would spend half an hour looking for it.

"Homework," I said gloomily. "If I wasn't dead, I'd have a splitting headache by now."

"What the hell are you reading?"

"Listen to this: *By definition, the church and the Undead are doomed to be enemies. See index vii, xxiii, and xvii.* I spend so much time looking up the damn footnotes I have no idea what the hell I'm reading."

She walked over and stared at the volumes. "Jeez," she said, sounding impressed, which was a rare and wonderful thing with her. "What are these?"

"Supersecret vamp stuff. Apparently there's undead artists, writers, bankers, valets . . . blah-blah. And they keep producing stuff like this after they're dead. Wonder if there's an undead bestseller list?"

"How long you been at it?"

"Half an hour! It's been endless. I'm so ready for a break."

"Well, good, because I had regular coffee instead of decaf and I'm wide awake. Let's go do something."

I shrugged. I really wasn't a late-night party girl. Although maybe now that would change.

"Aw, c'mon!" Jessica was begging. "We haven't done something fun, just us, since you—well, you know."

Since I died. Right. "Fair enough." I tossed the book aside, wincing as it slammed into the carpet. "Is there anything good playing at the Hype?"

The Hyperion was an open-all-night movie theater that showed cheapie movies. You could see a movie for two bucks, but it was a movie that opened eight months ago. Usually they got movies right around the time the video store did. And it was always funny to see previews for movies that had been out for three months. Still, two bucks!

Jessica smirked at me. She was looking efficient and businesslike in her gray Armani suit, black hose, and black pumps, but the smirky grin sort of ruined the effect and made her look like a smug first-grader. "You'll never guess."

"Probably not, so why don't you tell me? And don't smile like that, it gives you crow's feet."

"Does not. Go on, guess."

"Uh . . . *Gone with the Wind?*"

The smirk vanished. "Shit, no! Why would I want to watch a movie that glorifies—"

"Oh, here we go."

"—slavery while elevating the rich plantation creeps to the status of demigods?"

"First of all, they're not demigods. They're as flawed as people can be—the heroine's a jerk, for God's sake. Margaret Mitchell makes no secret of the fact that Scarlett O'Hara is vain, willful, obstinate, selfish . . ."

"Oppressive."

"Yes, yes, all right. But Mitchell also points out that Scarlett treats her servants—"

"Slaves."

"Not after the Civil War ended, they're weren't. She treated them better than all the white people, even her own husband! Husbands."

"Yeah, but—"

"*And* the hero was a womanizing, cruel gambler who raped his wife when he got drunk. I mean, hello? These are flawed people. The slaves and servants, on the other hand, are almost universally good, long-suffering, and devoted to their families. The whole point of the book was that there was *plenty* of bad stuff perpetrated by the North. I mean, how many of the freed slaves really *did* get forty acres and a mule?"

This was an old and well-loved discussion. I think Jessica secretly liked the book—I'd found my copy in her room more than once—she just liked to argue about it. And most whites wouldn't dare defend it to her. Me, I had no shame. Also, she was wrong.

"It's a book that glorifies white people at the expense of blacks."

w"The vain white people who ended up alone and unhappy, or the white people who got the shit kicked out of them by the Union Army? Or the white people who starved to death during Reconstruction? Or—"

"All *right.*"

"You know, for somebody who could buy London, you're awfully touchy about slavery. I mean, no one in your family was ever a slave."

She sniffed. "You can never know my pain."

"The pain of being the first kid on the block to have her own Patek Philippe watch? You poor oppressed creature."

She giggled. "Thank God you understand. This is, of course, why I tolerate your bigotry and snobbishness."

I threw a sofa pillow at her. We had done this part of the dance, too, but with my undead reflexes she had no time to duck. The pillow hit her square in the face and knocked her back two steps.

"Help, help!" she said. "I'm being oppressed!"

"Thief! You stole that line from Monty Python."

"Now *there's* a movie. God, that was quick. I didn't even see your arm move."

"Sorry," I said, and I meant it. I could tell she was a little rattled. "I'll try to slow down a little."

"Don't," she said shortly. "I'll get used to it. C'mon, let's go."

"What *is* playing? You never told me."

"You'll like it. Come on. More research."

SHE was right. I liked it. But I wasn't about to give her the satisfaction of knowing she was right—she got that too often at the Foot and from the horde of adoring boyfriends.

"You know I don't like movies that have Roman numerals after the titles," I whined.

"Shut up. Those are the best ones. Besides, you're out a whole two bucks."

"Plus nine," I said, holding up my 7-Up, which was the size of a gallon ice cream container. I sipped contentedly while the opening credits for *Blade V: Return of the Vampire King's Nephew* scrolled down the screen. I tried to ignore the fact that my feet were sticking to the floor.

I'm afraid I laughed through most of the movie. In particular, when the hero leapt over a moody crowd of bad guys, had a sword fight in midair with the villain, and landed lightly on his feet all the way across the room just in time to prevent the heroine from falling to her death. Then he caught his sunglasses, which had been flying toward him (contemptuously tossed by the villain's henchman) in slow motion, and popped them on his head while the heroine gazed up at him adoringly. Shyeah! All he needed was a halo.

"Will you quit it?" Jessica hissed, elbowing me for the tenth time. "You used to think this stuff was scary."

"Well, now I think it's funny. Oh, look! Even though he emptied his pockets in the earlier scene, now they're bulging with extra bullets. How handy! It's *Treasure Island* all over again. Somebody shoot the head writer."

"Someone's gonna shoot *you*, you don't shut up."

"Hey, even better! Even though he parked miles away, now his car is waiting for him right outside the bad guy's lair. What, is it like the Batmobile? Does it come when it's called?"

"Go get another drink, why don't you?"

"I drink anymore I'll burst. As it is, I might actually have to use the bathroom."

The end came to a predictable, yet satisfying, conclusion, with plenty of room left for yet another sequel. I steered Jessica toward the back door exit.

"Why are we going out here?"

"I need to get some air." Which was a lie, but no need to scare her just yet.

"So, I guess you liked it. I mean, you laughed enough."

"It was great! I should do more research. Rent a bunch of old movies. You know, like classics. *Nosferatu. Dracula. Fright Night. Dracula*—the one with Gary Oldman running around in that little old lady hairdo. I don't know what was creepier, the way he licked blood off razors or the way he wore his long white hair in a bun."

Jessica cracked up. "Like Gary Oldman isn't scary enough!"

"Exactly. And what's that one with Eddie Murphy and Angela Bassett? Oooh, and *Vampires* with James Woods."

"I thought you wanted to watch classics."

"Those are. They're all from the last century, aren't they? And *Dracula 2000*. And—"

"I am *so* glad the millennium thing finally happened. I was getting really sick of movies sticking the number two thousand at the end of every damn title."

"Grump, grump, grump. Let's go down this alley."

"*Where* are we going?"

"I thought we'd take a short cut." The streetlights down in this neck of the woods were few and far between. Really perfect.

*Come on, guys, what do you want, a welcoming blare of trumpets?*

"Oh. Are you—uh—hunting?"

"No."

"Aren't you thirsty?"

"Yep."

"Why haven't you—uh—"

"Because it's gross," I said irritably, kicking an empty Budweiser can out of my way. It flew down the alley and smashed up against the far wall. "Look: I know I have to get used to it and I should just suck it up, no pun intended, but even though it feels really, really, really good—"

"It does?"

"Best sex you've ever had, times ten."

"Best sex I've ever had, or you've ever had?"

"Har-har."

"Well, there's a pretty big difference."

"Shut up! Besides, it doesn't matter. I still don't like the idea of it. Drinking someone's blood . . . ech."

"I don't blame you, Bets, but you have to," she said earnestly. "What if you get sick?"

"I don't think I can. But I can't put it off much longer, either. I haven't fed in a while. I'm unbelievably thirsty." My tongue felt like a little dry lump in my mouth. "You wouldn't believe how thirsty."

She shied away from me like a nervous horse. "Forget it! I'll kick ass for you, I'll throw money at you, I'll fight creditors for you, I'll buy your house to keep it away from the Ant, I'll help you defeat the forces of evil, but I'm not lunch!"

"Calm down before you have a stroke. I was thinking about the two guys who are following us."

"What two guys?" She started to crane her neck.

"Don't look, for God's sake. You'll tip them off."

"What two guys?" she asked, looking exaggeratedly casual.

"The two who followed us into the movie theater, loitered near the snack stand, then followed us into the movie, and were right behind us when we left."

"Wow. You saw all that?"

"More like smelled."

"Maybe they just want to pick us up. You know, for a date or something."

I snorted.

"It's not outside the realm of possibility," she said dryly. "I mean, people do go on dates. Besides you, I mean."

"I know, but these two smell like dried semen and pancakes. I'm pretty sure they're looking for trouble."

"Did the dried jizz tip you off, or the pancakes?" She was trying to joke, but her voice cracked on pancakes. "Should I call nine-one-one?" she asked, digging into her purse for her cell phone.

"No. Don't worry, Jess. I'd never let anyone hurt you. Especially not these two pukes. Just a minute." I swung around to face them. They probably thought they'd been moving quietly. "Back off, boys. We're in no mood."

"Give us the purses, bitch."

"Jeez, can't you count? She's the only one carrying a purse. And technically it's not a purse, it's a handbag."

"What's the difference?" Jessica asked curiously. I could tell she was taking heart at my complete lack of fear. Either that, or she was easily distracted. No, that was me.

"Well, a purse is more like a bag, and a handbag usually doesn't have a handle. I know it seems complicated, but it's really—"

"Bitches, gimmee your shit *now*."

I scowled at the interruption. Muggers were so rude! "No."

They both blinked at me. They were roughly the same height, a couple inches taller than me, and much broader through the shoulders. Neither of them had made acquaintance with soap nor razor in the past few days, and they reeked of desperation and trapped anger. And they were hungry. Starving, actually. Well, I could relate.

Jessica was unconsciously clutching her handbag—not her purse—to her chest and was watching the three of us like a spectator at a sporting event. She hadn't backed up, though—she was glued to my side. If I hadn't adored her before, I would have now. She was frightened, but she wouldn't run.

"Why don't you guys get lost?" I suggested, while they were

still pondering my refusal. Clearly this was the point where the woman in question handed everything over and then submitted to rape. They weren't sure how else to proceed. "You don't want to mess with us."

"Yeah," Jessica echoed loyally. "You don't want to mess with us."

"I mean, we'll fight, you'll lose, and then I'll have to eat you, which sucks because you're both just filthy. I mean, ech! It's called deodorant, gentlemen. It's not hard to find."

That was the end of the chitchat as they both charged me at once. I heard Jessica squeak and jump out of the way, which was smart, because the fur was about to fly. I was still reluctant to— er—what was the military term? Engage? But now it was out of my hands.

I was pretty nonconfrontational in life. I never liked to fight, unless it was a good old-fashioned catfight with lots of insulting nicknames. I certainly wasn't used to getting physical. But it was time to try to get over that, as well as my weird (for a vampire) aversion to drinking blood. If not for my sake, then for my friend's.

I'm sure they were moving very fast, but to me it looked like they were charging me through knee-deep molasses. I caught the wrist of the smellier one and yanked him past me, hard. He smacked into the alley wall and crumpled to a heap on the filthy floor. The other one I caught by the neck, shook like a terrier shakes a rat, then briskly bonked his forehead with mine. He sagged in my grip, unconscious. Thank goodness! The last thing I needed was this guy trying to hump me while I drank.

"Don't look, ith groth," I told Jessica, and then I sank my fangs into his neck.

He was gross, he was disgusting, he reeked, and it was just fine. His blood wasn't gross. His blood was like sweetly potent burgundy. His whiskers rasped against my cheek as I drank my fill. It was over in less than a minute.

I let go of him right about the time Jessica stopped throwing up. "I told you not to look," I said, hurrying over to her, licking the blood off my rapidly retracting fangs. I pulled her away from the wall she'd leaned against—yuck. It was so slimy, it shined. "Why'd you look?"

"It wasn't that. I mean, I looked, but it wasn't bad. There was hardly any blood. You know, because you drank—" She made a "hurp-hurp" sound and I stepped back in case she wasn't done barfing.

"I'm sorry," I said miserably. "I shouldn't have fed in front of you."

She straightened up and said with a familiar snap, "Don't be sorry. It was just that it was so fast." She looked up at me, her forehead shiny with sweat. "I mean, my adrenaline barely had time to get moving and it was scary but you weren't scared and then one of them was flying through the air and then it was over. I think it was more that than anything else."

"Oh. Are you all right?"

"I'm fine." She straightened up and added firmly, "Too much bad movie popcorn."

"I know it was stale," I said dryly, "but it wasn't that bad."

"I'm used to gourmet popcorn."

I laughed. "Jess, you're one in a billion."

"Fucking A right. Keep it in mind." She shoved her hand in mine as we stepped around our would-be assailants. Her palm was almost as cold as mine, and sweaty. I squeezed, and she squeezed back.

"Um, Betsy, is that guy going to end up like Nick?"

Good question. I thought about it. "I don't know. I don't think so. I mean, Nick liked me before. So the feeding—me biting him—meant more than it did . . . or should have, I guess is the way to say it. And it didn't seem to affect Marc. But this guy is a stranger."

"You're talking through your ass. You have no idea."

"None," I said glumly. "Thus Vampire 101 with Sinclair."

We went home.

# Chapter 23

"HERE I am, just wandering down a deserted street in the middle of the night. I hope I don't run into any trouble. Goodness, that would just ruin my whole evening." I strolled and hummed, trying to project Innocent Victim. I was certainly dressed for it—red linen A-line skirt, white blouse, red Ferragamos. Last year's, but it was dark in the alley—who'd know?

Five minutes went by, and my feet were killing me. "This is stupid!" I yelled to the shadows where Sinclair was lurking. "I'm not a goddamned worm on a hook. I gave up watching *Seinfeld* reruns for this? It's—aaiigh!"

Someone threw a brick wall on top of me—at least, that's what it felt like—and we hit the dirt—literally! Stupid Lake Street . . . filthy even after it rains. I smacked whoever it was on the side of the head and my hand instantly went numb. It was like slapping a brick. A dirty brick. I felt him slam my shoulders into the ground, and then I saw a flash of—fangs?

I shrieked like a fire alarm. Stupid Sinclair and his stupid Vamp 101! His big plan was to teach me more stalking, but I bet he didn't expect a vampire to grab me.

I articulated this stream of consciousness with, "Stupid!"

"Pretty," the thing that needed mouthwash crooned. "Don't scream anymore."

"Ha! I haven't even gotten warmed up! And cripes, do you need a bath." His mouth flashed down and I managed to get my arm up in time. He bit me anyway and I yowled. "Stop it stop it stop it!"

He licked his lips thoughtfully and stared down at me. He had shoulder-length hair that had last been washed when Bush was president . . . the *other* Bush. His eyes were the color of dirt, his cheeks were scattered with pockmarks, and his denim shirt had holes in the breast pockets. Still, that was no reason to let yourself go.

"What, Laundromats aren't open at night?" I griped.

"Who are you?" he asked at last, looking vaguely puzzled. "You're delicious, and fast, but you're not a vamp—"

He quit talking as he was jerked off me. I looked up to see Sinclair holding him off the ground by the scruff of the neck. I half expected him to start scolding my attacker. Bad undead night-stalker! Naughty!

I climbed painfully to my feet. "Finally," I said. "What were you waiting for, violins?"

The guy who'd jumped me was scary, but Sinclair was all towering fury in his black overcoat with flashing eyes. He swung, and the vampire went sailing into the nearest brick wall.

Quick as thought, Sinclair was there, picking him up off the ground and shaking him like a rat, then swinging again. He flew through the air with the greatest of ease and smashed into a Dumpster.

Sinclair picked him up *again*—I could barely follow this, he was moving so quickly—and again there was a *whoosh,* and a *thud.*

"This is the queen."

Whoosh! Smack!

"*My* queen."

Whoosh! Smash!

"Never touch her."

Whoosh! It was like being in a twisted Batman rerun. Blam! Smash!

"*Never* touch her."

"Okay, that's enough!" I yelled. My would-be bloodsucker was a huddled, bloody, garbage-y mess. The last toss had thrown him inside the Dumpster, and I jumped in front of it. Sinclair grabbed my shoulders and pushed me aside, but I clung like a limpet. "All right, okay, ease up. He made a mistake, let's not spread him into the road like undead jelly."

"He hurt you," Sinclair snarled. Literally snarled—his upper lip lifted away from his teeth and everything. "He bit you without permission."

"Hello, whose bright idea was this, anyway? And it's not like

I'm walking around wearing a crown. He had no idea who I was."
Shit, *I* had no idea who I was. "Just . . . calm down, okay? Take a
breath. Take ten. You're really freaking me out."

He stared down at me. "You need to rid yourself of this tender
heart."

"Hey, I'm hard as nails, chum. I just don't like the *noise,* is
all." Not to mention the *thud-squish* every time the vamp hit
something solid.

"He hurt you," Sinclair repeated stonily.

I held up my arm. "Oh, barely, you big mommy. See? It's
practically all healed anyway. Having to smell him was a lot more
traumatic. Did you *see* the state of his shirt? Yech."

He stared at the chubby flesh of the underside of my arm (note
to self: do more curls), then gently took it in his big hands. He
held my arm thoughtfully for a moment, then pressed his lips to
the wound.

"Uh." Why did I feel that tickling touch between my legs? He
was nowhere near my legs.

He lapped up the fast-drying blood, then pressed a kiss to the
rapidly healing wound.

"Er." I realized I was leaning closer to him, when I should
have been throwing him into the Dumpster with the other one. His
dark head was bent over my arm and I itched to run my fingers
through his hair. "Sinclair. Could you. Uh. Not do that?"

He was pulling me closer to him.

"Please?"

He was bending his head over mine, and I could see the savage
flash of his fangs in the lone streetlight.

"Pretty please with blood on top?"

He kissed me so hard I was pulled up to my tiptoes, forced to
cling to his shoulders for balance. This hurt (stupid pumps!), but I
didn't care. His tongue swept into my mouth and I tasted my own
blood. This was as provocative as if Sinclair had suddenly
stripped down to his privates in the alley.

I had fistfuls of his coat and was kissing him back. I could feel
my mouth get crowded and knew my fangs had come out . . . in
response to my own blood, how fucked up was that?

Kissing Sinclair was like making out with a sexy timber
wolf—he was licking my fangs and nipping me lightly and growling under his breath and it was . . . oh, it was really something.

Why wasn't I scared? I was in an alley with two vampires,

making out with a very bad man who was a lot bigger and stronger than I was. Someone who hadn't exactly asked for this kiss—just took what he liked. What was the matter with me? Why was I still kissing him? And why was I still having this internal monologue?

Sinclair had left my mouth, which felt rudely swollen, and was trailing kisses down the side of my neck. I could hear myself gasping—a good trick, since I hardly ever had to breathe.

He was cuddling me into his chest and kissing my neck and stroking my back, and I was loving every second of it. There was a split-second pause and then Sinclair moved in for a bite.

Luckily, half a second was all I needed. I let go of his coat and staggered backward, and when he reached for me, I grabbed his hand and pulled him past me, hard. He smacked into the wall behind us, bounced off, and whirled to face me.

"Making out ith one thing," I tried not to gasp, "but none of that thtuff."

"Mmmmm." He touched his mouth, bemused. His fangs were gone. Damn it! How'd he do that? "What's wrong with your voice?"

"Nothing." Let's—no. What can I say without s's? "I want to go home now," I said carefully. "I have had enough for one night."

"You didn't learn much," he pointed out.

*Just that you're about the best kisser in the world.*

"More than you think," I replied.

# Chapter 24

I woke *(rose?)* to see Sinclair standing over me. This was not the best way for me to start the day, which I believe I put across by screaming like a girl in the third grade.

"And a fine evening it is," he said by way of reply. He was splendidly dressed in black pants, a black mock turtleneck, and a black jacket. He was holding a glass of plum wine in one hand, and had his other hand buried in his pocket up to the wrist. He was *muy* suave, damn him, and I had the fleeting thought that he looked like a vampiric James Bond.

On Nostro and his minions, the all-black thing looked like a cliché. But Sinclair made it seem as though he was the one who started the trend, so on him it looked good.

It wasn't fair. I had to die to meet someone really fabulous, and it was someone I couldn't stand. I had no idea if I didn't like him because I wanted to jump his bones, or because he was an arrogant snot. Or both.

"You've gotta stop hovering over me when I wake up," I groaned, throwing back the covers and standing. His eyebrows arched at my pajamas—cream, with a pattern of salmon sushi and tuna rolls—but, thankfully, he didn't comment. "Seriously. You're gonna give me a heart attack one of these days."

"You slept well?"

"Like the dead," I chortled.

He leaned in close. This was extremely disturbing. What was more disturbing was how I wanted to grab him by the ears and plant one on that sinful mouth.

"Could you not crowd me the second I get up?" I bitched.

He ignored me. "I quite enjoyed our little . . . interlude last night."

"You would. Can you please do me a favor and at least ask before we lock lips?"

"No," he said carelessly.

I ground my teeth and shoved past him. He trailed after me like a big, muscular puppy. "Why in the world are you going into the bathroom?"

"Habit," I said, and shut the door in his face. Then locked it for good measure.

After my early evening ablutions, such as they were, I walked into the kitchen to see Sinclair listening politely to Marc, who was explaining how he'd saved dozens of lives in one measly ER shift.

"—and then all the other docs were like, 'no way, man, it can't be done,' and I'm all 'dudes, step back, I'll do it and damn the consequences,' and they're all, 'we're getting the hospital administrator, man,' and I'm all 'dammit, dudes, this boy will die without my help,' and they're all—"

"I thought you were doing paperwork last night," I said. "You know, catching up on your charts. Filing. Stuff like that."

Marc gave me a good glare for interrupting the fantasy. "This happened after I got caught up," he said stiffly.

"Sure it did. Why are you here?" I asked Sinclair.

"Who cares?" Marc asked. "Stay as long as you want."

"That was *not* an official invitation," I said quickly.

"Tina and Dennis and I require your services. Things are escalating with . . . a certain other party."

"You mean old Noseo is finally making a move?"

Sinclair also glared, clearly not caring for the way I blurted out vampire biz to mere mortals. "In a word, yes. We can discuss the subject further en route."

"Oh, come on, Sinclair," I whined, "why do I have to get involved? I just got up and now I have to rush off to the mansion of sin? Besides, I've got stuff to do today. Tonight, I mean."

"*Stuff?*"

"Yeah. I haven't been to the bookstore all week—the one time I got near it I got snatched away to that creepy mausoleum—*and* I need a pedicure. And I have to get some new clothes, because I don't have a lot of evening wear and these days I'm all about evening wear. Plus, it's practically summer and I haven't even *looked* at bathing suits. What's the matter?"

Sinclair had been rubbing his forehead, as if a killer migraine had just sunk its claws into his brain. "Elizabeth, Elizabeth. You are so young you make me tired."

Marc laughed.

"Uh . . . thank you? Anyway, I've got places to go, and your house is nowhere on the list."

"I must insist."

"Oh, jeez!"

"Probably vamp politics take precedence over a foot massage," Marc said between gulps of coffee.

"Oh, as if *you* know. Stay out of this."

Sinclair cleared his throat before Marc and I started throwing things at each other. "Your friend is correct."

"Dammit, dammit! Like I have any interest in this at all," I griped. "Because to be brutally honest—"

"Which you never are," Sinclair interrupted.

"—it's all so damned dumb. It is! I bet you think so, too, but you'll never admit it."

"No, never," he agreed.

"I can't think of a more annoying way to spend the evening," I griped. I hated, hated, *hated* having a plan for the evening only to find it completely trashed by someone else's stupid agenda. *Hated.* "I really can't!"

"Neither can I," Sinclair said dryly.

"You hush up. Do I at least have time for some juice?"

"If you hadn't taken five minutes to complain, we might have."

*"Fine."* I resisted the urge to kick one of the table legs. "Guess we'd better get going, get this over with. I—wait." I cocked my head toward the front door and saw Sinclair was doing the same thing.

"Cut that out," Marc ordered. "You guys are giving me the creeps. You look like a pair of golden retrievers."

"Someone is coming."

"It's—I think—" A tentative rap on my front door. I hurried over to open it. My father stood on the front step. "It's my dad!" I said aloud, both for Sinclair and Marc's benefit, and because I was *very* surprised.

"Hello, Betsy." He tried a smile. It didn't quite fit. "All right if I come in?"

I stepped back, pleased to see him while cursing his timing. He'd had all week to visit, and he picked now?

"Sure, come on in. Dad, this is my roommate, Marc, and this is my—uh—my—"

"Eric Sinclair," he said, extending a hand to be shaken. "A great pleasure."

"Meetcha," my dad mumbled, shaking Sinclair's hand as quickly as he could and then dropping it like a trout. "Um, Betsy, could we—?" He motioned toward the back of the house.

"Oh, sure. Guys, we'll be right back."

"Nice to meet you," Marc said.

"Time is our enemy," Sinclair added. Like any woman who'd hit the big three-oh didn't know *that*.

Back in my bedroom, I shoved my dry cleaning pile on the floor, clearing a space for my father to sit down. But he remained standing. He didn't look so good, either. He'd always been a handsome guy, and now that his thinning dark brown hair was liberally flecked with salt and pepper, he was right out of central casting for Distinguished Gentlemen. The Armani didn't hurt, either. But it didn't hide the crow's feet, nor did it cover up the red-rimmed eyes and lines of exhaustion around his mouth.

"What's up, Dad?" I sat down on my bed and rubbed my hands together. I could count on one hand how often he'd visited me. This did not bode well. "Everything all right at home?"

"Well, no. That's why I—your stepmother and I—well, I needed to talk to you."

"About?"

He blinked at me, and then burst out, "What do you think? You're dead, Betsy. We were at the funeral."

"No you weren't," I said automatically, trying to figure out where he was going with this. "It was canceled because I'd gone on walkabout."

"I know," he said bitterly.

"Really? Because it seems like a few of the details have slipped your mind."

He shook his head hard, like there was a fly buzzing around his ear. "You look like my daughter, and you've got her smart mouth, but Elizabeth is dead. My daughter is dead."

"Dad, I'm *right here*."

"And we have to move on," he continued stubbornly. "With our lives and—and things. So stay away, Betsy. Go be dead."

He started to walk to the door, but I was off the bed in a flash, had crossed the room and clapped my hand on his shoulder and pulled him away from the door in about half a second. I shoved him toward the chair, ignoring his frightened gasp.

"You've had your say—such as it is. Now it's your turn to listen to me." Had I ever been so mad? Right now, it was hard to re-member. I shoved my hands into my pockets. I didn't trust them. They wanted to fly to my father's face and pull the skin off in strips. They wanted to grab his throat and tear it open. "I always knew, deep down, you were a coward. You're famous for taking the easy way instead of the right way. At work, at home, with your wives—you always avoided conflict and took the low road. Well, I managed to love you anyway. But I'm not letting you do this."

"Elizabeth—please—" He was cringing away from me. I re-alized I was looming over him like a blond bird of prey, and backed up.

"I'm going to be at your place for Easter dinner. As scheduled. It's been like that for years, remember? *You* set it up. Mom got me for New Year's; you got me for Easter; Mom got me for Memorial Day weekend; you got me for the Fourth of July. Just because I was too stubborn to stay dead doesn't mean your wife is getting out of baking a ham this year. Assuming she can find the fucking stove."

I jerked him out of the chair and propelled him toward the door. "I'll see you on Easter, Dad. And don't lock me out, either. Trust me on this." I hissed the last bit directly in his ear. "You wouldn't like it."

I knew I sounded mean and tough, and I was glad, but I wanted to burst into tears. I always knew he was weak, but I assumed he'd at least be happy I wasn't dead.

Sinclair was still on his feet when I hauled my dad into the kitchen. "Ah, Mr. Taylor," he said politely, as if his damned super-vamp hearing hadn't picked up every word. "Allow me to see you out." He seized my father by the collar, crossed the room, and tossed him out the door like a naughty puppy. Then he shut the door with a satisfying bang.

Marc was staring at me. "What's wrong with your eyes?"

"What are you talking about?" I asked irritably.

"They're . . . they're all red. The whites are blood red."

"My contacts are bothering me," I snapped.

"But you don't wear—"

Sinclair had come close and was also peering into my face. "Hmm."

"Oh, cut that out," I snapped. "God, I am *so* pissed off right now!" I felt like I could pick up the entire house and throw it down the block. Or wear knockoffs! No, that was just my rage talking.

Marc was leaning as far away from me as he could. I had the

impression it was completely unconscious. "You're upset? How come?" he asked innocently.

"Give me a break. I know you must have heard."

"Well . . . it was kind of loud . . ." He smiled sympathetically. "What are you going to do?"

"Worry about it later. Are we going, or what?" I practically yelled at Sinclair.

"We are."

"Good night, Marc, you eavesdropping floozy."

"Knock 'em dead, Oh Majestic Queen of the Narcissistic Undead."

"As far as royal titles go," I said, following Sinclair out the door, "that one stinks."

On the way to the car, Sinclair tried. He really did. "Ah, Elizabeth, do you wish—?"

"I wish not to talk about it is what I wish, and I *really* wish you hadn't heard the whole damned thing."

"I apologize."

I waved a hand irritably and climbed into the passenger seat. "It's nothing new. You know? This behavior of his? Absolutely typical." I flipped the mirror down. My eyes were their usual blue-green. Marc must be snorting coffee grounds again. "I guess I never outgrew waiting for him to be a better man."

"Perhaps if you give him some time . . ."

"He's got two weeks. Then it's Easter. But for now, I guess we have bigger fish to fry."

He looked at me for a long moment, then smiled. "Yes, we do. But for now, I think you're remarkably brave."

"Oh, don't start with me. I could not be less in the mood."

But his comment cheered me up a little.


"I *won't.*"

"But you must."

"No!"

"Are you so anxious for Nostro to gain more power?"

"Why does this have anything to do with me?"

"You know why. We've risked ourselves for you, Majesty, many times."

"Thanks, but nobody asked you to. *I* didn't ask you to."

"You were foretold."

"Enough with that!" I was close to panic. I had thought this would be more Vamp 101, but instead it was an advanced course: "Why Betsy Has to Help Us Overthrow the Most Obnoxious Vampire in Four Centuries."

That's why they were so interested in me. Not just because I was the Queen, but because I was the Queen who brought all the tribes together, who ruled them as one. Like the speaker of the House, only way more bloodthirsty. More Book of the Dead crap, which Tina had been reading to me all night. It was like attending Bible school in hell.

I should have known not feeding with them would be a mistake. It was all very casual . . . in addition to Sinclair's harem, several "friends" lived at the mansion: women for him and Tina, men for Dennis. Any one of them (or any three of them) would have jumped at the chance to be my dinner, but the whole group-meal thing freaked me out. As did the blood-sucking thing, frankly.

Unfortunately, they were mighty impressed when I passed up the chance to feed. Too impressed. Between that and not burning to death the other day, everyone in the house was convinced I was the Queen. Except the Queen herself, of course.

"*Elizabeth.*" I blinked and noticed Sinclair was snapping his fingers in front of my face. "I've been calling your name for thirty seconds. Did you have some sort of attention disorder before you rose? You seem to have a difficult time paying attention."

I batted his hand away. "Never mind. Not only am I not El Vampiro Chosen One, or whatever, but I'm barely a vampire."

"You should probably make that feminine," Tina suggested gently. "La Vampira."

"This is no time for a language lesson," I said irritably. "Anyway, whoever you guys think I am—"

"Whomever," Sinclair said with a smirk.

"—I'm not her."

"She's got us there," Dennis said apologetically. "She really is a terrible vampire. Too dumb to go up in flames in sunlight, and not nearly ruthless enough."

"Shut up, Dennis. Although you've got a point," I added grudgingly.

We were in one of Sinclair's living rooms. He had three that I knew of. And probably his very own morgue in the basement. It was late—close to midnight. So, lunchtime, in vampire time. Tina, Dennis, and Sinclair had been taking turns explaining how the four of us were going to knock Nostro's block off. I wasn't buying it.

"Look, you guys. I'm a secretary." Whose father preferred her to stay dead. *Oh, stop that. Stay focused.* "If you need me to type a bunch of memos calling for Noseo's resignation, I'm your girl. You got a stack of filing you need taken care of before we can kick ass, bring it on. You want some office supplies? I'll fill out the paperwork in triplicate. But I'm not a kingmaker."

"You—" Tina began, but I cut her off.

"Shit, I'm a little new to the game to be choosing sides and overthrowing tyrants. A week ago I was still installing Netscape Navigator!"

"This pains me as much as it does you, Elizabeth," Sinclair said, picking up his wineglass and taking a distracted sip. "A woman of your erratic temperament would not have been my first choice. More damning, you are young—young when you died, and as a vampire you're a positive infant. But how much more do you need to see to believe?"

I sniffed. "Quite a bit more, actually."

He pointed to the Book of the Dead, which had its own nifty little cherry wood stand next to the fireplace. I'd been tempted to boot it into the flames more than once this evening. "Our book—our Bible, if you will—tells of a female vampire who will not be burned by the sun, who can control her thirst, who has dominion over beasts—"

"They're just dumb dogs!"

"—who is still beloved by God—which is why you can wear a cross around your neck."

"Still not buyin' it," I said stubbornly. "Coincidence."

"You can do all these things, Elizabeth. And what's more, you are yourself—I don't doubt that the woman before me is much the same as the twit who breathed a month ago."

"Hey!"

"You're vain, you think constantly of your own pleasure, you like your pretty things, you're fond of your creature comforts . . ."

"Oh, you're one to talk, Satin Sheet Boy!"

He remained unruffled, though Dennis had to force his laugh into a cough. "You have remained *you*. This is the most definitive proof . . . you can think of others—friends and strangers alike—before your own needs. Most vampires would drink from their own grandmothers if thirsty enough. Plus, people react to your charisma."

Tina and Dennis nodded, and I blurted, "But I don't have any char—"

"Do you really think if Dr. Marc had met just any vampire, he would have allowed her to feed from him, taken a meal with her, then moved into her home and done everything to help her?"

"That's different, that's—"

"Different, yes, but more than you know. He instantly wanted to be with you, and never mind the fact that he is not oriented to your sex."

"Oriented to my—now you're just getting weird."

"Your friend Jessica never once was frightened of you— correct? Not only did the book foretell your unique abilities, not only do we vampires know who you truly are, but ordinary people feel it, too."

"Marc's a nice guy who wanted to hang out with me, is all," I said defensively. "And Jessica's like a sister to me—of course she wouldn't be scared." But even as I said it, it didn't ring true. My own father was afraid of me—but not Jessica. Marc was ready to throw himself to a messy death—and now he was plotting with Jessica on ways to make me help the world. In the space of a week. *Less* than a week.

"Elizabeth, as difficult as you are finding this to believe, you were meant to help us destroy Nostro. To bring peace. That will benefit all of us, vampires and humans alike."

"But—"

"Your friends *and* your parents. If you are the queen," he added slyly, "you can be sure no one will turn your mother into a midnight snack."

I jumped up. "Is that a threat?"

"Of course not. Even now, Nostro could be sending the Fiends to your mother's house. He's very, very angry with you. Of course," he added, no doubt guessing I was ready to bolt from the room and put Mom up in a Super 8, "I made arrangements for her to leave the state yesterday."

"You . . . how?"

"I was very persuasive," he said, and smiled. It wasn't one of his sneaky nasty smiles, either, but a sunny grin that made him look years younger. "Never fear, she who bore you is safe. And quite a fascinating woman, I might add—she instantly guessed I was a vampire and, for a refreshing change, didn't scream the house down. She did, however, threaten to brain me with a gold-plated candelabra if I 'tried any funny stuff.' " He turned to Tina. "By the way, I promised her you would come by for tea some night . . . she has several questions about the war."

"Oh, the war," Tina said, rolling her eyes. She was sitting cross-legged by the fireplace and looked just as cute as a bug in a pink blouse and white capri pants. "That's all academics ever want to talk about. 'What was the Civil War *really* like? What did you think of General Grant? Did the slaves really want to be freed?' Ugh. Not to mention, I'm too young to remember! But no one listens."

I relaxed slightly. As much as I could ever relax in this place, anyway. I believed Sinclair. Don't ask me how I knew, but it was plain he was telling the truth. (Also, I wanted to go along on that tea party . . . I had a few questions myself.)

Mom was safe. But for how long?

And it was nice of him not to bring up my father with the others. It was embarrassing enough that Marc and Sinclair knew my dad didn't want me around. Which is why this whole queen thing was so *weird*. I mean, my *father* doesn't want me, but eighty zillion vampires do? Give me a break.

It wasn't fair. I didn't ask for this, and I didn't deserve it, either. But I didn't say so out loud. Nobody promised fair. I knew that by the time I was in junior high.

They were all staring at me like undead cats, so I cleared my throat and asked a question. "Does—does Nostro think I'm the Queen?"

"No. He thinks you are a rare vampire, the kind born strong, but he discounts all things in the Book of the Dead—he must, else he'd have to believe in his own downfall."

"So, why does he care?"

"Oh, he wants you," Tina put in quickly. "You think vampires are born strong every day? You think vampires *rise* every day?"

"Good point," I said. "I haven't the faintest idea how to make a vampire. It's probably not very easy."

All three nodded, and the effect was so compelling I almost nodded myself. Tina continued, "Nostro is a huge believer in population control, because it's a lot easier to control the vampires who are already here. Which reminds me, Betsy . . . why *are* you here?"

"Well, Sinclair showed up at my house—uninvited, as usual—and we—"

"No," Dennis interrupted. "Who turned you? What happened? We've all been wondering."

"We understand if it's a delicate subject," Tina added sympathetically. "Getting murdered isn't much fun."

"Oh, that. I wasn't murdered. I got run over by a car."

"An Aztek," Sinclair said, looking amused.

"Yeah. How'd you know? Never mind. Anyway, I woke up dead. But I was attacked a few months ago—I think by the Fiends."

Dead silence (really!) while they digested this. "So . . . the Fiends attacked you—were set on you, maybe? But you didn't die. Then, months later, you *do* die . . . but not by vampire. And now you're . . ." She trailed off.

"Has any vampire ever risen who wasn't turned first?" I forced a laugh. "I mean, it can't be *that* unusual . . . right?"

Another silence.

"Uh . . . guys?"

"How is it that the Fiends didn't kill you?" Sinclair asked.

"Beats me! They all swooped down on me like rabid flying squirrels, and I beat them off with my purse and yelled myself hoarse."

Tina hid a smile, but Sinclair was all Mr. Interrogator. "Where were you?"

"Outside Khan's. You know that Mongolian barbecue place?" Mmm . . . Mongolian barbecue. When I'd been alive, I would have killed for a plate of sautéed beef and noodles, with extra garlic sauce. "It's on 494, right across—"

"Mongolian barbecue?" Dennis asked.

"Garlic," Sinclair said.

"Of course!" This from Tina. "Did you like garlic in life, Majesty?"

"What's not to like?"

"Well, that explains it."

"Not to *me*."

"Some of the legends are true," Sinclair said. "We're actually allergic to garlic. It acts as a blood coagulant."

I must have looked as blank as I felt, because Dennis elaborated. "Tough to suck someone's blood if it's all clotted."

"Yuck!"

"Sorry," Sinclair said, sounding anything but. "I imagine you stepped from the restaurant, positively reeking of the stinking rose, and they couldn't bear it. But that doesn't explain . . ."

"Maybe the Book of the Dead . . ." Tina began.

Sinclair shook his head. "There isn't time. But it's interesting, isn't it?"

"Quite."

"What?" I said. "I figure, I was in the wrong place at the wrong time . . . twice."

"Or the right time," Sinclair said quietly.

"Cut it out, Mr. Mysterious, you're creeping me out. Let's talk about the Fiends. What is their deal? Are they rabid vampires or overgrown bats or what?"

"It's an . . . experiment, I guess you could say," Dennis said reluctantly. I saw Sinclair's lips go thin with distaste as Dennis continued. "Nostro's experiment. No one is quite sure what the purpose is. I'd say the kindest thing to do would be to stake the lot of them."

"Agreed," Sinclair said firmly.

"Whoa, wait!" I held my hands up like a referee. "It's probably not their fault. That crummy Nostro probably made them that way. Maybe they can be fixed."

"Again with that tender heart," Sinclair observed.

"Again, blow me. That's not it. I just—uh—think they might be good minions. That's all." Plus, they were just so pitiful. I should have hated them for landing me in this mess, but mostly I felt sorry for them. Poor ugly smelly things. Give them a bath, cut their hair, let them gambol in the park like undead puppies (on leashes, of course), who knew?

"We do need to get moving on this," Tina said, doing me the courtesy of ignoring my lameass minion excuse. "Nostro's given us a deadline."

"I still don't know why he cares so much," I grumbled.

"It's all about pride, Elizabeth. And an ego that monstrous won't face possible defeat . . . from any quarter."

Oh, yeah, *Nostro's* ego was huge. "Look, we can't just storm the castle, right? He's got a zillion followers."

"Cut off the head," Tina said coolly, "and the body will die. Better yet, the body will throw its allegiance to you."

I grimaced. "Swell."

"Majes—Betsy, I know this must be difficult." Tina gave me a warm, understanding smile, which instantly put me on my guard. "As you said, you've only been one of us for not quite a week. You should be adjusting to your new life, not plotting to overthrow despots."

"Yeah, exactly! *Thank* you!"

"But time is running out," she went on implacably. "We need your assistance on this as soon as possible."

"Why? What's the rush? He's been around for a few hundred years, but you guys have to kick him off the anthill this week?"

Tina and Sinclair exchanged a glance. "We just do," Sinclair said smoothly. "We'd like you to co-op—"

"Whoa, hold up there, Dr. Deception! What's going on? What haven't you triad of retards told me?"

"Oh, now, *that* was uncalled for," Dennis sniffed.

"Ah . . ." Tina looked at Sinclair again, who shrugged. "Well, Majesty, when I was at Nostro's—when I gave you the locket and we left his territory without permission—"

"Permission?" I practically shrieked. "He threw us in the pit to murder us!"

". . . that was essentially an act of war. And Nostro has given us until tonight to bring you back."

"Or?"

"Slaughter."

"We think he's getting ready to go to war anyway," Sinclair added. "You're his excuse. He has been growing steadily more unstable over the centuries. He came so close, so many times. If you read the books, you know."

Skimmed the books was more like it. But yes, I knew.

Sinclair was still droning away. "He is all bottomless ambition and cruelty. Now that he finally has a kingdom, he is wildly paranoid of anything that might take his power. You frightened him badly when you couldn't be hurt by holy water, and more than anything, he can't let anyone see his fear."

Well, that made a lot of sense. The biggest bullies in the world were the ones who were scared to death of losing their power base like my former boss. And Saddam Hussein. And Nostro.

Still, I wasn't sure what I could do to help them. I mean, I wanted to help. I'm pretty sure I wanted to help. But what could somebody like me do? Sure, these days I could take on a couple of would-be rapists, but a horde of evil vampires loyal to Nostro? Only if I could bring along a flamethrower.

I slowly tuned back in. Sinclair was *still* talking!

"I've tolerated him because, until now, we kept out of each other's way. I overlooked his misdeeds and he overlooked my freedom."

"That was swell of both of you."

"But your presence changes things. Complicates them, too. The time for apathy is done."

The time for what is what? Oh, who cared. "I don't know about all that, but I'll tell you what—I never thought I'd be scared of a bald guy in a bad tux. I mean, he's sincerely crazy. It's not just the numbers he controls and the bad clothes and the bald spot . . . he's creepy."

Tina nodded. "Probably a sociopath in life. Either that, or he went mad after he died."

"Yuck-o. And his history! Cripes, it's enough to give a troll nightmares. He doesn't care who gets hurt or killed as long as he can be the boss. He started trying shit when he was barely dead, you believe that? I'd never trust him to do the right thing on his own—and I sure don't trust him to do right by the vampires he forced to be on his side."

Sinclair nodded. Tina looked relieved and I could practically read her mind: *By jove, I think she's finally getting it!*

"He's always regretted letting me go," Sinclair explained. "Knowing me and mine aren't under his control eats at him. One day we'll come downstairs and find two hundred vampires waiting for us. I would prefer," he added dryly, "to be proactive."

"Yeah, but shouldn't we . . . I dunno . . . spy out the land, or something? I mean, we can't just go charging over there. Right? Hello? Anybody? Right?"

Tina spread her hands. "We're out of time."

"Oh, this is crazy! You guys are sincerely nuts, you know that?"

Sinclair cleared his throat. "Dennis?"

Instantly Dennis jumped to his feet, hurried out, and a moment later returned carrying four plain white shoeboxes stacked in his arms like a little column. He set the boxes down, then left again, and came back with six more. He spread them out in front of me and began flipping the tops off the lids.

I screamed. With joy. Flip! A pair of lavender Manolo Blahniks with the dearest three-quarter-inch heel was revealed. Flip! A pair of Beverly Feldman sandals in buttercup yellow. Flip! An ice-blue pair of L'Autre Chose slingbacks. Flip, flip! *Two* pairs of Manolo Blahniks, one black lace, one red leather. Gold Salvatore Ferragamo heels . . .

I moaned and pounced on them. They were all in my size! I tugged off my tennis shoes, yanked so hard my socks went flying over my shoulder, and slipped into the yellow sandals. Bliss!

"Mirror!"

"I can't believe we're bribing our future queen with designer shoes," Tina muttered.

*"Mirror!"*

"Over there," Sinclair said, and pointed. There was a mirror above the fireplace. I dragged a chair over, plucked the mirror from the wall, hopped down, and leaned it against the far wall. I peered at the reflection of my feet. I felt like Dorothy in the ruby slippers. Like Princess Di during her coronation! Like—like a vampire queen with a truly outstanding shoe collection.

"I have *never* looked more amazing."

Tina made gagging noises, which I, being a well-shod lady, ignored. I twirled in front of the mirror. "These are wonderful! How did you do it?"

"I saw your shoe collection when we were at the house the other night, and had my ladyfriends do some shopping while we slept. Mitzi sends her regards."

I made a mental note to check the rest of the shoes for scorpions. "These are so, so pretty! Amazing!"

"What a pity you can't keep them." Sinclair sighed theatrically and motioned to Dennis, who started putting the lids back on the boxes.

I nearly wept. "What? Why?"

"Well . . . you're so adamant about not helping us. Not being a kingmaker, as you put it. Very wise and practical, but of course useless for our purposes. Thus, Plan B must be put into effect. Perhaps Nostro will accept these as a token of peace."

Nostro? Nostro putting his nasty clammy fingers all over the buttery soft suede, the delicate embroidery? Giving them to Shanara? Using them for the Fiends to play fetch? Never, never, never!

"Don't touch! Bad vampire!" I snapped, and Dennis froze in mid-reach. "I'll help you. *And* I get to keep the shoes."

"Done and done," Sinclair said, his lips twitching as he tried not to smirk. I'm sure he thought I was vain and weak-willed and a complete idiot. Who cared? I was a vain weak-willed idiot with the season's coolest shoes.

I jumped off the chair, flung my arms around Sinclair, and kissed him full on the mouth. He was so surprised I nearly toppled him over. "Do I get a bonus pair if we settle Noseo's hash tonight?" I asked, peeking up into his dark, dark eyes.

"Kiss me like that again, and I'll buy you a baker's dozen."

I let go of him like he was hot—which he totally was, I mean, oofta!—and not without regret. Hugging Sinclair was like hugging a great smelling rock. I was willing to bet even the guy's earlobes were well-defined. "Better not tempt me. Okay, so, let's go get the bad guy."

"It's that simple?" Tina asked. She shook her head at us, grinning as Sinclair, with a bemused expression, touched his mouth.

"A deal's a deal," I said, admiring my pretty feet. Of course, we all knew it wasn't just about the shoes. At least, not entirely. Probably not entirely. But Sinclair was no fool—this was all the excuse I needed to do what seemed more and more like the right thing.

Plus, it made me feel loads better. Dad didn't want me around, but these guys needed me. Maybe I was worth something after all.

"YOU'RE going to help them overthrow Nostro, then." Dennis effortlessly lifted a full case of wine up onto the bar. I'd asked for more plum wine, and Tina and Sinclair were downstairs plotting strategy.

I had no interest in the gory details . . . I suspected they wanted me along more for the power of my pseudostatus ("We've got the queen on our side . . . surrender!") than any actual fighting or tactical skill I'd bring. At least I hoped so.

"Sure. Look: It's not that I want Nostro to stay in charge, because I don't. He's a crazy creep and he treats his Fiends badly and all the other vampires are scared shitless of him, except maybe for Sinclair. I mean, when the monsters are scared of somebody, they should probably get rid of that person, right?"

"Right . . ."

"I mean, did you read that book about him? Cripes, it read like a history text from hell. You read it, right?"

"Many times."

"Right. Yuck. Anyway, I was just hoping to stay out of vamp politics. But if they can use me to kick him off the mountain . . ." (and if I can increase my shoe collection by eighty percent) ". . . it seems like the thing to do." Hearing it out loud, I was actually more than half convinced. Okay, a quarter convinced. But progress was being made.

"What if you change your mind?"

I caught on. Dennis was leery about my one-eighty. Didn't want me chickening out when it got nasty, and leaving his friends high and dry. Completely understandable. I rushed to put him at ease. "Don't worry. I won't. Besides, I owe that creep for siccing Shanara on my friends. *And* for throwing me in the pit with the Fiends. And for the Maypole Massacre of sixteen-whatever."

"But you weren't even alive then."

"So? You *did* say you read the book, right? I almost threw up reading about that little dosey-do-and-swing-your-partners. Creep."

"He is a temperamental man."

"Yeah, like a rabid wolverine is temperamental. And frankly, I'm sick of worrying about running into some of his tribe, sick of being dragged to his various hideouts . . . yuck! This week would have been hard enough without being caught up in Nostro's war." Reciting his sins against me was getting me worked up. I vibrated with righteous indignation. This was starting to seem like a really good idea, and never mind the shoes.

"So your mind's definitely made up?"

"One . . . hundred . . . percent," I said emphatically. "You don't have to worry."

"Actually," he sighed, "now's when I have to *start* worrying."

I had just enough time to wonder why he was swinging a case full of wine bottles at my head when everything went bright white, then dead black.

# Chapter 25

**W**HEN I woke up I was horribly thirsty. I knew why. Dennis, that traitor schmuck asshole, had hit me so hard if I'd been alive it would have killed me. At the least, he probably shattered my skull.

While I was dead to the world my body healed itself, and now I was unbelievably thirsty. I cursed myself for turning down Sinclair's offer to share dinner. It had seemed so morally upright at the time, and now it was probably going to get me really dead.

I opened my eyes. I was in a windowless, cellar-like room. Cement walls and floors. Chilly as hell. Smelled like mud.

"Asshole," I croaked. I cleared my throat and tried again. "Asshole, you there?"

"Yes," Dennis said, with the nerve to sound apologetic. He straightened up from whatever he'd been doing and gave the chains around my ankles an experimental tug. "Sorry about that. For what it's worth, this is really for the best."

"Oh, okay, then I'll just stop worrying. Jackass. Just tell me *why,* you jerk. Sinclair takes good care of you. He's the good guy. I heard you and Tina have been with him for, like, forty or fifty years. So why the double cross? Were you always an asshole, or is it, like, a recent development?"

"Nostro is my sire." Dennis said that with a simple dignity that made me want to kick him. "Everything I am is because of him. When he asked me, years ago, to go to his enemy, how could I refuse?"

I tugged at my wrists. Nope. Don't know what I was chained up with—titanium? cold silly putty?—but it wasn't budging.

Wrists above my head, ankles spread wide . . . and this slab was really cold.

"Let me get this straight, jackass. Nostro ripped you open like a trout and drank from you like a fountain while you were alive, and from that you've inferred that you *owe* him?"

"It wasn't like that. He released me. He freed me."

"He turned you into a Happy Meal, and you were dumb enough to think it was a favor."

Dennis slammed the knife I hadn't noticed he was holding into my upper thigh. Yow! There was a 'chunk!' as the tip embedded itself in the slab of stone I was chained to. It stung like crazy, but I wouldn't give him the satisfaction of yelling.

"Ow!"

Okay, I'd give him a little satisfaction.

"I've been stabbed before," I sneered. "Barely a week ago, in fact. *And* I've been audited, *and* I come from a broken home. In short—no offense, shorty—you don't scare me." I wriggled again . . . no go. In addition to the indignity of being clobbered with a case of plum wine, dragged to the bad guy's hideout, and chained to a stone altar (did Nostro keep a hack scriptwriter on the payroll to feed him clichés?), my clothes were in tatters. Dennis had been busy with the knife before I woke up. "You'll have to do a lot better than that."

Dennis bent close to me, so close I could see the candlelight gleaming off the gel he used in his hair. It occurred to me for the first time that he looked like an egret. "I threw all your new shoes into the fire," he whispered in my ear.

I howled in agony and thrashed ineffectually. "Bastard!" I wept. "You'll pay for that."

He straightened up, lips tightening with disgust. "You make my gorge rise."

"I bet you say that to all the girls, you overly moussed nancy boy."

"You care more about your pretty fripperies than anything else."

Fripperies? That was a new one. And it was tough to argue, so I kept my mouth shut.

"*You,* the queen? Never. Not while I'm around to serve my master."

"I agree with you! Hey, I never asked to be the queen, jerkweed. It wasn't exactly on my top-ten list of things I'd like to do after I die. I'll renounce the throne, okay? I never wanted it anyway. And I'm pretty sure it's not mine."

"It won't work. They'll never let you alone." He sighed. We both knew "they" meant Sinclair and Nostro. "It doesn't matter now. You'll die. You'll never rule."

"Let me get this straight. You believe I'm the queen, even though your master doesn't. And the Book of the Dead was right, but you just don't like it? Not *too* pathetic."

I wriggled again, and again to no avail. I tried to ignore the image of lavender Blahniks roasting in the fire, turning black, the room filling with the stench of burning leather . . .

He snapped his fingers before my eyes. "Pay attention!"

"Whaaaaaaat?" I whined.

"Yes, you're right. I tolerated your presence when you had no intention of helping Eric Sinclair. When you were a cute young vamp for him to coax to his bed."

"Ewwww! Fat chance, shiny head!"

"What a liar you are! The entire staff knew you slept together."

"Yeah, but we just slept together. We didn't—you know. *Sleep* together."

He shook himself, as if the effort of talking to me was tiring him out. "However. The moment you changed your mind about joining with them to overthrow my sire—"

"It was clobberin' time. Yeah, I got that part. Listen, answer a question—how the hell do you kill a vampire? Specifically, how will you kill *me*? You can't toss me into the Pit this time, because the Fiends are scared of me. And you can't lock me in a room facing east and wait for the sun to do your dirty work. A holy water facial won't do it, either. Not that I would mind a facial, so if you think it'll work, go right ahead. Just go easy on the exfoliants; I have combination skin."

Dennis's brow wrinkled and he looked worried for a brief moment. Then he shrugged. He gestured to his left, and I looked where he was pointing. There were several swords propped in the corner. "Cutting off your pretty little head should do the job nicely."

I grimaced. Yeah, I didn't really see any way around that one. "You know something? I'm actually kind of glad it's come to this. Me or Nostro. Because I am sick to *death* of this shit—the kidnappings and the treachery and whose side are you on . . . it's so fucking childish. How can any of you stand it?"

"We know our place." He jerked the knife out of my thigh. "A pity you never did."

"Nobody tells me my place, needle dick." Hey, maybe I was

the queen! At the least, I wasn't in a hurry to get on my knees for Nostro *or* Sinclair. Bully for me. "Well, chatting's been fun, but we should probably get to it, right?"

He blinked down at me. "You *want* to have your head cut off?"

"Anything's better than lying here freezing my ass off and smelling your mousse. Suave is all wrong for your hair type, by the way. It's so fine and girly, you should use Aveda products."

He smoothed his sleek head and glared. "Never mind your silly jokes."

"I never joke about hair. Say, where *is* your psycho boss, anyway? I would've expected him to be in here with forty or fifty of his closest underlings, gloating nonstop and looking like a designer's bad dream."

Dennis grimaced. He probably thought it was a smile. My, my, he was getting good and pissed. Excellent. "He's killing Eric and Tina. But he'll be right along."

I quit smirking. Part of the reason I'd been so flip, other than the complete absurdity of my situation—I mean, come on, half naked and chained to a stone slab?—was because I'd been expecting Sinclair and Tina to rescue me.

"The day Nostro gets the drop on Eric Sinclair is the day I . . ." I couldn't think of anything absurd enough.

". . . get your head cut off," Dennis finished helpfully.

"Hmm."

"I signaled my tribemates, of course, as soon as I had you. Some of us brought you here, and the rest set fire to Sinclair's mansion. We had the place surrounded, and anyone who made it out would have gotten a holy water shower. Not that anyone made it out, I'm sure. Vampires are incredibly flammable."

I thrashed ineffectually. That gorgeous Victorian, crammed with priceless antiques. And my new shoes! And Sinclair and Tina, and their ladyfriends, and the guys who were in Dennis's harem! *And my new shoes!*

And it was all my fault. Sinclair and Nostro had been at war for years and years, but it was my presence that escalated the situation. They might have stayed at an impasse for another five hundred years. But for me. It was all my fault. And I'd never get the chance to make up for it.

"You fucker," I said helplessly.

"All's fair in love and etcetera," he said lightly. "I'm afraid I can't wait much longer for Nostro. Best to dispatch you and commence celebrating. Also—aaagggkkk!"

I stared. There was a long metal blade sticking out of the side of his neck. Just as my eyes had adjusted to what they were seeing, Tina wrenched the sword out of Dennis's neck and swung again. He ducked away from her. She instantly turned and smashed the sword down on the chains between my ankles. And again. And—

"Watch it!"

She spun and ducked, and Dennis's blade went whistling over her head. I kicked and wrenched as hard as I could. She'd weakened the chains, and if I could just—

I kicked free of the chains and flipped my feet over my head, quickly, to gain momentum. Now I was standing behind where my head and shoulders had just been. The chains were biting into my wrists, which probably would have broken if I'd tried this last week, but I ignored the pain. I braced my weight against the altar and pulled as hard as I could. There was a tearing—both of my flesh and the chains—and then I was free.

"Oh you fucker," I said breathlessly, turning. Seeing Tina alive helped me focus my anger on the lost shoes. Mighty would be my wrath! "Now you're gonna get—yuck!"

Tina was kneeling before me, holding Dennis's head by the hair and very plainly—yeerrgh!—trying to hand it to me.

"Majesty, I beg your forgiveness for the indignity you suffered and offer you the head of our enemy as—"

"Put that thing down," I said impatiently. "I can't talk to you when you're shaking his head like a damned maraca."

"At once, Majesty."

She dropped his head and I yanked her to her feet and gave her a hearty smack on the mouth. "That's for that whole nick-of-time thing you seem to have going on." I kissed her again. "And that's for cutting off the bad guy's head." *Mwah!* "And that's for being so cute." *Mwah!* "And that's for not being dead."

"Sure," she said, fending me off with an elbow. "You're all affectionate *now,* when there's no time. Let's go."

"Where's Sinclair?"

"We split up to find you. Since that honor was mine, I imagine he ran across Nostro instead. Now I have to show you to your people."

"My—" She tossed me a sword, then grabbed my arm and pulled me along so fast I stumbled to keep up. "My people?" I glanced back, more than happy to be leaving the cheerless little room I had wondered if I would die (again) in. Dennis's headless body was twitching all over, then shuddered and went still. It didn't turn into dust and whirl away, just lay there like a puppet with its strings cut. And its head missing. Another gross-out in a week filled with indignities.

"The only reason I got back here in time to help you was because I told Nostro's people you were the foretold queen."

"Yeah, but how'd you avoid being barbecued? Dennis seemed pretty sure you guys were ashes."

"The underground tunnel, of course," she said with bare impatience. She was still hauling me along like a sack of feed. "They blocked it, but poorly. Under normal circumstances they might have succeeded, but Sinclair was so angry you'd been taken—I've never seen him like that." She shivered a little. But maybe it was just the chilly room temperature.

"That Sinclair. A big mushy pussycat at heart. So everyone got out okay? That's so great! I mean, I thought you guys were all toast. Literally toast."

"Ah . . ."

"I was so bummed when he told me you were all dead! But I kept talking and stalling anyway, you know, like they do in the movies. It was all I could think of to do. And look how great it worked out!"

Tina looked at me for a moment that probably seemed longer than it was. "Karen's dead, Betsy."

I stopped short. Karen, burnt up? Burnt to *death?* And for what? Status and territory. Boys and their toys, fighting over *land.* Even though this city was plenty big enough for two head vamps.

What a fucking waste.

"I'm sorry," Tina continued when I didn't say anything. "I know you liked her. If it helps, the feeling was definitely mutual. You were all she could talk about the last couple days."

"I—I didn't know her. She made me tea, is all. But she was nice. I thought she was really nice." I was too numb from all the rapid events to say much more, but beneath the numbness I could feel anger stirring. It reminded me of black water moving under ice in January. When I stopped feeling numb, someone was going to pay through the nose.

"So . . . so you guys got out and came here. Piece of cake, right?"

Tina snorted. "Dennis left too quickly with you—a rather large error of judgment, which I'm happy to say cost him his head. Eric and I got out and came straight here, yes. I was prepared to fight my way in, but instead told everyone I ran across that I was there for their salvation and our queen. And, for a wonder, no one tried to stop me. That tells me they might be ready. If I show you to them, they may yet turn on him."

"Think so?"

"No," she said grimly, hauling me up a flight of stairs, "they're too frightened. To stop me, but also to help me. Though I've noticed that when we put you into the equation, interesting things happen. So we'll try. And if I see Nostro I'm going to have his balls for breakfast."

"Thanks for the visual."

"There!" She pointed; there was one hell of a brawl going on in the ballroom. At least thirty people were fighting and kicking and punching and clawing at each other. Nostro and Sinclair were probably in the middle of it.

Tina dropped my hand and waded in. I turned and ran. Past the ballroom, past the swimming pool, all the way outside. I knew what I wanted—now how to find it?

I stared in confusion at the grounds—just my luck, Nostro lived on a damn half acre. Where the hell were the . . . ?

A teeny, red-haired vamp scuttled around the corner right into me, clearly having no interest in joining the fight. When I seized her arm, she squeaked and shrank away from me.

"Where are the Fiends?"

"Please—don't—don't hurt me—"

"The Fiends, twit! Where does your boss keep them? I know they're locked up around here somewhere."

She blinked up at me and when I got a good look at her I felt sick. She couldn't have been more than fourteen when she died. She weighed, at rough guess, about eighty pounds. Scrawny as hell and with the biggest brown eyes I'd seen outside of a pet shop. A teenager forever. Perpetually in the throes of adolescence . . . I couldn't think of a worse fate. Sinclair was a pig, but he wasn't killing teenage girls. If I hadn't already made up my made to fight Nostro until he was in little pieces on the ground, I would have done it in that instant.

"Their cage is behind the barn," she said in a small voice. "I can show you just pleasedonthurtme."

"Relax, cutie. This is shaping up to be your lucky day. You'd better stick with me. It's dangerous in there."

"Oh, dangerous? Tell me! I thought the Korean War was bad." She relaxed a little as she realized I wasn't going to use my sword to cut off her head. "I'm—I'm Alice, by the way."

"I'm the queen, Alice." Korean War, let's see, that made her—forty? Fifty? I'd never get used to this. "It's nice to meet you, now come on."

The Fiends sent up an ungodly racket when they saw me. I groped and was relieved to find Dennis hadn't relieved me of my cross . . . he probably hadn't been able to touch it, or had forgotten about it. I flashed the Fiends and they went into their abject cringing routine.

Was I really going to do this? It could backfire and then I'd be fucked.

Well, I was fucked anyway. I took a deep breath, smashed the locks on their cage with a few punches—it hurt, but nothing compared to what it felt like when I tore my wrists free of the chains—and stepped inside.

"Uh . . . your—uh—your queenness . . . majesty or whatever . . . I wouldn't . . ."

"It's okay." At least, I hoped it was okay. If not, I wouldn't have long to regret my actions. About five seconds, tops. "I think I've got their number." I held out my torn, bleeding wrists. I could still bleed from a pulse point, it seemed, just not as well as when I was alive, and not as hot. The flow was thick and sluggish, and such a dark red it was almost black. It made me feel slightly sick to look at it.

The Fiends crawled toward me, sniffed me up and down, then lapped from my wrists. Their breath was cold. Their smell was indescribably bad.

"What are these things?"

"They're vampires who weren't allowed to feed when they rose." Alice was clutching the bars and watching us with big scared eyes. "They become animals when that happens . . . they lose their sense of self. All they know is hunger."

"Huh." I felt sorrier than ever for them—they'd once been *people!* Even if they were the authors of my new existence, I still felt bad. "Is it fixable?"

Long pause. "I . . . I don't know. No one has ever been able to—I mean, my lord Nostro wouldn't—"

"Say no more. And stop calling him lord. Alice, this appears to be working. So I'm gonna try something and probably I won't get killed. But I might. Hey, it wouldn't be the first time. Anyway, are you with me or against me? It's okay if you want to stay out here."

"Stay out here? And let you go in alone?" She looked woefully tempted for a moment, then shook herself like a dog. "I think—I think I'm with you." She stared at me through the bars, then lowered her gaze to my cross, which was still giving off its brave little light. It reminded me of the Snoopy nightlight I'd had as a kid.

She looked away, then looked back, as if drawn. She brought one hand up to cover her eyes, but it stopped halfway to her face. "You're so brave and . . . and strong. And it must be right, for how can you—"

"Today, Alice, could you answer my question today? I still have to save my new friends, kill Nostro, and get home in time to set the VCR to tape Martha Stewart."

"I'm your servant," she said softly. She squeezed the bars so hard I heard metal groan. "Forever and ever. Because you were nice and because you would have let me stay outside. Even if I won't. Stay outside, I mean."

"Swell. I think." Would I ever get used to people instantly throwing me their allegiance? Lord, I hoped not. "Here's the plan."

# Chapter 26

W**I T H** Alice and the Fiends hot on my heels, we charged back up to the house and ran into the ballroom. The Fiends appeared willing to follow wherever I led, which was a huge relief— I didn't relish trying to keep them all on leashes. And they hadn't tried to devour me, which was a big plus.

Nostro and Sinclair were still going at it so fast I couldn't see a thing. Just blurs of fists and the thuds of blows landing. For a wonder, no one else was fighting; most of the others were up against the far wall listening to Tina. Everybody looked scared.

"—not interfere! Whoever wins this will be our new lord and you *cannot* interfere! That was our law when mortals were still cringing in caves!"

Cringing in caves? Oh, very nice. Trust Tina to leave us all with a disturbing mental image.

"*I'm* going to interfere," I said hotly. Behind me, the Fiends were crowding me and rubbing against my legs. It was comforting, if unbelievably creepy. I pointed to the blur that was Nostro and Sinclair. "Sic him!"

Yowling and snarling, the Fiends rushed forward. So did I—in time to grab Sinclair and pull him out of the way. As quick as I was, a Fiend still knocked us sprawling and I caught a blow from Nostro that made my ears ring. I shook it off and rolled over on my back to watch.

You know in cartoon fights how all you can see is smoke and whirling limbs and stars and birds and stuff? That's what it was like. The Fiends were snarling, Nostro was screaming, and we were all staring. Then the Fiends started making wet noises, Nostro was gurgling, and then the wet noises continued. But Nostro wasn't making any more noise. Tough to do, when you're in pieces.

Dead silence, broken by me whispering, "That was for Karen, you piece of shit."

Nobody said anything. Thirty vampires were staring at me, and the triumph on Tina's face was almost too much to bear. Her face was like a beacon, beautiful and terrible at once. She didn't look like a preppy cheerleader just then, but like a warrior claiming victory.

I turned to Sinclair, sure one of his coolly sarcastic remarks would break the tension, and then I screamed and scrambled to my feet and tried not to puke, all at the same time.

Sinclair was horribly burned. Most of his left side was a blackened mess. All his hair was gone. His eyelids were gone. I could see the veins in the skin of his left arm as they tried to sluggishly move blood through his dead system.

Incredibly, he was *smiling*. His cracked lips pulled back and his teeth looked even whiter and longer against his burned flesh. I should have been terrified, but this was someone I knew, even if it was someone I didn't like. Much. I think.

"Victory," he whispered.

I burst into tears. Well, as much as I could, now that I couldn't cry real tears. Sure, victory, but at what cost? And what happened next? He was burned because of me, he'd lost his home—and most of his flesh!—because of me. Karen was dead because of me. And instead of recovering or feeding to get better or staying the hell out of the fight, he'd come running to my rescue.

"Sinclair—Eric—what—"

"He needs to feed," Tina said as Sinclair put a hand out and steadied himself by clutching her arm. "From you. Your blood will heal him quicker than anything else."

"It's a queen thing?"

She nodded, but she wasn't looking at me. Her eyes were big and sad as she stared at Eric. "Water will help—it facilitates the healing process. Then—"

"Right, right, you can explain later." I remembered them dumping Detective Nick into the shower. At the time I thought it was to get him clean. Now I wondered.

I gingerly grabbed Eric's right hand and pulled him over my back, fireman style.

"Oh, now I must object to this," he said to the back of my thigh.

"Shut up, Eric. It'll feel better soon . . . you must be in agony . . ."

"The lengths I must go to so you'll call me by my first name."

I made a sound, a cross between a laugh and a sob. Sinclair was an unwieldly package, but, thanks to my vamp strength, light as a page of paper. "Shut up, you jerk. This is no time for your nasty sarcasm."

"You must tell me how you turned the Fiends' loyalty from Nostro," he said conversationally, upside down. God, this was the weirdest day ever! "Such a thing has never been done before."

"You're always so nosy."

"You're always so intriguing."

I carried him to the pool room, then stood him up and steadied him.

"Really, this is all so unnecess—"

"Take a breath," I said, standing so close to the edge my toes dangled over.

"Why?" Sinclair asked, reasonably enough. Then we plunged into the deep end.

I had time to think, *oh, shit, the chlorine's going to sting him like hell*, but from the look of relief on his face, that wasn't the case at all.

I wondered why water helped. Was it because we were technically dehydrated? We didn't sweat or pee or cry, but dump us into a pool and everything got better? Weird. Maybe there was an explanation in one of those giant boring books I'd borrowed.

Sinclair pulled me to him gently and I went willingly enough. He was a blackened husk because of me; the least I could do was let him regain strength from my blood. I only hoped I had enough to do him any good. Was drinking from a vampire—from me?—so very different from drinking from someone who was still alive? Tina seemed to think so, and that was good enough for me.

I shivered as his teeth broke the flesh of my throat. It was like losing my vamp virginity. The water was deliciously cool as we floated near the bottom of the deep end. It was odd and delightful to be completely comfortable underwater and not have to worry about coming up for air.

I had my hands on his shoulders and, while he drank from me,

I could feel the skin on his back knitting together, reforming from nothing, could feel him regaining strength and vitality. He stroked my back as he fed, which was lovely—soothing and sweet and comfortable. *Being* lunch felt as good as *drinking* lunch. This was the pleasure of being taken, of being held by a creature much larger and stronger, a creature who could break you if he chose, but wouldn't. (Probably.) It was the pure pleasure of surrender.

Eric pulled back and smiled with a look of pure uncomplicated happiness. His face healed itself while I watched in shocked amazement. So fast, it was happening so fast! Then he was whole, perfect—a completely gorgeous male specimen. With really big canines. It had taken less than five minutes.

I laughed underwater and nearly choked. He pulled me to him again, not nearly so gently this time, and then his mouth was covering mine, his tongue was rubbing against mine, and his arms were around me, pressing me against him.

We kissed for an hour . . . or so it felt. He pulled me free of my rags and I helped him out of the burned tatters he'd barely been wearing. Mindful that he couldn't bear the cross, I took it off and let it float away, making a mental note to retrieve it later. When I touched his throbbing, firm length I was glad I was floating and not standing—I doubt I'd have been able to keep my feet. He was huge and beautiful and I wanted every inch inside me.

I was tired of fighting my attraction to him, tired of pretending I didn't feel it in my stomach every time he smiled. Love? I didn't know. I'd never known anyone like Eric Sinclair, who thought I was a hopeless twit but had fought for me, lost everything for me, and secured a throne for me.

His lips closed over one of my nipples and he suckled gently. Then his tongue rasped across the firm peak and I had to remind myself not to gasp underwater. His hands were everywhere, kneading and stroking my back, my buttocks, my thighs. Then he released me and dove.

My back arched as I felt him part me with his thumbs, as I felt his tongue burrowing inside me. I stared blindly toward the pool's surface while his tongue stroked and teased and licked and stabbed, while his fingers restlessly kneaded my thighs.

I wrapped my legs around his head and seized a fistful of his hair, fairly grinding his face into me. The sensations from his lips and tongue, coupled with the sensual feeling of the water caressing every inch of me, were putting me into ecstatic overdrive.

Then I felt his fangs pierce me, felt him suck gently, drinking from the very center of me, and I spun away into orgasm. Spun? No, was shoved, *thrust* into orgasm, and I screamed silently, staring at the gorgeous light on the surface.

He reached up, found my waist, and pulled me down to him, kissing me every inch of the way until his mouth was covering mine again.

*She's so beautiful she feels so good ah I can't I can't hold back I have to have her have to be inside her oh Elizabeth my darling my own oh oh oh . . .*

I froze. I was hearing thoughts, but they sure weren't mine. And it wasn't like he was taking over my brain, it was more like I was . . . eavesdropping. Since when could I read his mind? Anyone's mind? Could he hear me?

*Eric, I have a galloping case of VD, that's not going to be a problem, is it?*

Nothing; he kept kissing me and was now sucking my lower lip into his mouth. I reached for him, found his enormous length, and stroked gently.

*Now I have to now take her touch her now have her now oh please don't let me hurt her oh Elizabeth my luminous queen I'd die for you . . .*

He pressed forward. I looped my legs around his waist—we were now drifting upside down—and slowly impaled myself on his length. It was tight—it was unbelievably tight—and splendid and amazing and wonderful.

I felt his hand in my hair, forcing my head up, and he watched my face as he came into me, inch by inch by inch.

*Don't stop,* I mouthed at him.

*Ah sweetheart as if I could . . .*

And still he came forward, kept pushing into me. He buried his face in my throat as he forced himself to enter with excruciating slowness, forced himself to hold back for fear of hurting me.

Which was all very nice, except I wanted to come again. Wanted to feel him all the way up inside me. Wanted to feel him in my *throat,* wanted to ride him until I was screaming and clawing, wanted to see his eyes roll up and feel him spasm against me. I wriggled closer and he shuddered; I bit him on the throat and he shoved, seating himself within me with one thrust.

I squirmed against him, enjoying the sensation of being pinned, impaled. Fucked.

*No oh no don't don't I'll hurt hurt I'll hurt her ah ah AH AH ELIZABETH YOU FEEL SO GOOD . . .*

I locked my ankles behind his back, dug my nails into his shoulders, and shoved back at him. I bit him again, on the other side, and he writhed against me. We thrust against each other . . .

*Can't stop can't stop can't can't Elizabeth oh Elizabeth you feel alive to me you feel like no one else to me Elizabeth*

. . . almost battling beneath the water, surging and thrusting and writhing against each other; his mouth found mine again and he kissed me so hard one of his canines pierced my lower lip.

*MORE MORE MORE MORE MORE MORE MORE*

I came so hard I saw spots—or maybe that was the pattern on the pool vent—came so hard I could feel myself clenching around him . . .

*ELIZABETH! ELIZABETH! ELIZABETH!*

. . . felt him shudder as he found his own release. It was—it was like being alive again!

His grip tightened, his tongue thrust even deeper into my mouth, and then he was relaxing, relaxing and slipping out of me, smaller and softer, but still formidable.

I started to pull away—float away, actually—but he grabbed me back and held me for a long moment while we drifted toward the surface. I couldn't hear him in my head anymore, which made me sad.

Love? I had no idea. But it had sure been something.

# Chapter 27

I nearly yelled as my head broke the surface. The pool room was filled with dozens of vampires, all waiting patiently. I dove back down, swam around for a few minutes, found Sinclair's sister's cross—easier than I would have believed!—and put it back on. I lurked on the bottom of the pool for another minute, then gathered up my courage and swam back to the surface.

Yep, they were all still there. Nuts. I treaded water and tried to think about where I'd get some clothes. And about what they must have seen. They were all staring down at me and were completely expressionless. God knew what they were thinking. First dead, then a vampire, then a queen, now a whore. What a week!

Tina knelt by the pool and held up a robe. I swam to her and got out, let her help me into the robe—ewww, a polyester-cotton blend, but I was in no position to be picky—and got it belted in about half a nanosecond.

Sinclair, that shameless hussy, had no problems with modesty. He simply lifted himself from the pool and stood before our audience, splendidly naked. While I stared, the teethmarks on his throat and shoulders healed. Nothing else happened, but I still stared.

"Behold," Tina said loudly, "your Queen and her consort!"

The assembled vampires cheered, but it was a subdued hoorah. More like a communal "Mm-hmm." They probably thought the new boss was the same as the old boss.

It was so obvious they were still afraid. I felt bad for them, but what could I do but try to prove I wasn't a balding sociopath? Maybe after they got to know me they wouldn't be scared anymore. And—wait a minute.

"Uh . . ." I raised a finger.

"Nostro is no more," Sinclair said sternly (and nudely). "The Fiends are under my Queen's command. As are all of you."

"Uh . . . Eric?"

"Any who do not wish to swear allegiance may leave now, tonight. We will not force your hand; you are free to come and go as you wish. Those dark days are over. But any who remain, and swear loyalty to her Majesty the Queen, will be under our protection so long as we live."

Consort?

"Consort?" I asked. I was having a hard time catching Tina's eye, all of a sudden, and why should that be? "Tina? Consort? What?"

Vampires all over the room were kneeling, were brushing their foreheads against the tile, but I had no eyes for them. And still, Tina wasn't looking at me. *"What's going on?"*

A few of the closer vamps cringed away from me—a good trick in mid-kneel—and Tina coughed, while Sinclair turned to give me a thoughtful look. Then he smiled at me. Why should his smile be scary now, of all times?

"Hello? Am I in the room? Is someone gonna answer me? Consort? What's going on?"

Tina coughed again. "We—ah—didn't get a chance to finish explaining the prophesies from the Book of the Dead. Because Dennis—and we just didn't."

"Soooooooo?"

"But you were foretold, and Nostro's downfall was foretold, and Eric being—uh—being your King was also—"

*"What?"* I could actually feel my eyes bulge. "What did you say?"

"She said Eric being your King was also," Alice piped up helpfully from somewhere behind me.

"Quiet, you. Tina, explain. *Now.*"

"*'And the first who shall noe the Queen as a husband noes his Wyfe after the fall of the usurper shall be the Queen's Consort and shall rule at her side for a thousand yeares.'* At least," she added, "that's as close as I can recall. It goes on in the same vein for quite a bit, no pun intended. I'll show you the appropriate passage when we get back."

*"What?"* I actually swayed on my feet. Sinclair steadied me. I yanked my arm away and nearly fell back into the pool. "I'm the queen and Sink Lair is the king? Since fucking when?"

"Since fucking," Sinclair said helpfully.

"Why didn't either of you tell me? Why didn't you warn me? For a thousand years? What?"

"Well," he who was on my permanent shit list said reasonably, "if I said, 'Elizabeth, dear heart, I want to make love to you, but just so you know, I'll come to the crown right after I come in you,' then I wouldn't have gotten to see you naked."

Tina accurately read the look on my face, because she quickly stepped in front of Sinclair and spread her arms protectively in front of him. The jerk just looked amused, and stared at me over the top of her head.

"That's not why, Majesty. You've touched him deeply, which is why he's being flip." Then, under her breath to Sinclair, "Cut it *out*." She gave me a big, fake smile. "It was foretold, that's all. Just like your ascension to the throne. There's nothing any of us can do about it."

"Want to bet?"

Sinclair spread his arms wide. "Sweetest, you sound so cross. We have a coronation to plan, so put on a smile. Also, as soon as I rebuild my home, you'll move in, of course."

*"Want to bet?"*

"Well, perhaps later, then. After the . . . er . . . happy surprise has worn off."

"You said!" I jabbed a finger toward Tina's chest. She flinched, but held her ground. "You said if I became Queen I could get rid of Sinclair!"

"You wanted to get rid of me?" The asshole had the audacity to sound hurt.

"I didn't think Sinclair would end up being your consort," she said weakly, but I knew she was lying. She might consider me her queen, but Eric was her sun and moon, closer than any brother. What he wanted, she would get for him. She revered me, but she loved him. "But now—the book was right. It's been right about everything. And—and we just have to accept it, is all."

"Accept my ass!"

"Well, if you—" Sinclair began.

*"You shut up.* I'm going home!" I said loudly. I tightened the robe's belt. How was I going to do that? I had no keys, no car, no driver's license, and no underpants. Fortunately, I was too furious to care. "Both of you stay the hell away from me—*I mean it!*"

Tina bit her lip and stared at the floor, but Finklair smiled at me. "Impossible, my Queen. You and I have a kingdom to run."

# Epilogue

So, I'm the queen of the dead. As if it's not hard enough adjusting to the fact that I killed the bad guy—and I'm not the only one amazed, believe me—now I'm a dead monarch. And the lout I'm hopelessly attracted to, yet despise, is my king. For all intents and purposes, we're stuck for the next thousand years. A thousand fucking years! We'll be running longer than *The Simpsons!* Every time I think about it I want to shove somebody—a specific somebody—through a wall.

A week ago my biggest problem had been losing my job. Ah, for the sweet freedom of those days. Now I had to worry about running a kingdom of vampires, keeping my hands off Sinclair (because, oh God, I still wanted him, would do just about anything to feel his hands and—other things—again), giving Tina the cold shoulder until I decided to forgive her, keeping Jessica and Marc from starting their new crime fighting business (HELP, Inc.), and helping thousands of vampires adjust to being in charge of their own destiny.

I also had to find time to rebuild my relationship—such as it was—with my father and the Ant. While it was convenient that they were pretending I wasn't an ambulatory dead girl, I couldn't let things go on like that. If I had to get used to my father's trophy wife, he could get used to my return from the dead.

Not to mention finding permanent suck buddies and a paying job—I was undead and unemployed, and couldn't live off Jessica's charity forever. The very idea was ridiculous. But convincing her of that was likely to be the most difficult task of all.

I put Alice in charge of the Fiends . . . they were still at Nostro's place, but they had more room to run, and hopefully some genius vamp would be able to fix them. I was resisting pressure from almost everyone to have them staked. It was tough saying no—it was tough getting used to the idea that I was in charge. I was the youngest vampire by several decades, and it was just too weird.

I'd insisted on giving Karen a proper funeral, which apparently went against all vamp rules. Like I gave a fuck. But I put my foot down, and it was surprisingly well attended. Not bad for a midnight service.

I didn't speak to Sinclair or Tina during the service, but took the urn home. It's sitting on my mantel right this minute. A reminder to me that collateral damage is never acceptable.

My mom was also at the service. She was completely taken with Sinclair. He really swept her off her feet when he swooped in like a dark angel to whisk her out of harm's way. She thinks the fact that Sinclair is the king is just dandy. I tried to explain his trickery, sneakiness, and out-and-out dishonesty—without actually mentioning the pool boinking—but it fell on totally deaf ears. "You know, Betsy, just because you're undead doesn't mean you have to be unwed."

Yeah, sure. I planned to *stay* unwed, for a thousand years to be exact. Having that wretch Sinclair as a consort was bad enough; I wasn't about to become the little undead woman.

I'd also run into Nick recently, in one of those funny coincidences that often happen in the suburbs—we both happened to be grocery shopping at the same Rainbow Foods.

He had looked a little better, and seemed only mildly surprised to see me in the fresh-squeezed juice department. He had no memory of reading about my death, or of our time together. So that was one worry off my list.

Now if I could just get Sinclair to quit dropping off pairs of designer shoes. In his last card he said he would drop off a pair a day until I forgave him. I'm up to fourteen pairs of Pradas, eight pairs of Manolos, and six Ferragamos.

Maybe I'll forgive him . . . eventually.

I'm still waiting for this season's red Jimmy Choo slides.

# Undead and Unemployed

*For my former bosses: Jim, Linda, Bob, Vince, Maggie, Neil, Kathy, Pat, Jeff, and Ron. Some of you were terrific, some of you I suspected were sociopaths, but all of you taught me something.*

# Acknowledgments

As always, this book would have been more difficult without the help of my husband, Anthony, who keeps the kids out of my hair when I'm on deadline, reads everything I write, and thinks I'm gorgeous. He's right, of course, but I appreciate the reminder. He also comes up with the "Undead" titles and believe me, some of them are a real scream.

Thanks also to my family, who are staunchly supportive and, I swear, get more excited over these book deals than I do.

Thanks also to Cindy Hwang, whose edits usually include "More Sinclair!". Fans of the vampire king have her to thank.

And special thanks to the Magic Widows, my book club and dear friends, who listen tirelessly to my book ideas and plots for taking over the world.

And the first who shall noe the Queen as a husband noes his Wyfe shall be the Queen's Consort and shall rule at her side for a thousand yeares.

—The Book of the Dead

If that rat bastard Sinclair thinks I'm going to be his wife for a thousand years, he's out of his fucking mind.

—From the private papers of Her Majesty, Queen Elizabeth I, Empress of the Undead, Rightful Ruler of the Vampires, Consort of Eric I, Lawful King

# Prologue

*Police interview of Robert Harris.*
*June 30, 2004*
*55121 @ 02:32:55–03:45:32 A.M.*
*Filed by Detective Nicholas J. Berry*
*Fourth Precinct, Minneapolis, Minnesota*

AFTER being treated at the scene, Mr. Harris denied the offer of hospital care, and consented to accompany the responding officers, Whritnour and Watkins, to the precinct for an interview.

The interview was conducted by Minneapolis Detective Nicholas J. Berry.

Robert Harris is a fifty-two-year-old Caucasian male who works for Bright Yellow Cab as a taxi driver. Mr. Harris was on duty during the events transcribed below. Mr. Harris has passed a breathalyzer; labs are pending on possible drug use.

DETECTIVE BERRY: Are we ready? Is the tape . . . okay. Would you like something to drink? Coffee? Before we start?

ROBERT HARRIS: No thanks. If I have coffee this late, it'll keep me up. Plus, y'know, with my prostate, it's just asking for trouble.

DB: Can we discuss the events of this evening?

RH: Sure. You wanna talk about the Twins getting their asses kicked, or why I was dumb enough to take a job where I haveta sit all the time? Goddamned hemorrhoids.

DB: The events—

RH: Sure, you wanna know what I meant by that story I told those fellows, the ones who took care of me. Nice enough fellows, for a coupla flatfeet. I don't mean no disrespect by that, either. I mean, that's why we're here, right?

DB: Right.

RH: Because you guys think I'm crazy or drunk.

DB: We know you're not drunk, Mr. Harris. Now, earlier this evening—

RH: Earlier this evening I was sittin' on my ass, thinking about my kid. She's nineteen, goes to the U.

DB: The University of Minnesota, Duluth Campus.

RH: Yup. Anyway, that's why I pull so many second shifts, because cripes, those books are expensive. I mean, a hunnerd and ten bucks for a book? One book?

DB: Mr. Harris—

RH: Anyways, so there I was, mindin' my own business, eating my lunch. Course it wasn't exactly lunchtime, cuz it was ten o'clock at night, but when you're on second shift, you do what you can. I was sittin' at Lake and 4th. A lot of the cabbies don't like that neighborhood, you know, because of all the Negroes. No offense. I mean, not that you look it, but—

DB: Mr. Harris, I'm not African American, but even if I were, I'm sure I would devoutly wish we could stay on course.

RH: But you never know these days, am I right? Goddamned P.C. Nazis. A man can't speak his mind anymore. I got a friend, Danny Pohl, and he's just as black as the ace of spades, and he calls himself a-well, I'm not going to tell you what he says, but he uses it all the time. And if he don't care, why should we?

DB: Mr. Harris . . .

RH: Sorry. Anyway, so I'm in this neighborhood, which, yeah, some people say ain't so great, and I'm eating my lunch—ham and Swiss with mustard on Wonder Bread, in case anybody needs to know—when all of a sudden my cab was on its side!

DB: You didn't hear anything?

RH: Son, I didn't have a single hint. One second I was eating, and the next I was lying on my side and all the garbage on the floor was raining down on me and I'd dropped my sandwich and the side of my head was resting on the street. I could hear somebody walking away, but I couldn't see nothing. But that wasn't the worst of it.

DB: What was?

RH: Well, I was still trying to figure out what happened, and wonderin' if I could get the mustard out of my new workshirt, when I heard this really loud scream.

DB: Was it a man or a woman?

RH: Tell you what, it was hard to tell. I mean, I know now, because I saw them—both of them—but I didn't know then. Whoever was yelling was having their legs pulled off or something, because they were shrieking and crying and babbling and it was the worst sound I ever heard in my life. And my daughter's tone deaf and is always takin' up new musical instruments. Like that time with the tuba. But that was nothing compared to this.

DB: What did you do then?

RH: Well, shit, I climbed out of the passenger side of my cab as fast as I could, what d'ya think? I was a medic in the war— Vietnam, that was. I hung it up after I got back stateside and I never went to a hospital again, nope, not even when my wife, God rest her, had Anna. But I figured I could maybe help. My cab was insured, I didn't mind about that, but someone was really in trouble and that was a lot more important. I thought maybe somebody had backed over their kid by accident. Some of those alleys are pretty dark. Hard to see stuff.

DB: And then?

RH: Then the bus pulled up. It almost hit my cab! And that was weird, because it was pretty late for the buses to be running, and this one was empty except for one passenger.

Then this gal jumps out. And the bus just sits there. I seen the bus driver just staring at the gal like she was made of chocolate ice cream. And then I got a good look at her.

DB: Can you describe her?

RH: Well, she was tall, real tall—'bout my height, and I'm just shy of six feet. She had light blond hair with them streaky—what d'you call 'ems? Highlights! She had kind of reddish highlights, and the biggest, prettiest green eyes you'd ever seen. Her eyes were the color of them old-fashioned glass bottles, those real dark green ones. And she was real pale, like she worked in an office all the time. Me, my left arm gets brown as a berry in the summertime, on account of how it's always hanging out my cab window, but my right arm stays real white. Anyway, I don't really remember what she was wearing—I was mostly looking at her face. And . . . and . . .

DB: Are you all right?

RH: It's just this part's hard, is all. I mean, this gal was maybe five or six years older than my daughter, but I—well, let's say I wanted her the way a man wants his wife on a Saturday night, if you know what I mean. And I'd never been one to horndog after kids young enough to be *my* kid, and never mind that my wife's been dead for six years. So it was kind of embarrassing, too, that even though those awful screams were still sort of echoing in the air, here's me all of a sudden thinking with my dick.

DB: Well, sometimes, under stress, a person—

RH: Wasn't stress. I just wanted her, is all. Like I never wanted anybody. Anyways, I stared at her but she didn't pay me no notice. Gal like her, she probably gets old coots like me staring at her twenty times a day. She didn't say nothing to me, just marched back toward the alley. So I followed her. There was a couple of street lights back there, so I was finally startin' to be able to see stuff. Made me feel a lot better, I can tell you.

And just like that, before we could even get there, the screams stop. It was like someone had shut off a radio, that's how sudden it was. So the gal, she starts to run. Which was funny to see, because she was wearing these teetery high heels. Purple, with bows on the backs. She had teeny feet, and these pretty little shoes. It was kind of funny to see that.

DB: And then?

RH: Well, she could sure move in them shoes, and that was a fact. She musta been a real track star or something. And I was right behind her. And we get to the alley, and right away I seen it was a dead end, and I didn't want to go too far in. It's funny, I never think about the Nam no more, but that night it was like I'd just gotten back home. Man, I was noticing *everything*. I was really wired.

DB: Could you see anyone in the alley?

RH: Not at first. But then the gal says, real loud but firm, you know, like a teacher, "Let him go." And then I seen there were two guys and they weren't standing ten feet away!

Don't know how I missed them before. One of them was this little short squirt, but he was hoisting a guy bigger than me, holding him up off the ground! He was slamming the guy into the brick wall real hard, and the big guy's head was sort of lolling all over the place, and he was out cold.

But then, when the gal talked, the little guy let go, and the guy who'd been doing all the screaming hit the bricks like a sack of sand—I mean, he was *out*. And the little guy marches up to us, and all of a sudden I was just scared shitless.

DB: Did you see a weapon, or—

RH: Nothin' like that. He was just . . . bad, I guess. He was about a head shorter than me and he had kind of gray skin. And one of those little black mustaches, real thin. Me, I think a man should grow a real soup strainer or nothing at all.

Anyway, he looked like a little punk, but there was somethin' about him—I just wanted to get away from him. It was like somethin' inside me knew he was bad, even if I couldn't see for myself exactly what it was. And let me tell you, I watched my own dear wife die from cancer of the stomach. She went an inch at a time and it took eight months. I didn't think nothing would ever scare me after watching that. But that guy . . .

DB: Do you need a break, Mr. Harris?

RH: Hell, no, I wanna get this over with. I promised I'd come down and tell you, so here I am. Anyway, this guy, he gets real close, and he says, "This is none of yours, false queen." And the way he talked—it was real old-fashioned. Like, I dunno, like people talked maybe a hundred years ago. And his voice—Jesus! I got goose bumps all over. I wanted to run, but I couldn't move.

But the gal didn't seem to care. She straightens right up and says, "Oh, blow me. Get lost, before I lose my temper."

DB: "Blow me"?

RH: Sorry, but that's what she said. I remember it real well, because it was a shocker. I mean, I'm a big guy, and *I* was scared. She was a kid, and she didn't sound scared at all.

DB: Then what happened?

RH: Well, the little mean guy, he looked like he was gonna fall over. I was shocked, but he was . . . well, he was *really* shocked. Like no one had ever talked to him that way in his whole life. I dunno, maybe no one had. And he says, "My meals are none of your business, false queen." That's what he kept calling her—"false queen." Never did hear her name.

DB: "False queen."

RH: Yeah. And she says, "Sit and spin, jerk off." Seriously! Then she says, "You know as well as me that you don't have to scare 'em or hurt 'em to feed, so cut the shit." Or maybe it was "cut the crap." Anyways, she was ticked off.

DB: And then?

RH: Then he grabs her! And his lips peeled back from his teeth, like a dog getting ready to bite. *Just* like that, our neighbor's dog Rascal went rabid last summer, and before I shot the poor dog, he looked just as crazed and out of control as this guy.

And before I could help her—I was scared, but I didn't want her to get messed up, I mean, I woulda done *something*—she whips out this cross and jams it onto his forehead! Just like in the movies! And man oh man, I thought the *big* guy was a screamer. This guy, he yowled like his lungs had caught fire, and all this smoke starts pourin' off his forehead, and oh, Lord, the smell. You wouldn't *believe* how bad it smelled. Like pork on fire, only the pork had been spoiled first. God, I'd like to puke just thinkin' about it.

And he let go of her and kind of staggered backward, and she steps up just as cool as a cucumber and says, "You'll pick this gentleman up and you'll take him to the hospital. And you'll pay for the bill if he doesn't have insurance. And if I catch you feeding like this ever again, I'll shove this cross right down your throat. Got it, or should I get out the hand puppets?"

And he sort of cringes away from her and nods. She was so stern and beautiful, he couldn't look at her. Shit, *I* could hardly look at her! And then he picked up the big guy, who was still conked out, and sort of ran out of the alley with him.

Then the gal turns to me and kind of sighs, like she's real tired. Then she says, "Did you ever get stuck in a job you really hate?" And I allowed as to how that had happened to me once in a while. Boy oh boy, she was somethin' gorgeous.

DB: And then?

RH: Then she asks am I all right. And I say I am. And she says for me not to be scared. And I say as long as she's there, I won't be. And she gave me a big smile for that one.

So we started walking out of the alley, and she sees my cab laying on its side. And she looks all disgusted and says, "Jeez, what an infant." I guess she meant the guy who ran away. And she walks over—this is the part you're interested in—and kneels down, and slips two fingers underneath my cab, and lifts it back up until it's on its wheels again.

DB: She lifted your cab upright?

RH: Yup.

DB: With one hand.

RH: With two fingers. I know how it sounds. It's okay. The other cops didn't believe me, either.

DB: And then what happened?

RH: Then she looks at me with those pretty green eyes—except now they were more hazel then green, which was kinda strange, I dunno, maybe her contacts fell out—and says, "I think it'll still run. Sorry about your trouble." And I tell her it's okay. And she climbs on the bus—which was still waiting for her by the way, which could be the weirdest thing that happened tonight—and waves good-bye to me. And then the bus drove away. Ran down a mailbox and through a red light, too.

DB: That's it?

RH: Ain't that enough? It was some night. Tell you what, that gal was something else. I don't *never* want her mad at me.

DB: Because of her strength?

RH: No. Because I wanted her, but I was scared of her, too. I'm just glad she turned out to be nice. Because what if she was like that little guy in the alley? The vampire?

DB: You believe the man was a vampire?

RH: Shit, who else would scream and be burned by a cross? What I'd like to know is what *she* was.

DB: You believe in vampires, do you?

RH: You've been a good listener, son, and I appreciate it, but I want you to pay close attention to just one more thing. I was in a war when I was just a teenager. And I found out that the guy who don't believe his eyes is the guy who goes home in a bag. So, yeah. I believe in vampires.

Now, I mean.

END INTERVIEW
03:45:32 A.M.

# Chapter 1

W H E N I'd been dead for about three months, I decided it was past time to get a job.

I couldn't go back to my old one, of course. For one thing, I'd been laid off the day I died, and for another, they all still thought I was six feet under. Plus, a job during daylight hours just wasn't going to work anymore.

I wasn't starving or homeless, at least. My best friend, Jessica, owned my house and wouldn't let me pay rent, and she had her team of super accountants pay the other bills despite my strenuous objections. I sure didn't need to grocery shop for much except teabags and milk and stuff. Plus, my car was paid off. So my monthly expenses were actually pretty low. Even so, I couldn't live off Jessica's charity forever.

So here I was, on the steps of the Minnesota Re-Employment Center. They had evening hours every Thursday—thank goodness!

I walked through the doors, shivering as I was greeted by a blast of air-conditioning. Another thing about being dead that nobody warned me about was that I was cold pretty much all the time. Minneapolis was having a severe heat wave, and I was the only one not hating it.

"Hi," I said to the receptionist. She was wearing a stiff gray suit and needed her roots done. I couldn't see her shoes, which was probably just as well. "I came to the unemployment center to—"

"I'm sorry, miss, that's RE-Employment. Unemployment centers are an anachronism. We're a responsive twenty-first-century re-employment one- stop center."

"Right. Um, anyway, I'm here to see one of the counselors."

For my audacity, I spent the next twenty minutes filling out paperwork. Finally, my name was called, and I was sitting in front of a counselor.

He was a pleasant-looking older fellow with dark hair, a gray-flecked beard, and chocolate brown eyes, and I was relieved to see the wedding ring as well as the photo of his pretty wife and *de rigeur* adorable kids. I fervently hoped he had a happy marriage, so he wouldn't make a fool of himself once my undead charisma smacked him in the face.

"Hi, I'm Dan Mitchell." We shook hands, and I saw his eyebrows go up in surprise when he clasped my clammy palm. "Elizabeth Taylor, right?"

"That's me."

"Are your eyes all right?"

I was wearing my sunglasses for two reasons. One, the fluorescent light hurt like a bitch. Two, men didn't fall under my spell if they couldn't see my eyes. The last thing I needed was a slobbering state employee humping my leg.

"I was at the eye doctor's earlier," I lied. "He put those drop things in."

"Yeah, been there. Elizabeth Taylor—just like the movie star!" he enthused, obviously having no idea people had been drawing that conclusion since the day I'd been born.

"Betsy."

"Betsy, then." He was flipping through the reams of paperwork I'd handed him. "Everything looks right . . ."

"I hope so. I'm here for Unemployment—"

"We're the RE-Employment Center," Mitchell said absently, still flipping.

"Right, right. Anyway, I need a new job, and while I'm looking, I'd like Unemployment Insurance. In fact, I have a quest—"

Mitchell looked vaguely alarmed. "Um . . . I need to stop you right there. We can't do that here."

I blinked. Not that he could tell behind the Foster Grants I was wearing. "Come again?"

"We're a re-employment office. That's what we do."

"Sure, okay, I get it, but don't you . . . ?"

"If you want unemployment benefits, you need to call the hotline. Or use the Internet. I'm sorry, but we can't answer your question here."

"Let me get this straight. This is the place I go to when I'm unemployed . . ."

"Yes . . ."

"And you have unemployment benefit applications here—"

"Absolutely!"

"But you don't have any staff here who can help me get unemployment benefits."

"Yes, that's correct."

"Oh, okay." This was weird, but I could be cooperative. Probably. I leaned back in the uncomfortable plastic chair. "Okay, so, can I use your phone to call one of these hotlines?"

Mitchell spread his hands apologetically. "Ah, jeez, you know, we used to let people do that, but some folks abused the phones, and so—"

"So you're telling me I can't call an Unemployment Hotline using a telephone in the Unemployment Office?"

"Well, technically, remember, we're not an Unemployment Office anymore"—I suddenly wondered if a vampire could get drunk. I decided to find out as soon as I got out of this bureaucratic hellhole—"and that's why we can't let you do that." He shrugged. "Sorry."

I whipped off my sunglasses and leaned forward, spearing him with my sinister undead gaze. It was a rotten thing to do, but I was desperate. "I need. To use. Your phone."

"No!" He hunched over and clutched the phone protectively to his chest. "It's against policy!"

Amazing. I was sure my vampire mojo would leave him putty in my hands, but apparently his bureaucratic training was stronger than ancient evil.

"You'll just have to go home and contact them on your own dime," he snapped.

I stomped back to the waiting area. Outrageous! I wasn't just any undead tart, I was the queen of the vampires!

"Don't forget to fill out a customer satisfaction survey on your way out!" Mitchell yelled after me.

*God, kill me now. Again, I mean.*

# Chapter 2

 T+Iⵉⵉⵉⵉⵉⵉⵉⵉⵉⵉⵉⵉ flashing red lights in my rearview mirror produced their usual result: a surge of adrenaline, then annoyance. I hadn't been going *that* fast. And it wasn't even a patrol car pulling me over. It was a Chrysler, for God's sake.

One of the many people dedicated to ruining my day got out of the car and started toward me. He didn't have that slow, arrogant strut that staties have. In fact, he was jogging. I recognized him at once and groaned.

Nick Berry. Detective Nick Berry, to be exact, and absolutely the last person I wanted to see. We had an embarrassing episode last spring, and I lived in fear that, one of these days, he'd remember I was dead. Or at least, remember he'd been at my funeral.

He slipped into the passenger seat. "Hey, Betsy. How's it going?"

"You're abusing your authority as a sworn officer of the law," I informed him. "I wasn't even barely speeding."

"Yeah, yeah. Listen, where were you the other night?"

"Which one?"

"Saturday?"

*Uh-oh.* "Home," I said, putting plenty of fake curiosity in my tone. "Why?"

"I don't suppose anybody could back you up on that one?"

I shook my head. "Marc was at the hospital, and Jessica was probably at home—I didn't see her that night. Why? What's going on?"

Nick leaned back, easing his feet through the garbage on my passenger side floor. He didn't know how lucky he was. It had

been a lot worse when I'd been eating solid food. "Cripes, don't
you ever clean out your car? How many shakes do you drink in a
week?"

"None of your business. Now go away and catch bad guys."

"I'm going to need a tetanus shot when I get out of here," he
complained, kicking an empty 7-Up cup off the end of his boot.

"Seriously, Nick, what's up? I mean, if you're not giving me a
ticket—"

He shook his head. "It's stupid."

"Well, I figured."

"No, really stupid." While he babbled, I let my gaze roam over
his blond hair, his swimmer's build, his chiseled features—then
jerked my gaze back to the road where it belonged. That's how
we'd gotten into trouble the last time. I'd been newly undead and
unbelievably thirsty, he'd been handy, I'd drunk his blood, and
he'd been lost. For a long time. Sinclair had to step in and fix it. I
still had no idea what—if anything—Nick remembered.

". . . and this nutty old cab driver described you. I mean, not
that there aren't about a zillion blondes in Minneapolis, but still.
The description fit you pretty well. It was the shoe thing, actually,
that caught my—"

"Well, obviously it wasn't me," I lied. "Doy."

"Doy? Haven't heard *that* in about fifteen years. But anyway, I
think you might be right. The whole story was just . . . I think the
guy was . . . I don't know. Maybe some of it was real, and some of it
he imagined, or made up to get attention. He seemed like a lonely
guy." Nick was rubbing his temples in a way that made me distinctly
nervous. "I . . . sometimes I have dreams and they *seem* real . . ."

"That happens to everybody." Should I zap him with my vamp
mojo? Would it interfere with whatever Sinclair had done, or
would it make things better? "Maybe you need a vacation."

"That was a funny thing that happened to you last spring," he
said, changing the subject. At least, he *thought* he was changing
the subject. "I mean, not everybody has a mix-up like you do."

"I still say it was my stepmother playing a joke. It's not like
she wouldn't want to see me dead."

"Yeah, but going to the extent of a fake funeral—or was there
a funeral?" He was rubbing his temples so hard, they were getting
pink. "I dreamed about it, but mostly I . . . I . . ."

"Nick, for crying out loud!" I said loudly, hoping to snap him
out of it. "I've got stuff to do. So are you going to get out of here
or what?"

His hands fell to his lap at once, and he seemed to shake off the trance-like state he'd fallen in. "So sorry, Betsy," he said sarcastically. "What, there's a shoe sale somewhere?"

"As a matter of fact, there is. Look, I hope you catch the bad guy—"

"Yeah, yeah, I'm sure you're on pins and needles. Never mind. Saw your car and couldn't resist. But, I gotta get back to it."

"Okay. Nice to see you again."

"You, too. Stay out of trouble." He smiled at me and climbed out of the car, unaware of the straw sticking to his heel. "Have a good one."

"Bye!" I called, and waited until he pulled out in front of me before I got my car moving. It was just as well; I was shaking like a leaf. Poor Nick was crawling all over the truth, and didn't have a clue. I wished I could confide in him, but enough people knew my dirty little undead secret as it was.

Besides, once I *had* confided in him. And it had been an utter disaster. I wasn't making the same mistake twice.


AN hour later I was at the finest, most glorious place on the planet: The Mall of America. Or, if you're a shopper, Heaven on Earth.

I decided to trudge through the first level of Macy's to cheer myself up, and then drown my sorrows in two or ten daiquiris on the fourth floor.

Like any great idea, the Mall (never "the mall") is something familiar, made bigger. A lot bigger. Everyone has parked in a lot and walked into a store. Here you had to walk a long, long time to get to the store, is all. It helped to memorize the state you were parked in. You know how most parking lots can name their sections after two or three animals? "Oh, honey, don't forget we parked in the marmoset lot." The Mall was so big, they couldn't use animals. Animals are puny. They used states. And not little states like Rhode Island, but big honking states like California and Texas.

I parked in Texas and crossed the small side street to Macy's. As always, I was struck by the beauty of the building. The red brick and soaring windows reminded me of—don't laugh—a church. And the star they used instead of the apostrophe in Macy's seemed so heavenly.

Once inside, I inhaled the sweet smell of perfume, leather,

cotton, and floor cleaner. Before I'd been laid off I was a secretary. Now I was jobless, unless you counted the whole queen of the vampires gig, which I certainly did not, not least because it didn't pay for shit. Besides, most days I doubted I was the queen. Certainly the other vampires I'd been crossing paths with lately didn't think so. And Sinclair . . . Never mind about Sinclair. I wasn't going to think about that jerk.

I zoomed in on the shoe department like a blonde homing pigeon. Shoes, shoes everywhere! Ah, sweet shoes. I truly think you can take the measure of a civilization by looking at its footwear.

Because I was in a department store, I was enveloped in its time warp. So although the fourth of July was less than a week away, the shoe department had all their fall colors and styles on display. That was all right. I already had twenty-two pairs of sandals.

I eyed the row of Kenneth Cole boots, finally taking down a vibrant red pair and feeling the leather. They'd look terrific with my black duster, but I already had a pair of red boots. Hmm . . . should that make a difference?

I also checked out the Burn footwear. They were supposedly all made by hand—and for two hundred dollars a pair, they'd better be—but I'd never tried a pair. Maybe when I got a job, I'd treat myself, give them a try.

Typical of Macy's, the saleswomen were all ignoring me because I wasn't waving fifty dollar bills at them. I tapped the nearest one on the shoulder. "Excuse me, could I see the new Etienne Aigners?"

She looked at me over the tops of her black cat's eye glasses. A much too harsh a color for her face, by the way. They made her pale skin look even paler, and her brown eyes kind of muddy. "I'm sorry, miss, we don't have any."

"Oh, sure you do. I understand if you haven't had time to go through them and put them on display, but I'd just like to see them."

I could see another saleswoman and a balding man in a gorgeous Armani suit watching us from a distance. He was holding a clipboard and wearing a Macy's name tag. The woman beside him was staring at her coworker, who'd obviously woken up that morning with a need to be unhelpful.

"We really don't have any—"

"Who do you think you're talking to?" I asked impatiently. "The Aigners have been out for six days. You probably got them four days ago. I just want to see if he put out a lavender pump like he was supposed to."

"Listen, you—"

*"Brigid."*

The saleswoman cut herself off and looked over at the guy who'd been watching. I'd heard them coming, but she hadn't, because she jumped and looked terribly guilty. "Yes, Mr. Mason?"

"Please come to my office. I need to talk to you. And Renee"—he turned to the other saleswoman—"please take our customer in the back and show her the Aigners."

"Ha! I mean, thanks."

"This way, miss," Renee said, smiling. She was shorter than me by a good four inches, with brown hair and red highlights, and hazel eyes that looked at the world through classic wire rims. She had lots of freckles and natural, high color. She was wearing a red-and-black plaid suit, black tights, and Nine West black flats. Pretty, in a "brainy girl who grew up to be classy" kind of way.

She walked me through a door in the back of the shoe section and then let loose with a stream of giggles. "Holy cow! You really told Brigid. She's toast. She was supposed to have that display up the day before yesterday."

"Don't ever get between me and a new line of shoes," I said. "Others have found that out to their sorrow. I guess I should follow that up with an evil laugh, because it sounds sort of ominous."

Renee snorted and escorted me past the discount racks. The Aigners were scattered all over the floor, mixed in with Nine West's crap from last season.

"Oh, the humanity!" I gasped when I saw the mess.

*"Big* trouble," Renee muttered.

"Help me straighten this out!"

"Uh . . . okay. I mean, you don't have to. They're just shoes."

I swayed on my feet, and didn't trust myself to reply. Instead, I got to work, and Renee helped.

Within ten minutes, we had all the Aigners lined up like dead soldiers, close to the door. They were a little dusty, but no major damage. The Nine Wests I'd kicked into the far corner. Alas, no lavender pumps. Just as well; I couldn't afford to buy shoes today, anyway.

"That's better," I said, dusting off my hands. I heard the door open behind us but, since Renee didn't react, I didn't turn. Jeez, how in the heck did I get along before, without vampire hearing? "It won't take long to get these to the floor."

"You know a lot about shoes," Renee said, staring. "I didn't even notice the Jude pumps had gotten mixed in with the others, and I've been here four months."

I tried not to shudder at her ignorance; it wouldn't be nice. Luckily, the dude rescued me. "Excuse me, ladies. Find everything you needed?"

"Unfortunately, no. Maybe he'll do it next season."

"Mmmm." His name tag read John Mason, Store Manager. He looked like my dad's accountant . . . balding, glasses, good suit, great shoes. He smelled like Calvin Klein's One and baked potatoes. "We are now short a sales associate for the shoe floor," he announced. Renee pursed her red lips in a silent whistle and rolled her eyes at me, where Mason couldn't see. "Are you by any chance looking for work?"

I stared. John Mason, Store Manager, was a genius or a telepath. "Yes, I am! What a coincidence, I mean, that you would ask me!"

"Not really." He pointed to my purse, where the paperwork I'd gotten from the Re-Employment Center was sticking out. "Would you like to work here? Not on commission," he added sternly. "I can pay you nine dollars an hour."

"Wh—sure! When can I start?"

"I'll need you here every evening, Wednesday through Saturday," he warned.

"You bet! I can only work nights, anyway."

"Well, then."

Before I could kiss him on the mouth, Mr. Mason had walked me over to Human Resources and gotten me my paperwork. I was a little worried at first—I had died three months ago, after all. Would my social security number work?

It did. Thank you, government backlog!

The paperwork finished, Mr. Mason handed me my name tag and bid me good night.

Betsy Taylor, it said.

Macy's, it said.

BetsyTaylorMacy's. Wow. Oh, just . . . wow. Really totally wow.

Outside the store, I did a little skip step of joy . . . and nearly sailed over a car by mistake. I probably could have pulled that off even if I hadn't been dead.

Wow! Me, working for Macy's! That was like a fox working for a chicken farm. It just didn't get any better.

# Chapter 3

𝓛 hurried home to Apple Valley to tell Jessica all about my new job. But the unbelievable stench assailed me on my front step, and I almost couldn't make myself go inside.

I fidgeted on the front step for a minute, debating, and finally told myself, well, you defeated the most evil vampire on the planet just a couple of months ago, so you can do this, too.

I opened my front door and followed my nose to the bathroom, where my best friend was lurched over the toilet.

"Still have the flu?" I asked sympathetically.

"No stupid questions from vampires," she groaned. She retched again. I observed she'd had chicken soup and toast for lunch. "Use your super strength to pull my head off my shoulders, please."

"For crying out loud, Jess, how long you been in here?"

"What day is it?"

I noticed that she hadn't had time to turn on the bathroom light in her headlong gallop, and had initially missed the toilet. Oh, well. The wall needed re-painting, anyway.

When she was finished scatter-puking, I picked her up like a big doll and carried her to the guest bed. Before I'd become a vampire, there was no way I could have done this. Jessica was a few inches shorter than me, and about as pudgy as a stop sign, but she was gangly and hard to move around. Now, of course, it was cake.

I brought her a glass of 7-Up and a wet washcloth. She cleaned herself up as best she could, and then I picked her up and ran back into the bathroom so she could throw up the soda.

"Maybe it's time to go to a hospital," I said nervously. She'd been barfing for two days.

"Marc·can give me a shot when he gets home," she said. She sounded hollow, because her head was all the way inside the toilet bowl. Luckily, she'd gotten her hair cut last week.

Marc was my roommate, a resident at the Children's Hospital in Minneapolis. He'd moved in the week I woke up dead. Jessica had a gorgeous, chic little seven-room place in Edina, but she spent most of her time at my place.

"Is there a reason you're being sick here," I asked, "instead of at your place?"

"You don't know how lucky you are," she replied, ignoring my question, "being dead and all."

"Right now I agree with you. Hey, guess what? I got a job."

"That's nice." She looked up at me. Her brown eyes were sunken. She'd looked better on the day of her parents' funeral. "Why are you just standing there? Why aren't you killing me?"

"Er, sorry." I took a breath through my mouth. Luckily I only had to do that about twice an hour. "You know, this sort of reminds me of your twenty-first birthday. Remember?"

"The night is"—she *hurped-hurped* for a second, then continued—"a blur."

"Well, you were mixing crème de menthe with vermouth, and then you started with Jack Daniels and tequila. I tried to get you to slow down, and you told me to shut up and get you a Zima with a bourbon chaser. Then—"

"Stop!"

"Sorry." Yeah, not the brightest move. But that was the last time she'd been this sick. "If you were a guy, or gay, I could hypnotize you into passing out. I guess I could try hitting you over the head with something . . ."

"Just help me back to bed, dead girl."

I did. I was ready to *hurp-hurp* myself, and wanted to go back to Macy's in the worst way.

Instead, I tucked Jessica back in—she dozed off while I was pulling the blankets up to her chin—and left her to start cleaning.

I found some clothespins in the kitchen junk drawer. Don't ask me why—I didn't have a clothesline. Junk drawers are a miracle in themselves. The stuff that turns up in them—why were there coupons for free bird seed? I didn't have a bird.

I found with the clothespin over my nose, and Playtex rubber gloves on my hands, and by thinking about the spring line of Ferragamos, I could scrub the bathroom without yarking up the blood I'd drunk about three hours ago. My donor had been an amiable car thief who'd been fumbling with the steering column of a Pontiac Firebird when I found him. After I'd taken what I needed, I called him a cab. It was bad enough I was a lamprey on legs; I wasn't going to be an accessory to grand larceny.

I was rinsing the mop in the toilet when I heard a knock. I hurried to the living room and opened the door before Jessica could wake up.

Tina stood there, looking all big-eyed and hopeful. She took one look at my ensemble and slapped a hand over her mouth to stifle the giggles.

"Get lost," I suggested. I still wasn't speaking to her. Thanks to her, and Sinclair, I was the queen of the undead. A small fact they'd hidden until after Sinclair and I had made love. There could be no forgiveness!

"Please can't I come in, Majesty?" she asked, lips twitching madly.

"No. And don't call me that." Still, I stood there with the door open. I'd liked Tina the moment I met her. Of course, whenever someone saves my life on first acquaintance, I tend to feel warm toward them.

And except for her unwavering loyalty to Sinclair, which made her do the most annoying things (see above: the whole queen of the vampires thing), she was pretty cool. Old— something like a hundred and some years—but cool. She didn't act or talk like an old lady, though she could be stiff sometimes. And she looked like a *Glamour* cover girl with her long blond hair, high cheekbones, and pansy eyes, so dark and enormous they seemed to take up half her face.

"What on earth are you doing? And what is that stench?"

"Cleaning up," I replied nasally. I plucked the clothespin off my nose. "Jessica's got the flu."

"I'm sorry to hear that. The flu. I haven't had that in . . ." Her eyes tipped up in thought. "Hmm . . ."

"Fascinating. Look, the bathroom smells like someone died in there. I'm not exaggerating—I would know, right? We both would. So, I have to get back."

"Let me do it," she suggested.

"Forget it," I said, startled. Yech! A job I wouldn't wish on my worst enemy. Or Sinclair.

"Such work is beneath you."

"I'll be the judge of what's beneath me, missy," I snapped. "And as it happens, cleaning up puke is right up my alley."

"I insist, Majesty."

"Too bad. Besides, you can't come in without my permission. Ha! And again I say, ha."

She raised her eyebrows at me, dark and delicate as butterfly feelers, and stepped over the threshold.

"Well, nuts."

"Sorry. Old wives' tale. Besides, Eric and I were in and out of here a couple of times this past spring, remember?"

"I've been doing my best to forget all about last spring." I handed her the clothespin.

"Besides, if you think about it, it makes no sense," she said gently. "Why wouldn't a vampire be able to come and go as she pleased?"

"Spare me the lecture. And if you're going to barge in, make yourself useful. You want to clean? Be my guest."

She moved forward so eagerly, I actually felt bad for a few seconds. She was so desperate to get back in my good graces.

Not my problem.

"So, what d'you want? Why'd you come over?"

"To beg your forgiveness again," she replied soberly.

"Scrub first," I advised. "Then beg."


TINA made about as much noise as a ninja, but Jessica sat up anyway when we walked into the bedroom. "Whu?" she asked muzzily. "Tina? That you?"

"Poor Jessica!" Tina hurried to the side of the bed. Her delicate nostrils flared once, and then she was smooth-faced and polite. "If memory serves, the flu is dreadful." She put a hand on Jessica's forehead. "You must feel awful."

"I do, but that feels great," Jessica groaned. "Your clammy dead hand is just the ticket. How come Betsy let you in? Thought she was still ticked off at you and King Gorgeous."

"Do *not* call him that," I muttered.

"She took pity on me. Go to sleep, darling," she soothed. "When you wake, you'll feel much better."

Just like that, Jessica's eyes rolled up and she was out, snoring blissfully.

"Damn!" I was impressed in spite of myself. Tina was bisexual; I figured that's why she had power over men *and* women. "Nice work! I didn't know you could cure the flu."

"Thank you. Scrub brush?"

"Next to the toilet. But seriously, this is just too sad. You must have more important things to do than clean my bathroom," I commented, following her to said bathroom. "It's almost the weekend, for God's sake."

Tina flinched at "God". Vampires were so touchy about organized religion. "Actually, I did have some news."

"Sinclair has turned into a pile of ash?" I asked hopefully.

"Ah . . . no. But it's funny you should say that. We're getting reports of quite a few staked vampires."

"So?"

She looked at me.

"Ah, no," I whined. "What, this is *my* problem?"

"You're the queen."

"Oh, so I have to protect the city's vampires?"

"The world's vampires, actually," she said gently.

Good thing I was standing near the tub, because all of a sudden, I needed a place to sit down.

# Chapter 4

"So, somebody's been running around killing vampires?"

"Yes. More than one somebody, most likely. We suspect a hit team."

" 'We' being you and Sinclair."

"Yes."

I drank the rest of my tea and got up to fix a fresh cup. The bathroom sparkled like something out of a toilet bowl cleaner commercial; Tina could scrub like a fiend. Did fiends scrub, I wondered idly. Note to self: find out.

"Look, Tina, no offense, but I'm not sure this is necessarily a bad thing."

"No offense taken," she said dryly.

"I just don't think it's my job to protect the city vampires, is all. Shit, I've been protecting the city from *them*. What is it about upright wood ticks that they have to hurt their food? Huh?"

She stared at her cup and didn't answer.

"I mean, just the other day, I'm minding my own business, when I have to pull a bloodsucker off his lunch. Not only did he rough up his meal, but he tipped over a city cab and scared the shit out of the driver just for the hell of it. Just because he could."

Still, Tina said nothing. I knew her blood donors were one hundred percent willing, but it was still embarrassing to be associated with the bad guys.

I jumped into the silence. "So, I'm betting this hit squad or whatever has a legitimate beef with the undead. Right? Right. Now *I* have to get involved? What the hell for?"

Tina was silent for a long moment, then finally said, "You're young."

"Oh, sure, throw that in my face again."

But she had a point. Four months ago, I'd been a live nobody. Now I was a dead monarch. But I still remembered what it was like to breathe and eat and run around outside in the daytime. Would I have cared *then* that someone was killing vampires?

Nope.

To be perfectly honest, most vampires were assholes. I couldn't begin to guess how many people I'd saved from being munched, all because vamps had victim issues. It was like, once they rose from the dead, they spent the rest of the time getting even for being murdered.

"I imagine you feel . . . torn," Tina said.

"More like annoyed and pissed off."

"But the fact remains, someone is killing your people."

I didn't say anything. Sadly, Tina didn't take the hint. Instead, she continued, "We need to put a stop to it at once."

I sat down across from her with my fresh cup of tea. "Oh, man," I sighed. "Look, let me think about it, okay? I just got a new job, my roommate's sick, my dad's scared of me, my car needs an oil change, we probably have termites, Jessica's house-hunting behind my back, and it's almost the weekend. I'm just so busy right now."

"You have a job?"

"Uh-hum." I tried to look modest. Not everybody could land the job of a lifetime. "Selling shoes at Macy's."

Another long pause. "You'll be working at a mall?"

Tina wasn't as fawning or floored as I expected. Weird. "Not *a* mall, *the* Mall, and yeah, so my plate's kind of full right now. Plus, I have to work tomorrow. At Macy's. At *the* Mall. So maybe we could pick this up later?"

She drummed her fingers on the table and stared at me. "I suppose I could get together all the information we have and bring it over later for you to look at."

"Oh, just sum up. Write me a memo."

"A memo."

"Yup." I stared at my wrist. Forgot to put on my watch again, darnit. "My, my, look at the time! This has been great, but I've got to scoot."

"You're as subtle as a brick to the forehead. I'll be back."

"That's just swell. An undead Terminator, just what I need in my life. Give Sinclair a nice kick in the balls for me."

She sniffed. "No need to be rude."

Of course, she was dead wrong. Where Sinclair was concerned, there were all kinds of need.

# Chapter 5

*Four Days Later*

"UM, Mr. Mason, d'you have a minute?"

We were back in the employee section, and I was standing just outside the boss's cubicle. Tastefully upholstered in blah gray, there wasn't a single picture, kid's drawing, party invitation, or softball sign-up sheet tacked to any of the cube walls. Except for a computer, his work space was clear. The place was as Spartan as a monk's cell. It was impressive and creepy at the same time. "If you're busy, I could—"

"I am, Betsy, but I'm glad you came back here . . . I need to speak with you." He took off his glasses—was it, like, a rule that if you were in management you wore glasses?—gestured for me to sit, and then polished the frames on his sweater which, weirdly, was tucked into his slacks. "But first, what can I do for you?"

"Uh, well, my paycheck seemed a little light. Not that it wasn't a kick to have a check from Macy's, because it was. But still . . . I was expecting a bit more. I was thinking maybe you guys didn't have all my hours on there, or something."

He held out his hand, and I gave him my pay stub. He scanned it once, then handed it back. "Well, there's fica, federal tax, state tax . . ."

"Right."

"And your employee discount."

"Right. What?" Damn! I'd bought a few things to celebrate my new job, but I had no idea I'd spent four-fifths of my paycheck before I even got it. Damn you, indigo blue high heels from Liz Claiborne!

"Oh," I said, sounding just so intelligent, I was sure. "I forgot about that. Sorry to bother you."

"A moment, please, Betsy. How do you like being on the Macy's team?"

"Are you kidding? It's great! It's like a dream come true!"

"I'm glad. And with one or two small exceptions, it's a pleasure to have you working here."

"Uh-oh," I said dolefully.

He smiled. "First let me say your knowledge of fine footwear is unparalleled by anyone in the store, excepting myself."

I modestly brushed my bangs out of my face. *Excepting myself, my ass. But be nice*. "Thanks."

"However . . ."

"Oh, here we go."

"I've noticed you try to talk a . . . a certain type of customer . . . out of their purchases."

I didn't say anything to that, and fought the urge to squirm in my chair. The fact was, if someone came in wearing shoes that were terribly beat up, I was loathe to sell them one of my finely made babies. Who knew what could happen? Once the shoes were out of the stores, they were beyond my protective sphere. I had to look out for my leather charges!

"Well," I finally said, "I don't like to be one of those pushy sales types."

"That is admirable, but nor should you be one of those sales types who doesn't sell shoes. Keep it in mind, please."

"Okay," I said humbly. For a minute I toyed with the idea of hypnotizing him into letting me sell to whomever the hell I wanted, then rejected the plan. I never liked forcing people to my evil will and only did it in emergencies . . . like when I was starving, or needed to cut in line at the movies.

I vowed I'd sell to the next person who asked me for help. No matter how ratty her sneakers, no matter how tatty her heels, no matter if her eye shadow had creases at the lids and her lip liner didn't match her lipstick, I'd sell her something fabulous and keep a smile on my face at the same time, even if I needed to rush into the employees' lounge and throw up afterward.

I marched back out onto the sales floor, my gaze darting about for a likely customer. Ah! There was one, and she was actually pretty well-dressed—linen jacket and navy slacks. Good shoes—

Manolos, circa 2001. She was about my mom's age, and was looking at the Beverly Feldman boots.

"Hi," I said brightly. She jumped and nearly fell into the display. I grabbed her elbow and steadied her—a little too firmly. Her
feet actually left the floor for a moment. "Whoa, there. I didn't
mean to startle you."

She turned to look at me, her eyes so wide I could see the
whites all the way around her pupils. I heard her heartbeat suddenly pick up a double-time pace, and felt real, real bad. "Don't
*do* that, dear! I didn't even hear you come up behind me!"

"I'm sorry." *Nice work, Betsy, you retard. You've gone from refusing to sell to your customers to scaring the shit out of them.
Stupid undead quiet feet.* "I didn't mean to scare you."

She was peering up at me. "Why are you wearing sunglasses?"

"I have weak eyes," I lied. "The fluorescents really kill. Uh . . .
I just wanted to know if you had any questions."

"*I* have a question."

All the hair on my arms stood straight up and I nearly shuddered. I knew that voice. Eric Sinclair, bad-ass vampire and all-
around sneak. And my consort, God help me. How's this for
ludicrous: most of the vampires think I'm their queen, and that
Eric's their king. *My* king.

I straightened up and stared off in the distance, cocking my
head attentively. "Yes, Satan?" I turned slowly, and faked a big
smile for Sinclair. "Oops! Sorry, Sinclair. I got you mixed up with
someone else."

He was standing by the tree of shoes I'd made out of Liberty
ankle boots, arms folded across his chest, mouth a slash of disapproval. As always when I saw him, my undead heart went pitter. A
true irony: I'd had to die to meet someone truly spectacular, and it
turned out I couldn't stand him.

He was dressed in black linen slacks, a dark blue shirt, and
loafers without socks. He was wearing a black suede jacket that
looked like a Kenneth Cole.

As always, his charisma was like a rough wave. I had to actively resist the urge to cross the six feet between us and put my
hands in his jacket, ostensibly to check the label. He was still the
best-looking guy I'd ever seen, all rangy height and powerful
build and black hair, and the blackest eyes. The eyes, in fact, of a
devil.

Not to mention the devil's mouth. The man could kiss, and
that was a fact. It was one of the more infuriating things about

him. He'd never asked to kiss me. Not once. Just took what he liked. I hated him, and I hated myself for wanting him.

"I simply didn't believe it."

"What? I wasn't paying attention."

The moment had probably seemed longer than it was. I hadn't seen him since the night we had killed our common enemy, Nostro, and, er, coupled. What can I say, it had been a weird week.

I turned back to my customer, who was staring openmouthed at Sinclair. Her breathing had all but stopped. Her heartbeat was still galloping away. I gave her a poke. "We have several lovely boots in that style."

"I was certain Tina had been mistaken."

"Or I could go get some more from the back."

"So I came down to this capitalist hellhole to see for myself."

I turned. "Do you mind? I'm—*aagghh!*" He'd crossed the distance between us with his usual spooky speed, and when I'd turned I'd nearly run into his chest.

"This is intolerable."

"Pal, you don't know the half of it," I said to the buttons on his shirt. I put my hands on his broad chest—ooooh, mama!—and shoved him back a step. "Get lost, I'm working."

"My queen," he said, glaring down at me, "does not work."

"This one does," I said shortly. "And do you hear yourself? Jeez, I knew you were an ancient motherfucker, but even you must know women can have jobs now. And dammit! You made me say 'motherfucker' at work."

"No consort of mine is going to peddle footwear for minimum wage," he snapped. "Get your things right now. You're coming back to my-our-home, which you should have done three months ago."

"What home? Last I looked, your mansion was a pile of ash." I ignored the stab of guilt. Sinclair's thirty-room haven had been torched the night I got snatched by the bad guys and practically beheaded. Then I killed the bad guy and boinked Sinclair. Like I said. Crazy week. "There's no way you rebuilt it in three months."

"True," he admitted. "I'm keeping a suite at the Marquette for Tina and the others."

"Vampires are staying at the Marquette Hotel?"

"The concierge service is excellent," he said defensively. "And your place is at my side. Not in this monument to consumer greed, waiting on . . . on *tourists*."

"What are you, the Fred Flintstone of vampires? Clearly

we've never met, or you forgot everything you knew about me." I clasped his hand and shook it like a Republican, which I was. His hand was cool, and twice as big as mine. "Hi, I'm Betsy. I'm a feminist, I work for my money, and I don't take orders from long-toothed jerk offs. Nice to meet you."

He had a familiar expression on his face—anger warring with a smile. "Elizabeth . . ."

I controlled a shiver. Nobody said my name like he did. First of all, nobody called me Elizabeth. And nobody did it with such a rich, rolling tone, either. He said my name the way diabetics talked about hot fudge sundaes. It was flattering, and distracting beyond belief.

I'd been shaking his hand, but now he was gripping it in both of his. This was nerve-racking, to put it mildly. I could pick up a car, and had. Sinclair was at least twice as strong. "Elizabeth, be reasonable."

"Not in my job description. Go away."

"You succeeded admirably, you know. I've come to you. You've won. Now return with me and"—he leaned in closer. His black eyes filled my world—"we'll discuss things."

I tried to pull my hand away, with no luck. I resisted the urge to brace my foot on his knee and kick free.

"I had all the discussions with you I care to have had," I squeaked firmly, hoping I didn't sound as rattled as I was. Have I mentioned that on top of everything else, Sinclair was really good at discussing things? You could say those one-on-one naked chats were his specialty. "You tricked me and you used me and you suck. Literally. And my getting this job doesn't have a damned thing to do with you, you conceited twerp."

"Then why are you here?" he asked, honestly puzzled.

The man was impossible. "Because I have to work, idiot! I have bills to pay."

He let go of my hand and straightened. This was both a relief—he wasn't looming over me like a gorgeous Bela Lugosi—and a disappointment. "I have money," he said, trying a smile. It looked ghastly, because I knew he was forcing himself not to throw me over his shoulder and head for the fire exit.

"Goody for you. It's not mine, you know. Nothing of yours is mine."

"Such lies."

"Will you stop it? Now get lost, I have two hours to go on my shift."

"I command you to resign your post."

I burst out laughing. I actually had to lean against him to keep from falling down. It was like leaning against a great-smelling boulder. Finally I wiped my eyes and said, "Thanks, I needed that. Long day."

"I was serious," he said stonily.

"So was I! Now get lost, you sneaky creep. Go find some other bimbo to lie to."

"I never lied to you."

"Why, you're lying right now! Ooooh, you've got nerve coming out your *ass*. You—"

"Ahhh . . . Betsy? Is there a problem?"

We both turned. Sinclair let out a small, exasperated growl at the interruption. As if he didn't have enough odious qualities, he was unbelievably arrogant and felt strongly that peons should keep their distance.

My boss, Mr. Mason, was standing by the cash register. He was holding one of his clipboards—he had at least five, each with a different color pen attached to the clasp by a color-coordinated string—and looked icy cool, as usual. I didn't think the man could sweat.

"There's no problem, Mr. Mason. This"—Asshole. Degenerate. Devil. Plague on my life. Lawful consort—"fella was just leaving."

Mason coughed into his fist. "Do you need a break in the green room?"

"Green room" was the code for "do you want me to get Security down here to kick his ass out, righteous?" This showed Mr. Mason was a man of high intelligence. Humans got the creeps around run-of-the-mill vamps. Something about us just set their radar off. Sinclair wasn't run of the mill. Women wanted him, and men were scared shitless of him. Deep down in their brains, they knew exactly what he was. But the women—and a disturbing number of men—ignored the part of their brain that told them to get away and stay away. Mason wasn't doing that.

"No, no," I said hastily. God knew what Sinclair would do to the rent-a-cops. "Really, everything's fine. My . . . uh . . . friend was just leaving."

"This is your supervisor?" Sinclair asked, barely glancing at Mason.

"Ind-may your own usiness-bay. Bye!"

Sinclair locked gazes with Mr. Mason. "Fire her."

Mason's eyes went blank and shiny, and he actually swayed before Sinclair. He was like a bird being hypnotized by a cobra!

I kicked the rat fink right in the ankle, bruising the hell out of my foot. "Don't you dare!"

"Betsy . . . so sorry . . ." Mason slurred, "Cutbacks . . . budget . . . exemplary performance . . . really quite knowledgeable . . . but . . . but . . . regret . . . regret . . ." He was so distressed at being forced to do something against his natural instincts, I expected him to say "Does not compute!" and start sputtering smoke.

"Go back to your cube and forget this ever happened!" I snapped. I whipped off my glasses—Macy's was divine, but the lights were fierce—and let the full force of my undead mojo, which was considerable, if I do say so myself, flare out. "Do it now!"

Mason ran out. He did it stiffly, his arms never moved from his sides. I watched him go, appalled, and then rounded on Sinclair.

"If you ever—*ever!*—do that again, I will kick your ass severe."

"Do tell."

"I mean it! Don't be coming into my workplace and making me say 'motherfucker' and hypnotizing my boss. *Now get lost!*" I could feel my face trying mightily to get red. Since my blood flowed sluggishly at best, all that happened was that I got a headache.

"You'll need my help again."

I made throwing up noises in response.

"Oh, I think so," he said coolly, but his eyes were glittering in a way I didn't like. And where were *his* sunglasses? "Your very nature assures it. As always, I am at your service. But . . ." He rested a finger on my nose. I jerked away. "There will be a penalty to be paid."

"Yeah? Will I have to listen to you whining about prophecies and concierge service? Because if that's the penalty, I'd rather eat glass than take your help."

"Agreed." He gripped my arms and lifted me up until we were eye level. This was startling, to say the least. My heart was probably pounding at ten beats a minute! I heard a double *clack!* as my shoes fell off my feet. "Before I go . . ."

He leaned in. I leaned back. It wasn't easy, since my feet were a good eight inches off the floor. "You put your face on mine, I'll bite your lips off."

He shrugged. "They'll grow back."

"Yuck! Put me down."

He sighed and set me down. "Until you need me, then." He turned around and walked out of the shoe department.

I yelled after him, "Don't hold your breath, loser!" Although he certainly could. For hours.

Strong words. But it took me an hour to stop shaking. It hadn't been easy, pulling back from that kiss.

Plus, believe it or not, I really hate confrontations.

I turned back to help my customer, but she was long gone. In fact, the entire shoe department was empty except for me. Great.

Damn you, Sinclair.

# Chapter 6

"IT'S official," Marc announced. "We've got termites."

"Jeez, let me take my shoes off, willya?" I tossed my keys on the hall table and kicked off my heels. "Good morning to you, too."

"Sorry. I got the report this afternoon while you were snoozing, but I had to leave for the hospital before I could talk to you about it."

I followed him into the kitchen. He was wearing his scrubs, and had probably only beaten me home by about half an hour. He was letting his hair grow out, I noticed. It wasn't quite so brutally short. And he was gaining weight, thank goodness.

When I first met Dr. Marc Spangler, he was on a ledge ready to splatter himself all over Seventh Avenue. I talked him down and bullied him into moving in with me. He decided that living with a vampire was a small improvement over some cop scooping him up in a bucket.

He had my tea all set up for me. I'd never had a roommate before, and I sure liked it. It was really convenient living with someone who could answer the phone during the day while I was sleeping the unholy sleep of the undead. And it worked for Marc, too. I refused to charge rent, so he paid the utilities and ran my errands when he was off-shift. I had always figured doctors made more money than secretaries. I was wrong.

"Termites, huh?" He tried to show me an odious yellow paper, but I waved it away and sat down at the table. "I didn't think people got termites anymore. I thought that was, like, a '50s thing."

"Actually, they cause more damage than all other natural disasters combined."

"Somebody's been spending too much time on the Web again."

"I didn't feel like downloading more porn." He grinned, which made his green eyes sparkle. That, along with the goatee, made him look like a friendly demon.

That was probably why I liked him from the start. I only knew two people who had green eyes, true green eyes, not the lame hazel color like I had. One of them was my mom.

"Get rid of the bugs, but the house is wrecked. It's gonna cost big bucks to repair."

"Well, shit."

"Right."

"There must be something we can—did you bat your pretty eyes at the bug guy?"

"Like Scarlett O'Hara. Believe me, it was my pleasure . . . the guy was *built*. But alas, he was mostly immune to my charms. Wouldn't budge on the quote, or the bad news. Got a date Saturday, though."

"Are we sure they're termites? I thought those little bugs flying around were ants."

"Nope. *Insecta Termitidae*. In other words, we be fucked."

I sipped my tea and drummed my fingers on the table. Maybe it was time for a change, and God had visited upon me *Insecta-*whatever to get the message across.

"Maybe Jessica—"

"Shhhh!" I hissed.

"Maybe Jessica what?" the lady said, walking into the kitchen.

"Forget it," I said. "What, did I miss a memo? Are we having a meeting?"

"Actually, yeah." She yawned and grabbed the bread, then dropped two slices into the toaster. She was wearing her usual workday uniform—blue jeans, a T-shirt, and sandals. Her coarse black hair was skinned so tightly back from her skull, her eyebrows were forced up in a look of perpetual surprise. "Pretty inconvenient, too. I hate setting my alarm for two A.M."

"Cry me a river. You don't think I miss feeling the sun on my face once in a while?"

"Oh, bitch, bitch, bitch," she replied good-naturedly.

"We got the report, and it's like your guy thought," Marc said.

"Wait a minute. 'Your guy'?"

"Jess paid for the exterminator consult," Marc explained.

I let my head drop into my hands. "Marc, we can't depend on Jessica to bail us out every time we have money problems."

"We can't?"

"Marc!"

"Yeah, but . . ." He shrugged. "She doesn't care. She's got more money than she could spend in thirty lifetimes. So why should we care if she wants to help us out? It's not like she'll miss it."

"Uh, guys? I'm right here. In the room."

"Well, she's not paying to fix the house," I declared, wiping tea off my chin, "and that's that."

"Well, what do you want to do? We can't sell the house until the termites are kaput. I guess we could get an apartment . . ."

"Or a suite at the Minneapolis Marquette," I muttered. The smell of sweetly toasting bread was making me nuts. Item Number 267 that sucked about being a vampire: food still smelled great, but one bite and I'd puke. I was strictly a liquid diet girl now.

"What was that?" Jess asked, fishing her toast out of the toaster, juggling them over to the table, and sitting down.

"Guess who came to work tonight to order me to quit and move into the Marquette with him?"

"Eric Sinclair?" They said this in identical, dreamy tones. My best friend and my roommate had a severe crush. Then Jessica giggled. "Eric came to Macy's? Did he burst into flames the moment he passed the first cash register?"

"I wish. He tried to hypnotize my boss into firing me."

"Did you kill him?" Marc asked.

"I wish. Then I had to work overtime, and then I had to . . . well, never mind . . ."

"Suck blood from a would-be mugger?"

"Would-be rapist, but never *mind,* I said. I swear, the bad guys in this city are such idiots. When they see me throw their buddy ten feet, why do they assume I can't do the same thing to them? Anyway. Then I came home to the termite report."

"It's probably just as well," Jessica said with a mouthful of toast. I shook crumbs out of my eyes as she continued, "It's not like you were in love with this house. Maybe it's time for some new digs."

I didn't say anything, but I gave it some thought. I'd had the house for years . . . since I flunked out of college. My dad consoled me with a check for twenty thousand dollars, and I used it to put a hefty down payment on my little three-bedroom cottage. I'd outgrown the place years ago, but was too lazy to go through the work of selling and upgrading.

"I've got some thoughts about that," she continued, taking a swallow of my tea. "You own the house free and clear, right?"

"You know I do," I replied, exasperated. "You're the one who paid off the mortgage when I died."

"Right, slipped my mind."

"Sure it did."

"Well, I vote we get my bug fella to spray. Then we list the house for pretty cheap. In this economy, in this suburb—"

"Oh, here goes your anti-Apple Valley rant."

"I'm sorry, I just think towns without a personality are lame," she said with the full snobbery of a twenty-nine-year-old billionaire. "It doesn't even have a real downtown. It exists because of Minneapolis. Bo-ring."

"Snot." I *liked* Apple Valley. If I wanted to go to the grocery store and the movie theater and get a hair cut and have a pancake breakfast and grab the latest J. D. Robb, I could do it all within the same half mile . . . and most of it in the same strip mall. "Big-city snot."

She tipped her fingers at me—the nails were painted lime green, I noticed with a shudder—in a mock salute. "Anyway, I figure we could get one-fifty for it, easy. Even with termite damage. And we turn around and use it to put a down payment on something more fitting for our needs."

"*Our* needs?"

"I'm getting rid of my apartment. Marc and I talked about it, and we agreed I should move in, too."

"Did I miss another memo?"

"No, just a meeting. We had it during the daytime."

"I wish you'd stop doing that," I grumbled. I thought about protesting, but Jess was over here so often, she'd practically moved in, anyway. I figured I knew why, too. My death had really shaken her up. She didn't like letting me out of her sight anymore.

And what did I care? The more the merrier. Ever since I found out monsters really do exist, I hadn't been crazy about coming home to an empty house.

"So we're agreed? We'll fumigate, list the house, and find something a little bigger. Don't worry about a thing, Bets. Marc and I will house-hunt during the day."

I drank my tea.

"Bets?"

"What, you want my approval? I'm just the figurehead."

"Well, that's true."

"But you're sure cute," Marc teased. "Even if your Macy's name tag is upside down."

* * *

A few nights later, I woke up to a world of sky blue. I had a moment of total confusion—had I fallen asleep outside? Then I realized Marc had written a note on a Post-It and stuck it to my forehead while I slept. Bastard.

> *Supervamp: We accepted the offer on the house, and Jessica's found us a new place. Meet us at 607 Summit Ave, 10:00 P.M. to check out the new digs.*

Oh, Lord, what did she do? I crumpled the note in my fist. Summit Avenue? I did *not* like the sound of that.

I looked around my room. There were six empty boxes stacked neatly in the corner. An unsubtle hint to pack.

I showered, changed clothes, and brushed my teeth. I had no idea if other vampires still brushed their teeth, and I didn't care. Think of the morning breath of someone who drank blood for supper! I flossed, too. And used mouthwash, although the sharp medicine-mint smell was enough to make me gag.

I was getting ready to walk out the door (after tripping over the boxes in the living room), when I heard a tentative tap and opened it to see Tina standing on the step.

"Thank you *so* much for siccing Sinclair on me," I said by way of greeting. "He came to my work!"

"He did?" she asked innocently. She was dressed like a crime-about-to-happen in a red pleated miniskirt, short-sleeved white sweater, black tights, and black flats with silver buckles. Her light blond hair was caught back from her face with a red headband. She looked about sixteen years old. "Now that I think about it . . ." She pursed her red lips thoughtfully. "He mentioned he might go to the mall to see you."

"Nice try, but I'm not buying it. He doesn't take a dump without running it by you first."

"Actually, it's been several decades since either of us had to—"

"You look really cute, by the way." She was sly, but she had great taste in clothes.

She smiled, then shrugged. "I have to go out later."

"Do not tell me." Tina had a trio of devoted blood donors, but occasionally she liked to get something different off the menu. "I absolutely don't want to hear it."

"I won't. Also, here is your memo." She handed me a thick manila envelope.

"This feels like a lot of pages," I said suspiciously, weighing the stiff packet in my hand.

"I summed it up as best I could. There are photographs as well."

"Well, I'll read it when I—"

"Tina?"

"Yaagghh!" I dropped the envelope. It hit the floor with a flat thump. A second head had appeared around the door—another blond cutie—but I hadn't heard a thing. It was pretty hard to sneak up on me. Nobody alive could do it, but old vampires could.

"I'm so sorry," the cutie said. Her eyes were big. "I beg your pardon, your Majesty. I did not mean to startle you."

"Don't call me that. And you didn't startle me, you scared the shit out of me. How old are you?"

This wouldn't be very nice under normal circumstances, but vampires loved to show off how decrepit they were.

This one was no different. She straightened proudly, and good posture did wonderful things for her. She was tall—almost as tall as me, and a good head taller than Tina—with shoulder-length hair so blond it was really almost silver, and eyes as blue as the sky on Easter Sunday. She was pale, of course, but on her it looked good. Her coloring was so fair, it demanded pale skin. She was wearing khaki shorts, a dark pink shirt buttoned at the throat, and leather sandals. She smiled tentatively.

"I'm seventy-eight, Majesty."

"Riiiiight. Well, you don't look a day over twenty-two. And don't call me that. Who are you?"

"This is Monique Silver," Tina said quickly. "She came to pay her respects to Nostro, and found a new regime in charge. There's another vampire in town, but"—Tina glanced over her shoulder—"she wouldn't come in. In fact, she's walking back to the hotel."

"She's shy," Monique said helpfully.

Tina snorted, but didn't elaborate. "Anyway, Monique's staying with us at the Marquette."

I smiled, but I didn't like that one bit. Tina staying with Sinclair was no big deal. They were practically brother and sister, and Tina didn't swing that way anyway. But I didn't care for the idea of this *Penthouse* centerfold sharing a bathroom with Eric Sinclair.

"Nice to meet you. Hope you weren't fond of ole Notso." I said this with some anxiety—what if she had been?

Her warm smile put me at ease. "Indeed, no. In fact, I'm grateful to you. We all are . . . Betsy?" Her eyebrows—so pale and fine they were almost invisible, which made her face look like a sexy egg—arched.

"Betsy," I said firmly. "No Majesty. Thank God you catch on quicker than Tina."

They both flinched at "God" and Monique actually fell back a step. Well, she better get used to it.

"I'd invite you guys in, but I have to be—"

"Going somewhere?" Tina tilted her head. "Don't you need to feed?"

"Later, maybe."

"You haven't fed yet? And don't plan to?" Monique's eyes were big with surprise.

"I try to put it off as long as I can."

"Oh, now, surely you're not still reticent about—"

"Want to come with?" I asked abruptly, to forestall the lecture. Tina and Sinclair thought it was exquisitely stupid that I hadn't embraced my inner vampire. "I'm checking out the new house Jess picked out for us."

"You're moving?" Monique asked as I locked my house and trotted toward the car.

"Have to. Termites. And I would appreciate it if that little piece of info didn't fall into Sinclair's shell-like ears," I told Tina. "It's none of his damned business."

"Of course, Majesty."

"Quit it."

"Of course, Majesty."

"I hate you," I sighed, opening the door for Monique.

"No you don't," Tina replied, barely suppressed laughter in her tone, "Majesty."

# Chapter 7

"GOODNESS!" Monique said.

"Wow," Tina said respectfully.

I slumped so hard against the steering wheel, my head activated the horn for a brief honk.

I should have known. I should have known! Summit Avenue was one of the oldest streets in St. Paul. It was absolutely packed with mansions. And 607 Summit Avenue was a doozy. White, except for black shutters. Three floors. An amazing front porch right out of *Gone with the Wind*. And the detached garage was as big as my current house.

"Dammit, dammit." I climbed out of the car, and Monique and Tina scrambled after me.

"Just how much money does Jessica have?" Tina asked in awe. It was taking forever to get to the door via the front walk.

"Too much." I was stomping so hard, I could actually feel my heels leaving marks in the concrete. I eased up. Damn sidewalk was probably five hundred years old. "Way too much."

"I think it's perfect. It suits your rank much better than—"

"Stop." I pounded on the front door, then opened it and crept in, instantly intimidated.

It was worse than I feared. The first thing I saw was the sweeping staircase, eight feet wide, shined to a high gloss, and winding up out of sight. The front hall was as big as my living room. The place smelled like wood and wax, cleaning supplies and old, old carpet.

"Jessica!" I yelled. *Ick-uh, ick-uh, ick-uh* echoed up and down the hall.

"You're going to live here?" Monique asked, goggling.

"Shit, no. Jessica!" *Ick-uh! Ick-uh! Ick-uh!*

She and Marc appeared at the top of the stairs, and galloped down to us. "Finally! You're late. What do you think?" she said. "Isn't it grand?"

"Wait'll you see the dining room table," Marc added. "It has seventeen leaves!"

"Jessica, it's too big. There's three of us, remember? How many bedrooms does this place have?"

"Eleven," she admitted. "But that way we don't have to worry about where to put up guests."

"And, we all get our own bathroom," Marc added.

"And probably your own kitchen!" Tina said, eyes gone huge as she stared at the castle Jessica had bought with the money she'd found in her car seat cushions.

Sensing my mood (not a great trick), Jessica said sternly, "Oh, come on. Open your mind. It's big, but it's just a house."

"The governor's mansion is across the street!" I yelled.

"Just look around," Marc coaxed. "You'll like it."

"You guys . . ." I heard myself getting shrill and forced my voice into the lower registers. They'd probably worked hard, and the place had cost her a bundle. The closing costs alone had probably been six figures. It made me uncomfortable as hell, but I didn't want to come off as an ungrateful jerk. "It's not a question of liking, okay? I mean, I can see it's amazing and gorgeous and stuff."

"Thank goodness," Marc said.

"It's beautiful, okay? There's nothing wrong with it. But it's a question of affordability and practicality. Come on, how much is it?"

"Well, we're renting it for now, until they track down the owner."

"Jessica . . ."

"Three thousand a week," she admitted.

I nearly fainted. "The money from my house won't even cover a year's rent!"

"So you *can* do math in your head," Marc teased. "I was wondering."

"Have you lost your mind?"

"Which one of us are you talking to?"

"Look, this is way more in keeping with your station, anyway," Jessica said, striving to sound logical.

"What station?" I glowered at her warningly. We didn't talk about the Queen Thing. She knew I didn't like it and was trying to find a way out of it.

"You know what station," Jess said sternly. *Traitor!* "With the king dropping by—"

"Do not call him that," I said through gritted teeth.

"Wow," Marc said, peering at me. "Your eyes are getting all red again. And . . ." He looked past me. I'd heard Monique and Tina back up a step, but I was too irked to care.

"Sinclair, all right? With Sinclair and Tina and . . . and other people"—she nodded at Monique—"well, you really need a decent house. Something that shows people—"

"That my roommate pays all my living expenses. Come on, this place isn't me."

"It's private . . . we're the last house on the block, and the only thing in the back yard is the Mississippi River. It's large and private, and there's a terrific security system in the garden. And you need privacy, Bets, even if you won't admit why. And it's big enough for you to entertain."

"Can't we just get a condo in downtown Minneapolis or something?" I whined.

"Vampire queens do not live in condos." Monique said it, but Tina and Jessica nodded emphatically.

"Look, we gotta live somewhere," Marc broke in. "Right? I mean, your house is gonna collapse in on itself if those bugs keep chomping. So, give the place a try for a few weeks. That's all we're asking."

Sure they were. Like I was going to pack and move my stuff twice in the same season. Jessica was bossy, which I was used to and could fight, but Marc was the voice of reason, against which I had no defense.

"You have to admit," Tina added helpfully, "it's an amazing house."

"So? If I'm the queen, how come I don't get to make any of the rules?"

Jessica grinned. "It's not your worry. We'll keep you informed."

"It's like, Jessica's the Bruce Wayne to your Batman," Marc added. "You can go out and fight crime, and she can pay the bills."

"Bruce Wayne and Batman were the same guy, idiot."

Jessica and Tina laughed together, which was annoying. At least Monique was remaining respectfully silent.

"Hi, Tina, I didn't get a chance to say howdy before," Marc

said. He put out his big paw and shook Tina's teeny delicate hand. It was almost funny. I mean, Marc was tall, slender, and in pretty good shape, and he towered over Tina. But Tina and Monique could break all the bones in his hand with a single squeeze. And he knew it. Jessica did, too. They didn't care, either.

They were adjusting to this vampire stuff a lot faster than I was.

"Give me the tour," I said, surrendering. Marc was right. We had to live somewhere. And Jessica could buy every house on the block by barely cracking her credit line at the bank. There were lots of reasons to complain, but her financial situation wasn't one of them. "Let's see what you've signed me up for."

TINA and Monique left when the real-estate agent arrived, which was just as well. One hungry bloodsucker was plenty for the tour.

The agent was a perfectly pleasant older woman with gray hair and a truly awful tweed suit (in July!). But she scored points because, even though we all knew she was looking at a hefty commission, she didn't slobber all over us. And she knew plenty about the house. Marc whispered to me that she was probably around when it was built in 1823.

I *hee-heed* into my palm while May Townsend ("Just call me May-May, dear.") droned on about the exquisite woodwork, the fine craftsmanship, the fact that termites hadn't devoured the place, the pure privilege it was for low-life primates like us to walk on the hallowed floors. I thought about eating her, but frankly, the tweed smelled. She must have had a cedar closet at home.

"As I told you over the phone," May-May was saying while we trudged down from the third floor to the second, "most of the furniture comes with the house. The owners are in Prague and, frankly, would be interested in selling."

"We're renting," I said firmly, before Jessica could say anything.

"Very well, dear. This is the master bedroom," she added, opening the door to soaring ceilings, a bed the size of my kitchen, and huge windows. "It's been fully updated and the attached bath has a Jacuzzi, pedestal sink, and—"

"I call it!" Marc said loudly.

"Like hell," Jessica snapped. "I think the person who stands a chance of actually entertaining in their room should get it."

"Well, that lets Betsy and you out," Marc sneered. "When was the last time you got laid?"

"None of your damn business, white boy."

"Hand-stenciled wallpaper, unique to the time period, and note the gold leaf in the corners—"

"Since I've been shanghaied into this place," I interrupted, while May-May droned on about the authentic wood in the authentic floorboards, "I'll take the master bedroom. It's not like you guys don't have a dozen other ones to choose from."

"Ten," May-May corrected.

"Whatever."

"No fair!" Marc cried.

"It's that, or back to Termite Central." Finally, I was throwing my weight around . . . and actually getting my way! "Uh, hey, Marky-Marc, why don't you and May-May go check out the pedestal sink?"

"Why? If I don't get to use it, I—hey!" I gave him a gentle shove in the direction of the bathroom, sending him sprawling, and the real-estate agent dutifully followed. I didn't care if Marc heard, but my undead state was none of May-May's business.

"Uh, Jess," I asked quietly, "who's gonna take care of this mountain? Marc and I work nights, y'know, and you weren't exactly born with a silver broom in your mouth."

"I'll get a couple of housekeepers," Jessica assured me. "And we'll get someone to take care of the lawns and garden."

"I can take care of the lawn!" Marc yelled from the bathroom.

"Oh, you're gonna mow two acres every week?" Jessica yelled back. "And stop eavesdropping! I'm trying to have a private conversation here!"

"Maybe I will! Mow, I mean."

"Let's try to keep the helpers to a minimum," I said anxiously.

"Don't worry, Bets. No one's gonna find out unless you tell them."

"Find out what?" Marc asked, coming back into the room.

"That she's as dumb as she looks," Jessica said cheerfully, neatly avoiding my kick.

"Ready to inspect the first floor?" May-May asked brightly. I wasn't, but trailed behind them dutifully.

# Chapter 8

JESSICA was as good as her word. I hadn't even gotten unpacked before I started seeing people in and out of the house, or Vamp Central, as Marc liked to call it. There were at least three housekeepers and two gardeners; Jessica hired them from The Foot, her nonprofit job-finding organization, so it worked out well for everybody.

The fridge was constantly full of pop, iced tea, cream, veggies, and supper fixings. The freezer bulged with ice cream and frozen margaritas. But the helpers were so circumspect, I hardly ever saw them. And if they thought it was weird that I slept all day and was out all night, nobody ever said anything to my face.

It was funny how much unpacking depressed me. We'd been in such a hurry to get out of Termiteville, I'd sort of thrown my stuff into boxes without really thinking about it. But while I was finding places to put things away, I was forced to really look at the junk I'd gathered over a lifetime.

The clothes and shoes and makeup weren't such a big deal, though I was so pale these days, I hardly ever wore anything but mascara. The books were something else.

My room had, among other things, amazing bookcases built into the corner, and while I was unpacking boxes and putting books away, I realized the gap between my old life and my new one had gotten huge without my noticing. It had been such a crazy summer, I hadn't really noticed that there hadn't been time to do any re-reading of old favorites. And now there never would be.

All my favorites: the Little House series, all of Pat Conroy's work, Emma Holly's erotica, and my cookbook collection—they were useless to me now. Worse than useless . . . they made me feel bad.

I loved *Beach Music* and *The Prince of Tides* because not only could Pat Conroy write like a son of a bitch, he had the soul of a gourmet chef. The man could make a tomato sandwich sound like an orgasm you ate. And my days of eating tomato sandwiches were long gone.

How many times had I escaped to my room with a book to avoid my stepmother? How many times had I bought a cookbook because the glorious color pictures literally made me drool? But it was done, now. Tom, Luke, Savannah, Dante, Mark, Will, and the Great Santini were all lost to me. Not to mention *The All-American Cookie Book, Barefoot Contessa Parties,* and all of Susan Branch's stuff.

I put the books away, spine-side in, so I wouldn't have to look at the titles. Normally I kept too busy to feel bad about being dead, but today wasn't one of those days.


I saw the kid for the first time when I was vacuuming the inside of my closet. This was the third time in five minutes—no way was I just dumping my shoes into a two hundred year old closet that smelled like old wood and dead moths. Thank goodness I didn't have to breathe!

Handi-vac in hand, I backed out of the closet on my knees and nearly bumped into her. She was curled up like a bug in the chair beside the fireplace. One of fourteen. Fireplaces, not chairs. I had no idea how many chairs there were. Anyway, she was watching me and I was so startled I nearly dropped the vacuum.

"Yikes!" I said. "I didn't hear you come in."

"My mama says I'm quiet," she replied helpfully.

"You have no idea. It's tough work, sneaking up on me. Although," I added in a mutter, "more and more people seem to be doing it all the time." I raised my voice so the kid wouldn't get freaked out by the blond weirdo talking to herself. "So, your folks work here?"

"My mama used to."

"Used to? Then what are you—"

"I like your hair."

"Thanks." I patted my blond streaks and tried not to preen. Ah, dead, but I've still got it. "I like yours, too."

She was just about the cutest thing I'd ever seen. She had t. face of a patient doe, all wary and cute, with big blue eyes and ı spray of freckles across her nose. Her blond, curly hair was pulled back from her face in a blue bow that matched her eyes, and she was wearing striped overalls rolled to the knees, pink anklets . . . and saddle shoes!

I edged closer to get a better look at her footwear. "Aren't you bored to death?" I asked. "Clunking around in a big house like this? Where's your mom?"

"I like it here now," she replied, after giving my question some thought. "I like it when people are here."

"Well, you're gonna love it now. My friend Jessica hired a fu— uh, an army. Say, sunshine, where'd you get the shoes?"

"My mama bought them for me."

"Where?"

"The shoe store."

Rats. "I like them a lot," I said truthfully. "My name's Betsy."

"I'm Marie. Thanks for talking to me."

"Hey, I just live here, I'm not a rich snobby jerk like you're probably used to. Uh . . . do you know how to get to the kitchen from here?"

Marie grinned, showing a gap between her front teeth. "Sure. I know all the shortcuts. There's a secret cave between the kitchen and the second dining room!"

"*Second* dining room? Never mind. Onward, Marie. I gotta get some tea in me before I do something somebody'll regret."

Before I could take her hand, I heard thundering footsteps, and then Jessica burst into the room, waving the telephone. "Gotta go—Marquette—Tina's in trouble," she wheezed, then collapsed until she was partially lying on my unmade bed. "Cripes! I think there's a thousand stairs in this place."

"You of all people don't get to complain about how big this place is. What are you talking about, Tina's in trouble?"

"Sinclair—on the phone—" She held it out to me.

I grabbed it. "This better not be a trick," I snarled into the receiver.

"Get here now."

I ran.

I T was a good trick, not screaming and then barfing when I saw what had been done to Tina. Luckily, I'd been audited (twice!),

...d was the child of ugly divorce proceedings, and had loads of practice keeping my dinner down.

"Another one of your tiresome ploys for attention," I said.

Tina tried a smile, and I hoped she'd knock it off soon. Half her face was in tatters. In fact, half of her bad self was in tatters. She floated listlessly in the tub, which was full of pink water.

Don't ask me why, but when you immerse a sick vamp in water and add baking soda, they get better quicker. Amazing! The stuff can make cakes rise and de-stink refrigerators. It made no sense to me, but I was pretty new to the game to be questioning undead physics.

"Jeez . . ." I croaked the word out, then cleared my throat. "Who did this? Are you—of course you're not okay, but—does it hurt?"

"Yes."

"What happened?"

"Just that whole tiresome humans killing vamps thing," she replied.

That stung. "Well, shit, Tina, I didn't think they were going after the good ones!" While I was waving my arms around and generally working up a good spate of hysterics, Sinclair appeared with his usual spooky speed and grabbed my wrist.

I had time to say, "Wha—?" before he nicked my wrist with the knife I belatedly noticed he was holding. "Ow!" I said, yanking my wrist away, but it was all for show. It was so fast, and the knife was so sharp, I'd barely felt it. Well, at least he didn't bite me. "You want to ask before you start gouging me?"

Tina turned her head away and ducked under water. "And you stop that!" I said, bending over the tub and gingerly prodding her head. I wiped my wet hand off on my jeans. Yech! "I know what I'm supposed to do, dammit. It's just nice to be asked, is all," I added, glaring at Finklair.

"Stop wasting time," he said, typically stone-faced, but his eyes were kind of squinty. I knew he adored Tina. She had made him, and they had a bond I respected, even if I didn't understand it, and thought it was extremely weird. "Let her feed. Now."

"No," Tina gurgled from the bottom of the tub.

"I said I'd do it," I snapped. "Will you sit up so we can get this over with?"

A bubble appeared, but Tina didn't move.

"This is your fault," Sinclair said coldly. The situation was so alarming, I just now noticed he was wearing cherry red boxers and nothing else. "Now fix it."

"My fault? I'm not the one who decided to give Tina a haircut . . . all over! Don't get pissed at me. I came as soon as you asked me to. Not that you exactly asked."

His hand clamped onto my shoulder, which instantly went numb. "Tina is well aware of your childish aversion to blood drinking. She's playing the martyr, and I won't have it."

"Hey, I'm with you! Get her out of there and let her chomp away. I'm on your side."

If he'd been alive, his face would have been the color of an old brick. Each word was forced out through his teeth. "She will not obey me in this."

"Oh, so that's why your boxers are in a bunch? Great color, by the way, they really bring out your—ow! Lighten up, I think I just lost all the feeling in my left arm."

"Fix it," he said implacably.

I kicked the tub. "Tina, get out of there."

A sullen glug.

"This is the queen speaking!" I managed not to laugh. Queen of shoes, maybe! "Now sit up, will you?"

"Don't ask," Sinclair hissed in my ear. "Command."

"Stop that, it tickles. Teeee-naaaa!"

She sat up. "I don't want you to," she lied. "You think it's barbaric."

"Stop being such a baby," I said, though she was one hundred percent right. "What's the alternative? You live in the tub like an undead anatomy project and slowly heal over the next six months? The maids will have a fit."

Her nostrils flared and I realized that blood had been trickling down my fingers the whole time I was arguing. I turned around, put my hands on his rock-hard chest, and pushed and kicked and shoved until I finally slammed the bathroom door in his face.

"I really can't stand that guy," I sighed, rolling up my sleeve.

"Liar," she said, and grinned at me.

"Could you not do that until your face grows back? No offense."

"Oh, Majesty," she sighed as I knelt by the tub. "I'm so sorry to ask this of you."

"Don't be a moron. I'm just glad you're alive, so to speak."

She gripped my arm and lapped the blood off my fingers, then sucked on my wrist until I couldn't see tendons or raw wounds, until she was beautiful again. It didn't take long. I was always amazed at how quickly vampires healed. It rarely took more than a few minutes. And, weirdly, my blood sped things up considerably. If Tina had fed off a human, it might have taken the better part of the night to recover. More crap I didn't understand . . . and frankly, I was afraid to ask too many questions. Tina might answer them.

"So," I said brightly. "Got any other plans for the evening?"

"After a near-death experience, I like to relax by scrubbing a tub."

"I'd help, but forget it. I've got nineteen of my own to worry about."

# Chapter 9

We stepped out of the bathroom just as what's-her-face, the cutie from the other day, rushed into the suite.

"Tina, thank goodness!" she cried, her shiny blond hair in wild disarray. She looked and smelled like she'd been rolled in a McDonald's Dumpster. A mustard packet was sticking to her left cheek. "I thought they'd killed you!"

She ran to Tina and sort of fell on her, hugging her and kissing her. Yech. Good thing Tina wasn't dressed yet; she'd never get those stains out. I gathered from the babbling that the bad guys had jumped both of them, but Tina had led them away from Monique.

"Dumbass," I commented.

"I quite agree," Sinclair said, scowling. He rooted around and found one of his robes for Tina, which he held open for her. When she had it tied around her, she pretty much disappeared into fluffy black terrycloth. "You should have both stood your ground—or both run."

"I know, I know," Monique interrupted before Tina could open her mouth. "I wanted to fight but Tina—"

"And you shouldn't have left my friend and saved yourself," Sinclair continued in a voice that made dry ice seem warm and accommodating.

We all gulped. Then I patted Sinclair's arm. "All's well and all that, Eric. Everybody's okay. That's the important thing. Right? Eric?"

His eyes uncrinkled and he almost smiled as he looked down

at me. "Why do you only call me by my first name in moments of crisis?"

"Because that's about the only time I don't feel like strangling you," I said truthfully. "Now don't fuss at Monique. Tina's a grown woman—a very grown woman, I might add, she's, like, a hundred years old, and if she wanted to play decoy that's her lookout."

Monique didn't say anything, but she threw me a look of pure gratitude.

"The important thing," I said emphatically, "is getting to the bottom of this. Tina's one of the good guys. She didn't deserve to have some vampire hunter after her. So I guess we better figure out why." Did I really just say we had to get to the bottom of this? I felt so stupid, bossing around people who were at least fifty years older than me.

Now if I could only remember where I'd put the memo Tina gave me . . .

"Attend, please," Sinclair said, and grabbed my elbow. Eh? He pulled me across the room and through the far door, which he promptly shut.

"What?" I whined.

"You have decided to hunt down the killers?"

"Killers, plural? Yikes. I mean, sure, I guess."

"You require my help?"

"Yes," I said, not liking where this was going. "Are we going to hang out in the dark and ask each other obvious questions? Because this is weird, bordering on creepy."

He smirked at me and held out something. I looked at it. It was one of the hotel's drinking glasses.

"What's—oh."

*What had I said at Macy's? "I'd rather eat glass than take your help."*

*Well, shit.*

"Fine," I said, grabbing the glass. God knew when he'd palmed the thing, the sneaky motherfucker. "Here goes." I stared at it. I had no idea if biting into it would hurt. But I was about to find out. At the very least, gulping down chunks of glass would make me throw up. I mean, risotto made me puke, for crying out loud.

Never mind. Quit stalling. I raised it to my mouth, closed my eyes, opened my mouth . . . and bit down on air.

Sinclair was holding the glass again. It was uncanny how

quickly he could move. He was like a magician. An evil magician in boxers. "You were really going to eat it?"

"I *said,* didn't I?"

"You're either the most amazing woman I have ever known—"

"Well." I patted my bangs back into place and smiled modestly. "Or the most asinine."

"I hate you."

"You keep saying that," he said, drawing me close. For a wonder, I let him. Long night. Plus, he smelled great. And felt great. Cherry boxers. Yum. He dropped a kiss to the top of my ear and I effectively fought a shiver. "But you keep coming back."

"Curiosity killed the cat."

"Not yet. Come, let's rejoin the others."

"Yes," I said, massively disappointed he hadn't been more grabby, and mad at myself for being disappointed. "Let's."


"ᖴOᑌᖇ." Tina said. "Four dead so far. Again, I mean."

"I, uh, lost my memo."

She made a sound that was suspiciously like a snort. "Fine, I'll sum up for you. A group of humans has been going around targeting lone vampires and cutting off their heads, or staking them, or both."

*Ick. Both?*

Monique spoke up. "At least we learned something: it's not one person, it's a team."

"I never thought it was one person," Sinclair said.

"No, I wouldn't think so, either. I mean, come on. One regular guy or gal wreaking all this havoc? No chance." I stretched out my feet. Ack! Scuffed toes! I'd have to give this pair away. "How do we know it's not a group of *vamps*?"

"Blood samples found at the scene were live."

"Oh, ugh!" I cried. "You mean, if someone took my blood right now—"

"You'd be dead. At least, under a microscope. Try to stay focused, Elizabeth."

"I am. Yuck-o. Do we know why? Other than the obvious."

"The obvious?" Monique asked, looking cutely confused.

"Vampires are assholes." At their stares, I elaborated. "Look, I'm sorry, but it's true. You guys grab poor unsuspecting slobs off the street and chomp away. I'm amazed this hasn't happened earlier."

"It's happened," Sinclair said coolly, "all through the ages." He'd slipped on a pair of black slacks, but was still disturbingly shirtless. "And no one in this room behaves in such a fashion."

"You gotta admit, that makes us pretty rare."

"No, I don't think so," Monique said seriously. "Most vampires outgrow the need for the hunt. It's much easier to keep sheep."

"To what?"

I saw Tina make a slashing motion across her throat, and Sinclair shake his head; Monique was oblivious. "Sheep!" she said brightly. "You know. Two or three people who are devoted to you and let you drink whenever you need to."

"We're getting off the subject," Sinclair said quickly.

"The hell we are!"

"Later, Majesty," Tina said, glaring at Monique, who was looking amazed. "You can tell us all how awful we are *later*."

"How can we draw this team out into the open?" Tina asked.

"Well, bait, of course," Monique said.

Sinclair nodded approvingly. "They appear to strike every other Wednesday, for some reason."

"Maybe they all have jobs," I said, "and they can only get Wednesdays off."

"More likely," Sinclair said kindly, "those days are significant. For example, they might be on the occult calendar."

"So," Tina continued, "two weeks from now, we'll see if we can't catch them."

I barely contained my sneer. "Just like that, eh?"

"Well," Tina said reasonably, "chances are, they're not a bunch of old folks. The attacks are too ferocious and quick, for one thing. It's probably a bunch of young adults . . . I'll bet a thousand dollars not one of them is legal drinking age."

"Did you see any of them?" Monique asked.

"Too busy fighting, and running. They were well equipped, I'll tell you that much. I certainly did not linger."

"Good thing," I said, impressed. "I mean, even with not lingering, you got ripped up pretty good. I'm really glad you're okay."

"Why, Majesty," Tina teased, "I didn't know you cared."

"Cut that out, you slut." Tina had made no secret of the fact that she'd jump into my bed anytime. This rattled me, because A) I was straighter than a laser beam, and B) even laser beams get curious. One time in college, a bunch of my sorority sisters and I got really drunk and . . . well, anyway, sometimes I was curious. Best to keep her at arm's length. I had enough trouble keeping Sinclair out of my bed. "Your seductive ways won't work on me."

"Weapons?" Sinclair asked with a trace of impatience.

"Guns, stakes, crossbows, knives, masks. But as I said, I'm sure they're young. They felt young. They moved young, and smelled young."

"Smelled?" I asked.

"Lots of Stridex," she explained.

I stomped on the giggle that wanted out. Killer teens with acne! Sounded like a movie of the week.

"So right away, we've got an advantage."

"We do?"

"We're older, smarter, and trickier," Sinclair said, sounding way too smug for my taste.

Tina and Monique nodded.

I rolled my eyes. "Well, then, those poor guys don't have a chance, do they?"

"Exactly," he replied, totally missing my sarcasm.

# Chapter 10

"**MARIE**!" I yelled. "Are you here?"

I doubted it. It was almost eleven o'clock at night. But her folks kept odd hours, because she usually—

"Hi."

"Oh, good." I popped out of my closet. "Have you seen my purple Arpels?"

"Are they the ones that look like fairy shoes, or the ones that look like ballet slippers?"

"Slippers."

"Uh-huh. The left one is under your sink, and the right one is under the bed."

"Dammit!"

"Well, you were so tired last night," Marie soothed. The kid loved overalls and hairbands; she was always dressed the same way. Must be a stubborn little tick at home. "You just sort of threw everything off you and fell into the bed."

"Stop spying on me, you little turd."

She giggled. "Don't call me that!"

"Yeah, yeah." I hunted around—lo! My shoes were exactly where she'd said. "Where is everybody?"

"Um . . . Dr. Marc is working, and Jessica's sleeping."

"Oh." Bo-ring.

"There's new stuff in the kitchen," she said helpfully. "Jessica told the pantry manager to get you some white tea, and she picked up fresh cream at the farmer's market."

"Really? D'you know how rare and expensive white tea is?

I've been dying to try it. Oooh, and fresh cream! Come down, I'll fix you a cup, too."

She shook her head, which didn't surprise me. Marie was one painfully shy kid. Except around me, for some reason.

I quickly got dressed in khaki shorts, a red sleeveless mock turtleneck, and slipped into black flats. I ran a brush through my hair. It was staying exactly shoulder-length, and my highlights were staying exactly as high-lit as they'd been the day I died. One less thing to worry about. Besides, I was too chicken to try a haircut—what if I was stuck with it forever? Well, maybe a trim . . .

"I'll bring up a cup for you," I promised on my way out the door.

"I'm not thirsty," she called after me.

It took ten minutes to find the kitchen. I'd been living here for days, and still got lost. Thank God for my vampire nose, or I'd probably never have found it.

There was a note from Jessica on the table.

*Bets, the owner called again. VERY anxious to sell to us. Keeps dropping the price. I'm seriously considering it. What do you think? J.*

"I think it's too expensive, is what I think," I said aloud. Might as well have the argument by myself. It was the only way I'd win. "The three of us rattle around in here like dried peas in an empty can. Also, I'm getting sick of the smell of old wood."

"Bitch, bitch, bitch," Jessica yawned, slouching into the kitchen in her jade green silk pajamas. They set off her ebony skin superbly. Bitch.

"Well, it's true." I didn't add that the place was starting to grow on me, and for once, it was nice to have all the closet space I needed. "Can't sleep?"

"No, I set my alarm so I could talk to you."

"Oh. Thanks. But you need your sleep."

She shrugged. "I'll take a nap this afternoon. You're not working tonight, right?"

"Nope, I've got the next two days off. Although how Macy's will run without me remains a mystery. Are you really thinking about buying this place?"

"If the owner keeps dropping the price, it's a major steal. And you have to admit, it's beautiful."

"Agreed." I poured myself a glass of chocolate milk. Screw tea . . . took too long. "Beautiful and big. I may have to buy more shoes just to fill up my closet."

"God help us. So, what's new? Besides the fact that you're the only vampire in the world with a milk mustache?"

"Well, we've got some little scumballs killing vamps, and I was kind of torn about that until they tried to take out Tina—"

"She okay?"

"She's fine now." I omitted the gross blood drinking details. "My boss is going on vacation and is leaving me in charge of the department."

"God help us."

"Oh, quit saying that. And we're setting a trap for the killers the day after tomorrow. Also, I'm thinking of calling Child Services for Marie."

Jessica yawned and got up to make coffee. "Who?"

"This little cutie who's always hanging around. I don't mind, she's not bratty or anything, but cripes, the kid's *always* here. No matter what time it is. I'm sure her dad means well, taking her on his jobs, but this is ridiculous."

"Well, don't go flying off the handle and getting Child Services involved. You could call Detective Nick, maybe have him— No, don't glare. You're right, bad idea."

"It makes me nervous enough knowing we're living in his jurisdiction. I keep expecting him to show up on our doorstep yelling, 'You're dead and I forgot all about it!' " I shivered.

"He doesn't have a chance against Sinclair wiping his memory. But back to the kid . . . I could talk to her dad," she suggested. "Who is he?"

That stumped me. "You know, I never found out. I'll go ask her. She's probably still in my room. I'm sure the little brat's trying my shoes on when I'm not there."

I hurried back to my room, but Marie was gone, and didn't come out when I called her.

# Chapter 11

"BUT why do *I* have to be bait?" I whined.

"Well, you fit the profile."

"What, I'm a vampire?"

"Yes," Monique said.

"I'm the *only* vampire who can do this?"

"Yes," Tina said.

"I don't care for this idea myself," Sinclair said. Yay, Sinclair!

"If I'm bait, that will seem awfully suspicious," Tina said. "The same with Monique. We barely got away, but now we're strolling around, unconcerned? Unlikely. And Eric, you're a little too formidable to be really good bait."

"Thank you," he said.

"Barf," I said. "Aren't there any other vampires you can pick on?"

"Well, there's Sarah . . . but she keeps pretty much to herself. She has for the last fifty years."

"Who's S—"

"And . . . you *are* the queen," Monique interrupted apologetically. "It's sort of your responsibility."

"Scratch the 'sort of'," Tina replied, "and replace it with 'entirely'."

"Whatever happened to 'they will come over you over my dead body, your Majesty?' I mean, jeez, that was only three months ago."

"That was different," Tina said with maddening calm. "You were unaware of your responsibilities then."

"Oh, blow me. Okay, okay, I'll do it. I assume I'll have back-up?"

"Of course!" Monique said warmly. I smiled at her. At last, someone who appeared to care if I was chopped into pieces. "We'll all be watching and waiting. And if the four of us can't handle a group of youths . . . well, we should all just stake our-selves right now."

"Pass," I said, although, worriedly, Tina and Sinclair were nodding. "Okay. What do I do?"

SIX hours later, I'd had enough. "This isn't working!" I yelled. "And the sun's coming up soon! A total wasted evening, losers!"

Sinclair materialized out of the shadows, effectively scaring the crap out of me. While I gasped and grabbed my chest, he said, "It appears you are correct. We'll have to try again later."

"Well, dammit," Tina said from behind me. I yipped and spun around while she continued. "I want to get these little thugs *now*."

"Soon," Sinclair soothed. He slung a companionable arm around her shoulder. He practically had to bend over to do it; she was really short. "Let's head back to the hotel and get some rest. Where's Monique?"

"Here," she said from across the street. She quickly crossed against the light—vampires were total renegades—and joined our little huddle. "This is unfortunate. I had hoped—"

"Next time," Sinclair said.

"Oh, crap! We're gonna trash another evening by doing this again?" I grumped. "Gosh, I can't wait. Remind me to get that night off, by the way."

Sinclair muttered something in response, but I didn't catch it. Lucky for him.

"Great shoes," Monique said, pointing.

"Yes," I said, pleased. I was dressed in black—a cliché, but it seemed appropriate for the evening shenanigans—except for my shoes. They were clear Lucite wedges with a butterfly in each heel. Normally I try to avoid plastic shoes, but this time I made an exception. "Aren't they great? Sixty-nine ninety five, with my discount."

"Are those real bugs?" Tina asked.

"No," I said, offended.

"Oh, that's right. You're in P.E.T.A."

"Not anymore. They were getting a little extreme. I mean, I'm as against spraying shaving cream into a rabbit's eyes as the next person. But they're trying to prevent AIDS research, which I think sucks."

"How nice," Sinclair said silkily, "that your politics are as changeable as your wardrobe."

"Uh . . . thanks?" *Was that a compliment?* "But I still wouldn't walk around with real bugs in my shoes."

"Are they comfortable?" Monique asked. "They're so high."

"Comfort is irrelevant! A small price to pay."

"This is enthralling," Sinclair said, "but the sun will be up soon, and I would rather not be burned alive while you ladies discuss footwear."

"Picky, picky. I'll see you guys later."

"I'll walk you to your car," he said quickly.

I laughed. "Why? What could possibly happen to me? The bad guys aren't coming out tonight . . . or if they did, it wasn't around here."

He hesitated for a long moment—had he been hoping for a grope in the parking garage?—then said, "Very well. Good night."

"'Night. G'night, Tina. Bye, Monique."

Five minutes later, I was in the US Bank parking ramp. My car was the only one on level three. Good thing I was already dead, or I'd be really creeped out. Minneapolis was pretty low-crime compared to most cities, but it didn't do to tempt fate.

I unlocked my car and was about to open the door when I noticed— Argh! Was that a *scuff* across my toes? Two pairs in one week! My vampire lifestyle was ruining my footwear, and I just would not stand for it.

I bent over to get a closer look, and heard a *whummm-thud!* I straightened up in a hurry and saw a thick wooden arrow quivering in the metal between my window and the roof of the car.

I whirled. There was a kid—eighteen, nineteen—standing beside one of the concrete pillars, holding a crossbow. I heard the click as he popped another arrow into place, and sidestepped just as the punk blew out my driver side window.

"Cut that out!" I shouted. "What's the matter with you?"
*Move.*

I ducked again, and the kid jumped behind the pillar as two more arrows sailed past him. Great. There was one behind me, too.

"What, you were too good for our trap?" I called out. "I wasted my entire evening and you show up *now?* Next time"—I could actually see the kid's arrow coming at me in not-quite-slow motion, and sidestepped again. Guess my undead adrenaline was kicking in—"make an appointment."

"Give it up, you vampire whore," someone called from behind me.

"Oh, that's nice," I snapped. "You don't even know me!"

I heard muffled footsteps. They were good, I hadn't even noticed I was walking into an ambush. But now I was noticing everything. I figured there were at least three people on this level with me, maybe four.

I had the strong urge to move again—thank you, inner voice—and this time three bullets stitched my car door. Then another smacked into my shoulder.

"Owwwww!" I complained. It felt like getting bopped with a baseball bat. It hurt for a few seconds, then my shoulder went numb. "Lucky for you guys I've got a million other T-shirts at home. What did I ever do to you?"

The ones behind me were muttering to themselves, and the kid by the pillar—a blue-eyed blonde right out of Surfing Central Casting—looked amazed. He stared and stared, appearing to be waiting for something. What? For me to blow up? Were the bullets special?

"Duds," the woman called from somewhere.

Finally, he said, "Stand still, you fucking bloodsucker."

"Are you on drugs? Do I have Giant Moron written on my forehead?"

"No," my would-be killer admitted.

"And will you stop with the wrecking of my car? I have to make this one last at least another year." Luckily, Fords were built tough. "Who are you jerk offs, anyway?"

"We're the Blade Warriors," a woman called from behind me. She was pretty well hidden; I had no idea what she was wearing. I rolled my eyes, and the kid by the pillar stopped in mid-reload to stare at me again. "We kill vampires."

I snorted. Teenagers! Well, at least they'd stopped shooting at me. "The Blade Warriors? Seriously? You guys actually thought that up and said, 'yeah, that name doesn't blow, we'll go with that one'?"

There was an embarrassed silence.

"And as far as killing vampires goes," I continued smugly, "you're sort of sucking at it. How much ammo have you wasted on me?"

"You'd know about sucking," Blondie sneered.

"Hey, I'm not the one running around in Kevlar with crossbows in the middle of the night like a geek loser. And four against one? Not *too* lame."

"But you're a vampire!" the woman protested. She was about ten feet closer. Oh-ho. Keep the dead chick talking while the other three sneak up on me. "You kill people!"

"No I don't. I've only killed one person in my whole life, and he was already dead. I *told* you guys you didn't know anything about me. What, because I'm a vampire I automatically deserve to be shot with arrows?"

"Well . . . yes."

"Bullshit. You're teenagers, but I'm not trying to kill *you*. Although if you keep shooting up my car," I muttered, "I might."

Having finished my speech, I figured it was time to get gone before my luck ran out. Thank goodness, I was parked on the right side of the ramp. I swiftly crossed the six feet to the wall, dodging another bullet and two arrows on the way, and without another word to the Loser Warriors, vaulted over the ledge and plummeted three stories to the street below.

# Chapter 12

I limped down the street, grabbed the first homeless guy I saw, apologized profusely, and hauled him behind a dumpster for a rejuvenating snack. As always, drinking blood felt physically wonderful, while emotionally I was disgusted with myself.

After a few seconds (it never took long), I left my smiling, sleeping blood donor asleep on a pile of cardboard. It was a warm night; he'd be okay. Unless you knew he was there, you couldn't see him.

My shoulder healed like magic before I even left the alley, and I was amazed to feel the bullet pop free of my flesh and fall into my bra.

I fished it out and stared at it, but I don't know a bullet from a dildo, so I tucked it back in and resolved to show it to Sinclair later. Or maybe Nick Berry . . . a cop would know all sorts of stuff about bullets. If I dared involve him in this.

I made it home just before dawn—thank goodness for late night taxis!—and realized when I tried to pay the fare that I'd left my purse in my car. So I zapped him with the old vamp mojo, ignoring the stab of guilt, and he drove off thrilled to his toes.

There was, of course, the expected uproar when I walked in. Marc and Jessica were both yelling at me at once, and while Jessica punched buttons on her cell phone, Marc nagged me into stripping off my T-shirt so he could check my wound.

"Huh," he said, poking my shoulder like I was a side of beef. "I don't see a thing."

I coughed but didn't elaborate on how I'd cured myself. "Who are you calling?" I asked Jessica.

"You know who," she said, then barked into the phone, "Betsy was attacked. She's here now."

"Aww, no, not Sinclair! That's all I need." I looked at my watch. "He probably won't have enough time to get here, anyway."

"Yeah, he's pretty helpless, that one," Marc said. He wadded up my shirt. "Might as well toss this, chickie, it's ruined. What was it like, getting shot?"

"What kind of a dumbass question is that from a guy who went to medical school? It hurt!"

"I mean, is it different for a vampire, do you think? I've seen lots of bullet wounds at the hospital, but none that healed in an hour."

"How should I know? I've never been shot before. I mean, I could see the bullets coming at me—"

"Cool, like in *The Matrix*?"

"No. They were like baseballs thrown hard. I could dodge them, but I really had to be on my toes."

"Thank God you're all right," Jessica said. I blushed with pleasure, and then she wrecked it by adding, "you idiot. What were you *thinking?*"

"Hey, don't yell at me! I was *thinking* of going to my car and driving home," I said. "I'm the victim. So what, exactly, is my crime?"

"I'm gonna strangle that Sinclair," she muttered. When Jess got mad she sort of did this thing where she sucked on her cheeks, which threw her cheekbones into sharp relief. She looked like a pissed-off Egyptian queen who needed a few milkshakes. "Dragging you into this . . . putting you in danger . . ."

"This wasn't part of me being bait. This was after. The . . ." I could barely get it out without giggling. "The Blade Warriors were waiting for me in the parking ramp."

Marc's eyebrows shot up and he and he and Jessica traded a glance.

"I know how it sounds," I said.

"Bad," Jessica replied.

"*Real* bad," Marc elaborated.

"I was talking about their name, but you're right, that's not too cool. An ambush. Huh. Look, I'm going to grab a quick shower; I feel sort of yucky. We'll talk more in a few minutes, okay?"

Annoyingly, they waited outside my bathroom while I freshened up. At least Marie wasn't here—it would have been too awful to explain the evening's occurrences to a little kid.

I stepped out of the bathroom in clean cotton shorts and a new T-shirt, and started back downstairs. Jessica and Marc didn't wait, they pelted me with questions during the long journey to the main living room.

"How did you get away? Tell me everything," Jessica ordered finally, when she noticed I was ignoring everything she and Marc were saying. "Start with, 'I went diddy-bopping out the door six hours ago like a big blond idiot,' and finish with 'and then I walked in all bloody and tired-looking'."

"Can't it wait?" I griped. "I'm just going to have to tell it all to Sinclair again. Ugh, what a night. I'll be glad when it's tomorrow. Tonight, I mean."

Just then, the front door was thrown open, hard enough to make us all jump, and lo, there was the prince of darkness.

"Are you all right?" Sinclair demanded, crossing the room in swift strides and peering at my face.

"Please, come in," I said sarcastically. "Don't forget to wipe your feet. And I'm fine. There was no need to rush over here. Where are your shoes?"

Jessica coughed. "I sort of promised him I'd keep him apprised."

I forgot about the fact that Sinclair was in a suit, a topcoat, and bare feet. "You did *what?*"

"Never mind that now," Sinclair said impatiently. He was running his hands over my face, my neck, my shoulders, my arms.

I slapped his hands away when he started to raise my shirt to look at my stomach. "No, let's talk about that *right* now." Before I could work up a good rant, I realized I was suddenly very tired. Extremely tired. I shook my head to try to throw it off, and realized that it was a lot lighter outside. "Uh-oh," I managed, just as Sinclair and the living room tipped away from me, and the carpet rushed up to my face.

"I hate that," I said, exactly fifteen hours later. I opened my eyes and was startled to see Sinclair with his jacket off, sitting in the chair beside my bed, reading. "Jesus!"

He winced. "Please don't call me that. Good evening."

"This is so bogus! How come *you* don't have to sleep all day?"

"I'm quite a bit older than you are. Now." He slapped the book shut. I saw it was one of Jessica's collection of antique school books. Dumbest hobby ever, except maybe for golf. "Tell me everything that happened last night."

I ignored the command. "Did you sleep at all?" I asked suspiciously. Oh, I knew him of old.

He smirked. "I did rest beside you for a few hours."

"Pervert!"

"No, but if I was such a thing, taking advantage of you would have been simplicity itself."

"Have I mentioned how much I strongly, *strongly* dislike you?"

"Ah!" he said, looking pleased. "We're making progress. From hate to dislike."

"Strong, strong dislike. Where are my roomies? I don't want to have to tell this story a thousand times."

"We're here," they chorused, walking into my bedroom.

"And so am I," Tina added, trailing them. "Are you all right, Majesty?"

I'd given up on trying to get her to call me by my first name. I ignored Marc's chortle and replied, "I'm fine. I only got shot once."

A muscle jumped in Sinclair's cheek. Weird. I'd never seen that before. "They shot you?" he asked with scary calm.

"My car's a lot worse off than I am, believe me. Which reminds me, we have to go get it tonight. And my purse. In all the excitement—"

"From the beginning, please."

I told them. I didn't leave anything out. And nobody interrupted, not once, which was a brand new experience.

"They knew you were a vampire," Tina said when I finished. She looked very, very troubled.

"Uh, yeah. Good point. *How* did they know? I mean, most vampires don't even believe it."

"And how did they know about the other vampires?" Marc asked.

"Well, it must be . . . I mean, maybe a vampire is siccing these guys on us?" I guessed.

"Probably a vampire," Jessica said at once. "Who else would know who's dead and who's not?"

Sinclair nodded. "And they were waiting for you." He looked cool as a cucumber, but his hands kept opening and closing into fists. "They knew you were coming."

"Apparently so." I hadn't really had time to think about how weird that was. "Quit doing that, it makes me nervous. Oh! I almost forgot!"

I jumped out of bed and practically ran over to my dresser, where I'd placed the bullet after tossing my clothes in the hamper. "I have a clue!" I said proudly, holding it up.

"That's great, Nancy Drew," Marc said with fake enthusiasm.

"Shut up. Check this out, you guys." I gave it to Sinclair, who examined it briefly and passed it to Tina.

"This is a hollow-point," she said, very surprised.

"Yikes," Jessica said. "A vampire gun expert."

"I like to keep busy," she replied mildly. "I'll take a look at it later."

"I was thinking we could show it to Nick," I said.

"Detective Nick Berry? I don't think that's wise at all," Sinclair said. "Best he stays out of our business."

"He might already be in it. He pulled me over the other day and had all sorts of questions. Don't worry," I said, because Tina and Sinclair both looked alarmed, "your mojo's holding. He didn't remember about me being dead and all."

"Still, he sought you out," Tina said, looking troubled.

"It was just a coincidence," I said uneasily. "He recognized my car and pulled me over."

There was a short silence, broken by, "You should rest," Sinclair ordered, getting up from his chair. "Spend the night in bed."

"I spent the *day* in bed, and that's plenty."

He ignored me, as usual. "Tina and I will put our heads together and—"

"I'm *fine,* how many times do I have to tell you? Stop clucking. And I have to work tonight, I can't stay in bed."

"You will not be going to work."

"The hell!" I glared up at him. "Stop trying to boss me around, when are you going to learn?"

Jessica cleared her throat. "Uh, Betsy."

I ignored her. "I never listen—"

"I have learned that."

"—and it just pisses me off."

"Bets."

"Frankly, you could do worse than listening to me," Sinclair snapped back. "This *faux* independence of yours is growing tiresome."

"Faux?" I cried. That meant fake, right? Probably. Stupid French! "Listen, jerkoff—"

"Betsy!" Jessica seized my arm in a grip that would have hurt like hell if I'd been alive. "Girl talk," she said to the room at large, then dragged me into the bathroom.

I extricated myself, with difficulty, from her grasp. "What? I'm in the middle of something, here. What did you have to say to me right this second?"

She lowered her voice; we were both well aware of vampire hearing. "I wanted to stop you before you said something worse."

"Girlfriend, I haven't even gotten started—"

"Okay, I know you don't like him—or you think you don't like him, I haven't figured out which—but Bets! It was the most romantic thing ever. He caught you before you did a nosedive into the carpet. I mean, you started to go down and he *moved*. Then he sort of scooped you up and carried you up to bed, although how he knew which room was yours is sort of a mystery, and he never left your side."

"Ew."

"No, the opposite of ew. I came up to check on you guys about lunchtime and you were both . . . uh . . . dead to the world, and he had his arm around your shoulders and you were sort of cuddled into his side."

"I was not!" I said, shocked. Was I so shameless in my undead sleep?

"Bets, you totally were. And then, when I checked on you a few hours later—"

"Jeez, couldn't stay away, could you? Not too creepy."

"Hey, it's interesting. Anyway, Eric was awake, and he asked if he could borrow one of my old books, and nice as you pleased, asked for a cup of coffee."

"You're not a waitress."

"No, but I'm a good hostess. Anyway, it was . . . it was kind of nice. He was really nice. And he's nice to you."

"No, he isn't!"

"I think you should treat him better," she said firmly.

Traitor! I took a deep breath, which made me dizzy. "And *I* think . . ."

But we were interrupted by a knock on the bathroom door, so we went back out to my room. To my surprise, Sinclair and Tina were gone.

"He sort of stomped out," Marc replied in answer to my unspoken question. "And she said good-bye, very politely, and followed him." He shook his head. "Are you really going to work tonight?"

"You bet."

"It's just . . ." Marc looked worried, which for him was pretty rare. "Those warrior guys knew who you were. They might be tracking you."

That was a startling—and unpleasant!—thought. "I don't think so," I said after a minute's thought. "How would they know where I work?"

"They knew where you parked," he pointed out.

"I *have* to go. Otherwise, Finklair will think I dodged work because *he* said to."

"Perish the thought," Jessica said. "God forbid you should take the advice of an older, experienced, extremely intelligent man."

"I'd do anything that guy asked me," Marc said admiringly. "What a hunk! Oooh, and he's all intense and stern, but you just know that once you got him between the sheets—"

"Stop!" Jessica and I said simultaneously.

"You know it's true." He wiggled his eyebrows at me. "In fact, Betsy, didn't you find out for yourself not too long ago?"

"I don't want to talk about that," I said firmly. "He tricked me. He knew if we had sex, he'd be the king."

No, I didn't like to talk about it. But I sure thought about it a lot. Not only was it the most pleasurable sexual experience of my life, it had been *so* intense. Because, for a while there, while he was inside me, I was inside *him*. I could read his mind. And his thoughts . . . his thoughts had been very nice. While we were having sex, at least, he had really liked me.

Maybe loved me.

"Come on," Marc was saying in his coaxing doctor voice, "it was three months ago. And there have been compensations, right? I mean, Sinclair and Tina are cool, and it's obvious they really like you. What's so bad about that? When are you going to let it go?"

"A thousand years," I said, trying not to show how upset I was getting. Marc, who had a huge crush on Sinclair, just didn't get it. And Jessica thought I should be nice to him. Nice! "That's how long I'm stuck in this gig. Thanks to *him*."

"Well, I know, and I'm sorry. Don't cry about it," he said, kindly enough. "But there's worse things than nice vampires thinking you're in charge, right?"

"I don't want to talk about it anymore."

"Okay," Jessica said at once. She was glaring at Marc. "You don't have to if you don't want to. Look, why don't you get dressed for work? I'll make you some tea, and then we'll go get your car."

I sniffed. "Okay. Actually, I'll come down with you. I want tea right now . . . I'm dying of thirst. Don't look at me like that."

"Sorry," they said in uneasy unison.

"Oh, please. Like I'd ever bite either of you two dorks," I muttered. "I'm gonna change my clothes, and I'll be right down."

They left, and I thought I heard the front door open, but I was too annoyed to really care. More visitors—great! Well, bring it on.

I turned around to go to my dresser and nearly fell over Marie. "Jeez, don't *do* that!" I practically yelled. Okay, I did yell. "Sugar, would you mind clearing out? I've had a rotten evening and it's barely started. Go find your dad, or something."

"Sure," she said, staring at me with big, solemn eyes. "But I don't think you should open the door."

Yeah, yeah, whatever. She was gone when I came out of the bathroom, and I changed into a clean blouse, khaki shorts, and slipped on a pair of black sandals. I ran a brush through my hair and decided that would do, and decided to head downstairs.

I opened my bedroom door, and got the surprise of my life.

# Chapter 13

FROM the private papers of Father Markus, Parish Priest, St. Pious Church, 129 E. 7th Street, Minneapolis, Minnesota.

Killing the Evil Ones is not as satisfying as I had assumed it would be. And I can hardly believe I am thinking such a thing, much less writing it down. When I am long dead, these papers will belong to the Holy Church. What will they think of me, and however will I explain myself to my Heavenly Father?

At first, I thought God was acting through our employer. I am beginning to wonder if that was the devil, speaking to me in the voice of my pride. Because many things I have long believed may not be true. And if that is the case, what will become of me? What will become of the children? They say all things work toward God's will . . . perhaps even the Undead do, as well.

The money, the equipment, the skills of the Blade Warriors . . . every vampire the children found was dispatched. I assumed we were doing great good. We are commanded not to kill, but are these things not already dead? I thought God was acting through me, through the children, but now . . .

It started to go bad when the two females escaped. Both were beautiful, looked young, and had the strength of ten tigers. Although we inflicted great damage on the smaller, dark one, she eluded us in the end. It was the first time we had been unable to do our duty, and it weighed heavily on the boys. Ani was more sanguine, but even she couldn't hide her distress.

Then there was the vampire in the parking garage.

Except was she?

Our employer had never been wrong. But this woman—she did not hiss and snarl when cornered, she did not try to bite. She seemed puzzled, and annoyed, and although she moved with the grace of a jungle cat she did not try any tricks of the dead—the hypnosis, the mind-bending, the seduction. Instead, she yelled at Jon and mocked the rest of us. She made us feel foolish and worse, we feared we were foolish. And after taunting us, instead of engaging, she fled. And we learned something more—heights are a vampire's friend.

Ani found the purse in the woman's—the vampire's—car. And that was another thing. This vampire had a car, a job, and a life. She was carrying full identification, right down to her library card.

Vampires, going to the library.

The name was right—Elizabeth Taylor—but nothing else fit with what we knew of the Undead.

We could all feel doubts start to creep in. In our business, that is fatal.

Jon proposed a simple yet daring plan. And so it was that the next evening, we found ourselves on Summit Avenue, in the state's capital.

To our great surprise, the front door was unlocked. There were several cars in the driveway, and when we stepped inside we could see a cook hurrying through the entryway with bags of groceries. She gave us a single, disinterested glance and disappeared through an archway. We heard a car start outside and Wild Bill went to check. When he returned, he informed us the gardener had just left.

"Weird" was Ani's comment. She was a philosophy major at the University, and we had deep respect for her mind. "The vampire's driving a beat-up Ford, but she lives here? And what are all these people doing here? Do they know? And if they do, are they with her? Or prisoners? There aren't any marks on them, and they don't look like they've been snacked on . . ."

Before we could answer—and troubling questions they were—a lovely young African American woman came hurrying down the steps, and behind her was, of all things, a physician! He was a sharp-looking young man with dark hair, wearing light green scrubs and looking quite surprised to see us.

"Oh, great," the woman said. She was thin to the point of emaciation, but lovely just the same. Her ebony skin had reddish undertones, and her cheekbones made her look almost regal. Her eyes flashed dark fire as she hurried toward us. And, oddest of all, she seemed familiar to me. "Don't tell me, let me guess. The Blade Warriors. I have a huge bone to pick with you."

"That was our friend you ganged up on," the doctor added. He was right on her heels as they rapidly approached.

This was a bit nerve-wracking. We were quite helpless around humans—we certainly wouldn't kill them! But we had never met a vampire with human friends before.

And where had I seen the woman?

"Maybe they're pets," Ani muttered behind me.

"Maybe you're trespassing," the woman replied coldly. "You assholes are on private property. Mine. So get the hell out, unless you're here to apologize to my friend. In which case, you can still get the hell out, because we don't want to hear it."

"The door was unlocked," Jon pointed out.

"So it's not breaking and entering," the doctor said, grinning. "It's just entering."

His little joke caused most of us to relax a bit, but the young woman remained unmoved. "You guys get out of here," she said with clear warning in her voice. "I'm going to count to three. Then I'm loading the shotgun. Then I'm filling the waterguns with bleach. Then I'm releasing the hounds. Then—"

"Jessica Watkins?" I asked, utterly surprised.

She blinked at me, just as surprised. "Yeah. So?"

"I'm Father Markus. You donated half a million dollars to my church." At last, at last I had placed her! I hadn't recognized her in faded jeans and a Gap T-shirt, because I usually saw the lady at fund-raisers, when she was dressed in formal attire. "This is a surprise. It's good to see you."

Taken aback, she let me shake her hand. "Uh, yeah. Good-good to see you, too. Um. What are you doing with these idiots?"

"These are my children," I corrected her firmly.

She leered. "Oh, you're one of those priests, eh?"

Although the Church's reputation had suffered griev-
ously the last few years, I did not rise to the bait. "I take care
of them," I explained patiently, "and they look after me in my
old age. We do God's work."

"Not today, Father! Betsy never did a single thing to any
one of you. Leave her alone!"

"We're here to solve a mystery," I said. "We're not quite
sure your . . . your friend is . . . is who we think she is."

"So you come to my house at night, bristling with
weapons? I'm surprised you didn't show up at noon like true
cowards," she said, her imperious voice dripping with scorn.
She was her father's daughter, all right. The man had been
known to make other CEOs cry just before taking over their
companies.

"We would never," I said, offended. "Even the undead
deserve to be dealt with honorably."

"Outnumbered five to one and cornered and staked to
death? Father Markus, I never dreamed you were such an
asshole."

How that stung! I was a good man, a good priest. I helped
hunt the Undead. I saved lives. I was not an asshole.

As was her wont, Ani stepped in when she felt someone
was being disrespectful. "Don't talk to Father Markus like
that," she said in warning. She was a tall woman—easily my
height—with jet-black hair cut just below her ears, and
lovely, tip-tilted almond-shaped eyes. Her mother had been
Japanese; she had never known her father, but from her build
and coloring, we guessed he was Northern European. Her
limbs were long and slender, and she was one of the fastest
runners I had ever seen. She had been considering the
Olympics when we found her. "Not unless you want to eat
teeth."

"Ani," I murmured.

"Going to stake regular people next, you bimbo?" Jessica
snapped. "You come into my house hunting my friend, you
don't even knock, you bring guns and knives into my home,
and now you're threatening me? Girlfriend, you should have
kept your ass in bed today."

The children were shifting uneasily, and I couldn't blame
them. Hunting the Undead was one thing. Arousing the ire of

the city's—the state's!—wealthiest citizen was quite another. Even without her money, Jessica Watkins would have been formidable. As I said, she was her father's daughter.

"Look, let's make a deal," the doctor said, neatly breaching the awkward silence. "Father, why don't you go upstairs to Betsy's room—"

"Betsy?" I repeated.

"—and toss some of your holy water on her. That should do the trick, right?"

"Marc," Jessica began, but he shook his head at her.

"Well." I coughed. "It will likely burn her severely. It could even kill her. Or blind her. Your friend."

"It's a risk we're willing to take," the doctor said cheerfully.

"We're going with him," Jon said.

"Fine, but the toys stay down here. Just holy water. Ought to be enough for big-shit vampire killers like you guys, right?"

His words were rude, but he was still grinning at us in a friendly way. I tried to find the trap, but I couldn't see it. "Right."

"So, then. Go on up. We'll wait." He looked disturbingly cheerful, but, as I said, I couldn't see the problem.

The children dutifully unholstered guns and unsheathed knives. There was quite a pile on the lovely cherry table when they finished unloading. As for myself, my cross and holy water had always been all I needed. The Undead always went after one of the children; they tended to steer clear of me.

"Right, then." I took a deep breath. "Let's go. But first . . ." The children dropped their heads obediently, and I closed my eyes. "O Heavenly Father, please guide my hand and keep our family safe. In Your name, Amen."

"Amen," they echoed. Interestingly, the doctor and Jessica also said Amen.

"Third floor," he said helpfully. "Fifth door on the left. Watch the seventh step, it squeaks."

I couldn't help but stare at him, and knew my bewilderment must have shown on my face. Odder and odder. But we had our duty, and even had permission to finish it.

I pulled the cork from the bottle of holy water and led the way upstairs.

# Chapter 14

ℒ opened the door and, to my total amazement, got a vial full of water thrown in my face. For a moment I just sputtered. Then I started to sneeze.

Oh, great. Holy water! The stuff was worse than hot pepper. I sneezed and coughed and gasped until my vision finally cleared.

There were several people crowded in the hallway, but I focused on the tall, old one in black, the one staring at me and holding a cross out.

"Thanks very much!" I snapped. "What'd I ever do to you, jerk? Here I am, minding my own business, and you throw holy water in my face! Look at my hair! And my *shirt!* Dammit, I just put this on!" I shook water off my feet—lucky for these guys they were last season's sandals—and shouldered my way past him and the other weirdos. "Is this what they teach you in Jerkoff School? Do *I* come to *your* house and throw water on *you?*"

"We . . . uh . . ."

"Well, come on." I stomped down two levels and heard them sort of shuffling after me. Nobody was talking. Which was probably just as well, since I wasn't done yelling. "And another thing! Haven't you heard of knocking? I mean, how long were you lurking in my hallway, anyway? Not *too* creepy."

Marc and Jessica were waiting for me at the foot of the stairs. Marc was smirking, and Jessica was glaring. At least all was right with those two.

"Problems?"

"You wouldn't believe it!" I ranted. "I open the door, and big idiot in black here throws holy water on me!"

"Not surprising. Marc told him to," Jessica said.

"You *what?*"

"We weren't sure," big idiot in black said, looking confused and scared and apologetic, all at the same time. "We weren't sure . . . we thought you were a vampire."

I was a heartless denizen of the undead, and I was unmoved. Who cared if he strongly resembled somebody's grandpa? Okay, *my* grandpa. "I *am* a vampire, dumbass! I ought to pull all your teeth out and play craps with them."

"But . . . but that's impossible!" one of the dorky teens blurted. I glared at him . . . and recognized him.

They all took a big step back as I rounded on them. "I know you guys! You're the Broody Warthogs!"

"Blade Warriors," one of them, the surfer dude from last night, corrected in a mutter.

"You shoot up my car and now you're *here?*" I whirled on Marc and Jessica. "They didn't hurt you guys, did they?"

"Never," the big idiot in black said, sounding—the nerve!—offended. "We only kill the dead."

I finally realized the black suit was actually a priest's outfit, and so resisted the urge to pull his head off his shoulders and use it as a soccer ball. Would I go to hell for calling a priest a dumbass? Even if he was one? A problem to worry about later.

"You guys . . ." I took a breath, ignoring the wave of dizziness that caused, and forced calm. "We've been looking for you guys."

"I'll bet," the woman said. She was super pretty, and big—my height—but looked mean, like a tall, evil Lucy Liu with a bad haircut. "I'll just bet."

"Hey, you think we're not gonna notice if you guys are running around slaughtering vampires?" I lied, because, of course, I hadn't. "Hardly! You're in big trouble."

Oooh, wait till Sinclair found out I caught the Word Barriers! All by myself!

"I don't think—" the priest began, trying yet again, but I was still too annoyed to let him finish a sentence.

"What's the matter with all of you? What'd I ever do to any of you?"

"Well," big idiot in black said. "Ah. That is to say . . . nothing."

"She isn't a vampire," surfer guy insisted.

"She is," shorter geek with black hair moussed in spikes and tipped in white insisted.

"Is not!"

"Is!"

"Isn't!"

"Is!"

The Lucy Liu knockoff stepped to the big table in the entry-way, pulled a knife as long as my forearm out of a heroic pile of weapons, and handed it to Marc, handle first, much to his surprise. "Would you please," she asked pleasantly, "drive this into my ear until I can't hear anymore?"

I couldn't help it. I laughed. And, as always, it was hard to hold onto my mad when I was giggling. Ridiculous, but there you go.


"I still say she's not a vampire," Wild Bill, the kid who had the armadillo haircut, insisted half an hour later. He had cream on his lip, but I wasn't going to tell him.

"You'll just have to take my word for it," I said. We were in the Tea Room—one of the tea rooms—and Jessica was playing hostess to the people who had tried to kill me. Well, I guess it was slightly more civilized than biting them or pulling their arms off. "I really am. And we'd better figure out how to get along."

"You can't blame us for being surprised," Ani said. Her name was Ani Goodman. Wasn't that a great name for a vampire hunter? Give the girl a decent haircut, and she would be a force to be reckoned with. "It's just that you're awfully . . . uh . . ."

"Vain," Marc said.

"Shrill," Father Markus added.

"Annoying," Jessica piled on.

"Did someone already say vain?" Jon, the leader who looked like a surfer, said.

"You guys are hilarious." I crossed my arms over my chest and crossed my legs for good measure. "If everybody's done having a good chuckle at my expense—"

"*I'm* not done," Marc said.

"This is awkward," Father Markus said.

"No kidding!"

"Because until now, we have felt we were doing God's work."

"Oh. I thought we were still talking about me."

"I'm sure we will be, soon enough," Ani soothed, and Jessica cracked up. They traded a look, and the mood of the room shifted a bit more toward the "can't we all get along?" side.

"The vampires we killed—they were abominations." Boy, that Father Markus would *not* be shaken off a subject. "But now, given recent events . . ."

I squirmed. I knew how bad vamps could be. But I was the queen—laughable as the idea was—and I had a responsibility here. Too bad I hadn't the faintest clue what it was.

"So you guys just woke up one day and decided to start staking vampires?" Marc asked. He leaned over and stuffed half an éclair into his mouth. I nearly drooled . . . the pastries looked sooooo good. Custard squirted out the end and puddled on his plate. I looked up and realized Jon was watching me watch the pastry. I tore my gaze away and contented myself with another gulp of tea. "What, it was in your horoscope or something?"

"No," Jon said. "Father Markus knows tons of people from his parish work, people the rest of us have never met, people from all over the world."

"Well, that's true," Markus coughed modestly.

"And a few months ago he started getting these e-mails, and then money started showing up in our account for weapons and stuff, and then we'd get a list of names and addresses. Hangouts, like . . . and we'd go to work."

"How'd they know about you guys? How'd you even learn to fight?"

"They are orphans who avoided the system," Father Markus said quietly.

"So?" I asked, puzzled.

"Grew up on the streets," Ani said with her mouth full. She swallowed her sugar cookie and continued. "Good place to learn how to fight."

"I caught Jon and Bill trying to boost my tires behind the church," Markus said fondly, "and brought them under my wing. And they brought me the others."

"Awww, that's so cute. Not that we give a shit." I snickered. So much for being a good hostess. "Who's financing you?" Jessica asked.

The Weird Warriors looked at each other. "Well, the thing is," Father Markus said delicately, "we don't know. Our—"

"Puppet master," Jessica said.

"—patron wishes to remain anonymous."

Jessica rolled her eyes at Marc, who shrugged. I thought it was kind of weird, myself, but didn't say anything. With Jessica in the room, I didn't have to. "Uh-huh. So, you guys get everything you need to kill vampires, somebody just hands you all that stuff on a plate, and you don't question it, you just start killing them off?"

"We questioned it at first," Ani said. "But we were more easily persuaded when the first vampire nearly killed Drake."

"Who's Drake?"

"Drake doesn't run with us anymore. He's trying to learn how to walk again."

"Oh," Marc and I said.

"Anyway," she said briskly, "after that, it was easy. We certainly didn't question the morality of it. Most of the time when we cornered a vampire they were about to eat somebody. Or were actively hurting someone just for fun."

I squirmed, but didn't say anything.

"Until we ran into you, that is."

At last, I could say something in defense of vampires. "Actually, until you ran into Tina and Monique. They got away, too. And FYI, they're good guys! Not that you bothered to check."

"Look, we're sorry," Jon said, crumbling his vanilla biscuit in his agitation—what was he thinking? *I* wasn't going to vacuum, that was for sure! "But who checks the bona fides of the undead? They're vampires, *ergo* they're evil, *ergo* they should be killed."

"I've got your *ergos* right here," I muttered. Unfortunately, he had a point. Not that I could tell them that. In fact, what could I tell them? Should I even be talking to them? Was I supposed to be killing them right now? I'd never killed anybody alive before.

And how could I kill them when they were drinking orange pekoe tea and eating cookies with us? Should I wait until they finished, or jump them when they were getting refills? Being a soulless denizen of the undead was *really* hard sometimes.

While I was pouring more tea and contemplating mass murder, I heard a door slam open one floor down, but didn't say anything. We had enough problems without more uninvited guests.

There was a *tap-tap* on the window behind me, and I turned. And nearly spilled my tea. Tina was looking through the window, which was disturbing because we were two stories up.

*We're coming,* she mouthed. *Stay calm.*

"For heaven's sake," I said, standing, crossing the room, and opening the window. Everyone else jumped, and Jessica let out a little scream when she saw what was on the window. I realized I was the only one who'd heard Tina knock. "Come in here and have some tea like a civilized person. Eww, you're just sort of hanging on the house like a blond moth! Get in here."

She glared at me but clambered in. Then she glared at the Warriors. "We're here," she said with great dignity, "to rescue you from certain death."

"Biscuit?" Ani asked sweetly.

The door to the tea room slammed open and, big surprise, there was Sinclair. Uninvited, as usual. He didn't stand still very long; the next thing I knew he had picked Jon up and was shaking him like a broken pepper grinder.

Pandemonium. Spilled tea. Biscuits on the floor, where they promptly got stepped on and ground into the two-hundred-year-old carpet.

I jumped in front of Sinclair, arms spread, just in time to get another face full of holy water. I shook my head to clear my eyes, then grabbed Jon and wrenched him out of Sinclair's grip. A little too hard; the guy went sailing over the back of two chairs and hit the corner with a thud that shook the teacups.

"Stop it, *stop it!*" I yelled. "This isn't helping, you retard!" Then I spun and sneezed on Sinclair's lapels.

The two little guys—Wild Bill and Devo—were cowering behind Father Markus, who had his cross out, but Ani looked ready to rumble as she studied Sinclair and clutched a butter knife.

"It appears her Majesty does not need saving," Tina said, and *she* was studying Ani.

"No shit. Thanks for noticing. Why don't you guys sit down, take a load off? Have some tea, and a cookie if they aren't all squashed."

"Why," Sinclair demanded, whipping out a black handkerchief and wiping my face, "are you having tea with the vampire killers?"

"Because they're too young to drink alcohol?" I guessed.

Tina brought her hand up to cover a grin.

"Hey, I recognize you!" Ani said suddenly, staring at Tina.

"No you don't," I said quickly. "Never seen her before. Got her mixed up with another bloodsucker."

"Of course she does," Tina replied. "The last time I saw her, she was on the business end of a crossbow and I was running for my life."

Interestingly, Ani blushed. Sinclair, who'd been holding my shoulder while he wiped all the holy water off my face, suddenly tightened his grip and I yelped. "Don't start, don't start again!" I yelled, waving my arms frantically. "Let's sit down and talk about this like civilized people!"

"Why?" he asked coldly.

"Uh . . . because I asked nicely?"

He stared at his handkerchief which, now that it wasn't touching me, was starting to smolder. So, once holy water was, like, off my person, it could hurt a vampire? Weird! He tossed it in the wastebasket and scowled at the Blond Warriors.

"As my queen commands," he managed to spit out through gritted teeth, to my surprise and everyone else's relief.

# Chapter 15

"**YOU** guys get that you're just a loaded gun someone else is aiming. A tool, a big, dumb, tool." Jessica popped another cracker into her mouth, chewed, then added, "You get that, right?"

"That's not true," Wild Bill whined.

"Sure it is. You guys weren't even a team before the Puppet Master came along. Now you're running around staking dead people. And you don't even know why."

Sinclair nodded approvingly and sipped his Earl Grey. The vampires were comfortably spread out on one side of the table, and everybody else was crammed together on the other side. Father Markus had hung his crucifix around his neck, keeping it in plain sight, which made the other vamps a little antsy. They kept trying to look at him, and then their gaze would skitter away.

Across the table, the others jumped a foot whenever Tina or Sinclair reached for more tea. It was kind of funny.

"So who *is* the Puppet Master?" Tina asked. "Don't any of you have any idea?"

"No," Ani replied.

"Oh, come now."

"I swear! Everything's been anonymous. We assumed it was some rich vampire victim. You know, someone who lost a loved one to . . . to one of you."

"Ennnnhhhhh! Thanks for playing . . . what do we have for her, Johnny?"

"Quit doing your game show host schtick, Marc," I ordered. "You're confusing the vampires. They're not big TV watchers."

"Certainly not daytime television," Sinclair sniffed.

Marc smirked. "My point is, I doubt it. Remember, guys, we were talking about how it had to be a vampire, because he knew who was dead and who wasn't? How would a regular person know that? It's not like Eric keeps a list . . . oh, John Smith rose from the dead, better write that down."

"No," Sinclair said, and he was actually smiling. Thank God. "I don't have a list."

"Actually, *I* was saying that," Jessica said, "and you're right. The bad guy's one of you," she said, pointing to the vampire half of the tea table. In fact, she was pointing right at me, and I batted her hand away. "You've got to figure out who, and why. And ouch, not so hard, Bets."

"Sorry. I get nervous when people make announcements about killers and then point at me. So, why? Why would a vampire want to kill other vampires?"

"If we knew the why, we'd know the who," Tina said, sounding like an undead Dr. Seuss.

"You at least know where your funding comes from," Sinclair said. It wasn't a question.

"All funds required for our activities are wired from a Swiss bank account," Father Markus explained.

"Ah, the Swiss," Tina muttered. "Accommodating financiers to Nazis, third-world dictators, and vampire killers."

Nobody said anything to that.

Father Markus cleared his throat. "All our instructions and intel arrive via anonymous e-mails."

"Intel?" I smirked. Someone's been watching too many *Alias* reruns.

"Devo is our computer expert, but even he has been unable to trace the e-mails."

"Oh, you bothered to try?" Sinclair asked politely. Even seated, he dwarfed everyone at the table. "I thought you had just taken your marching orders and off you went like good little meat puppets."

"Sinclair!" I gasped. Meat puppets? Where had he picked *that* up?

"So who's a suspect?" Jessica asked quickly. She got up to pace, which was always annoying; but she'd been doing it for fifteen years and wasn't likely to stop now. "I mean, assuming you guys are interested in finding out."

"Of course we are," Father Markus said, offended.

"Why?" Tina challenged. "We're still vampires. You're still our food."

"I am not, young lady," Father Markus said sternly, which was a laugh, because Tina had about ninety years on him. "And it's one thing to assume you're doing the Lord's work, and another to find out you're being used and you don't know why, or by whom."

Tina actually looked chastened; Sinclair mostly looked amused.

"What, find out?" Marc shook his head. "You always knew you were being used. You just didn't care until an upstanding citizen pointed it out."

Father Markus shrugged, but his color was high, like he was embarrassed but didn't want to say anything else.

"So, we think it's a vampire," Jessica said, crunching crumbs into the carpet as she got up to pace. *Dammit!* "Well, there's a pretty good suspect right here in this room."

"Who?" I asked, surprised.

"Me," Sinclair said.

"Well, if you've been sending us all that money," Ani said sweetly, "thanks."

"Oh, come on. Sinclair the Puppet Master? Well, okay, *that* makes sense, but he wouldn't kill vampires. Right? Right."

"Why not?" Marc asked. "No offense, Sinclair, but you're not exactly the type to enjoy competition."

"You are a keen observer, Dr. Spangler."

Marc glowed under the sarcastic praise. *I* wanted to know how Sinclair knew Marc's last name . . . I'd never told him.

"And now that Nostro's dead," Marc continued, like a gay, male, younger version of that old lady from *Murder, She Wrote,* "you can thin the herd a little more. And you can sure afford to finance the Blade Warriors."

"That's ridiculous!" I said hotly. "He's a loathsome crumb and an overbearing control freak, but he wouldn't start slaughtering his own people."

"Thank you, Elizabeth," he said politely.

"Well, he might," Tina said with her trademark ruthless honesty, "but he'd do it himself. He wouldn't farm the work out to a bunch of pimply . . . um, to other people."

"Also," Sinclair added quietly, "I would never harm the queen."

I grinned in spite of myself. *He likes me, he really really likes me!*

"Then there's you, Bets," Jessica said, and my grin fell off my face. "It's pretty well known you hate being the queen, and that you can't stand most vampires. Plus, you're not exactly the type to get your hands dirty. It'd be just like you to hire a group to do the work for you."

I wanted to say something like, "Knock it off!" or "Drop dead!" But nothing she had said was untrue. So I just drank tea and glared.

"Except she has no interest—or participation—in vampire politics. And she wouldn't know who was a vampire and who wasn't. Not to mention, she doesn't have the money to fund this operation. Which brings us," Sinclair added lazily, "to you, Jessica."

"Oh, come on!" I yelled.

But Jess was unfazed. "True, I'm a pretty good suspect." She started ticking the reasons off on her long fingers. "I've got the money. I'm sympathetic to my friend's plight—namely, that she doesn't want to be queen of the vamps. I don't much give a crap if vampires get killed or not—sorry, guys. I'm rich enough to be able to hide my tracks. Except there's one problem."

"She isn't the one," Father Markus said.

"No?" Jessica smiled.

"No," he said firmly. "I've known your family since you were small, Miss Watkins. It's not in you."

"You knew my father, right?" she said, hanging onto her smile.

"I did. It's not in *you,*" he repeated stubbornly.

"Hello?" a voice said, and then Monique stuck her head through the doorway. Tina and Sinclair didn't move, but the rest of us jumped a foot. "Did I miss anything?"

"Who is *that?*" Jon slobbered.

"Never you mind. What are you doing here, Monique?"

"Nobody was at the hotel, so I made an educated guess. What's going on? My, what a beautiful room." She settled herself between Tina and me, looking adorable in beige capris and a red sleeveless sweater.

"We're trying to figure out who the Puppet Master is," I explained. "Um, Monique, you're not rich, are you?"

She was pouring herself a cup of tea, and didn't spill a drop. "Oh, good gosh no," she said mildly. "Not compared to some." She raised her eyebrows and nodded at Sinclair and Jessica.

"And what of the good Detective Berry?" Sinclair asked.

"What, Nick?" I was totally surprised. He wouldn't have occurred to me in a million years.

"Isn't it true that he's reappeared in your life after a three month absence? And as a member of the police force, he has access to information the rest of us can only dream of."

"Yeah, but . . . he's so nice."

"He didn't look terribly nice when he was drooling and cringing and crawling around your carpet last spring," Tina said frankly.

"But he doesn't remember any of that!"

"Doesn't he?"

I fell silent; I had no idea what Nick remembered.

"After his experience with us, he has good reason to hate vampires," Sinclair added.

"The trouble is," Tina said, "we have too many suspects. It could be any one of Nostro's followers. Betsy isn't exactly . . . ah . . . acknowledged by all of us as the rightful queen."

"Mongrels," Monique said under her breath.

"Some vampires might perceive that as a chance to seize power," Tina continued.

"Which eliminates the number of suspects to about three hundred," I said glumly.

"More like two hundred thousand," Sinclair corrected.

"That's how many vampires are running around on the planet?" Ani asked, looking appalled.

"Give or take a few hundred."

We batted the subject around a while longer, but soon enough it was close to four in the morning and we decided to call it quits. Also, we were out of tea and the rest of the cookies were squashed.

Tina and Sinclair left first, giving the Blade Warriors their backs, which was a major diss, but I kind of liked them for it. I wanted to know how they'd known to come back earlier tonight. I started to follow them out when Ani grabbed my arm.

"Uh . . . Betsy . . . Betsy's okay, right?"

"It's my name," I said, puzzled, as Marc and Jessica filed past us, arguing, as usual.

"I was . . . uh . . . I was wondering about Tina."

"Tina?"

"Short, good legs, blond hair, big pretty eyes—Tina."

"Oh," I said, catching on, "*that* Tina. What about her?"

"What's her, you know, her situation?" Ani was practically jumping from one foot to the other—I wondered if she'd had too much tea. "Is she with that Sinclair guy?"

"Uh, no." *I am. Sort of.*

"So what's her story?"

"She's a hundred-year-old vampire who could eat you for

breakfast before snapping your spine like a drumstick," I said, deciding to nip this in the bud right now. "She's loyal to Sinclair, fierce as shit, stubborn as hell, and a killer on a liquid diet. That's her story."

"Right, but is she seeing anyone?"

"Ani, you're a vampire killer!"

"Well, you guys have spent the whole night explaining that some of you are good," she snapped back. "You're the furthest thing from a vampire I've ever seen. You're like those cheerleaders I went to high school with. I think in the interest of live-to-undead personal relations—"

"Oh, ick. Go away. No, she's not seeing anyone. But being that the last time you two met, you tried to cut her head off, I foresee problems in this burgeoning relationship—*aagghh!*"

Tina had stuck her head through the door. Dammit! I was tying bells to her *and* Sinclair. "Ani, dear, you left your headlights on," she said. "I thought you might like to know."

"Thanks!" she said, leaping past me and practically knocking me into the table. "I'll take care of that right now. And I . . . I've been meaning to talk to you. To . . . um . . . apologize for trying to kill you and everything."

"That's all right, dear. You didn't know any better."

"Right! That's exactly right! I thought all blood suckers were heartless killers, but I see now that maybe I was wrong." The door slammed behind them, but I could still hear Ani. "Maybe we could talk it over a cup of coffee or something . . . sometime . . ."

"Ick," I said again, but who was paying attention? Nobody.

# Chapter 16

I opened my eyes to see Marie hovering over me.

"You've got to stop doing that," I said, throwing back my comforter with a groan.

"I'm bored."

"Well, sugar, what the hell am I supposed to do about it? Go find your dad."

"And you never wake up when I talk to you."

"Never mind about that." I yawned. Another night in the salt mines. "Scoot, I've got to get dressed for work."

I jumped in the shower, got cleaned up, and dressed for work. Marie had indeed scooted, and for a change I had my bedroom to myself.

Jessica tapped on the door while I was putting on my mascara, and I yelled for her to come in.

"Evening, dead girl. Um. Why are your books all facing the wrong way?"

I shrugged.

"Fine, be mysterious. Sinclair called. He's bringing some people over tonight."

"That's nice. I'm not going to be here, though."

"Ooooh, the diss *du jour*."

"It's not a diss; I've got to work. Besides, it serves him right for not even asking if he can come over."

"Yeah, that'll learn him. Listen, are you going to keep an eye on the Blade Warriors, or what?"

"Me?" I said, appalled. And what was I thinking when I

bought navy blue mascara? The new black, my foot. My eyelashes looked cyanotic. "Why the hell would I do that?"

"Well, you want to make sure they're not going to run around axing any more vamps, right?"

"Why would they? We explained all that last night. About how they're toys in the hands of a fiendish master, blah-blah, time to stop killing dead people and figure out what's going on."

"I still think someone should keep an eye on them."

"*You* watch the zit brigade."

"Oh, that's nice," she said, but she laughed.

"Not a single one of them can walk into a bar and legally order a drink. I didn't like hanging around with teenagers when I *was* one."

"Says the former Miss Burnsville."

"I can't help it," I said with great dignity, "if my fellow inmates liked me more than I liked them."

"Maybe you can channel the Warriors' energy in a new direction," she suggested.

I nearly put my eye out with the mascara wand. "Maybe *you* can, you're so worried about it. I'm in charge of the dead people, not the live ones."

"Well, I think they're looking for direction." She added slyly, "Jon's already called for you five times."

"What, during the day? Idiot."

"I think he's got a crush."

"So that's where you're going with this. Great. Just what I need."

"Hey, there's worse problems to have."

"Name one."

"I can't right now. But I'm sure something will come to me," she added cheerfully.

I was in a fairly foul temper when I stomped out of the house. Unfortunately, I wasn't quite quick enough. I ran into Sinclair, Tina, Monique, and a vampire I didn't know on my way to the car.

"How nice of you to come out to meet us," Sinclair said. "Are you feeling all right?"

"I'm on my way to work." I glanced at my watch. "In fact, I've got about twenty minutes to get there. Bye."

"This is Sarah," he continued as if I hadn't spoken. "Sarah, this is Elizabeth the First, our sovereign."

The First? I was a First?

Sarah nodded coolly. She was short, about Tina's height, with close-cropped brown hair and brown eyes with green flecks. She was wearing black slacks, a sleeveless black turtleneck, and croc-odile flats. Her slacks were belted, also via crocodile. Sharp!

"Sarah's in town to pay her respects," Tina said, breaching the silence.

"Hardly," Sarah sniffed. Tina jabbed her in the side with her elbow, but Sarah's expression didn't change.

"Nice to meet you," I said, trying to lighten the tension. One thing about dead people, once they'd been vampires for a few de-cades, they really figured out the style thing. "Great shoes."

"You killed Nostro." It wasn't a question.

"Well, yes."

"*You* did."

"Sarah . . ." Sinclair warned.

"Hey, it was self-defense! Sort of. Okay, not really. I mean, it was self-defense in the sense that he eventually would have tried to kill me again, and he'd already tried to kill me twice—or was it three times?—and I sort of caught him between attempts, but it's not like I started anything. *He* started it! And I didn't exactly do the deed myself, you know. I mean, I was responsible and all, because I set the Fiends on him, but I didn't actually bite his head off."

Sarah was staring at me. Tina was staring at the ground and nibbling on her lower lip, and Sinclair had his eyes closed.

"What?" I griped. "I'm just telling her what happened. And now I really, really have to go. Go in if you want, Jessica's home, but next time call first so I can be home when you come over." Ha! Not likely. But it was the polite thing to say.

"I'm not going in that house," Sarah said.

"What have you got against my house? Are you the one Tina and Monique tried to bring over the other night, but you got pissy and walked away?"

"I did not get pissy."

"Okay, whatever." God, what a weirdo! "Never mind, I don't want to know. Listen, I'm going to be late."

"So you keep saying," Tina teased, "but I notice you're not go-ing anywhere."

"We have pressing business," Sinclair-the-killjoy reminded me.

"Give me a break. You guys don't need me to figure out who the Puppet Master is. Go talk to the Warriors some more."

"Actually, they're meeting us here." He whipped out a card.

From where, I had no idea—he wasn't wearing a suit jacket and his shirt didn't have any pockets. "We made the arrangements last night, and Jon gave me this."

"They've got business cards?" I rolled my eyes. "Jesus, why am I not surprised?" They all flinched. "And will you guys stop jumping like you've been goosed every time I take the Lord's name in vain?"

"Some things you cannot order," Sarah said, still ice-cool.

"Yeah, well, okay. Bye."

I walked past them and felt their eyeballs on me all the way to my car. Which was just as unpleasant as it sounds.


"YOU don't want that one," I whispered. "They say it's hand-stitched, but they lie."

"Oh-ho," my would-be shoe buyer said. "Tricky tricky."

"You might try one of the Pradas," I suggested. "I know she's really ubiquitous, but she deserves it. Look at the design! It's like a kimono for your foot."

"It's nice, but—"

"Holy God, it's true. You really do work at Macy's!"

I turned. Jon, weirdo leader of the Blind Warriors and surfing beach escapee, was standing by the cash register, staring at me with his mouth open so wide, I could see his fillings.

"What?" I snapped. Then, mindful of my customer, I forced a smile. "I'll be with you in a minute."

"No rush. I've got plenty of shoes," he retorted, grinning.

I turned back to my customer, who was determinedly jamming a size seven Escada onto her size nine foot. "Stop that," I said. "You'll ruin the lacing. Let me get you one in your size."

"This-is-my-size," she puffed.

Fine, enjoy blisters the size of plums. "I'll be over here if you need me," I said sweetly, then seized Jon by the elbow and hustled him over by the boots. He yelped as his feet left the floor. I put him down and hissed in his ear, "What are you doing here?"

"Wanted to see if it was true," he whispered back, his breath tickling my ear. "Are you sure you're a vampire?"

"You would not believe how many people ask me that."

"I'll bet," he said, staring at my name tag.

"What do you want?"

"Are you going to eat your customer?"

"No!"

"Don't yell, I was just asking. Can't we all just get along?"

"Says the vampire killer."

"I've reformed," he said, sounding hurt.

"Hmmm."

"Why are you wearing sunglasses inside at night?"

"Because I'm a big Corey Hart fan?" I guessed.

His blank stare reminded me that I was dating myself. Obviously the boy wasn't up on his '80s pop. "Never mind. Did Sinclair put you up to this? Oh, God—he's not here, is he?" I looked around wildly, but only saw retail customers.

"Is he your boyfriend?"

"Are you in law school? What's with the twenty questions? And no, he is not."

"Because he sort of acts like he is."

"One of the many, many reasons why I despise him. Now will you take a hike? You should be meeting with Sinclair and Tina and figuring out who sent you out to kill us, not bugging me."

He shifted from one foot to another. "Well . . . Ani's there, she's the brains, not me."

"Ani, the brains?"

"So I figured I'd come and see you. But if you really want me to go."

"Finally, he catches on! Yes, I really want you to go. Thanks a ton for stopping by," I said, giving him a gentle shove in the direction of the exit. "Bye!"

He turned and started walking backward, his hands stuffed in his faded jeans which were, I might add, about three sizes too small. His blond hair gleamed under the fluorescent lights, and even from eight feet away I could see how blue his eyes were, and how well he filled out his T-shirt. He practically radiated Good Boy Vibe. "I'm sorry I tried to kill you," he called, still walking backward.

I mimed locking my lips shut and throwing the key over my shoulder. He flashed another grin—product of a really excellent dental plan—turned around, and left in the direction of Orange Julius.

Nice kid. If Jessica was right, and he did have the hots for me, I'd have to squash him gently. For one thing, he was ten years younger. For another, he was alive. For another, I was a vampire and he was a vampire killer.

Besides, between work, and the queen of the dead thing, and fending off Sinclair, I just didn't have time to cram a boyfriend into my schedule.

Too bad.

# Chapter 17

My cell phone rang while I was on 494 West. I kept forgetting to change the tones, so it burbled "Funkytown" at me when it rang.

"Hello?"

"Hey, where are you?" Jessica. "I'm entertaining Sinclair and Tina all night, here."

"I care! It's their own fault for not calling ahead. I'm on my way to check on the Fiends."

"Ooooh, cool. When are you going to bring me to meet them?"

"Never."

"Oh, come on!" she whined.

"Forget it. They're too dangerous."

"You say that about all the fun stuff," she pouted.

"Oh, yeah, real fun. Crazed bloodsuckers who are more animal than human. Hey, trust me on this, if they weren't my responsibility, I wouldn't go near them."

"Fine, fine. Catch you later."

"Give Sinclair a smack for me." I disconnected and tossed my phone onto the seat beside me. It was too bad I couldn't grant her request, but I wasn't about to take chances with her life. Even if she did have my car windows fixed while I was sleeping.

I pulled up to Nostro's house. He'd made the Fiends, as a sort of twisted experiment, and we still kept them at his house. Why not? He sure didn't need it anymore.

The Fiends were what happened when you didn't let a newborn vampire feed. They went out of their minds with hunger and lost most of their I.Q. Not to mention their ability to walk on two legs and bathe regularly. It was disgusting and sad at the same time.

I went around to the barn in the back—probably the only barn in Minnetonka—and observed the Fiends gamboling in the moonlight like big undead puppies. They rushed over to me when they smelled me and I patted a couple of them, feeling stupid. They had once been human, and I felt ridiculous treating them like pets. Of course, they acted like pets—hideously dangerous, unstable, bloodthirsty pets—but never mind.

"Majesty!"

Alice hailed me and hurried across the wide yard. She'd been about fourteen when Nostro had turned her, the big jerk. Perpetually in the throes of adolescence! Talk about your fate worse than death.

"Hi, Alice." She was looking especially cute in a blue jumper and a white blouse. Her curly red hair was caught back in a blue headband. Bare feet. Toenails painted sky blue. "How's it going?"

"Fine, Majesty."

"For the millionth time: Betsy."

"They seem happy to see you," she said, avoiding the whole name issue.

"Yeah. They look good. You're doing a great job."

Alice glowed. Or maybe it was because she'd recently fed; her cheeks were positively rosy. As for the Fiends, they drank pigs' blood, and the weekly butcher's bill was high indeed. This was extremely weird, as every vampire I'd ever met, including me, needed "live" blood.

Maybe because the Fiends were barely human, so to speak, they didn't have to have the stuff right from the source.

"I think they're getting better," Alice said. "I left them some books and they didn't shit all over them this time. They did nibble on them, though."

"I don't need to hear this. But thanks anyway. How are you doing?"

"Oh, well, you know," she said demurely. She gestured at the giant, empty house. "It's a little lonely out here once in a while, but Tina keeps me company."

"Well, jeez, Alice, you're not a prisoner. You can leave whenever you want. You don't have to live out here."

"This is my job now," she said seriously. "It's the most important thing there is."

"That's the spirit." I guess. "Uh . . . thanks again."

"I'm here to serve, Majesty."

"Cut that out. You have everything you need here?"

"Yes, of course," she said cheerfully.

It didn't look like it to me, but I suppose after living under Nostro's regime, playing zookeeper to a bunch of feral vampires was a walk in the park. Me, I'd have been bored out of my mind by now. But Alice never complained, and when I made noises about getting another vampire to take over Fiend duty, to give her a break, she practically cried.

"Well, I'll be out next week. You've got my cell. Call if you need anything."

"I certainly will, Majesty."

I sighed. "And work on the Betsy thing, will you?"

She just smiled.

"They should all be staked."

"Jesus!" I nearly jumped into Alice's arms. She put out a hand to steady me and then, as if afraid of touching my exalted self, pulled back. "Sinclair, I swear to God, if you don't stop doing that . . ." In the moonlight he looked like a moody devil.

"Majesty," Alice said, tipping her head deferentially.

"Alice," His Majesty said.

"What the hell are you doing here?" I asked, undeferentially.

He shrugged.

"Well, that was helpful. I was just about to leave. Don't be staking the Fiends after I go."

"I'll come with you."

Great. Why was that thought equally thrilling and annoying?

"See you, Alice."

"Majesties."

"Good night, Alice."

The Fiends whined when I left, but then I heard a splash and heard slurping—*yeerrgghh!* Feeding time at the zoo. I hoped Alice hadn't gotten her jumper all bloody.

Sinclair caught my hand and held it as we walked back to the cars. Awwww, just like an undead couple going steady! "There's been another killing," he said.

I nearly tripped over a gopher hole. "What? When? Why didn't you say anything a minute ago?"

"Tina and I think it's best to keep it from the other vampires until we find the culprit."

"Oh." Too bad they hadn't kept it from *me*. "Anybody we know?"

"No. A woman named Jennifer. Rather young for a vampire, in fact, Tina found her death certificate and it was less than twenty years old."

"A mere infant. Huh, that's weird. Jon didn't say a word tonight about killing somebody else. I'll strangle the little creep!"

Sinclair's grip tightened, ever so slightly. "You saw Jon tonight?"

"Yeah, he came to bug me at work."

"I'll speak to him about that."

"You will not," I said, irritated. "What, you're the only one allowed to bug me at work? And let go of my hand."

"Yes. And no."

"We're getting off the subject."

"A hazard in any conversation with you. But you're quite right. Jon and Ani swear they had nothing to do with it."

"You think they're on the up and up?"

"Yes. Tina concurs. Also, she was with Ani most of the evening."

"That's never going to work, FYI," I predicted. "Ani won't be Tina's pet, and you can't tell me Tina's looking for a girlfriend."

"I can't?"

"Plus, hello, they have *nothing* in common. Not to mention the age difference. The *hundred-year* age difference."

"I don't know that an age difference is so insurmountable," he said carefully, then added, "It's really none of our business."

"Oh, shut up. And let go of my hand!"

"I decline. Stop squirming. At any rate, this Jennifer is dead. Someone is still killing."

I kicked at a tuft of grass, which went flying like a divot on a golf course. "Well, at least the kids didn't screw us over. So now what?"

"Now we must examine the body. Maybe we'll find something we missed before."

I stopped short. Sinclair kept going, so I was nearly yanked off my feet. "Nuh-uh, count me out! *So* not on my to-do list for the night!"

"It's your responsibility," he said implacably.

"Forget it! Seriously, Eric, dead bodies creep me out. I can't even watch *Night of the Living Dead* by myself."

He rubbed his forehead as if a killer migraine had sprouted. "Elizabeth . . ."

"You're not really going to wreck my evening like this, are you?" I begged. "I just can't think of anything worse."

He laughed. "Sometimes . . . frequently . . . you're too adorable."

"Now who's getting off the subject? Like I haven't noticed you've led me to your car and are stuffing me—watch the hair!" I warned as he put his hand on my head and tucked me into the passenger side of his Lexus. "Dammit, Sinclair, this isn't over!"

"You can finish it," he said, climbing into the driver's seat, "on the way to the morgue."

FOR that extra creepy touch, the morgue was—get this—in my basement. That's right: *my* basement.

"Just kill me now," I muttered as we descended the stairs.

"Well, where else should we keep the body?" Marc asked, reasonably enough. He'd been key in the evening's body-snatching activities—people hardly ever questioned a doctor's movements. "The Marquette Hotel?"

"Anywhere but our damned house!"

"Oh, you're always complaining."

"Since April," I said darkly, "I've had a lot to complain about."

Marc pondered that one, then finally said, "True enough."

There was quite the party in the basement, though it took a while to find them—the basement ran the length of the house. There was a room on the far end that I'd never been in before, and that's where Tina, Monique, Sarah-the-weirdo, Ani, Jon, and Jessica were waiting for us. Oh, and the dead body. Can't forget that.

"I object again," Sarah said by way of greeting.

"Be quiet," Sinclair ordered.

"What is your problem with our house?" I asked, puzzled. "I mean, I get that you don't like me, if you were fond of Nostro, which calls your taste into severe question, by the way. But what have you got against my digs?"

"I used to work here," she said distantly. "I didn't like it then, and I certainly don't care to be here now."

"Well, sor*ry!* Nobody's making you stay."

"Untrue," Sinclair said, fixing Sarah with his dark gaze. She instantly stopped bitching and stared at the floor.

I wondered what the big deal was. Then it hit me: Sarah didn't like me, wasn't crazy about the fact that I'd killed Nostro, and had recently blown into town. If she had money, that made her a pretty good suspect. No wonder Sinclair wanted to keep her close.

Sarah looked up and said, "Nostro made me."

"Oh." Well, that explained it. He'd been an utter shit, but his vampires were weirdly loyal, especially the ones he made himself. It made zero sense to me, but what did I know about vamp politics? Nada.

"I had no real love for him," she was saying, "but he deserved my loyalty. He gave me immortality. He made me a goddess among men."

"And a weirdo among the rest of us." Her little revelation had just put her at the top spot of our list of suspects. I wonder if she knew? "Well, we'll just have to agree to disagree, I s'pose."

"I rather doubt that."

"Thank you all for coming," Tina said, cutting Sarah off as she opened her mouth again. "Especially on such a grim errand."

"I told you we needed a big house," Jessica whispered in my ear.

"Yeah, but . . . for this?"

I stepped closer. The dead vampire, Jennifer, was stretched out on the beat-up wooden table in the center of the room. In two pieces.

I gagged and turned my face away. I felt Sinclair rub my back and, weirdly, I took strength from that, and after a minute I was able to look. I wasn't the only one affected. Jessica was so pale she was more gray than brown, and Tina's big eyes were pools of sadness.

"Before you ask," Jon said, looking annoyingly unmoved, "we didn't cut off her head."

"If I thought you had," Sinclair said pleasantly, "there'd be another body here in two pieces."

"Don't start, you guys," I said automatically, as Jon paled and twitched toward his knife. "Don't you guys have *any* ideas? Anything at all?"

"This is the first killing that didn't happen on a Wednesday," Tina said.

"We always got together on Wednesdays," Ani said. She was walking around the table, inspecting poor headless Jennifer. "It was the only day all our work schedules lined up."

"Ah-ha!" I said. "See, that was my theory all along. Remember, the night Tina and Monique got attacked?"

"Yes, yes, you're very clever," Sinclair said absently. He was prowling right behind Ani, also looking at the body.

"Don't tell me," I said to Jon. "Radio Shack."

"How'd you know?"

"Just a wild guess, Geek Boy. And what the hell's a Devo?"

"He's our computer expert. He—"

"She's been shot," Sinclair said.

"*And* beheaded? Talk about overkill," Jessica muttered. I shuddered.

"With vampires, it's best to be sure," Ani said, almost apologetically.

"Which reminds me," Tina said. "The bullet one of you shot into Her Majesty the Queen. It was a hollow point filled with holy water."

"No wonder it stung like crazy," I commented.

"And you *survived?*" Monique practically gasped. "I can't believe it!"

"Oh, well, you know," I said modestly. Monique was looking at me with total admiration, which was a pleasant change. Most vampires looked at me like I was a bug.

"Yes, our Elizabeth is just full of surprises," Sinclair said, ruining the moment with his sarcasm. "Which one of you Warriors thought up that charming little gift?"

After a moment's hesitation, Ani slowly raised her hand. She blushed as Tina looked at her reproachfully.

"Hmmm."

"Come on, take it easy on her," Marc said. "You have to admit, it's sort of brilliant."

"Yes, we have to admit that," Tina agreed. "I'll see if the bullets are still in the body. And if they're the same kind, we'll know that the Puppet Master—for want of a better phrase—killed Jennifer. Which is interesting."

I raised my hand. "Um, why?" It was much more gross than interesting, if you asked me. Which nobody had.

"Because we've—the Blade Warriors—agreed to stop killing vampires until we figure out who's been pulling our strings," Jon cut in. "I mean, we all talked last night, after we met you guys—"

"And had tea with us," I said with a triumphant look at Sinclair.

"—and decided to hold off for a while."

"For a while?" Tina and Sinclair asked in unison, equally sharply.

Jon ignored them. "We sent our boss an e-mail last night. But it looks like he's still killing vampires. Or he's found someone else to do it." He spread his hands, puzzled. "Well, how come? Is he targeting specific vampires, or is he an undead serial killer, or what? I mean, he had to go out and stake this vamp the minute he got our e-mail. Why?"

"If it's even a he," Monique piped up.

"Good point, uh—"

"Monique."

Jon could hardly take his eyes off her, which wasn't surprising. She was really beautiful, and dressed to kill in an Ann Taylor suit, black stockings, and black pumps. Her hair was almost silver against the black of the suit.

Frankly, I had met very few ugly vampires. One, to be exact. And he was more unwashed than unattractive.

Which made sense—every vampire I'd met had been a murder victim, killed by another vampire. And vampires seemed to seek out good-looking people to snack on. I guess because drinking blood seemed so sexual . . . most people wanted to boink good-looking partners. And most vampires wanted to drink from cuties.

Monique was gorgeous, there just wasn't any two ways about it. Tina wasn't exactly hard on the eyes, either. I could see that even Jennifer had been beautiful, though her long, brown hair was matted with blood, and—

"Wait a minute. Don't talk, don't talk!" I clutched my head and writhed.

"What the hell's wrong with you?" Marc asked.

"I know that look," Jessica said. "She's got an idea. Or she needs an Ex-Lax."

"Am I the only one who noticed that all the murder victims are women?" I cried. "Say it isn't so!"

Tina looked startled. "Well . . . yes, I suppose so. That's another thing they all had in common, besides taking place on Wednesdays, and—"

"Don't you guys think that's a little weird?" I asked Tina and Sinclair. Then I rounded on Jon and Ani. "Don't *you* guys?"

"It—uh—didn't make much difference to us," Ani coughed. "We figured you were all bad."

"We're feminists," Jon said, totally straight-faced. "Killing female vamps didn't bother us at all."

"This could shed light on the motive," Sinclair said.

"Ya think?" I asked sarcastically.

"The women all look different, right?" Jessica asked. "So it's not like the killer's going after a certain type. I mean, if he targeted Betsy *and* Tina *and* Monique . . . you three don't look a thing alike. You're not even the same build."

Meaning I'm a disgusting hulk who towers over the delicately built Tina and Monique . . . thanks.

"It's getting kind of late," Monique said after a long silence in which I contemplated my enormous bulk and the others contemplated who-knew-what. "Maybe we could pick this up tomorrow night?"

I had just gotten there, but I wasn't going to argue. Unfortunately, Monique's suggestion meant three nights in a row with these killjoys, trying to solve murders. I stifled the urge to remind them I was a former secretary, not a former homicide detective.

"Does someone have a knife?" Tina asked. "I'd like to see if I can get one of the bullets out."

"Oh, I'm so out of here," I said, turning away. Last straw, last straw! Overload! "Tina, you seriously need a hobby."

"Right now," she said grimly, "my hobby is catching whoever is doing this. I'll take up sewing later."

"I'm holding you to that," I muttered.

Sinclair handed her a pocket knife, which she unfolded with a loud *click*. The blade was almost four inches long—Sinclair was clearly a big believer in the Boy Scouts' Motto. Tina bent over Jennifer's body and started probing at her chest.

I practically ran up the stairs.

# Chapter 18

ON followed me all the way up to my bedroom. "You know," he said, stiff-arming the door open when I tried to close it on him, "I'm the one who talked the Warriors into backing off you guys."

"That's super. Your good citizenship medal is in the mail. Why don't you go home and wait for it?"

"It's just that after meeting you it didn't seem right."

"Okey-dokey. 'Night!"

"Yeah, um, listen, you don't need to bite anyone or anything, do you?" He sounded weirdly hopeful; I almost hated to tell him I didn't. And what kind of behavior was this for a vampire killer? "Did anybody ever tell you, you've got the prettiest green eyes?"

"They're not green; they're mold colored. Jon, I'm trying to get ready for bed, here," I said, trying to keep the exasperation out of my voice. "When the sun comes up, if I'm not in bed I'll keel over wherever I'm standing."

"Really? Like, no matter what you're doing, you'll just fall down asleep? Like, totally helpless and all?"

"It's not as exciting as it sounds." I put my hand on his face and gently shoved him backward. "So, good night."

"I'll see you tomorrow," he began, and then he was suddenly jerked out of sight. Then Sinclair was shouldering his way past me and kicking the door shut behind him.

"For crying out loud," I started in, "when did my bedroom become Grand Goddamned Central?"

Sinclair leaned against the door and crossed his arms over his chest. "I insist you discourage that infant immediately."

"In case you weren't paying attention, I *have* been. It's not my fault he's interested in vampires."

Sinclair snorted. "He is not. He's interested in you."

"Well, what am I supposed to do about it?" I bitched. "I've got enough problems right now."

"Problems, coupled with the prettiest green eyes," he said dryly.

"Eavesdropper! Go away, I have to get ready for bed."

"You're not going to wear those silly sushi-print pajamas, are you?"

"Hey, they're comfy. Go away."

"Remind me to buy you some decent night attire."

"I'm having bomb dogs sniff over anything you buy me." I tugged at the door knob, but he wouldn't budge. I slapped at his shoulder. "Will you get out of here? Don't you have to get back to the Marquette before you burst into flames?"

"Oh, I don't know," he replied casually. "There's plenty of room here. I thought I might stay."

I knew it, I *knew* living in a mansion was a bad idea. There was no graceful excuse to get out of having an overnight guest.

"Fine, whatever, but you're not sleeping in here."

"No?"

"No!"

"I'll go back to the Marquette," he suggested, "for a kiss."

"Fine, *fine,* jeez, you're so annoying." I snatched handfuls of his hair, jerked his face down to mine, kissed him on the bridge of the nose, and let go. He tried to grab me, but I was wise to his ways, and dodged his hands. "Now go away. Deal's a deal."

"Hmph." But he left. Thank goodness! I think

I woke up the next night and lay there for a minute, feeling anxious but not sure why. Then I remembered: murders, playing detective, Jon and Sinclair. And that was just the stuff on the top of my brain.

Marie was sitting in the chair beside my bed, looking reproachful.

"What?" I asked.

"You used to be around here a lot more," she said wistfully.

"Sorry, sunshine. There's stuff going on . . . never mind." I wasn't going to talk about beheadings with a kindergartener. Instead, I sat up and swung my legs over the side of the bed. "You see anything wrong with these pajamas?"

"No. I like them."

"Exactly!" Stupid Sinclair. "Well, I have some stuff to do tonight, but maybe tomorrow we could—ow!" I'd tripped climbing off my bed (it was the size of a train car) and fell into Marie.

Actually, I fell *through* Marie. It was like plunging into a lake in February. I hit the carpet with a thump and could see her little feet, sticking through my arm.

"Jesus Christ," I said, and it was a good thing I didn't need to breathe, because right now I was breathless.

"Don't be mad," Marie said anxiously. "I didn't want to tell you."

"Oh my *God*. You're . . . you . . ." I waved my hand through her head. Holy shit on toast! There was a ghost in my bedroom!

I scrambled to my feet and lunged through my bedroom door, totally ignoring Marie's pleas to come back. Good thing the door was open, or I would have crashed through it. I nearly knocked Jessica down the stairs and went straight out the front door, where I slammed into Sinclair so hard, I bounced off him and lay on the sidewalk like a stunned beetle.

"I thought you were going to get rid of those ridiculous pajamas."

I jumped up and practically climbed him like a tree. "Eric, Eric, the worst, the absolute worst . . . in there . . . in my room . . ." I pointed to the house.

He grabbed my arms. "What's wrong? Are you hurt? Did someone touch you? Is Jon here? I'll pull out his carotid if he—"

"My room . . . in my room . . . up there . . . Marie . . . in my room—"

"Majesty! Calm down. What's wrong?" Tina, running up the sidewalk. They must have just pulled up. Nice! Don't call or anything, you guys. Even in the midst of total panic, I felt annoyed. "Did someone try to kill you again?"

"I wish! In my room, there's a dead girl in my room!"

"There's a dead girl out here," Sinclair said, puzzled.

"Not me, fool!"

"Come on. Show me." He tucked my hand into his and started up the walk.

I yanked on his hand so hard he nearly fell over backward. "No! I can't go back in there, Eric, I can't! I'll go stay with you at the Marquette, okay? Only let's go right now, okay? I'll drive. Let's go! Okay?"

Eric's dark eyebrows shot up so high, I thought they'd leave his forehead. "Well," he said slowly, "if you feel that strongly about it . . ."

"Don't you *dare,*" Tina said. "Opportunistic bastard. She doesn't know what she's saying."

"Is that any way to talk to your king?" he asked, sounding wounded.

She snorted. "When the king's acting like an ass, yes. Come on, Majesty. Let's go see your dead girl."

"You guys are insane! I'm not going back in there ever again!"

"What about your shoes?"

Good point. I had to get them out! I didn't know if Marie could slime them with ghostly protoplasm, but I wasn't about to take the chance. "Will you come with me?" I asked, trying not to sound as pathetic as I felt. "Both of you?"

"Yes, of course." Sinclair patted me. Too bad I couldn't work up much mad about it—I had bigger problems. "Don't be frightened. I can hardly believe this is the woman who set the Fiends on Nostro."

"*Totally* different."

"Frankly, I always thought you were too flighty and capricious to ever feel true fear."

I jerked my hand out of his. "Fuck you, too."

"Ah, that's better. The true Queen has rejoined us."

Jessica opened the door, disheveled and annoyed. "You nearly killed me!" she yelled. "What the hell's going on?"

I was shivering like a wet dog. "You won't even believe it."

She followed the three of us up the stairs, bitching nonstop, until I got to my room and rushed through the doorway before I could lose my nerve. Marie was still in her chair, but her lower lip was pooched out and she glared at me.

"There! Dead girl!"

"What are you talking about?" Jessica asked.

Sinclair shook his head. "I don't see anyone, Elizabeth."

I pointed. "But she's *right* there. In the chair by my bed. See?"

They were all staring at me. So was Marie, for that extra creepy touch.

I tried again. "She's right over there. Overalls, headband. Saddle shoes! How can you not see those darling shoes?" I turned to Tina and Sinclair. "You guys see her, right? Super vampire vision, or whatever?"

"No," Tina said apologetically.

"Sure you do. She's right there!"

"I'm sorry, Majesty. No." Then Sinclair, still staring, struck her on the elbow, and her eyes widened. "Yes."

"You guys are nuts," Jessica said. "I'm straining my eyes so hard I've got a headache. There's nothing there."

"There is," Sinclair said. "A girl-child. Blonde. Big eyes. Messy hair."

"Ha! So you *do* see her!"

"We see her," Sinclair said carefully, "because you have willed us to."

Oh, now what bullshit was this? "What are you talking about?"

"You've forced us to see," Tina explained.

"What are you guys talking about?" Jessica practically yelled.

Just then, Marie burst into tears. "Stop it!" she sobbed. "I hate that! I hate when people talk about me like I'm not here!"

"Jeez, hon, don't do that," I said quickly.

"What?" Jessica asked.

"She says she doesn't like it when we talk about her like she's not here."

"Tell her we're sorry," Jessica said, rolling her eyes.

Marie cried harder. "I can hear *you*."

"Jessica, get lost," I snapped. "You're not helping at all."

"Gladly! Hallucinating bloodsuckers I do *not* need. Plus, I missed my nap today and I'm getting sick of these midnight meetings." She stormed out, slamming the door behind her.

"Marie." I was finally starting to calm down. I mean, the kid was dead and all, but she hadn't scared me on purpose. And she was so little. "Marie, why didn't you tell me you were . . . uh . . ."

"Because I knew you'd be like this," she said, still crying.

I couldn't stand it. The poor kid! Dead and stuck in this oversized starter home with *me*. For eternity!

I swiftly crossed the room, knelt, and hugged her. And nearly let go of her. It was like embracing an ice sculpture. But at least I could touch her now. "Don't cry," I said into her teeny, perfect, ghostly ear. "We'll fix it."

She sniffed and hugged me back. Pretty good grip for a little kid, too. "No you won't. Nobody can."

"We're not like the other people who have lived here," Sinclair commented.

I turned and looked at him, pulling Marie into my lap. "What, you can hear her now?"

"Yes. She was very faint at first, but now I can hear her and see her perfectly well." He was giving me the strangest look. "Thanks to you."

"Oh, stop it. Listen, Marie, is there a reason you're stuck here? Do we need to find your . . . uh . . . bones or something?"

"No."

"It's okay, we don't mind looking."

"The perfect activity for a Sunday night," Sinclair muttered.

I ignored him, warming to my subject. "Yeah, we'll look. Then, when we find your . . . when we find you, we can give you a proper burial, and you can go to Heaven!"

"I'm buried in the front yard," she said. "Under the fence on the left side, by the big elm tree."

I tried not to barf. Bodies of little girls in my front yard! Jesus! "Well . . . uh . . . that's . . ." I was totally at a loss for words.

"Marie," Tina said, squatting until they were eye level, "why are you here, darling?"

"I'm waiting for my mom."

"And when did you . . . when did people stop being able to see you?"

Marie looked confused. "I'm five," she finally said. "I've been five for a long time."

Tina tried again. "What year were you born?"

"My birthday's in April," she said proudly. "That's the diamond month! April tenth, nineteen forty-five."

There was a pause, then Tina said tactfully, "Well . . . sweetie . . . chances are your mother is already dead. Why don't you try to find her? I'm sure she's waiting for you."

"She's not dead," Marie said solemnly, her big teary eyes fixed on Tina's dark gaze.

"How d'you know?" I asked curiously.

"Because I'm still *here*."

"And you've been here . . . all this time?"

She nodded.

"Holy shit," I commented. It was just like that little weirdo in *The Sixth Sense*! I saw dead people!

Now it made sense. The way the house kept changing hands. The owner's desperation to sell. The continually plummeting price. The way Marie wouldn't eat or drink with me. The way she was always around, no matter what time it was. Maybe ordinary humans couldn't see Marie, but some of them must have known something was wrong, because this house had been on the market for ages.

"Can we . . ." I swallowed. "Can we dig you up and put you somewhere else?"

Marie shrugged.

*Memo to me: Dig up dead kid ASAP and move her OUT OF FRONT YARD.*

"This is all very interesting," Sinclair commented, "and bears further scrutiny, but we have work to do."

"Eric Sinclair, you heartless bastard!" I covered my mouth. "Oh, shit, I shouldn't have said that. Oh, *shit,* I shouldn't have said *that!*"

Marie was giggling through her fingers. "It's all right," she told me. "I know those words. One time when the workmen were fixing the basement and one of them dropped a cement block on his foot—"

"Never mind, I can guess the rest."

"It's not personal, dear," Sinclair told Marie gently. "But we have more time-sensitive matters to attend to."

"Jerkoff," I coughed into my fist.

"She's been here for over half a century," he pointed out. Then he looked directly at Marie. "No one will forget about you."

"It's all right," she said at once. "Betsy can see me. She could always see me. And she can *touch* me. You'll come back, won't you?"

"Bet on it. Besides, I have no choice. I live in this fu— this mausoleum. But *no* creeping around and scaring the crap out of me anymore, agreed?"

"Hmph. Okay."

"It *is* fun to watch her jump," Sinclair told Marie, who laughed again.

"What's the rush?" I asked. "Did somebody else get . . . uh . . . did something else happen?"

"There are a few vampires in town who wish to pay their respects," Tina explained.

"Ugh."

"Sorry. And the bullets I . . . ah . . . found last night did match the ones the kids were using."

"Oh-ho."

"So we have things to discuss."

"Right." I turned to Marie. "Boring grown-up stuff, sorry. But I'll be back."

"I'll be here," she said, without the slightest trace of irony.

# Chapter 19

THE berating started as soon as we left the house. "How could it have escaped your notice that Marie was a ghost?" Sinclair asked. "You've lived in this house how many weeks now?"

"Hey, I've had a lot of things on my mind," I said defensively. "What, I'm gonna interrogate a five-year-old? Besides, she never told me."

"But didn't you realize that she always wore the same outfit?"

"Clearly, you haven't known a lot of kids. They can be stubborn little ticks. Heck, when I was in second grade I wore the same pair of shoes for two months."

"I have to admit, I never thought I'd see something like that," Tina said as we all piled into Sinclair's convertible. At least it wasn't red. For a taciturn dead guy, he could be a flashy son of a bitch. "And I've lived a long, long time."

"See what? A ghost? Yeah, it was weird, all right. Man, I'm still creeped out about it."

"Well, try to get a grip on yourself," Sinclair advised, starting the engine, which kicked over with a rumbling purr. "It's inappropriate for the queen of the dead to be afraid of ghosts."

"I must have missed that memo," I grumped.

"I've never seen a ghost before tonight," Tina commented.

"Nor have I," Sinclair added. He backed out of the driveway without looking. Showoff.

"Really? But you guys are so much deader than I am." Hmm, that didn't come out quite right. "I mean, you've been around longer." Way, way, way longer.

"Being able to see and speak with the dead—all dead—is strictly a province of the Queen. And, if she chooses, her Followers."

"Seriously? Huh. How d'you know?"

"Foretold," Tina and Sinclair said simultaneously.

Then Tina added, "It was in the Book of the Dead. 'And the Queene shall noe the dead, all the dead, and neither shall they hide from her nor keep secrets from her.' Like that."

I nearly hit the canvas roof. "Goddamn it. Goddamn it!" Sinclair almost drove off the road and Tina cringed, but I was too mad to care. "I'm *so* sick of this! Something completely weird happens to me, and you guys are all, 'Oh, yeah, that's in the Book of the Dead, too, did we forget to mention it?' Well, no more! We're sitting down *right now* and reading the whole nasty thing from beginning to end. Where is it? Is it at the hotel? Let's go find it right now."

"We can't," Sinclair said.

"Why not?"

"Because to read it too long in one sitting is to go insane."

"Oh, that's your excuse for everything," I snapped. I crossed my arms over my chest and wouldn't speak to them until we got to the hotel.

THREE unproductive hours later, I stomped up the sidewalk and through the front door, and immediately threw myself face down on the couch in the entry hall.

"What a fucking disaster," I said to the cushion.

"What's the matter?" It was Marc, standing somewhere to my right. "Are you okay?"

"No."

"They'll come around," Tina said apologetically. "They just need time."

"Ha!"

"What's wrong?" Jessica, hurrying down the stairs. It was amazing how, even though I couldn't see them, I knew exactly where they were. It was amazing that it was almost dawn and they'd been waiting up for me. It was also amazing that this eighty-year-old sofa smelled like popcorn. "Was there another killing?"

"No," Tina said. "We met some other vampires tonight, ones who recently came into town. It . . . ah . . . didn't go well."

"Quite right," Sinclair said, sitting down beside me. "And that's very interesting."

I flopped over and glared at him. Interesting my ass. "How?"

The vampires—there were about half a dozen of them—had done their best to ignore me, and it was so damned chilly in that room from their hostile vibes that I got the shivers.

Oh, they were perfectly deferential to Sinclair, and there was all sorts of "My King" this and "Your Majesty" that, but nobody talked to me at all.

"They're just jealous," Tina said, before Sinclair could answer. She sat down in the chair opposite the couch—this entryway was practically a fourth living room—and looked at me sympathetically. "No vampire in the history of human events has been able to do what you do."

"So?"

"Betsy, you wear a cross around your neck as everyday jewelry! Half the time I can barely look at you."

"Oh, *that* makes me feel better."

"You know what I mean," she said gently. "And in their defense, this has happened very quickly. Many of them have been under Nostro for a hundred years or more. You've been in power for three months."

"So has Sinclair," I pointed out. "And nobody has been giving him the deep freeze."

"Uh," Tina replied, and that was about it.

"They're jerks, but you knew that," Jessica said. "Why's it getting you down now, all of a sudden?"

"Good question. I dunno. It's been a sucky week. And I forgot I was supposed to work tonight. That's twice I had to blow off Macy's. My boss is *not* pleased. And they—the other vamps— they were really cold to me. It was like Antarctica in that hotel room."

"Actually, this is very promising," Sinclair said. "We have our motive."

"What? We do?"

"I was curious to see how out-of-town vampires would react to you, which is why we needed you tonight. And it's patently clear you have aroused much resentment in the vampire community."

"Buncha crybabies."

"I suspect there is a price on your head. In fact . . ." He paused; he had everyone's full attention, and probably found it surprising. "In fact, I suspect these murders are part of a plot to put you out of the way."

"What?" Marc, Jessica, and I all yelped in unison.

Tina was rubbing her eyes. "Oh, shit," she said quietly. "Yes, it fits, doesn't it?"

"Is that why all the other victims were women?" Marc asked skeptically.

Jessica jumped in with, "But why kill other vamps at all?"

"Practice," Tina said. "Working their way up to you, Majesty."

"That's the worst thing I've ever heard!" I sat up in horror. "You guys can't be right. No way!"

"It sort of makes a ton of sense," Jessica said quietly.

"No. That's . . . that's just wrong. On about thirty different levels." Killing people to get in the habit of it? Working their way up to me? I was suddenly swamped with guilt. Poor Jennifer! She wasn't even a true victim; she was *practice*. "Nostro was in power for about a billion years and nobody tried to off him; I'm around since springtime and it's open season?"

"In a word, yes."

"But—"

"You're very threatening to many vampires," Tina said. "You go your own way. You aren't dependent on anyone's protection. You don't need shee . . . ah, human companionship. We have to feed every day, Majesty. *Every* day. As best I can determine, you can go as long as a week without feeding." Actually, my record was ten days, but that was nobody's business. "You are immune to sunlight—"

"If I'm so immune, how come I go down like a rookie boxer whenever the sun comes up?" I grumbled.

"Everyone needs to rest sometime," Sinclair said, managing to sound smug and soothing at the same time.

"Crosses, and holy water," Tina continued to drone. "The Fiends, whom you did not make, obey your every whim. You have a wealthy benefactor. The king . . ." She trailed off, and it was like she rearranged what she was going to say, because she just finished with, "The king is fond of you also."

Yeah, fond like a wolf is fond of raw beef. "So? Why do they care? It's not like I was overly involved in vampire politics."

"Not yet," Sinclair said.

"Oh. This sucks. This totally and completely sucks. The vampires all hate me and everyone's trying to kill me!"

"Not all," Sinclair said, totally straight-faced. "However, this brings up a vital point: you need a guard. Humans during daytime hours, and loyal vampires in the evening. The Puppet Master isn't likely to stop anytime soon."

This was getting better and better. If I was still alive, I'd have a splitting headache by now. I flopped back down on the couch and sighed. "I just can't believe it." But that was a lie. Tina was right; in a really really bad way, it *did* all fit.

"Keep Sarah close," Tina said after a long silence.

"I concur; she's a good suspect."

"She's a weirdo is what she is, and what are we going to do?" I put my hands over my eyes. "Oh, man, I really need to get out of here." I jumped off the couch and began to pace. "This has been the suckiest week since I died, I swear to God!"

"D'you want to go to Heaven?"

I was touched by the offer, and not a little surprised. Jessica hated shopping, and she practically loathed the Mall of America. I guess when you can buy every single thing six times over, it takes some of the fun out of window shopping.

"No. We can't, anyway . . . it's, like, three o'clock in the morning. The Mall's closed. Even the bars are closed."

"We could go bowling," Marc suggested brightly. "There's a really good twenty-four-hour lane not five minutes from here."

"B-bowling?" The room began to swim. I sat down before I fell—almost in Sinclair's lap. "You mean . . . with . . . with borrowed shoes?"

"What's the *matter* with you?" Jessica snapped at Marc. "Are you trying to make her more upset?"

"Jeez, sorry! I forgot how weird she was about her footwear."

"I'll be all right," I said faintly as Sinclair fanned me with a couch pillow. "I just need a minute."

"The Puppet Master doesn't have to cut off your head," Marc said. "He just has to put you in secondhand shoes. You'll off yourself in despair."

Sinclair laughed, and I snatched the pillow out of his hand and smacked him in the face with it.

# Chapter 20

MARIE was waiting for me when I finally went up to my room. I was glad to see her—I'd thought of a couple of things to ask her after we left earlier. And I'd do just about anything, even interrogate the ghost of a kindergartner, to take my mind off the problem *du jour*.

"Still haunting my room, huh?"

"I am not! I just like it in here."

"Uh-huh. Listen, I wanted to ask, how did you . . . uh . . . end up like this?"

She frowned, and a cute vertical line appeared between her eyebrows. "Gee. Nobody's ever asked me that before. O'course, nobody's really talked to me before you came."

Yeah, that whole queen of the dead schtick had all sorts of fringe benefits. I forced a smile as she continued. "Well. My mommy was working here. We used to sleep in Jessica's room. You know, when Mommy was done working. And once, a bad man came. I heard him come. I woke up and I ran out and saw him hurting Mommy, so I ran over to kick him, and he threw me really hard. And after that, nobody could see me anymore."

She must have hit her head and died, I thought. And then the asshole who tossed her like a tiddlywink buried the body in the front yard. Too bad nobody saw him and called the cops.

And why was that tickling my brain? There was something there, and I just couldn't get to it. Dammit! Why was I great-looking instead of a genius? Usually I didn't mind, but nights like this . . .

"Oh," I said finally, because really, what was there to say? "Well, thanks. I was just wondering."

"I wish my mom would come. I want her real bad."

For sixty years she'd been wanting her! Poor kid. It's funny how that's what was keeping her in the house where she'd been murdered. In the books the spirit can't rest until the killer's been brought to justice, or whatever, but this ghost was just hanging around, waiting for her mom.

In a minute, I was going to start bawling.

"Want to see my new dress?" I asked finally, desperate for a subject change. "I got it on sale. Sixty percent off!"

"Sure."

While I was doing my impromptu fashion show for Marie, I had a brainstorm. *I* would be her mom! I couldn't have kids of my own—I didn't pee anymore, much less ovulate. But I could look after Marie and maybe if she got used to me, she wouldn't miss her mom so much.

This was the most cheerful thought I'd had in a while. The whole "you'll never have a baby—ever" thing had been kind of bumming me out. Not usually, not even every day. But every once in a while that dark thought would sneak back and catch me by surprise.

Not that I wanted to have anyone's babies. Not anyone's in general, and certainly not Sinclair's. Like he could knock me up with his dead sperms, anyway. But still. It would have been nice to at least have the option.

But now I *had* options. I would . . , I would . . . I would adopt ghosts!

Well, okay. Like any plan, it needed work. What the hell, I had time.


THE next night, Jessica and I pulled up outside my father's house. It was much too big for two people, tucked away in the fashionable suburb of Edina, and was too expensive for the housing market. Which made it perfect for my stepmother, Antonia Taylor, aka the Ant.

"Bet they don't have termites," I muttered, staring at the house.

"What?"

"Never mind."

We got out of the car and headed for the front door. Before Jess could knock, I put my arm around her shoulder and said, "I apologize in advance for everything my stepmother's going to say, and everything my father *won't* say."

"That's all right."

"Thanks for coming with me."

"No problem, I'm looking forward to it," she lied. We both knew it was going to be a miserable evening.

It was the traditional Taylor 4th of July BBQ. Due to my father's hectic work schedule—he was the CEO of a company that manufactured sponges—it was taking place on July18th.

The Ant used this party as a chance to show off, so all kinds of people were invited: rich, poor, coworkers, family members, friends, politicians. Jessica got an invitation in her own right because she was rich, which cancelled out the fact that she was black.

"Seriously," I said again, knocking. "I'm very sorry."

"Oh, relax. Think she'll offer me fried chicken and watermelon again?"

I groaned, then forced a smile when my stepmother opened the door.

She blanched when she saw me. This wasn't atypical behavior; I'd have been shocked if she'd smiled. Or even remained expressionless. I'd never been able to forgive her for shattering my parents' marriage, and she'd never been able to forgive me for returning from the dead. It made holidays uneasy, to say the least.

"Happy Fourth of July," I said dutifully.

Ant nodded. "Jessica. Thanks for coming." She left the door open and marched away.

"She thinks your name's Jessica," Jessica stage-whispered.

"Very funny." I followed the Ant into the house. Where, to my total astonishment . . .

"Mom?"

"Hi, sweetie!" My mother put down her drink—Dewar's and soda, from the smell—and threw her arms around me. It was like being embraced by a pillow that smelled like cinnamon and oranges. "I was hoping you were coming." She gave me a hearty smack on the cheek, then grabbed Jessica and gave her the same treatment.

Jess hugged her back, delighted. "Dr. T! What are you doing here?"

A fair question. The Ant despised my mother, and the feeling was heartily mutual. They took great pains not to be in the same town, much less the same room in the same house. I couldn't imagine the bizarre-o set of circumstances that led to my mother's presence in my father's house.

"Don't you remember? I got promoted last month."

"Sure, you're head of the department now." My mom was a professor at the University of Minnesota. Her specialty was the Civil War, specifically the Battle of Antietam. Yawn. "You boss around all those little professor weenies."

"Which rates me," my mother said, smirking, "my own invitation to the Taylor Barbecue Fete."

I rubbed my temples. The Ant's social climbing knew no boundaries. Now she was inviting history professors! This made no sense. Moron. Profs hardly ever got rich. And they could be death at parties. Not *my* mom, of course. But still.

"Thank God," Jessica was saying. "Someone I can talk to who won't mistake me for the help."

"Oh, hush, Jessica, nobody thinks you're the help. Except . . . well, never mind."

"It's swell to see you here," I finally said.

My mom blinked up at me. I'd been taller than her since the seventh grade. "What's wrong?"

"Bad week," Jessica said, snagging a waiter by the elbow and relieving him of a glass of wine. "Undead politics. You know."

"And how's Eric Sinclair?"

"Annoying," I said, grabbing my own waiter. This one was carrying Bloody Marys. I took a gulp and grimaced. I'd like to get my hands on the jerk who decided it was a good idea to wreck tomato juice with vodka and hot sauce. "Arrogant. Obnoxious. Doesn't listen. Shows up uninvited."

"The king of the vampires," my mom murmured. She tried a leer, and failed, instead looking like the Before picture in an antacid commercial. My mom was short, plump, and had white, curly hair. She'd looked like a television grandma when she'd been in her thirties. "And he's quite fond of *you*, sugarlump."

"Barf," I said, and finished my drink. I scooped a cup of punch off the tray of yet another waiter—how many caterers did the Ant hire, for God's sake? For a "casual barbeque"?

"Err . . . perhaps you should slow down, honey. You're driving, right?"

"Mom, do you know how much booze a vampire needs to drink in order to get tipsy?"

"Well, no."

"Neither do I." A fine night to find out! I finished that drink, too, and downed the rest of Jessica's wine. "Anybody see my dad?"

"He's in the corner with the mayor. Good luck de-ensconcing him. Sweetie, are you really having such a hard time? Do you want me to come and stay with you for a few days?"

I actually shuddered. That's all I needed, my mom running interference while Sinclair and Jon pursued me, the Puppet Master tried to stake me, and the ghost of the dead kid ran around in my room singing "Mary Had a Little Lamb" until I thought I would about go out of my mind.

"Maybe next month, Dr. T," Jessica said quickly, seeing as how I was about to pass out from stress. "It's just . . . complicated right now."

"Never mind, Mom," I said, as nicely as I could. My mother, unlike *some* parental figures I could mention, was totally behind my undead status and tried her best to help me out. She was actually glad I was a vampire; she told me she didn't worry about me being mugged or raped or anything these days. It wasn't her fault my life was so unbelievably—what was Jessica's word?—*complicated*. Yeah, like the wake of a tornado is complicated.

"I think I'm here tonight for another reason," Mom went on, in a lower voice. "Your stepmother appears to be practically bursting with a secret. I suspect The Big Announcement will be tonight."

"Ugh." Oh what, what now? She'd bullied my dad into buying a plane for her shopping trips? She was trying to start another charity ball? "I don't suppose we could leave now?"

"We didn't have to come at all," Jessica pointed out.

I shrugged. In April, when I'd been newly risen, my dad had made it clear he considered me dead, and if I didn't have the good manners to *stay* dead, I should at least stay away. And I'd made it equally clear that I was his daughter, and it was his job to love me, dead or undead. We'd existed in a sort of uneasy truce ever since. I'd been here for Easter dinner a couple months ago, and was here now for the July BBQ. Like it or lump it.

"Have you . . . uh . . . eaten tonight?"

"I'm fine, Mom. Don't worry about it."

"Because I had an idea. Be right back."

She trotted off in the direction of the kitchen, all plump efficiency and speed.

"I cannot believe your stepmother invited your mother to her party."

"I can't believe Mom came!"

Jessica gave me a look. Above the kitchen racket, I heard a blender kick into life. "Of course she came. She wanted to make sure your dad and your Ant were being nice to you."

I smiled for the first time that night. Jess was probably right. My mom looked pleasant, but could be a pit bull if she thought I was in trouble.

Before we could speculate further, Mom returned with what appeared to be a dark chocolate milkshake.

"It's roast beef," she confided, and I nearly dropped the glass. "I thought, since you can't eat solid foods . . . but you can drink . . ."

"Hmmm," Jessica said, looking at my beef shake.

"Excuse me, ladies, but if you'd take your seats." The waiters were escorting all of us to the big table in the dining room. Interestingly, Ant had seated us at the head of the table, beside her and my dad. Weird! Usually she wanted me as far away from her as possible. Hell, I'd been seated at the kid table until I was twenty-six.

"Hi, Dad," I said, as my father sat down across from me. He flashed me a shaky smile and accidentally knocked over his wine glass.

"Darren," my mother said politely. "You're looking well."

My father smoothed his combover while a waiter righted his glass and blotted the wine stain. "Thanks, Elise. You too. Congratulations again on the promotion."

"Thank you. Doesn't Betsy look charming?"

"Uh, yeah. Charming."

"Thanks, Dad," I said dryly.

"Antonia," Mom said, as the Ant hitched her chair forward in a series of mini-scoots. "Lovely party."

"Thank you, Mrs. Taylor."

Hee! My mom, out of stubbornness and spite, had kept her married name after my dad had ditched her.

"Dr. Taylor," my mom corrected sweetly.

"Jessica," the Ant said. "How are you?"

"Fine, Mrs. Taylor."

"I heard you sold your downtown condo . . . friends of mine almost bought it. Where are you living now?"

"In a mansion on Summit Avenue," she said bluntly, because she knew it would drive my stepmother insane with jealousy. The Ant had been angling for a Summit mansion for years. But, well-to-do as my dad was, that was out of their reach. My mom hid a smile as she went on. "It's much too big for us, of course, but we're managing."

"Oh, err, Betsy's with you?"

"Sure. We're roommates. Along with Marc, our gay pal"—the Ant was a rabid homophobe—"and of course we needed the space because of all the vampires dropping by." And a rabid vampire-phobe.

My mom snorted into her drink. Typical of society parties, nobody noticed what Jessica said, so it wasn't like she'd blown my cover. Besides, even to me, it sounded unbelievable.

I picked up my glass of roast beef and sniffed. Didn't smell too bad. Actually, it smelled kind of good. And the glass was comfortingly warm.

"You tell 'em our news, Toni?" my dad asked, still grimacing over Jessica's announcement.

"News?" my mom asked politely.

"Oh, yes." For the first time all evening, my stepmother looked straight at me. The force of those blue eyes (contacts) and that blond hair (bleached) and those red lips (Botoxed) made me drain my glass of my roast beef in a hurry. Too bad there wasn't some gin in there, too. "Darren and I have exciting news. We're starting a family."

"Starting . . . ?" my mom asked, puzzled.

Jessica's eyes widened. "You mean you're—"

"Pregnant," the Ant said, triumph and hate ringing in her voice. "I'm due in January."

I leaned over and threw up the entire beef shake on my mom's lap.

# Chapter 21

"**How** could she?" I moaned. "How *could* she?"

"Because she's jealous of you," Jessica said bluntly. "She has been since the day she moved into your dad's house. She probably thought she was well rid of you back in April. But you were too dumb to stay dead. So, she figures, 'I'll have my own kid, and then I'll get my share of the attention *and* Betsy's.'"

Yep, that was the Ant, all right. To a T.

"I admit," Mom said, "I was surprised. I hadn't expected Antonia to go that route." She laughed suddenly. "Your poor father!"

"He deserves it," I said. I was slumped over in the passenger seat, praying for death. I'd refused to put my seat belt on. Right now, I'd welcome a trip through the windshield. "He picked her. He married her."

"And he's been paying for it ever since, Elizabeth," Mom said in her "don't argue with me" tone. "It's time you grew up and let it go. If *I'm* not angry anymore, why are you?"

"Shut up."

"Beg pardon, young lady?"

"I said, we've showed up. We're here."

My mom gasped as we swung into the driveway. I couldn't blame her. I still half-expected to get thrown out of the mansion myself whenever I ventured past the main hall.

"Oh, Jessica, how marvelous! I suppose it's ridiculously expensive."

"Yeah," she said modestly.

"My goodness! What a palace!"

Jessica, I could see with a sour eye, was lapping this up. I didn't say anything, though I sure felt like it. Jessica's parents died when she was a kid, my mom was the closest thing she'd had to a maternal-type, and Jess adored her.

"Come on up, I've got some sweatpants I can let you have." Mom's skirt was, of course, ruined. Beef shake, bile, and cashmere . . . not a pleasant combo.

"It's really not nec—"

"What, you're going home in your pantyhose? Give me a break. Come on."

"Vampires," Mom whispered to Jessica, "are so touchy."

"I heard that," I snapped.

"Did you really?"

"It sucks," Jessica murmured back. "I can't cut a fart on the third floor without Bets hearing it on the first."

"Goodness."

As we stepped into the entryway, Marc was walking through carrying a pitcher of iced tea. "Hi, Dr. T. Hey, just in time, you guys! Your guests are here."

"What guests?"

"Um, let's see." Marc started ticking them off on the fingers of his free hand. "There's two of the Blade Warriors, the king of the vampires, the vampire who made *him,* the local parish priest, and one other vampire. Sarah something."

"Great," I griped. "Am I the only one who calls if I'm going to show up at someone's house uninvited?"

"Apparently so," Sinclair said, appearing from nowhere as usual. My mom jumped about a foot. So did I. "Dr. Taylor. A pleasure to see you again."

Mom practically swooned when Eric took her hand in both of his and bowed over them like a dead Maitre d'. "Oh, your Majesty. Nice to see you, too."

"Eric, please, Dr. Taylor. After all, you're not one of my subjects. Pity," he sighed.

"And you must call me Elise," she simpered.

"And I must vomit. Again," I announced. "Will you two stop making googly eyes at each other for five seconds?"

"Forgive my daughter," Mom said, staring raptly up into Sinclair's eyes. "She's normally much more pleasant. She's had a rough night."

"Of course, as she is your daughter, I expect great things of her."

"Why, Eric! How sweet. Betsy never told me you—"

"Seriously, you guys? I'm gonna barf again. So cut it out."

"I will also," Sarah said. I turned; she was standing in the entryway to the second living room. "If we're finished for the evening, I'd like to go."

"No," Sinclair said.

"Yes," I said at exactly the same time. "In fact, why don't *all* of you go? I'm not in the mood."

"Get in the mood. We have serious business to attend to." The frost in his voice melted as he turned puppy eyes to my mother. "Serious vampire business, dear lady, or of course I would insist you join us. We could use a fine mind like yours."

"I want to go!" Sarah shouted. Actually shouted! I thought I was the only one who yelled at Sinclair. "I want to go *now!*"

"What's your problem?" Marc asked. The iced tea pitcher was sweating like Rush Limbaugh in July, and dripping on the floor. He looked around for a piece of furniture less than two hundred years old to set it on, in vain. So he grimly hung onto the pitcher. *Note to self: Buy coasters.* "I heard you don't like this place. What's your damage?"

"If you must know," Sarah said, biting off each word like she'd probably like to bite off Marc's fingers, "I had a daughter once. And she was . . . well, she died. Here. In this house. And I don't want to talk about it and I don't want to be here."

She took a step forward and walked into Sinclair's outstretched arm. I actually heard my jaw muscles creak as my mouth fell open. "You *what?*" I practically screamed.

"A child? A blond girl?" Sinclair asked sharply.

I shouldered him aside. "Is her name Marie? Does she wear headbands to keep her hair out of her eyes? And saddle shoes with anklets? And overalls?"

Sarah burst into tears. This was more shocking than when she yelled at Sinclair. "You know about her? How did you know? Who told you? Don't talk to me about her, I don't want you to do that!"

"Sarah, she's buried in my front yard!"

"She's what?" Jessica asked sharply. "You're forgetting to share again, dead girl."

"Come on!" I pointed up the stairs. "To the vampire bedroom!" I whipped around, which made my mom just about fall over. I must have been moving too fast for her to track again. "Mom, I gotta take care of this right now, okay? We'll talk later, okay? Only this is important. Okay?"

"Of course." She hugged me. "Go do your work."

"*Mom.*" I wriggled free. "You're embarrassing me in front of the other vampires."

I dashed up the stairs.

I burst into my bedroom, with entirely too many people hot on my heels. "Marie!" I bawled. "Marie, come out!"

She faded into sight. I'd never seen her do it before and let me tell you, it was weird. At first I didn't think she was in the chair, and then the chair looked a little blue around the edges, and then it was like a faded Marie was sitting there, and then a regular Marie was sitting there.

"What?" she asked, looking puzzled. Then she looked past me and her eyes went huge. "Mommy!"

I turned; Sarah would need my help. "Sarah, you can see the ghost if—"

She knocked me into Tina as she lunged past. "Sweetie bug!"

Tina steadied me and muttered, "Sweetie bug?" at the same instant. I felt her pain; it was all I could do not to snicker, too.

Sarah tried to hug Marie, but ended up nearly falling into the chair instead. This did not forestall a lecture. "Mommy, where have you been? I've been waiting and waiting!" Marie had her hands on her hips; she was the picture of outraged patience.

Sarah backed off and tried to answer, but cried harder instead.

"Marie," Sinclair asked, "what did the man who knocked you down look like?"

"Don't ask her about that," Sarah ordered. Her voice was still thick, but her maternal hackles were raised. King or no king, Sinclair wasn't going to cause her kid any pain. I really liked her for it. I felt bad about all the times I blew her off as an icy weirdo. "You don't have to, anyway. It was Nostro. He killed her. And turned me."

"And you were mad at me for killing him?" I asked, aghast.

"It's . . . complicated," she said, my least favorite word of the week.

I heard a *snap* and looked; Tina had picked up the chair and broken one of the legs off of it. "Stop that, the thing's probably worth six figures," I ordered. "Well, now what? I mean, they're reunited." Did this mean Sarah was going to move in, so she could be close to Marie? Shit, I hoped not. If I let one vampire move in, I'd have to let 'em all in!

Sarah was waving her hand through Marie's head.

"Mommy, come *on*. What's taking so long? Let's go!"

Sarah turned toward me. She had aged ten years in ten seconds. Her face was haggard and still she sobbed. "Betsy, my Queen, I need a favor."

"What?"

"Is it—I heard you think we have souls. That vampires have souls."

"Uh . . ." Where was she going with this? I was starting to get a really bad feeling. "Yeah, that's true. I mean, that's what I think."

"So it is true," Sarah said. "Because you're the queen. And your will is our will. So it says in the Book of the Dead."

*That* thing again. "Okay. I mean, sure, whatever you say."

"Yes. All right."

There was a pause, like she was nerving herself to say something. If she'd been human, she probably would have taken a steadying breath.

"Then I must ask a favor. I'd like you to kill me. Right now."

# Chapter 22

"**YOU** want me to do what?"

"I'll do it," Tina said quickly. I realized that the chair leg she'd been holding would make a good stake. Dammit! Three steps ahead of me, as usual. "The queen shouldn't have to undertake such a low task."

"Uh . . . still having trouble tracking, you guys . . ."

"Low task?" Sarah's eyes were blazing. "My death is not low! It will reunite me with my own flesh and blood, gone from me these fifty years."

"Guys?"

"I only meant . . . the queen doesn't have the stomach for such things," Tina added in a low voice. "But I don't mind, and I'll be glad to help you out."

"Oh." Mollified, Sarah backed off again. "All right, then."

"Sarah, are you sure?" I kept a wary eye on Marie and practically whispered the rest. "I mean, what if it doesn't work? What if you . . ." *Wake up in Hell,* I'd been about to say, but that probably wouldn't do. "What if I'm wrong?"

"You're the queen," Sarah said, plainly puzzled.

"Besides, you do believe it. In your heart of hearts," Sinclair said. I jumped; he'd been so quiet, I had forgotten he was still in the room. "You know you do. Else why wear the cross? Attend church?"

"How do you know I go to church?"

"Elizabeth, I know *everything* about you."

"Okay, now you've moved from annoying would-be suitor to obsessive stalker. But I'll deal with that later. Give me that thing."

Tina slapped the chair leg into my palm like a vampiric O.R. nurse. "Sarah asked me. So I'll do it."

"Thank you, Majesty."

Tina didn't say anything; she just bowed her head.

"Um, *how* do I do it?"

"Aim for the heart," Sinclair said. He touched a spot on Sarah's breast. "Dead center. As quick and deep as you can."

"And that'll . . . do it?"

"Yes. No vampire can recover from a wooden stake through the heart, even if you remove it afterward. She won't disappear like in a silly movie, but she'll be dead for-ever."

I gulped. "Okay. But first, Sarah, you should probably confess. You know, go see God with a clean slate."

Sarah cringed. "Can't I confess to you?"

"No, of course not. Just a second." I snatched open my bedroom door. Ani, Jessica, and Jon nearly fell on me. "Cut it out, you snoops. Father Markus!" I bawled. "Get up here! We need you!"

"I'll get him," Ani said.

"No, *I* will," Jon said, and they were in an instant and furious tussle. Fists flew and they were kicking and scratching like pissed-off chinchillas.

"Uh . . . Jessica . . ."

"Right," she said, stepping over Jon and Ani, locked in combat, and hurrying down the stairs.

"Okay," I said, popping back into my bedroom. "Jess went to get the priest."

"He's not going to touch me with any of his . . . his tools, is he?" she asked, actually trembling. The woman who yelled at Sinclair was scared of an old man in his sixties! "Or sprinkle me with . . . with anything?"

"No. He's just going to hear you out. Just tell him all the bad things you've done—"

"All?" she repeated, appalled

"Sum up, then," I said, exasperated. "Then I'll stake you through the heart and you and Marie can be together." And then I'll throw up again, and hide under my bed for the rest of the week. A fine plan!

Father Markus could move when he wanted; there was a quick tap at my door and then he poked his head inside. "You called for me?"

"Yeah. Thanks for coming so fast. C'mere, Father . . ." He shut the door and I quickly gave him the rundown. "So, if you could, you know, make her shiny for God . . ."

"I don't think he can," Tina said. "He can't make the sign of . . . make any signs, or touch her with anything . . ."

"And if she isn't a practicing Catholic, it would be inappropriate, to say the least. Frankly, it's inappropriate anyway, given her . . . ah . . . status." Markus looked around nervously, unfolded his bifocals, and slipped them on. "Are you sure there's a ghost in here?"

"Trust me. Well, just do the best you can." Could a priest do Extreme Unction on a vampire?

Father Markus smiled at Sarah, who was cowering away from him, and I noticed for the first time what a nice face he had. It was long and mournful, like a priestly basset hound, but when he smiled he showed a deeply sunk dimple in each cheek, which was awfully cute.

"Sarah, child." He slowly reached for her hand. She flinched, then let him take it. "Are you heartily sorry for all the sins you've committed, both in life and in death?"

"Yes."

"And do you accept our Lord Jesus Christ as your savior?"

"Eric Sinclair is my Lord," she said, glaring. "And Betsy is my Lady."

"In the afterlife, dear?"

"Well, I suppose so," she grumped. "I mean, if He'll have me."

"Very well, then. I commend your soul to God." He made the sign of the cross over her head and she flinched behind her upraised arm, but nothing happened. She didn't burst into flames or anything like that. I have to admit, I was relieved. I mean, that would have just wrecked the whole evening.

"Thanks, Father," I said.

"Do you need—"

"Bye."

Tina held the door open, pointedly.

"But I'm curious—"

"Vampire business, I beg your pardon," Tina said politely. Then she fixed Ani and Jon with such a withering glare that they instantly lunged for the stairs. Father Markus crept out, throwing one last glance over his shoulder as the door shut.

"Okay." That sounded good; I'd try that again. "Okay. Here we go. Um, Sarah, stand over here." I steadied her against the wall. Then I moved her—my shoes were behind that wall. "Okay, here we go. Um. Okay." I made a practice jabbing motion where

Sinclair had pointed. Oh, Lord, how did I get myself into these situations? "Okay."

"Wait!" She grabbed my wrist.

"Oh, thank God."

"No, it's not that. I haven't changed my mind. My clothes. I have a closetful of Armani that I'll never use again. Tina knows where I live. They'll be yours now. You're taller, but we've got the same body type. You can alter most of it."

"Armani?" I flung my arms around her and kissed her chilly cheek. "You won't regret this, I promise."

"Then *get it* done. Please."

"All right, all right."

"Mommy?" Marie, sounding worried.

"Be with you in a minute, baby," Sarah replied, too brightly. Then, hissing, "Do it!"

I did it. I slammed the table leg into her, harder than I had to. I was so afraid I'd wimp out and bungle the job, I overcompensated. The table leg went through Sarah, and through the wall. I let go of it, and Sarah stayed pinned to the wall like a beetle to a card.

And she was gone. I knew she was gone, I could feel it. And if I hadn't been able to feel it, I could sure see it. Her eyes, which had been slitted in rage against my slothful slowness, were glazed over. She was twitching all over like a landed trout, but I knew those for what they were—death spasms.

I turned away, morbidly afraid I was going to barf again. I felt Sinclair's hand on my elbow. "Steady," he murmured. "It was well done. And look!"

I looked. Marie had an expression of intense surprise on her face; she was staring at her hands, which were transparent. She looked up at me and smiled, showing a gap where she'd lost her baby teeth. "I'm going to see Mommy now, B—" Then she popped out of sight.

There was a long silence while the three of us tried to think of something to say. Finally, Tina spoke up. "I'll dispose of the body."

"Vampires have cemeteries?" I asked shakily. I *felt* shaky, like any second I would fall flat on my face.

She smiled. "Yes."

"Okay. Um, listen. It's been a really long night. An unbelievably long night. Tina, I'm your queen, right? I mean, you've always believed it."

"Of course, Majesty."

"Okay, well, will you do me a really, really big favor? Will you go downstairs and make the Blade Warriors go away, and tell Marc and Jess and my mom I'll see them tomorrow? Because I'm just not up for company right now."

"At once, Majesty." She picked up my hand and—weird and disturbing—kissed it. "You did good." She smiled and her whole face lit up. "You did great."

So how come I felt like a total shit?

I heard Tina tugging and pulling. I refused to look. Then she carried the body out. Sinclair held the door open for her, then closed it behind her. Naturally, he assumed "I don't want company" didn't apply to *him*.

"Well, that's that," I said, staring at the spot where Marie had just been.

"Yes, I suppose so."

"I'm really happy for her."

"As am I."

"I mean, she missed her mom so much, she hung around here for half a century. Years and years! And now they're together. That's good, right?"

"Right."

I burst into tears, and suddenly found myself leaning on something hard and covered with cotton—Sinclair's chest. His arms were around me and he was stroking my back. "Elizabeth, don't cry, sweetheart. Everything you said was right. Everything you *did* was right."

"I know," I wailed into his lapel.

"There, now. You made the hard choice, and that's always difficult." He kissed the top of my head. "But you were a queen to Sarah when she needed you, and Marie couldn't have asked for a truer friend."

He was being so sweet, I cried harder.

"Elizabeth, why do you always smell like strawberries?"

The abrupt topic change startled me in mid-sob. "It's my shampoo."

"Well, it's lovely."

"Also, Jessica threw a strawberry at me earlier. It was the garnish in her daiquiri at my dad's house, and it got stuck in my bra, and I didn't have time to change before you guys came over. I mean, I fished it out, but there was juice and seeds everywhere."

"Well, that's . . . that's lovely, too." I could feel his chest shaking with suppressed laughter.

I jerked back and slapped his shoulder. "It's *not funny,* Sinclair. I'm having a crisis, here."

"Yes, I'm beginning to recognize the signs."

"It's just, I would have looked after her, you know? I had this plan. I mean, I'll never have a baby. So I thought I could sort of take Marie under my wing. And I got used to having her around. She was always around."

"Yes, it must have been unbelievably nerve-wracking."

"No, it . . . I thought, that was okay, right? I mean, once I got over being creeped out by the whole ghost thing. But now I'll . . . I'll never see her again." Just the thought made me cry harder. "That's the only way I'll ever have a kid, is if some other kid gets *murdered* in my house and hangs around!"

"Elizabeth, that's not true."

"It's just been the crappiest week!"

"Yes, it's been difficult for you, hasn't it, poor darling?"

"Yes! And someone's trying to kill me and my house is too big and the other vampires hate me and I'm going to have to crush Jon like a bug one of these days so he quits hanging around and I can see dead people and I think maybe the gardener's a ghost too and my stepmonster's pregnant with my half brother or sister."

He looked at me soberly. "No one will dare to harm you while I'm around." Then, "Who did you say was pregnant?"

"Never mind. You know," I sniffed, "you can be really sweet when you're not driving me up a tree."

"Why, you stole the very words from my mouth," he teased. "Also, I never thanked you for saving my life."

"What? When?"

"When that infant tossed holy water at me. You jumped in front of me and got soaked. Remember?"

"Oh. That. Well, you know," I shrugged. "It was nothing to me. I mean, I knew it wouldn't hurt me. Besides, I wouldn't want anything to happen to that pretty face," I teased.

"Indeed not." He caressed my cheek and I noticed again how very, very black his eyes were. Meeting his gaze was like looking up at the winter sky.

When he leaned in and pressed a kiss to my lower lip, I grabbed his lapels and kissed him right back. He smelled so good—all crisp cotton and his own secret smell. I, of course, smelled like squashed strawberries. Well, he seemed to like it. Also, his tongue was in my mouth and I didn't mind a bit.

"I suppose you'll be ordering me out now," he murmured, breaking the kiss and nipping lightly at my throat, but not breaking the skin. It made me shiver and lean into him.

"Well, I really should. I mean, it's a rotten thing to do."

"What is, darling?"

"I'll just be mean to you again tomorrow. It's rotten to let you stay the night."

He laughed against my neck. He hardly ever laughed, and when he did it was always startling and kind of fun, like finding a ripe orange in your mailbox. "I'll risk it," he said, and shrugged out of his jacket.

I stood back and watched him disrobe. It was amazing how quickly the clothes were flying off him. God, he had a great body. A farmer's son, Sinclair had been in excellent shape when he died. His shoulders were so broad he had to have his suits tailor-made, and his arms were tautly defined with muscle. His chest was lightly furred with black hair, tapering to a narrow waist and long, muscular legs. And he was very happy to see me.

"This doesn't mean anything, does it?" I asked, although it was suddenly hard to talk . . . my tongue felt too thick for my mouth. "There's not another little passage in the Book of the Dead that maybe you forgot to mention? If we have sex again does this make you, like, super king forever and ever?"

"No." He turned me around and unzipped my dress. He nuzzled the back of my neck. "You're . . . ah . . . not planning on talking the entire time, are you?"

I whipped back around. My dress fell to my feet in a silk puddle and I saw his eyes widen appreciatively—for a change, I was wearing matching underwear. Pale green, with monarch butterflies. "What's *that* supposed to mean?"

"Oh, nothing. Chat away, dear. I'll be all ears." He laughed again and hugged me to him. This was quite interesting, as I could feel his hard length pressing against my lower stomach, so I decided to forget about being annoyed. "Oh, Elizabeth. I'm really, really quite fond of you."

"Yeah, I can tell. Well, I like you, too, Eric, when you're not being a shit."

"In other words, when I'm buckling under. A fine platform on which to base a thousand year relationship."

For once, that thought wasn't completely terrifying. And he

was so strangely cheerful, it was perking me right up. Frankly, I'd never seen him in a better mood. The man must absolutely love getting laid. "Let's just take it one day at a time, all right?"

"As my queen commands," he said, and scooped me up, and tossed me on the bed. "Also, I like your butterflies. But I think they should be on the floor, don't you?"

And in a moment, they were.

" WOW."

"Yes."

"I'm panting. I'm actually out of breath, and I don't need to breathe. Day-amn!"

Sinclair stretched, then pulled me to his side and pressed a quick kiss to my breast. "Art comes in many forms."

"Oh, so you're an artist, now?"

"Yes."

I snorted, but didn't disagree. He'd been hungry, and skillful, and very, very good. Of course, he had about sixty years of experience. My throat still stung where he'd bitten me, but I wasn't holding it against him. I knew he'd been completely unable to help himself.

I wondered if he hurt where I'd bitten him.

I lay there next to him and tried to think about how to tell him my dirty little secret. Because it had happened again. When we were making love, I could read his mind. But I knew he couldn't read mine. I'd tried to send thoughts to him before, but with absolutely no reaction. And I wasn't smart enough to figure out a tactful, nonthreatening way to share this with him.

*Say, Sinclair, did you know that when we're having sex, I can read your every thought and desire? This isn't going to bother someone as tightly controlled as you, is it?*

Pass.

"Say, are you sure you want to spend the night? What if the Puppet Master makes another go at me?"

"Let him try," Sinclair said, pulling the comforter over us. "I've been fantasizing about pulling his head off for the last few days."

"You know, *most* people fantasize about getting married, or building a dream home, or going on vacation somewhere nice."

"I think about those things, too," he said seriously.

"Oh, is this the part where we share intimate small talk and fall in love?" I teased.

I could feel him studying me in the dark. "No," he said finally. "Go to sleep."

Sure! It'd be so easy, because it wasn't like I had a ton of stuff on my mind or anything. Shoot, I was still replaying the really excellent sex I'd just had. *Really* excellent.

I could still feel his hands on me. Actually, his hands *were* on me. But earlier, they'd been everywhere. And he'd kissed me everywhere, too. He'd been like a starving man in an Old Country Buffet restaurant.

And I mean *everywhere*. Sinclair had practically taken up residence between my legs. When his tongue had snaked inside me, I'd just about gone out of my mind. He licked and kissed and sucked, and I was so busy begging him not to stop that at first I thought he'd been talking out loud.

*"Don't bite her, don't bite, don't bite, don't bite . . ."*

"What's the matter?" I'd gasped.

"Nothing. Hush," he'd said, and flicked my clit with his tongue.

*". . . bite don't bite don't bite don't bite don't don't don't . . ."*

I grabbed his shoulders and tugged until his chest was settling against mine. "That's nice," I had managed. "Are you going to fuck me now?"

I expected a sarcastic response or one of those annoying "as my queen commands" sneers, but instead he shoved my legs further apart with his knee and surged inside me. I could practically feel him in the back of my throat; he was really hung, and that was just fine.

*". . . bite don't bite don't bite don't bite don't you'll scare her don't bite don't . . ."*

I wrapped my legs around his waist, urging him closer as he stroked, and pressed his face into the side of my neck. The muscles in his shoulders were rigid with strain; they felt like rock beneath my fingers.

Then I bit him. He stiffened in my embrace and shuddered all over; his cool, rich blood flooded my mouth and the sensation of taking from him while he took from me tipped me over into orgasm.

I barely felt his teeth break my skin; I was shuddering around him and realized that high whimpering sound was coming from me.

We were rocking together so fiercely my giant, heavy bed was actually moving; the headboard was slapping the wall and I imagined the house was probably shaking, too. At least, it should have been. It felt like the universe should be affected by what we were doing; it wasn't just a couple of lonely people having sex. For the first time, I had a real sense of who we were, and what we were about. The king and queen of the dead were making love so fiercely, chunks were falling out of the wall.

*Elizabeth!*

"Eric," I'd managed.

He thrust once more, harder than he had before, the head-board gave a final slam, I came again, and so did he. His grip tightened until it was just short of painful, and then he was licking the bite mark on my neck, and I was gasping and out of breath.

"Jesus!"

"I've asked you before not to call me that," he said, and we both cracked up.

Yeah, it had really been something. The question was, could I now read anyone's mind during lovemaking, or just Eric's? And how much longer should I keep this to myself?

I heard a *crack* and flinched; Sinclair had snapped his fingers in front of my face. "Are you in there? I've been saying your name for the last ten seconds."

"Sorry. I was thinking. And don't do that; you know I hate it."

"Thinking about?"

"Actually, about how amazing you are in bed." Well, it was mostly the truth. "I hate to tell you anything that'll make your head bigger than it already is, but yum!"

"Thank you," he said politely, but he sounded pleased. "Of course, you bring out the best in me. Your body is a feast."

"Well, I'm trying to slim down. Seriously, you're the best I've ever had."

"Oh? Out of, say, how many?"

"Forget it, pal. We're not doing this."

He yawned and cuddled me into his side. "Why not?"

"Because you'll win. You've been having sex a lot longer than me."

"True. But I'm curious about the others you've invited into your bed."

"Let's just say I could count them on one hand and leave it at that." Actually, three fingers. But that was none of his business.

"Practically a virgin," he mused.

"Oh, hush up. Hey, is it getting lighter in here or is it just *mmmmmm* . . ."

The last thing I remember was Eric chuckling as I sank into unconsciousness. Stupid sunrises!

# Chapter 23

I opened my eyes and was not at all pleased to see Marc standing over me. His mouth was hanging open and he was gaping down at me. And presumably, Sinclair, who had at one point kicked off the covers.

"What?" I leaned over Sinclair, grabbed the comforter, and spread it over us. "Somebody better be on fire, pal."

"Huh? Oh. Uh . . . sorry, the reason I came up here has been driven completely out of my head by the sight of your cellulite."

"I don't have any," I snapped.

"Neither do I," Sinclair said. "Good evening, by the way."

Jessica walked in. She slowed as she saw Sinclair next to me, then pretended like she hadn't just had the crap shocked out of her and strode briskly over to Marc. "Are you going to give her the phone or what? It's your boss," she added to me. "He sounds pissed."

I grabbed for the phone, which wasn't easy because Marc was still staring, and I had to wrestle it away from him while remaining modestly covered.

"Hello? Mr. Mason?"

"Elizabeth. You were supposed to be here an hour ago."

Shit! What day was it? What *time* was it? Wait a minute . . . "Mr. Mason, I switched with Renee for tonight. She's covering my shift."

"Oh? Because Renee isn't here, either."

Well, hell, go yell at *her*. "Mr. Mason, I'm not on tonight."

"The schedule disagrees."

"Yeah, but . . . we switched!"

"I see. Do you think you could come in for a couple of hours, since Renee seems to have forgotten your . . . ah . . . arrangement?"

"Sure," I said quickly. I was going to have to do some serious damage control on this one. "Be there in an hour."

"Good-bye, Elizabeth."

"Shit!" I said as he hung up. "He thinks I'm lying to cover my ass."

"And what an ass," Sinclair said admiringly.

"You stop that. Dammit, now I've got to go in and be all nicey-nice and kick Renee's butt up to her shoulderblades when I see her."

"At the same time?"

"Dammit!"

"Mason takes you for granted," Jessica declared.

"You're sweet, but I haven't been a very good employee lately, what with my—"

"Secret vampire life?"

"Well . . . yeah."

"Slut," Marc coughed into his fist.

"I am not! I've only had sex twice in the past . . . what year is this?"

Sinclair laughed.

"You guys go away," I ordered. "I have to grab a shower and get ready for work."

"The Blade Warriors are here," Jessica said, rolling her eyes. "Well, one of them."

I rubbed my temples. "It's Jon, isn't it?"

"If Jon's the one who looks like he should be on a beach with Gidget and her pals, yes."

Sinclair growled. Actually growled, like a wolf or something! "Send him away," he ordered.

"Calm down, O king of the dead people," Jessica said, smirking. "As it happens, he's insisting on talking to Bets, here."

"I could not care less. Send him away."

"Stop ordering my friends around!" I rested my chin on my fist. "Nuts. Well, I can't talk to him right now, I've got to get to work. I'll have to see him later. Nobody's died, though, right?"

"Not yet."

"Cheerful thought," I muttered, standing. What did I care? Jessica'd seen me naked about a million times, and Marc was a lot more interested in how Sinclair looked. "All right. I'll catch you guys later."

"Oh, come on," Marc whined. "We want to hear about what happened up here last night. Specifically, why Tina came down the stairs carrying a dead vampire. And why you didn't wake up by yourself."

"Later," I said firmly, and walked into the bathroom.

I was rinsing shampoo out of my hair when I heard someone pull back the shower curtain. "You'd better be anyone but Eric Sinclair," I said without opening my eyes.

"You'd prefer Marc? Or perhaps Jon?"

"Ugh, and again . . . ugh." I finished rinsing and opened my eyes. Eric was splendidly nude (still!), standing in front of me with his hands on his hips, smiling. "He's just a kid with a crush."

"You sound unsurprised."

"For some weird reason," I admitted, "teenage boys really like me."

"I can't think why," he said, idly tweaking my nipple.

I slapped his hand away. "What's got you in such a good mood? That's the second smile this morning. Evening, I mean."

"Oh, I guess I'm just an evening person." He grabbed me to him and rubbed his chest across mine. "More of that strawberry shampoo, I see."

I tried to wriggle away, but I was too slippery. I was like a trout in a live well. Nowhere to go! "Cut that out. I don't have time for your shenanigans. I'm late already." But hoo, man, was I tempted! No. I couldn't. My job in Heaven depended on *not* getting sweaty with Eric right now. Dammit! "Did I say I'm late? Because I really am."

"Spoilsport," he said, but he released me. "Why you insist on dashing off to a meaningless—"

"Don't start."

"I wasn't," he said, having the gall to sound wounded.

I tossed him the soap, which he snatched, one-handed, out of the air. "Sure you weren't. Lather up, big boy, and then it's time to hit the bricks."

"You can make getting clean sound so . . . dirty."

I laughed in spite of myself. "Don't start, I said!"

"I hear and obey," he replied, and then squeezed my shampoo bottle—*when* had he grabbed that? Strawberry gel arched out and splattered across my breasts.

I cursed, and ducked under the spray again to rinse. Then we ran out of hot water—stupid ancient water heater!—and we were both cursing.

\* \* \*

ℐ was headed down the back stairs—the quickest way from my room to the driveway behind the kitchen—when I heard Jon's plaintive, "But she *likes* me. I can tell!" and froze in mid-step.

I started to creep back up. I'd take the other stairs, go around the front way, but Jessica's words glued me to the spot.

"Jon, she's not just a vampire. Although that would be problematic enough, don't you agree? You and your little group of nerd hoods kill vampires."

"Only the bad ones," he said. "We voted. Sinclair and Tina and Betsy and Monique are off-limits. We were still trying to figure out about Sarah when she . . . well, whatever you guys did to her. But if we catch a vampire trying to hurt or kill a human, he's fair game."

"Spare me your twisted machinations. And you might want to run that plan by Sinclair."

"He's not my boss!"

"Okay, okay, don't burst a blood vessel. My point is, Betsy's not just *a* vampire, she's the *queen* of the vampires."

"So? She doesn't even like that job. And the way I hear it, it's an accident that she's even queen, anyway. She'd get out of it if—"

"Yeah, but she can't."

"If she really wanted to—"

"No, really, she can't. I guess the vampires have this book with all their laws and prophecies and stuff in it, and according to that book—which is like the vampires' bible, so they pay attention to it—Betsy's the queen and Eric Sinclair is the king."

"So?" Sulky now, not that I could blame him. It's not like Jess was telling him anything he wanted to hear.

I heard her shift her weight and almost grinned. She was losing her patience, and trying her best not to lose her temper as well. "So, it's like they're married. In the eyes of vampire law, they *are* married. Not only are you lusting after a vampire, you're lusting after a married one."

"So?"

"Don't be such a moron. They've got a kingdom to run, Jon, and in case you haven't noticed, the king is crazy about her. He'll pull your head off if you try anything. And be fair, it's not like Betsy's encouraged you. Right?"

Sullen silence.

"Besides . . . I think . . . maybe . . . she loves him, too."

"No."

I nearly fell down the stairs. Damn right, no!

"Oh, it's the best kept secret in the world. Even from her! But I guess my point is, why don't you drop this whole thing? She'll just keep rejecting you. Or, Eric will pull your head off. So we're looking at a lose/lose situation, right?"

"I'm still asking her out."

I heard a whoosh as Jessica threw her arms in the air. "Fine, get your head handed to you, see if I care."

"If she says no, she says no. But I'm asking anyway."

Great. Well, I'd field that one when I came to it. As for right now, the front stairs awaited. And so did Macy's!

I actually laughed while pulling out of the driveway; I couldn't help it. The idea was too absurd. Me, in love with Eric Sinclair? And *him* in love with *me?* Even sillier.

I drove him nuts. I knew it. He knew it. We all knew it. The only reason he even liked having me around was because I was the queen. Beyond that, we had nothing in common. Ab-so-lu-te-ly nothing. It was silly enough that we were destined to rule at each other's sides for, like, a zillion years. He had to be as annoyed about that as I was.

My cell phone buzzed. *Boop-boop-boo-BOOP-BOOP-boop bip boop boop!* Stupid "Funkytown" theme; I've got to get that changed. I fished it out of my purse. "Hello?"

"As usual," Jessica announced, "you've left an enormous mess for me to clean up."

"Sorry about that, but I had to get to work."

"And *what* did you do to Sinclair? He's humming! And he did the dishes! 'High time to earn my keep,' he says, and then he mojo'd the housekeeper into taking a nap. You should see the guy in Playtex rubber gloves."

I cracked up. "You're making that up."

"Who could make something like that up? And he shows no desire to leave, either—usually he does a fade when he finds out you've left. Not tonight. I keep tripping over the guy. It's creepy, but interesting."

"Yeah? Who's all there?"

"Everybody. Jon, Ani, Father Markus, Tina. Oh, I almost forgot the best part! After doing the dishes and rearranging your bookcase—all the titles are facing the right way, now—"

"Goddamn it!"

"He runs into Jon, who has got it *bad* for you, FYI—"

"I heard."

"Anyway, I figured they'd sort of growl at each other and beat their chests like gorillas on the Nature channel, but Sinclair just smiled at him and patted him on the head. Patted him on the head! Good thing I hid Jon's crossbow in the fridge or there'd have been real trouble."

"That *is* weird," I admitted.

"Weird, shit. It's bizarre and unprecedented, is what it is. You must have knocked his brains loose."

"Jessica!" Then I snickered. "Okay, well . . . maybe I did."

"What, did you grow an extra breast or something? And don't think I didn't notice the big chunks that fell off the ceiling in your room. I'm telling you, I've never seen this guy in such a good mood."

I swerved to avoid a red BMW—I hate those 'I've got a yellow light so I have the right of way' drivers. "Look, we had a nice night, okay? A very nice night. I was upset about the Ant, you know, and having to stake Sarah—"

"*You* killed her?"

"—and all the stuff that's been going on lately, and he, you know. He made me feel better."

I could feel Jessica leering through the phone. "I bet."

"Oh, stop it."

"Well, watch out for Jon-boy. He's determined to ask you to the sock-hop, or whatever kids his age do for fun."

"Sock hop? Cripes."

"Should have stayed dead," Jessica advised, "like a normal person."

"Oh, shut up."

"Spray it, don't say it," she said, then hung up on me so she could get the last word. Jerk.

# Chapter 24

"*I'm fired?*"

"We're going to have to let you go," Mr. Mason explained. "When you're here, Elizabeth, you do fine work, but of late you've become unreliable."

"But . . . but . . ." But I can't help it. But I'm the queen of the undead, and queens didn't get fired! But I've been really busy trying not to get murdered! But the new Pradas are coming in next week and I desperately need my employee discount! But I've never been fired by someone wearing a turtleneck in July! "But . . . but . . ."

"Besides, don't you have more pressing business to attend to?" he added kindly. "You've got a killer to catch, and a consort to satisfy."

"Yeah, that's true, but—*what?*"

"You shouldn't be here, Majesty. Everyone appears to grasp this but you."

I gaped at him. Started to speak, couldn't, gaped some more. Tried to talk again. No luck. I had been struck mute with shock, just like when Charlize Theron won the Oscar for Best Actress.

He opened the lone manila folder on his otherwise spotless desk, and withdrew a paycheck, which had a blue piece of paper stapled to it. Termination form. Argh! "Here's your final check. And good luck catching the killer."

"Mr. Mason!"

"Oh, I'm not a vampire," he said, correctly reading my bulging eyes and sprung jaw. "I'm Kept."

"You're what?"

"I'm a sheep," he clarified. He tugged at his cashmere turtle-neck, baring his throat. There wasn't a bite, but there was a pretty good bruise. "At first, when you came here, I thought it was a test. Or a joke. Then, I realized you were serious. You really wanted to work here. I couldn't think why. Finally, I realized I must fire you for your own good."

"Thanks tons," I said, starting to recover from the shock. "Jeez, why didn't you tell me sooner?"

He coughed into his fist. "I assumed you were smart . . . er . . . I thought you knew what I was."

I snatched my check and stood. "Well, you were wrong about me, mister! So there!" Wait a minute. Oh, never mind. "This is just perfect. The perfect end to a perfect week."

He spread his hands apologetically. "I do apologize. And I wouldn't advise trying to snare me to get me to re-hire you. After all this time, I'm immune to everyone but my master."

"But . . . but if you know me, you must have recognized Eric Sinclair. And he zapped you pretty good."

"His Majesty the King," Mason said carefully, "is a very pow-erful vampire. You're quite right; I could not resist falling in thrall."

"Thrall? Falling in thrall? I don't know what the hell you're talking about, but I'm leaving before I pull your head off your shoulders and use it for a soccer ball."

"And I appreciate it. It really is for your own good, you know," he called after me as I stomped out. I made a rude gesture queens probably weren't prone to. Felt pretty good, though.

l trudged out to my car, which was parked in Georgia. Stupid gi-gantic Mall of America parking lot. What a rotten week. I couldn't imagine it getting any worse. Well, I suppose I could get decapi-tated. That might be worse. On the other hand, my troubles would pretty much be over.

I rested my forehead on my car roof. The body shop had done a good job of patching up the bullet holes and arrow gouges. And it ran like a dream. Too bad I just didn't have the energy to fish out my keys and get in. I'd probably run over a little kid on the way home, or have to break up another vamp/human unfair fight. Something. Something bad, guaranteed.

I heard a car pull up behind me, but didn't turn. What fresh hell was this? Probably the Ant, loaded down with crucifixes and baby formula.

"Majesty?"

I turned; it was Monique. She had opened her car door, a sleek black Porche, and was half-in, half-out of it. She looked gratifyingly concerned, which cheered me up a little. "What's wrong, my Queen?"

"Everything!"

She blinked at me.

I started banging my head against the roof. It didn't hurt a bit. "Every single thing in the whole world, *that's* what's wrong."

"Majesty, you're denting your car roof," she observed.

"Oh, who cares? I'd elaborate on my grotesque and numerous problems, but then I'll probably start to cry, and it'll be really awkward."

"I'm willing to take a chance. Why don't you leave your car and come with me? We can get a drink and you can tell me who you want me to kill."

"Don't tease me," I sighed. "And that's the best offer I've had all day. Okay."

I abandoned my car without a thought and practically jumped into Monique's Porsche. "Let's book."

# Chapter 25

"**THAT** does sound bad," Monique admitted when I finally wound down. She downshifted to make the yellow light, which showed off what pretty legs she had. Black miniskirt, black heels, white blouse with lace cuffs. Tarty, but trendy. "But at least the king is firmly in your corner."

"Ha! Firmly in my pants is more like it."

"Ah-*hum*. So . . . how is he?"

"Annoying."

"I mean . . . are his sheet skills adequate?"

"I have to admit," I admitted, "I've never heard it put quite like that. And yeah. They're more than adequate. I mean, he's really fine. Whoo! I could sweat just thinking about it. If I still sweat."

"Do tell!"

To a near stranger? Even a nice one? No thanks. "But it doesn't mean anything to him. He just likes sex. You should have seen what he was doing the first time I went to his house!"

"He seems," Monique said carefully, "to be an acceptable consort."

"Sure, if you don't mind being bossed around. And condescended to. And hugged when you're upset. And made love to until your toes curl. And-uh-look, let's talk about something else."

"As you wish." She wrenched the wheel as we turned onto Seventh Avenue—practically on two wheels, yikes!—and pulled up outside a small brownstone with a screech. I thought it was an apartment house, but the doors were propped open and there was a line of extremely hip-looking people stretching down the sidewalk. The red neon sign over the doors read SCRATCH.

"Oh, dancing?" I asked, brightening. "I love to dance."

"This is my club. I've been longing to show it to you."

"Oh, yeah?" Well, that explained the nice clothes. And the Porsche. "I didn't think you were from around here."

"I have properties all over the country. It's amazing what you can do when you've got seventy years to get it done."

"Good point," I said, as a valet held the door open. He was wearing black cargo pants, tennis shoes with no socks, and a white t-shirt with green lettering: GO FANG YOURSELF. Very cute. He smirked at me as he slammed the door shut and another valet drove Monique's car away. "So, this is like a vampire club?"

"Mostly. Come along, Majesty, let's get you a drink."

"Sounds good to me." We brushed past the waiting crowd and I followed her like a sheep to slaughter. Hmm. I *was* following her, and I certainly didn't mind, but why did that corny saying creep me out all of a sudden?

And why, now that Monique and I had entered the club, had everyone stopped dancing? And why were they all staring at us?

"You know," Monique said, turning to me, "you really don't deserve him."

"Who?" I asked dumbly. Sheep to slaughter? Where had I heard that before? Mr. Mason, of course. He said he was Kept. A sheep. And where had I heard that icky term before Mason? From Monique, the night Tina and she were attacked. She said it was much easier when you kept sheep, instead of hunting all the time. And Tina and Sinclair had blown it off, hadn't wanted to explain. Too late now. Too bad for me. "Who don't I deserve?" Except I had a horrid feeling I knew exactly who she was talking about.

"The king, of course."

"Yeah, of course. Uh . . . you didn't put Mr. Mason up to firing me or anything, did you?"

She just looked at me.

"Yeah. 'Course you did. He lied about Renee not coming in, so he could fire me and get me out of the building. And then . . . uh . . . he tipped you off, I guess, so you knew where I'd be, and now we're here. In your place."

"I knew you were foolish," she sighed as several hands grabbed me from behind, "but I didn't think you were a moron."

"What's the difference?" I yelled as I was dragged to the middle of the dance floor. Unfortunately, I didn't think it was because they wanted to do the Lambada with me. "And who's a moron? I figured it out, didn't I? Hey! Cut it out! Hands to yourselves, creeps. Monique, what the hell . . . ?"

Monique disappeared behind the bar, and reappeared with a wicked-looking stake as long as my forearm.

"And here I thought you were mixing me a daiquiri."

"This is your cue," she said, as if explaining to a slightly retarded student, which I resented the hell out of, "to say something obvious, like, 'you're the killer.' "

"Well, you are! I can't believe it! The *one* new vampire I meet who's actually nice, and you're going around killing vampires!" There were still about ten hands on me and they held me firmly. Where was Sinclair when I actually wanted him around?

"Yes," she said, sounding bored. Gosh, it was too bad I wasn't able to capture her full attention. I was getting so mad, I felt like biting myself. "I had this insane idea that you might be difficult to bring down. So I wanted the Warriors to get some practice. Then . . . *then,*" she added, and her lip curled, and she looked truly furious for the first time, "that idiot, that infant, that moron, Jon, fell under your spell. And he wouldn't kill you for me anymore. And he persuaded the others to stop, too."

I shrugged modestly. It wasn't my fault I had unholy sex appeal. "Too bad, you cow. And will you guys get *off?*" I yanked and pulled, to no avail. Were they rubber vampires, or what? "*And* you set yourself up to be attacked, to throw suspicion away from yourself."

She yawned. "Mmm-hmm."

And it worked, too, dammit. I'd never considered Monique for a second. I was too busy keeping a wary eye on Sarah, who was worth about twenty of this treacherous bitch. To think I staked *her* and decided to go party with Monique. God, I was really too stupid to live sometimes. However, it didn't look like that was going to be a problem much longer.

"Well, now you're gonna get it. I guess. Yeah! Big trouble, Monique." As soon as I freed myself from the grip of the Rubber-Maid Undead. "Any second now, and I'll . . . uh . . ."

"So, I'll kill you," she finished, perking up, "and Sinclair will be in need of a new consort, and of course Tina won't do. They're more like siblings, have you noticed? And Sarah's dead, and there aren't many of us who are suitable, you know."

"So that leaves you, huh?"

"That leaves me."

"But aren't there thousands of us?"

"I can assure you, Eric Sinclair will find me the most viable choice."

"And the fact that he has a consort right now," I said dryly, "isn't an impediment, or anything."

"Impediment! I'm amazed you didn't need a flashcard to use the word."

"Hey, hey! Assaulting me is one thing, but watch the nasty comments."

She stalked toward me, stake in hand. I became morbidly aware that we had an audience. Besides the vampires hanging onto me with grim determination, there were about twenty more on the dance floor who were staring at us. No help, I figured. They belonged to Monique. Or they didn't think I was a real queen. Either way, it amounted to the same thing. Well, at least she was still talking, even if she was waving that stake around like a band leader's baton. Classic James Bond villain mistake. I hoped.

"Waste of resources."

"What? I wasn't listening."

She gritted her teeth. "I said, I am appalled at the waste of vampires and resources. I should have taken you myself, the moment I came to town. I had no idea you'd be so easy."

"Hey! What'd I say about the nasty stuff?"

"To think I was paying the Blade Warriors to practice, to hone their skills, to work their way *up* to you. What nonsense! You didn't really kill Nostro, did you?"

"What?" The abrupt subject change took me by surprise. "Is that why you thought I'd be such a toughie?"

She gave me a withering "of course" look.

"As a matter of fact, I *did* kill him, so there." Alas, like little George Washington, I could not tell a lie. "Well, sort of. I set the Fiends on him, and they ate him." The Fiends! What I wouldn't give to see their snarling faces right now. "But listen, Monique. You don't have to stake me to get Sinclair. You can *have* him."

"I disagree."

"No, really!" I couldn't believe this. First he tricked me into boinking him. Then I found out I was his undead little woman for a thousand years. Then he tricked me into boinking him again. Well, sort of. Now this nutty bitch was going to kill me to have him for herself! Oooh, if I lived through this, he was getting a piece of my mind.

A pox on you, Eric Sinclair!

"Seriously. I don't want him, I never wanted him." Okay, that last one was a small lie. I mean, I *wanted* wanted him, you know, like you want a juicy steak, but I didn't want to be married to him, not without him at least asking. Which he never did. Not once. Was that so much to ask? A marriage proposal? I didn't think so. Not that anybody asked my opinion. Oh, God forbid, anybody should ask my opinion!

". . . is devoted to you."

"What?"

"Will you pay attention? In case you haven't noticed, you're in dire straits."

"Yeah, yeah. I've been there before. Look, we can work this out. Sure, you're a crazy cow bent on my destruction, but can't we get along? I mean, if my parents could work things out, anybody can. You can have Sinclair on Mondays, Wednesdays, and Fridays, and I—"

She lunged forward with a scream of frustration—I'll admit I have that effect on people—and buried the stake in my chest. It hurt like a son of a bitch. And then I died. Again.

# Chapter 26

**FROM** the private papers of Father Markus, Parish Priest, St. Pious Church, 129 E. 7th Street, Minneapolis, Minnesota.

Moments too late! I suspect that's why we were all so slow to react. It didn't seem real that we hadn't arrived in time to save the day. The children, especially, had no real experience in failure. The cavalry always arrives in time, at least in the movies.

Jon had followed Betsy all over town, of course—foolish boy, we had all warned him it was hopeless—and something about the club put him on alert. Possibly the way all the vampires waiting outside ran off for no apparent reason. They must have sensed something in the air—shifting allegiences, perhaps. It didn't matter now.

The important thing was, Jon called us when he got to Scratch. It didn't take long for us to arrive, in terms of mileage. In terms of time, of course, it took just a few moments too long.

When the woman who had been pulling our strings killed Betsy, it was like all the light went out of the room. Exactly like that. We were so shocked, nobody moved.

And Betsy was still, so still. It seemed ridiculous that those green eyes would never again flash fire, that her red lips would never form the words idiot or moron or asshole ever again.

Then Eric Sinclair, as formidable and frightening a creature as I have met in my long days, just went to pieces. It would have been touching if it hadn't been so terribly, terribly sad.

He cradled her in his arms and sank to the floor. His coat billowed around them as they fell. He whispered her name, over and over, and caressed her face with trembling fingers, and blocked all of us out.

Our former employer, Monique, tried to explain herself. She could smell death in the air—her own, as well as the Queen's. We were all standing in silent judgement, but she must have known it wouldn't last. That we would soon be moved to action. She had been caught out, her true colors revealed at the worst possible moment, and she knew it as well as we did.

It was the usual, tedious motive: she explained that she had coveted Eric, who by vampire law belonged to Betsy. So Monique had formed the Blade Warriors to get Betsy out of the way.

Was she crazy, I wondered disapassionately, or just driven? Had years of feasting on humans warped her conscience until hiring children to kill her own kind actually seemed like a fine plan? I didn't know. And at the moment, frankly, I didn't care.

But she might as well have been speaking to a boulder. Despite her pleadings for his attention, Eric Sinclair simply rocked Betsy in his arms and wouldn't look up or speak.

Tina, however, had no such compunctions. She was as angered and shocked as any of us, but she was not frozen to inaction. I have long been fascinated by how different vampires are on the outside from their true selves. Tina had always looked like a charming sorority girl to me.

Not tonight.

She led the charge, and in minutes, a vicious fight was raging all around us. I pulled Marc and Jessica behind me— they were too stunned to fight—and held out my cross, but I needn't have bothered. I could see several of Monique's minions were slipping out the back, avoiding the fight entirely. Wise of them. Because when Mr. Sinclair recovered his wits, this would not be a good day to be on Monique's side.

Being human, I of course could not track much of the fight. It was a physical impossibility. There would be a flash of silver or a blurred fist, and then a vampire's head would be rolling on the floor, or a body would sail through the air. And the children, as always, acquitted themselves well.

Finally, only Monique was left, and Jon, who had tears in his eyes, pulled his knife and marched toward her. He ignored us, he ignored everything. He swung it back, and I heard him say, "This is for Betsy, you bitch," only to be stopped in mid-swing by Tina's sharp, "Hold!"

For she had moved with that eerie, inhuman quickness, and was now holding our common enemy at swordpoint—Ani's sword, in fact—and had an arm out to prevent Jon from getting closer.

Monique had been backed into a corner, and Tina, despite her fragile looks, was formidable. Ani was backing her up, but it appeared to be entirely unnecessary.

"We'll let the king decide her fate," Tina said, and that was that. Even Jon, heartbroken, could not argue with that command.

I noted much of the heart had gone out of Monique's group when Eric Sinclair arrived. It made sense, though it was unfair and unkind to dear Betsy. Because if she hadn't seemed especially royal or noble—although she was, if one cared to take the trouble to really see her—there was never any question of Eric's right to the throne. And nobody wanted to mess with the most powerful vampire on the planet. Especially when he had just lost his consort to treachery and betrayal.

The last of Monique's vamps slipped out, and we let them go. We had been woefully outnumbered, and weren't unaware of the depths of our luck.

While Tina held Monique at bay, the rest of us crouched around Betsy. There was no blood and, as I wrote earlier, the whole thing didn't seem quite real. She did not look like a dead woman. The stories were wrong. The movies were wrong. She wasn't a pile of dust, she wasn't a wizened mummy. Her eyes were closed, though she had that vertical wrinkle in the middle of her forehead which usually meant she was annoyed. She looked as though her eyes would pop open at any moment and she would demand tea with extra sugar and cream.

After a long moment, Marc, ever the practical physician, asked what we should do. Jon did not answer him, and Tina just shook her head. Monique tried to speak, and stopped when the swordpoint pressed into her throat.

As for the rest of us, we knew it was hopeless. Vampires

did not come back after being staked with wood. It was impossible—even those formidable night creatures had to follow their own rules. But none of us had the heart to let Marc and Jessica in on this fact. We were just using this time to begin to recover from the shock.

It had been, as the deaths of all charismatic individuals are, too sudden, too quick. We wanted time to grieve.

Jessica was straightening out Betsy's bangs, which were quite disheveled, and I could see her tears dripping down on Betsy's still face.

"Oh, Bets, Bets . . . it's not fair. We figured it out. If we'd just been here a minute sooner . . . we could have saved you! We *should* have!"

She was young.

"I just can't do this again," Jessica wept. "I wasn't supposed to have to go through this anymore with you. You've got to stop dying on me!"

"Well, forget it," Marc said abruptly. He put his hand on the stake protruding between Betsy's breasts. Jon put out a hand to stop him, but Marc shook his head so hard, his own tears flew. "I can't stand to see her like this, you guys. Like a bug tacked to a fucking board. It's not right, and I'm not havin' it."

And, with a wrench and a grunt, he yanked the stake out of her chest.

Betsy's eyes flew open, which of course, startled everybody.

# Chapter 27

ℐ felt a sharp burning in my chest, heard my shirt tear, and opened my eyes to give whoever-it-was a piece of my mind.

"Owwww!" I complained. "Dammit, this is a new shirt!"

There was a *thump* as Sinclair dropped me. Why he'd been holding me I had no idea—his sneakiness and hidden agendas were boundless. "Elizabeth," he said, and I was startled to see his lips were dead white.

"Owwww again! What'd you do that for?" I rubbed the back of my head. "What are you guys all staring at? You're freaking me out." And they were! I was looking up at a moon of faces, and every one of them had their mouths hanging open. I was afraid if I stayed where I was, I'd get drooled on.

"Buh," Jon said.

"Yeah, okay. What happened? Where's that sneaky cow, Monique? Oooh, she's toast! Did you guys know she was the bad guy? She totally is! She tricked me into coming and partying with her. Except some party—she *staked* me in the chest. I mean, who *does* that? And it hurt like hell! And what took you guys so long? Why am I lying on this disgusting floor? Sinclair, help me off this floor right now."

"Buh," Jon said again. Not sure what the boy's problem was, but right now I had bigger fish to fry.

"You're alive!" Jessica blurted. "Again."

"Look at this hole in my shirt," I complained. "Does she think cotton grows on trees? Wait a minute. It does, doesn't it? Or does it grow on bushes? Either way, I . . . mmph!" I beat at Sinclair's

..lder until he stopped kissing me. "Dude! Time and place, ..ay? Now let me up."

He hauled me to my feet and Jon threw his arms around me, which made me stagger. Then Sinclair peeled him off me and started making that peculiar growling noise again, and Jon sort of bristled back, and Jessica snapped at them both to cut the shit, but I didn't care because I spotted Monique, who was backed up in a corner and had a sword at her throat, courtesy of my new best friend, Tina.

"Ha!" I said, yanking the stake away from Marc, who let out a yelp and then pulled a splinter out of his palm. "Stake *me* in the chest, willya? And you *ruined* my shirt."

I marched over to Monique, who managed to look amazed, scared, and pissed, all at the same time. "False queen," she said defiantly as Tina stepped away. Made me sort of nervous. I kind of wished that the sword was still pointing at my nemesis *du jour*. "You'll never rule."

"Tsk, tsk. Someone skipped her Book of the Dead bible lessons. Apparently I *am* ruling. It's just, losers like you didn't get the memo."

"You're talking too much," she said. "You always do."

"Awww, that hurts, Monique! It gets me right here." I touched the gaping hole in my shirt. "Where's the love? Say, while I'm thinking about it, you dropped something over there." I hefted the stake. "I think I'll give it back. If you don't mind."

"You don't have the—*urk!*"

"Oh, gross!" Jessica cried, turning away.

"Sorry," I said, stepping back and surveying the staked Monique with—I admit it—not a little bit of satisfaction. "What can I say? Death is messy. And she had it coming." I tried not to sound as whiney and defensive as I felt.

Because she *did* have it coming. For what she made the Blade Warriors do to all those other poor vamps, never mind what she did to me. Let her explain herself to the devil, if she could. *I* didn't care.

"Nicely done," Sinclair commented. He was looking a little better—not so deathly pale (for him)—which was a relief. And he wasn't growling at Jon like a rabid bear anymore.

"I wanted to do it," Jon pouted.

"It was sort of my job," I explained. "You can kill the next evil vampire serial killer."

"Oh." He visibly perked up. "Okay. I'm glad you're not dead for real."

"Me, too," Marc and Jessica said in fervent unison.

"Yeah, um, what's up with that? Monique's not going to come back like I did if I take that stake out, is she?"

"Of course not," Tina said, sounding shocked. "No one ever does. I mean . . . besides you. No one has ever . . ." She trailed off and shook her head, looking mystified, which for someone that smart, was a pretty rare thing.

"And that's interesting, isn't it?" Sinclair asked.

"Interesting," Jessica said, still looking a little green around the gills, "is so *not* the adjective I'm thinking right now." She shook a finger under my nose. "You . . . you . . ." She didn't have to say any more. I could tell she had been through hell again.

He ignored her. "I don't believe the Book of the Dead mentioned just how . . . unkillable . . . Elizabeth seems to be."

"Well." I shrugged. "You know. Hard to keep a good woman down, and all that."

"Particularly now," he said dryly, "with all your new possessions."

"What?"

"By our law, when you kill one of us, their possessions become yours."

"No way. Really? What about their families?"

"Vampires don't have families," Tina explained patiently. "Except for you, apparently. Didn't you wonder why Nostro's house never sold? It's yours."

"Sweet! First Sarah's Armanis, now this! Did you see Monique's Porche? Mine, all mine!" I stopped, because Marc and Jessica were giving me funny looks. "I mean, not that I killed her just to get the car, or anything." That was just a sweet, sweet bonus.

"No," Tina said, giving me a funny look of her own, "but I think that's the story we'll spread."

"How come?"

"We'll have to," Sinclair said, "until you work up some ruthlessness. Otherwise, this problem will keep coming up. Others will assume you're an easy kill, and will try for your crown."

"Who cares? She's obviously unkillable."

"Nobody is," Father Markus objected. "Not even Christ."

"Besides, I'm plenty ruthless," I protested. "I killed two vampires this week! *And* I put the milk back last night when there was just a tiny bit left."

"That was you?" Marc asked.

"Although . . ." I nibbled my lower lip, thinking. "I didn't kill
.. Mason, and I sure should have."

"Mason? Your supervisor at Macy's?"

"Yeah, he's Monique's evil minion! He totally set me up.
Fired my ass, then tipped her off so she could scoop me up like a
minnow in a bait shop. Jerk."

"Really." Sinclair's eyes went flat. "Elaborate." He made me
tell him the whole story, and then he took me over it one more
time. Everyone was appropriately outraged on my behalf. It was
great!

"I can't believe your boss tried to kill you, too," Jessica said. "I
mean, I know they're trying to keep the unemployment rate down,
but that's ridiculous."

"Most people think their bosses are out to get them. But mine really was! Eh, never mind him . . . now what? I mean, besides changing my shirt. This is just"—I looked down at myself—"yech."

"We have much to discuss," Sinclair announced.

"You're right about that," Tina said, looking disturbingly fer-
vid. "What does this mean? For all of us, and for our queen?"

"It will make for some fascinating additions to my papers,"
Father Markus admitted. He looked like he could hardly wait to sit
down at a desk and write. Bo-ring.

"Majesty, you're with us again! Unprecedented! And—"

"Look, you two . . . I realize you can't help being total buzz
kills, but we're not having any big panel discussion tonight. It's
Friday, I've shrugged off death's clammy embrace—"

"Again," Ani said.

"—and I want to dance!"

"I could use a drink," Jessica admitted, "or five."

"Me, too," Marc chimed in. He wiped sweat off his forehead.
He and Jessica still looked really rattled. "It's really stressful,
watching you come back from the dead."

"I'm sorry," I said humbly. "It's been a bad week for everybody, I guess."

"No more of this getting killed crap," Jessica ordered.

"Hey, it's not exactly fun for me, either! It's not like I'm doing it for the attention." There was an annoying, pointed silence.
"I'm not!"

"Where are you going dancing?" Ani asked.

"Nowhere you can get in," Jessica said shortly. "This is strictly
a roommates-of-Betsy unwinding thing."

"I'm a roommate of Betsy," Sinclair said mildly.

"I guess we could go to Gator's," I said. Then the words sunk in. *"What?"*

"Oh, did I not mention it?" He looked so innocent; b wouldn't melt on his fangs. "We're leaving the Marquette; it's longer adequate for our needs. And after some discussion of th problem earlier this evening, Jessica has kindly agreed to be our landlord."

*"You're moving in?"* I was going to faint. I was going to throw something. I was going to get new sheets. "You . . . I . . . you . . ."

Jessica spread her hands and shrugged. I shot her a murderous glare. All that "she's in love with him and she doesn't know it" talk I'd overheard! And she'd been planning *this*.

I never should have slept with him again. Jessica wouldn't have jumped to dumbass conclusions if she hadn't seen us in bed together. Oh, I knew it! I knew I'd be sorry for that moment of weakness, but even I couldn't have foreseen this. *Nothing good comes of having sex with Eric Sinclair!*

I put a hand up, rubbed my forehead. "I really need that drink now."

"We're in a bar," Jon pointed out.

"Forget it, you little weirdos," I said rudely, including Ani in my diatribe. "A) I'm not partying in dead Monique's tacky club, and B) you guys aren't even drinking age. So you're not coming."

"Oh. Almost forgot." Jessica fished in her pocket, then stretched something shiny toward Eric and Tina. "Here's your house key."

I snatched it from her and ate it. I gagged, but it went down.

"Oh, very mature," Sinclair sniffed, but I could sense the smirk lurking.

"Don't talk to me." I paused, to see if the key was going to come back up. It was staying put, for now. "And *you* . . ." I grabbed Jessica's ear and she yelped. "Come on. I'm driving my new Porche somewhere and you're gonna explain yourself." After I threw up the key.

"It just makes fiscal sense . . . if you look at the numbers I'm sure you'll—let go!"

"He can sleep in my room," Marc offered.

"I suppose I should say something negative about vampires living in sin," Father Markus said, "but that seems to be the least of your problems."

"Actually, I've already picked out the room next to Elizabeth's—do not attempt to grab my ear," he added quickly as

...ied in his direction. "Unless you wish to be put across my

'Oh, is that what you guys are up to when the sun goes ...wn?" Ani teased, as Jon reddened and looked away.

I got out of there, dragging Jessica and Marc, before my head exploded.

# Epilogue

So now I'm living with stupid Sinclair and stupid Tina in a gigantic mansion that I can't afford. *And* I'm undead and unemployed. Again.

Okay, well, Tina's not so stupid. In fact, I kind of like her when she's not startling me with her core of utter ruthlessness. Plus, she makes a mean strawberry smoothie. Even Sinclair drinks them! I guess he really loves strawberries. I gotta change my shampoo.

Strange vampires keep dropping by to show tribute. Apparently Monique's little coup failure has been making the gossip channels, because dead people are falling all over themselves to stop by and say howdy. For some reason, they bring blood oranges. Sinclair says it's tradition. I say it's cracked. The fridge is full of the damned things.

I thought Marc and Jessica were nuts to open their—our—home to more vampires, but Marc earnestly explained that he doesn't think of Tina and Eric as undead. I bet he'd change his mind if either one of them ever got hungry enough.

As for Jessica, she's made up her mind that as long as Sinclair and I are meant to be, we might as well start getting used to each other. And it'd be rude to leave Tina out, since she and Eric are practically brother and sister. Thus, we are now roommates. I searched her room, but could find no evidence of drug use.

It's unbelievably nerve-wracking to come downstairs and find Sinclair already in the tea room, reading the *Wall Street Journal* and getting a smirk ready.

Not to mention, I've been fighting the almost constant tempta-

ɔ sneak into his room wearing nothing but a smirk of my
. But I realized my lesson in Monique's club: nothing good
ɪ come of having sex with Eric Sinclair. And as for the gentle-
ɪan in question, he's been . . . well, a perfect gentleman. Dammit.

He and Tina brought the Book of the Dead to the house, where
we keep it in the library on its own little mahogany book stand.
Jessica tried to read it and got a three day migraine for her pains.
She also jumped at small noises and wouldn't eat for most of
those three days. Now she stays the hell away from the library.

I'll get to the book myself someday, but for now I'm trying
lighter fare. Let Tina and Sinclair manage the thing, if they could.

When I rose a few nights ago, there was a copy of Pat Conroy's biography, *My Losing Season,* on my chest. It took me a
week to read it and the best part was, there was no mention of
food anywhere. So I put it on the shelf with my other books.
Guess a door I thought was closed had swung open again . . . I
was sure glad.

I tried to thank Sinclair (I knew Jess hadn't done it; she'd have
made sure she got the credit . . . but I bet she gave him the idea),
but he gave me a look like he didn't know what I was talking
about, so I dropped it.

Jon left town. He said he wanted to get back to the suburbs to
see his family, but I think, and Jessica concurs, he couldn't stand
the thought of Sinclair living with me. Which made two of us,
frankly. He promised to come back at the end of the summer, and
I actually find myself missing the little weirdo.

Ani hangs around most evenings. I think she and Tina have
something going, but they're discreet. Still, they're both doing a
lot of wandering around the mansion, humming. And the goofy
smiles are annoying.

Sinclair was right: Monique's stuff came to me. It was true. She
really did have several properties all over the world. And *two* cars!

What the hell I was going to do with a club in Minneapolis, a
spa in Switzerland, a private school in England, and a restaurant in
France remains beyond me. I don't know a damn thing about managing multiple businesses. I guess I could go get a job at one of
them. Maybe I'd try to run Scratch . . .

Detective Nick Berry's peripheral involvement in the whole
nasty business was that rarest of things. A true coincidence. The
cabbie I'd saved had just happened to give his report to Nick. Nick
had just happened to see my car a few days later and pulled me

over. I was glad. I'd messed up his life once before; I wou
hated to find it a ruin again.

Mr. Mason disappeared. I didn't even know about it until ᴵ
the blurb in the paper. He had no family, and his own boss was
one who finally reported him missing; how's that for sad?

Gone without a trace, until they found a few pieces of him in
his apartment a month later. Inside a suitcase, which he'd apparently been in the middle of packing when . . . when whatever happened, happened. I asked Sinclair about it, and he just turned the
page of the *Journal* and didn't answer me. So I didn't bring it up
again. Felt a little sorry for Mr. Mason, though. After all, he *did*
give me a job at Macy's.

Went to see the Ant, with a Calvin Klein onesie for my future
half-sibling. Sort of a "can't we pretend we don't hate each
other?" ice breaker. She "accidentally" spilled red wine on it.

I'm worried about the gardener. Nobody else talks about
him, and when I describe him I get a lot of funny looks. Jessica
says she did hire someone to take care of the lawn and
flowerbeds, but it was a young woman in her twenties. This guy's
old, really old.

I'm pretty sure I'm the only one who can see him.

I'm scared to go talk to him, but one of these days I plan to get
it over with. Whatever his deal is, hopefully I can help, and he'll
vamoose like Marie did. I miss *her,* but creepy old guy ghosts staring up at my bedroom window whenever I look out I do *not* need.

I did a lot of thinking about what happened that night in
Monique's bar. The whole day—week!—had a fairly nightmarish
quality and sometimes it's hard to remember all the gory details.
Whenever I try, my mind veers off to sweater sales and leather
gloves. All the winter stuff is in the stores now, and I need to
stock up.

Jessica asked me about it, and Tina did, too, but Sinclair
avoided the subject entirely, and I wasn't sure why. I told them the
truth—I didn't remember much between getting staked, and Marc
pulling the stake out.

What I didn't tell them was the one thing I *did* remember: Sinclair's voice floating out of the dark, coaxing, commanding, and
saying the same thing over and over again: "Come back. Come
back. Don't leave me. Come back."

Weird. And sometimes I wonder if I dreamed it. Or halluci-
nated it. Or, most amazing of all, if he really said it. God knows I

...going to ask him . . . I was still building up my courage to ...the dead gardener.

...o, either I can't be killed, or the king of the undead brought ...back by the sheer force of his will. Either way, something to ...ink about.

But not today. Neiman's is having a sale, and I desperately need a cashmere cardigan. I'd prefer red, but I'll take any primary color. Jessica's paying! She says it's a "congrats on coming back from the dead again" present.

Works for me.

# Author's Note

PRETTY much without exception, the events in this book are entirely made up. Vampires don't stay at the Marquette Hotel; nor do they work the cash registers at Macy's.

However, as of the time of this writing, if you go to a Work-Force Center in Minnesota, they aren't allowed to answer questions about unemployment insurance. And at some centers, you really aren't allowed to use their phones to call someone who can. Honest.

Also, visitors to Summit Avenue will note that the house across from the governor's mansion A) isn't Betsy's, and B) isn't at the end of the block. Artistic license, which is a fancy way of saying I was lazy.

# Undead and Unappreciated

*For my brother-in-law, Daniel,*
*who never complains.*
*No matter how often I try*
*to drag good gossip out of him, dammit.*

# Acknowledgments

This book would not have been possible without . . . me!

Also my husband, my PR person, my sister, my parents, my editor, my girlfriends, my agent, the copy editor, the cover artist, the sales reps, the marketing team, the book-sellers, the makers of Godiva chocolates, and my readers.

But mostly me.

# Author's Note

Of course, the devil's daughter doesn't really live in a suburb of Minneapolis. She lives in a suburb of Saint Paul. Duh.

Also, Betsy researched the Web for nondenominational wedding information and relied heavily on http://www.maggiedot.com/7Destiny/. Many thanks to the Reverend Marcia Ann George.

The Queene's sister shalt be Belov'd of the Morning Star, and shalt take the Worlde.

—THE BOOK OF THE DEAD

Make a searching and fearless moral inventory of yourself.

—ALCOHOLICS ANONYMOUS, STEP FOUR

Will you still need me, will you still please me, when I'm sixty-four?

—JOHN LENNON AND PAUL MCCARTNEY

# Prologue 1: Secrets

ONCE upon a time, the devil was bored, and possessed a not-very-nice pregnant woman, and ran that woman's body for about a year.

The devil still drank and smoked, but only in moderation. The devil was good about taking prenatal pills but grumbled about the inevitable constipation.

And eventually, the devil gave birth to a baby girl.

After a month of diapers, night feedings, colic, laundry, spilled formula (the devil hated to breast-feed), and spit-up, the devil said, "Enough of this," and went back to Hell, which was infinitely preferable to living with a newborn.

The devil's daughter was adopted and grew up in a suburb of Minneapolis, Minnesota. Her name was Laura, and she liked strawberry ice cream, and she never, ever missed church. She was a very nice young lady.

But she had a terrible temper.

# Prologue 2: Problems

*Thunderbird Motel*
*Bloomington, Minnesota*
*8:57 p.m.*

"OKAY. guys, let's set up here . . . Charley, you okay here? You got light?"

Her cameraman looked up. "It's shitty out here. Should be better inside."

"We won't film out here . . . we'll go inside the conference room. So, you're sure this is okay?"

The representative, who was smooth and sweatless like an egg, clasped his hands together and nodded slowly. Even his suit seemed to be free of threads or seams. "People need to see that it's not a bunch of chain-smoking losers who are afraid to go outside. There's doctors. There's lawyers. There's"—he stared at her with pale blue eyes, pilot's eyes—"anchorwomen."

*Subtle, jerk.* "Right, right. And we'll put all that across." She turned away from the AA rep, muttering under her breath. "Fuckin' slow news days . . . give me a war update anytime . . . okay! Let's get in there, Chuckles."

Charley knew his stuff, and with the new equipment, setup was not only a breeze, it was relatively quick and quiet. The conference room looked and smelled like a thousand others; sparse and scented of coffee. Interestingly, none of the room's inhabitants looked at them directly. There was a lot of coffee drinking and low chatting, a lot of nibbling on cheese and crackers, a lot of quiet milling and sideways glances.

They looked, the newswoman thought to herself, exactly like the man said. Respectable, settled. Sober. She was amazed they'd agreed to the cameras. Wasn't the second A supposed to be for *Anonymous*?

"Okay, everyone," the rep said, standing in the front of the room. "Let's get settled and get started. You all remember Channel 9 was coming tonight to help raise awareness . . . someone watching tonight might see we're not all villains in trench coats and maybe will come down."

"I'll start, and then we've got a new person here tonight . . ."

Someone the reporter couldn't see protested in a low yet frantic voice, and was ignored—or wasn't heard—by the rep. "I'm James," the rep continued, "and I've been sober for six years, eight months, and nine days."

There was a pause as he stepped down, then a rustle, a muffled, "Oof! Stupid steps." Then a young woman in her midtwenties was standing behind the small podium. She squinted out at the audience for a moment, as if the fluorescent lighting hurt her eyes, and then said in a completely mesmerizing voice, "Well, hi there. I'm Betsy. I haven't had a drink in three days and four hours."

"Get on her!" the reporter hissed.

"I'm tight," Charley replied, dazzled.

The woman was tall—her head was just below the NO SMOKING ON THESE PREMISES sign—which put her at about six feet. She was dressed in a moss green suit with the kind of suit jacket that buttoned up to her chin and needed no underblouse. The richly colored clothing superbly set off the delicate paleness of her skin and made her green eyes seem huge and dark, like leaves in the middle of the forest. Her hair was golden blond, shoulder length and wavy, with lovely red and gold highlights that framed her face. Her cheekbones were sharp planes in an interesting, even arresting face.

Her teeth were very white and flashed while she spoke.

"Okay, um, like I said, I'm Betsy. And I thought I'd come here . . . I mean, I saw on the Web that . . . anyway, I thought maybe you guys would have some tricks or something I could use to stop drinking."

Dead silence. The reporter noticed the audience was as rapt as

Charley was. What presence! What clothes! What . . . Were those Bruno Maglis? The reporter edged closer. They were! What did this woman do for a living? She herself had paid almost three hundred bucks for the pair in her closet.

"It's just . . . always there. I wake up, and it's all I think about. I go to bed, I'm still thinking about it."

Everyone was nodding. Even Charley was nodding, making the camera wobble.

"It just . . . takes over. Totally takes over your life. You start to plan events around how you can drink. Like, if I have breakfast *here* with my friend, I can hit an alley afterward *there,* while she's going uptown. Or, if I blow another friend off for supper, I can reschedule on *him* and get my fix instead."

Everyone was nodding harder. A few of the men appeared to have tears in their eyes! Charley, thankfully, had stopped nodding, but was getting in on the woman as tightly as he could.

"Get the suit in the shot," the reporter whispered.

"I'm not used to this," the woman continued. "I mean, I'm used to wanting things, but not like *this*. I mean, gross."

A ripple of laughter.

"I've tried to stop, but I just made myself sick. And I've talked to some of my friends about it, but they think I should just suck it up. Ha-ha. And my new friends don't see it as a problem at all. I guess they're, what do you call them, enablers." More nods all around. "So here I am. Someone with a problem. A *big* problem. And . . . I thought maybe coming here and talking about it would help. That's all." Silence, so she added, "That's really all."

Spontaneous, almost savage, applause. The reporter had Charley pan back, getting the crowd's reaction. She wasn't sure the rep would let all their faces be shown on the ten o'clock news, but she wanted the film in the can, just in case.

She wanted Charley to get the woman walking to the back of the room, but when he panned back, she was gone.

The reporter and her cameraman looked for the gorgeous stranger for ten minutes, with zero luck. Neither of them could figure out how a woman could just disappear out of a small conference room.

Gone.

Shit.

# Chapter 1

$\mathcal{I}$ took another slurp of my tea (orange pekoe, six sugars) and stuck out my left foot. Yep, last season's Brunos still looked great. Hell, they could be from the last decade and still look great. Quality costs . . . and it lasts, too.

Marc Spangler, one of my roommates, slouched into the kitchen, yawning. I withdrew my leg before he tripped and brained himself on the microwave. He looked like pan-fried hell, which was to say, he looked like he just came off shift. Since moving in with an emergency ward physician, I've discovered that your average doc comes off shift grimier than your average garbageman.

I greeted him warmly. "Another hard afternoon saving lives and seducing the janitor?"

"Another hard night suckering poor slobs out of their precious lifeblood?"

"Yep," we both said.

He poured himself a glass of milk and sat down across from me. "You look like you need some toast," I prompted.

"Forget it. I'm not eating food so you can get off on it second-hand. 'Ooh, ooh, Marc, make sure you smear the butter allllll over the bread . . . now let me smell it . . . don't you want some sweet, sweet jelly with that?' I've gained seven pounds since I moved in, you cow."

"You should have more respect for the dead," I said solemnly, and we both cracked up.

"God, what a day," he said. His hair was growing in nicely (he'd gone through a head-shaving phase this past summer), so now he looked like a clean Brillo pad with friendly green eyes. I wished my eyes were like that, but mine were murky, like fridge mold. His were clear, like lagoon water.

"Death? Bloodletting? Gang war?" Unlikely in Minnesota, but he looked pretty whipped.

"No, the fucking administration changed all the forms again." He rubbed his eyebrows. "Every time they do it, there's a six-month learning curve. Then when we've figured out who has to sign what and in what order, they change them again. You know, in the name of efficiency."

"That blows," I said sympathetically.

"What about you, what'd you do? Chomp on any would-be rapists? Or was tonight one of the nights you didn't bother to get anything to eat?"

"The second one. Oh, and I crashed an AA meeting."

He was halfway to the fridge for a milk refill and froze like I'd yelled "I see a Republican!" "You did what?"

"Crashed an AA meeting. Did you know they film those now?"

"They *what*?"

"I was kind of nervous because I didn't know if I'd have to, y'know, prove I was a drunk or if they'd take my word for it, or if I needed a note from a doctor or bartender or something, and it was kind of weird with the camera lights and all—"

He was giving me the strangest look. Usually I got that look from Sinclair. "It doesn't work like that."

"Yeah, I know, I found out. Really nice bunch of people. Kind of jumpy, but very friendly. Had to dodge the reporter, though."

"Reporter—" He shook his head. "But Betsy . . . why did you go?"

"Isn't it obvious?" I asked, a little irritably. Marc was usually sharper than this. "I drink blood."

"And did it work?" he asked with exaggerated concern.

"No, dimwad, it did not. The reporter and the lights freaked me out, so I left early. But I might go back." I took another gulp of tea. Needed more sugar. I dumped some in and added, "Yep, I just might. Maybe they don't teach you the trick until you've gone a few times."

"It's not a secret handshake, honey." He laughed, but not like he thought what I'd said was funny. "But you could try that, see how that works."

"What's your damage? Maybe *you* should have a drink," I joked.

"I'm a recovering alcoholic."

"Oh, you are not."

"Betsy. I am."

"Nuh-uh!"

"Uh-huh."

I fought down escalating panic. Sure, I hadn't known Marc as long as I'd known, say, Jessica, but still. You'd think he would have brought something like that up. Or—ugh!—maybe he had, and I'd been so obsessed with the events of the past six months I hadn't—

"Don't worry," he said, reading my aghast expression and interpreting it correctly. "I never told you before."

"Well, I . . . I guess I should have noticed." I could put away a case of plum wine a month, and Jessica liked her daiquiris, and Sinclair went through grasshoppers like there was gonna be a crème de menthe embargo (for a studly vampire king, he drank like a girl), but I'd never noticed how Marc always stuck to milk. Or juice. Or water.

Of course, I'd had other things on my mind. Especially lately. But I was still embarrassed. Some friend! Didn't even realize my own roommate had a drinking problem. "I guess I should have noticed," I said again. "I'm sorry."

"I guess I should have told you. But there didn't ever seem to be a good time to bring it up. I mean, first there was the whole thing with Nostro, and then all the vampires getting killed, and then Sinclair moved in . . ."

"Ugh, don't remind me. But . . . you're so young. How did you even know you were one, much less decided to stop drinking?"

"I'm not that young, Betsy. You're only four years older than me."

I ignored that. "Is that why you were going to jump off the hospital roof when I met you?" I asked excitedly. "The booze had driven you to suicide?"

"No, paperwork and never getting laid had driven me to suicide. The booze just made me sleepy. In fact, that was the whole problem. Sleep."

"Yeah?"

"Yeah. See, being a med student isn't so bad. The work isn't intellectually hard or anything—"

"Spoken like a math genius."

"No, it's really not," he insisted. "There's just a lot of stuff to memorize. And they—hospitals—can't work a student to death.

But they can work the interns and residents to death. And the thing is, when you're an intern, you're always short on sleep rations."

I nodded. I'd faithfully watched every episode of *ER* until they killed off Mark Green and the show started severely sucking.

"So it was normal to go forty, fifty hours sometimes without sleep."

"Yeah, but don't patients suffer because of it? I mean, tired people fuck up. Even someone who didn't go to Harvard Medical School knows that."

Marc nodded. "Sure. And it's not news to administration, either, or the chief residents, or the nurses. But the fuckups are blamed because a babydoc—that's what the interns are called—did it, not because he did it because he hadn't slept in two nights."

"Bogus."

"Tell me. They're supposed to limit the amount of hours you work, but it's not enforced. After a while you get used to it. You can't really remember a time when you weren't dog-ass tired. It starts getting hard to sleep even on your nights off. You're so used to being awake, and even if you do fall asleep, you know a nurse is going to wake you up in five minutes to handle a code or an admit, so why bother going down in the first place, and you just . . . stay awake. All the time."

He went back to the fridge, refilled his milk, took a sip, sat back down. "So, after a while I started having a few shots of Dewar's to help me get to sleep. A while after that, I started thinking on shift how great that shot of Dewar's would taste when I got home. A while after *that,* I started drinking whether I needed to get to sleep or not. And after that, I started to bring my old friend Dewar's to work."

"You drank . . . at work?" *And you drink blood,* I reminded myself. *Let's not start pointing fingers.*

"Yup. And the funny thing was, I remember the exact day I figured out I had a problem. It wasn't all the empty bottles I was recycling every week. It wasn't even the nipping at work or showing up at the EW with a hangover almost every day.

"It was this day I was working in Boston when I was asked to work a double, and I realized by the time I got off, all the bars and liquor stores would be closed. And I only had half a bottle of Dewar's at home. So I started calling around—to a bunch of my friends to see if one of them would run out and pick up a couple of bottles for me.

"And none of them would do it. Understandable. When a pal

calls you up practically in the middle of the night because he's desperate for his fix, you're not gonna help him, right? But the weird thing was, I was calling these people at eleven thirty at night, and none of them thought it was weird. That's when I knew."

"So what happened?"

"Nothing dramatic. Nobody died or anything. Nobody who wouldn't have, even if I'd been Marcus Welby and stone-cold sober. I just . . . stopped. Went home—"

"Dumped out the half bottle."

"Nope, I saved it. It was . . . like a charm, I guess. As long as . the half bottle was there, I could fool myself into thinking I'd have a drink later. That was my trick. 'I won't have anything tonight, and tomorrow I'll reward myself with a big drink.' And of course, tomorrow I'd say the same thing. And I'm two years sober next month."

"That's . . ." What? Weird? Cool? Fascinating? "That's really an interesting story."

"Yeah, I can see the tears in your eyes. Which one did you go to?"

"What?"

"Which AA meeting?"

"Oh. Uh . . . the one at the Thunderbird Motel. On 494?"

"You should go to the one at the Bloomington Libe. Better stuff to drink."

"Thanks for the tip."

He drained his milk, gave me a milk-mustache smile, and slouched off toward his bedroom.

I drank cup after cup of tea and thought about Dewar's.

# Chapter 2

ERIC Sinclair, king of the vampires, was back from Europe the next night, I was sorry to see. It had been a relatively uneventful six weeks despite—or because of—the vampire king's voyage to Europe. I had been careful not to ask questions, because I didn't want him to misconstrue my interest in his activities as interest in him. On the top of my brain I figured he might be abroad to check on his holdings—they were on the vast side. On the bottom, I just didn't want to know.

"Welcome back," I said to Tina, his sidekick and oldest friend. Really old . . . like, two hundred years or whatever. "Die," I told him.

"I did that already," he replied, folding the newspaper and setting it aside. "And I have no plans to do it again, not even for you, darling."

"I'll see you later, Majesties." Tina bowed and walked past us, out the room.

"Hi and 'bye," I said. "Why can't you follow her example?"

"Miss me?"

"Not hardly." This was sort of a lie. Eric Sinclair, at six foot huge, was an imposing presence. It wasn't just that he was big (broad shoulders, long legs) or great-looking (black eyes, dark brown hair, succulent mouth, big hands). He was charismatic . . . almost mesmerizing. You looked at him, and you wondered what it would be like to feel his mouth on you in the dark. He was sin in a suit.

"Come and sit down," Jessica said. "We're having a late supper. Really late."

"Jess." I sat. "How many times do I have to say this? You don't have to adjust your mealtimes just because the three of us sleep during the day."

"It's no big deal," she replied, which was a huge lie, since it was three o'clock in the morning, and she was finally having supper. Or a really early breakfast.

"You're so full of it." I poured myself a cup from the ancient tea service that had come with the house. Like just about everything in the place, it was a zillion years old and worth about that many dollars. I was almost getting used to using antiques every day. At least my heart didn't stop if I dropped something.

"I missed you," Sinclair said, as if I'd been having a conversation with him. "In fact, I was most anxious to return to your side."

"Don't start," I warned.

"No, start," Jessica said, slicing her roast beef. The smell was driving me crazy. Oooh, beef! I barely knew ye. "It's been creepily quiet around here lately."

"And I think it's time we addressed our current . . . difficulty."

"It is?"

He meant the fact that we were king and queen together, technically husband and wife, though we'd only had sex twice in the last six months.

"You can't turn back the clock, Elizabeth. Even one such as you has to bow to logic."

"Don't be a putz," I told him. "Pass the cream."

"I'm merely pointing out," he said, ignoring my request—both of them, come to think of it—"that you cannot be a little bit pregnant or go back to being a virgin. As we've already been intimate, and are married by vampire law—"

"Yawn," I said.

"—it's pointless not to share a room, and a bed."

"Forget it, pal." I got up and got the fucking cream myself. "Do I have to recap?"

"No," Sinclair said.

"But you will," Jessica added, not looking up from buttering her green beans.

"I slept with you once, and got stuck with the queen gig. Slept with you again, and Jessica invited you to move in."

"So, by that logic, I should give up intimate relations with Jessica," Sinclair pointed out, "not you."

"What kind of logic is that?" Jessica asked, almost laughing. "nd you can just dream on, white boy."

"All of you, shut up and die."

"What'd *I* do?" she cried.

"You know what you did." I gave her a good glare, but she knew me too well and wasn't impressed. I decided to change the subject before we got into a real fight. Everybody knew my views on the subject. They had to be as tired of hearing about it as I was of bitching about it. "Where's Tina off to?"

"Visiting friends."

"I thought that's why you guys went to Europe."

"It's one of the reasons." Sinclair sipped his wine. "Marc is working, I assume?"

"You assume right. For once," I added, just in case it went to his head. His pointy head.

He ignored that, like he ignored 90 percent of what came out of my mouth. "I brought you something."

I was instantly distracted. And mad at myself for being distracted. And wildly curious . . . a present! From Europe! Gucci? Prada? Fendi?

"Oh, yeah?" I asked casually, but I nearly spilled hot tea all over myself, my hands started shaking so bad. Armani? Versace? "What'd you bring me, soap?" I tried to squash my soaring hopes. "It's soap, isn't it?"

He took a small, soap-sized black box out of his pocket and slid it over to me. I wasn't sure whether to be dismayed or excited. Small box = not shoes. But it could mean jewelry, which I liked as much as the next dead girl.

I flipped it open . . . and almost laughed. Strung on a silver chain—no, wait, it was Sinclair, and he never did anything halfway, so it was probably platinum—was a tiny platinum shoe, decorated with an emerald, a ruby, and a sapphire. The stones were so tiny they looked like a buckle on the shoe. It was just too adorable. And probably cost a fortune.

"Thanks, Sinclair, but I really couldn't." I slapped the box closed. I had drawn a line in the sand a few months ago, and it was tough work, sometimes, staying on my side of the line.

If I let him give me presents, what next? Sleeping together? Ruling together? Rewarding him for being sneaky? Turning my back on my old life and forging through the next thousand years as the queen of the vampires? Lame. And again: lame.

"Keep it," he said mildly enough, but was that a flash of disappointment in his eyes? Or was it wishful thinking on my part? An if it was, what was the matter with me? "You might change your mind."

"If you ever come to your senses," Jessica mumbled to her green beans.

The thick, awkward silence was broken when Marc walked into the dining room. "Great, I'm starving. Is there any more beef?"

"Tons," I replied. "You're home early."

"Deader than hell at work, so I got off early. By the way, you've got visitors."

"Someone's here?" I put my hand on the necklace box . . . then took it away. What was I going to do with it? I didn't have pockets. Just hold it in my hand? Sinclair wouldn't take it back. Maybe leave it on the table? No, that'd be kind of bitchy. Right? Shit.

Why did he have to do this stuff? He must have known I wouldn't have accepted it. Right? Shit. "I didn't hear the doorbell." Stick it down the back of my pants and smuggle it out of the room? Hide it in my bra?

"I caught them on the porch. It's Andrea and Daniel. They said they need to ask you something."

I stood up, glad for a chance to get away from Awkward Dining 101. "Well, let's go see what they want."

"Don't forget your necklace," Jessica said brightly, and I almost groaned.

# Chapter 3

ANDREA Mercer and Daniel Harris were waiting for me in one of the parlors, and I was glad to see them. Not just because of the distraction. I really liked them.

Andrea was a vampire, like me, and a young one, also like me. She'd been killed on her twenty-first birthday, about six years ago, and was starting to get a handle on the thirst.

Daniel was her boyfriend, a regular guy and an outrageous flirt, and I got a real kick out of spending time with them. They were total opposites: she was serious and moody, and he was fun and irreverent. But you could tell they really loved each other. I thought that was pretty cool.

"Your Majesty," Andrea said, standing the minute she saw me. I waved her back down and sat down myself.

Daniel yawned and sprawled on the settee. He was a tall, blue-eyed, good-looking blond with the shoulders of a quarterback . . . put him in a horned helmet, and he'd be the spitting image of a marauding viking. He didn't stand when I entered, which was refreshing. "Betsy, babe. You guys can't have meetings at a decent hour?"

"Bitch, bitch, bitch," I said good-naturedly. "What's up, you guys?"

"Thanks for seeing us," Andrea said.

"No, thank *you*," I mumbled. If not for them I'd still be smiling awkwardly at Sinclair and trying to figure out where to stuff the necklace.

"We'll get right to it, ma'am. Daniel asked me to marry him."

"What? Seriously? That's great! Congratulations!"

"Thanks." Andrea smiled and looked at the floor, then back up at me. "And the thing is, we'd like you to do it."

"Do what?" Get married? According to some, I already was married.

But not according to me. As happy as I was for Andrea, I was suddenly so jealous I was ready to spit on her Payless-clad toes. Why, why, *why* couldn't Sinclair have *asked* me to marry him? Why did he have to trick me? Why did he bring me presents instead of apologizing and trying to make things right? If he loved me, he had a crummy way of showing it. And if he didn't, why did he fix it so we were stuck together for the next thousand years?

"To marry us," Andrea was saying. Oops, better pay attention. "To perform the ceremony."

"Oh." This was a new one. As the queen, I could do all sorts of things other vampires couldn't do. Handle crosses, drink holy water, accessorize. But perform vampire wedding ceremonies? "Uh . . . I'm flattered but . . . can I do that?"

"Yes," Sinclair said from two feet behind me. I nearly fell off the couch. The guy couldn't make noise when he walked like anybody else, oh no. Six foot four and as noisy as a cotton ball. "As the sovereign, you can perform any ceremony you wish, including weddings."

"Oh. Jeez, you guys, I don't know what to say . . ."

"Say yes," Daniel said. "Because we can't get a priest. And Andy's got her heart set on you doing it, don't ask me why."

Andy (not that anybody else could get away with calling her that) nodded. "That's true."

"Which part?" I teased.

"All of it. Will you help us?"

"But . . ." But I didn't know how. But I wouldn't know what to say. But it would be really depressing for me to marry another couple, knowing I would never have a proper wedding. But it was ridiculous, having a secretary perform the wedding ceremony. "When's the big day?" I asked, surrendering.

They looked at each other, then back at me. "We figured we'd leave that up to you," Daniel said. "You know, with your busy queen schedule and all." Typical guy.

"When do you want to get married?" I asked her. She'd have picked out a date the second he proposed.

She hesitated for a second, glanced at Daniel, then said, "Halloween."

"Oh, cool!" And it would be. *So* cool. A Halloween wedding

ceremony . . . with vampires! Plus, more than two weeks to figure out exactly what the heck I was supposed to do.

Daniel looked vaguely alarmed. Again, typical guy. "That's kind of quick, don't you think?"

"That's okay," I said, trying to catch Andrea's eye while she glared daggers at her beloved. "Yeah, okay, that'll work. Do you want to have it here?"

Again she hesitated, and again she glanced at Daniel, who shrugged and relaxed back on the couch. "If that wouldn't be too big an imposition, Your Majesty."

"It's no trouble. It's not like we don't have the space. Besides, we haven't had a decent party here in . . . ever." I started to cheer up a little, picturing myself in a severe black suit and pumps in maybe a dark purple. Or burnt orange, for the holiday? No, purple.

"Thank you so much," Andrea was saying—oops, they were leaving. All business, that was Andrea. Plus Daniel was still yawning. It couldn't be easy, adjusting to the undead's schedule. I used to waitress at a truck stop during graveyard shift (years before I knew what the graveyard shift *really* was), and no matter how much I slept during the day, I always wanted a nap around four a.m. "We'll be in touch."

"No problem," I replied, walking them to one of the house's sixty doors. "Talk to you soon. And congratulations again."

They said their good-byes, the door shut, and I turned to see Sinclair had followed me. "He asked her to marry him?" he asked, staring after them thoughtfully.

"Yeah," I replied. "You should try it sometime." Then I walked past him and marched up the stairs to my bedroom.

# Chapter 4

WHICH was really stupid, because I had work to do tonight. I had to check on Scratch and the Fiends. So I pushed up my bedroom window, popped the screen, stuck a leg over the windowsill, and jumped.

One of the few nice things about being dead is it's pretty much impossible to die again. So a three-story fall was no problem at all. It didn't hurt; it didn't even knock the breath (what breath?) out of me. It was like jumping off the bed.

I hit the grass, rolled, stood up, shook the dead leaves out of my hair, examined the grass stain on my left knee . . . then remembered I'd forgotten my keys and my purse, and went to ring the front doorbell.

*Finally,* I was in my car, headed to my nightclub, Scratch.

It wasn't really mine. Okay, it was, by vampire law, which was confusing. The way it worked was, if you kill a vampire, all their property becomes yours. Vampires generally don't have kids or families to leave stuff to, and probate only happens during daylight hours anyway. So, I'd killed this rotten vampire, Monique, and she owned, like, eight businesses, and now they were all mine, but the only one I was really interested in was Scratch. I had Jessica's accountant put all the others—the school, the French restaurant, the Swiss spa (that one hurt to let go)—up for sale. Tried to, anyway. It was complicated not least because I couldn't prove I legally owned them. And, like a stubborn ass, I didn't want Sinclair's help. If they sold, I'd worry about what to do with the money later. Meanwhile, I was trying to hang on to Scratch, but it wasn't easy.

I was glad Monique was gone—well, dead. And not because I got her car and her businesses. Not *just* because of that. Monique had been bad, even for a vampire. She'd tried—repeatedly—to kill me, but worse, she'd killed other vampires to get to me. And she'd ruined my shirt. She had to go.

I'd been a secretary and office manager for years before I died, so managing a nightclub—handling the paperwork, anyway—was something I could actually do. Probably. If the other vampires would give me a chance. Trouble was, they hated my guts. I guess employee loyalty was big in the vampire world. They were pretty pissed that I'd offed the boss.

Not that any of them told me that in so many words. No, they kept their gazes averted and didn't speak to me unless spoken to. This made it easy to give orders but tough to strike up a conversation.

So I pulled up outside the club—it looked like an old brownstone, except with valet parking—and went inside. Deader than shit (no pun intended), as usual.

"Okay, well," I told one of them . . . I was having the worst time remembering their names. Probably because they never volunteered them. And vampires didn't go for those blue and white HELLO MY NAME IS ———— stickers. "We've got to get customers to start coming here again."

"Your Majesty knows how to do that," he replied, staring over my shoulder, which always made me think there was a monster sneaking up on me. Maybe there was. He was about my height, and about my coloring—blond, with light eyes—long slender fingers, and (no joke!) a slight overbite.

"Don't start up with that shit," I told Slight Overbite. "I mean a way to get customers where eighty people don't die a week."

See, the way the vampires liked to run things, they could have "sheep," a detestable word that meant a human slave/partner, and they could drink blood right out on the dance floor, and if a regular person got on their nerves, bye-bye regular person. Forget it! It was morally wrong, and I'd never get OSHA off my ass.

"That was under the old management," I told him. "We've been over this. Look, we can run a profitable nightclub for vampires without having to be horrible to regular people."

"We can?" he asked, now looking around at the totally deserted dance floor.

"Oh, shut up. Look: put your thinking cap on your tiny little head, because we're doing it. If you were a dead guy, wouldn't you like to hang out in a place where you won't get hassled?"

"Yes. And where I could drink and have fun."

"No, *no*. I mean, yeah, drink, have a daiquiri, have three, go crazy. Not . . . you know." I made a slashing gesture across my throat.

He shrugged.

"We're *going* to make it work, Slight Overbite," I reminded him. This had been my mantra for the last three months.

He shrugged again.

"MAJESTY!" Alice cried, running out to greet me. At least somebody was happy to see me tonight. Well, that wasn't fair. Andrea and Daniel had been happy to see me. They'd even *come* to see me. Well, to ask a favor. Still, it was nice to have any kind of company. "Welcome! You should have told me you were coming."

"How's it going, Alice?" As always, I admired her undead creamy complexion (she'd been turned into a vampire after puberty but before adolescence really got its claws into her, so no zits, ever). "How are the Fiends doing?"

"Really well," she enthused. "One of them escaped, but I got him back before he killed anyone this time."

I shuddered. "Good work. Is it the same one, the one who keeps getting out?" Nostro's property—another vampire I killed, and don't go making assumptions, because I'm not that kind of queen—had a high fence around it, but the Fiends were weirdly clever. More animal than human, they were vampires who hadn't been allowed to feed and had gone feral. This happened under previous management, you understand.

Anyway, I didn't feel right about staking them—it wasn't *their* fault they'd gone insane with a supernatural hunger for blood— and resisted heavy pressure from Sinclair and Tina to put an end to them. Alice was my Fiend keeper. She kept them clean, kept them fed, kept an eye on them, kept them from feasting on the local children.

"It's George," Alice confirmed. "He's a free spirit, I guess."

He was an insane nutty vampire who forgot how to walk upright, but never mind. "I can't believe you've named them. Sinclair freaked when you told him. Run them by me again."

"Happy, Skippy, Trippy, Sandy, Benny, Clara, Jane, and George."

I laughed. "Right, right. Good job." I tried to sober up. Poor things. It wasn't right to laugh at them. "So, you got George back?"

"Yes. He wasn't out for long this time. If you're looking for him, he's right behind you, Majesty."

I whirled. I loathed how vampires could sneak up on me, and the Fiends were . . . well, fiendish. George looked exactly like the others, with raggedy long hair, long filthy nails (Alice did her best, but like all of us, she had her limitations), unkempt and hungry-looking, with filthy clothes.

Though, thanks to Alice, they didn't look quite as wild-eyed as usual. They scuttled like dogs . . . she was trying to remind them how to walk upright, but they always toppled over, then scampered away. The others stuck around, since they were being fed, but George was a wanderer.

Right now, he was inching toward me and sniffing the air. The Fiends, luckily for me, were weirdly devoted. In fact, they'd devoured Nostro for me. (I tried to delegate when I could.)

"Quit that," I told him. I never knew how to speak to them. It was wrong to treat them like pets, but they weren't exactly human, either.

"Stop running away. Be good and listen to Alice."

"I don't exactly talk to them," she explained. "But I appreciate the support, Majesty."

"How's the house? Everything running okay?" I was talking about Nostro's sprawling mansion and grounds, which—have I mentioned this?—were all mine since I'd axed his sorry blood-sucking butt this past spring. You couldn't pay me to live in the creepy place, though, so Alice was my caretaker. Unlike *some* unnamed employees of a certain nightclub I could mention, she was helpful and nice. "You'd tell me if you needed a hand, right?"

"Oh, yes, Majesty," she lied. It was a point of pride with Alice that I relied on her so heavily to take care of the Fiends for me. She'd never admit to needing help. Yes, George got out once in a while, but if not for her, they'd *all* be out, all the time.

Sure, I felt bad about the two guys he'd eaten, but since the guys in question had been devoured while attacking lone women on the street, not *too* bad. "Of course, I would let you know. But everything's fine." She looked down at George, who was nibbling on his palm and looking up at the moon. "We're all fine."

# Chapter 5

ℒ stared at the baby shower invitation. It was pink (yurrggh), and sparkly, and seven inches high (how did she find envelopes to fit?) and in the shape of a baby carriage.

*Come and celebrate!*
*Antonia's having a baby!*
*(Baby registry at Marshall Field's,*
*612-892-3212, please no green or purple)*
*4:00 p.m., October 7th*

"Bitch," Jessica commented, reading over my shoulder. "She's having it during the day, when you can't come."

"Not that I'd want to," I sniffed, but the fact was, the baby-to-be was my half sibling, poor thing.

"Whatcha gonna get her?"

"The Ant? How about a brain aneurysm?"

Jessica walked past me and opened the fridge. "You have to get her something. I mean, the baby something."

"How about a new mother?"

"She's registered, anyway."

"Not *too* gauche, putting it right on the invitation. With color preferences!"

"Yes, yes . . . how about a portacrib?"

"A what?"

"It's a crib that folds up and you can take it around."

"Why," I demanded, gesturing for her to pour me a glass of milk as well, "would you want to take a crib around?"

"That way, if the baby comes to visit, it's got a place to sleep."

"You think the baby will make a break for it so soon?" I answered my own question. "Of course it will. Poor thing will probably sneak right out of the hospital nursery."

"Will you be serious, please?"

"I can't. If I think about it seriously, my head will blow up. It's just one more awful thing in my life right now—physical proof that my father is still having sex with the Ant."

"It must be hard to take," she agreed, "on top of being dead and all."

"Tell me." I took a gulp of milk. Being dead, being Sinclair's consort, living in this museum-sized mausoleum, trying to run Scratch (it was the only money I had coming in), trying to keep the Fiends on a short leash (literally!), trying to make nice with Dad and the Ant, and finally . . . "So, check this. Andrea and Daniel are getting married."

"And you're performing the ceremony."

"How'd you know?"

"Sinclair told me."

"Look, I forbid you to speak with that man."

"I'm his landlord," she reminded me. "We were making polite conversation while he wrote out his rent check."

I snorted. Like she needed the money. Jessica was rich. Not "compared to the rest of the world everyone in America is rich" rich. *Rich* rich. Like, Bill Gates tried to get her to loan him money for a new start-up rich. She turned him down politely, via email. Said it was her way of evening up the universe.

"This whole thing is ridiculous, you know. It's ridiculous that we live in this place. It's ridiculous that *he* lives with us. It's ridiculous that you're charging him rent, and it's really ridiculous that he pays it. You two have all the money in the world, and you're just trading it back and forth."

"Like baseball cards," she suggested.

"It's not funny, Jessica."

"It's a little bit funny. Besides, what was I supposed to do? After Nostro burned down his house, he was living on hotel room service. And it's not like we didn't have the space."

I had nothing to say to that, just gulped more milk and slumped at one of the kitchen stools. The room was laid out like an industrial kitchen, except the whole second half had a big table with chairs, and there was a long counter that ran a fourth of the length of the room, also with chairs. It was by far the most inviting room in the house, which is why I usually hung out there. I just didn't feel right in one of the parlors or the library.

Besides, the Book of the Dead was in the library. Like last year's *Vogue*s weren't bad enough.

"Someone's at the door," I said, wiping off my face.

"Oh, there is not."

"Jessica, there totally is."

"No way. You know, you're like one of those annoying yappy little dogs . . . every time a car rolls by outside, you freak out and decide someone's coming up the walk and ringing the—"

Bonnnnnnng-BONNNNNNNNNNGGGGG.

"I hate you," she sighed, getting up.

I checked my watch. It was almost six o'clock in the morning . . . probably not a vampire. They didn't like to be running around so close to sunrise. As a rule, they were more flammable than gasoline. Or was it inflammable? I always got those two mixed up. My D in chemistry had never served me well.

Sinclair walked in, winding his watch.

"You really need to get something battery-operated," I told him.

"My father gave this to me. And speaking of fathers . . ."

"Don't tell me." I covered my eyes. Should have covered my ears instead. "Don't even tell me."

"Guess who decided to stop by?" Jessica asked brightly, walking back into the kitchen. That was quick—she must have sprinted there and back.

I dropped my hands in time to see a tall, good-looking older man walking behind her, puffing to keep up, his dark brown hair heavily flecked with salt, the golfing pants tightly cinched at the waist with an alligator belt, the pink plaid complemented by the pink Izod shirt.

"Dad," I said with as much enthusiasm as I could muster, which wasn't a lot. He'd obviously stopped by en route to the links, which should have been touching, but wasn't.

"Betsy. Err . . ." He nodded at Sinclair, then his gaze skittered away. This was a pretty typical reaction when a guy met Sinclair. Women looked away, too . . . but always looked back.

"You look nice." I pointed to the corners of my eyes. "Get something done?"

His crow's feet had radically depleted, and he nodded. In fact, he looked better than he had in years. I was so happy my death wasn't, y'know, weighing heavily on him or anything. "Yes, your stepmother had me go see Dr. Ferrin. He does the mayor, too," he added, because he couldn't help himself.

Like Sinclair or Jessica cared . . . or needed it themselves. I looked at him but, as usual, Sinclair didn't take the hint. In fact, he was—oh, Lord!—sitting down at the table and making himself comfortable.

"I see you got the announcement," Dad said, glancing down at my mail, scattered across the counter. I'd always assumed being dead cut down on junk mail, but like so many things I'd assumed about death, I was wrong.

"Invitation," Jessica piped up, also sitting down. "Not announcement. Invitation."

"Well . . . but you can't come . . . because it's . . . you know . . ."

"I would be happy to go instead," Sinclair said with all the warmth of a rutting cobra. "In fact, it would be appropriate if I did. Why . . ." He grinned, which was horrifying, but also kind of funny. "I'm practically a member of your family."

I actually felt sorry for my dad; for a second I thought he was going to faint, just do a header into my mail pile. Sinclair, as an ancient dead guy, could walk around during the day, provided he stayed inside. Maybe he could borrow a fire blanket for going to and from the taxi.

A mental image of big-shouldered Sinclair in one of his sober suits, sitting primly on one of the Ant's overstuffed couches, a pink ribboned gift in his lap . . . it was too much.

I was annoyed with the big goober, as usual, but it was kind of cute the way he stuck it to my dad on my behalf. Talk about the son-in-law from hell.

"You gonna be okay?" I asked Dad, fighting a grin. Jessica, I noticed, had given up that fight.

"I—I—I—"

"You could wear the black Gucci," Jessica told Sinclair. "I picked it up from the cleaner's yesterday, so it's all set to go."

"Kind of you, dear, but I have told you many times, you are not an errand runner."

"I—I—I—"

"I was there anyway, getting my own stuff." She shrugged. "No trouble."

"You are too kind, Jessica."

"I—I—I—"

"It's all right, Dad," I said, forcing myself to pat his shoulder. "I won't let him come if you don't want him there."

"But I adore baby showers!" Sinclair protested, having the gall to sound wounded. "I find them scrumptious."

"I just . . ." My dad took a deep gulp of air and tried to steady himself. I stopped patting. "I just wanted to make sure you got the . . . the announcement. But I also wanted to remind you . . . your stepmother is very delicate . . . very . . . under a lot of stress, you know . . . the baby . . . and the spring carnival . . . she's chairwoman . . . and I don't think . . . don't think . . ."

"Stress." Jessica snorted. "Yeah, that's the problem. What's the shrink du jour say?"

"Dr. Brennan comes highly recommended," my father said and, because he couldn't help it, added, "He's very exclusive *and* expensive, but he made room on his calendar for Antonia. He feels she should avoid stress and . . . and unpleasantness."

"Maybe she should stop looking in the mirror," Jessica suggested, and I chewed on my lower lip, hard, so I wouldn't laugh. I had to admit, I was getting more yuks out of this predawn meeting than I'd had in about a month. Maybe it was a good thing Sinclair was back.

What was I thinking?

My father turned his back on Jess but said nothing. She was black, which meant he had a hard time taking her seriously: but she was also the richest woman in the state, so he couldn't afford to totally blow her off. It was a tricky balancing act, one he usually fucked up. "You understand what I'm saying, don't you, Betsy?" he almost pleaded.

"Sure. Send a gift, but don't visit."

Sinclair was on his feet, but my dad, who had his back to that part of the room, didn't notice. Poor survival skills—outside of the boardroom—that was my father. Jessica reached out and tugged, hard, on his jacket, but Sinclair didn't budge.

"It's okay," I added, waving Sinclair back down—but he still didn't budge, the stubborn tick. "I didn't want to go, anyway."

Dad relaxed and smiled at me. "Well, of course, that's what I assumed."

"Of course." I gave him a wintry smile in return, which, I was glad to see, backed him up a step. "Thanks so much for stopping by. My love to what's-her-name."

"Betsy, you've never understood Antonia—"

"I understand her fine."

"No, I don't think someone like you could ever understand—"

*"Mr. Taylor!"* We all jumped. The crockery had practically rattled. And my dad had nearly swooned again. "I demand you retract that statement *at once,* or I will be forced to—what are you doing?"

Jessica had jumped on Sinclair's back in an attempt to forestall the lecture (or possibly the maiming). She was clinging to him like a skinny black beetle, all arms and elbows and knees, and he shook his head, which nearly dislodged her. "Really, Jessica. Could you climb down?"

"Promise you won't finish that sentence," she whispered in his ear. "Take it from me. It won't do any good, and it might make things worse. She can handle him."

Anybody else would have said something like, "Hello, I'm standing right here!" but my dad, the master of ignoring what was in his face, didn't say a word. He brushed a piece of lint off his shirtsleeve and examined his Kenneth Coles, which were glossy with shoeshine, while my best friend climbed my consort like a premenstrual monkey.

"I certainly will not. She is my consort and my queen, and he is treating her like—"

"So," my dad interrupted, cutting Sinclair off, which nobody ever got away with except me, "I'll tell Antonia you said hi."

"Why?" I asked, honestly curious.

You have to understand, it's not like my dad was incredibly brave or anything. He had a pissed-off billionaire and a vampire king in the room, but it didn't faze him, because it was beneath him. He could just close his mind to anything remotely unpleasant—or even interesting. I'd gotten used to my father's oblivious ways by the time I was thirteen, when I realized he'd tossed my mom, and the Ant was going to be my stepmother. Since he was the only dad I had, I put up with a lot. But, to be fair, so did he.

"It won't be like the last time," my dad continued, sounding almost cheerful. "She was all alone last time, but this time I'm here, and she'll have all the support she needs. I just wish you could understand what she's been through, how hard she . . . she . . ." He trailed off as I stared at him, as he realized he'd just made a fuckup of truly heroic proportions.

"She's been pregnant before?" I asked, almost gasped.

Jessica *did* gasp. "Get out of town!"

"No—no, she didn't . . . I mean, I wasn't—she wasn't—we—we—"

"Was there a baby?" Sinclair asked quietly, and good as he was, my dad couldn't ignore that and turned around to face him,

moving stiffly like a puppet whose strings were being jerked.
Which probably wasn't that far from the truth.

"Yes."

"And"—Sinclair took a step closer (Jessica was still hanging
on to his back, gaping over his shoulder at my dad) and looked
down at my father—"were you the father?"

"Yessss." My dad sounded drugged. But then, anybody did
once Sinclair got close enough. He was the best I'd seen at it. I
could only entrance men, but he could do anybody.

"Where is the baby?"

"Antonia didn't tell me . . . didn't . . . we weren't together, and
she gave it . . . she didn't . . . she . . ."

"You better stop," I said. "He's about to blow all his cylinders."

"Quite right," Sinclair said. "That would be truly terrible."

I gave Sinclair a look, then took my dad by the shoulders.
"Dad. Dad! Listen. You came over and made sure I wasn't going
to come to the shower."

"Yes, I made sure of that," he agreed, focusing on me at once.
"Antonia insisted."

I gritted my teeth. *Bitch!* "But I didn't want to go anyway, so it
all worked out fine."

"Yes, you refused to go, so it really was all for the best."

"And I looked like hell."

"Yes, you looked terrible, being dead isn't agreeing with you
at all, not at all, just like Antonia said it wouldn't."

"Now go golfing and," I added spitefully, "stroke three figures."

"Ouch," Jessica said as my father marched out.

"I am just not believing this," I said, massaging my temples.
"Like I don't have enough to worry about. I can't believe he let
that slip."

"You have that effect on men," Sinclair said kindly. "They always reveal more than planned to you."

I shrugged but was inwardly pleased. "How long has he been
carrying this secret around? Why did he just happen to blurt it out
while you and I were in the room? Jessica, would you climb down,
for heaven's sake? I'm dying to know the rest. I mean, I might
have a brother or sister running around *now*."

"This doesn't bode well for your stress levels," Jessica commented, letting go of Sinclair's neck and dropping to the floor.

"We will find out more. Your father has incomplete information anyway. We should go directly to the source."

"Antonia," Jessica and I said at the same time.

# Chapter 6

SINCLAIR'S convertible was ridiculously crowded. He was driving, I was riding shotgun (finally, a perk to our "relationship"), and Marc, Jessica, and Tina were in the backseat.

Tina had come because . . . well, she always came with Sinclair when we were doing vampire stuff. The two of them went way back—in fact, she'd turned him. She was like his combination best pal/secretary/enforcer/confidant. Which was fine with me, because I sure as shit didn't want to do any of those things.

We had decided Marc should come along because we planned to drag all the gory details out of the Ant, and you never knew when a physician might come in handy.

Jessica, however, had blackmailed her way along. Sinclair had a lot of odious qualities, I'll be the first to say it (again and again); but one thing he liked to do was keep my friends out of vampire issues. And I couldn't really blame him . . . you just never knew when a totally normal vampire errand would end in a bloodbath with severed-limb soap.

Jessica never accepted these excuses. She put her size-nine foot down and that was the end of it. The clincher was when she told Sinclair it would be a shame if anything happened to any of his European suits while they were at the dry cleaners.

"In the old days," he'd replied, "errand runners were actually helpful." But that was all he'd said about it; Sinclair was always impeccably dressed, and had all his stuff tailor made. It wasn't being rich and wanting the best; his shoulders were too broad and his waist too narrow to buy off the rack. I could only imagine what his clothes cost. I had the feeling he would have let Jess ride in the passenger seat if she'd threatened his best Gucci.

So it was crowded, but almost nice. If it weren't for where we were going.

"It's just a word," Marc was insisting. Oh, not this again. Jessica hated "African American," but she wasn't too crazy about the *N* word, either. "It's lost all meaning. This isn't the nineteenth century. Or even the twentieth."

"I don't think we should be talking about this," Tina said, shifting so Marc's elbow wasn't on her eyebrow. She was teeny, but it was a tight fit back there.

"No, it's fine," Jessica replied.

"Of course it's fine, we're all civilized ad—well, we're all adults. Tina, I swear, you're the most politically correct dead person I've ever known."

"I just don't think this is an appropriate discussion for—for us." Tina had been born around the time Lincoln freed the slaves, so she had perspective the rest of us didn't. She was pretty close-mouthed about the whole thing.

"No, no, no," Jessica said, and I curled my fingers around the door handle, just in case. I knew that tone. "In this day and age, there are quite a few more important things to worry about. It *is* just a word. It's totally lost its meaning." Sinclair was looking up at her in the rearview, and Tina was edging away. Only Marc, who couldn't smell emotions, was oblivious. "Now go ahead," she continued calmly. "You just call me that *once*."

Silence. Followed by Marc's meek, "I didn't mean we should go around calling other people that. I just think—I mean I don't think—not that anyone should call you—or call anyone—"

"Will you stop already before one of us has to knock you unconscious?" I asked.

Jessica snickered, and that was the end of the discussion for that week.


W€ pulled upside my dad's Tudor (four thousand square feet for two people!) and piled out of the car. It was full dark, about nine o'clock at night. My dad had left town that afternoon for a business trip, and the Ant would be alone.

This information was helpfully provided by my mother, who supported my vampiric pursuits and helped me out whenever she could. Sometimes it's like that, I've noticed . . . one parent is almost too great, and the other one's a shit. I had my mom so high up on a pedestal, the poor thing probably got oxygen deprived.

I rapped twice, then opened the front door. Unlocked, of course . . . it was a pretty nice neighborhood. Very low crime. My dad didn't even lock his BMW when he left it in the driveway. As far as I knew, they'd never been robbed. Of course, if my funds ever ran low, that might change.

"Hellooooooo?" I called. "Antonia? It's me, your favorite stepdaughter."

"And by favorite," Marc added, stepping into the foyer behind me, "she means hated." He seemed to be bouncing back nicely from his humiliation in the car . . . but then, he was pretty irrepressible. Once you overlooked the whole attempted-suicide thing. Come to think of it, it was an *attempted* suicide . . .

"You haven't even met her," Jessica said as we all crowded into the small hall.

"No, but I've heard the legend. Frankly, I'm skeptical. Can she live up to the hype?"

"I have to admit," Tina said, "I'm curious, too."

"She knows you are a vampire, but the front door was unlocked." Sinclair sniffed. "Either she's unbelievably arrogant or unbelievably dim."

"You can't be here!" my stepmother said by way of greeting, running down the stairs like Scarlett O'Hara with a blond wig and frown lines. "I didn't invite you in!"

"That only works on black people," Jessica said.

Tina's eyes went wide, the way they do when she's concentrating on not laughing. "I'm afraid that's an old wives' tale, ma'am."

"Always a pleasure, Antonia," I said dryly. "Wow, you've gained a *ton* of weight."

She glared blondly. Her hair was the perfect color (and possibly texture, but I wasn't planning on touching it) of a cut pineapple. She had on more blue eye makeup than a seventies disco queen, and her lipstick was a shade redder than her lip liner. Nine o'clock at night, home alone, husband out of town, and in full makeup. And black miniskirt. And white silk blouse, sans bra. Unreal.

"You get out of here and take your friends with you," she said. She had been born and raised in Bemidji, but popped her consonants like she'd spent one too many years at an East Coast finishing school. "I told your father I don't know why he doesn't just wash his hands of you, and I'll tell you to your face. And another thing: I don't want you around the baby; I don't care if you're the big sister of the baby or not; you should have had the decency to stay dead like any normal person would stay dead."

"She *does* live up to the hype," Marc said, goggling at her.

"I couldn't agree with you more on that last one," I said. "This is Marc, my gay roommate." The Ant was, among other charming things, a homophobe. "And this is Sinclair and Tina." What they were was obvious. "We're here to ask you a few questions."

"Well, I'm not talking to you. I can't believe you had the nerve to even come here like a normal person when you're . . . you're . . ."

"A Republican?" I asked, possibly starting to enjoy this.

"We just have a couple of questions, and then we'll get right out of your hair," Jessica said. I could tell she was dying to say what she was about to say. "About the baby you *already* had."

The Ant, unfortunately, wasn't taken by surprise in the slightest, which meant my dad had warned her about his little slip. That was annoying. And surprising. My dad was pretty firmly under the Ant's manicured thumb. He lived in fear of her surgically plumped lips tightening in anger.

Instead, she took a breath and may have frowned, but she was fairly heavily Botoxed so it was hard to be sure. "You just mind your own business and get out of here, because it's nothing you need to worry about, and I can't believe you came all the way down here just to ask me about that. It's ancient history."

"All the way down here?" Marc asked. "You live in Edina, not darkest Africa."

"And are we going to stand in the foyer all night?" Jessica complained.

"I'm surprised we got this far," I replied.

"No, you're not staying in here all night. In fact, you're leaving right now." She dug around in her pocket and then whipped out a cross she had obviously made out of popsicle sticks. "The power of Christ compels you! The power of Christ compels you!"

I burst out laughing, even as Tina and Sinclair both took a big step back and looked away.

"I *told* you," Jessica said, "that only works on black people."

"How come you get to make those kinds of jokes?" Marc whined.

"Think about it, Marc," she replied patiently.

"Get out of my house, you rotten undead things!"

"She did the exact same thing when the Boy Scouts came around selling Christmas wreaths," I explained to the others, then took a step forward and snapped the cross away from her. "Where did you make this, shop class? You couldn't be bothered to go to a jewelry store and buy a nice one? I'm amazed you didn't make my dad cough up four figures for a diamond encrusted model."

"You get out of my house," she snapped. "You're not supposed to be able to do that."

"Tell me about it. Listen, we're going to ask you about my dad's other baby, and we're not leaving until you tell us everything."

"I'm not telling you rotten dead things a single detail. You're getting out and I'm going to sleep."

"Oh," Sinclair said, stepping forward once I'd put the popsicle sticks in my purse, "sleep will be the furthest thing from your mind in a few moments, Mrs. Taylor."

# Chapter 7

I came back down to the living room after a refreshing five minutes of putting the Ant's perfumes in the dryer and pushing Spin. Antonia was sitting on the far end of the couch, leaning forward, and staring raptly into Sinclair's face. Her hands were palm down in her lap, and she was compulsively scratching at the leather, but she never looked away from his eyes.

I felt kind of weird about this whole thing. Why, exactly, were we doing this? I wasn't even sure how I felt about it, but here we were anyway, digging around the Ant's substandard brain. And why was Sinclair so interested? Didn't he have king stuff to worry about? A suit fitting somewhere? Jerk training to attend, or teach? But here he was, sitting on the denim footstool, holding the Ant's human hands in his and getting everything out of her. Everything.

". . . and then I tried to get him to propose, but he wouldn't do it, he was afraid Betsy would get mad at him if he left her mother, so we broke up."

"Yes, but the baby?" Sinclair asked.

"The baby . . . the baby . . ."

"Man, she is getting freaked," Marc muttered to me. "Look at her."

I looked. *Scratch, scratch* went her nails against her leather miniskirt, and the corner of her mouth was sagging like she'd had a stroke.

And I could smell her anxiety. It was like burning glue.

"I don't remember . . ."

"Antonia, you remember," Sinclair assured her. "You just

haven't thought of it in many years. On purpose. Did the baby live?"

Her mouth hung open, and she moved her lips like she was trying to answer him, but nothing came out. Finally she groped and found Sinclair's hands, and the rest of her sordid tale just . . . just poured out. Like vomit.

"It wasn't me, it wasn't me! I got pregnant to get married, but it didn't work, and then the baby was here, and *it wasn't me!*" She wasn't just yelling, she was shrieking it, screaming it, and now her nails were digging into Sinclair's hands as she hung on for dear life. "It was supposed to work, and *it didn't work,* and I didn't know what happened, so I dropped her off . . . went to the hospital and left her in the lobby . . . nobody was around, but I knew someone would probably find her . . . so I put her down and never . . . never . . ."

"Jesus," I said, startled.

"The last time the Ant was this upset," Jessica whispered to me, "you came home a day early from summer camp."

"It's all right, Antonia," Sinclair soothed. "Of course it wasn't you. Who was it?"

"I don't know, I don't know." She bowed her head, and a dry sob escaped. "I was pregnant and then I wasn't and the baby . . . the baby . . ."

"Antonia, what day did you find out you were pregnant?"

"Halloween. Nineteen sixty-five."

"And what day was the next day? The day you woke up and the baby was already there?"

"August sixth, nineteen sixty-six. She was—she wasn't a newborn. I don't know how old she was, but she wasn't a newborn."

Dead silence while we all processed this. Marc hurried to Sinclair's side and whispered a question to him.

"Antonia, we're almost finished—"

"Good," she snapped, still looking at the floor. "I'm not telling you another thing."

"Yes, fine, Antonia, look up at me—that's better. Antonia, is there a history of mental illness in your family?"

"We don't talk about *that.*"

"Of course not, only nasty people talk about *that.*"

She was nodding so hard her hair actually moved. "Yes, that's right, that's exactly right, only nasty people—whiners, and—and—"

"But who was sick? In your family?"

"My grandmother. And both of my aunts. Not my mother, though, not *mine*."

"No, of course not. And you're different from them."

"It's just my nerves," she explained. "I just have very delicate nerves. *She* doesn't understand."

"No, she's not really the understanding type, is she?"

"Hey," I protested mildly.

"Anybody else would have stayed dead," the Ant went on, sounding aggrieved. "She didn't even have the class to do that. Has to be different—and—different—and has to rise and be a vampire. A vampire! She broke her father's heart."

"Class?" I yelped. "Oh, being undead is, what, classless now? And it's not like I had a choice, you tiny-brained, idiotic, shallow, Botoxed, gutless, chinless—"

"She lives with that rich Negro," the Ant confided. "And they're *not* married. Get what I'm saying?"

I slapped my forehead. Negro! Who even uses that word?

"I didn't know I was gay," Jessica commented.

*Oh, Lord, let me die now again.*

"Antonia, where did you leave the baby?"

"There was no baby."

"No, of course not. Certainly not *your* problem anymore. But where did you leave her?"

"She didn't cry when I left her," the Ant said steadily. "She was warm. I had—I had lots of towels and I could spare some. I put them in the dryer first."

"Of course you did, you're not a monster."

"*She's* the monster."

"Yes, she's terrible, and where is the baby?"

"Children's."

"Saint Paul," Marc whispered.

"All right, Antonia. You've been most helpful."

"Well, I try to donate to The Jimmy Fund when I go to the movies," she said.

"Oh, that's excellent. And you won't remember anything."

"No, I certainly will *not*."

"You'll go upstairs and get ready for bed. And you'll sleep like a baby."

"Yes, like a baby."

"Like the baby you callously abandoned," he said and abruptly let go of her hands.

\*   \*   \*

"—A sad woman," Sinclair commented when we were all outside again.

"Very sad," Tina agreed. She glanced at me out of the corner of her eye, which was as creepy as it sounded. "Very difficult."

"I've got privileges at Children's," Marc said. He was well into junior Sherlock Holmes mode, I was annoyed to see. "I bet we can track this baby down. And I bet I can get a crack at the Ant's med recs, too. Or at least try. I can try."

"Why do you want to see *her* records?" I asked. We weren't ready to get in the car yet, so we were sort of loitering outside on the front lawn.

"Because nobody blacks out for ten months unless something is *really* wrong. You heard her. One minute she was pregnant, the next she 'woke up' with a crying baby. So . . . what happened during that ten months?"

"I think I know," Tina said quietly.

"Tina," Sinclair said.

"Eric," she replied. She almost never used his first name.

"Tina?" I was surprised. Tina hadn't looked this nervous when Nostro threw us into the pit with the Fiends. But she was younger then. In a manner of speaking. "Hey, are you all right? Did you forget to have a snack?"

I noticed she had knotted her fingers together like kids playing "this is the church, this is the steeple" and now spoke to her knuckles, fast, without pausing. "My Queen, I always liked you personally, but now I am filled with admiration because you're not psychotic after being raised by *that woman*."

"Awww," I replied. I almost smirked. "That gets me right here, Tina."

"It's true," Sinclair said. "It's a miracle you're not *more* vain, shallow, and ignorant."

"Thanks," I said. Then, "What?"

# Chapter 8

"**WOW**!" Jessica said, shaking her head. "I heard it with my own ears, and I still don't believe she did it. Man, that's cold. Even for her."

"Most disagreeable," Sinclair agreed.

"Well . . ." Marc hesitated, then dunked his cookie into his tea until half of it dropped into the cup with a small plunk. Yech! I could never understand why he drank his cookies instead of eating them. "I'm not the biggest fan of Betsy's dad and stepmom, but if Antonia had a family history of that sort of thing—fugues or whatever—think how she must have felt. One minute she's pregnant, the next she's lost almost an entire year." He shook his head. "She must have been scared shitless."

"Anybody would have been," I added, "but her especially because of her family history." I noticed everyone was staring at me. "What? I can put myself in her shoes. Her tacky, plastic shoes. I don't like her, and I definitely don't think she should have dumped my kid sister off in a hospital lobby, but I still feel kind of bad for her."

"Humph," Jessica said. She wasn't eating or drinking anything, just sitting at the table with the rest of us, her bony arms folded over her chest. "Listen, Tina, you were saying you thought you knew what happened the nine months the Ant was non compos mentis?"

Tina didn't say anything. After a moment, it got awkward.

"Uh, Tina? Hello?"

Sinclair sighed.

"Uh-oh," Marc said to his tea.

"Elizabeth," he began. "There is something I must tell you."

I carefully set down my cup. This never, *ever* boded well. It was never 'I bought you six dozen flowers and forgot you don't like yellow.' It was always stuff like 'By the way, now you're the queen' or 'Hey, I'm moving in.'

"Hit me," I said. I would have taken a deep breath to brace myself, but that would have just made me dizzy.

"This is . . . a private matter."

"Right," Marc said, standing and pulling Jessica out of her chair. "We'll just go."

"Right," Jessica said, catching on. "We'll, uh, be dusting something. In one of the rooms." They hurried out, and I heard her whisper, "She'll tell us later anyway."

"Possibly not," Tina said.

"I had an ulterior motive when we went to your stepmother's house."

"You *did? You* did? An ulterior motive? *You?* No way!"

"The Book of the Dead talks about your sibling."

"How do you know? I thought if you read that thing too long, you lost your mind."

"I have been reading bits and pieces of it over the last several decades."

I digested that one. "Okayyyyyy. So the Book knew I had a sister roaming around the wilds of wherever." Then it hit me, what he was saying. "*You* knew I had a sister."

"Yes."

"You knew I had a sister." I guess I felt like if I said it out loud enough, it would be less painful? "You *knew* I had a *sister.*"

"Yes. Until today, I had thought the sibling in question was the baby your stepmother is carrying now." Then he added, totally calmly, "I was working my way up to telling you."

"Eric!" Jessica shouted from the hallway. "Work *with* me!" She raced in, Marc on her heels. "What is the *matter* with you? I fix it so you can move in, but this is the sort of thing that makes her nuts. Crazy, *in*sane!"

"I think it's safe to say," I said through numb lips, "that I'm feeling a little insane right now."

"It's just that you had so many other things to worry about," Tina said quickly, trying to cover Sinclair's ass as usual. "Being sovereign and solving the murders from this summer and the—the house situation and the other vampires not respecting your position and all of that. That's why he had to go to Eur—never mind.

He—we felt you had enough on your plate without worrying about your sister being the daughter of the devil and taking over the world."

I had been holding my teacup in both hands and accidentally squashed it like a bug. Jessica winced. Marc just stared at all of us. *"What?"*

Tina bit her lip. "Oh dear."

"Thank you for your assistance," Sinclair replied dryly.

Jessica dumped the cookies and crackers off the silver tray, walked around the table, and cracked Sinclair over the head with it. With a hollow *bonnnng!*, the silver dented. Sinclair didn't turn, just kept his steady, dark gaze on me.

"Lower," I said.

"You're so evicted," she told him.

# Chapter 9

I̶T was going to be sunrise soon enough, so I figured I should change into shorts and a T-shirt. What I really wanted to do was talk to Jessica about all that had happened that night, but she'd disappeared after assaulting Sinclair. There was still time to track her down . . .

I decided to cheer myself up by wearing my bargains, a $180 pair of white-and-black loafers. I'd be the best-dressed dead girl in the house. Then when I rose tomorrow night, I'd be ready for action. What kind of action, I had no idea. I'd worry about that then.

Meanwhile, I paired the bargains with black anklets, a black and white skirt, my cashmere mock turtleneck (a gift from Jess . . . the thing was practically indestructible in the hands of a good dry cleaner), and my black wool blazer. I checked myself out in the mirror and thought: adorable. I immediately felt better.

I guess this sounds kind of shallow, but it's harder to be depressed when you put yourself together as best you can. To put it another way, my life might be in the toilet again, but with my hair combed, my eye shadow coordinated, and my bra matching my underpants, I was ready for whatever the world threw at me.

I walked out of my room, down the stairs, down about six hallways, and into the kitchen, where Marc was eating Cheerios. I could hear Jess rummaging around on the other side of the room.

Without looking up from his cereal he said, "Nope."

I trudged back to my room, but not so quickly I couldn't hear Jessica talking to Marc.

"What was that? Where'd she go? I was looking for her."

"She's too tall to pull off the schoolgirl thing."

"I thought she looked cute."

"She looked like a blond zebra. Look, I'm her friend; it's my job to tell her this stuff."

"It's your job to pay rent. It's *my* job to tell her that stuff. You're a picky bitch," Jessica replied.

"Now who's spouting clichés? I'm gay so I'm bitchy?"

"No, you're gay *and* you're bitchy. I think she's had a tough enough week. And it's only Tuesday!"

"Right, so the last thing she needs is a fashion clashin' . . ." He trailed off (or I got far enough away) and I shut my bedroom door.

Nuts. Well, switch to leggings, stick with the mock and the blazer, and change into sandals. No, it was thirty degrees outside. Not that I was going outside. But you weren't really dressed until your toes had something under them. Penny loafers, I guessed.

I was just putting my bargains back into the closet when there was a knock at my door.

"Come in, Jess."

"Well, I thought you looked cute," she said by way of greeting.

"I think he's right. I'm too tall. You'd look good in that outfit. You want it?"

"No thanks. I want to talk about what happened earlier—" She glanced out the window. "You got time?"

"Yeah, half an hour, at least." I never saw the sun, though it couldn't hurt me. One of the perks of being the vampire queen. "Ugh, how awful was that whole thing?"

"No wonder Sinclair was so interested in tagging along to-night," she added, sitting next to me on the bed. "He knew, and he didn't tell you. Didn't warn you or anything."

"I *know*! See, see? Everyone's all 'Oh, give Sinclair a chance, he's not so bad' because they don't see the evil, dark, yukky, nutty side of him. He is the Almond Joy of my life."

"Honey, I'm convinced. That was pretty sneaky, even for him. Are you okay? It must have been a shock. You want another cup of tea or something?"

"No." I wanted not to be dead, but of course that wasn't hap-pening anytime soon. No point bitching about it right that minute. But knowing me, I'd get back to it later. "I'm so full of tea I'm seeping. Thanks for smacking him for me."

"It was either bonk him on the head or stab him with his own butter knife."

"That could have been fun. And thanks for evicting him."

"I don't think it'll work." She frowned. "He won't leave."

"Vampires and cockroaches. They're impossible to get out of the ducts."

"So, what? What does this mean?"

"I have no idea. I was starting to get used to the Ant being knocked up."

"Lie."

"Okay, you're right, I was still kind of freaked. But now I'm sort of getting used to the idea that I've got another sibling, never mind that she's the daughter of the devil. Not the Ant. The *devil*. But—and stop me if you've heard this before—what am I supposed to do about it?"

Jessica shrugged.

"There's gotta be more to it than that. I suppose I'll have to go to him and get the rest of the story."

"Screw that."

"Amen." I flopped down onto my bedspread. "I knew it was too quiet around here," I mumbled into my pillow. "Something was bound to happen. I was expecting zombies to come out of the walls or something."

"Bets, I think it's time."

"No."

"Yes, it is. You need it, and you're ready."

"It's too soon."

"I know it's scary," she said, rubbing my back, "but you'll feel better. You know it's the right thing to do."

"I'm not ready," I replied, scared.

"Yes. You are. It's okay, I'll be there with you."

I shook my head, but she wouldn't be dissuaded.

*The next evening . . .*

"Oh my *Gawd*," the pedicurist said. "*What* have you been *doing* with your *feet*?"

"She's been dead for the last six months," Jessica said helpfully from the opposite chair.

"I don't *care*, that's no *excuse*. Gawd, they're like *hooves*. You've got to take better care of them. What about that cucumber cream I gave you last spring? It doesn't apply *itself*, y'know."

"I've been busy," I said defensively. "You know, with stuff." Solving murders. Trying to run Scratch. Restraining myself from jumping Sinclair's bones. Not that I wanted to do that anymore. I think it would be fair to say my desire for him had been thoroughly squashed. I didn't want those big hands on me or those firm lips on me or that big—anyway, squashed, thoroughly squashed.

"*Everybody's* got stuff, you've *got* to take care of your *feet.*"

"And they'll take care of you," Jessica and I chorused obediently.

The pedicurist was sawing at my heels with a pumice stone. "Right! See, girls, you listen to me. Never mind about *stuff*. Foot care *has* to come first."

"Uh-huh." Maybe I could take her a little more seriously if she'd been out of high school more than twenty minutes. "I'll keep it in mind."

"Okeydokey then."

Jessica rolled her eyes at me, and I grinned back. "For a rich girl, you've got tough feet."

"Off my case, blondie. Yours aren't better."

"Yeah, but—"

"Didn't we just establish that there's nothing—not a single thing—more important than foot care?"

"Give me a break," I muttered.

The pedicurist dipped my feet back in the swirling water, then shook the bottle of nail polish. "Good choice," she told me.

"I like the classics," I replied. Revlon's Cherries in the Snow. A great, dark red. I didn't like dark colors on my fingernails, but I liked them on my toes all right.

"There, now," Jessica sighed as her pedicurist rubbed her toes. "Told you. You needed this."

"I'm not arguing. Heck, for a couple of minutes I forgot about the whole my sister is a child of Satan thing."

"How are *her* feet?"

"Not as good as yours," I told the girl, which was probably the truth.

WHEN I rose the next night, my feet were bare and unpolished. Unpumiced. They looked exactly the way they had the day I died.

I cried for five minutes—not over my stupid toes but for what it meant—and then I went downstairs and locked myself in the library with the Book of the Dead.

# Chapter 10

I picked up the wing chair from beside the fireplace (carefully . . . the thing was probably ten times older than me) and jammed it under the doorknob. It wasn't likely anyone was going to come looking for me—Tina and Sinclair were avoiding me entirely, and Marc and Jessica were probably asleep—but I wasn't taking any chances.

I was pretty damned sick of, "Oh, did I forget to tell you? That was in the Book of the Dead, too." I was going to sit down with the awful fucking thing and read it cover to cover. No more surprises. No more worrying about Sinclair holding out on me.

No having to go to Sinclair to get the whole story.

I picked the thing up off the stand, already grossed out. It was bound in human skin, how perfectly yuck-o, and felt warm to the touch, though that was probably because it was only a few feet away from the fireplace.

The Book. If the Bible was the Good Book, then this thing was the Terrible Bad Book. It supposedly had all sorts of vampire factoids within its nasty binding, and Sinclair had rescued it from his blazing mansion and stuck it in my house. We all avoided it like nobody's business. At least, I used to think so. But apparently Sinclair had been coming in the library and reading bits of it now and then. And keeping the good parts to himself, the treacherous prick.

I sat down, looking at the cover for a moment. *Tabla Morto.* The Book of the Extremely Creepy. Was that Latin? I didn't know from Latin. I peeked in the back . . . Was there an index? Could I look up "Betsy's sister" and save a lot of time? Nope, just a bunch of really disturbing pictographs back there. Never mind; I wasn't here to save time, I was here to save aggravation.

*Chapter one, page one, here I come.*

I wasn't scared. It was just a book. It couldn't hurt me. Nothing could hurt me. Except stupid Sinclair. No, that wasn't true. I was mad because he was keeping secrets, that was all. My king shouldn't keep secrets. *The* king shouldn't keep secrets, is what I meant.

The king. Sure. Some king. Fat lot of help he was to me, or anybody. Okay, there was that whole fighting for my crown and almost dying incident, but he wanted power, not me. He knew stuff, private stuff about me, but instead of sitting down for a helpful chin-wag *with me,* he kept secrets and was all, "Don't read the Book too long in one sitting or you'll go insane." If that didn't work when I was a freshman in bio, it wasn't going to work now.

> "Shalt be Vampyres and shalt be a Queen and King of Vampyres. But first the Vampyres will have no rule and shalt be chaos for twelve and a thousand yeares."

Right, right, I was following. That was Nostro and all the other little tin-pot dictators making Fiends and generally being disgusting. There really weren't any bosses until Sinclair and I came along. Which was weird, if you sat down and thought about it. Human beings had always had bosses . . . kings, queens, presidents, loan officers. Vampires managed to avoid them, by accident or design, until I came along.

See, what happened was, one vampire would intimidate and torture a bunch of others until he or she was ostensibly in charge, until another, jerkier one came along, and the whole thing started all over again.

Maybe they weren't so different from humans after all.

> "After chaos shalt be the Pretender, destined to dust. A Queen shall ryse, who has powyer beyond that of the vampyre. The thyrst shall not consume her, and the cross never will harm her, and the beasts will befryend her, and she will rule the dead. The Pretender shalt overstep and the Queen will overcome."

Hmm, how 'bout that? I shallll overrrrrcommme . . .

"And the first who shall noe the Queen as a husband noes his Wyfe shall be the Queen's Consort and shall rule at her side for a thousand yeares.

"And the Queen shall noe the dead, all the dead, and neither shall they hide from her nor keep secrets from her."

Yeah, yeah, I knew all this. Tina and Sinclair had told me this around the time Nostro bit true dust. And what they didn't tell me I found out on my own—apparently I could see ghosts. Unlike Haley Joel Osment's claims, they *did* know they were dead.

As for keeping secrets, the Book of the Yukky was wrong, wrong, wrong. That's all the dead did these days.

"The Queen's sister shalt be Belov'd of the Morning Star, and shalt take the Worlde."

Beloved of the morning star? I figured that was fancy talk for the devil. Take the world? Take it where? Take it over? Ack! So not only did I have a secret evil sister, but she was fated to take over the world, just like I was fated to rule the vampires with Sinclair?

Damn. Quite the family tree. What was up with my dad's genetics?

And what was the big deal? Why not tell me? Okay, it sounded bad when you just blurted it out: "You're the queen; if you have sex with me, I'm the king; your sister is the devil's daughter and might or might not take over the world. Cream and sugar?" But was that really so fucking hard to say?

I was starting to get a headache, which wasn't uncommon since I had been reading for . . . what? I looked at my watch. Jesus, I'd been locked in here for three hours! And I'd read maybe ten pages. I didn't have this much trouble with an Umberto Eco novel.

It was the text. It was almost impossible to read this archaic crap which, I might add, had never been spell checked.

And the headache. How could I concentrate when my head was throbbing like a fucking rotten tooth?

*But you don't get headaches anymore.*

It was so fucking hard to concentrate.

*You haven't had a headache since you became a vampire.*

The light in here was bad, too. In fact, the light was fucking terrible.

*A Vampyre.*

Queen this and Vampyre that and secret sisters; it was all such a payn in the ass.

*The Queen of the Vampyres.*

Well, back to it. This nice warm book—at least my hands weren't cold for a change—wasn't going to memorize itself.

"... and the Morning Star shalt appear before her own chylde, shalt help with the taking of the World, and shalt appear before the Queen in all the raiments of the dark."

*But it is nothing to worry about. In fact, you need not worry about a thing. Not one thing. The devil won't be as bad as you think; mostly that whole Lord of Lies thing is all hype.*

*And your sister might be a problem, but nothing you can't handle. What you should really handle is Eric Sinclair, because while he's a pain in the ass, he's also going to come in pretty handy, so you should stay on his good side.*

*Also, why are you wasting your time with all the sheep? For crying out loud. This is your damn house, and the sooner the lice crawling around on top of it figure it out, the better.*

Hmm. For an evil book written by an insane vampire who could see the future . . .

*How did I know that?*

. . . written in blood and bound in human skin, this thing was making a lot of sense.

*So just do your job . . . be the boss, run things your way, and rip the throat out of anyone who forgets who's in charge.*

You know, I *had* been letting things slide a little.

I couldn't believe I'd been worried about reading the Book of Good Sense! Finally, I was seeing things clearly. It was all so obvious. The first thing I had to do was go down to Scratch and tell Slight Overbite that he'd been 100 percent right about the best way to run a vampire watering hole. Then I'd—

"Betsy! Are you in there? What are you doing?" *Wham Wham Wham!* "There's something wrong with the door!"

—clean up my house. That was so fucking typical. Nothing going on in this room was any of Jessica's damned business, but she was nosing around banging on doors and demanding answers. I'd been putting up with it for too long, and I was done now.

I got up from the small couch, slapped the book closed, laid it tenderly on the stand, and walked over to the door.

"Bets! What's going on? Are you okay? You're not doing anything weird and vampirey in there, are you?"

I grabbed the chair blocking the door and tossed it so hard it crashed into the far side of the room. I noticed I'd yanked it so roughly it had bent the knob. Oh well. Plenty more where those came from.

I jerked the door open.

"Is everything—" Her eyes widened. "Are you okay?"

"Fine," I said, then slapped her so hard her head banged against the doorframe and bounced off. She staggered and almost lost her feet, grabbed for my shoulder to steady herself, thought better of it, and leaned against the door. One hand flew to her cheek, and the other flew to the side of her head. I smelled the blood before I saw it start to trickle through her fingers.

"Betsy, wh—why—wh—"

"Don't bother me when I'm working again, or you'll get another one."

"But—b—b—"

"And I wouldn't advithe interrupting me, either," I told her sweetly. Her eyes were so big, her fear was so big. It was awesome. And ohhhhh, the blood. Just going to waste running through those annoying veins. I smacked her again, and it was kind of funny to see she couldn't dodge it in time, didn't even know my hand had moved until her other cheek started to throb. "I have to thay, I thould have done thith yearth ago."

"Betsy, what's *wrong*?" she cried, and I decided not to kill her. She was irritating, and I'd probably get her money when I pulled her head off—she didn't have any family—but even though she was scared shitless, she was wondering what was wrong with me.

*What* is *wrong with you?*

I decided I would keep her around; it'd be good to have a sheep who worried about my well-being no matter what I did to her.

And ohhhh, the blood. Did I mention the blood just going to waste?

"Nothing'th wrong," I told her, almost laughing at her terrified expression. "Not one thingle thing." Then I seized her shoulders, jerked her toward me, and took a big yummy chomp out of the side of her neck.

She screamed, and her hands came up, too late—way too late. It almost took the fun out of it; she was so slow. Her hands beat against me while I drank, but I didn't even feel it; instead I was thinking, *Blood taken by force tastes better.* It was weird, but there it was. I didn't make the rules.

I let her go when I was done, and she hit the carpet so hard she raised a cloud of dust. She crawled away from me, sobbing, and curled up under one of the end tables. I licked her blood from my fangs and felt them retract . . . one of these days I was going to get the hang of this, by God. Sinclair could make his come and go whenever he wanted.

*Ummm . . . Sinclair.*

"So, let's recap," I told her, bending down so I could see her under the table. "Don't interrupt me when I'm working, don't cut me off . . . really, just leave me alone unless I need you. In fact, it's probably better not to speak until spoken to. I'm glad we had this little chat," I finished cheerfully. It was good to get the new ground rules out into the open. "I'll see you later. Oh, and I'll need a check for three thousand dollars. There's a sale at Marshall Field's."

I left, carefully shutting the library door behind me. Oh, goody, the doorknob worked, even if it was bent on the inside. I should reward myself for not wrecking it.

Make it four thousand dollars.

# Chapter 11

ℒ bumped into Marc on the way to my room to get shoes and car keys. He was scruffy (it was amazing how someone with such brutally short hair constantly looked like he needed a comb) and his scrubs were a mess.

"Why are you here?" I asked him.

"I'm pulling a double tomorrow, so Dr. Abrams let me knock off early." He peered at me. "You've got blood on your—"

"No," I said, "I mean, why are you *here?* Sucking off me like a big leech? You've only got your father, he's *sick,* but instead of tending to *your* business you're hanging around here butting into *my* business, paying—what?—two hundred bucks a month to live in a mansion? You hate your job, you hate your life, you haven't had a *date* in all the time I've known you, never mind a relationship, and the only way you can feel like you're worth anything is to tag along on vampire errands. Pathetic, Dr. Spangler. Really really lame."

He was gaping at me, which was pretty funny. Finally he said, "I don't hate my job."

Good comeback . . . not! "Move, Dr. Leech," I said, and shoved past him. Lucky for him I was full. I made a mental note to throw his ass out tomorrow, after he'd had a day to mull over each and every truthful observation I'd made. Maybe he and Jessica would get together and cry on each other's shoulders. That could be funny.

I got to my room and kicked my Manolos out of the way. Ridiculous! Teetery high heels—when would I wear lavender pumps? I'd thought to wear them when I married Andrea and

Daniel, but not only were they totally stupid shoes to wear in my position, I sure as shit wasn't going to let a vampire marry her sheep. They were food, not partners. What had I been thinking when I congratulated them? *Congratulated?*

I decided to take it easy on myself. Okay, I hadn't been thinking, in fact, I'd been running from my destiny. I hadn't figured it out then, but I had a handle on it now. It was the difference between being a young vampire and a queen.

I opened my closet door and pawed through the orderly piles of shoes. Yellow leather sandals—idiotic. Red knee-high boots—gaudy. Roger Vivier evening pumps beaded with turquoises. Turquoise! I hated turquoise, but I'd dropped almost a thousand bucks on a shoe decorated with that ridiculous rock. Fontenau heels in piss yellow . . . which I could only wear with black. Manolo Blahnik pumps in basic black . . . I could have gotten black pumps at Wal-Mart for twenty bucks!

Marabou mules. Emma Hope slippers. Japanese smiley face slippers—*smiley faces!* Leather golf cleats in tan and white . . . I didn't play golf. Cowboy boots . . . I didn't have a horse! I didn't even like to go out to the garden.

What was wrong with me? I'd pissed away thousands of dollars on stuff that went on my *feet*. My money problems would have been solved ages ago if I'd just stuck with flip-flops.

I finally found a pair of old green rubber boots I wouldn't be annoyed to be seen in and tugged them on, then clomped out the door in search of my purse. The mansion was worthy of my station, but it always took a while to get organized and out the door. Maybe I'd have elevators installed. And those concave mirrors they had in convenience stores. It would be nice to see who was coming down the hall.

Speaking of surprises, I rounded yet another corner and there was His Majesty King Sinclair coming toward me. He was impeccably dressed in trademark temperate colors: dark slacks, black belt, black shirt, black wool greatcoat. The dark clothes made even his eyes seem black, like a starless night in the middle of winter; I couldn't tell where the irises stopped and the pupils began.

There was some color in his cheeks—not a chill from being outside like you'd expect from a regular guy, but because he'd recently fed. I wondered who he'd bitten. Normally I tried not to think about it, but since he'd ditched the harem (in a needy attempt to get on my good side) he had to be hard up for blood.

Maybe he pounced on muggers and rapists, like I did. Of

course, due to recent eye-opening events, I was a little more broad-minded now about the quality of victims. Really, if they were on the street, they were fair game. It's not like they died from it or anything. Well, they might now. But I had other things to worry about.

"You're looking yummy," I said, reaching out as he neared and stroking the lapel of his coat. "As usual."

"So are . . . you . . ." he replied slowly, stopping in midstride and giving me a closer look. "You smell like blood. You've spilled some on your shirt."

"Silly me."

"And are those rubber boots?"

I edged closer. "Don't you think there are more interesting things for us to talk about than footgear?"

His gorgeous brow wrinkled. "Er . . . well, yes, frankly, but—"

I pulled him close and kissed him on the mouth. His firm, yummy mouth. Ooofa. How had I kept my hands off him all these months? His room was five doors down from mine, not five miles.

His hands were instantly all over me, slipping up the back of my turtleneck and clutching my shoulders. Oh, good, he wasn't going to be difficult.

I ripped through his coat and shirt, and we lurched back and forth in the hallway, clothes tearing, tongues exploring. We crashed through a door—and I don't mean we bumped into it and it flew open. I mean we left splinters and fell over a chair or something—I dunno, I wasn't taking a fucking inventory, I didn't even know what room we were in—and then we were rolling around on the dusty carpet.

His throat was right over my mouth while his hands were busy below my waist, tearing through my clothes to give himself access, and I couldn't resist and bit him. He stiffened above me, and I nearly groaned as his warm sweet/salty blood filled my mouth. His hands moved faster, the tearing got louder, and then he was shoving his way inside me, filling me up, and I rose to meet him and then pulled back from his neck.

I licked his throat, and he seized me by the hair, jerked my head to one side, and sank his fangs into my neck. His rough urgency shoved me over into orgasm, and I brought my knees up and met him thrust for thrust. I had another one and was trying for big number three when he shuddered and his head dropped to my shoulder.

"So," I said after a moment, "you're gonna need a new coat."

He laughed. "Among other things."

I stuck out my arm and looked at my watch over his shoulder. "Well, we've got about an hour until the sun comes up. I was gonna run down to Scratch, but I guess I could do that tomorrow."

"Is it time for the tiresome small talk?"

"I was thinking it was time for the oral sex."

He rolled off me, jumped to his feet, picked me up in his arms, and galloped to my room.

# Chapter 12

"**DARE** I ask what prompted this change of heart?" he asked after slamming the door shut with his heel and dumping me in the middle of the bed.

"It's boring," I replied, removing the shreds of my clothes. "Besides, you shouldn't look a gift horse in the crotch."

"A cliché that should be cross-stitched onto a sampler, no doubt." He was hopping on one foot as he frantically tried to remove his shoe, and I laughed at the sight.

I had a thought, there in my head and almost gone, but I groped for it and got it. I wondered why I hadn't been able to read Sinclair's mind during sex, as I had always been able to do so before.

Well, my head had been a lot emptier before. There was room for him in there while we were boning away. But there wasn't room for him anymore. That was all right with me, though. A lot of things were going to be different from now on.

Finally he was rid of the stupid things and joined me on the bed. "I am glad you're here," he told me. "I've waited a long time."

"Lover, the waiting's over. I think it's safe to say I'm finally in a position to appreciate all your excellent qualities."

And speaking of positions, we sixty-nined for a while—the cool thing about being a vampire? You don't need to stop to catch your breath. He was all the way down my throat and it didn't bother me a bit. We'd have to find someone to come in and fix the headboard, though . . . it was cracked right down the middle. One of us had kicked it—well, at one point we'd both kicked it.

After a while I climbed on top of him (Heigh-ho Silver,

awaaaaay!) and was happily bouncing my way toward yet another orgasm when I heard the unmistakable sound of a car pulling into the drive.

"Who's that?" I asked, looking at my watch again. Hmm. Fifteen minutes until sunrise. Vampire?

"Tina," he groaned. "Do you think you could focus on the matter at hand, darling?"

Tina! Little Miss "You're the Queen but Sinclair's my boy" backstabber. So quick with the "Your Majesty" routine and so quick to sabotage me, leave me in the dark, do anything she could, every damn time, to make sure Sinclair came out on top.

I needed *him;* I sure as shit didn't need her. She was old—the oldest vampire I knew—and she was dangerous.

I had to get rid of her.

I dismounted and groped for my robe, which was hanging off the door to the master bath. No time to get properly dressed; I wanted to take care of this *now*.

"Elizabeth!" Sinclair sounded equal parts aggrieved and surprised. "Do you have an appointment you've forgotten?"

"Yeah." *Just a little something I should have done six months ago.* "I'll be back. Don't finish without me."

"But—" I was already hurrying down the hallway and didn't hear the rest. Sex with him was always super, and I'd get back to it soon enough, but this was a lot more important. The last thing I needed in my house was an infinitely old, infinitely crafty vampire who didn't have my best interests at heart.

Besides, there were plenty more where she came from. Younger. Less dangerous. Certainly less annoying. And my boy Sinclair wasn't going anywhere. He practically had a leash and a collar.

I caught up with Tina in the front entryway; she had just shut the door. I guess I'd really jammed down those stairs.

"Good morning, Your M—" Then she screamed. Possibly because I'd taken the small gold cross out of my robe pocket and thrown it at her.

Sinclair had given me the delicate necklace a few months ago (it had formerly belonged to his ages-dead baby sis). I couldn't wear it around the house; it hurt Sinclair and Tina to look at it, not to mention any vampire who wanted to come calling.

But (and this is the dopey part) I liked to keep it close. So it was usually in the pocket of my jeans or, at bedtime, my robe.

"Tina, in case you haven't noticed, I've had just about enough of your shit."

"Don't—don't—" She'd dodged and was cringing in the corner. "Don't do that!"

"Don't ever tell me *don't*." Hmm, that had sounded more menacing in my head. Oh well. She'd catch up with current events soon enough. Out with the old, in with the new. And all that.

"What's happened?" she cried.

I sent a fist looping toward her face for an answer, but she was too quick, and next thing I knew I was wrist-deep in the wall.

"Dammit!" I pulled my hand out and shook the plaster dust off. When I had someone call the headboard repairer, I'd also have them get a wallpaper hanger in here and have someone build a new door.

But first, back to the business at hand. I looked around for the cross. I could jam that sucker right through her forehead and bye-bye Tina; she'd die screaming and that was fine, as long as she died.

Ah! There it was, on the floor beside the small table we dumped our house keys on. I bent for it—and Tina grabbed my shoulder and pulled me back so hard I went sailing into the opposite wall.

"Hey!" Now I *really* wanted to kill her. "You keep your hands to yourself, you fucking cow."

"I'm sorry, Majesty." She was standing perfectly still, well to the left of the cross. She watched me carefully and with interest, like a cat watches a mouse hole. "But I'm not going to let you kill me. I want to help you. What's wrong?"

"Help me by standing still," I replied, and launched myself at her. And got a kick to the chest for my trouble, and broke a chair as I hit the ground.

Damn! "You've kept in shape the last hundred years or so."

"It's one of the advantages of being immortal," she said calmly. It was actually sort of impressive how quickly she'd gone from flabbergasted surprise to cool assessment. Like I needed another reason to kill her. "Plenty of time to learn how to fight. What's happened?"

"Nothing much. Got some light reading done earlier tonight. The good news is, I know all about my sister. The bad news is, you're gonna have to go, Tina. Sorry."

"She's gone crazy, Tina, watch out." I looked. Jessica was standing in one of the doorways, gray-faced and bloody. She had a palm pressed to her forehead, stanching the yummy flow of blood. How had I let her sneak up on us? Son of a bitch! This house had too many people in it, and all but one or two were gonna have to go.

Jessica swayed a little and clutched the doorframe to steady herself. "I mean really crazy. I think—I think she read the Book for too long."

"I gathered. Oh, Majesty." Tina shook her head. "What are we going to do with you?"

This was annoying, to put it mildly. "You, shut the fuck up. And get lost; this is vampire business. And *you,* stand still." I crossed the room too quickly for Tina to see—except she did see and easily avoided me. That was okay; it brought me much closer to the cross. I bent to get it. I'd ax Tina, and then I'd tool up on Jessica so bad, she'd be more worried about her iron lung than ratting me out ever again.

I heard the *whoosh* a split second before I felt the impact. The sun must have come up early, because my skull was filled with light.

Then the sun fell down. And so did I.

# Chapter 13

I groaned and opened my eyes. The hangover was incredible. Had I read a book or downed a liter of vodka?

The light made me blink, and I tried to process the eighty zillion thoughts rocketing through my head. There was one tiny bit of good to come out of the whole mess: I knew a lot more about the devil's daughter. But there were other issues I had to—

Wait a minute.

The *light*?

I looked. I was in a small room on the west side of the house; there was no furniture, but it had a good solid oak door. In fact, it was going to be the wine cellar until Sinclair pointed out that we couldn't keep wine in a room with so much light, the big know-it-all. So the bottles had been moved to the basement, and this room had stood empty and . . .

The light.

It was the sun.

I climbed to my feet—I was still in my robe—and walked over to the window.

The sun.

I stared. Then I stared some more. The big golden ball was just about level with the tree line; it looked like late afternoon to me.

I hadn't seen the sun since my thirtieth birthday, way back in April.

I'd read the Book of the Dead and let it turn me into a real asshole. That was bad. Very, very bad. But in return, I could now wake up when it was still daylight out. That was good. Very, very good.

And since I was the Queen and the sun didn't burn me, I could *go out*. Walk around and feel the light on my face, the warmth.

I tried to pull the window up, but it wouldn't budge. The mansion had so many rooms and there were so few people living in it, the window probably hadn't been opened in fifty years or more.

Too impatient to mess with prying, too wild to get outside, I broke the window with my fist and punched out the bigger pieces. Then I dove through it, feeling like Starsky. Or Hutch—which one was the blond again?

I thudded to the ground two stories below, spat out the dirt, and flopped over on my back to soak up the sunshine. The grass was chilly (it was a mild October for Minnesota, but it was still October), but I didn't care. The sun wouldn't be up much longer, but I didn't care. I had some tall apologizing to do, but—well, I cared about that, and I'd get right to it, too.

In a minute.

*Thank you, God. Thank you so much! I totally don't deserve it. But thanks all the same.*

Thoughts of the previous evening's activities kept crowding into my brain, wrecking my sunbathing. Unfortunately for me, the Book didn't provide amnesia.

Last night's itinerary flashed through my mind. Trying to kill Tina—who had handily kicked my ass. It was embarrassing to get stomped by someone half my size, but I was glad I hadn't succeeded. Those awful things I'd said to Marc . . . He'd been a good friend to me, and I'd called him Dr. Leech.

And Jessica . . . *Oh, Jess. I screwed up so bad. I'd set myself on fire before I'd hurt you again. You're the best friend a vampire could have.* Yeah, that sounded good. Repeat as needed. And repeat. *God, if she just hears me out, I'll apologize for the next thirty years. Just please, please let her listen.*

And Sinclair. I groaned and threw an arm over my eyes. Skanky villain sex with Eric Sinclair! That was almost as bad as feeding off of Jessica. I was mad at myself for using him and mad at him for letting me do it.

And for *not noticing* I was evil! How could that little fact escape his attention? The sucker noticed when a fly landed a block away, but he didn't realize I'd turned into SuperBitch?

I sat up, annoyed and dismayed, and heard the unmistakeable *cha-chik!* of a shotgun shell being chambered. I'd been on enough duck hunting trips with my mom to know what that sounded like.

(Those were my pre-PETA days, just like now was post-PETA; they were getting a little extreme for my taste.)

I looked around. Marc was standing about twenty yards away, holding my old twelve-gauge. What was that statistic? More people who kept guns in their home were fated to be the victims of that gun than victims of other violence?

Since I was right in his sights, I silently vowed to pay more attention to such statistics in the future.

"Uh, I'm not dangerous anymore," I said.

"Mmmm," he replied. He wasn't wearing scrubs or shoes, just jeans and a Tori Amos T-shirt. He either didn't have work or he'd taken the day off to deal with his psychotic undead roommate. "You all right? Did you cut yourself going out the window?"

He wanted to know if I was all right! It was almost enough to make me overlook the shotgun. "No. I mean, no, I didn't cut myself, not no, I'm not all right. I *am* all right. Now, I mean."

"Eric heard you go out."

"Okay. Uh, what are you planning on doing with that thing?"

"Well." He took a step closer, but the barrel didn't waver. "It won't kill you, but we figured it would slow you down. You can dodge bullets, but Tina doesn't think you can dodge buckshot."

"Tina's probably right. Is she okay?"

"Sure." He smirked a little. "She won the fight, in case you don't remember."

"I remember." I sighed and rested my head on my knees. "I remember everything, unfortunately. I guess now's a good time to start with the groveling. I'm sorry for what I said to you, Marc." I looked up at him. "I didn't mean it. I'd be pretty upset if you moved out."

"Uh-huh."

"Really, Marc. I'm really sorry. I screwed up."

"Okay." The gun stayed up.

"Is—is everybody else inside?"

"Yeah. Tina's still resting, but Eric and Jess and I are all awake. We were trying to figure out—never mind."

Trying to figure out what to do with me when the sun went down and I was still evil. I almost smiled; bet Sinclair didn't expect me to get up at four o'clock in the afternoon.

"It wasn't much of a prison cell," I couldn't help pointing out. "It had a glass window."

"We were counting on the effects wearing off."

"Well, is it okay if I go in?"

At last, the shotgun came down a little. "What are you going to do?"

"Grovel until I make it right. Oh, and yell at Sinclair. You believe he didn't notice I was psycho?"

"Yeah, well . . . he's kind of upset, too."

"*He's* upset?"

"Yeah."

I couldn't help but notice Marc hadn't put the safety on. He might believe I was back to myself, but he wasn't going to take any chances. It made me sad; he'd never been especially wary around me before.

I wondered what else had changed.

# Chapter 14

"LOOK who's feeling better!" Marc called as I hesitantly entered one of the tea rooms.

"Uh, hi," I said. Then, "What is *that* doing in here?"

I didn't mean Sinclair (though, after last night, I wasn't especially thrilled to see him, either). I was pointing to the Book of the Dead which, incomprehensibly, was on the table next to the bowl of sugar cubes.

"I, too, decided to do some light reading," Sinclair replied. He looked like he was playing statues; he was sitting stiff as a board. "Of course, I stopped after a couple of pages."

"Look, you were right, okay? I shouldn't have read it. Big, dumb, lame mistake."

"Really dumb," Marc added helpfully.

"Really dumb," I agreed, still looking at Sinclair. "And you shouldn't have had sex with me."

"*You* had sex with *me*," he pointed out, having the nerve to sound annoyed. "And you left early."

"Well, yeah, because I was totally evil! And you didn't even notice!" Hmm, my groveling wasn't going quite the way I planned. Still, I couldn't help being upset. "How could you not notice?"

He stood. It was easy to forget what a big guy he was when he was sitting down all prim and proper at tea. But when he flashed to his feet—too quick for most people to track—he towered over everyone else. Marc actually flinched, not that I could blame him. I felt a little like flinching myself.

"I take it to mean," he said quietly, "that the only reason you chose intimacy with me—repeatedly—is because you were out of your head?"

"Well . . ." Boy, did that sound bad. And he looked—not crushed, but like he was getting ready to be crushed. "Uh . . . it's not like I don't think you're a great-looking guy, Eric. I don't think finding each other attractive has ever been the problem." I'd been so focused on what I'd done to Marc and Tina and Jess, I hadn't really thought about how Eric might feel about it. I mean . . . he was a guy. He got laid. A couple of times! I thought he'd be generally okay with it and would scold me about the Book but . . . I didn't think I'd hurt his feelings. Hell, I didn't think I could hurt him at all.

He was the king of the vampires, for goodness' sake.

"Anyway . . ." I was still trying to figure out how to finish the sentence without hanging myself or hurting Eric worse than I already had.

"Oh, hey, look at this," Marc said too heartily. "A shotgun! This isn't mine. I'll just put it back in your closet, Betsy. Well, maybe *my* closet." Then he hurried out.

"Put the safety on when you unload it," I called after him.

"Never mind," Eric said quietly, and I whipped back around. He had sat down again when I wasn't looking. The moment, whatever it was, had passed. "You have answered my question, whether you meant to or not."

"Eric . . ."

"Elizabeth, it has not escaped my notice that you are awake."

"Right. Can't get anything past you." I sat down across from him. "I was outside getting some sun when Marc came to get me. I've got some tall apologizing to do, I know. Where's Tina?"

"Still resting." He was giving me the weirdest look. "Until the sun sets, of course. You say you were *outside*? I heard the glass break but I could hardly believe—"

"Yeah. It was great! I wish you could come out with me; the sun felt so good."

"The sun would incinerate me in a nanosecond."

"Right. Sorry about that. I haven't been out during the day in six whole months, so I was glad to get out of here, believe me."

"Tina," he said, still looking at me like I was a strange new species of bug, "has not seen the sun in well over a hundred years."

"Well, I'll tell her all about it. After I, you know, make things right. Although I'm not sure how much I've got to make right with her; she *did* kick my ass pretty good. You should have seen it," I joked, trying to lighten the mood a little.

"I missed it, as I was waiting for you to return to bed," he said coldly, and I almost cringed.

"You—" I tried to fix it. Couldn't think of a way. I finished the sentence, hating how I sounded like a sad little kid instead of a grown woman. "You really didn't notice?"

"I was . . . distracted. I can assure you, it will never happen again."

His face was so still, so cold. I had to get out of there. Now. This very second. "Where's Jessica?"

"Hiding from you, of course." He grabbed the Book and stood. "I should put this back. Since you appear to be back to yourself, there is no need for further research. Good day."

And that was that.

# Chapter 15

"***JESSICA?***" I softly tapped on the door with my knuckles. "Jess? It's Bets. Can I come in?"

Silence. I could hear her moving around in there, but she wasn't talking. Ugh. I could take anything—death, torture, knockoffs—but the silent treatment.

"Jess? I fucked up, honey. Really really bad. I'm so sorry. Sorry for hitting you and biting you and saying all those rotten things." Listing my sins made me feel worse, if possible. "Can I please come in?"

Nothing. And who could blame her? I wouldn't talk to me, either.

"Jess, let me in, sweetie. Wouldn't you rather see me groveling in person? And I've got a good grovel going, you really don't want to miss it."

Nothing.

"Well." I coughed. "I wanted to tell you I'm not evil anymore and say I'm sorry for—you know. For everything. I'll—uh—I'll be around if you need to talk. Or something. Okay? Okay. Well, I'm gonna go now."

I paused, waiting for her to dramatically fling open the door and holler for me to wait. That's what always happened in the movies. Then I turned around and walked down the hall.

This was gonna be much, *much* harder than I thought. I'd fucked it up all the way around, all because I'd decided to read the Book of the Dead instead of rereading *Gone With the Wind*. I felt like Scarlett after the Yankees went through Tara, except less attractive.

Marc and Tina were at the foot of the stairs, talking. I resisted the urge to eavesdrop—I'd made enough mistakes in the last forty-eight hours—and slowly walked down to meet them.

"Feeling better, Majesty?" Tina asked. Her smile looked real. Marc seemed okay, too. His shoulders were a little set, but he looked relaxed enough.

"Um, yeah. Listen—"

"I'm glad you're all right now. And I must apologize for taking liberties with your person. I—"

I grabbed her little paws and looked down into her big pansy eyes. "Oh, Tina, I'm the one who owes *you* the apology. I suck!"

The corner of her mouth twitched as she attempted to extricate her hands. "Majesty, you do not."

"No, I totally do. I feel so bad that I tried to kill you. I'm *glad* you kicked my ass. Humiliated, but glad. I didn't know you could fight like that!"

She laughed and brushed her straw-colored bangs out of her eyes. "Luckily for me. I must admit, I had a bad moment when you threw your necklace at me."

"Well, I'm really sorry."

"I, also. I am glad," she added with touching sincerity, "you are better."

"Oh, I'm completely evil-free."

"And . . . you rose while the sun was up."

"Yeah. Turn evil, get a new power," I joked. "It's like the worst trade-off ever."

"Hmm," she replied, giving me the same look Sinclair had. It wasn't much fun when *she* looked at me that way, either.

"You should have seen her rolling around in the grass like a big blond puppy," Marc said. "It was pretty hilarious."

"You hush," I said, but I couldn't help smiling. It felt good after recent events.

# Chapter 16

"**WELL**. I do have some good news!" I shouted. "I know how we can track down my sister!"

"Why are we having a meeting in the hallway?" Sinclair asked, looking up from his notes for practically the first time all night.

"So Jessica stays in the loop, duh," I replied. "Anyway, I thought we could track my long-lost sister down and ask her not to take over the world! Okay? I mean, something good came out of the fuckup du jour, right?!?"

Marc rubbed his ear. "How do you want to start?"

"Well, I know she was born right here in the Cities, on June 6, 1986!"

"Six six eighty-six?" Tina asked. "That's interesting."

"It's lame, is what it is! What, we're in *The Omen* now?!? But anyway, we can narrow it down to all the baby girls born to the Ant on six six eighty-six, and how many of them can there be? One, I'm guessing!"

"I don't think you have to *scream*," Marc said. "Her door isn't that thick."

"Do you think you can get the records? You said at the Ant's that you'd try!" This meeting was making me tired. And why wouldn't Sinclair look at me? I figured he was still pissed about the other night. Not a word about how he didn't even notice I was evil, natch. I started to get freshly annoyed and tried to squash it. I was in no position to play the victim. "Marc?!?"

"Shit, I heard you." He rubbed his ear. "Yeah, I don't think that'll be too hard."

"What about confidentiality issues?" Tina asked.

"What's that you say?" I shrieked. "You want to know how we get around confidentiality stuff?"

They both looked annoyed, and then Marc answered her. "Well, let's put it this way. Normally I don't like to go snooping around in charts that are none of my business. But to find Satan's daughter and save the world, I'll make an exception. And Tina, if you or Eric come with me, I'm sure we can get past the clerks."

"All right," Tina said.

"Do you want me to come, too?" I screamed.

"It's not necessary," Tina said, leaning away. "We'll tend to this errand for you, Majesty. Besides . . ." She eyed the closed, locked door to Jessica's bedroom. "You have other things to worry about."

"Right! Well, here's what happened! In case you were wondering!"

"*I'm* wondering how long this meeting will last," Sinclair muttered.

"The devil got really bored down there in Hell and decided to come to Earth for a while! And she possessed the Ant when she was knocked up! And then she went back to Hell!"

"You know all this?" he asked, looking up again.

"Yes! The Book told me! I mean, it didn't *tell* me, I sort of read about it and then just knew the rest!"

"So your stepmother actually *was* the devil for, what, almost a year?"

"Yes!"

"That's amazing," Tina said, wide-eyed.

"Not so amazing! What's amazing is that she was possessed by Satan for almost a year and nobody noticed anything unusual!"

What was that? I thought I'd heard a muffled laugh from the other side of the door. I listened hard, but I couldn't hear anything else. Nuts.

"I have to admit, that's a new one on me," Marc said. "But you don't seem surprised."

"I grew up with the woman. So the devil thought she was the perfect vessel . . . I guess you called it, Marc." My voice was getting tired, so I was talking normally for the moment. "She lost nearly a year of her life, and when she came back to herself, she must have totally freaked. Dumped the baby, tried to get things back to normal. Then later, she managed to talk my dad into marriage. So she got what she wanted, eventually."

"But at what cost?" Sinclair asked. He was sitting cross-legged on my right side and turned to give me a look that was almost scorching. Then the moment passed, and he was back to his notes.

"Right," I said uneasily. "Okay! So, Satan went back to Hell, the Ant broke up my parents' marriage, my sister was dumped into the foster care system, and now we gotta find her before she takes over the world!"

"An interesting agenda," Tina said, bringing up a small hand to cover her smile.

"For all the good it will do," Sinclair said, "your sister is fated to rule the world. As you will recall from your own late reading, there is not a lot of gray area in the Book. I doubt anything we can do will prevent the daughter of the devil from doing that which she pleases."

"Well, we're gonna try!" I hollered back. "We can't not try!"

He shrugged. "As you wish."

Damn right, as I wish. Now if I could just tear him away from his precious note-taking, things might start getting back to normal around here. What the hell was so damned engrossing, anyway? His last will and testament? His grocery list? I leaned over and peeked, but he was writing in a language I didn't know.

"Okay, meeting adjourned!" I shrieked. "Unless anybody has anything to add?" I half-turned and watched Jessica's door, but it didn't open.

So that was that.


THE next afternoon, I drove to my mom's office at the U. Tina wasn't up yet, Jessica was still avoiding me, Marc was off somewhere, and if I was exposed to much more of Sinclair's cold shoulder, I was gonna get frostbite.

We'd find out later tonight what, if anything, Tina and Marc had found out, but for now, the waiting was driving me nuts. The whole situation was driving me nuts.

So, like any insecure, lonely, friendless vampire, I wanted my mommy.

She'd had the same dumpy office for twenty years—tenure didn't mean a decorating budget, apparently—and I made my way there in no time. DR. ELISE TAYLOR, HISTORY DEPARTMENT was etched on the glass part of the door. Her specialty was the Civil War, specifically the battle of Antietam. Like I hadn't had my fill of *that* by the time I was ten.

I could hear her talking in the hallway long before I saw her silhouette against the door. She had half-opened it and was still haranguing her colleague:

"I'm not going to the thing, and you can't make me, Bob, you absolutely can't."

Then she saw I was waiting for her. Her mouth popped open, and her green eyes bulged. Her snow-white hair was straggling out of its usual neat bun; it was her post–sophomore Civil War 124 look. Then she shut the door on poor Bob and ran to me.

"Betsy! You're up!" She looked out her window, looked back at me, looked out the window again. "My God, what are you doing up?"

"Surprise," I said, holding out my arms. She jumped into them—I'd been a head taller since I was twelve—and gave me a squeeze. "I thought I'd do the pop-in."

"I love the pop-in if it's you. So what's happened? Is this part of being the queen? Oh!" Her hand went to her mouth. "I just realized . . . this means you can go to Antonia's baby shower."

I grinned. "Thanks. I totally hadn't thought of that until now. Heh."

"So . . . what's happened?"

I ended up telling her most of it: reading the Book, and going crazy, and what I had done to Jessica and Marc and Tina. I left out what I'd done to Sinclair. Mom didn't need any updates on my sorry sex life. Besides, she was so fond of Sinclair she'd probably be annoyed with me. I also left out the daughter of the devil angle. Mom was broad-minded, but it was best to give her the info in digestible chunks.

". . . and Jess is still hiding from me—she sleeps at night now, behind a locked door. She used to stay up all night because I was up all night. I really screwed the pooch, Mom. Pardon my French. I think the worst part is, I'm in a mess that's totally of my own making. Sinclair warned me about the Book, but I didn't listen. And Jess paid for it. Everybody paid for it."

"You did, too, honey," my mom said, her eyes soft with sympathy. Ahhhh. A mother's love . . . it was like slipping into a sauna—warm, yet hard to breathe. "You're still paying for it. Of course, Jessica is upset. But you've been friends since the seventh grade. A little felony assault isn't going to change that."

"Do you think so?"

"Yes," she said firmly, and I started to perk right up. "Your friendship survived death. It'll recover from this. Just keep apologizing. Do it every single day. Besides, a little remorse will do you good, dear."

"Thanks, Mom."

"I take it Tina and Marc have forgiven you?"

"Yeah, seems like it. Tina never seemed mad about it in the first place, and Marc's a little tense around me, but he treats me nice and all. It's just Jessica." And Sinclair. But there was only so much I could stand to tell her about my own piss-poor behavior.

"Honey, it wasn't your fault. It was that Book. Bound in skin and written in human blood, you say? It must be ancient . . . possibly predating—well—everything." Her eyes were seeing me and far away at the same time; I'd seen that look before. "What I wouldn't give to—you say you keep it in your library?"

"Mom. Seriously. If I see you near that thing, I'll throw it in the fireplace. I might do it anyway. No Book for you." So she'd know I wasn't kidding, I went Soup Nazi on her. We were both gigantic *Seinfeld* fans. *"No Book for you!"*

"Betsy, you can't." She was all somber and reproachful. Not a big fan of book-burning, my mom. "It's literally priceless. Think of what we could—"

"It's a priceless pain in my big white butt. You don't go anywhere near it, get me? The thing's been around forever, and even Sinclair hasn't read it all—just enough to torture me with. I mean it, Mom. Promise you won't try to check it out."

"I promise if you promise not to burn it."

"Fine, I promise. And thanks for the escape hatch, but I can't blame the Book for how I acted after. Nobody stuck a gun in my ear and made me read it. It was my choice. And I've *got* to make it up with Jess."

"Well, keep trying to apologize. You'll have more time to do that, now." She looked out the window again.

I leaned down and rested my head on her shoulder. "Yeah, you're right. I'll keep at it."

She rubbed my back, and we watched the sun go down together.

# Chapter 17

"It took some doing," Marc said into the baby monitor, "but we got it figured out. Over."

"It's not a walkie-talkie, and you're not a trucker," I said, exasperated. "And how much doing could it have taken? You started last night."

"Hey, next time *you* track down Damien. Whose name is Laura, by the way."

We were in the kitchen—everyone but Jessica—and I was getting the scoop on my lost-now-found sister. The three of them were unanimous in their dislike of screaming at Jessica's closed door, so Marc had picked up a set of baby monitors. He'd popped one into Jessica's room that morning, while she was out and the rest of us were conked. She couldn't have minded—we didn't find the monitor in little pieces in the kitchen garbage, at least.

Wait a minute.

Laura?

"Satan's kid is named Laura?"

"Laura Goodman." Tina giggled.

"That's pretty dumb."

"Almost as ridiculous a name as Betsy for a vampire queen," Sinclair commented.

Was that a nasty comment or a nasty-nice comment? Was he getting over being mad? And why did I care so much? *He* was usually on *my* shit list.

I had to admit, I didn't much care for the role reversal. But what could I do? I had the distinct impression that apologizing for having sex with him would just make everything worse. And things were plenty bad enough, thanks. "So, what else did you guys find out?"

Plenty, as it turned out. Laura had been adopted about ten seconds after the Ant had dumped her, thank goodness, by the Goodmans, who settled with her in Farmington, where she grew up. Even better, Laura was a student at the U of M and had an apartment in Dinkytown. My mom could probably help me out a little there.

"It wasn't even very hard to find this stuff out," Marc added. He turned to Tina. "My review is tomorrow. Will you please come to work with me?"

She rolled her eyes and laughed again. "Oh, Marc."

"Well, I suppose it wouldn't have been," I said. I had great respect for Tina's sinister powers. Hey, trying to kill her could be seen as a compliment! A sad, lame compliment. "If there's someone out there Tina can't put the vamp mojo on, I haven't met them."

"Less mojo was needed than you would believe. Everyone was very open about . . . well, everything. The adoption and where she is now and what she's doing. We've even got her phone number."

"Well, good." I guess. That was good, right? Right! Time to regain control of this meeting. Assuming I'd ever had it. "So I guess we'll . . . what? Go see her? Track her down in the root of all evil—Dinkytown, is it? Tell her we're onto her, and she'd better not fulfill her destiny or we'll . . . what?"

"One thing at a time," Sinclair said. Since he was having very little to say these days, I was glad to hear him piping up. "We must find her first."

"Together?"

He speared me with his dark gaze. Which was as uncomfortable as it sounds. "You shouldn't speak to Satan's own by yourself. Of course, I will come with you."

"Of course." I smiled at him, but he didn't smile back.

"Meeting's over," Marc told the baby monitor. "Over."

# Chapter 18

"SHE volunteers at the church," I said. "Oh. My. God! She *volunteers* at the *church*!"

"No matter how many times you say it out loud," Sinclair said, "it still seems to be true."

We'd been shadowing a group of kids—all girls in their late teens—for the last two hours. I wasn't sure which of them was my sister—there were three blondes, two brunettes, and even a strawberry blonde in the group. They'd gone from the U (my mom had most helpfully provided Laura's class schedule, breaking about twenty school regs in the process) to an apartment house in Dinkytown, and now they had all trooped into the local Presbyterian church.

"They're like a flock," Sinclair observed.

"That's just what girls do at that age." Heck, any age. "They travel in clumps. Like hair!"

"Charming."

We were in Sinclair's Passat. I know, I know . . . the king and queen of the vampires, tooling around in a blue Passat? He was keeping the really good cars—the convertible (a Mustang ironically a convertible), the Spider, the various other pretty cars that I didn't know the names of—under wraps for the time being.

Maybe he had hauled the good ones out before to impress me, and now that he was done with the mating dance, it was Passat time.

Ridiculous.

Right?

"I'm going in," I said. I waited for him to caution me, to warn me not to be heedless, to be careful, to insist I wait until the devil's spawn was in a place he could go, too.

Instead, I got, "That seems wise. We really must find out more about this girl."

"Well, so I'll go in. Wait here for me, okay?"

"Mmmm." He was squinting at the church again; I could have started disrobing, and he probably wouldn't have looked away.

"Hey, how come the devil's kid can go in a church and you can't?"

"Ask her," he suggested.

"I think I'll work up to that one," I replied and climbed out of the Passat to cross the street.

I opened the door and walked into the church, hoping Sinclair was noticing the awesome way I could do just that. Yay, the queen!

Argh, again, why did the queen *care*? Was the queen at heart a pathetic loser who could blow off a guy while he was all over her, but the minute he started ignoring her couldn't stop thinking about him? And why was the queen referring to herself in the third person?

But I had to admit, I'd been so focused on being mad at Sinclair for various sins against me, I'd sort of gotten used to him being around. Being concerned about me, always ready to take one for the team, that was Sinclair all the way. When he wasn't being sneaky and withholding.

*Focus, idiot.* Instead of the main part of the church, the part with the pews, I was in a dining area with tables and chairs all over. The gaggle of girls was in the far corner, chatting and giggling, and one of them—the tallest, the blondest, the prettiest—waved at me, said something to her friends, and walked over.

Too late, I realized I had no cover story. At all.

"Hi," she said, smiling. She was wearing a white button-down, crisp and spotless, with khaki pants and loafers. Beat up, ancient, cracked, yukky loafers; no socks. Her hair was long and fine, the blond strands looking like rough silk, and caught away from her face with a white headband. Her eyes were a perfect, clear blue, the exact color of the sky. Her skin was also irritatingly perfect, creamy with peach highlights, and not a freckle in sight. No makeup—she didn't need it.

And she was smiling so pleasantly at me, in her casual

running-around clothes, that I instantly knew she was one of those beautiful girls who didn't know they were beautiful. It took all of my powers as the queen of the undead not to instantly hate her.

"Why are you and your friend following us?"

"Uh . . ." Because, as king and queen of the vampires, we feel that you—or one of your friends—as the devil's daughter (and worse, the Ant's daughter), should be stopped from ruling the world. Welcome to the family! Now get the fuck out. "We're . . . we're looking for Laura? Laura Goodman?"

"I'm Laura," she said, holding out a slim, pale hand for me to shake. I took it, being massively unsurprised. She was too tall (as tall as me!), too pretty, too perfect. And you know what they said about the devil taking a pleasing form. "What can I do for you?"

"Well . . . the thing is, I—"

"Laura!" One of her gaggle was calling over to us. "You coming? This dance isn't going to plan itself."

"Be right there," she called back, and turned back to me. "You were saying?"

"It's kind of a private thing. Do you have any time later tonight? Or tomorrow? Maybe we could have some coffee and talk?"

"Okay," she said, and she wasn't giving off scared vibes, which was good. Really trusting . . . or really scarily powerful with nothing to fear from the likes of me. "How about lunch tomorrow? Kahn's?"

"Ohhhh, I *love* Kahn's!" So we couldn't go there. If I couldn't eat the awesome garlic noodles with scallions and lamb, I wasn't going to watch someone else do it. "But lunch is bad for me."

"Well, I've got class tomorrow until four thirty . . ."

"How about Dunn Brothers, at five? Right around the corner?"

"All right, then." She shook my hand again. "It was nice to meet you . . ."

"Betsy."

"Right. See you tomorrow for coffee."

"Bye," I told my sister and watched her walk back to her friends.


"SO she's this wretched evil beast who's fated to rule the world *and* she's a natural blonde. Just ridiculously pretty—hair, face, long thin legs, okay clothes, terrible shoes. And sweet as sugar, so far. When she turns into her horrible demon self it should be something to see . . .

"I didn't see much resemblance to the Ant or my dad, except for her being tall like me, and blond. But that's not too hard; we're in Minnesota, not Japan. I dunno. I'm having coffee with her tomorrow, trying to suss out her evilness . . . so I guess that's everything."

I clicked off the baby monitor and then remembered, so I turned it back on. "Almost forgot, I told Sinclair all about this, too. Sun's not going to be down all the way by five—I swear, vampires must have thought up daylight savings—but since it hasn't kicked in yet, he can't come. He didn't even seem to mind that he couldn't be there again. I guess he's still pretty pissed at me. Not that I blame him. Or you," I added hastily. "I can't seem to fix it with either one of you. And it's weird—it's bugging me that he's being so chilly and distant. And it's bugging me that it's bugging me. I can't apologize, and I can't pretend nothing happened. I guess . . . I guess I'll just focus on other stuff. Oh, my mom's having me over for supper the day after tomorrow, and she says you should come, too. If you want."

Silence.

I clicked the monitor off again and went up to bed.

# Chapter 19

THE devil's own—Laura Goodman, college girl about
Dinkytown—breezed into Dunn Brothers at two minutes after
five. She waved at me, paused to speak to the counter guy—who
was slavering like a beast, I couldn't help noticing—and then
came over to me.

"I'm so sorry I'm late," she gasped by way of greeting, shaking my hand again. "I'm really, really sorry. Have you been waiting long? I'm sorry."

"It's fine, Laura. By my watch you're right on time." She
seemed so contrite, so sincere, I found myself rushing to reassure
her. "Have a seat."

"Thanks. My cocoa's coming."

"Don't like the hard stuff, huh?" I asked, indicating my own
doublechocolattespressowithextrafoam.

"Oh, I try not to drink caffeine after lunchtime," she replied. "I
have to get up early in the morning for work."

"You've got a job, too?"

"Too? Oh, that's right." She smiled at me. It wasn't a grin, it
wasn't a smirk, she didn't raise an eyebrow knowingly. It was just
a nice smile. "You were following me half the night yesterday."

"Well, yeah," I admitted. "I guess it's no good pretending I
wasn't."

"My father says liars are fated to believe their own lies, so it's
probably good you're coming clean."

"Yeah . . . your father. Uh, listen about that . . ."

She leaned forward and took my hand in hers, then dropped it.
"Gosh, your hand is cold! You should have another hot drink."

"Sorry. I have bad circulation."

"No, *I'm* sorry. I hope I didn't make you feel bad. I shouldn't have just blurted it out like that."

"Don't worry about it, Laura." She was too good to be true! Minnesota nice was one thing, but Laura was in a class by herself. "Listen . . ."

She leaned forward, perfect gorgeous face lighting up. "This is about my family, isn't it? My birth family." She paused, then added, "Sorry about interrupting."

I blinked in surprise. "How'd you know?"

"Well." The counter guy brought her a white coffee cup the size of my head, absolutely brimming with whipped cream and swirled with chocolate syrup. She smiled up at him and cupped the biggest cocoa in the world in her hands. "I was thinking about you last night, after you left. And you're tall, like me—in fact you're about an inch taller. My whole life, I've never met a woman taller than me. And you're blond, and we both have light-colored eyes . . . and you were so mysterious, but so nice . . . it just got me thinking."

"Oh, so you know you're—that you were adopted?"

"Yes, of course. Mama and Dad told me all about it, about how of all the babies in the world, they chose me." She was still smiling, clearly happy at the memory. "God brought me to them."

"Right." God. Uh-huh. "Well, I recently—like, this week— found out about you, and I did some detective work." With vampires. And a certain dark book bound in human skin. No, *not* chemistry. "And I tracked you down and—I don't know." I really *didn't* know where I was going with this. "I just wanted to meet you and then I guess . . ."

"You're my sister, right?"

"Half sister," I hastened to correct. I did not have a single drop of blood in common with the Ant *or* the devil. Biologically, Laura was the Ant's own blood daughter, but without the interference of Satan, she never would have been born. It was enough to make me want to lunge for the Advil. "We have the same father." *And I'm so, so sorry about that, Laura.*

"Well, I'm just so pleased to meet you!" Impulsively, she leaned over further and flung her arms around my neck. I almost broke her arms before I realized she was hugging me, not attacking me. "I really, really am," she gushed. She was so close I could smell—vanilla? I'd smelled it before, natch, but being in a coffee shop, I'd assumed . . .

"Well, thanks," I said, gently extricating myself. "It's nice to meet you, too. Has anyone ever told you, you smell like cookies?"

"I use vanilla extract instead of perfume. It's cheap, and they don't test it on bunnies," she told me soberly.

"Huh. That's kind of clever, actually."

"People tell me that a lot." She sipped her cocoa and continued, oblivious of her whipped cream mustache. "I'm at the U on scholarship. Hmm, what else should I tell you? What do you want to know?"

"What are your folks like?"

She wiped the cream away with the back of her hand, then wiped her hand on the napkin. "They're wonderful. Dad is the minister at the Presbyterian church in Inver Grove—"

"Your dad's a *minister*?" I tried to dial back my total amazement and shock. I thought the *devil* was supposed to be in the details. "That's—really cool."

"Uh-huh. And Mama takes care of the house, and me. She's in school now, too! Now that I'm out of the house, she thought it would be a good time to finish up her nursing degree. We're students together at the U! Oh, you have to come over! They would love to meet you."

"That would be"—extremely weird; incredibly uncomfortable; horribly inconvenient right now—"great."

"What about you, Betsy? What do you do?"

As God was my witness, I had no idea what to say. I just couldn't blurt it all out to her. She was such a sweetheart, I didn't want to wreck her evening. Day. Month. Life. I resolved to take it one step at a time. "I'm—I run the—a—nightclub. A bar, actually. It's called Scratch, and I own it."

"You *own* it?"

"Well, it was left to me. By someone—" Who I staked. "Anyway, that's really my thing. I mean, that's what I do." That didn't sound suspicious, right?

"I'd love to see it sometime."

"Well, maybe I'll bring you by." Ha! The devil's daughter, checking out my undead nightclub. "You seem to be—I mean, you seem kind of together about all this."

I had to admit, this was so not what I expected. I expected threats, mustache-twirling death threats. Not a pleasant coffee in Dinkytown. The Book had warned me about her but hadn't mentioned what an innocent she'd be.

"Mama and Dad were very open about my background," she was explaining.

*Not that open, honey.* "Yeah?"

"And now that I'm out of the house, I was going to do some detective work of my own. I love Mama and Dad—of course!—but I was curious, you know? I had a lot of questions, but I didn't want to be disrespectful."

"Sure, I can totally get behind that."

She smiled at me gratefully. "Anyway, you just saved me a whole lot of work." She seemed so nice, so grateful, that I couldn't help returning her smile.

"It's just so nice to meet you."

"It's nice to meet you, too."

"I've always hoped for a sister."

"Actually, me, too. My folks split up when I was a kid—"

"I'm really sorry."

"Thanks. Anyway, I was pretty lonesome, and if it wasn't for my friend Jess, I don't know what—" Talking about Jessica made me feel like choking up. How could I tell Laura the truth . . . about anything? About what I was, how I'd been such an asshole, how she was supposed to be an asshole, too, and by the way, please don't take over the world. "We're kind of in a fight right now," I finished lamely.

"If I can ask . . . Betsy, I hope you're not offended . . ."

"Go ahead. I've butted into your life."

"Well . . . when your folks split up . . . was it because of me?"

"Oh no no no," I assured her. Then, "Well, maybe. A little. It wasn't your *fault.* I mean, you were just a fetus. But I guess when my mom had proof my dad was cheating . . . things sort of went downhill."

"Oh." She looked down at her lap. "I guess I don't really know how to feel about that. I'm sorry my birth father was faithless, but if he hadn't been . . ."

"Don't beat yourself up," I advised, in big sister mode. "Trust me, you'll screw up in your life enough without taking the blame for something that isn't your fault."

She looked up from her hands and smiled again. "I really—oh golly, who is *that*?"

I looked. Eric Sinclair, walking in . . . but not to order coffee, I bet. I realized the sun had fallen down while Laura and I were chatting.

"That's my—" I took another look at Laura's perfect beauty, the way she was goggling at Eric, remembered (like I could forget) his recent disinterest in me, and said it. "My boyfriend." Except that wasn't right, either. According to the Book, he was my consort, my husband, my king. I'd always felt just the opposite, that he wasn't anything to me—just another vampire in a city full of the darn things.

"He's your *boyfriend?*"

"Yep, that's my steady sweetie." I was digging myself quite the hole with my big fat mouth. But no matter how nice Laura was, I did not want the devil's daughter to know the king of the vampires was available. And vice versa.

"Elizabeth." Suddenly, Eric was right *there*, standing beside our little table by the window. I jumped and nearly threw my coffee into the window. He was holding a large foam cup with a straw sticking out of the cover, a cup that smelled like strawberries. The man was a nut for his smoothies.

"Hi, Sin—Eric. Ah, Eric, this is my sister, Laura. Laura, this is . . ."

He raised an eyebrow.

"Eric," I finally said. That wasn't a horrible weird awkward pause, was it?

"Charmed," he said.

"Hiya," she replied, dazzled. She shook his hand and gasped again. "Boy, you both have freezing cold hands! I guess you two are a pretty good match."

"Right!" I said. "That's what made us perfect for each other: clammy extremities. Laura and I were just catching up with each other."

"Pull up a chair," she invited. "Have you been dating long?"

Sinclair lifted the other eyebrow at "dating." I couldn't blame him. We had done quite a few things together, none of which could be classified as a date. "Six months," he said, sitting down. Then he paused, and added, "You smell like sugar cookies."

"She uses vanilla extract for perfume," I explained. "It's better for our animal friends."

"Oh, yes, our animal friends." He barely seemed to notice my explanation. "My, my, Laura Goodman. I must say, that is a charming name for a charming young lady."

"Eric's old," I broke in. "Really really old."

"Er—really?" Laura asked. "Gosh, you don't look even out of your thirties."

"Tons of face-lifts. He's a surgical addict. I'm trying to get him help," I added defensively when they both gave me strange looks.

"I was just telling Betsy that my parents would love to meet her, and you must come, too."

"I would be delighted, Laura."

"Yeah," I said, watching the two of them stare at each other over foam cups. "That'd be swell."

# Chapter 20

"I'm so sorry to bother you with this." It was the third time Alice had said it. "But I thought you ought to know."

"It's okay, Alice. It's not your fault. They're not animals, they're people. It's stupid to pretend they don't have human brains. I should have figured that out a long time before now."

"It's not your fault, Majesty. The fault lies with me. It's—"

"They should be recaptured and staked," Sinclair said, sounding bored.

"We've been over this," I snapped back.

"I suppose we have."

I didn't agree with his kill-all-Fiends mind-set, but his boredom with the subject wasn't much fun, either.

"It's not 'they,'" Alice supplied helpfully. "It's just one."

"Let me guess: George?"

"Yes, ma'am."

"Swell." The perfect end to a perfect night. The devil's daughter turned out to be sweet as cream, Sinclair gave off the distinct impression that he'd like to sample some of that cream, I was in hell, and George had gone on the lam again. "Just great."

"We'll find him again, ma'am."

"Okay, well, call me if he turns up."

"At once, Majesty."

"We'll keep our eyes peeled, not literally. Meanwhile, let's think of a better system to keep him. The others don't seem to want to get out, but George does, so let's figure out why and fix it so he can have what he wants here on the property. It's not the best plan in the world, but it's what we'll start with."

"Yes, Majesty."

"Swell," Sinclair said, and gave me a thin smile.


"W+H-A-T the hell are you doing following me around?" I griped. We'd driven back to the mansion in our cars, and I was bitching Eric out on the front lawn. "Like dealing with the spawn of Satan isn't touchy enough without you popping up like a jack-in-the-box with fangs."

"I wasn't following you," he pointed out coolly. "I was following her."

Nuts. I'd been afraid of that. "Why?"

"She is a fascinating creature. I had no sense of deceit from her, did you?"

"N—"

"All that potential power, that world-building power, wrapped up in a lovely package. A genuinely nice girl with no clue of the unholy power she could wield." He was practically rubbing his hands together. "To harness that power . . . if I could just—"

"We," I said. "If we could just."

"Yes, yes. Really, an engaging dilemma."

"That's just super," I said, managing to keep the acid bitterness out of my tone. Pretty much. "Look, one thing at a time. We've got to make nice with Jessica and find George."

"As you have made clear in the past," he reminded me, "those are your problems, not mine."

For a second I couldn't say anything; it felt like cold dread just—just grabbed my heart. Six months of pushing him away, and when I succeeded, I was sick about it. Which was sick

And as upset as I was, I was also mad. Okay, I'd screwed up. He was an eighty-year-old dead guy. Like he'd never made a mistake in all that time?

When I finally found my voice, I went on the attack. Anything was better than feeling like the biggest loser in the world.

"*Listen,* jackass. Do you think you can stop sulking for five fucking minutes and *help me*? Is that too fucking much to ask? If you won't admit you're mad, then you'd better be on board with the dark evil stuff like usual. You can't have it both ways."

He looked down at me, totally unmoved. "You . . . would . . . be . . . *amazed* at what I can have." Then he turned away.

I grabbed his sleeve and tried to pull him back. "Don't walk away from me, you—"

"Did you hear something?" he asked, shaking free of me with no trouble at all. "There's—" Then he was gone, knocked a good six feet sideways by something.

"Eric!" I called, like every useless movie heroine in the history of cinema. I charged over to grab whatever had tackled him. "Let go!" *And thanks!*

I leaned forward to seize whatever by the back of the neck—assuming it had a back of a neck—when suddenly it got off Sinclair and stood.

And stood. And stood. It was tall, even slumped over. Long dirty clots of hair hung in its face, and its clothing—filthy jeans and a T-shirt of no definable color—was in rags. Bare feet. Filthy toes.

"George!" I gasped.

"How completely fabulous," Sinclair said, getting up off the ground and brushing himself off. There were leaves in his hair, but *I* wasn't going to tell him. "I assume he followed us. Or tracked you."

"Tracked *me*?"

"They are uncommonly attached to you, in case you've forgotten their devotion when they killed Nostro," he snorted, as if I *could* forget.

"Aw, shaddup. George, you were very very bad to run away from Alice." I shook my finger under his nose. It was a little disconcerting the way he followed my finger with his muddy gaze. "Very bad! But you were very good to stomp Sinclair when he was being a dick, so I think we'll call this a wash."

"What?" Sinclair scowled. "How can you say—"

"Pipe down, ass hat. You know what, George? Let's call Alice and have her come get you. Good, good Fiend!"

"No, no, no," Sinclair began. At least he was evincing some interest again—interest that didn't threaten the hell out of me.

"And while we're waiting, you can have a shower."

"Elizabeth, I must protest."

"Really?"

"Yes."

"Hate the idea, do you?"

"Completely."

"Good enough." I took George's cold, grimy hand, and he followed me.

# Chapter 21

$\mathcal{I}$ didn't dare bring him into the main part of the house—Jessica and Marc were probably around, and I didn't quite trust George enough to just let him go like that movie *Born Free*. So I brought him through one of the basement doors, helped him strip, and stuck him under the shower we had down there.

He seemed to like it, creepy darkened basement notwithstanding, first standing like a hairy lump and then stretching a bit under the beating warm water. I dared leave him for just a moment, superspeeding my way through the house to grab some of Marc's clothes. Marc, shaving, didn't hear me or see me, and I'd explain later.

George was shaking his head under the spray so his long strands flew when I got back to the basement, and I let him enjoy the shower for another ten minutes. I almost couldn't bear to turn it off; seeing him clean and almost happy gave me a glimpse of the man he once had been.

Not a bad-looking one, either, under all the mud. Tall and thin, with long arms and legs that were sleekly muscled, and a broad back and a *great,* tight butt. Very pale, of course, but a clean, open-looking face with thin lips. He looked like a swimmer, in fact, all gangly limbs and big feet. And big, uh, other things, but I was trying to stay clinical.

"So, why'd you come after me?" I asked.

No answer, big surprise.

"It's creepy," I added, "but kind of cute. You must have thought I was in danger from Sinclair." I snickered, remembering seeing Sinclair practically knocked out of his loafers on the front lawn. "Well, Alice is on her way, so you'll be back home soon."

When the water started to get chilly, I shut it off and draped George in a humungous beach towel. Impersonal as a nurse, I briskly dried him off, helped him get dressed in a set of Marc's scrubs, then combed out his long hair. Under the light, it was past his shoulders—which was weird, vampires couldn't grow their hair—and brown with gold highlights. It must have been long when he'd died. What had he been? Rock drummer? Motorcycle racer?

"There now!" I said, stepping back to admire him. "You look great. If you can just resist rolling around in the mud, you could almost pass for an ordinary creature of the night."

"Majesty?" I could hear Alice calling me—I must not have heard her car over the sound of the shower. "The king said you were down here."

"Yeah, come on down, Alice." She tentatively crept down the stairs, obviously ready to be yelled at. It was tough work reminding some of these guys that I wasn't Nostro with red highlights. "Look who I found! Doesn't he look great?"

She stared. "George?"

"In the undead flesh." I reached up—way up—and tousled his hair. "He must have followed me home. Or picked up my scent and followed that. You should have seen him tackle Sinclair. It was great! Disrespectful," I added with mock severity, "but great."

"Again, Majesty, I'm so s—"

"Alice, for crying out loud. You've got your hands full, I know that. In fact, I should get you some help." What other vampire could I trust with such a tedious but important, job? Maybe I'd find one at Scratch.

"He looks"—she was circling around him, a good trick since she had to actually go through the shower to do it—"different. It's not just being clean. He's been clean before."

"It's the scrubs," I decided. "They make him look smarter."

"Nooooo, with all respect, I don't think that's it." She looked at George, then me, then George. I waited to hear her theory. Alice looked like a demure fifteen-year-old in her plaid skirts and head-bands, but she was really, like, fifty years old. And no dummy, either. "Ah, well."

That was her big theory?

"We've taken up quite enough of your evening, Majesty. Come on, George." Alice put her hand out and clutched his forearm, which he yanked back so quickly she almost fell into the shower. He didn't growl at her, but he showed his teeth.

"Uh-oh," she murmured.

"Maybe he wants to stay here with me," I said, a little surprised.

"I don't think it's a maybe. Perhaps if you helped me get him out to the car . . ."

"You know what? Let him stay."

"Majesty, you live in the city. I'm not sure that's wise. He might—"

"He's had plenty of chances to pounce—heck, he didn't do anything to Sinclair except knock him out of the way. I know! I'll let him feed on me and then he can just stay in the basement for a couple of nights."

"*You'll* let him feed?"

I didn't take offense at Alice's reaction. It was well-known that I wasn't the biggest pro–blood giver among vampires. Except with Sinclair, the whole thing kind of squicked me out.

Well, Sinclair was over! The past! I was going forward, not back. And while I was at it, the hell with Jessica, too. I had two new friends: the devil's daughter and George the Fiend.

It sounded so ridiculous I didn't dare dwell on it; instead I chomped on my own wrist until my sluggish blood started to flow, and held my arm out to George.

"Thish thould do it," I slurred. *My life isn't horrible and weird. My life isn't horrible and weird. My life—*

"I must admit," Alice commented, her red hair seeming to glow against the gloomy basement bricks, "when I rose this evening, I hadn't foreseen any of tonight's events."

"Thtick with me, bay bee." George had grasped my wrist, lapped up the blood, and was now sucking like a kid with a Tootsie Pop. "Ith a new thrill every minute."

Alice reluctantly left, I managed to get my arm back, and then I made George a nest in one of the empty basement rooms—one of the inner windowless ones—with a bunch of clean towels. I went upstairs to find a pillow, saw the usual unrelieved darkness outside was now a dark gray, and hurried back down, hauling a wool blanket out of one of the linen closets on the way. George was already stretched out on the towels, sound asleep.

I left him the pillow, locked the door—compassion was one thing, carelessness something else—and went up to my room.

It had been an unnatural night, that was for sure. Good in some ways—bad in others, and, ultimately, challenging.

# Chapter 22

" . . . So that's the really bizarro thing," I told the baby monitor. "She's not this incredibly evil creature out to rule the world. She's a perfectly nice college kid. An education major, for God's sake! She wants to teach kindergarten when she grows up. If you cut her, she'd probably bleed maple syrup.

"So anyway, on the one hand that's a relief, but on the other, I can't just let her run around being unconsciously evil. I guess I better tell her. One of these days. And how do you tell someone that their mom is the devil? It would have been hard enough to tell her the *Ant* was her mom.

"And let's not forget what the Book told me. The devil's supposed to show up. She's—I guess it's a she—she's supposed to show up to Laura, poor thing, and to me. 'In all the raiments of the dark,' whatever that means. So I can't dick around with warning Laura. Right?"

Silence. Was Jess even listening to her baby monitor? I had no way of knowing. Her car was in the garage, but who really knew?

"Right," I finished. "Well, so that's what's been going on. That and there's a Fiend living in the basement, so don't go down there during the day. In fact, don't go down there altogether. Listen, if you want to meet Laura, just let me know. She's really a sweetheart. She's having me over for supper pretty soon. And Sinclair, unfortunately, but I'll worry about that later. Well, 'bye."

I snapped the monitor off and just sat at the kitchen counter for a minute, thinking. Tina came in and nodded respectfully; I sort of waved at her and kept with the pondering.

Jessica was still mad . . . and worse, scared. She'd been mad before, plenty of times, but she'd never hidden herself away for days (nights) at a time. Her method was normally to tell me at length, loudly, how and where I'd fucked up, repeat as needed.

My sister was running around the campus of the University of Minnesota, totally unaware she was going to try to take over the world one of these days. Sinclair was still giving me frostbite every time he looked at me. The Ant was still pregnant. Only Marc seemed unchanged by it all and, frankly, with his work schedule, he had never been around all that much to begin with.

My cat Giselle walked into the kitchen, ignored both of us, and headed to her bowl. I didn't bother trying to pet or cuddle her. Giselle and I had a strict working relationship. I worked to feed her, and she worked on ignoring me. Plus, in a house this big, days would go by when I didn't see her. I made sure she had food and fresh water, and she ate and drank and did her own thing.

Well, at least someone else's life was unchanged.

"Everything sucks," I announced. "Again."

"I'm sorry to hear that, Your Majesty." Tina glanced up from *Outdoor Life*. She was a gun nut, that one. "I'm sure you'll find a way to make it all right again."

"All right *again*? Tina, when has it ever been all right?"

"A poor choice of words," she admitted, turning a page. Reading upside down, I could see the title of the article: "Tracking Antelope in Big Sky Country."

"And as nutty as everything is, I've got the nagging feeling I'm forgetting something." I thought and thought. "What the hell is it?" Monique? Dead. Sister? Friend. Scratch? Still in the red. But that reminded me—Monique had hired a bunch of pimply faced vampire killers last summer. To be honest, once they'd stopped trying to cut my head off, I'd sort of forgotten about them. "What are the Blade Warriors up to these days?"

"Jon is still at his parents' farm, Wild Bill is out of town at the SciFiConBiTriCon, and I have no idea what the others are doing. Frankly," she admitted, "once they stopped trying to stake us, I instantly lost interest in their activities."

I could relate. "Except for Ani," I said slyly.

Tina smiled. "Well. We had to go our separate ways, but she was a very charming girl."

"Right. Charming. We *are* talking about the girl who has more knives than shirts, right? Don't answer. Okay, so it's not that. What *is* it?"

"Well, you were planning to shop for new shoes for Andrea

and Daniel's wedding," she pointed out. "With all the goings on, perhaps you haven't had—"

"Andrea and Daniel's wedding!" I nearly shouted, then rested my forehead on the cool marble counter. "Aw, fuck a duck."

"I take it you've remembered what you had forgotten?"

"When is it?" I asked hollowly.

"Halloween. A week from tomorrow."

"Swell." Jessica was supposed to help me shop. Maybe I'd turn on the baby monitor and remind her. No, she knew. Unlike me, she had a great memory. She was just ignoring it. Not that I could blame her, but the cold shoulder *was* getting old.

"Aha!"

"I tremble to ask."

"I'll ask my sister to go shopping! You know, one of the few people on the planet who don't think I'm scum."

"Majesty—"

"Don't bother, Tina. And don't mind me. I'm sort of neck deep in self-pity right now."

She smiled sympathetically. "I'm sure you'll work everything out. Who could resist you for long, my queen?"

"Thanks. That's a little creepy, but thanks. I—"

Suddenly, so fast I could barely follow it, Tina's hand dropped to the knife block, she pulled out a wicked long butcher knife, and whipped it underhand toward me in one smooth motion. I squeaked and got ready to duck (to try to duck), when I realized she hadn't been aiming at me.

George the Fiend blinked at us from the kitchen doorway, a knife sticking out of his chest.

"Damn," she swore, getting up. "Majesty, get back. I'll—"

"You'll stop throwing sharp things at his heart, that's what you'll do!" I leapt up and went to George, who didn't seem especially fazed. "He's okay, Tina, he's not here to hurt us. Jeez, good thing it's not a wooden stake."

"I never even heard him approach, blast it." Tina wasn't this upset when she called Sinclair on keeping secrets about my sis. "I was trying to buy time for you to get away. I would have found something suitable in another few seconds."

"That's comforting." Okay, it wasn't, but what else was I supposed to say? "Good work. Except don't throw knives at him anymore."

Tina's dark eyes were practically bulging. "My queen, what is he doing in our kitchen?"

"He must have gotten out of the basement. Stop me if you've heard this before, but George is the Houdini of feral vampires. I'm gonna have to get him a straitjacket or something. And a cowbell." I patted him soothingly, then grasped the handle of the knife, gritted my teeth, and pulled. It stuck to his breastbone for half a second, then slid out. Yecccccch!

George the Fiend hummed a little but otherwise stood still for it. He didn't bleed.

"My goodness," Tina goggled. "He didn't even notice!"

"Yeah, he's the Fiend you love to stab. Poor George, does it hurt? Of course it doesn't hurt. You'd probably be screaming like a third-grade girl if it hurt. Listen, you're supposed to *stay* in the *basement.*"

"He's not bleeding," she said, coming over to inspect the stab wound.

"Well, he's dead."

"We do bleed," she reminded me. "Not much compared to a living, breathing human, but we do." She bent forward . . . then jerked back as George growled at her.

"Better not," I said. "I think he only likes me. And Alice. But then, she feeds him." And so did I, I remembered suddenly. I'd let them drink my blood the night we killed Nostro . . . and again last night.

"He's dangerous," Tina nagged.

"Yeah, yeah, thanks for the update. Listen, they're Fiends because Nostro let them rise but not feed, right?"

"Yes."

"Well. I *have* let them feed. I mean, Alice feeds them buckets of blood from the butcher, but it's not live blood. They're the only vampires that can subsist on—what would you call it? Dead blood? Unfresh blood? But maybe that's what keeps them like animals. I fed George last night, and here he's walking around and—well, being creepy, but look! He's not crawling. He's *walking*. He stood in the shower last night, too," I remembered.

"I see where you're going with this."

"Good, because I don't have a clue . . . I was just thinking out loud."

I looked at his chest again. "See, he's not bleeding, not like you or I would. Maybe he has to—I dunno—build up? Maybe I can cure him!"

"And maybe you should think this over some more before . . . oh, Majesty," she scolded as I chomped on my own wrist again.

"As you would say, this is so totally the opposite of thinking this over."

"Where's your spirit of adventure?"

"It wore off during World War Two," she replied dryly. Meanwhile, George was obligingly sucking on my wrist, still humming.

"That almost sounds . . . familiar."

"It's the Beastie Boys! 'Brass Monkey'!"

"Is that good?"

"Dunno, but it's a song. He's standing, and he knows rap songs." It was working! I would cure him, I'd cure them all. And Laura wouldn't take over the world. And Sinclair would forgive me and want to sleep with me again. And Jessica would stop being mad and scared and go shopping with me. Everything was working out great!

"Isn't tomorrow your stepmother's baby shower?" Tina asked, and I instantly sank back into a funk.

# Chapter 23

"... AND then I graduated valedictorian at my school and got to give the speech to all the kids, and then I got a job volunteering at Goodwill, in addition to my jobs at Target and Super-America, while I waited to start at the U in the fall."

I stifled a yawn and shifted the phone to my other ear. If you'd ever told me the devil's daughter would be nice, but dull . . . "Yeah, then what happened?"

"Well, that's about it. I mean, I'm still in school. Nothing much has happened to me yet."

*Give it time, sweetie.*

"What about you, what have you been doing? You're—what? Twenty-five?"

I laughed. "Actually, I turned thirty in April. And I've had kind of a checkered career. Model, secretary, waitress . . ."

"And right now you own a nightclub?"

"Right now, yeah." I'd just looked over the books the other night, in fact. We were definitely in the red—I was shocked at the price of booze, not to mention utilities—but so far I had been able to borrow from Peter to pay Paul. Without Jessica's help, I couldn't much longer. But it was hard enough to ask her for a loan when she *wasn't* pissed and terrified. "I guess we'll see how that goes."

"So, tell me about my birth mother and father."

That was the *last* thing I wanted to do. I downed my hot milk in a hurry and tried not to drop the phone. She'd called me about a minute after I'd woken up that afternoon. Three thirty in the afternoon, yippee! A new record. Maybe someday I'd manage to wake at lunchtime. "Uh, well . . . gee, so much to tell. Where to start. Ah . . ."

"Do you think I could meet them sometime? I wouldn't want to push my way into their lives. I understand they gave me up because it was what they thought was best for me. I wouldn't want to intrude or make them uncomfortable in any way."

"Don't forget, Dad didn't even know you existed until after you were adopted." Why had I said that? Did I want her to like Dad? Maybe I was so dreading telling her about the devil, I wanted her to have something nice to hold on to.

"That's true, Betsy. And I know my mother was alone . . . poor thing, she must have been so worried when she found out. No one to turn to . . . maybe her minister was able to counsel her."

Her minister, her bookie, whatever. "Yeah, the . . . poor thing." Suddenly, a wonderful (or terrible) idea came to me. "Listen! Do you want to meet them both? This afternoon?" The shower started in . . . I checked my watch. Twenty minutes. Well, we'd be fashionably late.

Laura's happy squeal was answer enough.

"SHE'S pregnant again?" Laura asked, staring at the Ant's too-big-for-two-people house. "At her age?"

"She's not that old, remember." I checked my lipstick in the mirror. Next to Laura's breathtaking, fresh beauty, I don't know why I bothered.

She looked wonderful; her hair was in two golden braids today, the ends brushing the tops of her breasts, her bangs perfectly level with her eyebrows. She was wearing a clean white blouse (she must have a closet full of them) and a navy A-line skirt. No panty hose, and sensible black flats. Isaac Michener, good. The Target collection, bad. She looked like an extra on *Touched by an Angel*. And I felt like a before on *Nip/Tuck*.

"I'm so excited!"

"Oh, she will be, too," I lied. "Let's go."

We knocked politely but, since it was a party, opened the massive front door and went right in. The driveway was packed with cars, and I could hear the gabble of voices off to the right.

The Ant came hurrying out to greet us, the smile vanishing when she saw it was me. She glanced over my shoulder to the windows on either side of the door, confirming the sun was still up, looked back at me, looked out the window.

"Surprise!" I burbled.

"Congratulations," Laura said.

The Ant swallowed her tongue and forced a grimace that I suppose was technically a smile. "Thank you for coming," she managed. "Betsy, you know where to hang up your coats."

Laura handed me her knee-length mustard-colored trench coat. (I know it sounds awful, but on her, it worked. She probably could have worn the kitchen curtains and it would have worked.) I slung it into the hall closet.

"Gifts . . . gifts can go in the living room. There's a table."

"We didn't bring a present," I informed her gleefully. "Just our bad old selves."

"We have a gift," Laura corrected me. Now that I'd relieved her of her coat, I saw she was holding a small box of Tiffany blue, with the standard white ribbon.

Relief washed over the Ant's face; I could almost hear her thought: Not a total disaster after all! She practically snatched the present out of Laura's hand and ripped the ribbon off. Inside was a sterling silver baby spoon.

"Why, this is—it's very nice. Thank you, er—"

"Laura Goodman, ma'am. I'm a friend of Betsy's."

"Well, you might as well come in and have some cake," she almost snapped. To Laura, she added warmly, "So nice *you* could come."

Big surprise, Laura the Great had won over the second most evil creature in the universe. And where'd the present come from? She was a college student on scholarship; I doubted she kept a closetful of Tiffany baby gifts around.

Sixteen thousand years later, it was almost seven o'clock, and guests were pulling on their coats. Laura and the Ant were chatting like old pals—Laura seemed to think everything about her birth mother, from the bleached hair to the fuzzy pastel sweater to the knockoff pumps—was just swell. Me, I was ready to bite everybody in the room just for the relief of the screams. It was the usual collection of wannabe socialites and poseurs. Believe me, a bite on the neck would doing every one of them a favor. The fact that they all didn't recognize me—or pretended not to—was one of the nicest things that had happened all week.

"Come by anytime," the Ant told the devil's daughter. She didn't say anything to me, but her look spoke volumes.

"That was *great!*" Laura yammered on the way back to the car. "Wow, what a gorgeous house! And she's so nice! And pretty, don't you think she's pretty? I wish I could have told her the truth—I feel so bad about lying. And to a pregnant lady!"

"You didn't lie," I said, wondering why there was never a pack of feral vampires around when you needed them. "We *are* friends. Just ones who haven't known each other very long."

"Oh, Betsy." She slung an arm across my shoulders and gave me a one-armed hug. "You're the greatest. Thank you so much for bringing me here today."

"Umf," I said, or something close to it. "Listen, can I ask you something?"

"Sure. Anything."

"How'd you have a present all ready to go?"

"Oh, I bought that a long time ago," she explained with awe-inspiring (yet slightly nauseating) earnestness. "I always knew I'd meet my birth mother someday. The spoon was actually for *me*—you know, like a gag gift. But it works even better to give it to my future brother or sister. Just think, I was an only child my whole life, and now I'll have two siblings!"

"That's super," I said. I'd been half-hoping for an evil explanation but was yet again disappointed.

"Well, I have homework to do, so can I trouble you to take me back to my apartment?"

"Why? It's still early." And I had nothing to do. No one to go home to. Tina had given George a dozen balls of yarn—balls of yarn—and he was busy unrolling them and rerolling them when I left. Tina had stayed behind, amused, to watch him (at a prudent distance). Marc had work, as usual. Jessica was gone—her car was, anyway. Sinclair was somewhere, but I wasn't about to go looking for another dose of chill nasty.

"Gosh, Betsy, I don't know . . ."

"Oh, come on. You're not at the minister's house anymore, Laura, time to let your hair down. Literally—those braids are a little 2002. Or 1802. I know! We'll go to the Pour House. We can drink daiquiris, talk about boys, go crazy."

"I can't, Betsy."

"Pleeeeease?" I wheedled.

"I mean I really can't. I'm not twenty-one. I'm not allowed to drink."

"Oh, that." I pushed away federal law with a wave of my hand. "I can get you in, don't worry about that." One peek at my mold-colored eyes, and no bouncer would be able to resist.

"No, Betsy," she said as firmly as I'd ever heard. "It's against the law."

"Fine, fine." I sighed, then brightened. "I know! Let's go shopping! The mall will be open for another couple of hours. I've got a wedding to go to; we can look for an outfit and shoes and stuff."

"I can't," she said apologetically. "I don't have any money. And it wouldn't be right to—"

"That's okay, I—" Didn't have any money, either. Normally Jess would go with me, and she'd either pick up the tab outright or we'd work out a deal—I'd put in a few days at The Foot, her non-profit org, in return for a cashmere sweater or pair of sandals. "Uh . . . hmm . . ."

"Maybe we should call it a night."

"Yeah, okay." I was disappointed at the sorry state of affairs my life had come to, but there was no use taking it out on Laura.

Not to mention, she was a nice kid and all, but she was no sub-stitute for my friend. Or Sinclair. I'd been wrong to use her as a distraction.

"Wait!" I said, almost driving into a streetlight. "I've got it! We'll go to Scratch."

"Your club?" she asked doubtfully.

"Yeah. And I won't sell you a drop of booze, I promise. We'll just check it out, and then I'll take you home." What recently learned lesson about how you couldn't swap friends like baseball cards?

"Well . . ." She was weakening! Either my fiendish undead pow-ers of persuasion were working on her, or she had any kid's curiosity about how the inside of a bar looked. "Maybe just a quick look . . ."

"Yippee!" I called, and wrenched the wheel to the left.


"WOW," Laura goggled. "It's in here? It's so nice!"

"Here" was a well-kept brownstone; in fact, the place looked just like somebody's home. Now that I knew it was a vampire bar, I knew why: the more innocuous the surroundings, the better.

"I'll just park out front," I said, and set the emergency brake. Nobody was going to tow it in *this* neighborhood.

I walked in, Laura right on my heels, and was a little bummed to see how dead the place was. Of course, it was early—only about seven thirty—but still. Except for a couple of vampire waitresses, and Slight Overbite manning the bar, the place was deserted.

"How's business?" I half-joked when Slight Overbite left the bar to greet us.

"The same, Ma—"

"This is my sister, Laura," I interrupted. "You can just call her Laura. Laura, this is—" It occurred to me that I'd forgotten his name again. "This is the guy who looks after the bar for me when I'm not here."

"Klaus, ma'am." He bent over her little white hand, and when he looked up at her from that position, an alarming amount of the whites of his eyes showed. It was like looking into the face of a corpse. "Charmed."

Laura, thank God, didn't notice Klaus's extreme yukkiness. And, even better, seemed immune to his charm. Of course, Klaus wasn't all *that* charming, but still . . . "Hi there," she said, shaking his hand. "It's real nice to meet you."

I practically jerked her away from Slight Overbite, who was looking as though all his Christmas wishes were coming true at once. What had I been thinking? Bringing my sweet little sister to a bar run by vampires? Sure, I was the head bloodsucker, and she wasn't in any danger, but still. Exposing her to Klaus and the sullen waitstaff . . . I was out of my mind.

"Ah, Laura."

I spun around, and there was Sinclair, looming over us like a big black bird of prey. "Elizabeth," he said, obviously noticing me for the first time. At least he'd remembered my name.

"Hi again," Laura said, dazzled. And who could blame her? That hair, those eyes, those shoulders . . . yum. To think that it had all been mine, and I'd thrown it away by . . . uh . . . sleeping with it. I guess.

"What are you two doing here?" he asked, a shade of disapproval in his deep voice. I knew "you two" meant "Laura." I wasn't about to explain that desperation and loneliness had driven me to yet another boneheaded move. So I did what I always do:

"Why don't you mind your own fucking business for *once*?" I snapped. "If I want to take my sister to my place of business, that's my own damned business and not any of your business." Was I overusing the word *business*? Fuck it. "So mind your own business."

"Betsy!" Laura gasped.

"Quiet, you." Lectures from the spawn of Satan/Ms. Goody-goody 2005 I *so* did not need.

"It's inappropriate for her to be here, and you know it. What were you thinking?"

"That you should mind your own business?" *And stop following my sister?*

"I think I'd like to go home now," Laura said primly.

I opened my mouth, but Sinclair beat me to the punch. "Allow me to see you home, Laura," he said, proffering his arm for her to take.

"Oh. Well . . ." She glanced at me—for approval or help, I wasn't sure—and I shrugged. "All right, then. That's very kind of you."

"It's my great pleasure."

They walked out.

That was it. My life was now officially horrible. Worse than horrible. I'd be tempted to jump off a cliff, except I knew I'd survive it.

"Give me some Dewar's," I told Klaus.

"I can't," he replied smugly. "You haven't paid the liquor bill, and we're out."

Of course we were.

Depressed beyond all measure, I drove home.

# Chapter 24

BEFORE I could drive myself through a plate glass window, my cell phone rang. Jessica? I clawed it out of my purse. "Hello? Jess? Hello?"

"Hi, Betsy. It's me, Nick. Berry," he added, like I could forget. Nick was a Minneapolis cop.

"Oh, hey." I was disappointed but worked on not showing it. "Who's dead now?" I joked.

"Several people, but that's not why I'm calling. Listen, I haven't seen your new digs, and I just got off. I thought I'd come over and say hi."

"Oh. Look, I'm glad to have you over, Nick, but why now?"

"Well . . ." I heard an odd sound in the background and realized he was chewing on a Milky Way. Nick abhorred donuts. "This is going to sound a little out there, but I haven't been able to get you out of my mind lately. I mean, you gotta admit, that whole thing last spring where you almost died and they had a fake funeral and all—"

"Yeah, last spring was a real laugh riot."

"And then this summer with all the dead bodies—I guess the killer moved on, because there hasn't been one like it in about three months—but you were sort of in the middle of that, too—and . . . I don't know. I just thought it'd be fun to stop by, catch up."

"Well, sure." Come on into my parlor, big boy. Actually, the last thing I wanted was the cop who had known me in life nosing around in Vampire Central after my death, but I couldn't think of a way to say no without arousing his suspicions. "I'm on my way there now. I'm guessing there's no need to give you the address, seeing as how you're the man and all."

"See you in twenty," he confirmed.


I hurried into the mansion to straighten up but realized Jessica's corps of home helpers (the cook, the gardener, the garage guy, the downstairs guy, the upstairs lady, the plant lady) was way ahead of me. The place was immaculate and freshly vacuumed. Marc's car was gone, but Jessica's was in the garage, so I darted up the stairs and knocked on her door.

"Jess? Detective Nick is coming over to play Welcome Wagon, which isn't much good in the way of timing, but seriously, when *is* the best time for a cop to come over? When you're not a vampire," I answered myself. "Anyway, if you want to come down, we'll be in"—Where? Where was a vampire-free zone?—"one of the parlors. I think."

I went to the basement and found Tina sitting a prudent distance away from George, scribbling notes, while he crocheted an endless chain in sunshine yellow. He'd churned out about thirty feet so far and didn't look up when I shrieked.

"You gave him a hook?" I could hear a car pulling in and didn't wait around for Tina's answer. At least George was occupied.

Nick was waiting at the door, and I played ditz and "forgot" to give him a tour. We ended up shooting the breeze in the small sitting room just off the front hall.

"This place is amazing," he said, staring. As always, he was easy on the eyes. My height, blond, broad-shouldered, tan. Ooooh, a tan! It was really great to see someone with real color in their cheeks. "You and Jessica are really moving up in the world."

"Ha!" I replied. "Jess pays for the whole thing."

"Well, yeah." He grinned boyishly. "I figured. Have you found a job yet? Not that you need one, I guess . . ." He gestured to the room.

I *didn't* need one since I had the whole queen thing going, but I wasn't telling him that. Likewise, I didn't dare tell him about Scratch. I couldn't prove to a live person that I legally owned it. I sure didn't need a cop snooping into it.

Nick wasn't just any cop. He'd known me in life but, worse, had fallen under my vampiric spell after I died. Sinclair had ended up making Nick forget quite a bit from last spring. But it was a worrisome thing sometimes; we honestly didn't know what he re-membered or if Sinclair's mojo would wear off.

"You look great," I said, changing the subject. "You're so tan! Where'd you go?"

"I just got back from Grand Cayman. Me and a bunch of the other guys saved up for about a year and a half. It's really not that expensive if you go in a group. Actually, that's sort of why I'm here."

"I can't go to Grand Cayman with you," I joked. I wasn't up to pushing the new sunshine allowances.

"No, no." Of course not. Why would a healthy red-blooded male want to date a corpse with badly polished toes? "One of the guys was looking for a new place to go to an AA meeting, and I knew from my brother that they had a good group at the Thunderbird—on 494? Anyway—"

"You were there the night I went," I said with a sinking feel-ing. It was definitely weird the way Nick kept stumbling back into my life. What were the chances?

"Well . . . yeah. And it's none of my business at all . . ."

"One of the *A*s stands for *Anonymous,*" I pointed out.

"Yeah, I know. My brother did the twelve steps a couple years ago. I just—I guess I was surprised to see you there," he finished lamely.

*He* was surprised! Was my luck *ever* going to take a turn for the better? "Well, it's nothing I like to talk about," I said, sort of telling the truth.

"Sure, sure, sure," he said quickly. "I understand. I just wanted you to know . . . well, sometimes it's a hard thing to talk about. It's like nobody else can possibly get it, right?"

"Right," I said, on surer ground.

"So I just wanted you to know that if you ever wanted to, you know, just talk . . ." He trailed off and smiled at me, which made the cute laugh lines in the corner of his eyes crinkle in a friendly way.

I nearly wept; it was beyond wonderful to have someone be nice to me, to be concerned with my problems. Well, that wasn't fair; Laura was nice, and Jessica *had* been concerned until I'd hurt her. It wasn't Laura's fault Sinclair was taken with her. What guy wouldn't be? And it wasn't Sinclair's fault he'd decided I'd given off negative vibes one too many times.

Poor Nick didn't have a clue, but he cared. That counted for a lot.

"That's so sweet of you. I really appreciate it." We'd been sitting next to each other on the little peach-colored love seat, and he was inching closer to me. Maybe he had an itch. "And I promise I'll keep it in mind. But I really don't want to talk about my dumb problems right now." My incredibly lame, stupid, dumb problems.

"I just—wanted you to know," he breathed, and then he kissed me.

Oh, yay! No, boo. No, yay! I let him go for a few seconds, quite enjoying the feeling of a warm mouth on my cool one. I could hear his pulse thundering in my ears. He smelled like chocolate and cotton.

It was actually kind of nice. He liked me. He'd always liked me. Of course, since I'd died he'd found me way more attractive, but I tried not to take advantage of it. Except for that one time. Which Nick didn't remember. I was pretty sure. But anyway . . . not taking advantage of innocent policeman.

Although without much difficulty I could. He was so nice, so great-looking, so earnest—and as a cop, he'd come in *real* handy. I could—I could—

*Take him.*

I could get rid of this annoying thirst for the moment, that's what I could do. I could—

*What are you waiting for?*

—get a little warmth, a little happiness, be needed, be touched, be wanted.

*It would be so easy.*

I jerked away, actually throwing Nick to the floor. It *would* be easy. Real damn easy. Which is why I couldn't do it.

Is that why I read the Book . . . to learn how to be an asshole vampire? Is that what I learned from hurting Jessica—take what I wanted when I could get it? Is that how my mom raised me? Is that the kind of queen of the dead I wanted to be?

"Jeez, I'm so sorry," Nick said from the floor, apparently overlooking the fact that I'd thrown him on his ass. His face was red with blushes. "I'm really sorry, Betsy."

"No, no, it's my fault!" I was shouting to hear myself over his pulse, which alarmed him. I lowered my voice. "Sorry. It's my fault." It really was. Nick had no idea why he found me so appealing. God knew it was a mystery to me most times, too. "Sorry again. You'd better go." I hauled him to his feet and showed him the door, over his protests and apologies. "Thanks for stopping by. Great to catch up! 'Bye."

I shut the door and leaned against it with my eyes closed. I could still hear his pulse, though that was probably my imagination.

It had been a near thing.

"Is your date over already?"

My eyes popped open. Sinclair was standing on the left side of the entryway; he'd obviously come through the back.

"That was—"

"I know."

"He thinks—"

"I know."

"But he's going now, I—"

"Yes, I imagine you took care of it. Good work," he added distantly.

"It wasn't—"

"I understand. The last thing you—we—need is a police offi-cer nosing about. And the quickest way to get rid of him—" Sin-clair shrugged. "Well, you did what you had to do."

"Eric—"

"I'll leave you to retire. Oh, and Laura and I are having coffee tomorrow evening. You need not join us."

He turned. And walked away.

# Chapter 25

$\mathcal{I}$ kicked my bedroom door open so hard, my foot went through it, and I spent a few seconds hopping in the hallway, trying to pull my ankle free.

I finally staggered into the room, pulled off my Beverly Feldman flats, and threw them into the far wall. The leather might get scratched, but I didn't give a fuck.

That's right. *"I don't give a fuck!"* I screamed. "It's not fair! It's not fair! I did the right thing, I sent Nick away! I could totally have boned him silly, but I took the damned high road and for *what*? To have that jerk make me feel *worse*? To be *more* lonesome?"

I was hurling clothes away like a madwoman, searching for my pajamas at the same time, and generally staggering around my room like a drunk.

I scooped up the Feldmans from their separate corners and went to put them away in their little cubby but ended up collapsing facedown on my closet floor, sobbing. I clutched the shoes to my (naked) chest and curled up (naked). I was probably getting tears on my Manolos, and I just didn't care.

"Betsy?"

I ignored it and cried harder. I was in no mood for the latest hell. Tina, telling me George had crocheted a ladder and was on the lam again? The Ant, telling me it was twins? The plant lady, telling me the plants were as dead as I was?

"Sweetie, why are you naked and crying in your closet?"

I cracked open an eye. Jessica was peering into the closet, a look of concern on her (bruised) face. "Go away," I cried. "Go away, you still hate me, I know it."

"Oh, shut up, I do not." She came into the closet, pushed suits aside, carefully moved shoes, and sat cross-legged beside me. "Come on, what's the matter?"

"Everything!"

"Right, but be specific."

"Sinclair doesn't love me anymore. I bet he doesn't even want to be the king anymore. I bet he's sorry he tricked me into the whole gig. And he's got the hots for my sister. My *sister*! Who's the daughter of the devil, but that's not even the worst part."

"What's the worst part, honey?"

"Everybody likes Laura, that's what."

"Everybody likes you, too. Even before you died you had this kind of cool charisma going."

"Yeah, but Laura has it in spades. She makes me look like Saddam Hussein. I mean, nobody can resist her."

"I'm sure that's not—"

"The *Ant* likes Laura!"

"Oh."

"And she and my dad are still wrecking my life—it was the longest baby shower ever. And I'm gonna have to file Chapter Eleven on Scratch. And she's—Laura, I mean—she's nice but she's no you. And then I could have had sex with Nick and he really likes me, but I love Sinclair so I sent him away, and Sinclair didn't even care and—and—oh my God!"

"Uh . . ." Jessica was obviously trying to puzzle out the babble.

"Oh my God! *I love Sinclair!* I love him! *Him!* That—that arrogant sneaky gorgeous cool sneaky—"

"Well, of course you do."

"See, this is the sort of information I could have used earlier," I said and cried harder.

Jessica was patting my back. "Come on, Bets, you knew deep down you loved him. Like anyone could move into your house if you really didn't want them. Like you'd put up with all that from just any guy. Like you'd *sleep* with just any guy."

"But he's such a jerk."

"Well, sweetie, you're not the easiest person in the world to get along with, either, sometimes." She grinned and touched her black eye. "And this isn't even for losing your *Simpsons Season Four* DVD."

"Jess—I'm so sorry—I feel so bad—" I gestured to my nudity, the closet, the cedar balls.

"I know, Betsy." She bent down and kissed me, right on the

temple. "I just had to sulk and, you know, heal up the last couple of days. I know you were sorry right after."

"I was, I was! I felt like dead dog shit. It's been the absolute worst week."

"Frankly, the only reason I've decided to forgive you is because I'm dying to meet the daughter of the devil."

"Oh, God, she's so boring." I sat up and wiped my dry (I didn't cry like a normal person anymore) eyes. "I mean, really nice. Don't get me wrong, she's a total sweetheart. You'll like her. But—"

"But she's no queen of the vampires."

"I haven't been much of a queen these days."

"That's not true. You read the Book so you could find out more about yourself, about the threat to the world—your sister. And you tracked her down and were ready to rumble, until she turned out to be nice. And you're helping George."

"You *have* been listening to the baby monitor!"

"Are you kidding? That sucker's been on twenty-four hours a day. I was afraid to sleep; I didn't want to miss anything."

"Everything's such a mess."

"Worse than usual," she agreed.

"What am I going to do?"

"Well, honey, sending Nick away was a good start. It's actually fundamental, when you get right down to it."

"Oh, I know," I said earnestly. She could have suggested I boink the Green Bay Packers and I would have agreed. I was so happy she was talking to me again. "Er . . . when you say fundamental . . ."

She rolled her eyes, but then she was used to explaining things to me. "You sent Nick away because you didn't want to hurt him or take advantage of him. That's the kind of person you are—the kind you've always been. A lot has changed, but not that."

"You're right."

"Also, the sky is yellow, the Ant is misunderstood, and David Evins was just a talented amateur."

"Now you're just being mean."

"Well, I gotta milk this for all I can. And Sinclair doesn't love your sister."

"Not yet," I said darkly. "Give him time."

"Look, I'm sure he's interested in her—"

"Wait till you see her. Just wait."

"Like he doesn't have pussy thrown at him from cars?"

"What a horrifying mental image."

"I'm just saying, the guy can get laid whenever he wants. But he wants you."

"No, he—"

"Whatever you did to him after reading the Book," she said, and I don't think she was aware that she was touching her bruised eye while she reasoned stuff out, "can't undo how he feels. I'm telling you—I've *been* telling you—the guy is totally gonzo nuts for you, has been since the beginning. He's giving you the chilly treatment because his feelings are hurt. If he really didn't care about you, don't you think he'd just have shut up and fucked you?"

"I did think that," I admitted. "But he wasn't happy I had sex with him; he was hurt. I couldn't get why he was acting so weird, and it's too late now. He's been hearing me diss him for so long, he's given up."

"For so long? You've been a vampire for six months, Bets. That's nothing to him, it's a baseball season. Like I said, he's interested in your sister, sure. She's the daughter of the devil! And he's the king of the vampires. So of course he's gonna want to, you know, look into it. But I bet he's just covering his bases—being Sinclair."

"A real match made in heaven. Sinclair the star fucker and the woman fated to take over the world."

"She *would* be a pretty good consort for him," Jessica admitted.

"Anybody but me, that's for sure."

"Now, come on. The Book hasn't been wrong about anything yet—"

"The Book just said we'd be consorts, it didn't promise a happily ever after. Plenty of kings and queens ran things while hating each other." I'd minored in European history; Diana and Charles's marriage foundering before her death was nothing, historically speaking. "If you'd just heard how mean he's been—no, that's not right, not mean exactly, more like he doesn't give much of a shit."

"I did hear. I was starting to tell you, I'd been coming down to leave a check for Cathie—"

"The upstairs lady?"

"No, the plant lady."

"Jess, you don't have to pay someone just to water the plants. Five people live in this house, for Christ's sake. I'm sure we can handle it without—"

"*Anyway,* I sort of overheard your little *tête à lame* with Nick. And then I sort of overheard you and Sinclair. He was pretty frigid," she added, giving me a sympathetic look. "I'm sure it's not a total loss. But you've got some work to do."

I was trying not to be devastated by the blast of common sense she was giving my system. "Look, it's all on me, okay? I get that. I couldn't think of how to make it right with him. And to be honest, I thought I had bigger problems. So I just sort of put it out of my head, and then it was too late." I shook my head. "I've always assumed he'd be around to be, you know, yelled at and taken for granted. And of course I was wrong. Nobody's going to put up with that forever."

"Well, look. Put Sinclair aside for the moment. Actually, don't even do that—he's all wrapped up in this. Betsy, you can fix this."

"I don't think it's as easy as you—"

"I didn't say easy, I said fixable. And even if you couldn't fix it, you're not going to be all naked and weepy and whiney in your closet. I mean, come on. Crying in the closet? Honey, you're the *queen* of the *vampires*. Get your big white butt up off the floor and get dressed and start kicking some undead ass. Even before you died, you wouldn't take this shit lying down. So go fix it."

"You're right! Except for that thing about my butt." I was on my feet, my hands balled into fists. Mighty (and naked) would be my wrath! Jessica was right, who did they think they were fucking with? "You're totally right. I've been bending over, and for what? Well, forget about it!"

"Right!"

"I'm gonna right some wrongs, I'll tell you that right now!"

"Right! That's the girl."

I checked my watch, currently the only thing I was wearing (unless eyeliner counted). "And I'll tell you what we're doing first."

"Besides putting on underpants?"

"Right, besides that."

# Chapter 26

"**YOU'RE** really gonna do it?"

"Bet your ass."

"It didn't really cause any of your problems."

"No," I agreed, "but it's dangerous. It's just lying around in the library for anybody to pick up and read."

"It's irreplaceable."

"So was the Nazi regime. Besides, I promised my mom I wouldn't burn it." We were standing on one of the big bridges connecting the suburbs with Minneapolis, and talking loudly to be heard over the hum of traffic. It was chilly—maybe forty degrees—but I was so hyped up I barely noticed. "So it's gonna sleep with the fishes."

I shoved, and the Book of the Dead went down and down (it was a high bridge), and then plopped into the Big Muddy.

"Huh," Jessica said after a long moment of watching it sink out of sight with nary a bubble. "I guess I thought it would float on a bed of pure evil, or whatever."

"It's made out of skin, not Gore-Tex." I brushed off my chilly hands. "Boy, was that a relief or what? I should have done that months ago."

"Yep, that's that." Jessica zipped her coat higher. "Now what?"

"I don't know, but it's gonna be something, you know, take-chargish."

"Oh, good."

"And stay out of the basement."

"I don't think George would hurt me. Not on a full stomach, anyway."

"All the same."

"Don't worry. One vampire attack a week is my limit."

𝓵 hadn't had much time to effect change in my life—I'd talked with Jessica for hours, then destroyed a priceless artifact, and that had pretty much burned up my night. But after sleeping through the next day, I rose around six ready to kick some passive-aggressive vampire ass. First stop: Scratch.

On the way out to my car, I thought about trying to find Eric and doing something embarrassing like telling him I loved him, but chickened out. Also, I wasn't sure it would change anything. The last thing I could stand was being a burden—on anyone. If he didn't feel the same way—or worse, if he once had but didn't anymore—I wasn't going to be all Scarlett O'Hara ("Where will I go? What shall I do?") on him.

But at least I knew, now. It was sort of a relief to have it at the top of my mind, instead of lurking deep in my subconscious. But realizing—okay, admitting—I loved Eric Sinclair didn't solve anything. Real life was messy, and loving him didn't magically undo the old problems and make everything wonderful and perfect. In fact, it sort of made a few things worse.

If you took anything wrong in my life—"I'm upset Eric tricked me and made himself king" or "I'm upset Eric didn't tell me about my sister and Satan"—and tacked on "and I love Eric Sinclair," it made things messier.

Irony: loving Eric Sinclair and having it be another on a long list of problems. But now was the time for action! I was all done crying naked in the closet, thank you very much. I would be the mistress—queen, if you will—of my own destiny!

Starting with Scratch. I knew that place could make money; the vampires were sulking and not helping me. I needed to put a little fear of the queen into the undead. And I needed to have Margarita Mondays.

I drove around for what seemed like half an hour, looking for a parking ramp that wasn't full, then finally gave up and parked in one of the handicap spaces just down the block. I felt a twinge of conscience but managed to squash it; being dead had to count as some sort of handicap. For the millionth time, I reminded myself to get a Manager Parking spot put out front.

I stormed through the door and stood in the nearly empty

(groan . . . on a Friday night!) bar. "All right, listen up!" I began, only to be cut off by Klaus.

"Oh good, you've decided to drop by," he snarked.

"Hey, hey. I've had other things going on."

"Other things besides being the queen."

"Well, yeah. I mean no! It's all sort of wrapped up in . . ." I trailed off. Why was I explaining myself to this yutz? This was not part of the Take Charge plan. "Listen, things are going to be different from here on out."

"You're right about that," a vampire I didn't know piped up from her seat at the bar.

"Who's talking to *you*?"

"The employees of Scratch are now officially on strike," Klaus announced. He looked at his watch. "As of 6:59 p.m."

"You're *what*?"

"On strike."

I was having trouble processing this. "You're *what*?"

"We have formed a union," he continued, "to demand proper working conditions."

"And proper working conditions would be . . . ?" I had a horrible suspicion what they were.

"We want sheep to be allowed here, we want to be able to drink blood on the dance floor—"

"And at the bar," another vampire said. He was a pale brunette in a denim jacket, sitting next to the woman who'd spoken up earlier.

"Right, at the bar . . ." Slight Overbite was ticking the demands off on his long, spidery (yerrrrggggh) fingers. "And if a sheep becomes difficult, or a human wanders in, we want to be able to have a little fun."

"Kill them," I clarified.

"Right. Also, we want a dental plan."

"Really?" I gasped.

"No." He grinned, a wholly unpleasant image. "That last one was a joke."

"This whole *thing* is a joke. You guys are seriously nuts if you think I'm going to allow *any* of that. In case you didn't get the memo, we are, as of Nostro biting the big one, a friendlier vampire nation."

"You'd pull our fangs," he spat.

"I'd have you act decently!" We were nose to upturned nose. "What *is* it with you guys? You're dead, so you have to be assholes?"

"We don't have to be," the woman at the bar admitted. "We just like to. You can't change hundreds of years of mystic evolution."

"Sure I can. That 'we're going to do it because we can' crap doesn't fly with me. Now: as for being on strike, you're not on strike, you're fired. I can get anybody to run this place. You don't like the working conditions? Fuck off and die. Again."

"This is your last chance to change your mind," Denim Boy said. Like I was scared of anybody wearing a Tommy Hilfiger knockoff.

"No," I said. "It's yours."

"You're not leaving us with a lot of breathing room," a new voice said. For a place I'd thought was practically deserted, there were a shitload of vampires suddenly around.

"Fortunately," Klaus said, "we don't need any."

Another vampire came out from the back, dragging—uh-oh—Laura. He had a bunch of her perfect blond hair in his fist, right by her skull, and she had both hands on his and was stumbling, trying not to trip.

"Surprise," she said, trying to smile.

# Chapter 27

"CHEATERS!" I cried.

"We were so happy to make your sister's acquaintance."

"I'll bet, ya big cheater."

"Eric canceled our meeting," she said, "and I had a free evening, so I thought I'd come and see you."

"Well, next time, call first."

"I got that," she said.

"It was almost too good to be true," Asshole said. "It's so rare to find a vampire with any living relatives. And to have one walk into our hands . . ."

"Right! Rare. Don't you guys think that's weird? I mean, look how young she is. She's not my great-great-granddaughter, she's my kid sister. Doesn't that tell you something about me? Like maybe you shouldn't be messing with me?"

"I figure they don't like their working conditions," Laura said helpfully, still clutching the vampire's hand. "But this seems kind of extreme."

"Maybe your *mother* could help us out," I said, then waited. We all waited. Laura looked puzzled—or maybe she was rolling her eyes, I couldn't tell. "You know, your *mother* could show up and, you know, give us a hand."

Nothing. Humph! Typical. The devil: never around when you needed her.

"Look, you don't want to do this," I told Klaus and the cow at the bar and Tommy Hilfiger. "You really don't."

"I think she's right," Laura said, practically up on her toes. "I think you should try a walkout first. I think hostage-taking should be a second resort. Maybe third."

The vampire jerked her head, and she cried out.

I rubbed my eyes. I had to admit, I hadn't foreseen this.

What should I do? What if I lied and told them they could have their sheep and their homicide and their kill-one-get-one-free Thursdays, got Laura out of danger, then reneged? Could a queen go back on her word? The other vampires might lose respect for me . . . well, more respect.

"Before we get into this any further, I just want to clarify: What exactly do you guys think happened to Nostro and Monique?"

"The king helped you."

"Okay. And, just for the record, do you see the king around anywhere right now?"

Klaus hesitated. "No."

"I better leave one of you alive, then. I'm getting really tired of this 'Sinclair must have helped her' bullshit. If one of you spreads the word about me, that would really help me out."

"Ouch! That *really* hurts," Laura said to the vampire fisting her hair. "Will you please let go?"

"Shut up, sheep."

"Are you particularly attached to this man?" Laura asked me.

"I've never even *met* him."

"Oh, okay. I really, really hope this doesn't give you the wrong impression."

"Wh—" was as far as I got before a shaft of reddish gold light burst from the vampire's stomach, and he evaporated. Or vaporized. Or something—he didn't even have time to scream, it was that fast.

*I* screamed. Not very monarchlike, it's true. But I couldn't help it. See, in real life, vampires didn't disappear when they were killed. They didn't collapse into a dramatic dust pile or burst into flames, short of direct exposure to sunlight. They didn't even die when you poked them in the gut.

You stuck a stake in their chests and/or cut their heads off, and they died forever. They didn't get back up. Well, I did that one time, but that was a special case.

But other than sunlight cases, there was always a body, no matter what you did.

Laura was standing by herself, patting her hair down with her right hand and holding a—I guess it was sword of sorts—in her left. Proof! Proof she was hell spawned . . . she was a lefty!

"Sorry about that," she said. "But I just couldn't stand to have his hands on me another second. Yuck."

"What is *that*?" I gasped.

She glanced at the flame-colored sword. It glowed with such heat, it was actually a little hard to look at. "Oh, this?" she asked, like I was asking her about a new bracelet. "Well. I can forge weapons from hellfire."

"And you can *kill* people with that?"

"Not people," she said helpfully. "I'll be glad to fill you in later."

"This—ah—this changes—changes nothing," Klaus said, looking like he was trying not to barf. I knew the feeling. "We still—we still—ah—demand—demand—"

"You have to get close with that," Tommy Hilfiger said. "You can't get us all in arrgghh!" He said "arrgghh" because, quick as thought, Laura's sword changed to a crossbow, and she shot Tommy from across the room. He vanished in a puff of light, just like the other one.

She lowered the crossbow to her side and looked modest. Which she actually pulled off. She was so beautiful, she looked like a fairy-tale princess. With a weapon of mass vampire destruction.

"Ha-*ha*!" I crowed. "How about that, Klaus the mouse? Hah? Hah?

"Wait a minute." I turned to Laura. "You know we're all vampires?"

"Sure."

"And you were going to tell me when?"

"I was waiting for you to tell *me*," she said, having the nerve to sound offended.

"But how did you *know*?"

"Sometimes I just . . . figure things out. I guess I get that from my mother." She looked disgusted, like having anything in common with her mother was a revolting thought.

"Your mother."

More disgust. "The devil."

"You know. Your mom. Is the devil."

"Her mom is the devil?" the lady at the bar asked in a hushed voice.

"And you let me take you to the Ant's baby shower and never said anything? And brought her a present? And had *two* slices of carrot cake? And *talked* to her?" I was trying to figure out which was more annoying: yet another vampire coup or Laura keeping her mouth shut all this time.

"Well, *you* never told me you were the queen of the vampires," she said hotly.

"That's totally a different thing!" I cried.

"I wanted to get a chance to meet the woman who carried me for nine months."

"And then *dumped* you at a hospital."

"Yes, but when you compare that to, you know, being Satan, it doesn't seem so bad. In fact, it's downright friendly."

She had me on that one. "Laura, don't you get what this means? Your *mom* is *Satan*!"

"Of course I get what it means. Besides, I don't think your parents define who you are," she reasoned.

I opened my mouth to yell some more, only to get cut off. "Excuse me," Klaus said, sounding peeved, "but you have other business to attend to right now."

"It's not more interesting than this, pal," I said. "Vampires being sneaky and up to no good is so *not* anything new."

"She's too dangerous," the woman at the bar said, "to live another five minutes."

"Which one of us is she talking about?"

"Does it matter?" Laura asked.

Klaus said something in rapid French—I think it was French. The door to the back room opened, as did the front door, and all kinds of waitresses and bartenders and bouncers started streaming in. They were all pale and twitchy and pissed-off.

"As far as plans go, it's not the worst one I've ever seen," Laura said. "But you'll die if you all try to jump us at once."

"You got what he said?"

"Oh, I'm really good at languages."

"Which ones?" I asked, curious.

"All of them."

Of course. "Look, she's right. Can't we sit down and discuss this like civilized dead people and hell spawn?"

"Please don't call me that."

"I'm sorry! Just please don't shoot me or stab me."

Laura looked mildly crushed. "I wouldn't do that, Betsy."

"Sorry again."

"You can't—" Klaus said, and then lunged at me. Aha! The old 'keep a placid look on your face and talk normally and then jump them' trick. Unfortunately, it totally worked; he bowled right into me, and we went sprawling backward, knocking a table aside. Several vampires, I was sorry to see, leapt onto us to help.

"Nothing—is—more—important—than—this!" Klaus shouted, punctuating each word by smacking my head onto the floor. It was fairly easy for him because he had both hands around my throat. The guy was quick *and* strong; he had a grip like an angry anaconda.

*"Au contraire,"* I gurgled, and then I couldn't say anything at all. What was he doing, strangling a dead girl? That couldn't really hurt me; it was mostly just annoying. *Must be plenty pissed,* I thought.

I was digging my fingers into his hands to pry them off, but his grip never loosened, and the flesh was just peeling away in strips. Blurgh! Death loomed (again), *and* I was grossed out. It was the worst week ever. Again.

# Chapter 28

"NOT like this!" a vampire I didn't know was shouting into Klaus's ear. "We can't attack the queen! We all agreed not to attack the queen!"

*Yeah,* I wanted to shout, but couldn't say a word. I just made an agreeable sort of peep while I clawed at his hands some more.

"She's not the queen," he muttered and jerked one of his elbows back, straight into Sane and Helpful Vampire's throat. It didn't appear to hurt the guy, but it knocked him back. Even better, it caused Klaus's grip to loosen. I managed to get my hands up between his and shoved and kicked at the same time. He didn't get off me, but his grip fell away.

"It's times like this when I like to say a prayer," I said, still kicking and clawing for all I was worth, trying to get out from under him. It was the Homecoming Dance all over again! "The Lord is my Shepherd, I shall not want. Also, God is great, God is good, let us thank him for this food. Also, Jesus loves me this I know, for the Bible tells me so." Since Klaus was now screaming and clutching his ears, when I kicked him again, he finally flew off me. I rose up on my elbows and finished triumphantly, "And *God bless this mess!*"

I was fresh out of Bible verses, but the damage had been done. Sane and Helpful Vampire had already flung the door open and was frantically gesturing for the others to follow him. Some did—I'd worry about them later—but a distressing number stayed. Including Klaus, who had backed all the way up to the bar, his face twisted with hate and fear, his hands still clamped over his ears.

Laura was coughing a little and waving her hand in front of

her face, and I saw that the half dozen or so vampires that had been around her were now—gone. Vaporized. All but the last one. Laura's crossbow was a sword again, and she blocked a fist with her forearm, then stuck the woman (formerly "the woman at the bar") right in the chest. Bye-bye, annoying barfly.

"Ha-*ha!*" I crowed, pointing. "How about that? Hah? *Hah?* Didn't figure on her being hell sp—I mean, the devil's daughter when you grabbed her, didja?" Another vampire had me by the hair and was yanking me backward, but I didn't care. *"Didja?"* I was practically delirious with triumph.

"Betsy—" was as far as my wonderful, supertalented, too-cool sister got before she had her hands full again. I noticed that in addition to the kickass hellfire weapons, she was a pretty fair hand-to-hand fighter. Sometime in the last few years while she was finishing Bible school and volunteering for church bake sales, she'd picked up a black belt or two along the way. Now if I could just get her to wear some decent clothes . . .

"Don't worry about me," I called, though my skull was throbbing like a rotten tooth. "Everything's under contr—yeeouch!"

"Shut up, bitch," someone growled.

"Oh, *you* shut up," I snapped back. "Do you have any idea how often this happens to me? It's almost boring." And terrifying. But mostly boring.

Two more—not that there were that many left, thanks to Laura and their cowardice—came straight at me, and I heard the ominous sound of a chair leg being snapped off. The other one had me in a firm grip, his arm across my throat, his other hand still in my hair. Holding me nice and still. Well, the joke was on him! Stakes in the chest didn't work on me, so there. Of course, it was going to hurt like hell, and ruin my shirt, and if they decided to give 110 percent and cut my head off after, that could pose difficulties. I could buy a new shirt, but I kind of needed the head I had.

I opened my mouth to torture them with more psalms, when Laura got to the one on the right—stab, poof! It was amazing. I could never describe how cool it was, not in a thousand pages. She looked like an avenging angel with her shiny hair and demure bangs, her nondescript clothing, and the sword that actually hurt to look at, held so comfortably in her fist.

The vampire on the left was suddenly yanked out of sight, and there was a sickening crunch as he hit the wall. Courtesy of—I nearly gasped—Eric Sinclair. He'd come out of nowhere— probably pushing his way past the stream of frantically exiting vampires—and just grabbed the nearest one and shoved. The vampire bounced off the wall and hit the floor, and I could see where his entire face had actually been pushed in by the force of smacking into the concrete. The worst part of it was, it hadn't killed him. He moved feebly on the floor like a stunned beetle, trying to grow his nose back.

"Oh, guh-*ross!*" I screamed.

"Wow," Laura goggled.

"Take your hands off her," Sinclair told the guy behind me, "or they'll write books about what I'll do to you."

The vampire let go of me so quick, he yanked out a handful of my hair. I yelped and shook free of him.

Suddenly, surprisingly, it was just the three of us in Scratch—two vampires had picked up the guy who needed a new face, and they scrammed.

Oh, wait—four. Klaus was in the corner, showing his teeth like one of those little ratty dogs that liked to challenge everyone from the mailman to the preschooler.

Sinclair turned to him, but I held up a hand. "Tut, tut, my good man. I'll take care of this. Strike on *me,* will you? Form a union in *my* club, willya?"

"For shame," Laura added.

"Shut up, devil's whore," Klaus spat.

"Don't you call her that!" I said, shocked. "She's the farthest thing from a whore in the whole world. You're just mad because death is imminent."

He snarled at me. It would have been scarier if Eric hadn't been right at my elbow. "This isn't over yet, *Betsy.*"

"Excellent," I said. "I would also have accepted 'You haven't seen the last of me' and 'You'll regret this.'" Then I picked up the discarded chair leg and ran it into his chest. (You'd think, since it was a vampire bar, they'd have metal chairs.) Sayonara, Slight Overbite.

Unlike Laura's more dramatic death-dealing, he just toppled over, which forced the stake farther into his body (ugh), and lay there like a big old dead bug.

Now that *that* was over with, I had several impulses. I picked one and rushed to Laura and hugged her. "Wow, Laura, you were amazing! I'm so sorry I got you into such a mess, but wow! How cool were you?"

"I hope you don't think I'm a bad person," she explained. "Violence isn't usually the answer. But they didn't seem amenable to listening to reason, and I didn't want you to get hurt."

"You didn't want *me* to get hurt? Laura, you're amazing! How did you do that? How come it's a sword sometimes and a bow some other times? Can it do anything else? Did your mother give it to you?"

She laughed and twirled the sword in a small circle so the hilt was in her palm and not her fist, then sheathed it at her right hip— except she wasn't wearing a sheath. The sword just disappeared. Except I had the distinct impression it was still there.

Waiting.

I turned to Sinclair. "And you! Not that I'm not glad to see you, but—"

"Elizabeth!" I eeped and nearly cowered away from him; I'd never seen him so furious. His dark eyes were slits, and even his hair looked angry—it was messy and I squished the urge to straighten it with my fingers. His white shirt was open at the throat, and he was sockless and coatless. He'd come in a hurry. "What were you thinking, instigating a brawl with two dozen vampires?"

"I didn't start it," I said, shocked. He was holding my shoulders, and his fingers were actually biting into me. "I told them they couldn't kill people, and then they went on strike! Which isn't as nonviolent as it sounds, by the way."

"You might have been killed," he said through gritted teeth. "You must never, *never* do such a thing again."

"But *I* didn't do anythinmmmmph!" He'd yanked me to him and planted one on me, effectively cutting off my protest. I was so surprised he was kissing me—surprised he was mad at all—I just stood there for a moment and took it. Then I managed to pull away—or at least pull my lips away. My head was arched back like a snake's, but our chests were touching.

"Wait, wait, wait. I'm really glad to see you. But I'm confused."

He quirked a small smile at me. "Thus, the universe resumes its axis."

"Never mind about the universe." I gave in to my impulse, managed to free an arm, and straightened his hair. "I thought you were making moves on Laura."

"I've been meeting with her," he replied, looking confused.

"Right, but I thought—you know, after what happened, after I made you have sex with me—"

"Twice," he added. I could tell he was trying not to laugh. "After you raped me twice. Well, one and a half times."

"Um, yeah. I thought you didn't like me anymore."

He looked astonished. "Didn't *like* you?"

"And then Laura—she's so beautiful and her breasts are so perky."

"Thank you," Laura called from behind the bar, where she was fixing herself a Shirley Temple.

"And you were so mean to me—"

"I was a little cold," he admitted, his grip loosening. He didn't let go entirely, I noticed.

"A little?"

"It hurt me that you only made love with me because you had gone insane."

"I can't hear any of this," Laura announced, dropping a cherry into her drink. "Just carry on like I'm not here."

We did. "I'm sorry. But I wouldn't want you to think I only want to have sex with you when I'm crazy."

"I don't. I hung on to the notion that you were motivated by more than the impulse to hurt. And, truthfully, I could never leave you. Certainly not after you were vulnerable to the Book. I thought it was odd that the devil's own should show up—was so easily found—right after you read the Book. I dislike coincidences. So I resolved to find out as much about her as I could."

"So they were like—like business meetings?" I was starting to feel dumber than usual. He was looking at me so earnestly, and he still hadn't let go. Maybe because I hadn't asked him to. "You weren't interested in her as, like, a date?"

"I couldn't be with *him*," Laura said, so shocked she actually set down her drink with a clunk and a slosh. "He's a vampire!"

"And I couldn't be with her," he said, "because she isn't you. Oh, and for your information, dear," he added mildly, glancing over at her, "once you go undead, you never go back."

"Yuck! And Betsy. I can't believe you thought I'd try to steal your boyfriend," she said reproachfully.

"Consort," Sinclair corrected.

"I'm sorry. To both of you, I'm sorry. I guess I jumped to some pretty dumb conclusions." I hugged him. "I've never been so happy to be wrong! And with all the practice I have, you'd think—"

He pulled back and looked at me. "Elizabeth, even if I did not adore you, you are my queen. We're fated to be together. I've known that since the moment I saw you in the crypt."

"That's so romantic," Laura sighed, rinsing her glass.

"Sinclair—Eric—" Why did the most meaningful moments of my life happen in front of witnesses? "I—I adore you, too. Well, I don't know if I adore you. That's not really the word I'd use. But I—I—" I managed to wrench it out. God, this was hard! "I love you."

"Of course you do," he said, totally unsurprised.

"*What*? I finally tell you my deepest, most personal feelings and you're all, 'Yeah, I already got that memo'? This, *this* is why you drive me nuts! This is why it's hard to tell you things! I take it back."

"You can't take it back," he said smugly.

"I do, too, take it back! And don't you dare kiss me again!" I cried when he leaned forward. "Why do you have to be so annoying and smug all the time?"

"Because with you by my side, I can do anything."

I calmed down a little. He was still acting way too superior, but that was kind of sweet. In a frightening, world-domineering way. "Well . . . well, I guess I don't take it back. Not entirely."

"Of course you don't."

I almost snarled. "I guess I really do love you."

"And I you, darling Elizabeth. I cherish you, my own, my dear one."

Okay, now I was *really* calming down. "Well. Okay."

"Where are the darned napkins?" Laura sobbed from the bar.

He reached out and smoothed a lock of my hair behind my ear. "You're wearing my necklace."

I touched the small platinum shoe he had given me when he got back from Europe—had it only been a few days ago? "Well, yeah. I wanted it tonight . . . for luck, you know?"

He smiled. "Were you really jealous? You thought I was wooing Laura?"

"Maybe a little. You're not smirking, are you?"

"No, no." He smothered a snicker. "I am sorry for giving you cause for doubt."

"Oh, like you didn't notice she's fantastically beautiful," I bitched.

"She is not you," he replied simply, which was flattering, yet slippery of him.

"Eric . . . the thing about doubt . . ." I groped for the words. This was my chance. Maybe my only one. He was an all-powerful vampire king, but he wasn't a telepath. "I would feel more—together—with you, I mean—if we—if you and I—if we got married."

"But we are married," he said, puzzled.

"Not Book of the Dead married. *Really* married, with a minister—well, a judge—and my mom there and cake and hymns—songs—and a ring and dancing."

"Oh." He looked sort of horrified. "Well. Ah. I see."

"You see? Now? Why not before? It's one of the things I complain about constantly."

"Question asked, question answered."

I let that pass. "Look, I know this is probably getting old, but I was kind of shoved into this whole consort thing. I don't know a lot about you; we don't have this deep, meaningful relationship."

"To be fair, I think that's just as much your fault as his," Laura said, munching on olives. When we both looked at her, she said, "I'm sorry. But that's the impression I got."

"*Anyway.* A real-person wedding would—I would really love that."

"But we are already married." Sinclair seemed to be having trouble actually grasping my essential problem.

"But I don't feel it."

"And a real"—the corners of his mouth turned down, as if he was contemplating a fresh dog turd instead of getting married—"wedding . . . would help you feel it?"

"Totally."

Sinclair clasped my hands. "You are so immature," he said, looking deeply into my eyes, "that you take my breath away."

I jerked my hands out of his grip. "Aw, shaddup. And you don't even need to breathe. Yes or no, pal?"

He sighed. "Yes."

I was shocked. "Really? Yes? You'll do it?"

"Of course. You had only to ask."

"*I* had only to ask? See, this is part of the problem. You—"

"Elizabeth, darling. Shut up." Then he kissed me again.

# Chapter 29

"**Y**OU'RE getting *married*?" Marc's jaw was hanging down. We were sitting in the kitchen having hot chocolate and toast. Jessica was sitting on Marc's other side, and Tina and Sinclair were sitting on my right. I nearly sighed with the pleasure of it; things were finally getting back to normal. "A wedding? A vampire wedding?"

"You keep saying that; you sound like a crackpot parrot."

"Better be a midnight ceremony," he shot back.

"Yeah, I guess. That's okay. We could do like a roses in the garden midnight theme, with masses of red and white flowers everywhere . . ." Was that a shudder from Sinclair? He was studying the financial pages and didn't appear to be paying attention, but I knew damn well he was listening to every word. I narrowed my eyes and started to say something but was foiled by Tina.

"When is the date?"

"We haven't decided yet. I thought Easter, but that—uh, well, maybe next fall."

"Autumn's good," Jessica said. "We'll need time to plan." That *was* a shudder! Before I could act, she went on. "But you're still going to live here, right? There's plenty of room."

"Of course," Sinclair said absently, turning a page. "This is our headquarters. I see no reason to leave. Though," he added with a sly look, "you might forgo rent as a wedding gift."

"Forget it." Jessica eyed my shoe necklace and grinned. "Well, maybe for a month."

"Can we get back to the death and betrayal and all that?" Marc broke in. He was so intent, he dropped his toast into his tea. Oh, wait. That was the way he ate it. Shudder. "So the workers at Scratch turned on you? And you *and* Miss Goody-goody killed them?"

"Don't call her that. And yeah, most of them," I clarified. "Some of them got away while the getting was good."

"They're like rats that way." Jessica saw the look Tina was giving her and added defensively, "Come on. They jump her when they think they can get away with it, then get the hell gone when it goes bad. It's not the first time, that's for sure. I *know* you're not getting all offended on behalf of all vampire kind."

"No," she admitted.

"Steps will be taken," Sinclair said, still not looking up from the paper. What an irritating habit. I'd have to work on that after the wedding.

"Indeed," Tina said. "With all respect, Majesty, I wish you would have said something when you left. You shouldn't have gone there alone. It's my place to take on danger."

"Which one of them are you talking to?" Marc asked.

I giggled but sobered up when Eric clarified. "There wasn't time," he said simply.

"How'd you even know to go there?" I asked. "I've been wondering about that for hours."

Jessica coughed. "I might have given him an earful."

"That's one way of putting it," he said, looking wry. "I didn't rush there to save you. I rushed there to—" He looked around at the group. We were all hanging on his every word. But then, he had that kind of effect on people. "That is a . . . private matter . . . between Elizabeth and me. Needless to say, I was annoyed to find the queen in trouble yet again."

"One more time, pal: Not. My. Fault."

"You always. Say. That."

"Well, maybe after the wedding the other vampires will respect you more." Marc saw the frosty looks and added, "Well, they sure couldn't respect her *less*."

Since I'd had that exact thought earlier, I was hardly in a position to bitch. About that. Instead I said, "I think what's the most amazing thing—"

"Besides planning to supervise an appetizer menu for people who don't eat," Sinclair muttered.

"—is how remarkable Laura was. You guys. You wouldn't have believed it. She was slaughtering vampires left and right. It was the coolest!" When Sinclair and Tina traded a look, I clarified. "Bad vampires. It wouldn't have been as cool if she'd been killing nice, gentle orphan vampires."

"With a sword made of light?" Tina asked.

"Uh, hellfire, I think. If we're getting technical. And sometimes it's a crossbow. And it appears and disappears whenever she wants it."

"That makes sense," Marc said. I couldn't tell if he was joking.

"But she's so nice," Jessica said. "I haven't met her yet, but that's all you and Eric talk about, how nice she is."

"Yes," Tina said, "and that's interesting, isn't it? Is it an act, do you think?"

"No," Sinclair and I said in unison.

"Hmmm."

Sinclair put the paper down and picked up a pen and scribbled more of that language in the margin. At least it wasn't a hate note. I was pretty sure. I'd never noticed he wrote everything down in Latin or whatever it was. "I suggest we get to know her better, and not just because she is family." He looked at me. "Will be family. After the wedding. The . . . wonderful, wonderful wedding."

"I'm having supper with Laura tomorrow," I said. "I figure I owe her a cocoa at the very least. I can ask her some stuff. But she seems kind of private."

Marc snorted. "I'll bet."

# Chapter 30

I paused outside Sinclair's bedroom. The sun would be up soon, and just thinking about the night's events (not to mention living through them) made me tired. But now what? I'd told Sinclair the truth . . . told myself the truth. I knew he shared my feelings. We were engaged. We lived together. We were apparently in love. So did we share a bedroom? Did we wait until our wedding night?

My unholy lust for Sinclair's delicious bad self aside, I wanted to share a bed with him. I wanted to make up for using him earlier, and I wanted to hear his deep voice in the dark. And in my head.

On the other hand, after what I'd done to him earlier, what right did I have to expect us to literally kiss and make up? If our situations had been reversed, I'd have held a grudge for at least a year. Maybe I should give him time.

On the *other* other hand, he had come to Scratch specifically to . . . what? Regardless, he'd saved my ass yet again. Maybe it was silly to be all "you can have space, big guy."

Oh boy, was I pooped. Screw it. I'd worry about it tomorrow night.

I turned away and plodded down the hall to my room. One thing—well, another thing—to worry about; I had the master bedroom, which in a place like this was really saying something. After we got married, Sinclair would probably want to share it with me. That could be a problem; he was as picky about his suits as I was about my shoes. There was room in my heart for Sinclair, but was there room in my closet?

I opened my door and gaped. Sinclair was in my bed, shirtless (at least!), blankets up to his waist, poring over all kind of dusty books. He looked up. "Oh, there you are. Ready for bed?"

I clutched the knob. Uh, the doorknob. "Don't you think this is a little presumptuous?"

"No."

"I debated outside your door and decided to give you space!"

"How sweet. Please strip now."

I snorted, torn between irritation, arousal, and plain old happiness. One thing about Eric Sinclair: he didn't dither. "Okay," I said, shutting the door. "But don't think it will be this easy every night."

"I'm counting on it, actually. Do you know, you're the only woman who has ever refused me?"

"No wonder you're such a pain."

"Tina had the same theory," he said thoughtfully. "But I dismissed it."

I pulled my T-shirt over my head, struggled out of my jeans, then stripped off my bra and panties. I shoved a few smelly books out of the way, ignoring his wince, and wriggled under the covers.

"Sushi socks?" he asked.

"What is it with you and Japanese cuisine? You don't like my sushi jammies, you don't like my socks . . ."

He smirked. "It's possible they're hurting the mood."

"Hey, it's chilly in here."

"If I warm you up," he said, pulling me against his chest, "will you take them off?"

"Done and done," I said, and opened my mouth against his. His hands circled my rib cage and then moved up, and it was all very fine. Whatever had happened between us, this moment seemed exactly right.

I reached down and felt him beneath my hand, already hard, and had a second to wonder—How *did* vampires get it up? Then I forgot about it as his hands cupped my bottom and pulled me closer, so close you couldn't have slipped a piece of Saran Wrap between us. He broke the kiss and pressed his lips to the hollow of my throat.

*Oh Elizabeth, Elizabeth, at last, at last.*

I nearly sighed with relief. I could hear him in my head again! I definitely wasn't evil anymore. Not that I had worried too much about it, but I *had* missed the intimacy of it.

"I love you," I said.

*Elizabeth, oh my Elizabeth.* His grip tightened, and after a long moment he murmured against my neck, "I love you, too. I've always loved you." *Always. Always.*

"You can bite me if you wa—" And then his teeth were in me, his tongue was pressed firmly against my throat, and we shuddered together. Only when Eric bit me did I feel like everything was wonderful. Only with Eric did I not mind being dead. In fact, being with Eric was the opposite of being dead.

"Oh, G—oh, thath good."

He stopped drinking so he could laugh, and I leaned down and tickled his balls. "Don't thtart or I'll thing a hymn."

"Anything but that, darling. You should practice more, get used to the scent."

"I only like doing that with you," I said, and he bit me again, on the other side.

*And I you, you are sweet, you are like wine, you are . . . everything.*

"Ummm . . ." I was shivering like I had a fever; God, I wanted him so much. "Come inside me now. I've waited long enough. Don't start about it being my own fault."

He laughed again and eased into me; I wrapped my legs around his waist and felt him slide all the way home. And oh, it was sweet, it was like wine, it was everything. I licked his throat and bit him, yes, it was like wine.

"Elizabeth," he groaned, thrusting hard. He grabbed my thighs, spread them apart for him, clamped down. Shoved, pushed, penetrated. And oh, it was good, it was so good. *Elizabeth, I love you, there's no one. No one.*

"Oh, boy," I gasped. That was it. That did it. I had thought my orgasm was way off, but it was just around the corner and when he said my name, when he *thought* my name, I could feel myself opening beneath his hands, his cock, his mouth, opening and coming, and it was more than fine, it was like coming home.

"Listen," he said, and his voice—it was trembling. I was shocked, even in the depths of my pleasure . . . I'd never heard him sound like that before. "Elizabeth. Listen to me. Don't do that again. Run off like that. Scare me again. Do you promise?"

Well, I didn't exactly run off, I was just trying to take charge of things, and I certainly didn't set out to scare him, but—

*"Do you promise?"*

"Yes, yes, I promise. I didn't mean to scare you."

*You are the only one who can scare me.* "All right," he said, and his voice sounded normal again, thank goodness. He reached down and gently thumbed my clit, and this time when I shuddered, he did, too.

IT took a long time for me to move, and I just sort of wriggled out from beneath him and flopped over like a fish. He groaned when I punched his shoulder to get him to give me a little room.

"Well, that was . . ." Orgasmic? Too obvious. Earthshaking? Too clichéd. Fantastically amazingly wonderful? Too needy.

He picked up my hand and kissed the knuckles. "Sublime."

"Ah! *Luh mot just.*"

He laughed. "Close enough."

I hesitated. It was obvious to me, and had been from the beginning, that he didn't know I could pick up his thoughts when we were having sex (when I wasn't evil). And I had never been able to figure out a way to tell him. He was so controlled, so cool and calm, I didn't know how to say it without freaking him out or making him mad. Hell, I could hardly explain it to myself; I'd *never* been able to read minds before, and I couldn't read anyone else's.

But now was the time. Things had never been better between us, more comfortable, more natural. In fact, I had never been happier, felt more loved, so safe. I would tell him, and he wouldn't freak out, and everything would still be nice between us.

"Good night, sweetheart," he said, and the sun slipped up in the sky—I couldn't see it, but I could feel it. I spun down and down into sleep.

And the moment passed.

# Chapter 31

"⎯⎯⎯⎯○." I cleared my throat. "How 'bout those demonic powers?"

Laura wolfed down the last of her blueberry muffin. We were at the Caribou Coffee in Apple Valley, snarfing down muffins (well, she was) and white tea. After last night, I'd been tempted to cancel on her and spend the night in bed with Eric, but how many half sisters did I have? One, so far.

"Betsy, do you have something on your mind?"

"No, no. Well, maybe."

Laura's big blue eyes shone with reproach, which would have made me feel worse if there hadn't been crumbs sticking to her lower lip. "Everybody has secrets, Betsy. You most of all."

I handed her a napkin. "Hey, I'm totally open about my disgusting covert vampire lifestyle."

She laughed.

"Look, I just met you a few days ago, right? Heck, I just *found out* about you a few days ago. I couldn't think of a way to blurt out the whole 'I'm dead' thing without weirding you out. Or making you think I skipped my meds."

"You'd be surprised what does and doesn't weird me out."

"Hey, I was there, okay? I would totally not be surprised. Well, not that surprised. Look, let's do a *quid po ko*, okay?"

"I think," she said gently, "you mean *quid pro quo*."

"Right, right. Let's do one of those. I'll tell you something weirdly secret about me, and then you do the same."

"Um . . ."

"Oh, come on," I coaxed. "We're sisters, we have to get to know each other."

She fiddled with her glass. "Okay. You go first."

"Okay. Um . . . last night wasn't the first time a bunch of moody vampires tried to kill me."

She nodded. "Thank you for sharing that with me."

"Now it's your turn."

"Ah . . . when I was eight I stole a plastic whistle from Target."

"Laura!"

She cringed. "I know, I know. I felt so bad about it afterward I told my mom and my minister. Who was also my dad."

"For heaven's sake, what kind of morbid confession is that? I'm talking about really awful sinful evil stuff."

"Stealing *is* a sin."

I rested my forehead on the table. "I mean really bad stuff. Not kid stuff. Because I have something to tell you, and I can't do it if I don't feel a little closer to you."

Her eyes went round with curiosity. "Why can't you?"

Because I sucked at telling people intimate things about themselves. "Because I . . . I just have to."

"Well, why don't you just go ahead?" She patted the top of my head. "Just get it off your chest. You'll feel better."

"Okay. Well. You know how your mom is the devil and all . . . ?" Her lips thinned, but I plunged ahead. "And you know how—wait a minute. *How* do you know your mom is the devil?"

"My parents told me."

"Your mom and the minister?" I was trying not to gape at her, and failing.

"Yes."

"How did *they* know?"

"She told them. I think she thought it would be funny. That they would get rid of me. And she . . . the devil . . . appeared to me when I was thirteen." I noticed she didn't say "my mother." In fact, her lips were pressed together so tightly, they had almost disappeared. "She told me everything. About possessing a—no offense, a woman of poor character—"

"None taken. At all."

"—and how it was my destiny to take over the world and how she was proud of me because I wasn't like anyone else—"

The milk glass broke in her hands. It had been mostly empty, but a little bit spilled onto the table, and I frantically blotted. Meanwhile, Laura was getting pretty worked up.

"And it's not up to her, you know? It's not up to her at all! It's my life, and I don't give a—a *crap* about destiny or any of it. It doesn't mean anything anyway! I don't have to be bad, and it's not how I was raised. S*he* didn't raise me, my mother and father did, and *she* doesn't get to decide how I live my life, and that's how it is, that's how it is, that is *exactly how it is!*"

This would have sounded like a normal antiparent rant from any teenager, except while she was shouting, Laura's honey blond hair shaded to a deep, true red and her big blue eyes went poison green. I was leaning away from her as far as I could get without actually falling on the floor, and she was screaming into my face.

"Okay," I said. I would have held up my hands to placate her, but if I let go, I'd be on my ass on the floor in Caribou Coffee. "Okay, Laura. It's okay. Nobody's making you do anything."

She calmed a little. "I'm sorry. I just—she makes me crazy. So crazy."

"It's okay."

"I'm not like that."

"Okay."

"I won't be like that."

"Okay, Laura." I watched in fascination as her hair lightened and lightened until it was back to blond, as her eyes went from squinty and green to big and blue.

"It's like I said before. I don't think your parents define who you are."

"Definitely not." I was trying to look around the coffee shop without her seeing. How had nobody noticed her transformation?

"I didn't mean to get you upset."

"It's not your fault." She was nervously picking up the pieces of the glass and piling them into a napkin. "I'm—I guess I'm a little sensitive on that subject."

*Well, I won't be broaching* that *one again, Red, not to worry.*

"So, uh, thanks again for your help last night." I tugged on a hank of her (blond?) hair. "I couldn't have done it without you."

She didn't smile back. "Yes, I know."

# Chapter 32

"I have *got* to meet this woman!" Jessica gasped.

"It was unreal," I announced. "Totally, massively unreal. Honestly, I was afraid to take my eyes off her. And then she got over it and she was as nice as chocolate pie again."

"Huh. Did scary magical stuff happen?"

"Nothing besides the evil hair and colored contacts. Oh, and she gorged herself on four more muffins."

"That *is* evil."

"I know! She's as thin as a stick."

Jessica handed George a navy blue skein of yarn. We were in the basement, where she had fixed up his little concrete room with curtains (duct-taped to the walls), a mattress, lots of blankets, and about sixty pillows. An entire corner of the room had been taken up with a rainbow of crochet chains. George only knew one stitch. Still, the fact that he was stitching and not stabbing was a relief.

He didn't seem to mind Jessica poking around in his room, though we were careful—she was never alone with him. As long as I fed him regularly, he didn't even sniff in her direction. So she read to him, brought him yarn, tempted him with smoothies (which he disdained), and in general found him fascinating. He was keeping clean, too, and showering on his own. I'd borrowed lots of clothes for him from Marc and Eric, though he refused socks and underpants. He took the yarn she offered, slipped off the paper covering, and started to roll it into a ball.

I finished Noxema-ing my face—I might be eternally young, but vampires got dirty faces just like everyone else. Those little disposable towelettes were a godsend; I kept a ton in my purse. "I guess we'll have to keep an eye on her."

"You didn't figure that out after the mysterious weapons of hellfire?"

"Yeah, but now I *really* want to keep an eye on her. I mean, it's great that she turned her back on her destiny—"

"But can you really?" Jessica asked quietly.

"Exactly. I mean, look at Eric and me. I swore we'd never be together, but—"

"Your inner whore would not be denied," she finished.

"That is *not* what I was going to say."

"Sure," she sneered.

"You know, you could go back to not talking to me again."

"You wish."

TWO hours later, I was just getting to the part in the movie where Rhett sweeps a struggling Scarlett up the stairs when the phone at my elbow rang. Oooh, Clark Gable! I was normally not a fan of facial hair, but he was the exception to the rule. Those lips, those eyes! And the phone was still ringing. Nuts. I had to do everything myself.

I picked it up, gaze still riveted to the screen. "Hello?"

"Good evening, Your Majesty. I hope you don't mind my calling instead of seeing you in person, but there's so much to do, I'm a little short on time."

"Who the hell is this?"

"It's Andrea," she said, sounding worried.

"Oh, right. That was a test, Andrea. And you just passed."

"Thank you, Your Majesty. I was just calling to make sure you had everything you needed for tomorrow night."

"Tomorrow night?"

"My wedding," Andrea prompted me thinly.

"Oh. Oh! Right! Your wedding. I totally didn't forget about it again. Wow, tomorrow's Halloween already, huh?"

"No. Tomorrow is the rehearsal."

"Right, right. Well, I guess we'll see you tomorrow."

"My father can't make it, and my mother is out of the country . . . " She trailed off. I happened to know (from Tina, who was a remarkably tactful but accurate gossip) that Andrea's parents thought she was still dead. Well, none of my business.

"Hey," I said suddenly. "Do you mind if my sister comes?" Laura would get a kick out of it, not to mention Operation Keep an Eye on the Spawn of Satan would be a lot easier. And if there was a sudden wedding coup, she'd come in handy. "It's up to you, it's your wedding, but—"

"Your—no, of course not. I'd be honored. Any of your family members are welcome."

"That's nice of you, but I put my foot down with my mom."

"Ma'am, that's not necessary."

"No, it totally is. She's looking at this from a cultural perspective, and I can just tell she's dying to corner Tina and grill her about Life Back Then."

"Truly, Your Majesty. I don't mind." Andrea sounded like she was cheering up. "Someone's mother should be there."

"Oh." When you put it that way. "Well, okay. I'll let her know. She'll be thrilled. Sincerely."

"That sounds wonderful." Yep, she had definitely cheered up. I felt a little better. It was bad enough that my dad knew I was dead and ignored me. What must it be like for her?

For that matter, what must it be like to outlive your whole family? Not that it was Andrea's problem yet, but it would be. It was Tina's and Sinclair's right now, and had been for years. Someday it would be mine. Mom, Dad, the Ant, Jessica, Marc . . . all gone. Laura, too? I didn't know. With her fiendish powers and low cholesterol, she could live for five hundred years.

I shook it off. "So we'll see you tomorrow, then. Say hi to Daniel for me."

"I will. Good night, Majesty."

I hung up and hit the Stop button on the DVD player. Yikes! The wedding! Time to go shopping before I forgot about it again.

# Chapter 33

SATAN appeared to me while I was sipping a medium Orange Julius and flipping through that month's *Real Simple*. There was a small sitting area near the Orange Julius stand (technically, it was Cinnabon's property) and I was relaxing and pondering where to go next—Nordstrom or GapBaby.

I'd found a black cashmere dress to go with my purple pumps, but I was still watching out for the perfect accessory. And there was the gestating baby to consider; it wasn't a minute too soon to try to counteract the Ant's tacky taste.

Suddenly, there she was, sitting across from me. The devil. Satan. The lord of lies. And it wasn't any big shock—I'd known it would be coming. And I instantly knew who she was. Some things you just know, the way you just know you shouldn't wear true black mascara because it makes your eyes look small and squinty.

The devil, in case you ever wanted to know, is a woman in her late forties. Today, she was wearing a dark gray suit that buttoned up the front and looked almost military, black panty hose, and plain black pumps. Her hair was a rich chocolate brown, with steaks of silver at the temples, and done up in an elegant bun. Her eyes were very black. Her ears weren't pierced; in fact, the devil wore no jewelry at all.

She studied me from across the table for a few moments. Finally she said, "You are the vampire queen."

It wasn't a question, so I guessed she wasn't taking a poll. I wiped my mouth. "Uh . . . yeah."

"Elizabeth Taylor."

"Yes." From pure force of habit, I checked out her shoes

again . . . then looked one more time. What I had first taken for plain black pumps were in fact Roger Vivier comma heels. Vivier customized footwear for celebrities; his shoes were literally one of a kind. Queen Elizabeth had worn a pair to her coronation. I was looking at hand-tooled shoes with garnets in the heels.

Circa 1962. Only sixteen pairs were made.

They were the holy grail of footgear.

"Wh—where did you get those?"

The devil gave me a wintry smile. "Would you like them?"

Yes! No. Would I sell my soul for shoes? Of course not. The very idea was absurd. And the gleam of the garnets didn't call to me, the very idea of selling my teeny little soul wasn't a bargain at any . . . no!

"And you are half sibling to my daughter, Favored of the Morning Star?"

"What? Oh, you mean Laura? Right, that's what the Book called her. I guess 'Spawn of Satan' didn't have as nice a ring to it."

The devil had a superb poker face. "The Book. You shouldn't have tried to destroy it."

*Tried* to? One thing at a time. "Yeah, well, it didn't go with anything else in the library."

"That sort of thing could be considered blasphemy. Consider the average Catholic's reaction if the Pope threw a first-edition Bible into the Mississippi River. Now consider the message you just sent to your servants."

"They aren't my servants."

"Wait."

"Look, can we get back on topic? You were asking about Laura? Thanks *so* much for helping us at Scratch, by the way."

"I'm more of a watcher than a doer," Satan admitted. "Besides, I knew the two of you would prevail. In fact, the two of you combined are virtually unstoppable. Virtually."

"Yeah, yeah."

This was the devil. *The* devil! The worst creature in the whole universe. The reason people killed their husbands and ran over little kids in the road and drank too much and did drugs and raped and murdered and lied and cheated and stole. So I admit I was a bit cautious, even if the devil did look weirdly like Lena Olin.

"He still loves you, you know."

"Yep, I sure do know."

"In case you were having doubts. It seems to me that it's been a rough couple of weeks for you, so I'll set you straight on that, at least: He will always love you."

"Yes, I know."

(Later, Jessica would ask me, "Who was she talking about?" and I would tell her, "God. She was talking about God." This weirded out the vampires, but Jess thought it was very fine. As for me, I'd always known the truth. Yeah, it had been a bad couple of weeks, but I'd never doubted *that*.)

She sniffed. "It's too bad. My daughter has the same problem. You could have been formidable. *She* still will be."

"I wouldn't bet the farm on that one."

"I love to bet." She studied me, her blue eyes narrowing. Er, hadn't they been brown a minute ago? "Definitely a shame. You might have been someone to contend with. You still could be, if you jettison a few silly ideas."

"Oh, I don't mind," I assured the devil. "That was never, you know, a career goal or anything."

"Humph." The devil narrowed her hazel eyes. "Your step-mother was the perfect vessel for me."

"Oh, I'm sure," I said truthfully.

"And your father is a fool."

Okay, now I was starting to get a little annoyed. What'd I ever do to the devil? Besides not be completely and foully evil all the time? And not sell my soul for her shoes? Which I hadn't entirely ruled out yet. "Are we going to talk about anything I haven't figured out for myself? Because I was sort of hoping this would be an interesting conversation. I mean, you *do* have a reputation."

The devil smirked. "Wretched child."

"Look, it's kind of weirding me out to be talking to you here."

"I have been here many times."

"Ooooh, wow, a commentary on our grasping culture and how the mall culture is secretly the root of all evil! I'd never pick up on *that*. I've seen freight trains that were more subtle."

The devil glared. "I was just making an observation."

"Yeah, well, make another one."

"You're one step up from being a moron."

"I'm rubber and you're glue," I told Satan, "and everything that bounces off me sticks to you."

She narrowed her green eyes and looked like she might come over the table at me. After a long moment, she said, "Look after my Laura, if you please."

"Well, sure."

"I have big plans for her."

"Okay. That's not humongously creepy or anything."

She crossed her leg and pointed her toe up, giving me a look at the sole of her shoe. Totally unmarked. Oh, God. They were in perfect shape.

"Last chance," the devil said.

"Get thee behind me, Lena Olin."

She disappeared in a puff of smoke that smelled like rotten eggs. No, really. She did. And I went back to *Real Simple*. It was either that or have hysterics in the food court, and I did have some pride left.

# Chapter 34

EXHAUSTED from shopping and my Orange Julius with Satan, I staggered into my room and saw the large box sitting on the end of my bed. It was a plain brown cardboard box, so I honestly didn't think anything of it. It was boot-sized, so I figured Jess had picked me up a pair of winter boots to kick around in while she was out and about.

I flipped off the top of the box . . . and nearly fell *into* the box. There, nestled in crisp white tissue paper, were Kate Spade's Mondrian boots, way out of my reach at five hundred bucks. A dream in buttery black and red leather, with an inch and a half heel, they looked sleek and cool just sitting there. I could practically hear them telling me "Vrooom, vrooom!"

"Oooh, oooh," I gurgled, totally beyond coherent speech. *Me likey!* I snatched them up—tissue paper and box and all—to my chest. "Ooooh!"

Instantly rejuvenated, I whipped around to dart out and show them to—well, anybody—and there was Sinclair standing in the doorway, smiling. His dark eyes sparkled and he said, "Since you seduced me, it seemed only fair that I seduce you."

"Oh, baby!" I cried, and danced across the room to give him a kiss.

# Chapter 35

"OKAY, so, to finish up . . ." I glanced back down at my notes. This wasn't as hard as I'd thought it was going to be; there weren't very many people there to worry about (which was both good and bad) and, frankly, I looked great. So did the bride, in a cream-colored sheath and a set of grayish pearls, bareheaded, with flawless makeup. Daniel was in a dark suit of some kind, but who cared? Weddings weren't about the groom.

Daniel hadn't told his dad (for obvious reasons, but still, it was sad), planning to later explain his "elopement" with the new Mrs. Daniels, who had a horror of sunlight. Andrea's family wasn't there. My mom and my sister were, as were Marc and Jessica, Sinclair and Tina. George was enchanted with his new #6 crochet needle, and refused to come out of the basement.

So I wasn't especially nervous, but I wanted it to be nice. "I did some research on nondenominational weddings . . . obviously nondenominational . . . and I found this on the Web. Okay, it goes like this.

" 'May the promises you make to one another be lived out to the end of your lives in an atmosphere of profoundest joy.' " I paused. Daniel and Andrea were positively google-eyed at each other, and Mom was sniffling like she always does at weddings.

All part of my diabolical plan, so I went on. "I thought that would be good advice for anybody, regardless of special, uh, circumstances. So now we'll do the vows, and then we'll have punch. Do you, Daniel, choose to marry Andrea? To speak words that will join you with her as your wife for all the rest of the days of your life?"

"I will."

"Do you, Andrea, choose to marry Daniel? To speak words that will join you with him as your husband for all the rest of the days of your life?"

I paused again. That was the big question. Andrea had a long, long life ahead of her. And Daniel was no sheep. How would they make this work? Would she try to turn him into a vampire? Would he allow it?

It was none of my business. Better to focus on the day and worry about that stuff later.

"I will."

"Then by the power invested in me, by me, I now pronounce you husband and wife. Bite away."

They ignored me and kissed, but that was all right.

"I have one more thing," I said. "From Shakespeare. Don't look so surprised, my search engine works. Anyway, as soon as I saw it I thought of you two, so I figured this would be a good place to mention it." I didn't mention it was from *Romeo and Juliet*; hopefully their romance would turn out better.

> *"With love's light wings did I o'erperch these walls,*
> *For stony limits cannot hold love out,*
> *And what love can do, that dares love attempt."*

I finished and looked up from my notes.

From across the room, Sinclair was smiling at me.

# Undead and Unreturnable

*In honor of my grandfather,*
*John Opitz,*
*who taught me to do the best I could without complaint.*
*Which, like all important life lessons,*
*is lost on me.*

# Acknowledgments

First and forever I must, must, must thank my children, who are brilliant, charming, and deft at entertaining themselves when Mom's locked in the office on deadline. They'd probably prefer my company to a few lines in a book, but as always, their expectations are too high; I'm just not that good a parent.

Another thousand thank-yous (to go with the kisses!) to my husband, Anthony, who came up with "sinister metrosexuality" and likes Betsy almost as much as he likes me. He puts up with the mood swings, speechifying, and ear-cutting that is part and parcel of living with a mass-market paperback author, and I adore him for it.

Thanks also to my PR person/best friend/evil sidekick Jessica Growette, who I swear lies awake at night thinking about how to get my name out there. Which is cool, if creepy.

The Magic Widows, of course, must also be thanked. I learn something every Tuesday. Even better, sometimes I retain it!

Special thanks to Carl Hiaasen, John Sandford, and Laurell K. Hamilton for continually showing me how it's done.

Finally, thank you to the readers who enjoy reading about Betsy's comings and goings and who wanted to know where she went next. Thanks for hopping in and coming for the ride.

# Author's Note

After seeing all the books, movies, magazines, and *National Enquirer* articles out there about serial killers, I got a little curious. After some research, I found that the actual number of estimated psycho killer nutjobs running around is anywhere between ten and five hundred. (For obvious reasons, it's tough to come up with an exact number.)

Let's say the experts are way off, and triple the guesstimate: one thousand, five hundred. There are about three hundred million people in the United States. So roughly .0000005 percent of the population is made up of serial killers. Needless to say, chances are you're not going to trip over one in your driveway.

Betsy, of course, has problems most of us will never, ever have to deal with. She and Detective Nick Berry win the serial killer lottery in this tale, but, like drinking blood and endless police paperwork, it's not something most of the rest of the population has to worry about.

Also, colic is bad. But it doesn't last forever.

FROM THE BOOK OF THE DEAD:

"And the Queene shall noe the dead, all the dead, and neither shall they hide from her nor keep secrets from her."

AND:

"And she will noe Evil in many forms, and defeat it should that be her will, and be the Protector and Avenger of all the dead, for as long as shalt be the will of the Queene."

"Just like a spider with a line of silk! Did you ever see them throw themselves out into space to weave? They're taking a chance, every single time. They got to do it or else they'd never create anything. But I bet it don't feel good, even to a spider."

—OLIVIA GOLDSMITH,
*Fashionably Late*

"It's not a bad little tree, really. It just needs a little love."

—LINUS,
*A Charlie Brown Christmas*

"There's more of gravy than of grave about you, whatever you are!"

—CHARLES DICKENS,
*A Christmas Carol*

# Prologue

FROM *the* St. Paul Pioneer Press
*December 15, 2005*

THIRD WOMAN FOUND SLAIN. Minneapolis, Minnesota.

The body of an Edina resident was found this morning at approximately six-thirty A.M. Cathie Robinson, 26, was found in the parking lot of the Lake Street Wal-Mart. Forensics show that she had been strangled. She had been reported missing on December 13. She is believed to be the third victim of the so-called Driveway Killer, who has so far claimed at least three local victims.

Detective Nick Berry, who has been working with the FBI since the second victim, Martha Lundquist, was found on November 23, said the investigation is pursuing several leads. "This is our top priority," Berry said. "Nothing else even comes close."

Ms. Lundquist was reported missing on November 8, and her body was found in the parking lot of a White Bear Lake Target store on November 10.

The FBI has profiled the killer, who appears to be choosing tall blond women with light-colored eyes and short hair. Although an arrest is "imminent," Berry warns Minneapolis women to use caution when leaving their places of business.

It is believed that the Driveway Killer has also struck in Iowa, Missouri, and Arkansas.

The FBI and local police believe that the first local victim was Katie Johnson, 27, who was reported missing on October 28 and whose body was found on November 4 in the parking lot of the Lakeville McStop.

*From the* Star Tribune
*December 17, 2005*

BORN, to Antonia Taylor and John Peter Taylor of Edina, Minnesota, a boy, Jonathon Peter Taylor II, at 12:05 A.M. on December 15 at Fairview Ridges Edina.

# Chapter 1

This is how my tombstone read:

ELIZABETH ANNE TAYLOR
APRIL 25, 1974–APRIL 25, 2004
OUR SWEETHEART, ONLY RESTING

"That's just so depressing," my best friend, Jessica Watkins, observed.

"It's weird." My sister, Laura Goodman, was staring. "That is very, very weird."

"Our sweetheart, only resting?" I asked. "What the hell's that supposed to mean?"

"I think it's nice," my sister said, a little hesitantly. She looked like a dirty old man's dream with her long, butterscotch-blond hair, big blue eyes, and red peacoat. You know how ministers' kids will sometimes go wild when they finally get away from their parents? Laura was the devil's daughter (no, really), so her way of rebelling was to be as nice and sweet as possible. A dastardly plan. "It's a little different. Most of the people I know would have gone with a Bible verse, but your mama certainly didn't have to."

"Given how things turned out," Jess replied, running a hand over her skinned-back black hair, "it's a little prophetic, don't you think?" As usual, when she put her hair up, she pulled it back so tightly, the arch of her eyebrows made her look constantly amazed. Though it's possible, given where we were standing, that she really *was* amazed.

"I think standing in front of my own grave is the last place I

want to be on the seventeenth day of December, is what I think."
Depressing *and* creepy. Must be the holidays.

Jessica sighed again and rested her forehead on my shoulder.
"Poor Betsy. I can't get over it. You were so young!"

Laura smirked a little. "Like turning thirty wasn't enough of a
trauma. Poor Betsy."

"So young!"

"Will you pull yourself together, please? I'm right here." I
stuck my hands into my coat pockets and sulked. "What is it, like
ten below out? I'm freezing."

"You're always freezing. Don't bitch if you're going to go outside without your gloves. And it's thirty-five degrees, you big
baby."

"Would you like my coat?" Laura said. "I don't really feel the
cold."

"Another one of your sinister powers," Jessica said. "We'll add
it to the list with weapons made of hellfire and always being able
to calculate a 22 percent tip. Now Bets, run this by me again . . .
how'd your tombstone finally show up here?"

I explained, hopefully for the last time. I had, of course, died
in the spring. Rose in the early dawn hours the day of my funeral
and gone on undead walkabout. Because my body was MIA, the
funeral was cancelled.

But my mother, who had been in a huge fight with my dad and
stepmom about what to spend on my marble tombstone, had
rushed to order the thing. By the time it was finished, no funeral,
no service, no burial. (My family knew the truth about what I was
now, and so did Jessica. My other coworkers and friends had been
told the funeral had been a joke, one in very poor taste.)

So anyway, my tombstone had been in storage the last six
months. (My stepmother had been pushing for plain, cheap granite, with my initials and my dates of death and birth; a penny
saved is a penny earned, apparently. My dad, as he always did
when my mom and Antonia were involved, stayed out of it.)

After a few months, the funeral home had politely contacted
my mother and asked what she'd like to do with my tombstone.
Mom had the plot and the stone paid for, so she had them stick it
in the dirt the day before yesterday, and mentioned it at lunch yesterday. You know how it goes: "Waiter, I'll have the tomato soup
with Parmesan croutons, and by the way, honey, I had your tombstone set up in the cemetery yesterday."

Jessica and Laura had been morbidly curious to see it, and I'd tagged along. What the hell, it made for a break from wedding arrangements and Christmas cards.

"Your mom," Jessica commented, "is a model of scary efficiency."

Laura brightened. "Oh, Dr. Taylor is so nice."

"And just when I think your stepmother can't get any lamer . . . no offense, Laura." The Ant was technically Laura's birth mother. It was a long story.

"I'm not offended," she replied cheerfully.

"Have you two weirdos seen enough?"

"Wait, wait." Jessica plopped the bouquet of cream-colored calla lilies on my grave. I nearly shrieked. I'd sort of assumed she'd picked those up for one of the eighty thousand tables in our house. Not for my *grave*. Ugh! "There we go."

"Let's bow our heads," Laura suggested.

"No *way*. You're both fucking ill."

"Language," my sister replied mildly.

"We're not praying over my grave. I'm massively creeped out just being here. That would be the final, ultimately too-weird step, ya weirdo."

"*I'm* not the one on a liquid diet, O vampire queen. Fine, if you won't pray, then let's book."

"Yeah," I said, casting one more uneasy glance at my grave. "Let's."

# Chapter 2

"GOOD evening, Your Majesty."

"Tina, baby," I called, dumping more cream in my tea. "Have a seat. Have a cup."

"How long have you been up?"

"Two hours or so," I said, trying not to sound smug. God had answered my prayers and lately I'd been waking up around four in the afternoon. Of course, I lived in Minnesota in December, so it was just as dark at four as it was at eight, but still.

"But you . . . you haven't seen the paper?" Tina sat down across from me, the *Trib* folded under her arm. She put it next to her and ignored the teapot. "Not yet?"

"I don't like the sound of *that*. Not one bit."

Tina hesitated, and I braced myself. Tina was an old vampire, ridiculously beautiful like most vampires, totally devoted to Sinclair and, to a lesser extent, me. She had made Sinclair, way back when, and helped us both win our crowns more recently, protected us, lived with us (not like that, ewww!) . . . she was like a major domo, except little and cute. So I guess she'd be a minor domo.

She had long, taffy-colored hair, which she usually piled up in an efficient knot, and enormous dark eyes. Big brownish-black anime eyes. Though she barely came up to my chin, she gave off an almost noble air. Like Scarlett O'Hara's mother Ellen, I'd never seen Tina's shoulders touch the back of any chair; I'd never seen her even slouch. She was also insanely smart and never forgot anything. She was a lot more queenlike than me, to tell the truth.

Anyway, my point was, she handled with aplomb the sort of

situations that would drive most of us clinically insane or at least irritable. And she was hesitating. She was *nervous*.

*Lord, help me be strong*. "I guess you better tell me."

She silently unfolded the paper and handed it to me. Births and deaths. I read the announcement. "Huh," I said with total unsurprise. "My brother was born days ago, and they didn't bother to tell me. How about that."

Tina was actually cringing in her chair and opened her eyes wide at my remarks. "That's . . . that's all? That's your only comment?"

"Oh, come on. I grew up with those people. This isn't exactly atypical behavior. I guess I better get over to the house and pay my respects. Let's see . . . we're supposed to meet with the florist tonight, but I seriously doubt Sinclair's gonna mind if I reschedule that . . . and Jess and I are supposed to have a late supper, but she won't want me to miss this . . . yeah, I'll go see the baby tonight."

Tina's perfect, smooth forehead was wrinkled in surprise. "I must say, Majesty, you're taking this much better than I anticipated."

"I was sort of expecting it. I've been keeping half an eye on the birth announcements . . . just haven't had a chance to get to them today. The baby's early . . . I didn't think the Ant was due until January."

"She might have gotten her dates mixed up," Tina suggested. "It's possible she miscalculated the date of her last menstrual—"

"I'm trying to kill my unholy thirst, here," I reminded her.

"Sorry."

I took another look at the paper. "So brother Jon. You know, the last baby the Ant had was the daughter of the devil. Wonder what you're gonna be like?"

# Chapter 3

"YOUR father's not here," the Ant said. Although she looked haggard, her pineapple-colored hair helmet was in perfect shape. She was clutching a baby monitor in her unpolished fingers, and a steady, monotonous crying was coming out of it. "He's not back until tomorrow."

"I'm here to see the baby, Antonia. You know, my brother? Congratulations, by the way."

She was still hanging in the doorway, keeping me standing on the front step. "It's not a good time, Betsy."

"It never is. Really, for either of us. You look terrible," I said cheerfully.

She glared. "I'm busy now, so you'll have to come back."

"Look, Antonia, how do you want to do this? I can keep calling and keep coming by and you can keep blowing me off, and I can bitch to my father who will eventually get tired of being in the middle and make you let me see the baby, or you can let me in tonight and get it over with."

She swung the door open wide. "Fine, come in."

"Thank you so much. You're too kind. So have you gained a ton of weight lately?" I asked, shrugging out of my coat. Then I remembered that I was constantly cold and wouldn't be staying long and put it back on. "Not that you don't look, you know, good."

"I have to check on Jon," she said, scowling at the monitor. "The doctor says it's colic. Your father left me with him."

"Yeah, that's kind of his thing."

"We named him after your father," she added proudly, if inanely.

"But Dad's name is John. With an H. The baby's name is Jon, which, as I'm sure you know, being his mother, is short for Jonathon, which is spelled totally differently." My lips were moving; could she understand me? Maybe it was time to get out the Crayolas.

She glared. "Close enough. He's Jon Peter, just like your father."

I gave up. "Which bedroom have you set up as a nursery?"

She pointed to the south end of the hallway at the top of the stairs . . . the bedroom farthest from the master bedroom. Surprise. I mounted the stairs, and she was right behind me.

"You'd better not bite him," she snarked, which I didn't dignify with an answer. The Ant felt (and said, loudly, all the time) it was really thoughtless of me to not stay dead, and felt my fellow vampires were a bad element. That last one was a tough case to argue against. "You just better not. In fact, maybe you shouldn't touch him at all."

"I promise, I don't have a cold." I opened the door—I could hear the baby yowling through the wood—and walked into the nursery, which was overdone in Walt Disney Pooh. "Ick, at least do the original Pooh."

"We're redoing it next week," she replied absently, staring into the crib. "All my Little Mermaid stuff showed up from eBay."

Yikes, no wonder he was screaming. I looked down at him and saw nothing special: a typical red-faced newborn with a shock of black hair, little eyes squeezed into slits, mouth open in the sustained *"EeeeeeYAH eeeeeeYAH eeeeeeYAH"* of a pissed-off young baby.

He was dressed in one of those little sack things, like Swee'-Pea, a pale green that made the poor kid look positively yellow. His little limbs didn't have much fat on them; they were sticklike. His teeny fists were the size of walnuts.

Poor kid. Stuck in this overly big house with a Walt Disney theme, the Ant as his mom, and green swaddling clothes. It was too much to ask of anybody, never mind someone who hadn't been on the planet for even a week. If I could have wept for him, I would have.

"Here," the Ant said, and handed me a small bottle of Purell.

I rolled my eyes. "I'm not contagious."

"You're dead. Ish."

I debated arguing but then just gave up and gave my hands a quick wash. Baby Jon wailed the entire time. I felt a little like wailing myself as I handed the bottle back.

I didn't ask if I could pick him up; I just did it, carefully supporting his head. (I remembered that much from my baby-sitting days.) He finished up a final *"EeeeeeYAH!"* and then just laid there, gasping.

"I don't want you to—" the Ant began and then cut herself off and stared at her son. "My God, that's the first time he's stopped crying in hours."

"I guess he likes me."

"Give him back."

I handed Baby Jon over, and as soon as he was out of my arms he started howling again. The Ant hastily handed him back to me, and he quit.

I grinned—I couldn't help it. A new vampire power! Newborns did my unholy bidding. Even better, the Ant was looking as green as Baby Jon's outfit.

"Well," I said loudly, because I'd handed him back again and I had to be heard over the shrieking, "I'll be going now."

"Wait!"

Heh.

# Chapter 4

I POPPED open the kitchen door and practically leaped into the middle of the floor. "I have returned!" I cried.

"Yeah, so have I," Jessica said. She was still in her caramel-colored coat, a man's coat that came almost to her ankles, and had her knitting bag in one hand and her gloves in the other. Nobody else looked up. Maybe I'd better rethink the dramatic entrance; too many people were used to it. "Thanks for canceling on me, you evil whore."

"Oh, come on, like you really cared that I went over there and bugged the shit out of the Ant. And I have to cancel on you tomorrow, too, because I'm"—I paused for dramatic impact—"baby-sitting my baby brother."

Jessica gaped. "You're doing what to the baby?"

Tina and Sinclair actually looked up. "We didn't catch that one, dear," Sinclair told me.

"You all caught it. You heard exactly what I said." I pulled my cold hands out of my pockets and blew on them, which did zero good. "Yeah, that's right. I'm baby-sitting. The baby likes me, and even though the Ant doesn't, she's desperate to get out of the house. So I'm going back tomorrow night."

"Back . . . into your stepmother's home."

"To be alone with her baby," Tina clarified.

"Your stepmother's baby," Sinclair added.

"I know! It's a Christmas miracle!"

"Well, I'll come with," Jessica decided. "Keep you company. And I'd like to see—John, is it?"

"Jon. Yeah. It'll be fun! Weird. But fun. We can zap some

popcorn and 'forget' it in the back of her closet." I tossed my keys on the counter and crossed the room. "What are you guys working on?"

Eric Sinclair leaned back so I could take a look. He was the king of the vampires, my lover, my fiancé, my nemesis, and my roommate. It had been, to put it mildly, an interesting year.

As usual, I was so distracted by Sinclair's essential deliciousness, I almost forgot to look at the book they were so engrossed in. He was just so . . . well, yummy. Yummy and great-looking and tall and broad-shouldered and so so fine. Should-be-against-the-law fine. Big hands. Big smile. Big teeth. Big everything. Oofta. After months of fighting my attraction to him, I didn't have to anymore, and baby, I was gorging. We both were. It was nice not to be looking at him out of the corner of my eye all the time. We were getting married. We were in love. We were supposed to be drooling all over each other.

I brushed some of his dark hair off his forehead, tried not to stare longingly into his black eyes, let my hand wander down to his lapel, and finally tore my gaze back to the table. In half a second, my good mood evaporated like the Ant's taste at a sample sale.

"What the *hell* is *that* doing here?"

"Darling, your grip—" He put his hand on my wrist and gently disengaged me, because I'd twisted the cloth of his lapel in my fist and, knowing him, he was less worried about the damage to his windpipe than ruining the line of his clothing.

"Don't get upset," Tina began.

"Ahhh! Ahhh!" I ahhh'd, pointing.

"The UPS man brought it," she continued.

Jessica and I stared at her.

"No, really," she said.

"The UPS guy brought *that*?" Jessica squeaked, also pointing at the Book of the Dead.

"And a box from your mother," Tina added helpfully.

"Christ, I'd hate to see what's in the other box!"

"I thought we—" Jessica glanced at Sinclair, who was as smooth-faced as ever, though his black eyes were gleaming in a way that made the hair on my arms want to leave. "I thought it was gone for good."

"Shit, shit, shit," I muttered. It was open—open!—and I slammed it closed. "Shit! Don't look at it. Shit! Why were you looking at it?"

"Oh, well, the best-laid plans and all of that." Sinclair smiled, but he didn't look especially happy. "Better luck next time, and by that I mean, don't you *dare* try it again."

Long story short: I'd read the Book of the Dead around Halloween and had gone nuts for a while. Really nuts. Biting and hurting my friends nuts. Even now, three months later, I was still so desperately ashamed of how I'd acted, I could hardly think about it. I had punished myself by wearing Kmart sneakers for a month, but even that didn't seem to strike the right note of penitence.

The up side was, now I could rise from my deep, dark slumber in the late afternoon, instead of being conked from dawn to dusk. But it wasn't enough of a trade-off for me, and I'd thrown the Book into the Mississippi River, and good riddance.

Sinclair had been coldly furious, and Tina hadn't been especially happy with me, either. Historical document, priceless beyond rubies, invaluable soothsaying tool, blah-blah. He hadn't shut me out of his bed, but the entire time we were having sex that night, he never stopped with the lecturing. And in his head (I can read his mind, though he doesn't know that—yet), he was pissed. It had been a new kind of awful. But at the time, I thought it was a small price to pay to be rid of it.

And now it was back.

"Shit," I said again, because for the life of me, I couldn't think of anything else.

"Well," Jessica said, staring at the Book, "I have some good news."

"This is a really good fake?"

"No. I've just finished my last crochet class. Now I can teach George another stitch."

"Oh." I managed to tear my gaze from the Book. "Well, that is good news. That's—really good."

"How was your grave?" Tina asked politely.

"Don't change the subject."

"But it's so tempting."

"What are we going to do with *that*?"

"Jessica already changed the subject. And I thought we'd put it back in the library."

"Where it belongs, and should never have been taken from in the first place," Sinclair added silkily.

"Hey, my house, my library, my book."

"Hardly," he snitted.

"Besides, it's *our* house," Jessica said, which was kind, because she paid the mortgage. Sinclair paid a pittance in rent, and I didn't pay anything. We'd used the proceeds from the sale of my old, termite-ridden place to put a partial down payment on the mansion.

"It's dangerous," I said, which was futile because I knew when I was beat.

"It's a tool. Like any tool, it depends on how you use it." Sinclair started to get up. "I'll remove it to the library."

"Nuh-uh." I put my hand on his shoulder and pushed. It was like trying to budge a boulder. "C'mon, siddown already. I'll put it in the library. I promise not to pitch it into the river on the way."

After a long moment, he sat. I awkwardly scooped up the Book (it was about two feet long, a foot wide, and six inches thick) and shuddered; it was warm. The vampire bible, bound in human skin, written in blood, and full of prophecies that were never wrong. Trouble was, if you read the thing too long, it drove you nuts. Not "I'm having a bad day and feel bitchy" nuts, or PMS nuts. "I think I'll commit felony assault on my friends and rape my boyfriend" nuts.

"I'm going to the basement," Jessica said after the long silence. "I'm going to show George the new stitch."

"Wait," I grunted, hefting the Book.

"C'mon, I want to show him now, so he can practice."

"I said wait, dork. You're not supposed to be alone with him, remember?"

"He's never hurt me. He's never even looked in my direction. Not since you keep him full of your icky queen blood."

"Nevertheless," Sinclair said, free of the Book and now picking up the *Wall Street Journal,* "you are not to be alone with him, Jessica. Ever."

She scowled, but she was scowling at the paper, which was now in front of Sinclair's face. I almost laughed. Dismissed. He did it to me all the time.

"Let me dump this thing in the libe," I said, staggering toward the door—it was hard to carry something and not gag at the same time—"and I'll be right with you. Anything's better than this."

"That's a bold statement," Tina observed, stirring her coffee. "Especially since you've recently been to your stepmother's."

"Har," I said, and made my way toward the library.

# Chapter 5

"**WELL**!" I said brightly, descending the stairs. "That was about the most disgusting thing ever."

"And you drink blood every week."

"Ugh, don't remind me. George? Honey, you up?"

We went to the other end of the basement (the place was huge; it ran the length of the mansion and, among other things, we'd had decapitated bodies down there as well as a body butter party) and found George in his room, busily crocheting another endless yarn link. Sky blue, this time.

He looked up alertly when we walked into his room and then went back to his crocheting. The scary thing about George was how normal he was starting to look. He was tall and lean, with a swimmer's build, shoulder-length golden brown hair, and dark brown eyes. When he'd been more feral, it was tough to see the man under all the mud. Now that he was on a steady diet of my blood, it was hard to see the feral vampire under the man.

He was too thin, but he had the best butt I'd ever seen, never mind that my heart belonged to Sinclair (and his butt). His eyes were the color of wet mud, and occasionally a flash of his intelligence gleamed out at me. Or maybe that was just wishful thinking.

He seemed only to like me, which was fair, because I was the only one who hadn't wanted to stake him and his fellow Fiends. The others were at a mansion in Minnetonka, being cared for by another vampire. Unlike George, the other Fiends had no desire to do anything but crawl around on all fours and drink blood out of buckets.

I wasn't really sure what to do about the Fiends, thus my great and all-encompassing "live and let die" policy. The asshat who used to run the vampires was a big experiment fan—you know, like the Nazis. And one of his favorite things to do was starve newly risen vampires.

Thus, the Fiends: feral, inhuman, and not so great with the vocalizing. Or the walking. Or the—anyway. They were monsters, but it wasn't their fault . . . the *real* monster had gotten to them first.

All I could do was try to look out for them . . . and keep George amused. Unlike the others, George liked to drink my blood every couple days or so. Unlike the others, George was walking.

It was very strange.

"Check it out, baby," Jessica said, bringing out a crochet hook of her own and showing it to him. Then she glanced at me. "Uh, he's eaten this week, right?"

"Unfortunately, yes." I glared at my wrist, which had already healed over. I only liked sharing blood with Sinclair; the rest of it sort of squicked me out. And I only did it with Sinclair during, um, intimate moments.

Sad to say, my blood (queen blood, sigh) was the only thing making George better. Three months ago, he was covered with mud, naked, howling at the moon, and eating the occasional rapist. Yarn work in my basement and consenting to red Jockeys was a big damn improvement.

"Like this," Jessica was saying, showing him what looked, to me, like an incredibly complicated stitch. But then, I'd tossed out my counted cross-stitch patterns at age sixteen after declaring them way too hard. Crocheting and knitting . . . yurrgh.

My mom tried to teach me to knit once, and it went like this: "Okay, I'll do it really slowly so you can follow." Then the needles flashed and she'd knitted half a scarf. That's about when I gave up on all crafts.

"And then . . ." Jess was murmuring, "through the loop . . . like this."

He hummed and took the yarn from her.

"What's next on the wedding agenda?"

"Um . . ." I shut my eyes and thought. My Sidekick was upstairs, but I knew most of the wedding details by heart. "Flowers. I'm still pushing for purple irises and yellow alstromeria lilies, and Sinclair is still pretending we're not getting married."

"What's the new date?"

"September 15."

Jessica frowned. "That's a Thursday."

I stared at her. "How do you know *that*?"

"Because it's the date my parents died, so I try to get out to the cemetery then. And I remember, last September was a Wednesday."

"Oh." We did not discuss Jessica's mother and father. Ever. "Well, what difference does it make? Like Sinclair cares? Like the other vampires do? Oh, what, we've all got to get up early for work the next morning?"

"How many times have you changed the date? Four?"

"Possibly," I said grudgingly. It had been, respectively, February 14 (I know, I know, and to give me credit, I *did* scrap the idea eventually), April 10, July 4, and now September 15.

"I don't understand why you don't just get it done, hon. You've wanted this how long? And Sinclair is agreeable and everything? I mean, what the hell?"

"There just hasn't been time to get all the details taken care of. I *have* been solving murders and dodging bloody coups," I bitched. "That's why I keep moving the date. There aren't enough hours in the day. Night."

Jessica didn't say anything. Thank God.

"Look!" I pointed. George was crocheting the new stitch she'd just showed him. "Wow, he's catching on."

"Next: the knit stitch."

"Can't you ever rest on your laurels? Let the guy make a blanket or something."

"And after that," she said confidentially, "we're going to start with reading and math."

"Oh, boy."

"He already knows how. He must. It's just a matter of reminding him."

"Yeah, that's what it's a matter of."

She ignored that. "So what else? Flowers? And then what? You've got the gown picked out."

"Yup. Picked it up last week. The nice thing about being dead is one fitting pretty much did the trick."

"Well, there you go. What else?"

"The tasting menu."

"How are you going to pull *that* off?"

"It's wine for them, juice and stuff for the rest of us." I heard myself say that and wondered: *Who did I think "us" was?*

"Oh. Good work. And?"

"The cake. Not for us." There was that word again! "But there will be some regular guys there. You, Marc, my folks."

"The Ant?"

"I'm inviting her."

"You are? Well, maybe she'll have a face-lift scheduled that day."

I perked up. "Maybe. You think? Anyway. I'm leaning toward chocolate with raspberry ganache filling, topped with chocolate-covered strawberries. And, you know, ivory basket-weave fondant icing."

"Stop, you're making me hungry."

"And I've been trying to get Sinclair to go tux shopping."

"Why? He's got a million of them."

"Yeah, but this is *the* tux. The mother of all tuxes. The wedding day tux. He needs something special."

"Maybe in a nice powder blue," she suggested.

I laughed. "Or canary yellow. Can you imagine? Wouldn't he just die?"

"Again. Actually, he seems pretty close to it. He, uh, doesn't seem all that interested in the details. I mean, more than most guys. Which is weird, given his cool metrosexualness."

I hadn't heard that exact term (which had been sooo trendy the year before but was now woefully overused) applied to Sinclair, but I only had to mull it over for half a second before I realized she was right. He had a big dick, adored women, didn't mind kicking the shit out of bad guys, insisted on redecorating all the parlors, was a foodie and a tea snob. Ah, the love of my life. Great in bed and would only drink tea from leaves, not bags. Whodathunkit.

I sat down on one of the chairs and watched George busily crochet. Speaking of metrosexuals. He'd already done four inches across.

"You know how it is. Sinclair's like a tick, he gets so stubborn. 'We're married by vampire law, a ceremony is redundant,' blah-blah."

"That's tough," she said sympathetically. She was digging around in her craft bag and tossing more skeins of yarn to George. A wool rainbow flew through the air: red, blue, yellow, purple. "But you know it's not a question of love. You know that, right?"

"I guess . . ."

"Come on, Bets. You guys got that cleared up at Halloween-time. He worships you. He'd do anything for you. He's *done* anything for you. It's not his fault he's considered you guys to be married for the last eight months."

"Mmm. Did you know, our wedding is going to be the first vampire monarch wedding in the history of dead people?"

"Something for the diary. Vampire *monarch* wedding?"

"Umm. Because vampires get married now and again. And a vampire/human couple will get married—like Andrea and Daniel. But I guess since the Book of the Dead claims we're already married, it's never actually been done."

"So?"

"Exactly," I said firmly. "Exactly! Who gives a damn if it's never been done? No reason not to do it. But I'm not taking his name."

Jessica burst out laughing. "I just realized. If you did, you'd be Sink Lair."

"Don't even tell me."

"Better not tell *him*. He's kind of a traditionalist."

Exactly what had been worrying me lately.

# Chapter 6

ONE of the ghosts came to bug me while I was updating my diary. I don't know why I bothered. I'd write full steam for about a week and then totally lose interest. My closet was full of ninety journals that were only used through the first fifteen pages.

Marc had just left after begging me, once again, to have a carrot cake instead of chocolate. The maniac. We exchanged cross words and then he huffed out. Jessica was asleep. (It was two A.M.) Tina was out on the town, probably feeding. (I was careful not to ask.) Sinclair was somewhere in the house.

And the ghost was standing in front of my closet with her back to me, bent forward like a butler bowing from the waist, her head stuck through the door. I don't even know why I turned around. She'd been as noisy as a dead battery. I just did. And there she was.

I sat there for a moment and took a steadying breath, ignoring the instant dizziness. This happened occasionally. Part of the queen thing. The first time I'd been scared shitless. Ironically, I was terrified of dead things.

I wasn't used to it, exactly, but at least these days I didn't go tearing out of the room to cringe in the driveway.

"Um," I said.

She pulled her head out and looked at me, amazed. "You have a *lot* of shoes."

"Thanks."

"More than Payless."

I concealed a shudder. "Thanks." We stared at each other. She was a small strawberry blonde, about five foot nothing, with her hair pulled up in an I-Dream-of-Jeannie ponytail. She was blue-eyed and had lots of caramel-colored freckles all over her face and hands. She was wearing beat-up blue jeans and a booger-colored turtleneck. Battered black flats; no socks. Freckles on the tops of her feet, too.

"I'm, ah, sorry to bother you. But I think I—I think I might be dead."

"I'm really sorry to have to tell you this," I replied, "but you are."

She sat down on my floor and cried for about ten minutes. I didn't know what to say or do. I couldn't leave, though that was my first impulse—to give her some privacy. But I was afraid she'd take it the wrong way.

I couldn't touch her—my hands went right through ghosts, and it was horrible. Like plunging your limbs into an ice bath. So a supportive pat or hug was out of the question. "There, there" seemed unbelievably lame. So did going back to my journal. So I just stayed in my desk chair and watched her and waited.

After a while, she said, "Sorry."

"You're totally entitled."

"I knew, you know. I just—hoped I was wrong. But nobody—you're the only one—nobody can see me. The EMTs couldn't see me, and the guys in the morgue, and my boyfriend."

"How did you know to come here?"

"I—I don't know."

"Okay." Dammit! If the ghosts knew, nobody was telling. I didn't know if there was a sign outside my house ("She sees dead people") that only the dead could see, or what. Not that it made much difference. But I was curious.

She sighed. "I was hoping you could do me a favor."

"Sure," I said at once. I knew from experience that it was just easier (and quicker) to give them what they wanted. Otherwise, they hung around and talked to me at the most awkward moments. Ever been interrupted by a ghost while you're washing your hair? Or going down on your fiancé? Awkward. "What can I do for you?"

"Well, the last thing I remember—the last time anybody else could see me—I had just run out of our apartment building. Mine and my boyfriend's. We had this big wicked fight because he thought I was cheating on him, but I swear I wasn't!"

"Okay."

"And if you could just—go see him? And tell him? I only had dinner with the guy twice. I wasn't going to do anything. It's

Denny I love. I'm so mad I didn't realize that before running out in front of the—anyway. I hate the thought—I *hate* the thought—of Denny thinking to the end of his days that the last thing I did was cheat on him. I mean, I can't sleep for worrying about it." She paused. "Not that I could anyway. I think. But it's really bothering me. It—it really is."

"I'll be glad to go see him. I'll do it first thing tomorrow night."

"I live in Eagan," she said. Then she gave me excellent directions, which I wrote down in my journal.

"No problem at all. It's done."

"Thank you so m—" Then she looked extremely surprised and popped out of sight. This was also expected. It was like whenever they got whatever-it-was off their chests, they could go to . . . wherever.

Poor thing. I was getting all kinds. At least she didn't feel bad about stealing or a dead mom or criminal assault or something awful like that.

I went back to my journal and realized she'd never told me her name—and I'd never bothered to ask. This bothered me a lot . . . was I getting jaded? Well, obviously I was, but how bad?

Dammit.

# Chapter 7

THE next night, I pulled back into my driveway after going about my little errand. The boyfriend—Denny—had been tearfully receptive to my news. That was the weirdest part of all the ghost stuff . . . not only did the ghosts feel better after they told me what they wanted, but whomever I told also felt better. Believed me, unquestioningly. None of that Whoopi Goldberg skepticism in *Ghost*. No, it was always, "Thank you so much, thank God you told me, now I can get on with my life, are you sure you don't want any coffee?" Very strange. But better than the alternative, I figured.

There was a shiny red Dodge Ram pickup in the driveway, parked crookedly, one tire actually in the grass. I had no idea who the hell it was—no one I knew drove a red truck—and wondered if I wanted to go in.

See, things started out innocently enough—a visitor, a comment, finding out a new vampire rule—and the next thing I know, I'm up to my tits in undead politics, or attempted revolutions, or dead bodies.

It had gotten so that I distrusted everything new, no matter how minor. And that was a *big* truck. Not minor at all. With a super-cab, no less. It could have brought five new troublemakers to my house, easy.

I looked at my watch. It was only six-thirty. But that meant Tina and Sinclair were up, at least. So if it was something annoying, I'd at least have help. Maybe I could fob the whole thing off on them.

Shit, maybe it didn't have a single thing to do with me!

Nah.

I let myself in the front door in time to hear a cracking adolescent male voice yell, "I'll go if Betsy wants me to go, so cram it, Sinclair!"

I knew that piping, wanting-to-be-deep-but-not-quite-making-it voice. Jon Delk, former head of the Blade Warriors, current pain in my ass. After the Warriors disbanded last summer, he'd gone back to the family farm. I hadn't heard from him since. What the hell could have brought him back? Nothing good, that's what.

"Tina," I heard Sinclair say casually, and because I knew that voice, I started running, "see our little friend out."

"Go ahead, vampire. You just lay one dead finger on me."

"Okay," Tina said cheerfully and then I burst into the kitchen.

"Stop it! Whatever it is, play nice, you bums."

"Betsy." His face—his young, wholesome, ridiculously handsome face—brightened when he saw me, and he smiled so wide his dimples showed. "Hey. Great to see you. You look great. It's really . . . uh . . ."

"Great?" Sinclair snarked, leaning against the counter with his arms crossed. Stretched out in front of him like they were, his legs looked a mile long.

His darkness was an odd contrast to Jon—I mean, everything about Eric was dark. The clothes, the attitude. Even the way he carried himself; like he could pounce on you at any minute.

Meanwhile, Jon was practically vibrating from trying just to stand still, and he kept raking his hands through his blond hair, which did nothing to straighten it. He was always in constant motion, while Eric could do statue imitations and win, every time.

Jon's blue eyes watched us all anxiously, but I could smell gun oil and leather, so I knew he was wearing a holster somewhere—probably his armpit. Guys loved the armpit holster, though my mom had taught me it was one of the worst places to carry a gun. You could never get to it in time.

And he probably had at least one knife on him. He looked like a corn-fed nineteen-year-old, and he was. But he had also teamed up with a bunch of loners and killed more vampires than most people would see in a lifetime.

Luckily, he liked me, and liking me had ruined his taste for staking vampires. I wasn't sure why, because most vampires were assholes, but I wasn't going to complain. I held out my hand, and Jon shook it with a sweaty palm. "It's nice to see you, too. Is anything wrong?"

"I guess that depends," he replied, glaring over his shoulder at the lounging Sinclair, "on who you ask."

"No, uh, new dead people, though. Right?"

He shook his head. "Nothing like that. Betsy, can I talk to you in private? Maybe in your room?"

"Our room," Sinclair corrected, and smiled when the blood rushed to Jon's face.

"Oh, so you've finally gotten around to moving your stuff in? You've only had two months."

*That* took care of the smile, I was happy to see, and sure, maybe I shouldn't have said it, but I couldn't stand to see them picking on a kid. It was the fifth grade all over again.

"The queen has many duties," Tina added, her legs scissoring in her lap as she crossed them and looked smug. "I don't think there's time to—"

"Butt out, Tina. And Eric—knock it off. Hello, guest in our happy home?"

"Uninvited guest," Sinclair muttered.

"You wanna go?" Jon challenged. "Because we'll go, partner. Anytime."

"As a matter of fact, I *do* want to go," Sinclair said, straightening up from the counter in a movement so abrupt, even I couldn't see it.

"No, *no*. You guys! Jeez." I turned to Jon, who had a hand out of sight under his jacket. "Don't you dare pull a gun in my kitchen. I'm the only one who can pull a gun in my kitchen. Let's go up." Men! Like rats fighting over a hamburger, I swear to God. "Tell me all about . . . whatever it is. We all wondered where you went after you left."

He was young enough that he didn't feel silly sticking his tongue out at them—but boy, he sure looked silly. Tina rolled her eyes, but Sinclair just stared at him like a snake at an egg. I bit my own tongue, figuring Jon had taken enough shit for one day.

# Chapter 8

I let him go ahead of me on the stairs, speaking of juvenile actions. I couldn't help it; he had the nicest butt. He favored faded blue jeans and big belts, shitkicker boots, and T-shirts. He looked like an ad for Wheaties.

We had barely gotten to the first landing when he whirled, grabbed my shoulders, and burst out, "Betsy, you can't!"

Startled, I grabbed his wrists. "What?"

"You can't marry *him*."

"That's why you're here?" I mean, liking me was something, but for heaven's sakes.

"You can't do it, Betsy." I was gently trying to loosen his fingers from my shoulders, but he clung like plastic wrap. "I know you, and it'll never work. You're good, and he's *not*. He's totally not. You can't marry him."

"Jon . . ." My God, was I going to have to break his fingers? "Personal bubble, Jon."

He let go. Whew. "Sorry."

"Jon, listen. I know Sinclair has done his share of—"

"Murderous disgusting blood-sucking deeds?"

"—uh—questionable errands, but he's not really that bad. I mean, Nostro was bad. Monique was bad. He's just trying to get along."

"Betsy, that's the dumbest thing I've ever heard. *He is a bad man.* If this was a western, he'd be the one wearing the black hat."

"Jon, you have no idea what bad really is," I said, as nicely as I could. "If you did, you'd know Sinclair wasn't it. The vampire world, like our world, isn't black and white . . . there's tons of gray areas. Sometimes you have to make a bad choice to do a good thing. He's done everything for me—he's been killed for me, and he's saved my life. I think he's saved my life. I mean, assuming I could even—never mind, we're getting off the subject."

"Betsy." Jon stuck his hands in his front pockets, past the wrist, and looked away. "Sometimes a guy will do things for a— for a pretty girl. I'm not saying I don't think he, uh, likes you."

"You're saying I'm too good for him."

"Well . . ."

"That's really nice." I meant it. It was the compliment of the month. It was the thing I would take out and reminisce about when I was an old lady. "But I know what I'm doing. And I love him. I bet that's the last thing you want to hear, but it's true. And how could I *not* get married to the guy I love?"

He winced and still wouldn't meet my eyes. "Maybe it's a trick."

"Like a vampire mojo thing? I only think I love him? I really only love his teeth and his dick?"

That did it; he glared at me, full in the eyes, and the blood rushed into his cheeks. "Don't talk like that. That's not what I—"

"Because, believe me, I resisted the dark side for as long as I could. Then I realized he really wasn't. Bad, I mean. Well, that bad." Did it sound like I was making excuses for him? I didn't mean to. It was just . . . difficult to put into words. How I felt about him. What he meant to me. Shit, I'd only admitted to myself that I loved him three months ago. "He just took a little getting used to."

"Betsy, I'm not saying I don't think it's a good match— although I don't."

Now I was confused. "So you *are* saying you don't think it's a good match? Right?"

He kept going, unfortunately. Full speed ahead, and damn the torpedoes. "I don't think he's a good *man*. For anybody."

"Oh, so if he was marrying, say, Tina, you would have come down here to warn her off, too?"

Stubborn silence.

"Jon, did you really come all the way from the valley to try to stop my wedding? Because you had months to do that, you know."

"Ani stopped by and she—we caught up on current events, I guess you could say. And—" He cut himself off, but I knew where he'd been going. *And as soon as I heard you were getting married, I got in my dad's truck and left.* Oh, boy. Poor Jon. Crushes were the absolute worst. I'd almost rather die again. It *felt* like dying again, when you heard the person you adored above all others had never, ever given you a thought like that, and probably never would.

"I'm getting married, Jon. On"—for an awful moment I couldn't remember the new date—"September 15. I'd love it if you could come. All the Bees are welcome."

He smiled. Well, his lips moved. We both pretended not to notice that his eyes had filled and he was sniffing like he'd instantly picked up a cold—or a cocaine habit. "That stupid name."

"Hey, you want to talk stupid? How about the Blade Warriors? I feel ridiculous even saying it to you. You're lucky I just use the first letter."

The Blade Warriors! Oh, boy. Like my life wasn't silly enough. This past summer a bunch of kids—yep, that's right, not one of them could legally drink—got together and started hunting down vampires. The scary part? They were weirdly successful. (Vampires were notoriously complacent.) The scarier part? I was able to talk them into not doing that anymore. The Bees (I tried not to use the stupid name) had scattered and gone their own way. And now one of them was back, almost literally in my lap.

"I don't know if I'll be able to come," he said, changing the subject . . . but not really.

"Well, either way. I'm just happy to have anyone there who has a pulse."

"Will there be a lot of vampires there?"

"Yes, and no. My wedding is not a research opportunity, get it? Throw rice and drink. No, you're too young to drink. Throw more rice. Have a Shirley Temple. Go crazy."

"So it's going to be a *wedding* wedding?"

"Sure."

He chewed on that one for a few seconds. "I've never heard of that before."

"Well, don't you start. Sinclair gives me enough grief."

He perked up. "Really? He doesn't like all the bells and whistles?"

"Oh, you know. He says because we're consorts there's no need for bouquet, maid of honor, best man toast, all that."

"Really?" I could see his dimples again. Odd, the things that depressed the boy and brought him back up. "You, uh, you need any help?"

"You mean planning? Or in general? Because the answer to both is, I dunno. September's a long way off."

"Well . . ." He looked around the foyer and then glanced down the stairs. "I don't have to be back right away . . ."

"Do you have a place to stay?"

"Not really. I was going to stop by the church, see if Father Markus could put me up for a few nights . . ."

"Is that supposed to be a hint? Because it sucks. Why don't you just shove me off the landing? It'd be more subtle."

He laughed. "Yeah, it was pretty lame. Can I crash here?"

"Of course you can. We've got more rooms than the Hilton." In my mind, I could already picture Sinclair's reaction. I probably wasn't going to get laid tonight, at the very least.

Well, tough shit. The kid had had a rotten enough day; I wasn't going to turn him out onto the street on top of all that.

"That's great. I'd—I'd really like to stay here." He glanced around the ancient staircase. "It looks interesting. Like something out of an old book."

"Yeah, interesting. Hope you like dust. But listen, we've got a feral killer vampire living in the basement, so don't go down there. Oh, and if you drink all the milk, you have to replace it."

"What?"

"I know, but see, we all like milk in our tea, and when we're out it's really—"

"Did you say *feral* killer vampire?"

"Right, right. But he's okay. Just stay out of the basement. I don't want you up to any of your old tricks."

"Anything else?"

"Yeah. Good to see you."

"Good to see you, too." He smiled at me like he meant what he was saying.

Damn dimples.

# Chapter 9

I tiptoed down the hall and quietly rapped on the door to Sinclair's closet room. It would have been his bedroom, except he didn't sleep in there; he slept with me. But all his clothes and such were in here. And I'm sure that meant something, but I wasn't going to worry about it now.

"Eric?" I whispered, knowing full well he could hear me. But I wanted to keep our impending chat as private as I could.

"Yes?" he whispered back.

"Can I come in?"

"Why?"

I spun around. He was in the hallway, grinning and carrying a foot-thick freshly wrapped pile of clean dry cleaning by the hangers. *Wooden* hangers. Wherever he went, it cost a friggin' fortune. "You know I hate, hate, *hate* when you sneak up on me. You know that, right?"

"It's possible you might have mentioned it once before." He leaned past me and opened the door and then courteously stood aside so I could go in. "What nasty business have you been involved in since we parted ways four hours ago? I can't imagine what else would bring you to my room. Have you finally given in to your primal urge to kill Antonia?"

"I wish."

"Perhaps you kidnapped Baby Jon for his own good, and now you're here to tell me I'm a new father."

"I really wish." I paused. Best to just get it over with. "I invited Jon of the Bees to move in with us."

He was taking each dark suit out of its plastic cocoon and

carefully examining it before hanging it on some kind of weird suit tree, and in the middle of the ritual he laughed. "What a coincidence. I invited the new pope for breakfast."

"No, really."

He glanced at me and frowned. It was a mild frown, but pretty much all the sun and joy were sucked out of the room when his smile went. "Elizabeth."

"I know, I know."

"Elizabeth. You didn't."

"I really kind of did."

His eyebrows had rushed together to become one overpowering, disapproving unibrow. "Well, I am sure, since the invitation came so easily and thoughtlessly tripping off your dulcet tongue, you can un-invite him just as easily."

"It's only for a little while. Just till he gets his shit together."

"Oh, so twenty years, then?" he snapped. He tried to stomp toward me, but dry cleaning bags were everywhere and he was momentarily snared. I chewed on the insides of my cheeks and stared at him with wide eyes as he stumbled toward me. *Don't laugh don't laugh don't laugh.*

His black eyes narrowed, and he stomped an errant bag, which deflated with a sad *whooooooooooofff*. "Are you smiling, girl?"

"No, Eric." Girl? That was a new one. "Listen, I could hardly turn him out into the street."

"Why not, exactly?"

"Eric! Come on. Look, I'll make it up to you."

"Too damned right you will," he muttered, and grabbed me by the elbows.

"You're just going to fuck me, right? You're not going to make me run a lint brush over all your suits or anything horrible like that, right?"

"Be quiet." He pulled me in for a savage kiss and then tossed me on the bed and landed on me like a cat. In a flash, one hand was up my skirt, divesting me of my tights, and the other was pulling at his own pants. And while he was busy with all that, his tongue was busy in my mouth. I tried to help, to move, but he was controlling everything, and so I lay there and, as they say to do, thought of England. Except I was really thinking about his big dick and drooling at what he was going to do to me with it.

He pushed inside me and I wasn't ready, but I didn't give a ripe damn. We both grunted as we tried to force friction where there wasn't much. He had stopped kissing me and had buried his face in my throat, and my legs were wrapped around his waist. His shirt was still buttoned, and we both had our socks on.

He finally slid all the way home and I was able to pump back at him, and we found a sort of rhythm. It was better, much better, *way* better—it was *fantastic*. I loved the way his hands felt on my body, strong and frantic, and the way his voice sounded in my head:

*Never let anyone else never never you're mine mine mine mine MINE MINE.*

Pretty much just frantic. Then he stiffened against me, and even though I was miles away from coming, I didn't mind. I knew he'd spend the next hour making it up to me.

He collapsed over me with a groan, and I laughed; my shirt was still on, too. But with scattered clothes and all the plastic bags, the room looked like Filene's Basement on the day of a really good sale.

"Don't laugh at me, you horrible woman," he said without heat.

"Sorry, Eric. That was a real good lesson you taught me. Consider me chastened. Also, the Minnesota Vikings are moving in tomorrow."

He groaned again. "You're trying to kill me. You should feel deep shame."

"Ha!" I looped my legs around his waist and tickled him behind his ear, in a spot I knew was sensitive. "Ready to go again?"

"Kill me," he mumbled, slowly unbuttoning his shirt, but he couldn't hide the gleam in his eyes, or the sudden, ah, surge of interest. "The state of Minnesota frowns on premeditated murder, you know."

"The state of Minnesota would frown on pretty much everything that goes on in this house." I pulled off my strawberry socks and threw them in the air. "Let's ride, partner!"

"They probably don't think much of suicide, either," he snarked, but then he was kissing me again, and I pretty much lost the rest.


"WHAT are you supposed to do again?" Jessica whispered.

"I told you, like, three times. Jeez, tune me out much?"

"There's a lot of trivia in your life I have to sift through."

"What am I, the six o'clock news?"

"Exactly!" she said, refusing to take offense. "Sometimes it's hard to remember what's important and what's not so much."

"Very nice! Here . . . one-ten, one-eleven, one-twelve." We

paused outside the closed door, which, like all nursing home doors, tried to look homey with cards and such, and was anything but. No matter what you did to them, they looked, felt, and smelled like hospitals.

I rapped gently and, when there was no response, pushed on the door. It wheezed open on pneumatic hinges, and I could see an old lady sitting on the edge of the far bed.

She smiled when she saw us, her gums looking just like Baby Jon's.

"Uh, hi," I said, creeping in like a thief, Jessica right behind me. "I'm Betsy. This is Jessica."

She cupped a hand over one ear. She looked like just about every old person in Minnesota I'd ever seen, which was to say white-haired, blue-eyed, skinny, and wrinkly. She was wearing those old-lady panty hose that rolled to the knees and a faded yellow housecoat, buttoned to her neck.

"Hmm?" she asked.

"I said . . ." I inched closer. The door sighed shut behind us. Thank goodness. A scrap of privacy. "I'm Betsy, and this is Jessica."

"Hmm?"

Oh, great. I leaned over until we were kissing distance. She smelled strongly of apple juice. It brought back awful memories of my candy-striper days. And God knew what I smelled like. Probably the Angel of Death. "Annie sent me!" I bawled. "She said to tell you—!"

She leaned closer. Now we were a fraction of an inch away from *actually kissing*. "Hmm?"

*"Annie said to tell you there never was a map!"* I screamed, ignoring Jessica's giggles. Great! Maybe some of the nurses on the first floor hadn't heard the first part of this extremely private conversation. *"But there was an account, and here's all the info you need to get into it!"* I handed her a folded piece of paper.

*"No se . . ."* She shook her head. *"No se, no se."*

"Oh, for fuck's sake." I resisted the urge to kick the bed through the window. "Annie never mentioned *this*."

Jessica was actually lying on the other bed, holding her stomach, in hysterics. "Louder, louder! *No se!*"

"Will you get off your ass and help me, please?"

"I took French. You know that."

"Thanks for a big fat goose egg of nothing. You are, without a doubt, the worst sidekick in the history of duos. Now what?"

Luckily, the old lady—gad, I had to remember she was a per-

son, she had a name (Emma Pearson)—she wasn't "the old lady."
Anyway, while I was bitching at Jessica, Emma had unfolded the
piece of paper I'd handed her, and her face broke into a huge
toothless smile. She said something excitedly in Spanish—I'd
only had a year of it in high school and all I remembered was
*dónde está el baño?*—and clutched my hand.

"Oh, *gracias,*" she said. "*Muchas muchas gracias.* I am thinking you so much. Thank you."

"Uh . . . *de nada.* Oh, I almost forgot . . . Annie is very, very
sorry she stole the money, and she hopes you have a lot of fun
with it. She's . . . uh, *lo siento.* Annie *es muy muy lo siento
para* . . . uh . . . *para* stealing? *El dinero?*"

Emma nodded, still smiling. I prayed she had the faintest idea
what I was talking about. If she didn't, Annie'd be paying me another little visit.

Then we just looked at each other. To break the newly awkward silence, I asked, "*Dónde está el baño?*"

She gave complicated directions, which was okay because I
didn't have to go anyway, and we left after much waving and
shouted good-byes.

"She didn't appear to get a word of that," Jessica observed,
pulling her checkbook out of her purse, groping for a pen, and
scribbling something. "But she seemed to know about the account."

"Maybe she reads more English than she speaks. Or maybe
she understands the words *First National Bank* and her own
name."

"Maybe." She ripped off the check—I saw it was for
$50,000—and casually dropped it into the suggestion box on our
way back to the car. "This place really needs new wallpaper. Who
picked mucous green?"

"You're asking me? This place is like my worst nightmare.
Look at all these poor guys. Shuffling around and just pretty much
waiting to die."

"There were some people in the game room," Jess said defensively. "They looked like they were having fun putting the big
puzzle together."

"Please."

"Okay, it sucks. You happy now? I wouldn't want to end up
here, I admit it."

"A problem you'll never have, honeybunch."

"Well, that's true. And neither will you."

I cheered up a little. No, one thing that was most definitely not in my future was spending my last days scuffing along in Wal-Mart slippers and eating applesauce.

"You remember that time you volunteered at Burnsville Manor in high school, and you only lasted a day because that old guy punched you in the knee when you tried to make him finish his—"

"Let's stop talking for a while," I suggested, and the cow had the giggles all the way back to the mansion.

# Chapter 10

"I'm sorry, I'm sorry," she gasped, *ten minutes later*. I couldn't believe she was still hee-hawing about ancient history. "It's just, you went there with such high moral intentions, and you didn't even last a single shift. And you limped for a week!"

"Rich people should never criticize the working class," I snapped.

"Hey, I work fifty hours a week at The Foot."

Dammit, she was right. It had always been something of a mystery to me why she bothered. She pretended like the nonprofit was a tax shelter and she needed the break every April 15, but we all knew it was a lie. Bottom line was, she liked going there, liked seeing her dad's money teach welfare moms how to program computers and get good jobs.

She ran the place with an ever-shifting staff, and me. I did the books when she was between office managers. I didn't much mind the work, but I didn't live and breathe it the way Jess did.

"She seemed like a nice lady."

"Jess! She didn't say five words to us the whole time. She could be a drooling psychopath for all we know."

"Do you think some of the ghosts are bad guys? And ask you to help other bad guys?"

"Great. Because I didn't have enough awful things to contemplate." Horrible thought! One I immediately shoved out of my head.

"Sorry. It was just an idea. Do you think there *are* any old psychopaths?"

"Sure. They're not all killers, you know. It's a psych problem, like schizophrenia. It's not just the property of thirty-somethings. The ones who don't get caught prob'ly get old like any of us."

"I read somewhere that there aren't nearly as many psychopaths—sociopaths?—out there as the media want us to think. Something like one tenth of one percent of the population is a deviant sociopath."

"Well, good. Like the vampires aren't bad enough. They all seem like psychos to me."

"Tough one to argue," she admitted.

"You're right, though! It seems like every book, movie, and made-for-TV miniseries is about a brave young woman—always a shrink or an FBI agent—tracking down a serial killer who has mysteriously targeted her. Or her family. Or her dog. And she, along with the brave hero, must alone face the threat of the drooling nutjob—"

"*Taking Lives* wasn't so bad."

"Oh my God!" I shrieked, nearly driving into a stop sign. "Worst movie ever! I almost gave up on Angelina Jolie after that one."

"Too cerebral?"

"Oh, yeah, real cerebral. Jolie has sex with a guy who may or may not be the villain." Hmm, that didn't sound like anybody I knew, right? Argh. I shoved that thought into the tiny corner of my brain where I kept all bad thoughts: Prada going out of business, Sinclair coming to his senses and leaving me, me leaving him, the Ant moving in. "Jess, I love you, but—"

"Here we go."

"—you keep your taste in movies up your ass. I'm sorry, but it's true."

"Says the woman who bought *Blade IV* on DVD."

"That was research!"

"Oh, research my big black ass. You've got a thing for Wesley Snipes."

"First of all, what ass? And second, do not." I had pulled into our driveway, and we were just sitting in my Stratus, arguing, when I noticed that in addition to Jon's truck, there was a navy blue Ford Escort in my driveway.

Cop.

Detective Nick Berry, to be exact. I didn't have to see all the Milky Way bars on the passenger side floor to know, either. He'd had the same car ever since I'd known him.

"What's he doing here?" Jess asked.

I brought my head down so fast on the steering wheel, the car honked. "What now?" I groaned.

"Hmm, someone else who's desperately in love with you stopping by unannounced," Jessica said with annoying cheer. "Must be Tuesday."

"This is a serious problem."

"Oh, will you spare me please? 'I'm Betsy and I'm an eternally beautiful and young queen with the coolest guy in the universe boning me every night, and whenever he gets tired, other guys are lining up to take his place. *Waaaaaah!*' "

I gave her The Look.

"Sometimes," she admitted, "it's hard to empathize with your problems. Like they weren't trampling over me to get to you when you were alive."

"That's not true!" I said, shocked.

"What's more irritating—being invisible, or you not having a clue about your effect on men?"

"Jess, stop it. The last word I'd pick to describe you is *invisible*. You've dated senators, for God's sake."

She dismissed the Democrat with the great hair with a wave of her newly manicured hand. "Fortune hunter."

"Well, that one guy, no kidding. Okay, maybe there were three or four. But I'm just saying, having these guys popping up is a serious problem. And remember—half the time it isn't even me, it's my weird vampire mojo that's bringing them in. Like they say, just because they don't seem like problems doesn't mean they really aren't. Problems, I mean. For example, I'd like to have your tax troubles—"

"No, you wouldn't."

"Okay, I wouldn't. But I'm just saying. There are things going on in your life that I wish were going on in mine. Like lunch. Chewing. Sunrises."

"I'm usually in bed by then," she confessed.

"Well, you shouldn't be. Enjoy them while you can." It wasn't like me to be so serious about any particular subject, and I think she got it, because she just nodded and didn't make with the jokes.

"Before I get caught up in whatever fresh hell this is, please don't let me forget I'm supposed to baby-sit Baby Jon tomorrow night."

"Jon the Bee, Baby Jon the baby. Like that's not confusing. And don't forget your dad, John the Eternally Annoying."

"Don't give me anything new to worry about, I'm begging you."

"Me? It's not me, honey."

I got out to face the new problem. Maybe Nick was only there to break up my wedding. Sad when that was the cheerful thought I clung to.

# Chapter 11

"I'M the local liaison for the Driveway Killer task force," Nick explained, fussing with his coffee and finally putting it down on the coffee table in front of him.

"Driveway Killer?"

"The one who's yanking these poor women right out of their own driveways, strangling them, and then dumping the nude bodies in public parking lots?"

"Oh, *that* Driveway Killer." It was embarrassing to admit, but I never watched the news and I never read the paper. Not before I died, not after. (Well, I skimmed the birth announcements, but only since the Ant's eighth month, and never since Baby Jon came squalling into the world.) I mean, seriously. Why bother? It was never, ever anything good. Even in Minnesota, which had a pretty low crime rate, even here they only wanted to talk about the bad. Only the bad. If I wanted to get depressed, I'd read an Oprah pick.

I mean, I never even checked the weather reports anymore. And I sure as shit didn't watch TV; I was a DVD girl.

So while Nick was looking amazed that I could live in the same state with rampant media coverage (was there any other kind?) of a killer, Jessica was just nodding. My massive ignorance of current events was nothing new to her.

"Yeah, I've read about him."

"Who hasn't?" I asked gamely.

They ignored me, which I deserved. "And you're on the task force?"

"Yeah."

"To catch a serial killer."

"Yeah."

She tried to muffle it, but the laugh escaped anyway. I knew why—what had we just been talking about ten minutes ago? It was ludicrous.

But not to Nick, who was blinking fast and, I could tell, about to ask Jessica just what the hell her problem was. And never mind that she was the richest person in the state.

"It's late," I said. "She's tired. We're all tired. Long day."

"Uh . . . yeah." He checked his watch. "After ten already."

"I'm so sorry," Jessica said quickly. "I wasn't laughing at you, and I wasn't laughing at those poor girls."

"No," Nick lied, "I didn't think so." He turned back to me. "Anyway, Betsy, I'm sorry about it being so late, but I know about the hours you've been keeping lately, so I took a chance and swung by."

"You're welcome anytime, Detective," Sinclair said from the doorway.

Nick, in the act of picking up his cup, spilled his coffee . . . just a bit, but enough to wreck last month's issue of *Lucky*. I sure couldn't blame him; Sinclair was about as noisy as a dead cat.

"Jesus! You scared me. Which is not something we hotshot Minneapolis detectives like to admit," he joked, trying to cover the fact that his pulse had gone from ba-DUMP . . . ba-DUMP . . . ba-dump to BADUMP BADUMP BADUMP BADUMP!

"I apologize. It's Nicholas Berry, right?"

"Nick. Yeah."

Jessica gave me a look while they shook hands and sized up each other. Nick was built like a swimmer—lanky, with lean lines and big feet. His hair was bleached by the sun—he liked to save up and go diving on Little Cayman—and he had adorable laugh lines in the corners of his eyes.

Sinclair was broader and taller, and much older, but Nick had a gun, not to mention youth on his side. So you never knew.

The problem with the polite hand-shaking and "How do you do's" was that they had met before. In fact, Nick had come to me right after I'd risen as a vampire. In a moment of *extreme* weakness, I'd gotten (nearly) naked with him and it had sort of driven him out of his mind.

Sinclair had had to step in and make things right, and had used his vampire mojo to make Nick forget everything about that night. That I was dead, that Nick and I had seen each other (almost) naked, that he'd been a wreck when I wouldn't bite him again, wouldn't eat, wouldn't sleep. Everything.

The problem was (one of the problems), Nick kept popping back into my life at the weirdest times. Tina suspected he knew more than he was telling. And I honestly didn't know either way. But it wasn't exactly something we could come out and ask him.

So we sat around and pretended he didn't know we were vampires. And we didn't know if we were all pretending. Usually Sinclair and Tina could smell a lie from a hundred miles away, but Nick was a cop. He lied for a living.

"I'm Betsy's fiancé," Sinclair was explaining. "Eric Sinclair."

"Oh." Nick's face fell a bit, and Jessica shot me another look. I felt like throwing my tea in my face, just for an actual *physical* problem.

"We're getting married on July 4th."

"September 15th," I said quickly.

"As I said," Sinclair continued smoothly, "September 15. We do hope you can join us."

"Uh, thanks. I'll—thanks." He looked down at his hands for a minute and then back at me. "Anyway. The reason I stopped by. This killer—he's targeting your type."

"He is?" I was beyond appalled. A type? Gross!

"Tall blondes," Sinclair said. "With blue or green eyes." When we all looked at him, he said, "Some of us read the paper."

"Not that they're hard to come by in Minnesota," Nick added, "and maybe it's just a, you know, coincidence of geographical type, but still."

"What does VICAP say about it?" Sinclair asked.

Nick shrugged. "The feds won't catch this guy, no matter how many forms we feed into the computer. He'll get nailed by good old-fashioned cops."

I hoped Vicap, whoever he was, didn't hear Nick running down the FBI. Besides, that's what they did, right? Catch psychos? Not that I doubted Nick's ability. But I was glad he had help on this one. And really really glad I wasn't involved.

"And I just wanted to tell you to watch your ass," Nick was saying to, uh-oh, me. Time to tune back in. "Don't get out of the car until you've got your keys organized. Don't linger in the driveway, messing with groceries and stuff. *Watch* the driveway. Check the hedges when you pull in. This guy, I'm sure he's snatching them while they're distracted. They don't even have time to hit the horn. Half the time, there were people in the house, waiting for her. So be alert. Pay attention."

"Okay, Nick," I said obediently. It was, of course, ridiculous and sweet at the same time. The last thing I had to worry about was a serial killer. But it was adorable that he'd come by to give me a heads-up.

Unless he was fucking with us because he knew . . .

No, no. That was the way Sinclair looked at the world, like it was a big ball of mean out to get him. I swore that no matter how old I got, I wouldn't always assume the worst of people. I'd try, anyway.

"Are there any leads?"

"Just between us?"

"Well, us and the *Pioneer Press*."

He didn't smile at my sucky joke. "We've got shit. No witnesses, nobody even out walking his dog. He's really lucky, the asswipe."

"You'll get him," I said helpfully. Rah rah, the cops!

"Yeah, we will, unless he moves on. But he's going to have to slip up first." Nick's laugh lines suddenly doubled, and he stared at the stained magazine on the table. "And for him to slip up . . ."

"You'll get him," I said again. "And it was, I have to say, it was so nice of you to stop by. I appreciate the warning, and I'll be careful."

"Yes," Sinclair said, walking to the doorway in an obvious gesture for Nick to leave. Awkward! "It was very kind of you to stop by and warn my fiancée. I can assure you I'll look after her very carefully."

Now, if anybody else in the world said that, it'd seem loving and concerned. When Sinclair said it, it sounded vaguely like a threat. Certainly it was weird enough for Nick to give him the 'raised-eyebrows tough-cop' look.

Then he got up (reluctantly, it seemed to me) and said, "You just moved to the area, right, Mr. Sinclair?"

"No," Eric replied. I noticed he didn't ask Nick to call him Eric. But then, except for my roomies, nobody ever did. "I've been here a long time."

"Oh, okay. Remember what I said, Betsy."

"I will, Nick. Thank you again for stopping by."

"Jess, walk me out?"

She looked startled but gamely jumped to her feet. "Sure. You can check the driveway for us."

"Already did," he said, smiling at me, "on my way in."

# Chapter 12

I had my ear jammed so tightly against the door between the parlor and the hall, I probably had splinters in my cochlea. (It was weird how things like my tenth-grade biology report on the inner ear stayed with me for, like, ever.)

"Thanks again for coming over," Jessica said, sounding resigned. I figure I knew why. Nick was about to hit her up for a contribution to the Policeman's Ball, or whatever. I felt bad—Nick's devotion to me *was* a little on the obvious side—but what could I do? What could she do?

"I was really glad to see you were up this late, too," Nick said. "I've been meaning to talk to you for a couple of weeks, but things—you know. Work."

"Sure," Jess said. "What can I do for you?"

"Well, the captain mentioned he saw you at the new Walker exhibit, and I know you're into that stuff. I don't know if you heard, but—you probably heard—there's a new Matthew Barney exhibit opening this weekend, and I was wondering if you'd want to go."

"That'd be really mmm hmmm hmmm bmmm."

"Quite rude," Sinclair commented.

"Shhhh!"

"Bmmm mmm hmmm mmm?" Shit! They were walking through the house. There were about eight doors between me and the front door.

"Darling, whatever it is, she'll tell you about it the second she returns."

"Yeah, yeah." I turned. Sinclair was in my personal bubble, as usual, looking amused, also as usual. "I was just curious, that's all."

"Nosy."

"Probing," I insisted. "Like a reporter."

He put his hands on my shoulders and picked me up for a smooch. My feet were dangling a good six inches off the floor as I kissed him back, more a distracted peck because I was wondering what the other two were talking about. He nuzzled into the base of my throat but didn't bite, which is about as loving a gesture a vampire can make.

I guess that sounds romantic and all, and it kind of was, but it was hard to just, you know, dangle there. So I oomphed and umphed and climbed him until my ankles were crossed behind his back and my arms were looped around his neck.

"How delightful," he said. "This is bringing something more interesting than current events to mind."

"Perv. Can you believe Nick just stopping by like that?"

Sinclair's mouth went thin. "Yes."

"Wasn't that nice?"

"Yes. Nice."

"Oh, take it easy. Threatened much? Dude, take a break, go look in the mirror, and then relax, okay?"

"I didn't win you only to have you be distracted by some living meat with a shiny badge."

I gaped at him. Okay, I knew Sinclair generally felt vampires were superior to regular guys, but . . . living meat with a shiny badge?

"You didn't exactly win me," was the best I could come up with. "I'm not a Lotto ticket."

At my expression, he added, "You know you're attracted to shiny things. If you were a raven, you'd snatch that badge and go put it in your nest."

"Wh—uh—" Okay. One thing at a time. "Okay, listen, the reason I was trying to hear is, I just—Jessica said the dumbest thing on the way here. How sometimes she felt invisible next to me."

"Who said what?"

"Very funny. Don't you think that's dumb? I thought that was dumb."

"Dumb," he agreed.

I tried to kick him, but my feet were, of course, behind him. "This is serious! A) it's so not true, and b) it's terrible that she thinks that. But I think I know why she's got such a silly idea in her head."

"Because you're the eternally young, beautiful vampire queen no man can resist?"

"No!" Aw. But no. "She hasn't gone on a date in forever; she hasn't had a steady boyfriend since—jeez, when *did* she break up with dave?"

"Elizabeth."

I rested my chin on his shoulder and thought. "Was it before or after my dad threw the Ant the anniversary party at Windows? Because he—dave—came with her for that, but was that their 'we really can just be friends' date? Or were they really still living together then?"

"dave?"

"Yeah, after they broke up we decided he didn't deserve to have a capital letter in his name. Anyway, I need to fix her up. Trouble is, I'm running around with gay guys and vampires."

"That is a problem."

"Ha! So you agree vampires make rotten dates."

"That is a subject for another time. However, I think this could be very, very good for us."

"What?" I felt his forehead. "Are you all right? Because it almost seems like you're not following this at all."

"So we, and by we I do mean you, dearest, need to be supportive."

"What?"

I heard rapidly approaching footsteps, and Sinclair set me down. So things looked relatively innocent when Jessica burst into the room and yelled, "Nick asked me out!"

Then, the scowl. "I know you bums were talking about me."

*could you agree to go out with him when you were sure he liked me?* I tried to find a nice way to sum up my weirded-outness in one sentence. It was tough work, being an honest friend. "—I haven't seen you this, uh, excited in a long time."

"I haven't dated since way before you died." She hugged herself and spun in a small circle. "And he's *sooooo* cute!"

"Exceedingly cute," Sinclair encouraged. "Quite very much cute."

I figured it out right then. Sinclair never did anything without about nine secret agendas. He wanted a cop on the string. Awfully handy. Of course, it was only a first date, but if things went well . . .

"I thought you didn't go out with white guys," I pointed out. It was a straw, sure, but I was desperate to clutch at anything.

"I thought *you* said that was bigoted, asshole-esque, and twentieth-century."

"Oh, you're going to start listening to me now?" I grumbled. "I'm not saying I wasn't right, but your timing's a little weird."

"Now that that's settled, we have to decide on the appropriate post-gallery activity."

"That's not all we've got to decide on," I muttered and was—surprise—ignored.

"Because Detective Berry did the asking, I think we can assume he will want to treat you to whatever diversion you select."

"Dude. You are getting *way* overinvolved in this. Do you obsessively plan our dates? Not that we've ever actually been on a date . . ."

"Shut up, Betsy. For just this one time, it's about me. Go on, Eric."

"So it must be something you both like, that will not be terribly expensive, and that will encourage him to see you again in a social capacity, but not be too intimidating or force a false sense of intimacy."

I hitched up an imaginary belt. "That's a tall order, sheriff."

"Dinner anywhere decent is out. So is coming back here for a drink; this house definitely sends a message. Your idea of fast food is Red Lobster, so that lets out activities that are, ah, middle class. Which means . . ."

Jess waited. I waited. What the hell, I was curious. He could write a book. Nobody was good at dating. Everybody liked advice about it.

"Coffee and dessert at Nikola's," he decided after a moment's thought. "The coffee is first-rate, the food is excellent, it won't be terribly expensive if you don't eat a full meal, and the biscotti is homemade."

"*Oooooooh.* Sinclair, you are *it.*"

"Yes," he replied smugly.

"I am so scared right now," I said.

# Chapter 14

BEFORE I could take Sinclair aside and ream him out for . . . well, everything, and before I could take Jess aside and get the real scoop, the doorbell rang.

"Jessica, I would very much like to continue this conversation," he said, "but I must ask you to excuse us."

*"Oooooh,"* she replied. "Vampire biz, huh?" The evening must be one shock after another, because I hadn't heard this many *ooooohs* in . . . ever. "Who is it?"

"No one," he said calmly, "I wish you to meet." He inclined his head toward the door to the stairs. "If you please."

I didn't know what to say, and I could tell Jessica didn't, either. After an awkward couple of seconds, she shrugged and trotted out.

"Scream at me for that," he said, walking toward the front door, "later."

I was sort of terrified to see who it was, and as usual, my imagination ran away from me, because it was a perfectly nice-looking (beautiful, really) older woman. She looked like a librarian in her lilac blouse, gray skirt, sensible panty hose, and black pumps. They were leather and unscuffed.

She herself looked to be in her fifties, with black hair streaked with silver, and a handful of laugh lines in the corner of both eyes.

Her eyes.

There was something weird about her eyes. Sinclair had eyes like that, sometimes. When he was pissed at what was going on (read: other vampires trying to kill me), his eyes went like that.

They were so black you couldn't see into them, like those sun-glasses state troopers wear. You looked in and—it's hard to explain—you only saw yourself. Most times I could see his softer side, his love and worry for me, his amusement, the good stuff. And the times I couldn't see those things, I usually had my hands too full to worry about it.

I stared at her, a little scared, and she bowed and said something in (I think) rapid French.

Sinclair gave her a smile that looked 85 percent real. "Good evening, Marjorie."

"Your Majesties."

"It's good to see you again."

"And you, Sir."

Sinclair bent and kissed her hand, European style, but before anybody could kiss mine, I stuck it out to be shook. She did, smiling at me, and I almost dropped her hand. She was cold, which I expected, and I couldn't see anything in her eyes but me, which I did not.

An old one, I decided. A vampire who has seen absolutely everything—*everything*. And doesn't give a ripe shit anymore. About anything. I pitied them as much as I feared them. And I felt pretty sorry for them.

"It's nice to meet you," I lied.

She inclined her head. "Majesty. We have met before."

"No, we haven't." I'd never have forgotten those eyes. Not even Nostro had eyes like those. No, we hadn't met. And after today, I hoped we never would again.

"I was in a group that came to pay tribute after Nostro's, ah, accident on the grounds. Perhaps you didn't notice me."

"No, definitely not." Then, because it's possible she was disappointed (but who could tell? she was a damn robot), I added, "Sorry if I missed you in the crowd."

"Quite all right, my queen. Of late you had . . . a full agenda."

I laughed unwittingly. The robot had been programmed to make amusing observations! "That's one way of putting it."

"Something to drink? We have a Chateau Leoville Poyferre you might like."

We did?

"My king, that is as tempting an offer as I've received all year, but I must return to my duties. I only came by to beg the queen a favor."

She did? At least she was speaking English.

"Well," I said, "come on in."

"Thank you, my queen."

TO save time, we took the parlor right next to the front hall, and ole Marjie got right to it.

"As you know, I am head of the library downtown."

She *was* a librarian! I pretended like I knew, and nodded.

"I am starting a newsletter for the vampire community."

"You are?"

"It was your idea, my queen. 'Fer cryin' out loud, why don't you guys get a newsletter or something, I mean, cripes.' "

Sinclair grinned. "It has the ring of authenticity."

"When did I say that?"

"On the occasion of our first meeting, which you do not remember."

"Well, excuse me, I might have had a few things on my mind that day! If you don't come right up and introduce yourself, don't bitch about me not remembering you!"

"I apologize again," Marjorie said tonelessly, "for all my shortcomings."

"And you're stealing lines from *Gone With the Wind!*"

At last, the robot loosened up a little. She even smiled a little. "You have seen the movie?"

"Only about eight thousand times. It's not in the book, but it's a great scene . . . the one where Rhett almost gets called out, but he won't fight because he knows he can totally kick everybody's ass, and killing Charles Hamilton would be annoying and a big waste, so he just bows and leaves."

"I think that touches on a rather large theme of the book *and* the movie," Marjorie said thoughtfully, crossing her ankles like a lady. "Because we see Rhett's bad side frequently, but usually we only see his good side in relation to Scarlett."

"Yeah, like when he brought her the hat after the blockades tightened, and stole a horse for her so she could get out of town and see her mom. Who was dead. But Scarlett didn't know that."

Marjie was smiling patiently through my excited interruption. "But here, he has a chance to shoot a man from his own hated planter class, in a way that is societally acceptable, and instead, he—"

"Vamooses to the library, which is where he meets Scarlett and all that other stuff happens."

"Love. Death. War." She sighed. "Those were the days."

I ignored the uber-creepiness of the psycho librarian and went on in the same, uh, vein. "You know, I never thought of it like that! That from the very beginning, he was redeemable."

Marjorie shrugged. "I have been reading that book since the year it was published, and every time, I find something new. Extraordinary!"

Well, shit! Anybody who liked *GWtW* couldn't be that bad. Right? Right. "Listen, I'm sorry we got off on the wrong foot. I'm terrible with names and faces, and I'm sorry I didn't remember you."

"That's quite all right, my queen," she said, and this time it seemed like she meant it. "As I am here to ask a favor, I'm hardly in a position to sulk."

"Yeah, well. Never stopped me. What's up?"

"Well, as I mentioned earlier, I'm the local librarian."

Local library? As in, there was more than one? "Sure, sure. I remember."

Sinclair shot me a look, which I pretended not to see. He hadn't said a word for a couple minutes, but he seemed relieved we weren't going to scratch each other's eyes out.

"And as I said, I will be starting a newsletter. It will be online and only viewable to vampires who have the appropriate passwords, etcetera."

"You're not worried about someone hacking into it?"

She smiled thinly. "No."

"Right. Okay, go on."

"I would like you to contribute to it, my queen."

"Contribute . . . you mean, like write something for it?"

"Yes, ma'am. Every month."

"But . . . come on, Marjie—"

"Marjorie." Sinclair and Marj corrected me simultaneously.

"—you must have a million people who can do this for you."

"That is not the issue, my queen. As you of course have discovered yourself, many of our kind are having, ah, difficulty accepting your new . . . position."

"That was supertactful."

Another tiny smile. "Thank you, my queen. I feel, and many of my counterparts concur, that this would be a way for the community to get to know you. Perhaps come to appreciate the . . . finer qualities that aren't, ah, immediately apparent."

"Wow." I was shaking my head in total admiration. "You

should work for the United Nations. Seriously. I mean, when *he* tries that stuff, I just get pissed."

Ole Marjie inclined her head modestly. Sinclair gave me a look but still didn't comment.

"What would you want me to write?"

"Oh, whatever you wish. Neighborhood observations, essays on the eternal struggle between man vs. vampire, the pros and cons of keeping sheep—"

"I've got it!"

"Ah, the sheep issue. I admit, it can be controversial—"

"Shut up about the sheep, Marj." Sinclair winced, but I didn't give much of a shit. "No, I'm going to do a Dear Betsy letter. What's the one thing I've wished I could have since I woke up dead?"

"A sheep?"

"Marjorie, enough! No, I wished there was someone I could ask about vampire stuff and I'd get the straight shit in return. Not political shit, not 'oh, it's okay if you kill people as long as you're aligned with so-and-so' stuff. *Real* stuff. It'll be a 'Dear Betsy' column. Ann Landers for vampires!" As Jess would say, *"Oooooooh!"* I could hardly sit still, I was so excited!

Sinclair was rubbing his eyes. Marjorie looked at him for help and, correctly guessing none was forthcoming, looked back at me. "Ah . . . my queen, I admit I had a more, ah, *scholarly* approach in mind . . ."

"Then boy, did you come to the wrong house. I didn't even finish college."

"Oh."

"I bet you did, though."

"I have fourteen Ph.D.s."

"Geek, huh?" Ack! Fourteen! No wonder I got her mixed up with a robot. "Anyway, back to me. When do you need my first column?"

"Ah . . . whenever you wish. The newsletter will be published on your schedule, of course, and—"

"I'll have it for you by the end of the week. There's not a moment to lose! Just think, there's new vampires walking around right this second who don't have a clue how to act!"

"And you will infect them all."

"What?"

"I said, it sounds like we'll have a ball. I shall go back to the library at once and . . . prepare."

"Great!" I jumped up. Sinclair slowly stood, like an old, old man. Marjorie stood the same way; it was weird. They both looked crushed and knowing at the same time.

He kissed her hand again. "Thank you."

"My king, I only do my duty."

"For coming by."

"Sir, I am your servant."

"Yeah, thanks," I butted in, because I had the weird feeling they weren't talking about what I thought they were talking about. "Send me your e-mail address, and I'll zap the column over to you in the next few days. I'm TheQueen1@yahoo.com."

Was that a shudder? Naw. My imagination was working overtime. And speaking of overtime, I could hear Marc park his shitbox car and come bounding up the walk. How he kept his energy after fifteen hours on his feet in the E.R. was beyond me.

He popped the front door open and spotted us in the entryway. He covered the distance between us with half of one of his characteristic long lopes, and his green eyes brightened. "Hi, guys!"

I was torn. On the one hand, as he was generally a depressed individual with big problems (gay, dying father, premature balding), I was always happy to see him happy. We had met when he was moments from throwing himself from the top of the hospital at which he worked too many hours. I talked him out of jumping and took him home. He'd been hanging out with us ever since. And in the past few months, he'd had his dad set up at a great private—I guess it was a hospice, except it was a private home, and the nurse who lived there only took care of three people. So it wasn't like being stuffed in a nursing home. Anyway, he'd gotten his dad squared away and visited him as often as he could stand (I guess it was kind of a strained relationship), he'd gotten a new boss at work, he was growing out his hair, and he'd had a date in the last five weeks.

On the other hand, I wanted him nowhere near Marjorie. Marc was like a puppy around vampires . . . had no clue how totally friggin' dangerous they really were.

"So what's doing? What are you guys up to? What's going on?" Arf, arf, sniff, sniff, sniff.

Marjorie's delicate nostrils flared. "Your pet smells like blood."

"Yeah, kid fell out of his tree stand and bonked himself a good one," Marc said cheerfully, ignoring—or not hearing—"pet."

"Bled all over me. I had to get a new scrub top, but man, do I need

a shower. Hi, by the way," he added, sticking out his hand. "I'm
Marc Spangler. I live here with Betsy and Eric."

She looked at the hand like he'd offered her a dead garter
snake, and I could feel my eyes widen, practically bulge in their
sockets. I got ready to rip her a new asshole—what was it with old
vampires and being so shitty to regular people?—when Sinclair's
hand clamped over mine . . . hard.

I yelped just as Marjorie decided to shake Marc's hand. "You
live here with them?" she asked.

"Yup," he replied cheerfully. "It's not home, but it's much.
Olivia Goldsmith wrote that, by the way."

"Mmmm. She's the one who died of liposuction, yes?"

"No," he corrected. "She died of complications after lipo."

"I see. If you live here with them, why do you go to a job?"

"Uh . . ." He actually thought it over for a couple seconds.
"Because I'm not a two-legged parasite?"

"Mmmm." She caught the neckline of his scrub top and
pulled; with a squeak, he bent down to her. He had a foot and
thirty pounds on her, but she manhandled him (no pun intended)
easily, like he was a mannequin made of feathers. "But you
*haven't* been bitten," she said to his neck. "Yet. Mmmm . . ."

I opened my mouth. *Take your fucking hands off him NOW*
was already in my head and trying to rush out of my mouth when
Sinclair squeezed again. I groaned instead; I could feel the little
bones in my hand grinding together. He wasn't hurting me, but I
sure wouldn't want to spend a day doing that.

"Marjorie, don't you have business to be about?" he asked
calmly.

Totally distracted, she looked up, and I was shocked to see
her fangs had come out. "Eh? Oh." It was obvious, when she let
go and Marc popped back upright, that she was massively disappointed. "Yes, of course. Forgive me. I haven't dined yet this
evening, and it's made me forget my manners. I will take my
leave."

"Nice to meet you!" Marc chirped. And as she bowed and then
let herself out the front door, I looked at Marc and saw it: he didn't
remember the last minute. He'd had no sense of being in danger,
no sense of inappropriateness or cruelty from Marjie. As far as he
was concerned, he'd met a nice older lady on his way in, and now
he was going to grab a shower.

"I think I'll go grab a shower," he said. "Later, guys."

I started to have a dim idea why Sinclair had a) gotten rid of

Jess, b) been polite under extreme provocation, and c) didn't let me hang myself.

"I hope you took a good look, dear," he said, listening to the car drive away. "Because that is the oldest vampire you're likely to ever meet."

"She's an asshole."

He shrugged. "She's old. It's . . . difficult to surprise her. You did, though." He smiled, and it was like the sun coming up on the last day of winter. "You did very well."

"It's hard to hate anyone who has such good taste in movies. Though if she'd put another hand on Marc, I would've had to bring down the spank."

He got this weird look on his face, like he was horrified but wanted to laugh, too. "You—you must not. Or, if you decide, you must discuss it with me first. Never touch her alone. Never, understand?"

"Okay, Sinclair. Because that's *sooooo* me. Maybe we can form a committee and vote on every single thing."

His eyes went narrow but he hung onto the smile. "Listen, please. She is old, as I have said, and she has many friends. Friends she made herself, if you understand my meaning. She is . . . I guess you would say she is set in her ways. The old ways."

"Yeah, I get it. She's old; she's a stubborn jerk; she thinks humans are moronic lunch boxes; she's got a million friends; and if she doesn't like me, she could cause a lot of trouble for me."

"Us," he corrected. "It's important to keep Marjorie and those like her on our side. When I went to Europe last fall . . ."

He'd never talked about the trip much. Brought me back a nice present and mentioned he'd met up with friends, and that was that. "Yeah?"

"Let's just say I was dismayed by how many vampires were *not* on our side."

"Yeah, but you fixed it, right? You always fix everything. Like tonight. And ow, by the way." I flexed my hand, which, if I'd still been alive, would have been throbbing painfully. "Next time just wave a hand puppet at me, willya? I *need* this hand."

"To write your 'Dear Betsy' column."

"Was that an eye roll?" I demanded. "Are you rolling your eyes at me, Eric Sinclair?"

"Oh, no, beloved. I would never so disrespect my queen."

I laughed. "You're so full of shit your eyes are brown."

"They *are* brown," he admitted, taking me in his arms. He

kissed me for such a lovely long time, I forgot about Margaret. Marjie. Whoever.

"This really isn't the time or place," I muttered into his mouth as he lowered me to one of the phenomenally uncomfortable couches in the parlor.

"I'll have ample notice if someone is coming," he said, pulling open my blouse and yanking my pants down to my knees.

"What if I'm the one coming?" I teased, caressing the bulge in his trousers.

He groaned. "Don't do that unless you want to be finished before we start."

"Eric, you're talking like a man who's being neglected."

He braced himself over the couch, unzipped his fly, pulled my panties aside, and slid into me, neat as a magic trick. "I am neglected," he murmured in my ear. "Whenever I'm not inside you, I'm neglected."

"That's really lame," I whispered back. I braced a heel on the couch arm and met his thrusts. "And we're gonna break this couch."

*Fuck the couch.*

That thought—cool and uncaring, but hot at the same time— pretty much did me in; I heard something crack in the couch and then I was coming, clutching at Eric while his voice ran through my head, a vivid whisper of longing.

*O my own my Elizabeth my Queen I love love love love . . .*

I hope he "loved" fixing couches, because that was probably next on our agenda.

He groaned and collapsed over me, which elicited a groan of my own. "Kill me," he mumbled. "I'm an old man, and you're trying to kill me."

"Hey, this wasn't *my* idea, pal. And you're still in your prime. Your immortal dead guy prime." I giggled.

"Are you laughing at me, darling?"

"No, Eric," I said gravely, biting my lower lip so I wouldn't do it again.

"It would crush my tender emotions to know you were laughing at me during this vulnerable time."

"I'd never do that, Eric. So what was it like, inventing the telegraph?"

He chased me up the stairs, and I made a mental note to have someone take a look at that couch later in the week.

# Chapter 15

I T was about five A.M., and I was getting ready for bed (finally! what a long, weird day) when there was a brisk rap-rap at my bedroom door.

"Come on in," I called, buttoning the last button on my new jammies. Aw, they were so soft, so sweet to the touch . . .

Jessica opened the door and stuck her head in and then groaned when she saw me. "Jeez, Betsy! I'll buy you friggin' decent pajamas, okay? You don't have to wear those pieces of shit."

"What?" I cried. "These are brand-new."

"Yeah? What's Sinclair say about them?"

"What part of 'brand-new' aren't you getting? He hasn't seen them yet."

"He sees those, the wedding's off."

"Oh, shut the hell up." I stepped to the mirror and admired the navy blue flannel and red polka dots. They were too long in the pants and arms (I'd found them in the men's section, where I frequently shopped because I was so fucking tall), but a few washings should take care of that. And they were *warm*. "You didn't come up here to critique my nightwear. At least I hope you didn't. Because, really, how lame would that be?"

"No, I sure didn't. But I could sure spend half the night doing it."

"This from someone who wears football jerseys to bed."

"Totally different thing."

"I think I liked it better when you weren't talking to me."

"Too late now. Listen, I wanted to catch you before you guys went to bed—where *is* Sinclair?"

"He made a beeline for the computer after ole Long in the Tooth and 'Tude left."

"Huh. He used to practically count the seconds before you went to bed so you guys could do it."

"We already did," I admitted, "after Maggie left."

"Yet another room you defiled. And Maggie would be the vampire he didn't want me to meet?"

I shuddered. "Don't bitch, J. He was right. She's creepy. She's got eyes like a doll's."

"Barbie Doll or American Girl?"

"Blank." I gestured to my face, trying to convey in five words or less how creepy the woman had been. "Shiny."

"Shiny?" I could see Jess was trying not to laugh. She'd never met Nostro. In fact, I was the baddest vampire she'd ever met, after I'd read the Book of the Dead and gone evil. Which was to say, she'd never met a really bad vampire.

"She almost chomped Marc, and not only did he let her grab him, he didn't remember that she grabbed him. Stay the fuck away, I'm serious."

"Well, if Sinclair's worried about her, that's good enough for me. I've got enough creepy vampires to worry about." She plopped herself into what I always thought of as Maric's Chair. "Listen, are you okay with me going out with Detective Nick?"

"If you're gonna date him, you should probably get in the habit of referring to him just by his first name."

She waved that away. "Yeah, yeah. Are you?"

"Sure. Yeah. It was just a surprise, that's all. A good surprise," I added hastily. "Sinclair's right, somebody should have snatched you up ages ago."

She smiled thinly. "Yeah, well. Nobody's gotten around to it yet."

"I was just thinking that it had been a while for you . . . wasn't dave the last guy you were with?"

She nodded, fiddling with the neckline of her shirt. "Lower-case dave, yup, I remember."

"Okay, then. Look, we know Nick's nice, he's great at his job, he *looks* . . . yum. Go for it. But . . ."

I trailed off because I was torn. Did I warn my best friend that my fiancé was going to do everything in his power to make that relationship work because he was sneaky and that's how he operated? Nick might like Jessica for herself (or not; we hadn't established that yet), but Sinclair liked Nick for his badge.

Or did I keep quiet out of loyalty to my fiancé, the vampire king?

"But . . . ?" Jessica prompted.

"But . . . you . . . should . . . wear clean underwear."

She gave me an odd look. "Thanks for the tip."

"I gotta admit, I was kind of surprised you said yes."

She shrugged and picked a cloth pill off the arm of the chair. She was very fidgety tonight. "I dunno. It's great being with you guys and all, and living here, but the excitement of being best friends with the queen of the vampires doesn't exactly butter my muffin at night, you know? I mean in bed. Because we're all up and running around at night. But you know what I mean, right?"

"Sure. I hope it works out."

"With Sinclair on my side, how can it not?"

"I know! My God, was that weird or what?"

"You boy has a sinister metrosexuality going on," she agreed, "and that's a fact."

"That's one way of putting it. Oh, and get this! I have a job again. I'm writing a column for the new vampire newsletter."

"*What* did you just say?"

"I know!" I plopped down on the bed and propped my chin on my elbows, slumber-party-gossip style. "Can you believe it? Talk about practical. How totally unlike vampires to do something that doesn't involve beheadings or the mass slaughter of innocents."

"Maybe," she suggested, "it'll be an evil newsletter."

"Great. Something new to worry about. Which reminds me—"

There was a tentative knock on my door, one I knew well. "Come in, Jon!"

"Ooooooh," Jessica said, not looking at me. "I forgot to ask you how Sinclair reacted to the news of his roommate."

"It wasn't pretty," I mumbled back. Then: "Hi, Jon! You caught us. Everybody's about ready to turn in."

"Yeah . . . I just got up, actually. This is the one time of day that our schedules actually mesh."

"How interesting," Jess said sweetly, "that you've planned that out already. You've been here . . . what? A day?"

He looked flustered (and adorable!) as he stood in my bedroom doorway, shifting his weight from one foot to the other. "Well, not the one time," he explained. "Because, you know, it's wintertime. So I'll still be awake when the sun starts to go down, and—"

"Jon. My girl has to get ready for bed, and her fiancé's gonna be here any minute. So what's up?"

Not for the first time, I had the impression Jessica didn't much care for Jon.

"I, uh, because I'm going to be in town, I had this idea. Actually, I got it at school. I'm taking a writing class at the U—"

"That'll come in handy on the farm."

"Jessica!" I gasped. What did she have against farmers? "Go on, Jon. We're *all* listening." I glared at her for good measure.

"Well, anyways, I was going to the U last year and then I went back home—"

"Which we already know . . ." Jessica prompted him by making the "speed up" motion.

"—anyway, today I re-registered, and one of my new classes is—well, last year I took a class called The Writing Sampler—and this year I want to focus on the bio class."

"—logy or graphy?" I asked, having trouble seeing where this was going.

"Oh. Biography."

"Is that the one where you write your life story?" I asked, delighted. Yes! Something to keep him busy, and off of me! And off Sinclair's radar, best of all. "What a great idea, Jon! You've lived an incredible life and you're, what? Fifteen?"

"Twenty," he said thinly. "And a biography is when you write about someone else."

"Uh-oh," Jess muttered.

"Oh. Then—oh. Oh! Uh . . ." I blinked rapidly and tried to keep my mouth from popping open. "Well, that's . . . really flattering."

"I think it'd be a great project."

"Jon, you can't write about her and then show it to all your little school chums. We're trying to keep a low profile, here."

"Oh, I know," he said with painful earnestness. "I already told my instructor—"

"You did *what?*" we screamed in unison.

"—that it was fiction. A fake biography about a fictional character. He loved the idea."

*Then he's missing the point of the class,* I thought but didn't say.

"I mean, come on, you guys. Who'd take it seriously anyway? 'Oh, here's a biography tell-all of a vampire who lives here in the Cities.' Of course he's going to assume it's a fake. In fact," he added proudly, "he can't wait to read it. Said in twenty years of teaching no one's come up with that idea before."

"You didn't come up with it, either!"

He ignored her and looked at me. "So will you do it?"

"Do *what*?"

"Tell me the story of your life."

I opened my mouth.

"No," Jessica said.

I looked at him.

"No," Jessica said. "Bets, I'm doing you the hugest favor of your life here, right now. No. I'm saving you so much trouble right now. From *people*. You know. No."

Jon glared at her. "It's not up to *you*."

"Isn't there a combine you should be changing the oil on?"

"Isn't there a benefit you should be chairing?"

"Come on, guys," I said automatically, thinking.

I knew what Jess was getting at; she was implying that Sinclair would totally flip his gourd. As he sort of had when I told him Jon was staying with us. What could be worse than that?

Aw, Sinclair wouldn't mind. He had more important things to worry about than Jon's schoolwork. Frankly, with vampires like Marjorie running around town, I was kind of surprised he even noticed Jon was here.

And Jon looked so adorably hopeful, so rumpled and sweet in his jeans and yellow "Luke, I'm not your father" T-shirt. And bare feet! My God, you could practically see the straw sticking out of his hair.

"Wellllllllllll . . ."

"No."

"Maybe we could try it," I said. "Just to see how it goes. Maybe a couple chapters."

"*Noooooooooooooooo!*" Jessica yowled.

That's when Sinclair walked in. "What is going *on* in here?"

# Chapter 16

"**J**ON wants to—"

"That was rhetorical; I heard the discussion on the way up the stairs." He strode into the room, put a hand on Jon's face, and shoved. Jessica darted to the door and actually had it open in time for Jon to stumble through it. She took one look at Eric, said, "Good night, guys," and went through the door herself, at a slightly more dignified speed.

"*Sinclairrrrrrr!*" I yowled. "You can't go around manhandling my friends that way. No wonder he doesn't think I should marry you."

"I know exactly why the infant thinks I shouldn't marry you." He had his back to me, staring at the shelves full of CDs. He'd been sleeping in here for a couple months, but he had yet to move any of his own things in. All his suits and underwear and toiletries (if a vampire needed such things) were in his own room down the hall.

Why had I never wondered what that meant before? That he came to fuck and then left? Unlike me, Eric could move around all day, provided he stayed out of direct sunlight. So I figured, anything was an improvement over all the fighting and massive sexual tension we'd always ever known. And because I assumed after the wedding we'd share a room, not just a bed.

I'd assumed other things before. About Eric. And been wrong.

Worst things first. "You're being a big baby about this. You were a jerk about him staying with us for a while—"

"We are not the Super 8 Motel."

"Says one of the three people who moved in without paying a dime for the place! Or asking me! *I* at least sold my house for the down payment."

"It is childish to pretend it's the same thing," he sniffed. "I was the king, moving to an appropriate domicile to be at my queen's side. Jon is sniffing up your back trail like an addled bull in the pasture."

Wow. He was *really* mad. The farm metaphors only came out when he was superpissed.

"Eric, he's, like, twelve years younger than I am! I'd never go out with someone like that."

He turned away from the wall of Cool. His night attire, I couldn't help but notice, was exceptional: black silk pajama pants. And nothing else. I wished we could quit arguing so I could see if his nipples tasted as good as they looked. "You're sixty years younger than I am."

Nipples be damned! "What?"

"I said, you're sixty years younger than I am."

"Wh—buh—" I honestly never thought of it in terms like that anymore. I used to, when I was a brand-new vampire and he wanted me to choose between him and Nostro, but then I chose, and it's never come up since.

Unless Sinclair thinks it's time to make another choice . . .

"Look, Eric, you're just being . . ." I flapped my hands helplessly. "Well, weird. You're being weird about this. It's you I love. Not Jon. Not Nick."

His eyes narrowed. "What does Nick have to do with anything?"

"I'm just saying! Everyone's so concerned about my love life, nobody's listening to me, to what I want. It doesn't matter how many Bees or cops end up living here; it doesn't change how I feel about you. I made my choice, *you're* who I want to be with. You! The sneakiest, creepiest, studliest guy I've ever known."

He unclenched a bit. "I suppose I must take that as a compliment."

"I don't care how you take it, but be nicer to Jon. Stop shoving him around; it just showcases your—I can't believe I'm using this word in reference to you—insecurity."

"That term is exactly why I haven't yet brought up the subject of your new sleepwear."

"What?" I spread my arms, like Christ on the cross. "You think I'm insecure and that's why I wear this stuff? You're on drugs! Don't you think the dots bring out my highlights?"

He grinned, started to say something, but then cut himself off and turned back to the wall of Cool.

"How have I not noticed these before?" he asked.

Because we appeared to be done fighting, I didn't say anything, but boy, I was thinking plenty. Like: *well, if you came here for anything but sex, you'd probably notice all sorts of cool things.*

"*Various Hits of the Eighties.* Cyndi Lauper." Sinclair was flipping through the top shelf of CDs. "*Greatest Hits of Duran Duran. All Dance Hits of the Eighties. Eighties, Eighties, Eighties. More of the Jammin' Eighties. Madonna: True Blue. The Pet Shop Boys. The Beastie Boys.*"

"What can I say? I'm eclectic."

"Yes. Eclectic. That wasn't the word that sprang to my mind, I admit."

"Don't tell me you're one of those music snobs." But of course, he was. Nothing in his car but Rachmaninoff.

"No, no. The wedding's off."

"What?"

"I said, you have to take that off."

"Oh." Weird vampire hearing. It was either really good or really bad. "Okay, okay. Do you want to borrow—"

"No!"

"All *right,* don't *yell.*" I moodily started unbuttoning my flannel top. "And stop pushing Jon around, I mean literally pushing him. How'd you like it if he put his big ole farm boy mitts on your face and shoved?"

"I would love that," Sinclair replied with scary sincerity.

"Is that the stench of a dead goat I smell, or your testosterone? Cripes, throttle back. Besides, you're missing my point. I'm in here with you, aren't I? I don't go to Nick's place or climb into Marc's bed—I notice you're not weird about Marc—"

"Is that supposed to be a joke? I'd be infinitely more worried about Marc if we were the same suit size."

Hmm, good point. Moving on! "Maybe one of my undead superpowers is to make gay people straight, but I don't see you worrying too much about it."

"No," he agreed, sitting on the edge of the bed and drumming the fingers of his left hand on his right knee. "I don't worry too much about it."

"Right!"

"Also, you are not undressing nearly quickly enough."

"And I'm not in the Bee's bed, wherever that one even is—"

"Second floor. Third one down the hall, right side."

"See? I should be worried about *you* sleeping with him, you're so obsessed."

"Territorial," he conceded. "Not obsessed."

"But it's you I want to be with—did we not figure this all out in October?" I waved my arms, which, as I was unbuttoning, flapped like a clothesline in a windstorm. "It's *your* voice I hear in my head, nobody else's. That should prove you've got nothing to worry about."

"What?"

Oh, fuck.

# Chapter 17

"**Now**, don't freak out." Stupid, stupid! I'd meant to tell him, but not like *this*. I was thinking more along the lines of giving him a giant cookie frosted with "I can hear you in my head, lover!" Maybe for Valentine's Day. Twenty years from now.

"What did you say?"

"Okay, it's like this." I hurried over and sat beside him on my—our!—bed, and flung my arms around his shoulders, which wasn't unlike hugging the big oak tree in the backyard. "When we make love, I can hear what you're thinking. It's in my head."

Nothing. He sat stiffly, like we were playing statues.

I hugged harder. "And the thing is, I've been trying to figure out the right time to tell you, and there just never was one. But now that I see how insec—how worried you are about our houseguest, I figured it would be a good time to *prove* my love and how much we are *meant to be together* because in my whole life and death, I never heard anybody in my head, ever, not one time."

If anything, he got stiffer. "You hear. Me. In your. Head?" he asked carefully.

"Yes. But only during lovemaking. Never before and never after. I mean, I have no idea what you're thinking right now. Although, uh, I can probably figure it out."

"For. How. Long?"

"Since that time in the pool—the first time. And right up until . . . well, earlier. In the parlor, after Margaret left."

"Marjorie," he corrected automatically. He pried my hands off him and pulled my arms away.

"Don't be mad," I said, probably the stupidest line ever, right up there with, "she didn't mean anything to me."

He left.

I sat there and stared at the open doorway. Okay, I knew he wasn't going to take the news well, and I told him in a shitty way. At least I hadn't told him out of spite. But still—he'd had no prep at all. And now he had left, walked out.

I got ahold of myself. I wasn't going to sit on the bed cowering and waiting for him to come back and yell at me, or possibly throw a credenza at me. I jumped to my feet and ran to the door . . . where I promptly smacked so hard into the returning Sinclair I hit the floor like a backhanded pancake.

"Damn," I gasped. "You must have really tooled up those stairs."

"This is no time for one of your amusing pratfalls," he snapped. He stepped over me (he didn't even help me up!) and dropped something big on the bed, something that gave off its own dust.

I was totally horrified to see it was the Book of the Dead.

"Get that thing off my sheets," I ordered. "I just got those last week at Target! They're flannel!"

He ignored me, bent over the book, and flipped through it. Finally (a miracle with neither a table of contents nor an index) he got to the yucky nasty page he wanted, straightened, and pointed.

"What? You want me to . . . forget it, no way. I'm done with that—hey!" He'd crossed the room in a blink, seized my arm, and dragged me over to the Book. "Okay, *okay,* don't *pull.* These are new, too."

I bent over the horrible, horrible thing, written in blood by an insane vampire who could see the future. And never spell-checked, I might add, just to add to the overall fun.

"Okay, here we go—here? Okay. 'And the Queene shall noe the dead, all the dead, and neither shall they hide from her nor keep secrets from her.' " I stood up. "Right, so? We figured that's why I can see the ghosts and nobody else can."

"Keep reading."

"Eric—"

"*Read.*"

I hurriedly bent back to the homework from Hell. " 'And shalt noe the king, and all the king's ways, for all their reign o'er the dead, and the king shalt noe hers.' There, cheer up!" I straightened (please God, for the last time . . . no more reading tonight). "See?

I know your ways, and you know mine. So . . . I mean, this is deeply meaningful because . . ."

"As you said. You can read my mind during . . . intimate moments."

"Yeah," I nodded. "I told you that. Remember? Told you? As in, didn't keep it a secret?" *For more than eight months?* Shut up, brain.

"I cannot read yours," he pointed out.

"Yeah, I figured," I confessed. "I tried to sort of, uh, feel you out a couple times. But I didn't get anything back."

He just stared at me. I knew that look: penetrating and faraway at the same time. There was some serious thinking going on behind those black eyes.

"Eric . . ."

He took a step back.

"Okay, you're mad. I don't blame you; it was a rotten way to find out. Only, I knew you'd be like this! That's why I was scared to tell you!" Worst. Apology. Ever!

"I am not mad," he said.

"Eric, you're the one I want to be with."

"The Book begs to differ."

"Jeez, we've only been together for two months . . . we've only *known* each other since April. Give me time to 'noe your ways,' dammit, and you need time to noe—know mine. Just because you can't—you know. Just because you can't right this minute doesn't prove anything. And I'm sorry, okay? I'm sorry I didn't tell you. I wanted to."

"I understand," he said with horrifying distance, "why you could not."

"Eric, *you're* the one I'm marrying!"

"I'm the one you keep changing the date on," he said. "Perhaps because you have realized I am not your equal? Being a soft-hearted wretch, I can see why you would not be up to the task of telling me face-to-face that your feelings had changed."

"That has nothing to do with it!" I screeched. "Oh my God, did you just call me a wretch?" A coward, too! He'd turned telepathy into an excuse to postpone the wedding? Men! "How you could jump to a conclusion like that?"

"Yes, you are correct, it is simply a wondrous coincidence."

"I'm just disorganized, moron! It's not a personal observation! See, see? This is why I didn't tell you, I knew you'd freak out and get pissed."

"I'm not pissed," he said coolly. And . . . he didn't *sound* pissed. He didn't sound like anything I could figure. I didn't know whether to run and put my arms around him, or jump out the window and get away from him. The four feet between us yawned; it could have been the edge of a cliff. "I'm . . . surprised."

He was a liar, that's what he was. Finally, I recognized the emotion. I'd never seen it on his face before, so no wonder it took me a few minutes: it was fear.

Not for me. I'd seen that before, plenty of times. No, this was something else. He was afraid, all right.

*Of* me.

# Chapter 18

Dear Betsy,

*I'm a new vampire (I was attacked and killed by another vampire while I was on my senior class trip, eight years ago), and I'm not sure exactly of the protocol now. Things were different under Nostro, but I'm not sure how things are with you. There's a girl in my life I "see" once in a while, and she lets me bite her, but she thinks it's just part of fun. Sometimes I'll make friends with a new girl and bite her a few times, too. It's hard because I have to feed every day, but I don't want to kill anyone. Do you have any advice?*

Chewin' on 'em in Chaska

Dear Chewin':

*Well, you've got the right idea, anyway. Don't kill them, not any of them, if you can help it. They can't help being alive any more than you can help being dead. I try to go out and bite bad guys . . . you know, someone who's trying to drag me into a dark alley to "meet" his friends, someone I catch breaking into my car . . . like that. I feel like they got punished for whatever felony they were attempting, and I got to eat. Try that for a while and see how it works.*

*If you ever meet that special someone, you could tell her your secret and maybe she could help you out. Also, as you get older, you won't need to feed as much. Cheer up. This, too, shall pass.*

"It's pretty good," Jessica said. "Because the newsletter is new, I guess you had to make up the first few questions?"

"Yeah."

"Well, pretty soon you'll start to get real letters, so that's okay. But this isn't too bad."

I started to cry.

"Jeez!" Jessica said, putting the paper down and hurrying over to me. "I had no idea you were such a touchy edit! It's great, it's really great for your first time. Lots of—uh—lots of good advice."

"Sinclair moved out of my room," I sobbed.

"Well, honey, I don't know that he ever actually moved *in*."

I cried harder.

"Uh, sorry. Did you guys have a fight?"

"A big one. The worst one."

"Worse than when you thought he was putting the moves on your sister?"

"I wish that's what it was," I wept.

"Okay. Is it something you can tell me about?"

"No," I sobbed. Sinclair's humiliation was still fresh; the last thing I was going to do was spread it around.

She had poured a fresh cup of tea for me—we were in the kitchen—and now sat down in the chair next to me. My feeble letter lay on the table between us. I'd been desperate to distract myself from the fight. Thus, Dear Betsy.

"Well, honey, is it something bad you did?"

"I didn't think so. I thought it was good. Proof of something good. But he didn't agree. And then he left. It's been two nights, and he hasn't been back; I haven't even seen him in the house. I've seen George the Fiend more than my own fiancé."

"Right, but . . . you're not going around killing Girl Scouts or anything, right?"

I shook my head. "Nothing like that."

"And you didn't read the Book . . . Betsy!" she nearly screamed at my feeble nod. "Did you turn evil again?"

"I wish. I only read the paragraph he made me. He was just making a point. And then he slammed it shut and took it away, and took himself away, too."

"Well, is it something you can say you're sorry for?"

"I don't think I can apologize for this. Besides, I already did. We were pretty mad, though. He might not have noticed. But it was a secret for a long time. I guess I can apologize for not telling him right away."

"That's a start, right?"

"He's afraid of me now," I practically whispered.

Jessica burst out laughing. She laughed so hard she actually slapped the table with her palm. "Scared! Sinclair! Of you!" Slap, slap. "Oh, that's a good one." She sighed and wiped her eyes. "Tell it again; I needed that."

I glared. "I'm serious, Jessica. The thing I told him made him be scared of me. In the past he thought it was cool that I could do things other vampires couldn't—"

"And let's not forget, he wasn't above using you to get what he wanted," she pointed out, her cheeks still shiny from laugh-tears.

"Yeah, I know. But he was never, you know, *scared* of the things I could do. Just . . . impressed, like. He thought they were neat, and he thought it was great that I killed Nostro and what's-her-name, and he thinks it's great that the devil is my sister's mother, but he was never afraid *of me*. I'm telling you. That's what's happened now."

"This thing—whatever it is—it's made him scared of you."

I rubbed my eyes (pure force of habit; I had no tears) and nodded.

"Okay, so you should apologize for keeping the secret and then you gotta wait for him to get over his bad self."

"Wait?"

"Honey, have you *seen* the man? Does he strike you as the type of fellow who's scared of anything, much less his own girlfriend? He's gonna need some serious time to get used to the idea."

"Wh—how much time?"

"You're immortal," she pointed out. "What's the rush?"

"But . . . wedding stuff. We've got to plan the wedding. I can't do it by myself."

"So postpone it again."

"I can't," I said, appalled all over again. "Oh, I just can't. He's got it in his head that—never mind. But one thing I absolutely can't do is cancel it. Full speed ahead on all wedding prep."

"Are you *sure* this horrible thing you've done, it's not evil? What am I saying, it's Sinclair. Evil doesn't scare him. He probably gets off on it, in his heart of hearts."

"Trust me. It's not evil." *Elizabeth, oh my Elizabeth . . . you are sweet, you are like wine, you are . . . everything. I love you, there's no one. No one.* Probably never hear that again, so get used to the mental playback, babe. "It's the total opposite of evil. I thought . . . I thought it was kind of wonderful. But he—he—"

I cried some more. It was lame, but I couldn't stop. Just when I thought that the *one* thing I could count on was Sinclair by my side no matter what happened . . .

"He's still here, though, right?" I asked, groping for a tissue, again out of habit. I was snot-free. "At the house? He didn't move out?"

"Not that I know of, honey. Probably just back to his old room while he sorts things out." I stared down at the table, and Jess smoothed my crumpled bangs out of my eyes. "Poor Bets. If it's not one thing it's another. You want me to stay in tonight?"

"Yeah, we could—no!"

"Oh, that's flattering," she grumbled.

"No, I mean . . . tonight's the big night. Your date with Nick. You can't miss it."

"I can reschedule," she said gently.

"My ass!"

"And that's one thing not on the date agenda," she said cheerfully. "He might have asked me out because he knows you're taken—"

"Am I?" I sulked.

"But one thing we're not going to do is talk about your ass. Nor your tits, nor your scintillating personality—which, I gotta tell you, ain't so great right now."

She was teasing and I smiled, a little. "No rescheduling. You're going. I'll—I'll find something to do."

On cue, the swinging doors on the east end of the kitchen whooshed open and Jon walked in like the world's youngest gunslinger. "Anybody up to telling me the story of their life?" he chirped, waving his Sidekick.

"Well," Jess told me, getting up from her seat, "if whatever you did was evil, and I'm not saying it was, because your word's good enough for me, but if it was, you're gonna be punished for it right about now."

# Chapter 19

"**H**ΛVE you, uh, seen Sinclair around tonight?"

Jon snorted. "Not hardly. We sort of stay out of each other's way. I get the feeling he's not too crazy about me staying here."

"Well, it's not his house, now is it?" I asked sharply. Oh, great. Yell at the kid because your fiancé's not talking to you. "Sorry. I'm grumpy tonight."

"Because you haven't fed?" he asked eagerly, Sidekick poised. I saw he had flipped it around so he could tap on the tiny keyboard.

"No. But I'll worry about that some other night. Listen, Jon, if I do this for you, you've got to do something for me."

"I understand Betsy." He looked around; yes, we were alone in the cavernous parlor. We'd moved there after the housekeeper got back from Rainbow and shooed us out. "I don't—uh—approve of that sort of—um—thing, but you're so—I mean, I'll make an exception for you." He bravely pulled off his T-shirt and inched closer to me. "Besides, it'll be good for the book."

"Ick! No!" I shoved him away, and he went flying over the end of the couch and crashed into the carpet. Dust flew. He coughed. I freaked. "Sorry, sorry, sorry!" I hurried around the couch and helped him up. "I didn't mean to shove you so hard."

"S'okay," he gasped, in the middle of a major coughing spasm. "M'sorry, too."

"It's my fault. I guess I was vague. No, I'm afraid the favor I've got in mind is a lot worse than sucking your blood."

"Whatever it is," he choked, "I'll do it. But first . . . you gotta get someone in here with a vacuum, I mean, right now."

"Who do you think you're talking to? Jon, I couldn't find the vacuum if you stuck a gun in my ear. Which if memory serves, you have."

He reddened and settled himself on a chair across from me. "That stuff's all over with, now."

"And we of the vampire community are grateful, believe me."

"We're talking about you," he said. "Why don't you start at the beginning?"

"Well, I was born in a small town in Minnesota, Cannon Falls, and I went to school at Cannon Falls Elementary, where Mrs. Schultz was my favorite teacher. We moved to Burnsville when I was—"

"No," he interrupted, "I mean, the beginning, when you became a vampire."

"Oh. Kind of a short bio. I mean, not much has happened to me yet. As a vampire, I mean."

He rolled his eyes. "Betsy, I really like you and you're cute and all, but you are *so* full of crap."

"I am not! I haven't even been a vampire for a year, is what I meant, and I was a human for th—for twenty-five years at least. Hell, the Miss Burnsville pageant was way more stressful than vampire politics."

"Yeah, I'll get some of that stuff later for fill-in," he promised, but he was lying. "Let's get to the good stuff."

I sighed. "All right, all right. The good stuff. Well, I guess the good stuff starts on the last day. And it sucked, let me tell you. In fact, the day I died started out bad and got worse in a hurry . . ."

# Chapter 20

"... AND then you jumped off the roof of the mortuary and got run over by a garbage truck."

"Jon, there's no need to read it back to me; I know the story."

He laughed. "It's an incredible story! I'm reading it back to be sure I'm not fucking up anything. As it is, no one's going to think this is real."

"Well, good." We were in the entryway, and I was shrugging into my coat. Laura was here, coming up the walk, and she and I were baby-sitting Baby Jon tonight. "Because the whole point is, you're *pretending* it's a real bio about a vampire."

"I know, I know, you only told me a million times. Let's see . . ."

"Jon, I gotta go. Can we pick this up tomorrow?"

"Yeah, let me just be sure I've got everything so far . . . you tried to drown yourself in the Mississippi River, you tried to electrocute yourself, tried to poison yourself with a bottle of bleach, and then stole a butcher knife and tried to stab yourself to death? Is that all?"

"Uh . . ." I wasn't about to go into the rapists I'd accidentally killed. "Pretty much."

Laura walked in—I'd told her weeks ago to stop with the knocking already—and said cheerfully, as she always did, "Good evening, darling sister. Ready to go?"

"Yeah." So, so ready. I wasn't up for another round of *This Is Your Life*. "Laura, have you met Jon? Jon, this is my sister, Laura."

She was having her usual effect on men, I could see: Jon had dropped his Sidekick. And hadn't noticed. Dust was probably cramming its delicate little circuits, and Jon hadn't noticed.

Instead, he was staring at my sister, and I couldn't blame him: she made Michelle Pfeiffer look like a hag. Tonight she was wearing moon boots (they were in, then out, and now in again, and I didn't care how often they came back in, I hated them, I wasn't a damn astronaut), black jeans, and a huge dark blue poofy parka that should have made her look like a blonde Michelin Man but, because God was cruel, did not.

"You never told me you had a sister," he said, looking deep into Laura's blue, blue eyes.

"You never told me you had a Jon." She giggled, obviously liking what she saw as well.

"I never told you I have a bleeding ulcer, either. Barf out, you guys. Come on, Laura, we'll be late."

"It was nice meeting you," she said, holding out a mittened hand.

"Meetcha, too," he mumbled, still gaping. He had goose bumps as big as cherries, but he didn't seem to notice he was standing shirtless in subzero cold.

"I hope to see you again soon."

"Blurble," he replied. At least that's what I think he said.

"Well, 'bye!" I said loudly—no mistaking *that,* I hoped. I practically pushed Laura out the front door and slammed it behind us.

"Oh, he was cute!" she was already gushing as we walked to the car. I trudged; she skipped. "Where do you know him from? Does he have a girlfriend? Of course he has a girlfriend."

"Laura, take a pill."

"Only if you stop being one," she snarked back. A mittened hand flew to her perfect, bow-shaped mouth. "Oh, I'm sorry! It's just . . . I'm a little nervous about tonight."

"Baby Jon won't bite. He doesn't have any teeth. He might puke on you, though."

"I've baby-sat before," she said happily. "It won't be the first time."

"Heck, I've been on dates that weren't so pleasant."

# Chapter 21

T HE Ant greeted us with, "Get inside quick! There's a killer on the loose!" She grabbed me by the jacket collar—the first time she'd touched me in years—and hauled me into the foyer. Laura hurried in behind me just in time to avoid the door being slammed in her face.

"Those aren't killers," I explained, unbuttoning my coat. "They're Cub Scouts. They just want to sell you some wreaths and wrapping paper."

"Very funny, Betsy." The Ant was quite the wreath herself in a dress of poison green, which she had trimmed with a glittery red belt two inches wide, long fake red fingernails, and large red hoop earrings. Her lipstick matched her accessories, and her eyelids were as blue as the Caribbean. Her fake eyelashes were so long I at first thought a couple centipedes had crawled up there and died.

"No, it's the Driveway Killer," she was insisting, helping Laura (Laura had that effect on people) off with her big puffy coat. "He struck again! Took one of my neighbors right out of her driveway. At first we thought she'd, you know, just left—her husband—" The Ant made the universal "drinky drinky" motion with her thumb and forefinger. "But then her body turned up in the parking lot of the Lake Street Wal-Mart. Lake Street! Can you imagine? How tacky!"

"Er," was all Laura managed. The Ant could tax even her formidable powers of niceness.

"I'm sorry about your neighbor," I said, and I meant it, though the sentiment was probably wasted on the Ant, who apparently thought where your body turned up was far more important than how you lived your life.

"She was just minding her own business, coming in the house—or going, we're not sure which—and he *grabbed* her. I've been scared out of my wits ever since!"

"That's hard to imagine," I said sweetly.

"So you have to be very careful around here, girls."

I assumed she was talking to Laura.

"If something happened to you, I don't know what I'd do."

I was, against all my better instincts, touched. "Aw, Antonia. I don't know what to say."

"We'll be careful," Laura promised.

The baby monitor was on the little table for the car keys, and we could hear a thin wailing coming out from it. "Please, please be careful! Nobody else will sit with Baby Jon while he's like this."

"Jesus, Antonia. He's got colic, not rabies."

"And I'm late."

"We got here right on time, so I don't want to hear anything out of you. When did he eat last?"

"The baby nurse left all that on a note on the fridge." The Ant was putting on her black wool coat. Her hair didn't move, which was a good trick considering it was shoulder length. "The party is supposed to be over around one."

"Where is Mr. Taylor?" Laura asked.

"Oh, he's . . ." The Ant made a vague gesture. "Don't worry, if I have too much to drink I'll get a cab."

"Thank goodness," I said. "If you get too blitzed, just take a nap in the driveway and wait around for company."

She glared. "I suppose you think you're being funny again."

I glared. "A little funny."

Laura walked in the direction of the kitchen.

The Ant left.

I went upstairs, scooped up my squalling brother, and snuggled him to my shoulder while he gasped and decided to knock off with the crying. My finely tuned vampire senses informed me he didn't need a diaper change.

We went back downstairs and caught up with Laura, who was standing at the main counter reading a careful, detailed note signed Jennifer Clapp, R.N.

"She has a baby nurse, and she needs us?" She clucked her tongue at Jon, who grunted in return.

"The nurse only works business hours. And my dad put his foot down about a night nurse when the Ant's home all day."

"Mr. Taylor said no to her?"

"It happens occasionally." Propping Jon's well-cushioned bottom on my forearm and his head on my shoulder, I opened the fridge and grimaced. It was full of skim milk, iceberg lettuce, soy sauce, Egg Beaters, and bottles of formula. If I was alive, that'd be a real problem. Poor Laura!

And "Mr. Taylor"? Laura's biological father. Nobody knew that little factoid but me, her, and the devil.

It was really complicated and would have even been silly if it wasn't so frightening. See, the devil possessed my stepmother for a while. And I think it's telling to report the Ant was (is!) such a miserable human being that *no one* noticed. I mean, how friggin' unbelievable is that? "Oh, you're evil and insane and running over pedestrians with your bicycle and granting evil wishes and encouraging people to jump off tall buildings . . . same old, same old, eh, Antonia?"

Anyway. So my dad's second wife was possessed by the devil for a while, yes, that's right, *the* devil, and had a baby, my sister Laura. And then went back to Hell.

The Ant, "coming to" with a drooly baby to take care of, promptly *dumped* Laura in the waiting room of a hospital and went back to her old life without looking back.

So—here's where it gets weird—the Ant and my dad are Laura's biological parents. And the devil is her mother. *And* Laura was adopted by the Goodmans (come on! The Goodmans?), and raised in the suburbs of Minneapolis.

Have I mentioned her unholy hell-powers, like the bow made of hellfire and the way she can eat whatever she wants and never get a pimple?

So. It was a little weird when she referred to our—*her*—father as "Mr. Taylor." It was always "Mr. Taylor" or "Betsy's father." I had no idea how to handle it, so I just let it go. Just another thing hanging over my head like a wobbly guillotine.

"There isn't shit to eat," I announced, shutting the door, "as usual."

"We can have a pizza delivered." She held out her arms, and I handed the baby to her.

"*I* don't care; I can't eat it anyway. It's you I'm worried about. I get desperate enough, I can always drink the bottle of soy sauce.

Mmmm . . . salty. Anyway, did you eat supper before you came over?"

"No," she admitted.

"God, how pathetic are we? Don't start," I warned the baby, who had stiffened in Laura's arms and looked ready to start with the yowling again. "I'm thirty and I'm baby-sitting and scrounging in the fridge for a meal. Next I'll be calling my boyfriend to tell him to come over so we can make out."

"At least you have a boyfriend," Laura pointed out.

I smiled sourly and said nothing.

"He's *sooooo* cute," Laura cooed. Tonight Baby Jon was wearing a T-shirt, Pampers, and thick green socks. He'd put on a little weight, but he still looked more like a hairless, angry rat than the plump Gerber babies I saw on TV. "Isn't he just the darlingest thing you've ever seen?"

"This is a scary side of you, Laura, and I thought I'd seen the really frightening stuff."

"*Goooooooo,*" she replied, tickling Baby Jon under his pointy chin. Jon glared at her and then the odor of his discontent filled the air. "Oooooh, someone needs a diaper change." She looked at me.

"Daughter of the devil," I said.

"Vampire queen."

"Okay, okay, I'll do it. Gimme him."

Jon chuckled when I took him back, which, given his age, I knew was impossible. He wasn't really laughing, just like he wasn't really glaring. Still, it was cute.

I pretended he really liked me, though at this age he couldn't pick me out of a lineup. I cuddled him close all the way up the stairs, when Laura couldn't see.

The truth was, nights like this were the highlight of my life right now. I jumped whenever the Ant called. Bottom line? Baby Jon was the closest I was ever going to get to having a baby of my own. No tears, no sweat, no periods . . . no babies.

Ever.

Sinclair and I could do a lot—would do a lot, if he ever got over our little problem of the month. But we couldn't make our own babies.

Jess told me over and over not to be silly, there were only a zillion babies in the world who needed good homes, and Marc backed her up with horror stories of abuse from the E.R. She was right—they were both right—and I tried not to feel bad.

But at thirty, I hadn't thought I was forever turning my back on having my own babies. It was funny . . . I'd never seriously thought about having a baby. I just always assumed I would. And then I died. Isn't that the way it goes sometimes?

"It's dumb," I told Baby Jon, stripping him of the nasty diaper and setting it aside (I would later place it beneath the Ant's bed, where she'd go crazy trying to find it). "Dead people can't do lots of things. Walk, talk, have sex. Get married. Bitch. I'm lucky I can do anything, instead of just hanging out in a coffin and slowly turning into fertilizer. So what do I focus on? The good stuff? The cool powers? No, I piss and moan because Sinclair can't knock me up. Does that make sense? Does that sound like a person who's counting her blessings?"

"Fleh," Jon replied.

"Tell me." I sprinkled him like salt on a roast, rubbed in the powder, and then put a new diaper on him. He sighed and waved his little arms, and I caught a tiny hand and kissed it. He promptly scratched me with his wolverine-like nails, but I didn't mind.

# Chapter 22

"I can't thank you enough for coming out," the Ant said. Again. To Laura.

"It was our pleasure, Mrs. Taylor. Your son is adorable."

The Ant looked doubtfully at the monitor, which occasionally vibrated with Baby Jon's snores. "It's . . . it's nice of you to say so. I hope he wasn't any trouble."

"He's *dar*ling!" Laura exclaimed, brushing spit-up off her shoulder.

"Yeah, a laugh a minute," I grumped. "And I'm busy tomorrow, so don't even think about it."

"I'm free," Laura piped up.

"That's all right, girls. My fund-raiser was postponed, anyway. And Freddy can come over then, anyway."

"Freddy?" I asked sharply. "Hooked-on-her-migraine-medication Freddy?"

"She's not hooked," the Ant, no stranger to substance abuse, insisted. "She just has a lot of migraines."

"I don't care if she has a lot of brain tumors! She's not watching Baby Jon!"

"It's not up to you," the Ant snapped. Then, "Who?"

"When is your meeting?" Laura interjected quickly. "I'm sure we can work something out."

The Ant puffed a strand of hair out of her face, which didn't move. "Laura, I appreciate that *you* are trying to do *your* best, but there's nothing to work out. I'll be the one to decide what's best for the baby."

I got ready to pull her head off her shoulders and kick it up the stairs, a grisly surprise for my dad if he ever got back, when Laura asked, "Like you decided before?"

*Whoa.*

"What?" the Ant asked.

"What?" I warned, frozen in the act of reaching for the Ant's tiny head.

"The baby. From before. You decided what was best for her . . . that you couldn't take care of her."

"Now?" I asked my sister, who had apparently gone insane when I wasn't looking. "You're picking now to do this?" Rotten timing: a genetic legacy poor Laura couldn't escape.

"I don't—I don't—"

I dropped my arms to my sides. The Ant had a whole lot more to worry about right now than beheading by stepdaughter.

"It was a good choice," Laura added, "if it was the one that was best for you. Still, do you ever wonder what happened to her? Do you ever think about her?"

"No," the Ant said, looking right into Laura's incredible blue eyes. "I never think of her. Just like when you aren't here, I never think of you. That was a long time ago, and I never think about how when you wear your hair pulled up, you look like my mother. The way she looked when she liked us more than the bottle. I never think about that, and I never think about her, and I never, ever, ever think about you."

"Oh," Laura gulped, as I fought not to fall into the hall plant. She knew! She knew! And she never said anything! "I see."

"You're a real nice girl, Laura. I was happy to meet you. I'm always happy when you can come by. But it's late, and it's time for you to get out of here."

"Of—of course."

"A heart-stopping pleasure," I said, following Laura out the door. "Just like always. You jackass."

The Ant didn't say anything. Just stood in the doorway for a long time. Making sure the Driveway Killer didn't get us. Or making sure we really left.

# Chapter 23

$W \in$ walked to my car. We got in. I started it up. We sat for a minute, waiting for the heater to kick in. (We weren't too worried about the Driveway Killer.) We pulled out. We watched the Ant shut her front door. (She must have frozen her treadmilled ass right off, watching us leave.)

I couldn't stand it half a second longer and blurted, "I can't believe she knew. I can't believe she knew! She probably knew the minute she laid eyes on you, since you apparently look like her dead alcoholic mother. And she just . . . just let us come over and baby-sit! All those times! And you were at the baby shower! You brought her a fucking present from Tiffany's!"

"She is . . . a strong woman," Laura said faintly.

"She is a *YAAAAAAAAAAAAAGGGGGGGGGGGGGGHHHH-HHHH!*"

"What? What?" Laura was twisting around in her seat, her hand on an invisible sword hilt. There was a sword there, but it only came out when Laura wanted it. And only she could touch it.

I looked at Laura, looked back up at my rearview mirror at the sallow blonde who was sitting in my backseat, and looked back at Laura. "Yuh—uh—I saw a squirrel."

Laura was looking straight into the backseat, on the floor, around the car. "For goodness's sake, where? Behind your brake?"

The blonde stared at me, and I tried to pull my attention back to France Avenue. "It just . . . scared the hell out of me. Popping up like that." I glared into the mirror. "Without warning."

"Sorry," the blonde said.

"Well, don't scare me like that!" Laura snapped. "It's been a stressful enough evening."

"Tell me about it," the blonde in the back said.

My heart was galloping along from the adrenaline rush (okay, adrenaline tickle, and "galloping" meant about ten beats a minute), which was stressful enough without having to watch Laura, the ghost in the back, and the road.

"Were you—did you—" I finally spit it out. "Were you planning this? Scratch that: how long have you been planning it?"

"I didn't really plan it," she confessed. "I *carpe'd* the *diem*."

"Well, Laura, I hope you—hope you know that for the—for your mother, that was pretty good. I mean, she was almost nice. Which for her, was *really* nice."

"Yes, I know."

"Just give her time. She'll, uh . . ." *Grow a soul?* "And Laura . . . don't take this the wrong way or anything, but if you were planning on saying anything to our father . . ."

"Christ," the woman in the back said. "This is better than *Days of Our Lives*."

"Shut up!"

"That's good advice," Laura said.

"No, uh . . . I mean, I wouldn't recommend . . . maybe not right now, anyway . . ."

"Don't worry," Laura said, tight-lipped. "I wasn't."

"That's a load off my mind," the dead woman in the back said.

# Chapter 24

"**W**ELL. it's been"—*Upsetting. Tense. If I was alive, I'd have shit myself at least twice in the last hour*—"really something."

"You're not going in?" Laura asked, pausing outside the front door. None of us used any of the side doors. I didn't know why. Yes I did. Nobody wanted to get mistaken for a servant. Even the servants (the housekeepers, the plant lady, the gardener) used the front door.

"No, no. I'm going to stay out here"—in the freezing, subzero temperature and bitter wind—"and get some fresh air." Even though I didn't breathe.

Laura's perfect forehead wrinkled. "Are you sure?"

"What," the ghost protested, "you're not going to let me in?"

"No, it's a real nice night. And I want to . . . look at the garden in the moonlight."

"You've got to be shitting me," the ghost protested. "I've been stuck outside for more than a week, and you're not letting me come in?"

"On second thought," I said, "I will come in."

"Let's hope you're a better hostess than driver," the dead woman bitched.

"You shut up. You're getting your way aren't you?"

"All I said was 'are you sure,'" Laura protested.

"Sorry, sorry. I'm pissed at the Ant on your behalf, and it's coming out at totally inappropriate times."

"That cow," the ghost said. "She let her little yappy dog poop in my yard every damn week. She thought I wasn't looking."

"Enough," I said.

"I agree," Laura almost snapped. "It's been a long night."

"Honey, you don't know what the hell you're talking about."

"Are you still planning on meeting up tomorrow?"

"Christmas shopping," Laura agreed, calming down before my eyes. At least her hair hadn't changed color, thank goodness. "I'll meet you here at six, all right?"

"I can't friggin' wait," the dead woman said.

"All right," I said. "Good night."

I watched Laura drive off in her smiley-face yellow VW, which her too-good-to-be-true-but-they-really-were-good adoptive parents had saved up for three years to buy her.

I looked at the ghost, who was a couple inches shorter than me, with dark blond hair pulled back in a short ponytail. She was wearing a faded green Sea World sweatshirt with the sleeves pushed up to her elbows and black stretch pants. Socks. No shoes or coat. But of course, she wasn't cold.

"Why don't you come in?"

"Why don't I?" she agreed. "Thanks for the ride. I thought I was going to be stuck in Edina forever. Talk about hell."

She walked through me into the house, which felt exactly like someone throwing a bucket of ice water in my face. "Dammit!" I gasped, lunging to shut the door.

"Sorry," she said smugly.

# Chapter 25

"YOU'RE back!" Jon cried.

"Jeez, let me get my coat off. And not now, okay?"

"Who's the hottie?" the ghost said, ogling. She passed her hand through his crotch, which, thankfully, he didn't notice.

"Stop that! It's against the law to do that even if you are dead."

"What?" Jon asked.

"I'm getting my thrills wherever I can," the ghost explained, "so off my case."

Tina had followed Jon into the entryway. "Good evening, Your Majesty. I was just on my way out."

"How many weirdos live in this place?" the ghost asked. "It's like *The Real World with Losers*."

"All those shows are like that," I told her. To Jon: "Seriously, not now. I've got some other errands and stuff to do before the sun comes up."

"Oh, don't mind me," the ghost sniffed. "I'm sure you'd much rather be getting naked with Super Hottie."

"I don't want to get naked with him, for the millionth time!"

I didn't realize it, but judging from the echoes in the entryway, I had screamed it.

"Whoa," Jon said, backing off.

"Excuse my boldness, Majesty, but do you have . . . a guest?"

*"Dah-DAH-DAHHHHHHH,"* the ghost hummed dramatically.

I put a hand over my eyes. "God, yes. And she's really annoying."

"Why don't you drop dead?" the ghost suggested.

"Too late," I snapped back. "See her, Tina? About this high . . ." I held my hand up to my nose. "Blond hair in a tacky ponytail, tacky sweatshirt, no shoes."

"If I'd known I'd have to walk around in sweat socks for eternity," the ghost protested, "I'd have dressed up a little."

"Ah, yes," Tina said, squinting and then brightening as the ghost slowly became visible to her. "Good evening, miss. My name is Tina; this is Elizabeth, The One."

"Wait a minute. I go days and days and no one can see me, and now she says so and you can, too?"

"She is my queen," Tina said simply.

"The way it works is, I'm a vampire—"

"Get out!" the ghost gasped.

"I swear!"

"I just thought you were a freak, like that kid in the movie. I didn't know you were, like, dead already."

"Well, I am, so let's not rub it in, okay?"

"Oh, I have to be sensitive to your feelings about being dead?"

"That's not what I meant," I said through gritted teeth. "And if you'll shut up a minute, I'll explain how Tina can see you. Not only am I a vampire, I'm sort of the boss of all of them. And one of the (dumb) rules is, if I see a ghost and tell a vampire to see the ghost, they can see the ghost."

"How totally lame," she commented. "It sounds made up to me."

"Well, it isn't," I snapped. "And you should be a lot nicer, in my opinion."

"Well, nobody *asked* for your opinion, honey. It's nice to meet you," she told Tina. "Can you help me?"

"*I'm* supposed to help you."

The ghost looked at me doubtfully. "Yeah, well, great. Looks like I've got all the help I need."

"Why don't we have a seat in the parlor?" Tina suggested.

"Yeah," I agreed. "Why don't we? It's the first room on your right." As we followed the ghost, I practically whispered to Tina, "Have you, uh, seen Sinclair tonight?"

"No," she murmured back. "I haven't seen him in two days. I did not wish to pry, but . . ."

"*Ooooooh!*" the ghost said loudly, phasing through the parlor wall. "More dramatic shenanigans."

I sighed and followed her. I took the door, though.

\* \* \*

"FIRST things first," the ghost said. She didn't sit down, but we did, so we were sort of staring up at her, craning our necks. "I'm dead, right? I mean, I'm pretty sure. But I just wanted to double-check."

"Yes," Tina said.

"We're sorry," I added. "For what it's worth, you were way too young. You look about my age."

"Don't flatter yourself; I'm only twenty-six. I mean, I was twenty-six." She sighed and looked through us. Literally. "I figured. The last thing I remember is this huge crash, this big light in my brain, and then all of a sudden I'm back in my neighborhood and nobody can see me. That damn dog of Antonia's pooped *through* me."

"How can we help you?" Tina asked, all business.

"Sorry about your dying," I added.

"I'll tell you how I can help," she said. "My name is Cathie Robinson, and I'm—"

"The latest victim of the Driveway Killer," Tina said. She looked at me. "The *Trib* ran a story when her—ah—when your body was found, Mrs. Robinson."

"In a parking lot, right?" she asked glumly. She sat down, phased through the couch, and disappeared into the floor. We heard a muffled "Shit!" and then she struggled back up into the parlor. "In a fucking parking lot!"

"Yes, I'm afraid so."

"Sorry," I said again, because honestly, I couldn't think of a thing to say.

"That piece of shit! That little *lowlife*!"

"Do you remember anything about . . . dying?" Tina asked tactfully . . . as tactfully as such a thing could be asked, anyway. "About where you were taken? About the killer?"

"Honey?" Cathie asked, fixing Tina with a sudden, piercing gaze. "I remember *everything*."

Tina smiled. It was awful; you could practically see her drooling at the thought of getting her fangs into the Driveway Killer. "Then at last, you're having some luck, Mrs. Robinson. A friend of ours is on the task force."

Cathie sighed and leaned back (carefully, so she wouldn't fall through the wall). "I knew there was a reason I was following you around," she told me.

"Tell us everything. We'll worry about the difficulties later."

"What difficulties? I'll tell you where he is—where he took me, anyway—and you go get him!"

"Our friend—the one on the task force—not only doesn't know we're vampires, he certainly doesn't know we can speak with the dead. Sharing this information with him without compromising our safety will be difficult."

"But we'll figure out a way," I hastily advised Cathie, who was starting to look superpissed. "Obviously, catching this guy is *primo numero uno* on our list."

"Well, I should fucking well hope so!" she snapped. "I left a family, you know. And I was a good girl—I should be in heaven right this minute. The only reason I'm still here is to help you catch that scumshit, that piece of shit jerkoff, that assface."

I was still admiring Cathie's rich and colorful vocabulary when I heard a familiar step in the hall.

"Tell Tina the whole story," I said hurriedly, leaping to my feet.

"Hey!" Cathie protested. "Where the hell do you think you're going?"

"It's much more important to tell Tina than me," I said, practically running to catch up to him. "She's, like, ten times smarter than me anyway."

"*That* I figured out on my own. But what's more important than this?"

*Dead people,* I thought, darting into the entryway. *They're the most selfish people on the planet.*

"Sinclair!" I hollered. "Wait up!"

# Chapter 26

"**WHERE-WHERE** are you going?"

"Out," he replied.

That much was obvious; he was wearing his black wool great-coat and his Kenneth Cole shoes, which were shined to a high gloss. He was tapping his black leather gloves impatiently into his palm while he politely waited for me to Get On With It.

"Out—how come?"

"I need to feed, Elizabeth," he said simply.

I almost reeled at the implications of that. Since we'd been to-gether, we sort of had an unwritten rule about feeding . . . we only did each other.

That was the trouble with unwritten rules. Anybody could rewrite them . . . or ignore them.

"But . . . don't you want to . . . with me?" I couldn't believe I was asking this; me, the one who was totally squicked out by blood-sharing. But the thought of him finding some pretty girl . . . dazzling her . . . taking from her . . . and she'd fall in love with him of course . . . and then what would he do? Keep her?

It wasn't like he hadn't done it before. Hell, he used to have a harem of girls who *looooooooved* it when he drank from them. He gave them all tons of money and sent them on their way when he moved in, and that was that. Nice and neat.

Except now . . .

His glove-tapping sped up. "I had assumed, after what hap-pened earlier, that such things were off limits. To both of us."

"Well, when you *ASSuME*, you make an *ass* out of *you* and *me*. So there!"

"What?"

"We just had a fight, that's all, just a stupid fight. It's not the end of everything. And frankly, I don't want you going out in the cold and biting some other woman, so there!"

"Another 'so there.' You must feel quite strongly about the situation."

"Well, you freaked out when Jon, who I have no intention of biting or boning, moved in. Now you're off to the races, and you're all surprised that I have a problem with it?"

His mouth tightened; it look more like a scar than lips I had come to know well. "That is hardly the same thing."

"Wrong, suck-o! It's exactly the same thing."

"Very well." In a flash—I could see what happened only if I replayed it in my head—he dropped his gloves, kicked out of his shoes, and dragged me up the stairs. In the time it took me to re-alize he had dropped his gloves, he had kicked my (our) bed-room door shut, jerked my head to one side, and sank his fangs into me.

I screamed, shocked to my toes at what he had done—no, *how* he had done it. I tried to get free, but he had one hand across my shoulders and the other hand was forcing my chin to the side, giv-ing him easy access to my jugular. Wriggling free was like trying to get free of a tree that had planted itself around me.

"Stop it, Eric, stop it, please stop it," I begged, and hated my-self for begging.

*Yes stop what are you doing why are you hurting her you'll have your pride and that's all you'll have so stop it stop it STOP IT!*

He pulled back and licked my blood off his teeth. He watched the small trickle of blood travel down my neck, caught it with a fin-ger, and licked that dry, too. Then he let go of me and I spun away.

I knew it was coming. He knew it was coming. And he stood still for it. Penance? I didn't give a fuck. I slapped him so hard he staggered back, bounced off the wall, and lay on the floor like a stunned cockroach.

I stood over him, saw his fangs were still out, and slapped a hand over the bite on my neck.

"I said I was sorry, okay?" I hated the way my voice shook. Why hadn't I seen that coming? Just how dumb was I? "I said it. And I'm done saying it. So you're either gonna get over it, or you won't. Once you decide *that,* move in here or don't. And I mean *move in,* none of this showing up at night for blood and sex and then leaving. But enough of this sulking and pissing and moaning, okay? Believe it or not, I've got bigger problems than your bruised ego. Now get the fuck out. Here, I'll help you."

I bent down, meaning to pick him up and throw him out the window—I was pretty sure I was strong enough to do it, and was dying to find out. I had also counted on Eric's weird contrite mood, which didn't last very long, as I found out when he yanked me down on top of him.

"I guess you didn't hear my speech," I said through gritted teeth. "I guess I gotta go through the whole thing again."

"I heard it. What are your bigger problems?"

"What is this, a quiz show? *Undead Wheel of Fortune?*"

"You said 'believe it or not, I've got bigger problems than your bruised ego.' " His eyes were about two inches from my own. I could smell my blood. I hated myself for wanting him to take another bite. "I was wondering what they were."

"After the stunt you just pulled? I'm not telling you a fucking thing, pal!"

"Because I am a king who does not 'noe' the queen's ways," he said quietly.

"No, jackass, because you just came up here and practically *raped* me because you're in a bad mood! I don't give a shit that you can't read my mind when we're boning, and frankly, you should be relieved! Do you really want all that stuff in your head?"

"It's only a matter of time," he said in a monotone that scared me to death. "If you wish, you may throw me out the window now."

"Sinclair!" I slapped him across the face, a sort of "wake up, you're on fire!" smack, but he didn't say anything. "Dude, you have got to pull yourself together!" *I really need you now. More than I ever did, so please, please get it together, I'm sorry, you're sorry, everybody's sorry, can we please be the way we were a week ago?*

"On the contrary, I have finally seen things for exactly what they are. It's . . . distressing."

"Eric, come on. It's been a rotten day, and you already scared the shit out of me once."

"Oh, that," he said absently. "I apologize. I was hungry, and you were annoying. It won't happen again."

*Don't say that! It wasn't what you did, it was how you did it, please don't say that!*

"I'll go," he said quietly, "but before I do, I'd like to remind you that it's very likely you could have a living baby with a living man. I know how fond you are of Baby Jon, and I'm certain you could have one of your own once you come to your senses and jettison me from your life."

"But—I could? But—but I don't want—"

Oblivious to my massive confusion, he sat up and gently picked me up off him, the way you shoo a ladybug off your hand when you're going inside, stood, placed me on the bed, turned, and left.

# Chapter 27

"**HEY**. wake up."

I burrowed farther under the covers, a big undead worm.

"Hey, Betsy. Wake up."

*"Hnnnnnnwwwww,"* I mumbled, which any sane person would translate as "Go away, I'm sleeping."

"Your sister is beating the living shit out of that vampire who lives in the basement."

*That* got my attention. I sat up and there was Cathie, shoeless and looking scared, sitting in Marie's Chair. "What? What are you talking about?"

"Your sister. She came over early, I guess for Christmas shopping? She went downstairs, and I was bored out of my tits, so I followed her. She started beating up that long-haired guy in the basement, the one who can't talk. I didn't want to ask your friends to step in—one of your roommates looks like she's on a date, and her date is actually here, wandering around waiting for her—"

"Christ," I groaned.

"—and you're the only vampire I could wake up."

I tossed the blankets back and glanced at the clock: 5:35 P.M. I'd slept late, but the others wouldn't be awake for a few minutes yet, not until the sun fell down.

"Nice pajamas. Did you get them at a garage sale?"

I started for the stairs at a dead run. I was out my door in half a second, on the stairs in another second, and pounding down the basement steps while the blanket was still falling to the floor upstairs.

I screeched to a halt in front of the long, bare area of the basement we called the sparring section.

Cathie had not been exaggerating. Laura *was* fighting George, and if he hadn't been dead before, he would be soon. It's not that she was such a good fighter—though she was—it's that he wasn't fighting back. Every blow she landed sounded sickening and looked worse.

"Laura!"

"Fight, you demon spawn, *fight!*"

"Laura, stop it!"

"You *fight* so I can send you to my mother. You *fight* so you can tell her I'm doing *just fine* up here and she need not interfere . . . *again!*"

Laura's hair, I was dismayed to see, was flame red—the color of sullen coals after a raging fire. Her eyes were the color of fall grass—green, but dying. Gone was the rosy-cheeked blond teen we all knew and liked. We were here with the devil's daughter now.

"Jesus," Cathie murmured, finally making it back down to the basement.

"I wish," I said.

"What's wrong with her?"

"She has parental issues."

"No, *I've* got parental issues. She is fucked up severe."

"Later. *Laura!*" I bawled. "Get off him right now! *Now* now, not in a minute now!"

"Stay out of this, Betsy!" she shrilled back. She smacked George another good one—I could only imagine how much it must have hurt her hand, judging from how it split open George's cheek—and he reeled and almost went down, but didn't fight back.

"Laura, I hate to pull rank on you, but I'm the queen, and that's a subject so get your *fucking hands off him right now!*"

She smacked him again—wham*thud!*—I couldn't *believe* it. Was I even in the goddamned room?

I raced around them just as her sword materialized on her hip. I couldn't look at the thing—it was made of hellfire and gave me an instant headache, it was like looking into the sun—so I averted my gaze and somehow—I'm still not quite sure how I pulled this off—somehow I was in front of George, my arms spread out protectively, and that's how my sister accidentally plunged her blade into my chest.

# Chapter 28

"**BETSY**? Betsy? Betsy?"

"*Glllkkkkkkkkkk!*"

*Is that me? No. Who's choking? It's not me, right?*

"Laura, I am quite fond of you—" Sinclair? What was he doing down here? And it sounded like he was throttling my sister . . . I had no idea how I felt about that, to be honest. Yay? Boo?

"*Ggggglllkkkkk!*"

"—yes, thank you, but if she dies, I'm afraid you will die as well. It's this odd little territorial tic I have. I realize it's a problem, and I'm dealing with it, but right now I must stand by what I said."

"Betsy? Can you hear me?" Marc! That was Marc. Excellent! Finally, he has a day off when it actually helps me.

"She's got a big fucking sword sticking out from between her boobs." That was Cathie. "Of course she can't hear you. Why am I even bothering to talk to you idiots?"

*I'm not dead!*

"I suppose it's no good looking for vital signs." Tina.

"Well, she doesn't have a pulse, and she's not breathing, so I'd say she's dead. Also, there's a big-ass sword sticking out of her chest."

"Duh!" Cathie shouted.

"But she's been dead before, so this is kind of a stumper for me."

Tina hmmmmed and then said, "For us as well . . . where's Nick?"

"Jessica's keeping him busy upstairs, thank God. Of all the stupid times for her to start dating again."

"Amen to that," I said and opened my eyes. I was startled to see Marc and Cathie had been right—there *was* a big-ass sword sticking out of my chest. I'd seen Laura stab vampires with it before, and they instantly disintegrated. I was sort of amazed to see I wasn't a pile of ashes. "Sinclair! Put her down. Laura, get over here. Get this thing out of me."

They both looked over at me, Laura's face so red it looked like she was going to pop a blood vessel. Which, given the firm grip Sinclair had on her throat, was probably imminent. He let go, and she hit the cement, gasping.

"I can't leave any of you people alone for one day without all hell breaking loose," I griped. "Where's George?"

"We put him in the shower to wash away the blood," Tina reported matter-of-factly. She was on one knee beside me and kept squeezing my arm as if to reassure herself that I wasn't going to disintegrate.

Laura had heaved herself to her knees and then her feet. If I were her, I wouldn't be so quick to turn my back on Sinclair, but she only had eyes for me as she staggered toward us.

"Betsy, oh Besty! Forgive me!" She tripped and fell but probably was going to get back on her knees anyway, judging from what came out next, which was: "I swear, you were not my target! I'm an unworthy treacherous bitch, one you have taken into your family, and I repaid you with—" She gestured at her sword. "Please, please, I beg your forgiveness. I—"

"Laura."

"Yes?"

"Can we do this after you've pulled this thing out of me?"

"Oh. Oh! Yes, of course. I—ah—no one's ever—" She grabbed the hilt with easy familiarity. "Either my sword passes harmlessly through them—it only disrupts magic—or it kills them. It's never . . . gotten stuck halfway."

I felt a little ill. "Well, can we get it un-stuck, please?"

"Yes, of course, but after causing you so much pain, I feel I must warn you it may hurt a bit—"

"Elizabeth!" Sinclair said sharply from his brooding corner. We all snapped around to gape at him; it was not a good thing when he raised his voice. "I must insist you cancel the wedding at once."

I gasped with fresh outrage. "And the hits just keep on coming! Cancel the weddi*arrrrrrrggggggggg*!" I clutched my chest, which was hole-free, thank goodness. "That *did* hurt, you cow!"

"Perhaps less," he said, looking vastly relieved, "as you were distracted."

"Yeah, thanks for 'helping' me by scaring the shit out of me," I grumped as Tina and Marc helped me to my feet. Marc felt between my boobs, which I didn't take personally, and then circled around to feel my back.

"How do you feel?" Tina asked anxiously.

"Pissed off! I've been up for, what, ten minutes? Cripes. This is worse than prom '91. Laura, you've got some big-time explaining to do."

"Close your eyes," Marc told me, "and think of England." Then he pushed my pajama top up.

"Ack! It's chilly in here, stop that." I jerked away from him. "I'm pretty sure if I had a big old stab wound in my chest, we'd all know it."

"I can't believe you aren't dead!" Laura exclaimed. "I mean, I'm happy and everything, but I've never seen that happen before." Sinclair came up to our little group, and she sort of shrank away from him. "I tried to tell you . . . before . . . I didn't mean to stab her. She got between us."

"Yesssssssssss," Sinclair purred. "And who were you trying to stab when she, ah, got between you?"

"It wasn't . . . it wasn't for real." Laura suddenly looked about twelve years old. The braids helped. So did the fact that she'd put her sword away . . . to wherever it went when she wasn't killing vampires with it. "We were just practicing."

"I guess what happened at the Ant's bugged you more than you let on," I suggested.

Laura shrugged. She wouldn't look at any of us. Her hair was blond again, and her eyes were blue. The blue of the Ant's mother, apparently, or the devil.

"He's a feral vampire," she pointed out defensively. "It's not like I could have really hurt him . . . done some lasting damage."

Lie.

"It was just a training exercise."

Lie.

"It has nothing to do with my family life," she insisted, the third and (hopefully) final lie.

"It—"

*You fight so I can send you to my mother!*

"—doesn't—"

*You fight so you can tell her I'm doing just fine up here!*

"—mean anything."

"Oh, boy," Cathie said. Tina glanced over at her, but nobody else had a clue. "Did you say she had some parental issues? Because that's a pretty fucking big issue right there. I mean, come on, Liz. You don't believe this happy crappy, do you?"

"Don't call me that. It's all right, Laura," I said after an awkward moment. My life: a series of awkward moments. "It was an accident. I know you'd never want to hurt me."

"Yes, that's just right," she said, guileless blue eyes swimming with tears. "I'd never ever want to hurt you. I'd die before hurting you."

"Really?" Sinclair asked, head cocked to one side.

"Let me, ah, just go check on George, and we can go finish our shopping."

Her face lit up. "You—you still want to?"

"Are you kidding? What part of 'thirty percent off everything in the store' do you not get? It would take a lot more than this to keep me away. I'll meet you out at the car."

"Oh," she said sadly. "I guess this is the part where you all talk about what to do about me."

"It's more like a Secret Santa thing," I said, pushing her toward the stairs.

# Chapter 29

"JESUS," I said, staring into the shower. "She kicked the living crap out of him."

"Yes."

"I don't suppose he said anything."

"No," Tina and Sinclair said in unison. Marc had gone back upstairs to take Jess aside and assure her all was well. Who knew what Nick was up to—hopefully not prying too much. Cathie, miffed we had let my sister "get away," had walked through a wall and went who-knew-where.

"Poor guy, minding his own business and she comes down here and starts whaling away on him."

I started to chew on my wrist—the usual quick pick-me-up for George—when Sinclair stopped me. "A large part of your sister's faith hinges on redemption. She does seem to feel badly about her part in this. So why not have *her* feed George for a day or two?"

"Oh, but that's pretty . . ." Diabolically mean. "Brilliant," I confessed. "Okay, I'll tell her that. She'll have to feed him, one way or another, until he's healed up from everything she did to him."

"And I—ah—must be sure that the—ah—" Tina was stammering like a blonde learning Latin. And I ought to know.

"Tina, what in the world is your problem?"

"The thing!" she blurted. "I must be sure the thing is also taken care of."

"What?" I asked, but Tina was already out of the shower room.

Leaving me with Sinclair, who wouldn't talk to me, and George, who couldn't.

Oh.

"Well." Cough, cough. "I guess I'd better get to shopping—"

"You seem to always be shot or stabbed or otherwise fatally attacked when I'm not around." And was that a smile, lurking in the corners of his mouth?

"Hey, I didn't do anything. I was minding my own business, and Laura stabbed me in the heart." Okay, even I knew how lame that sounded.

He *was* smiling. "Your sister will have some bruising."

"Okay. I'll break out the ice packs. For the record, I disapprove of the whole strangling thing."

The smile was gone, banished to wherever Sinclair's smiles go. "She is *extremely* lucky that's all she will have."

"Now, come on. It was an accident. You saw how upset she was after."

"She certainly *seemed* to be upset," he agreed.

"What? She was lying?"

"I don't know. That's part of what I don't like."

"Well, you shouldn't have picked her up like that and choked her like a rat, that's all I'm saying. Although it was kind of—never mind. Bad, bad Sinclair! But thanks for coming to the rescue. Again."

He sighed and brought me close to him; warily, I went. "No matter how angry I am with you, I cannot bear to see you hurt, or in trouble, it seems."

I felt like jumping up and down. I squashed the impulse. "That's because we're in *luurrrrrrrrvvvv.*"

He grimaced. "How enchanting."

"Listen, I've been thinking."

"How charming!"

"Shut your face. I really have. Been thinking, I mean. About the fight, and the things you said. Maybe we shouldn't get married," I said uneasily. The training of a lifetime of reading *Modern Bride* rose within me and screamed in horror, but dammit, this was bigger than what I wanted.

"Are you sure she didn't hit you on the head with that hellish thing?" he asked, feeling my forehead.

I slapped his hand away. "I'm serious. This sort of thing is always going to be happening to us. To our friends. There's always going to be some disaster that will threaten to ruin everything. You have to admit, this was minor, as far as this stuff goes. And worse is around the corner, guaranteed. Maybe . . ."

"No."

"I'm just saying . . ."

"You've said it yourself: you won't feel like you belong to me without this silly human ritual. So we are doing it, damn it all. And I am not going through a tasting menu again, or a flower meeting. No. Absolutely not."

"That's . . . so sweet," I said finally. "So you feel like you're not worthy of me, but you're insisting on a wedding, when before you implied that me changing the date means I secretly don't want to marry you. Is that about right?"

"Secretly or not, this human ritual obviously holds deep meaning for you. So we will do it. Then even you will admit you belong to me."

"Uh . . . we're not using 'obey' in the vows."

He smiled. "Aren't you in for a surprise, darling."

# Chapter 30

"**WHAT** just happened?" I asked Jon on the way to the front door. "Did we make up? Are we back together again? We were ever not together? Did he change his mind after he saw me get stabbed? Should I hold a grudge because of the whole felony assault thing in my bedroom? Or should we call it even because I smacked the shit out of him right after? And why am I asking you this stuff? Where's Tina? Where's Jess?"

"So it's true!" Jon cried, fumbling for his Sidekick with one hand and frantically brushing his shaggy bangs out of his eyes with the other. "Betsy, we've got to pick up where we left off."

"*Shhhhhh!*" I could hear Jess and Nick chit-chatting from the next room. "Not while Nick is here."

"Nick would be . . ." He consulted his tiny notes. "Detective Nick Berry. Ooh, yuck, that's inconvenient."

"To say the least. We're not sure what he knows, so for Christ's sake don't be babbling about vampires and swords and shit while he's around."

"Don't worry. You can count on me. You know you can."

"Well, thanks." I smiled at him. Then I frowned. "You know, I *was* excited about Jessica dating this guy, but now I'm starting to wonder . . ."

"But when can we get together again?" he whined.

"Come shopping with Laura and me. She knows most of my dirty little secrets. You wouldn't have to keep your mouth shut around her." And I had a feeling that what happened in the basement was going to be off-limits, conversation-wise, for a long, long time.

"Okay!" he said, and actually pumped his fist in the air. I cried dry tears over what a geek loser he was and went to get my coat.

*Dear Betsy,*
*I died about ten years ago, and as you know, basically all I've cared about since is the thirst. But things are different now. I've been keeping up with my hometown newspaper, and I've read that my dad is going to retire. He was only 39 when I became a vampire. He's never seen me since, and neither has anyone else in my family. What should I do? I know I'm supposed to keep a low profile, but I really miss my folks and would like to see what they've been up to.*
    *Sign me,*
    *Family Friendly in Fridley*

*Dear Fridley,*
*For crying out loud, go see your dad. If you don't want them to know you're a vampire, make shit up . . . you've been recruited by a secret government agency and that's why you went missing for so long. So secret you can't talk about it, or even stay very long, but they should be super-proud of you because you're out saving the world.*
    *Something like that. Trust me, they'll be thrilled you're not dead. They won't even think of awkward questions until you're long gone.*
    *Your queen,*
    *Betsy*

# Chapter 31

**W**⸤ had rolled past the third group of carolers when Jon made the comment, "This time of year must be hell on vampires. Literally hell."

I giggled. "Some carolers came to the house, and Tina and Sinclair ran down to the basement with their hands over their ears. And they don't go shopping with me, needless to say. A simple 'Merry Christmas' from a stranger gives them indigestion for the rest of the day."

At last, Laura laughed. She'd been driving like a robot: no speaking, no engaging, just stiff turns and shifts.

"But it doesn't bother you."

"Heck, no, I love this time of year."

"You're crazy to go to the mall the week before Christmas," Jon observed.

"Oh, shut up. What do you know about it?"

"I know I finished my Christmas shopping in October."

I shuddered. One of *those* freaks. More unnatural than the vampires, if you asked me.

"Is George going to be all right?" Laura asked timidly.

"Ah, George. Yes, let's get to it, shall we? Sinclair came up with a super punishment for you."

"Asshole," Jon muttered, almost too quietly for me to catch.

I decided not to be distracted. *Focus on the devil's daughter almost killing you and a helpless psycho vampire.* "He needs fresh blood—like, from a living vein—or he'll backtrack, forget how to walk, all that stuff. I've been feeding him, but guess what!"

"Oh no," she moaned.

"Can I watch?" Jon asked.

"That's right, for beating the shit out of a guest with no provocation, *and* trying to poof the vampire queen into tiny piles of ash, your grand prize is . . . letting George leech off you until all his wounds are healed! Thanks for playing."

She shuddered. "It's disgusting."

"Should have thought of that before you whaled on him." Ohhhh, Sinclair was a dark genius. This was great. She looked as appalled as I'd ever seen her.

"What if I won't do it?"

I shrugged. "Then have a nice life, and don't ever come back."

"You wouldn't! Over one of those—those things?"

"Laura."

"I'm sorry. I just don't see him the way you do. He's not a man, you know."

"Neither is the kid in the backseat—"

"Hey!"

"—but we let him hang around. Bottom line, Laura, I know I bitch about the queen gig, but the thing is, you can't just come into my house and beat the shit out of one of my vampires. You just can't. And don't pretend like you don't get it, because I know you do."

She didn't say anything. The silence got long, so Jon piped up with, "What happened after you realized you couldn't kill yourself?" and we picked up my life back in April.

# Chapter 32

SINCLAIR was waiting in my room when we got back from shopping. I greeted him with a screeched, "Don't look, don't look!" as I hustled my bulging bags over to my closet, threw them in, and leaned on the door.

"Dare I guess you bought me a gift after my dreadful trespass last night?"

"If you're admitting you were an asshole, I'm not going to argue, but I felt better about you after you throttled my sister into semiconsciousness. What can I say? I'm a sucker for the old-fashioned stuff." I realized I hadn't exactly answered his question, because I added, "The thing I had on layaway was finally paid off, that's all. Don't go reading anything into it."

"You've been with Jon, then?"

I groaned miserably and sat down on the bed to pull off my shoes. "Come on, Eric! Don't start up with that tired shit again, willya? I was also with Laura, but that doesn't mean I was the *ménage* in their *trois*."

"I think you mean you were not the *trois*," he corrected. "And I was not starting up that tired shit again. My irritation with Jon now extends far beyond his romantic intentions."

"Oh yeah? God, the mind reels. What's he done now, start up with *his* tired old shit? The Bees active again?"

"No. But his current activities are almost as dangerous to you. Your life story is not appropriate for publication, in any forum."

"But it's a joke! He's passing it off as fiction, a cute idea for a classroom project. The gag is that it's supposed to be about a real person, and some of us know it is, but everybody else thinks—"

"I'm aware of the purpose of the 'gag.' Which is what he makes me want to do, by the way."

"Why, Sinclair! That was . . . dare I think the word . . . a joke? A yarn, a tale, a comical story? Are you feverish, nauseous, cramping?"

"Furthermore, I suspect he has engineered this entire thing as an excuse to stay close to you."

I sighed and stuck my shoes in my closet, fast, so Sinclair wouldn't see inside the bags.

"Elizabeth? I breathlessly await your commentary."

"What can I say? Maybe it is. Maybe it's a little weird that out of all the projects he could have thunk up, the one he picked is the one that lets him follow me around and ask questions."

"Ah." He looked at me approvingly.

"Jeez, Sinclair, I'm not a genius, but I'm not in a coma, either! I've had guys like me before; I can recognize the symptoms, poor bastards."

"Yes," he said. "We are poor bastards."

I didn't know what to say to *that,* so I just continued my train of thought. "I don't know. Maybe I feel sorry for him. Maybe I thought I owed him a break. He came all this way and basically got his heart stomped. And the whole reason he quit staking vampires was because he liked me. I felt like I had to be . . . I dunno . . ."

"Magnanimous in victory?"

I shuddered. "Of course that just came tripping off the end of your tongue, Sink Lair, what a surprise."

I noticed he was in his usual spot when we chatted: arms crossed, leaning against my door (people did have a tendency to run in after just a brief knock or worse, no knock), head tipped to one side as he listened to every word that came out of my mouth. I pulled my frog socks off and tossed them in the hamper, but at least he didn't try to move farther away when I did it. I didn't think I could take that again.

"I would almost prefer that you disliked him," he commented. "Men have been able to cajole women into bed using nothing more than their pity."

"Oh, right!" I snapped. "Like there was ever a woman in the universe who fucked *you* because she felt sorry for you."

"I am hoping," he said, pushing away from the door and coming toward me, "there will be at least one. I behaved abominably."

"Yeah, you were a real dick." I was watching him warily. This was too good to be true! Not to mention a) nothing had changed, and b) I wasn't a faucet. "I'm glad you're sorry, but I can't just get over being upset"—I snapped my fingers—"just like that. I can't turn it on and off."

"I must beg your forgiveness," he said soberly. I realized for the first time that his hair—*his* hair—was messy, like he hadn't combed it in hours. It was as startling as if he'd gone outside without pants. "I know during lovemaking—it's the nature of vampires, I think—we have been . . . rough . . . at times, but that was no excuse for assaulting you."

"Damn right!"

"My only excuse—"

"Hey, I thought you said there *was* no excuse."

"—is that I was driven by fear, which is a new experience for me." He frowned. "An unpleasant one."

"Well." I sulked and allowed him to hug me. He did it carefully, like he was hugging a barrel of snakes. One open at both ends. "I did surprise you. And not in a good way. I really didn't mean to keep it a secret for so long, and I didn't mean to blurt it out that way."

"And you apologized, repeatedly, for that."

"Yeah, I did! What, so, you're not worried about that anymore?"

" 'That' being the frightening and unmanning way you can get into my head during our most intimate moments, while you yourself remain a locked door to me?"

"Well," I grumped, "when you have that attitude, anything's going to sound bad." Then I loosened up and kissed him on the chin. "Aw, come on. I wasn't a virgin when I met you, and I kind of liked that this was a 'first' with you. It helped me—it helped me decide a lot of things. A big thing, this October. I mean, you were aware I was going to stay with you forever, or leave forever, right?"

"Ummmm," he said, because he was nuzzling my throat. I flinched back a little, and he kissed me reassuringly in the same spot he had chomped me the night before. It had, of course, healed perfectly, but I couldn't help being twitchy.

"And part of the reason I decided to stay was because, in my head at least, you weren't sneaky and weird."

"It will take me some time," he said, working his way into my cleavage, which was as wonderful as it sounded.

"Time?" I laughed and clutched his head. "Sweetie, you're so quick to check the Book for every little thing, you forgot we're stuck with each for a thousand years."

"Anything's going to sound bad," he said, picking me up and tossing me on the bed, "when you put it like that."

# Chapter 33

H⊂ had come up for a kiss after spending an inhuman amount of time between my legs, and I was trying to figure out if you could actually die, yes die, by orgasm. It seemed likely. It also seemed like a great way to go.

*Can you hear me now?*

"Sinclair, we are not doing a cell phone commercial right now," I growled. "Now take that thing and stick it in me and let's worry about something else! Anything else!"

*But you can . . .* pausing for the thrust. I moaned when it went home, when he buried himself in me, when I could feel him everywhere . . . *hear me.*

"Yes," I groaned. "I hear you."

*And when I think about how precious you are to me and how I nearly broke your sister's back when I saw her sword between your breasts, you can hear that, too?*

Thrusting back now. It was weird, having a conversation like this. About this. But I was nothing if not adaptable.

"Yes, I hear you."

*All right, then. I can live with this.*

"It's nothing," I grumbled, "compared to what I have to put up with."

"I read your columns," he said, after.

I groaned and hid myself in the blankets. After a few seconds of digging, he found me and pulled me out. "Aha! I've been saying that in my head for over a minute, to no avail. So it really is only during—"

"I *told* you. Must we relive every fight, all the time? And I don't want to hear the editorial report on my columns."

"I liked them," he continued, ignoring my queenlike command. And was it my imagination, or was proof that I wasn't a constant telepath really cheering him up? "I thought they made much sense. They will, of course, cause a bit of a scandal among the older crowds—"

"They're not *for* the old guys. Those guys have already figured out all the rules. I gotta admit, I kind of get a kick out of writing them."

"Perhaps seeing the lighter side of the queen will appease some of the more, ah, some of the vampires who are more set in their ways. Particularly the European faction."

"I don't have any other side," I admitted. Then: "European faction?"

"Yes, that group of older vampires who was giving serious consideration to overthrowing you."

I sat up. *"What?"*

"Did you never wonder why I suddenly went to France last fall?"

"Well—yeah, but—at the time we were—I made it a point not to show too much interest in your activities because I was still mad at you for being a sneaky freak, and *this is the sort of thing I've been talking about!*"

"But I persuaded them not to revolt," he said, looking totally puzzled. "I fixed the problem for you."

"First of all, why can't they just mind their own business? They can worry about them, and I can worry about me. Jesus!"

"Because you killed two major vampires in three months, one of them the sitting power," he explained. "It was cause for concern."

"And second, *whyyyyyyyy* did you secretly go over there and then not say a word about why you were going and what happened when you got back? Instead it was all 'I miss you, Betsy, why won't you sleep with me?' "

"I did miss you," he pointed out. "And I *was* wondering why you wouldn't share my bed. Or vice versa," he added, looking down at my green flannel sheets.

"But this is the stuff I'm talking about!" I thrashed between my sheets like a landed bass. "You can't keep this shit from me!"

"But I fixed it," he said. Honest to God, he was completely bewildered. No doubt wondering why I wasn't on my knees fellating him out of pure gratitude. Men! "I fixed the problem. There was no need to bother you with any of it."

I fought not to choke the living shit out of him. "But it was *my* problem!"

"But when you didn't tell me about your sometime-telepathy—"

"That was a totally different thing! That was something I couldn't help, that I meant all along to tell you about, and eventually did, and understood why it was wrong to keep it from you, and we moved on!" I was stomping back and forth, wrapped in my comforter. "This was not sneaking off to Europe—"

"I never sneak," he said coolly.

"Oh, dude, you invented sneaking!"

"You knew where I was going. And you knew when I returned."

"Semantics! And here's a question, ladies and gentlemen—"

"Who are you talking to when you do that?"

"Why not bring me with? Huh? They were going to overthrow *me,* why not let me come over and plead my case?"

He opened his mouth. Nothing came out. I had either cornered him with my cementlike logic, or he didn't want to tell me he thought I'd fuck up the whole thing. Either way . . .

"Get out!"

"All right," he said mildly, climbing out of bed, "but you did state in your terms that I must move all the way in, or all the way—"

"I know what I said!" I kicked the duvet in a rage. "I don't care about that now! If I look at you another second I'll—I'll kick you in the gonads! Now get lost!"

He got lost.

# Chapter 34

"**W**—a—i—t a minute, wait a minute." Jessica made the time-out sign. "You made up after your other fight, but now you're fighting again?"

I nodded miserably.

"You guys. Seriously. I really think you should get married already—talk about prewedding jitters! You're tearing each other apart!"

"Perhaps my father could help," Laura suggested. "He has counseled many couples before their special day."

Oh, right. I could just see Sinclair and me sitting in the minister's office. "Thanks anyway, Laura."

"What are you doing here?" Jess demanded. She was jealous of any woman who took up my time, even relatives. "Weren't you just here?"

"I had to let George feed again," she said glumly. She pulled back her coat sleeve to show us the neat bite marks and reddened flesh. "He's pretty much healed up now."

"Oh. Well, good work." I tried an encouraging smile, which felt like an embalmed leer. "Don't almost kill him anymore. Let that be a lesson to you. Etcetera. Time to get back to my problems: can you believe that bum?"

"Well. He *did* go to Europe to keep a bunch of scary old vampires from coming over here and killing you," Jess pointed out.

"You just like him because his rent checks have never bounced."

"No, but frankly, I figure that other hurdle—whatever it was—if you got over that, you can get over anything."

"Excuse *me*," Cathie said, right next to my ear, and I yowled

and knocked over my tea. "But if we're going to get back to anyone's problems, we're getting back to mine."

"There's a ghost in the room," I told Laura and Jess.

"Oh, honey. Not this again." Jess didn't believe in ghosts
(funny 'tude for someone who lived with vampires). No matter
what I did, I couldn't get her to see them. So she just . . .

"I'm out of here." She got up, ready to put her cup and saucer
in the sink, when Laura opened her mouth. I shook my head, and
we sat in silence until Jessica left.

"What does it want?" Laura practically whispered.

"I can hear *her* fine," Cathie snapped.

"She can hear you fine," I translated. "She's the latest victim
of the Driveway Killer."

"The one who's missing? Mrs. Scoman?"

"There's another one?" Cathie cried. "Dammit, dammit! This
is why I'm floating around this dump, trying you to get your head
out of your ass! This is exactly what I was trying to prevent! Son
of a fucking bitch!"

"All *right,* don't *yell.*" I put my hands over my face and shivered for a minute. "She's mad because there's another victim."

"Well . . . another lady who's missing. She got pulled out of
her driveway tonight; they've already put an alert out on her."
Laura was obviously trying to sound encouraging to the dead
woman she couldn't see or hear. "She hasn't actually shown up,
um, dead."

"Then let's go get him! Right now!"

"She wants to go after the bad guy," I told Laura.

"Of course she does! It's Mrs. Robinson, right?"

"Yeah, yeah, let's go!"

"Wait wait *wait.*" Cathie, halfway through the wall, backed up
and looked at me. Laura, halfway to the door, also stopped.
"Where are you guys going? Do you know where he lives? All
Cathie knows is that she got conked in her driveway—that's not
exactly news. And she has a vague idea of being in 'some old
house' and then she woke up dead. We have to tell Nick all this
stuff—"

"How?" Laura asked. "Of course, you're right, we must tell
the law, but how will we explain our knowledge?"

"We could say we got an anonymous letter or something."

"Which he will then wish to see." Laura sounded apologetic to
be thinking up problems. "At least, I know I would."

"A phone call?"

"Why would they call you? Or me, for that matter?"

"Because Jessica's going out with him?"

"You could pretend to be a victim who got away," Laura suggested, "and then tell them everything the ghost tells you."

"That's not bad," Cathie said, "but there's no damn *time*. Don't you get it? He doesn't keep us very long; he's scared."

"Scared of getting caught?" I asked, *so* far over my head.

"No, scared of us. The victims. He'll kill her tonight and dump her in some awful public parking lot where everyone will see her naked and laugh and point."

"Nobody—" I began, shocked.

"No, that's what *he* thinks. It's what he wants. Now can we come up with how to explain it *later*? At least let's go drive to where I remember the house!"

"An address, anything?"

"No, but at least we can get in the area. Maybe I'll remember more. It's worth doing, goddammit!"

"You're right," I said, after I'd told Laura everything that had been said. "It's worth doing."

"Now, now, *right now*!"

"She's right," Laura said, and I assumed it was in response to what I had said, not because she could hear Cathie. "It's worth doing. Let's go at once."

# Chapter 35

"**BAD** bad bad bad bad bad bad bad *bad BAD* idea," I said again.

"Take a left," Cathie commanded from the back. "And enough complaining. I'm sick to death of the complaining."

"We're not cops! Okay? In this car is a secretary, a college student, and a part-time horse trainer."

"It would have been full-time," Laura said, "but now that I'm dead, that bum Gerry's gonna snake the slot right out from under me."

"We should have told Nick the whole thing and let him come into the neighborhood with about nine SWAT teams."

"Never mind how difficult that would be to explain," Laura began.

"Right, and scare the killer off with a bunch of uniforms running around!" Cathie snapped. "No, we have to catch that jerk. Driveway Killer . . . Driveway Asshole is more like it. Left!"

"Does anything look familiar to her?" Laura asked.

"No," Cathie said. "But I won't forget the smell in a hurry. It stank like nothing else has."

"He stank?"

"No, the neighborhood. Something chemical, something like—"

"The Glazier Refinery?" I read off the sign as we passed it. There were about two hundred smokestacks in the air, and they were all pouring out smoke that smelled like fake pizza.

Cathie retched in my backseat. Could ghosts puke? I tried to stay focused. "I guess this is the area."

"God, that smell! How could the cops not smell it on my—goddammit, because he strips them and then dumps them."

"Still, you'd think there'd be some clues," I said doubtfully.

"This isn't *CSI,*" Laura said, watching out the window. "Not that I watch the show—an hour of people finding new and interesting ways to kill each other? No thank you. But this is real life, not television. And it's a big metro area. Millions of people, doing millions of things, over a large square area. I've lived out here all my life, and I've never even heard of this place. I think when we catch him, it will be obvious what he was doing and where he was taking them, but we have to get him first."

"Whoa, whoa! You guys, I think we agreed—"

"I didn't agree to anything," Cathie said.

"—that this is a fact-finding mission. We're not here to bust the guy. We need something concrete to take back to Nick and then *they* can come get him. We're just nosing around for clues."

"And if we find him standing over a woman with a big butcher knife?" Laura asked.

"Actually," Cathie piped up helpfully, "he strangles us. With his belt."

I shuddered. "If worse comes to worst, we'll catch him. Don't sweat it, Cathie, Laura and I are totally capable of knocking a guy out and calling the cops. I'll distract him by letting him stab me multiple times and then Laura will kick the shit out of him. We'll just use a nearby phone and do the anonymous tip thing. If Mrs.—uh—"

"Scoman. You really are terrible with names," Laura chided me gently.

"I know. Anyway, if she needs to go to the hospital, we'll take her. We'll—look, we're putting the cart ahead of the horse, here. Let's see if we can find the damn house first."

"He took off his belt, and he strangled me until I shit myself." I was shocked to see Cathie had scooted way over and was whispering in Laura's ear. "He did it because he's weak and because he's afraid of women. And after I was dead, he took off all my clothes and made fun of my boobs."

"Cathie! I mean, jeez, I'm not saying you don't have a right, but cripes!"

"What?" Cathie was smack in my rearview mirror again. "I didn't say anything. I'm looking at houses."

"I heard her that time!" Laura said, excited. "Talking about her boobs and such. I think I'm getting a new power!"

"No," I said, kicking myself for ever thinking things were as bad as they could get. "I think your mother's here."

"What?"

"Surprise," Cathie said, and smiled.

"Mother!" Laura had twisted around in her seat and was glaring at the devil. "I can do this without your help!"

"I'm sure you can," the devil went on in Cathie's voice, smirking with Cathie's face. "But it seemed for a moment like you were going to take the coward's way out. Knocking him out and waiting for the police . . ." The devil rolled her eyes. "That's just sad."

"Go to Hell," Laura said through gritted teeth, and—I'm not how she did this from the passenger seat of a Dodge Stratus—pulled out her sword and stabbed Cathie with it.

Who promptly cried, "What the hell do you think you're doing, you morbid bitch?"

Laura looked at me. "Is she talking again?"

"Oh, yeah."

"Good." The sword disappeared. Laura turned back around. Nobody said a word for five miles.

# Chapter 36

"**YOUR** sword disrupts magic," I began, because some-body had to say something.

"Yes."

"So why didn't it 'kill' Cathie?"

"I don't know. I've only ever killed vampires with it. I tried to kill a werewolf once, but it just made her change back into a woman. She was so startled she ran away from me, and I never saw her again."

"There are werewolves?" Cathie asked. "For real?"

"You gotta be kidding me, werewolves. Like I don't have enough to deal with?" I bitched.

"It was only the one time," Laura said defensively. "I'm sure you'll never have to meet one. They're rarer than vampires, I bet."

"Let's for cripe's sake hope so. Cathie, is any of this looking familiar?"

"I only saw the house from the inside," she said apologeti-cally. "I remember what the inside looked like . . . and the smell of the place. I remember that."

"Oh, it's that one." Laura pointed to a nondescript split-level on the end of the block. It was tan with dark-brown trim. The driveway and sidewalks had been neatly shoveled.

"It is?" Cathie whispered, leaning forward so that her head popped through the seat between us.

"How do you know? Cathie, does anything ring a bell?"

"Just the smell. How does she know?"

Laura sighed, a dreadful sound, and looked at the nice little split-level the way I would look at a child abuser. "Is it a black house? All black, even the sidewalks? Even the snow around it?"

"No," Cathie and I said in unison.

"It looks black to me," Laura said simply.

# Chapter 37

"Hi. Eric? It's Betsy. Listen, don't freak out, but Laura and Cathie—never mind, long story—anyway, we think we've found where the Driveway Killer lives, so we're going to check it out. It's 4241 Treadwell Lane in Minneapolis. Anyway, when you get this, call me. Except I'm going to have my ringer turned off so we can sneak up on this guy if we have to, so don't flip out if I don't answer. Okay, love you, bye!"

"Are you happy now?" Cathie bitched. "Can you please get off your ass and help me, or do you have more calls to make?"

"Hey, you've seen the horror movies. The heroine never tells anyone where she's going—it's maddening. Or if she does remember she has a cell phone, it's always dead. Or she can't get a signal."

"Or her fiancé is on the other line and doesn't answer the call," Laura prompted helpfully.

"You shut up. And keep that thing put away unless we need it."

"We'd better not need it," she said as we parked a few blocks away and got out of the car. "It only disrupts magic; it doesn't do squat on regular people. Well, humans, I mean."

"Oh."

"I've been meaning to ask," she whispered as we snuck up on the split-level and Cathie ran through (literally through) snowbanks ahead imploring us to hurry, hurry, hurry! "I thank God every night that I didn't hurt you, but, uh, *why* didn't my sword hurt you? It should have killed you."

I shrugged. "Got no idea, doll. But one thing at a time."

"Oh. All right."

"Now remember," I whispered as we peeked into the front window. "Fact-finding. And if the woman's here, we'll save her."

"What if there's no woman here, just the bad guy?" Laura asked.

"You'll recognize him, right?" I asked Cathie.

"Too damned right I will."

"Okay, well, then we'll pull back and call the good guys and wait for them to come."

"What if he leaves before—"

"One thing at a time, okay? We don't even know if anybody's home."

"Nobody's in the living room," Laura observed.

"Just a minute," Cathie said, and flitted through the window. We hid (in plain sight, in the front yard), feeling like idiots (at least I did) while she phased through the house. She popped out through the garage and said, "He's not here. But there's a woman in the basement!"

"Pull up the garage door," Laura suggested.

"Everything's locked," Cathie fretted.

"I'm sure I can pull it up—" I began.

"But you guys," Laura protested, "he'll *see* it!"

"Who cares? Do him good to get a really big scare. Maybe he'll do something stupid."

"And maybe he'll run away and we won't catch him."

"Well, we can't just leave that poor woman down in the dark by herself, thinking she's going to die."

"Goddamned right!" Cathie said. "One of you break something and get in here! All I can do is float around going *boooooooooo*. Cross of Christ!"

I picked up one of the bricks lining the sidewalk and tossed it through the front window. The noise was tremendous. Not to mention the mess. Cathie and Laura stared at me, shocked.

"Maybe this way, he'll think it's just kids." It was lame, but it was all I had. "Maybe he won't think the cops are here if he just sees a broken window."

"Oh. Good one." Cathie floated approvingly away, and Laura carefully hoisted herself up and into the living room.

"Watch the glass," I warned her and then cut myself a good one and cursed. Luckily, I bled as well as I read: sluggishly.

"Down here!" Cathie called, and darted into a closed wooden door.

What's funny was, I was starting to get used to the smell of the refinery—we'd been driving around the neighborhood a good twenty minutes, after all. But Cathie was right, it blotted out everything else. If he was killing women in the basement, I couldn't smell it from the kitchen. I couldn't even smell the kitchen from the kitchen.

Laura and I hurried down the stairs, which were predictably dark and spooky until Laura found the light switch. Banks of fluorescents winked on, and in the far corner, we could see a woman with messy, short blond hair, tied up and gagged with electrician's tape. Her outfit was, needless to say, a mess.

"Ha!" Cathie screeched, phasing though the wood-burning furnace and zooming around in a tight circle. "Told you, told you!"

"It's all right," Laura said, going to her. "You're safe now. Er, this might sting a bit." And she ripped the tape off the woman's mouth. "It's like a Band-Aid," she told her. "You can't do it little by little."

"He's coming back—to kill me—" Mrs. Scoman (I assume it was Mrs. Scoman) gasped. "He said he—was going to use his special friend—and kill me—" Then she leaned over and barfed all over Laura's shoes.

"That's all right," Laura said, rubbing the terrified woman's back. "You've had a hard night."

"If those were my shoes," I muttered to Cathie, "I wouldn't be able to be so nice about it."

"Oh, your sister's a freak," Cathie said, dismissing ShoeGate with a wave of her hand. "I've only known her a couple of days, and I figured that one out."

"She's different and nice," I said defensively, "but that doesn't make her a freak."

"Trust me. Having been killed by one, I recognize the breed."

"You take that back! You can't put someone like Laura in the same league as the Driveway Asshole."

"Will you two stop it?" Laura hissed, struggling with the tape. "You're scaring poor Mrs. Scoman! And I am not in the same league as the Driveway Asshole."

"I just want to get out of here," she groaned. "I want to get out of here so bad. Just my feet. I don't care about my hands. I can run with my hands tied."

Then I heard it. "Move," I told Laura. "The—we have to go now."

Cathie darted up through the ceiling.

"What?" Laura asked.

I started to rip through the tape with a couple tugs, tricky because I didn't want to hurt Mrs. Scoman. "The garage door just went up," I said shortly.

Cathie swooped back into the basement. "He's back! And boy, he is freaked out. Keeps muttering about the damn foster kids, whatever that's supposed to mean."

"Hurry," Mrs. Scoman whispered.

"Please don't throw up on me. If I do it any faster or harder, I could break all the bones in your hands."

"I don't care! Do my feet! *Break* my feet! Cut them off if you have to, just *get me out of here*!"

"Carrie? Do you have friends downstairs, Carrie?"

"Oh, great," I mumbled. "The predictably creepy killer has arrived."

Cathie pointed at the man—I couldn't see him because we were as much under the stairs as beside them—walking down the stairs. "Time's up, motherfucker," was how she greeted him, and damn, I liked the woman's style.

"Why did no one think to bring a knife?" Laura asked the air.

"Because we're the hotshit vampire queen and devil's daughter, and we don't need knives. Unless, of course, the bad guy ties up his victims with *tape*. Then we're screwed." Ah! I finally got her feet free and went to work on her hands. Because she would have had to run past the killer to escape, I shoved her back down when she tried to scramble to her feet. "It's okay," I told her. "We've got it covered. We really are the hotshit—never mind. I'll have this off in another minute."

The killer turned and came into the basement. Saw us. (Well, most of us . . . not Cathie.) Looked startled, then quickly recovered. "Carrie, I told you, no friends over on a school night."

"My name isn't Carrie," Mrs. Scoman whispered. She wouldn't look at the killer.

Cathie stepped into his chest and stood inside him. "Asshole. Jerkoff. Tyrant. Fuckwad," she informed him from inside his own head. "Loser. Virgin. Dimwit. Asshat. God, what I wouldn't give to be corporeal right now!"

"It's overrated," I mumbled.

"I can't believe this loser's *face* was the last thing I saw."

"You aren't the foster kids," the psycho nutjob killer said, looking puzzled. "I thought the kids at the end of the block broke my window again."

"Score," I said under my breath, tugging away. "What did I say? Huh?"

"Yeah, you actually had a good idea," Cathie snarked. "And we're not calling the police right this second why again?"

"Why did you kill those women?" Laura asked, the way you'd ask someone why they picked a red car over a blue one. "Why did you steal Mrs. Scoman?"

"Because they're mine," he explained, the way you'd explain about owning a shirt. Everyone was being all calm and civilized, and it was freaking me the hell out. I could smell trouble. Not a huge talent, given the circumstances, but it was still making me twitchy as a cat in heat. "They're all mine. Carrie forgot, so I have to keep reminding her."

"Psycho!" I coughed into my fist.

"Did you really," Laura began, and then had to try again, "did you really strangle them until they pooped, and then make fun of them after you stole their clothes?"

"Laura, he's crazy. You're not going to get a straight answer. Look at him!"

Unfortunately, looking at him didn't help: he looked like a lawyer on casual Fridays. Nice, clean blue work shirt. Khakis. Penny loafers. Not at all like the slobbering nutjob he obviously was.

Then he fucked himself forever by saying, "It sucks when you get the bra off and find out they don't have a decent rack. I don't mind them lying about that other stuff, but tell the truth about your tits, that's what my dad used to say. Otherwise, it's like lying."

Then, of course, he was dead, because Laura leaned down, picked up a chunk of wood off the pile, and broke his head in half. I screamed. Mrs. Scoman screamed. Even Cathie screamed, but I think she was happy. I wasn't. I was in Hell. I think Mrs. Scoman thought so, too.

# Chapter 38

I used my vampire mojo to convince Mrs. Scoman she had escaped and had no idea why the killer was dead, or who had killed him. I reminded her to tell Nick and the task force the killer's address. We thought she'd make out okay . . . none of the killer's blood was on her. It was all over Laura.

"Okay," I said on the way home. "I'm a little concerned."

"I lost my temper," Laura said, looking out the window. "I'll be the first to admit it."

"Freak!" Cathie sang from the backseat.

"That's another thing," I snapped, glaring into the rearview mirror. "You're supposed to disappear and be in heaven or wherever you people go after I've fixed your problem."

"Yeah, I know, but I kind of like this."

"What?"

"This." She waved her ghostly hands through my head. I shuddered, and the car swerved. "How cheated was I? Repeat after me: promising life cut short."

"Yeah, but . . ." I paused delicately. "You're dead. It's time to move on."

"Look who's talking. Besides, I helped you, right? I could get into the house when you guys were standing out on the lawn like jerks. I think I could be pretty good at this. Anyway, I think I'll hang around."

"Oh, Christ on crackers."

"What?"

"Good to have you aboard!" I said with fake heartiness.

"She's still here?" Laura asked. "That's odd."

"Don't try to change the subject! You murdered that guy. He was just standing there, and you killed him!"

"Killed him dead," Cathie agreed. "Like a big blond roach motel. She's a freak, but I'm totally in love with your sister right now."

"You stay out of this."

"If you think about it, the whole thing is kind of my fault," Cathie confessed.

"Never mind! Laura, what were you thinking?"

"That I was very very very very angry? And it upset me to know he would be walking around breathing the same air as my folks?"

Points for honesty, at least. "Laura, it's like this. I don't know if you're having a bad month, or if certain prophecies are coming to light, or what, but I gotta admit, I'm concerned. Okay? I mean, I'm a vampire and I'm not going around—okay, I am, but that's a totally different thing."

"I know it was wrong," Laura said, looking at me with guileless blue eyes, "but you have to admit, it will be difficult for him to take off his belt and strangle any more women after today. Won't it?" She almost smiled, and was that a flash of green I saw in her eyes?

I decided it was my imagination.

Before I could take the issue further—not that I had the slightest idea what to say, not exactly having the moral high ground—the blue Mustang behind me flashed its high beams twice. Then it snuggled right up on my bumper, and my cell phone vibrated.

"Do they give dead people speeding tickets?" Cathie asked.

"That's no cop, that's my fiancé." I hummed the first few lines of "My Boyfriend's Back" and then answered the phone.

# Chapter 39

"ERIC, it was just an ordinary guy this time! It's not like I got tricked by vampires or got stuck in the middle of another coup."

He put his hands behind his back. I knew why; it was so he wouldn't choke me. "What is this aversion you have to waiting for my assistance?"

"It's not aversion. You're just never around when I need you. Hum. Okay, that sounded nicer in my head. Hey, I did call you. It's not my fault you didn't answer your cell."

"I was available twenty seconds later! You were physically unable to wait less than half a minute?"

"Well, I kind of wish we had, because the thing is . . . ." I burst into tears.

"Oh, Elizabeth, don't do that." He snuggled me into his arms. "Was I shouting? I won't apologize for worrying, but I will clarify: I was concerned, not angry."

"It's not that. Laura—she killed the bad guy."

"And that's . . . er, bad?"

"It's how she did it. He didn't even attack us or anything. He was just standing there. And there were all these piles of wood in the basement, because he has—had—a wood-burning stove, and she leaned over and picked up a big old chunk of wood, and just *beaned* him with it! And I heard the crack—I heard his head break!" I shuddered. "And brains—did you know brains are pink and red? Don't answer that," I ordered tearfully. "And all this *stuff* came out. And he was just . . . dead. And she didn't even care! Just said later that she lost her temper."

"That . . . is cause for concern," he said after a moment's thought. "I must admit, I have . . . dispatched . . . my share of societal burdens in my day. But Laura seems to be—"

"Going over to the dark side."

"Or something," he agreed. "But it could be argued that she saved lives."

"Definitely it could be argued. I guess Driveway Jerk had this thing for short-haired blondes because when he was a teen, this girl named—never mind, it's creepy and stupid at the same time. And he was just driving around, looking for the right type to be in the right spot at the right time! Tell me how *that* can be allowed to happen in a sane world. You could be putting your groceries away ten minutes later and not be killed."

"But you and Laura are in a sane world," he suggested. "Righting wrongs."

"I really don't think this is the tactic we should use when talking to her about this, okay?" I pulled away so I could look into his eyes. "And see this? How I came right home and told you everything and we're discussing it like sane people who talk to each other?"

"Well, I did follow you to be sure you were going to do that," he admitted.

"This, *this* is what couples do! *Kuh-MYUN-ih-kate*. Memorize the word, Sinclair. Practice it."

"Consider me chastened." He didn't look terribly repentant, though. "Getting back to the matter of your sister . . ."

"I don't know what to do. What can I tell her, killing is wrong? Of course it's wrong, everybody knows that. She knows it, too. The problem is, that only makes us the biggest hypocrites in the world. Not to mention, it's not like she killed a Girl Scout. She did the world a favor. So what do I say to her?"

"That you're watching," he said quietly. "We're all watching."

"I think I'll take the 'we'll be there for you' tactic on that one."

"Either way. Come here, now, darling, sit down." He rubbed my shoulders, and I sat on the bed. "You've had a tough week, haven't you?"

"It's my new worst week ever," I sniveled.

"Well, in light of our new 'tell all' policy, I have some news for you."

I sighed and rested my forehead on his shoulder. "Who's dead now?"

"The *Star Tribune* has picked up your 'Dear Betsy' column."

"What?" I jerked my head up. "There've only been, what? Two newsletters? And I thought that was impossible! Anybody seeing the newsletter!"

"Supposedly it was. Marjorie is beside herself. Heads will roll, I can assure you. Possibly literally. We suspect either a member of the *Tribune* payroll is a vampire, or an enterprising human hacked into her system and gave it to a reporter."

"So what's—what's going to happen?"

"Fortunately, feedback seems to be that it's not to be taken seriously. The editor thinks it is a joke, the readers seem to like it, and the readers who are vampires are keeping their mouths shut."

"So only a few people in the city know it's a real letter to real vampires?"

"Yes. And because Marjorie's discretion is on the line, she is moving heaven and earth to find out who is responsible. I imagine we'll have some answers on that in a short time."

"Well . . . I guess things could be worse."

"They are about to get that way, I assure you."

I groaned and flopped down on the bed. "This whole tell-each-other-everything debacle, you're punishing me for it now, aren't you?"

"Darling, you know I live to obey your slightest whim. When before, I sought to protect you from the problems of governing a nation, now I see it was merely my ham-handed way of repressing you. Well, those days are over!" he declared, over my moans of horror. "Whereas in the past I felt discretion was the better part of valor—"

"Oh, now you're just making shit up to fuck with me."

"—now all must be revealed, constantly."

"Look, I figured out that you don't keep things from me to be mean. You just can't help it."

"Ah, but starting now, I shall help it."

"I get that you think solving problems for me proves your worth."

He sniffed. "I wouldn't go *that* far."

"You can't help it, you're in *lurrrrrvvv*."

"Stop that. I was going to tell you, Jon has transcribed nearly the entire first draft of your little tell-all."

"I thought it was going to be, like, a paper."

"It's turning into a book, dear. Three hundred pages at last count."

"Oh, he told you this?"

"It's possible I had Tina hack into his Sidekick," he admitted.

"Nice! Well, this is nothing new, right?"

"Given the fallout from the *Tribune* picking up your column—"

"What fallout? I thought everybody agreed it was a joke."

"—I got Jon alone and convinced him he had never written the book, never had the idea, never had any interest in your life story."

"Oh, Christ."

"Then I erased it."

"Oh, Sinclair. Oh, boy." I put my hands over my eyes. "This is going to be a bad one."

"You may proceed," he said, "with the yelling."

I tried to get myself under control. *He did it out of love. Misguided, weird love, but love. He's trying to protect you. In a misguided, weird way.*

"Okay, Eric, that was bad. Pretty bad. And I think, after what Jon has done for us, I think you should undo your mojo."

"But I went to all that trouble," he explained patiently, like I didn't get what he had done, "to be sure he forgot everything."

"And now I want you to make him remember! Look, he'll flunk his class, among other things. You really want him moping around here because he got an F in bio or whatever the hell it's called? And second, I agreed to let him do this. So by you sneaking in and undoing it, I look bad. Really, really bad."

He looked at me for a long minute. "I admit," he said at last, "I had not considered it in those terms. Your authority should not be undermined. Even by me."

*Especially* by you, but that was a topic for another time.

"So you'll undo it?"

"I will try," he said. "And in the spirit of full revelation, I must tell you I'm not sure it will work. I've never tried to undo a mojo, as you call it."

"What, in your whole life you've never made a mistake?"

He smiled. "No, but no one ever asked me to go back and try to rectify my errors. No one ever dared."

"Probably why you've got such an attitude problem."

"Probably," he agreed, and pulled me into his arms.

I wriggled around until I was straddling him. "I don't know about you, but I haven't eaten in days."

"You've been busy," he said, and then he groaned as I found his zipper and pulled. "I must say, I didn't think I would enjoy this

full disclosure rule you've implemented . . . ah . . . don't stop doing that . . ."

"Aren't you funny," I said.

"Consider it an order from your king."

"I'm hysterical with laughter here." I wiggled down, pulled
down his pants as I went, and divested him of his socks. Frantic, I
yanked at his black boxer shorts until they were little cotton
shreds, took his dick in my hand, moved it out of my way, and bit
him right on his femoral artery.

His hands plunged into my hair and he made fists, almost hard
enough to hurt, but not quite. He was so good at that. At coming
up to the line but not crossing it. I tried not to think of all the practice he must have had to get so good.

His cool, salty blood nearly overflowed my mouth, and for the
first time in days, I wasn't morbidly thirsty. Instead I drank from
him and felt his cock pulse in my hand, felt him give way, felt him
helpless, literally helpless in my hand as he spurted all over the
sheets, as he gave control to me.

*I love you. Love you. Love you.*

And the worst week ever was redeemed.

# Chapter 40

"LOOK. you don't even have to *go* to the florist, okay? I've got a book full of pictures for you to look at."

"Darling, I trust your taste impeccably. I'm sure whatever you choose will be appropriate to the . . . lovely occasion."

"You're lying! You think I keep my taste in my butt!"

"I am certain," Sinclair said, totally straight-faced, "that I never used that phrase."

Tina, who had been coming into the kitchen to get God-knows-what, abruptly turned around.

"Freeze!" I shouted. "I've got a bone to pick with you, too."

"How can I serve you, my queen?" she asked, all innocent. When she wanted, she could look like a sixteen-year-old kid.

"How about not hacking into my friend's computers and helping Sinclair *eat* three hundred pages? How about that?"

Tina looked over at Sinclair, who had suddenly rediscovered that the *Wall Street Journal* printed stock prices. No help there.

"Look, I know you're the king's man—er, so to speak—and you feel like you can't say no to him, but—"

"It's not that."

"What?"

"Not entirely that," she amended. "If I may be frank, Majesty, I don't think his little school project was at all appropriate. You do have enemies, you know."

"Tell me about it." I glared at the two of them, the undead Frick and Frack.

"I mean human enemies. Why make things easier for them? There is a difference between dishonesty and discretion."

Oh, like either of those two would know. "Look, just leave my friend's stuff alone, okay? I've already talked to Sinclair about this, and he's going to undo the 'you are getting verrrrrrry sleeeeeepy' thing."

"He is?"

"I am," Sinclair said to the paper.

"Love," Tina said, gaping. "It's truly an amazing thing to behold."

"Shush, Tina."

"My king." Fighting a smile, she grabbed the mail and walked out.

"As for you. You don't even have to pick the flowers you like, okay? Just pick the ones you absolutely loathe, can't stand the sight of, and I'll be sure those aren't anywhere near you on the big day."

"Darling," he said, turning the page, "I just don't have intensely strong feelings for flowers."

"But you were raised on a farm! You must have *some* preferences."

"Darling, I have a penis. Ergo I have no preferences."

"When are you and your penis going to get with the program?" Jessica asked, coming in the door Tina had just left by. "Just do what she asks, and it'll all be over that much sooner. For everybody."

"Way to make it sound fun, Jess."

"It's *not* fun, Bets. Not for anyone but you." She pulled up a chair and sat down. Eric was looking at her with some interest.

"At last," he said. "Someone says it out loud."

"Eric, she's been planning this wedding since she was in the seventh grade. Honest to God. She used to bring *Brides* magazine to study hall, and she'd show me the dress, the tux, the cake, the flowers. She even had the name of your kids picked out. She *still* does that."

"Hey, hey," I protested. "I haven't looked at an issue of *Brides* in years. A year. Six months. Look, let's get back on track, all right? Sinclair? You look okay? You're kind of pale, even for you."

"No, no, I'm fine." He managed a smile. He *had* looked sort of ghastly while Jessica was laying it out. "You realize, after this . . . wedding . . . you'll also be 'Sinclair.' "

Oh. My. God. I actually had managed to put that *huge* problem out of my mind. It was easy, what with the ghosts and cops and serial killers on my radar. But now, it was *baaaaaack,* looming in my head like a big dead flower. For a second I was totally horrified. Then I recovered. "No, I won't. I'm keeping my name."

"No, you are *not*."

"Like hell!"

"Uh-oh," Jessica muttered.

"If I have to go through this farcical event, the very damned least you can do is be Mrs. Elizabeth Sinclair."

"What does *farcical* mean?" I asked suspiciously.

"Happy," Jessica said.

"Oh. Okay. Look, Sinclair, I realize, being a million years old, that you can't help being an ancient disgusting chauvinist pig. But you're just gonna have to get over it in this case, because this is the twenty-first century, in case you haven't noticed, and women don't have to submerge their identities with their husband's."

"The entire point of getting married," Sinclair began, "is to—" He cut himself off and tilted his head to the left. Jessica turned and looked, too. I couldn't understand what the fuss was about; it was Laura. She was, despite recent events, welcome in our home anytime.

She eased the kitchen doors open and stepped in. "*Helloooo?* May I come in?"

Jessica was staring. "What are *you* doing here?"

Then I realized. It was Saturday night. Laura always went to Mass on Saturday nights. Said it kept her out of trouble, plus she could sleep late the next day.

She shrugged and pulled up a chair. "Oh, you know. I just— didn't feel like going tonight."

I was trying not to stare, and failing. "For the first time *ever*. Your folks are gonna kill me! They're gonna think I'm a bad influence."

"You are," Jessica said.

"It's no big deal, everyone. Maybe I'll go tomorrow."

"Forgive us for staring," Sinclair said. "It's just that you are so . . . devout. It was a surprise, seeing you here when you are usually . . . elsewhere."

"It's no big deal," she said again, and everyone heard the warning that time.

Luckily (?), George the Fiend chose that moment to also walk into the kitchen. I guess we were having a party and nobody told me.

"Now what's *he* doing up here?" Jessica asked. "To think, I almost didn't come in here for a glass of milk. Look at all the stuff I would have missed."

"I dunno," I said, staring. George was dragging half the blanket he'd crocheted, hopped up on a kitchen stool, drank all my tea—the first time he'd evinced evidence in anything but blood—spat it out on the floor in disgust, and started crocheting again.

Laura cleared her throat. "I, ah, want to take this chance, Mr. George, to apologize for—for what I did the other night. I was picking a fight because I was angry at someone else, and that's a poor excuse. In fact, it's no excuse. So again, I apologize. I'm very, very sorry. And I'm sorry to you, too, Betsy, and you, Eric, for laying hands on one of your subjects."

I shrugged it off with a mumbled "Well, what are ya gonna do?" but Sinclair, doubtless used to this sort of thing, waved it off with a kingly, "Think no more of it, Laura, dear. We know your actions are normally above reproach."

Yeah. Normally.

"He seemed better after I fed him," Laura suggested.

I restrained the impulse to slap my forehead. Of course he was better, duh! He got better after drinking my blood—queen's blood. How much good would the devil's bloodline do him? He could probably do my taxes by now.

"That's the stuff I got him last week," Jessica said, staring at the lavender blanket, which was almost as big as my bed. "He must be just about out. I'll run over to the fabric store and get him some more."

"Red, please," George the Fiend said.

Pandemonium. Chaos. And no matter what we tempted him with, how much we cajoled, how often Sinclair ordered, or how often I begged, he didn't say another word.

# Chapter 41

"Is this the third date? Or the fourth?"

"Nosy bitch," Jessica laughed. She checked her diamond earrings for the twentieth time.

"Yes," I assured her. "They're still there." I'd been saving to get her the matching pendant at Tiffany's; the classic blue box was on the swag-draped parlor mantel right this minute.

Okay, Sinclair was helping me. Not that he was big into Christmas. But he liked the idea of giving Jessica an extravagant gift. It would be the first time we gave anybody a present together. "You look like a tasteful Christmas tree."

"Meaning my ass looks fat in this green dress."

"No, no. You just look very spirit-of-the-seasony."

"Did you ever figure out what to give Sinclair?"

"Yeah. I took back asking him to un-mojo Jon."

"So now Jon will"—Jessica thought this out—"not remember he wrote the book about you."

"Right. I mean, it's a rotten thing to do, but I can't just think of myself on this one. There's a bunch of vampires counting on me to look out for them—I finally figured that out when I saved George from Laura. Well, a few days after I saved George from Laura. Even if they don't know I'm looking out for them, I'm supposed to be. So . . . no book of my life."

"Well, if that's what being the queen means to you, then, because you're the queen, I guess that's it."

"Yeah, that's it. I mean, I can hardly marry Sinclair and protect vampires *and* not be the queen. Even for me, that's pretty stupid."

"*Stupid*'s a harsh word," she said absently, fluffing her lashes with mascara.

"Isn't Jon supposed to turn in his bio after Christmas break?"

"Yeah." I laughed evilly. "Sinclair's doing it for him. He'd better not fob it off on Tina, either. A history of the life and times of Grover Cleveland. Apparently Sinclair knew him." I laughed harder. The perfect punishment!

"You talk it out with Laura yet?"

"No." I quit laughing. "I don't know what to say without sounding like a jerk. I guess—I guess we're just hoping it was a slip. I mean, look who her mom is. She's bound to have a short temper. And it's not like the guy didn't have it coming."

"Is that what the party line is? He had it coming?"

"No," I almost snapped, "but it's the best I can do. I don't see Nick crying about it."

"Big-time promotion, probably," she admitted. "And that's what we're celebrating. The Task Force is just about done. Nick's going back to his everyday stuff. And the Driveway Killer's done. And the Scomans are going to have a great Christmas."

"Assuming she ever stops having nightmares."

"Your little ghost told you that? What a voyeur."

"I heard that!" Cathie said, and then popped back out, probably to nag (not that they could hear her) the guys putting up the tree. We were late with it this year, and out of deference to Sinclair and Tina, Jess, Marc, and I didn't join in the trimming festivities. It had been a big enough fight just letting Jessica order one and have it sent to the house.

Needless to say, those two would be avoiding the entire east wing of the house until after New Year's.

"Obviously, if she'd had to pick between her life and nightmares, it's an easy choice. Still, I wish we could have spared her the entire experience."

"Come on. You saved her. And the bad guy got his. And you're getting married! Probably."

"What?"

"Well, I'm pretty sure. And I'm finally getting laid."

"It's a Christmas miracle," I said with mock joy. "With devils and vampires and dead serial killers."

"It's just gotten so commercial," she agreed, touching up her lipstick. "Want to sneak down and put a cross on the tree later?"

"No, I'd better not. Poor things, they've already got the heebie-jeebies."

"Boy, there's a phrase I never thought would be associated with bad-ass vampires."

"Any kind of vampires. Anyway. We'll work on that for next year. If they're going to stay out of the room altogether, why *not* put a cross on the tree?"

She laughed and slung a black cashmere wrap over her bony shoulders. "Good point. Now, on a scale of one to ten, with one being ratty-ass you, and ten being Halle Berry—"

"Nine point six. Definitely."

"What a liar you are, my girl." She kissed me, leaving an orange smear on my cheek, and floated out on a cloud of Chanel.

# Chapter 42

*AND I in my kerchief, and Ma in her cap* . . . that was all of it I knew, unfortunately. My mom could recite the whole thing by heart, all twenty verses or however many there were. Jess, Marc, Jon, and I were heading over there tomorrow night for Christmas Eve dinner. She'd tell it to me then.

I shut my—our—bedroom door behind me and saw Sinclair in a miserable huddle in the middle of the bed. "It's here now, isn't it?" he asked. "I can feel it. Draining the strength from me."

"Oh, jeez, you're such a baby! It's just a Christmas tree. It's not a nuclear device."

He shuddered. "You say tomato, I say *toe-mah-toe*."

"It's not even that big!" I held my hand up to my waist. "It's only like this big. We had to put most of the decorations back in the attic."

"It's going down the day after tomorrow, right?"

"It just went up! Oh, while I'm thinking of it, I don't suppose you want to go to you-know-what Eve dinner tomorrow with my mom."

He grimaced, like he smelled something bad. "Your mother is a charming woman in all ways, and normally I would be delighted."

"Thanks but no thanks, huh?"

"I am not leaving this house until the twenty-sixth."

"You guys. I swear."

"You will never understand, which is both boggling and frightening."

"Uh-huh. You're probably too freaked to get it up, am I right?"

He cocked an eyebrow at me. "Not quite that freaked out."

# Epilogue

"THANKS for not un-hypnotizing Jon," I said drowsily, much later.

His chest rumbled beneath my cheek as he laughed. "Which reminds me, my report on President Cleveland is nearly finished."

"Ha! Serves you right. Thanks."

"There is one small problem."

"About your report?"

"No. Something else, I'm afraid."

"There aren't any *small* problems, good-looking. Hit me."

"Tina and I have looked everywhere, deleted everything we could. But it appears Jon made a hard copy of the book before I reached him. He did something with it. We aren't sure what."

"Why do I hate where this is going?"

"And if I ask him, really get into his mind and ask him, it could jeopardize—"

"The footprints you've already left," I said glumly. "You think he turned it in to his prof already?"

"I . . . hope so. Because otherwise, a book-length manuscript about our lives has gone missing. And if your column catches on, someone could see it and . . ."

"Well . . . it'll probably turn up. He was doing it for school; it's not like he had some sinister motive or anything. Right? Sinclair? Right?"

"Probably." Which is as close as Mr. Buzzkill would ever get to admitting nothing would probably come of it.

"Catchy title, though," he said as we both felt the sun start to come up on Christmas Eve. *"Undead and Unwed."*

"That title sucks," I said, and then it was morning, and everything went dark, and I went wherever it is vampires go when they aren't Christmas shopping.